UNANIMOUS PRAISE FOR VICTORIA CHANCELLOR!

MIRACLE OF LOVE

"...tender and spellbinding, a classic time-travel!"
—Evelyn Rogers, bestselling author of
Wicked

FOREVER & A DAY

"A mesmerizing adventure with star-crossed lovers who will leave your heart pounding!"
—Helen R. Myers, RITA Award-Winning Author

"Victoria Chancellor has penned an exciting, eerie and romantic tale of obsession, true love and sacrifice."
—*Romantic Times*

BITTERROOT

"*Bitterroot* is an absorbing time-travel...."
—Rosalyn Alsobrook, bestselling author of
Love's Image

"Victoria Chancellor works magic with her clear, crisp prose, drawing the reader deeper...a truly believable and heart-wrenching tale!"
—*Romantic Times*

Other *Love Spell* books by Victoria Chancellor:
BITTERROOT
FOREVER & A DAY

PASSION'S PRESENTS

He pulled out beautiful flowing fabrics, soft knitted garments, blouses with lace. Erina felt her eyes go wide, heard the soft sound of a sigh that came from her.

"What have you done, Mr. Kirby? I cannot pay for these clothes!"

"I don't expect you to." He placed two pairs of shiny slippers on the table beside the sofa. "But I'm tired of seeing you in a dress that would be more suited for a museum. So these are for you. There are some...undergarments in this bag. I wasn't sure of your...size."

"But I'll not be acceptin' clothes from you. That would be most...improper."

"Erina," he said, placing his hands on his hips again, "don't argue every point with me, okay? Pick your fights carefully. I'm bigger and more persistent than you, and in the end, I'll win."

"I wasn't aware we were havin' a battle, Mr. Kirby."

"And stop calling me 'Mr. Kirby,'" he said, stepping close to her. "That's what people called my father, and he's long gone. I'm Grant. Not 'mister.' Just Grant."

She tried to ignore his nearness. The clothes he'd purchased lay about the sofa, draped like a very decadent offering on his own personal altar. Well, she couldn't be bought for a few handfuls of garments.

"I'll not be familiar with you, Mr. Kirby. I'll not—"

His hands gripped her arms and before she could say another word, his lips sealed over hers.

Victoria Chancellor

Miracle of Love

LOVE SPELL ◆ NEW YORK CITY

*In memory of my father
Arthur V. Chancellor
1913—1995
A man with a great amount of faith
who enjoyed his life to the very end.*

LOVE SPELL®

October 1996

Published by

Dorchester Publishing Co., Inc.
276 Fifth Avenue
New York, NY 10001

Printed in the United States of America.

Acknowedgments

Special thanks to the staffs of UTMB ER and Pediatric ER, *The Galvestonian*, Galveston Historical Society, Rosenburg Library, Rev. William J. Bosworth of St. Mary's Cathedral, Monsignor John Bell of the Dallas Catholic Diocese, Galveston County Child Welfare, Jerry Goldberg for his real estate expertise, the CompuServe RWA Online Chapter for their support, my Catholic friends for their "technical" help, and especially Evan Fogelman, for suggesting a religious time-travel.

For more information on Galveston, read Gary Cartwright's wonderful *Galveston, A History of the Island* (Atheneum, New York 1991).

Miracle of Love

Prologue

September 21, 1996
Houston, Texas

Grant hadn't been in his Jeep Cherokee five minutes when the car phone rang. Either an emergency or a summons, since only a few people knew his number. He briefly considered letting it ring. Who could really need him at one A.M.?

As soon as the question formed, he knew the answer. He'd slipped away from a post-opera premiere party his mother was hosting. She'd wanted him to stay, but not as much as he'd wanted to get away. Just for the weekend. If he'd had more time, he would have flown to Colorado and climbed something tall and steep before the mountains became snowed in for the winter.

He answered on the third ring. "Hello, Mother."

"How did you know it was me?"

"Who else would be calling?"

"Brian, Dottie. I could name a half dozen."

"Yes, but I didn't just sneak away from them, and I doubt any of our properties are in serious danger in the middle of the night."

"Sneak away is right. I wanted you to stay in town tonight. I'm having a breakfast in the morning for the diocese outreach program. You know they want that old building just a block from the church."

"Yes, I know they do." He rubbed the bridge of his nose as he drove east on the loop toward I-45. "Tell Brian to get together with Dottie and see if we can get a good write-off for it. But don't tell the church until I see the figures."

"Really, Grant, I hardly think that one old building is going to affect our financial position."

"Let me see the numbers first, Mother."

"Very well," she said with a dramatic sigh. "I'll talk to Brian."

"Good. Is there anything else?"

"No. I just wish you'd be around this weekend. I wanted you to meet some of the opera board tonight, but you got away so quickly—"

"It's late, Mother. Believe it or not, I'm tired."

"I think you were looking for an excuse to leave."

"Would I do that?" Of course he would. She preferred to ignore his lack of interest in her social life. Oh, it was fine for her, but . . . sometimes he imagined his parents had found him under the fictional cabbage leaf. He didn't have the "normal" traits of a Kirby.

"Absolutely. I'll bet you wouldn't be too tired to climb."

"That's different. But I still wouldn't climb at one

o'clock in the morning with the kind of wind we're having tonight."

"I never win an argument with you anymore," she complained.

"Why does a simple conversation have to turn into a competition to see who wins?" He'd never understood that about his parents. When his father was alive they'd made these little power struggles into some kind of game. Grant wasn't amused by the pastime, however. He didn't want to play their game and, in refusing to be baited, often disappointed his mother.

He was sorry she felt that way.

"I have to go, Grant. My guests are still here."

"Have a good time, Mother. I'll see you next week."

"If you decide to come back to town, join me for brunch at the club on Sunday. The Peterson's daughter is back from Washington—"

"I'm going to be at the condo all weekend. Leave a message if you need me."

"Good night, Grant," she said with a resigned sigh.

"Good night, Mother."

Silence descended like the blackness of night inside the Jeep. With only the whine of the tires and the faint sound of air whistling past, he felt a profound sense of loneliness. He was doing what he wanted—getting away for the weekend—but that didn't mean he was totally content with his life. The problem with his getaway was that he'd made it a solitary pursuit. No one from Houston had ever been invited. Only a few people from Galveston had been in his condo.

He realized that his choice seemed odd to many people, since he didn't own a unit in one of his properties. He'd bought the twelfth floor, two-bedroom standard layout at the Galvestonian at the market price when he could have afforded the entire building. But if he lived in a Kirby Investment property, he'd be treated like the owner. Catered to, tainted by his status as "boss," so that he couldn't come and go as a regular guy. And more than anything he wanted to be an anonymous person when he escaped from his position as the CEO of a multimillion dollar real estate investment firm.

Grant flipped on the radio and listened to the late-night chat of a sports station. Bored, he selected a CD and slipped it in, relaxing to the melodic strains of U2. The miles slipped past under the hum of the Jeep's tires, and soon he was crossing the high bridge from the mainland to the island. A few more miles and he'd be at the East Beach condo.

A gust of wind buffeted the car as he drove across the bay. He'd heard on the local evening news that a cold front, unusual this early in the year, would come through during the morning hours. That meant no swimming in the gulf, but he didn't care. His condo was stocked with a variety of clothes; he could run or work out at the gym, or just lay around and watch college football on Saturday. On Sunday he'd check out the Oilers game, then drive back to Houston that night.

On Monday morning he'd be ready for the office again. Ready to don the suit, read the reports, have business lunches, and make million-dollar decisions. This weekend he was just Grant Kirby, a former geology major at Colorado State who liked to relax in his modest condo in Galveston.

Chapter One

October 8, 1896
Galveston, Texas

Erina O'Shea pushed open one of the tall, heavy wooden doors of St. Mary's Cathedral, just wide enough to see that the church was empty. It was near midnight; the priests and Bishop Gallagher were no doubt snug in bed, safe from the unseasonably cold wind that whipped off the gulf and across the island like the screech of a witch. Clutching her bundle close, she eased herself inside.

Neither the priests nor the bishop nor any mortal man could help her. Only God, if he chose . . .

Candles burned at the Blessed Virgin's altar, dancing long shadows up the wooden columns and across the many stained-glass windows. But the light didn't reach all the way to the ornate wood and smooth plaster of the ceiling. The night seemed to press down on her, even inside this sacred place, as though she couldn't escape its sheltering darkness.

She knelt at the back of the church, dipping her fingers into the holy water and quickly making the sign of the cross. Her breath came fast and shallow, or was it *his* breath, gasping in the night? She felt her heart hammering beneath her chest, pounding inside her head. As quickly as possible, she walked past the carved wooden pews to the front of the church, toward the only hope she could imagine.

Kneeling awkwardly with her bundle, she leaned briefly against the wide altar rail. The wood felt cool and smooth to her forehead. She wondered if she had a fever, or was the unnatural heat just a response to her fears?

After making the sign of the cross again, she lit a candle with a shaking hand and looked up into the eyes that seemed to blink and shimmer in the golden glow.

"Mary, Holy Mother," she whispered, "you are my only hope."

Beneath her breast, her bundle stirred weakly, then coughed. Erina looked down at the tiny, fragile body of her son.

"Hush now, Colin. I've come to pray for a miracle, and if the Blessed Virgin is listenin', a miracle you shall have."

Even in the faint light Colin's skin looked blue. His eyes seemed heavy, although not with sleep. He was so weak, had been since his birth almost two months earlier. The sisters at St. Mary's Infirmary had told her he probably wouldn't live. He'd been born a month early, a tiny baby who'd needed her love and care so desperately. The city physician wouldn't give her an authorization to admit Colin to the charity hospital because there was no hope. Inside his chest was a problem that no doctor or nurse could fix, since no one could operate on a beating heart.

She couldn't depend on the skills of man to save what God had made defective. No, she had to ask Mary for divine intervention. And even though Erina knew herself to be an unworthy sinner, perhaps the Blessed Virgin would intervene for the life of an innocent child.

With shaking hands, Erina placed her son on the altar rail, holding him steady with arms braced on either side of his body and hands clasped in prayer. As Colin breathed unsteadily and whimpered occasionally, she spoke aloud. "Holy Mother, you know what it is to lose your son. Please, save my baby. He's an innocent child, a victim of our sins, but innocent all the same. And you are my only hope."

She paused for a moment, watching Colin's nearly transparent, blue-veined lids close over his dark eyes. His tiny chest rose and fell with each breath. Two fists grasped his blanket, holding fast even in sleep. He was so perfect in every other way, such a bonny child—except for his heart. If only God would grant this wish and make him whole . . .

She looked up into the compassionate eyes of the statue, who seemed to stare back with calm assurance. "Please, Blessed Virgin, ask God to grant a miracle to save my son. Please, cause his heart to be healed. I ask this in the name of your son, who suffered as well, and as a mother who cannot bear to lose her own child."

Tears welled up in her eyes, but she blinked them away. She would stay on her knees all night and all day tomorrow if there was a chance of saving Colin. This was her only hope. The more he moved or cried, the worse his symptoms became. And he grew weaker every day.

Suddenly he began to cough, his little fists beating against his covers, his eyes squinting closed. Between his tears and the way he tried to draw his legs toward his chest, he could barely take a breath. Erina tried to comfort him, but he seemed past comfort or a mother's love. She wished she could somehow reach inside his chest and make his heart whole, but she knew that was impossible. Not even a skilled surgeon could do that.

The skin around his mouth began to turn blue as Erina soothed him against her breast. She watched him grasp her finger with his little hand, as blue as his lips.

"Please, Holy Mother," she pleaded, tears falling down her cheeks, "grant a miracle. Save my son. Please, please. I love him so . . ." She squeezed her own eyes shut, unable to continue, unable to watch the life gasp and wheeze from Colin's tiny body. When he was gone, she would be all alone. She couldn't face life without her child.

"Please," Erina said one more time, gazing into the serene features of the Virgin Mother. "A miracle . . ."

Suddenly all the candles at the altar seemed to flare to life at once, surrounding her in a light so white, she could no longer see. She clutched Colin tight, frightened even as she dared to hope. Had

Mary granted her wish? Was this healing blaze her miracle?

As abruptly as the light began, it ended. Darkness cloaked her, or was it just the absence of the miraculous light? Erina's eyes searched for the details of the altar, the statue of Mary, even the wall sconces at the back of the church. But nothing looked familiar.

In her arms, Colin wiggled, then began to cry. "Hush, my little darlin'," she crooned softly.

Slowly, Erina's eyes adjusted to the darkness. Strange shapes filled the room, with faint light from some unknown source providing soft illumination. Strange, tall draperies framed a huge window that stretched across one wall. Odd boxes with shiny black fronts were stacked on shelves. The only furniture that looked familiar were a sofa and two chairs, and even they seemed oddly formed.

She was no longer in the church, that was certain. But where was she? What had happened to them in that bright light? Had Colin been cured?

At that moment he jerked, his arms pumping, his legs drawn up to his chest, and Erina felt more tears form. *He wasn't cured.* How could his tiny body endure this any longer? She knew the answer; it couldn't. Despite her prayers, despite her hope for a miracle, despite the white light, he was still gravely ill. A miracle *had* occurred, but not the one for which she had prayed.

"Oh, my baby," she said aloud, trying desperately to comfort him. But he was past a mother's comfort.

Suddenly the room was filled with a golden light

that was not as bright as before. And Erina sensed another presence, even before she heard his harshly uttered words.

"Who in the hell are you?"

Grant jerked awake, not certain what had disturbed him. He only knew something was wrong. Something besides the cold front that had arrived in Galveston shortly after he had, very early Saturday morning.

He usually slept like a baby in the king-size bed, with the balcony door in his bedroom ajar and the sound of the surf, twelve floors below, lulling him to sleep.

Not tonight. The wind had screeched like a banshee, swirling cold air into the bedroom. Was that what had awakened him?

No, it wasn't the wind. It was a baby! And then he heard the indistinct murmur of a voice. It wasn't coming from outside, but in. Someone was in his living room!

Within a second he was out of bed, pulling on jeans and grabbing his cordless phone. He wasn't sure if he was going to call the police or bash the intruder—not the baby—over the head with it.

And how in the hell had someone gotten into his condo? The building was locked at ten o'clock, and he'd activated his own security system before going to bed. The only open door was the one on his balcony, and there was no way a person could get in that way—unless they were an experienced climber.

No one had walked through his bedroom. And

only an idiot would bring a baby along to a break-in.

He took a deep breath and flicked on the over-heads, flooding the living room with light. Standing between his couch and the dining table was a young woman—more of a teenager, really—dressed in a long, gray dress, clutching a baby to her chest. Her eyes were wide, dark, and luminous, her face flushed, her appearance disheveled. She resembled a young Audrey Hepburn, with long, curly black hair spilling from an old-fashioned, hooded cloak.

"Who in the hell are you?" he asked.

"Erina O'Shea," she whispered, apparently as surprised to see him as he was to find her in his condo.

He felt her eyes flick across his naked chest and stomach like the tickle of a feather. As she took in his low-riding, unbuttoned jeans, her eyes widened even more. "You don't look like an angel," she said, her voice soft and tinged with an Irish accent.

"An angel?" He laughed sarcastically. "Hardly." His eyes narrowed, and he remembered where he was—and that this young woman was trespassing in a seemingly secure condo. "What are you doing here and how did you get in?"

"I don't—"

The bundle whimpered weakly, then cried a pitifully thin wail, interrupting her explanation.

"What's wrong with the baby?"

"He's very ill." Her voice and face revealed a wealth of confusion and fear. "I asked the Blessed Virgin for a miracle, and she sent me to you."

Grant blinked, unable to believe his ears or his

eyes. A miracle? He was obviously having a major hallucination. He seriously doubted that any deity, especially the Catholic ones of his younger years, remembered his address or cared for his whereabouts. He certainly hadn't frequented their houses in the last ten years or so, except to attend a few weddings and his father's funeral.

"Please, sir, I need your help. My child—"

"I don't know a thing about kids. I don't have nieces or nephews. Besides, I'm the last person you should approach for a miracle."

"But Mary sent me to you for help. I prayed to her, and then I was here, and I'm so afraid that Colin will . . ."

She obviously couldn't continue, breaking eye contact and bending her head over the child.

Placing the phone on the entertainment center, Grant walked toward her. She was small and frail in appearance, but her eyes burned with motherly love and something he hadn't seen in ages—faith.

When he neared she shrank away. Ignoring her fears, he pushed aside the blanket covering the baby and immediately felt a jolt of panic. He didn't know much about babies or children, but he was damned sure they weren't supposed to be blue.

"How long has he been like this?"

"He was born with a heart condition, but he's been worse lately. There's times when he turns so blue. Oh, please, sir. Please save my child."

Her pleas prodded him to action. "He needs to be in a hospital, not running around in this weather."

"The doctors at St. Mary's Infirmary told me they

23

couldn't do a thing for him."

"St. Mary's Infirmary? What are you talking about? Why didn't you take him to UTMB, or Sealy, or a half dozen other places?"

"But—"

"Never mind." Grant ran into his bedroom, pulled a sweatshirt over his head, and grabbed his jogging shoes. He pushed his feet into them as the young woman watched with wide eyes, still standing in the same spot.

"Come on," he said, reaching for her arm. "I can get him there faster than the paramedics can arrive up here."

"But where—"

"Move it," Grant said sternly. "You should have taken him yourself." He couldn't stand the thought of this little baby suffering because his mother wouldn't take him to the hospital. Instead, she'd dragged him out on a cold, blustery night to break into a condo.

"But—"

He pulled her out the door and into the corridor, past the other doors and the bank of elevators that traveled to the lobby, then down the other hallway and into the garage elevator. He jammed his finger on the button and silently cursed each second that the doors remained closed.

Glancing at the baby again, he noticed the horrid color, the searching, deep blue eyes, the way the little tyke had drawn himself into a ball like a wounded animal. "I don't know how you managed to get inside my condo, but you should have expended your time and effort in getting your son to the hospital," he said harshly.

"I tried. The hospital said they couldn't save him," she replied, her voice ringing with distress. "I don't know what this place is. Where would we be goin'?"

"To UTMB. It's only a mile away."

At her baffled expression, he explained impatiently, "The University of Texas Medical Branch. UTMB."

"That's the place where they train doctors. I'd need a certificate from the city physician; he already told me Colin's case was hopeless."

Grant shook his head. He had no idea what she was talking about. "They'll treat him in the ER."

The baby whimpered again, but sounded weaker than before. Just then, the elevator doors eased open and Grant steered the woman inside.

"What is this . . . thing?"

What part of the world was she from that she'd never been in an elevator? Obviously Ireland, but they had tall buildings there, didn't they? Ignoring her frightened stance, he pushed the button for the garage. "Don't tell me you've never been in an elevator."

"I've heard of such."

"Who hasn't?" Damn. Why did elevators always travel twice as slowly when he was in a hurry? He counted to nineteen before the elevator reached the bottom floor.

The young woman stumbled as he pulled her down the concrete corridor toward the garage. "Here, let me take him," he offered, then wondered where that request had come from. How long had it been since he'd held a baby?

Years, maybe. He remembered one company picnic when a baby had been shoved into his arms, kicking and squirming. This baby settled limply against Grant's chest. He felt something inside him leap to life as the slight weight of the baby rested trustingly against him, looking up with those dark blue eyes. Could they even focus yet? What did the boy see and feel—and know about his condition? Somehow, Grant knew he had to save this child. . . .

"How old is he?" he asked as they reached the Cherokee.

"Nearly two months," she said breathlessly. "What is this?"

He looked at her over his shoulder as he unlocked the doors. "A Jeep. Get in and buckle up."

She stared at the vehicle as though it might bite.

"Get in, dammit. We don't have time for this."

"But where is the team? Shouldn't you hitch them first?"

He stopped himself from shaking some sense into her. "Are you nuts? Just get in the car. I'm trying to save your baby."

"I . . . of course," she said fearfully, easing awkwardly into the front seat.

"Put your seat belt on."

"I don't know what you mean." She turned those wide eyes on him again. They appeared almost black in the faint light of the garage.

"Hell," he mumbled, juggling the baby with one arm while he reached for the seat belt and strapped her in. Didn't she know how to do anything?

He thrust the baby into her hands. "Hold him. I don't have a car seat."

The baby was no longer crying, which was probably a bad sign, Grant thought as he jumped into the driver's seat and turned the key. The engine leapt to life, causing a gasp from his passenger.

"Hold on," he said, slipping the gear into drive and gunning the engine.

They raced through the sparsely populated garage, up the ramp, and onto East Beach Drive before she could say another word. He wanted to know how the baby was doing but knew he couldn't take his eyes off the road, not at this speed. Taking the turn at the end of East Beach way too fast, he felt two wheels leave the pavement as he steered south on Sea Wall Boulevard.

The woman screamed.

"What's your name again?" he asked, ignoring her unwanted commentary on his driving skills.

"Erina," she gasped. "Erina O'Shea."

"You probably don't know any more about emergency rooms than you do elevators and cars, do you?"

"No . . . no, I don't think so."

"Then let me do the talking. Just answer the doctor's questions about the baby—what's his name again?"

"Colin."

"Colin," Grant said, rolling the name off his tongue with a bit of the same Irish accent she used. He ran the red light at Ferry Road and cursed. He should have turned there.

Taking the next right, he careened down Harborside toward UTMB way too fast, but it was late, the streets deserted. He followed the red signs to the emergency room as Erina whimpered in the seat beside him and Colin remained way too quiet.

"Are you sure the Blessed Virgin wanted you to bring me here?"

The signs guided him in almost a U-turn and up toward the second-floor entrance. He roared up a steep incline, passing the Care Flight helicopter on its pad, and pulled to a stop in a spot near the portico marked ER VEHICLES ONLY.

"I have no idea. All I know is that this kid needs help, and this is the best place around."

"They'll save my baby?" she asked as he released her seat belt and grabbed the child from her arms.

"They'll do their best," he said, certain that they would. Galveston boasted some of the finest medical facilities in the country. He should know; one of the wings bore his family name. "Come on."

He heard her footsteps behind him as he ran toward the glass doors. Then he was inside, racing toward the triage desk with the unconscious blue baby held securely in his arms.

Erina followed the man into the strange building, with its lights that seemed to hide in the tall ceiling, yet illuminated everything so brightly. The smell was equally strange, unlike anything she'd sensed before. And the people! A few slumped in chairs made of painted metal and fabric; some walked around, wearing very plain white or blue clothing, cut in a style she'd never seen before. Doors led in different directions, some with neatly lettered signs and words she didn't understand.

"What might this place be?" she asked the man, grasping the soft fabric of his shirt as he stopped beside a desk.

"UTMB Emergency Room," he said over his shoulder.

"But that's not right," she said, gasping for breath. "The university building is red brick with arched windows. Not this . . . place."

The man ignored her. "There's something wrong with his heart, or his lungs," he said firmly to the nurse behind the high desk. "He needs immediate attention."

"Have a seat."

"No. I think he's stopped breathing. He needs to be seen—now!"

The redheaded woman talked into some device. Perhaps it was a telephone, which Erina had heard about but never seen. Few people in Galveston had a telephone.

"How old is he?"

"Almost two months," Erina said, shifting her weight from side to side as she watched her son, lying in the arms of the tall man.

"How long has he had this condition?"

"Always. He was born that way."

"Was he a full-term baby?"

"What are you askin' me?"

"Was he born at nine months?"

"No. Only eight months."

"And the delivery? Was it normal?"

"I . . . I suppose it was." In truth, she'd been too racked with pain to remember much of the blessed event. "Mrs. Abernathy delivered him."

The woman's head snapped up from her papers. "No doctor attended the birth?"

"No. I couldn't—"

She looked back down at the desk. "What previous treatment has he received?"

"Not a thing! The doctors were tellin' me there was nothin' they could do."

The woman looked up at her, frowning. Erina noticed that her red hair was cut very, very short, and she wore blue cosmetics on her eyelids.

"He has these . . . episodes. But saints preserve him, this one is the worst."

"Get him some help," the man said. "You can ask these questions later."

"We need background before we can perform any procedures."

"My God, he could die while you ask your questions!"

At that moment some more people with uniforms burst through two doors and reached for her son.

"No!" she cried, suddenly afraid that they weren't part of the miracle for which she'd prayed. What if they took Colin away and she never saw him again?

The man handed her baby over without pause. She grabbed for him, her eyes awash with tears. "Colin!"

"Erina, calm down." She felt his hands on her arm,

holding her fast. "They've got to take him to an examination room. And you've got to pull yourself together."

"I'm wantin' to go with him. Don't let them take Colin away!"

"They're only taking him inside to examine him. They'll need information from you, so you've got to calm down and answer the nurse's questions. Can you do that?"

She looked up at the man. He seemed so sincere, so certain. "I want to help my son," she whispered.

"Then go with him, but stay out of the way, and no hysterics. They need answers, and you're the only one who can give them."

"He'll be in crash room one. We need these forms filled out," the woman behind the desk said. "What's the baby's name?"

"Colin," Erina said, glancing back at the swinging doors.

"I'll take care of this," the man said. "Go see your son."

Erina paused for just a moment, afraid of these strange surroundings but more afraid for her baby. She walked quickly toward the doorway where he'd been carried.

"Colin O'Shea," she heard the man say.

She stopped and turned around. "No. Colin Patrick Kirby," she said. Dropping her gaze from the man's startled expression, she added softly, "His father's name is Kirby." And then she turned back and hurried through the doors.

Chapter Two

Kirby? What did she mean, his name was Kirby?
Grant felt as though he were in the midst of some
mysterious drama, yet he didn't know how or why
he'd become involved.

"Excuse me," the triage nurse interrupted, "but we
need to get some additional information."

"Sure." Grant shook his head, but he could still see
the image of Colin, his blue-tinted skin color revealing his failing heart. The poor little guy. Colin Patrick
Kirby. Was he the son of some relative, or had Erina
O'Shea picked the name because the Kirby family
was well known, socially responsible, and financially
secure?

"And what is your relationship to the patient?" the
woman asked.

"I . . . I'm not sure," Grant admitted.

"Does the mother have insurance?"

"I have no idea." He doubted she carried insurance. She didn't appear responsible to him, dragging
a sick baby around on a night like this, breaking into

his condo through who-knew-what-method. He couldn't imagine what kind of occupation or background would require her to wear such clothing. Maybe she was some sort of religious fanatic or cult member.

"Who is the responsible party?"

"I don't know. If she doesn't have the means, I'll take care of the child's expenses." Had he really said that? Grant closed his eyes and wondered again if he was hallucinating. No, he really was in the ER of UTMB, taking on the responsibility of a gravely ill child. He could afford it, of course, but he'd always confined his philanthropic efforts to writing checks to legitimate charities, not providing funds to babies with names and faces, and mothers with wildly curly black hair and eyes that revealed her very soul.

You're getting fanciful, Grant, he warned himself silently. *Get a grip.*

"And your name is?" the woman asked.

"Grant Kirby," he replied, distracted by his jumbled thoughts and still-racing pulse.

"Oh, Mr. Kirby. I didn't recognize you."

He ran a hand through his hair. He was accustomed to the mollifying or patronizing tone some people used when they discovered his name, even though the fawning made him uncomfortable. Being on the cover of the local Sunday magazine insert of the *Houston Chronicle* and various business journals hadn't helped his anonymity, either. "That's okay. I'm a little disoriented myself."

"I'll just place your name at the top of the form, and these can be filled out later."

"May I go back and see how he's doing?"

"Well . . . only relatives should be with the patients."

He took a deep breath. "I may be a relative. I'm not sure yet. But his mother . . . well, she needs someone with her right now."

"All right, Mr. Kirby. He'll be in crash room one. That's the one at the end of the hall, just a bit to the left. Don't get in the way," the woman said with a smile. "And I hope your—I mean, *the*—baby is going to be fine."

Great, Grant thought as he walked through the swinging doors. Now the entire hospital would think that he'd just brought his secret love child into the ER for treatment, along with the obviously confused, very young mother. Great, just great.

"Let's get him stabilized. Get that ventilator over here."

The nurse pulled a clear mask off Colin's face as someone else rolled more machines to the bed.

"Don't worry," another nurse said, brushing past her. "The machine will breathe for him. He'll get more oxygen that way. And we're running other tests—X rays and an EKG—to see what's wrong."

Erina folded her arms across her chest, then stuffed a fist in her mouth to stifle a scream as the doctors inserted some sort of device in her son's throat. She didn't understand what they were doing. They'd already warned her to stay back, that interference could jeopardize the care her son received. As difficult as that was, she'd refrained from crying, or asking questions, or snatching Colin from the table and running out the door.

She'd grabbed his blanket instead, holding it in her empty arms, letting her baby's familiar smell fill her senses.

She shook from her fears, and from this unknown situation in which she found herself. These men didn't look like the doctors she'd seen before. The nurses didn't resemble the nuns at St. Mary's, or any other women she knew, with their short skirts and trousers like men's.

"We need your signature on this form." The redheaded nurse who had been behind the desk shoved a piece of paper at her, then handed her a dark, narrow object. "Sign here."

"I need a pen."

The woman looked strangely at her, then did something to the object, causing it to click, and placed it in her hand. "Read it and sign. We need your consent in writing."

"But the other doctors said—"

"Ms. O'Shea, I'm not sure why your son hasn't received any previous care, but he has a serious heart condition. We need to get him admitted."

"But what can they do for him?"

"We don't know yet. The important thing is to get him stabilized, so he's not deprived of oxygen for long periods of time. If his problem is congenital, he may need surgery."

"On his heart? But how can that be?"

"It's done all the time."

"And this can fix Colin's heart? And my son . . ."

"The survival rate is good. There are no guarantees, but we'll do everything we can to repair his heart."

Tears came to Erina's eyes as she looked down at the form before her. She couldn't read the words at this moment, but did that matter? They were going to save her son. She stroked the instrument across the paper, surprised to find a thin line of blue ink. With shaking hands, she signed her name. Anything to save her son.

The woman hurried away, form and miraculous pen in hand.

What kind of world was this? Where had Mother Mary sent her?

Just then the doctors rolled another piece of equipment toward the bed.

"Clear," someone said.

A whirring noise came from the machine. Erina jumped backward, right into something solid and warm.

Strong hands closed over her upper arms. "What's going on?"

"They're goin' to do something called 'stabilize' to him. Then they might have to operate on his heart." Erina glanced back over her shoulder, into the worried face of the man who'd been chosen to save Colin.

He seemed so concerned, so caring, even though he'd been wakened in the middle of the night and didn't know her or her son.

In the background Erina heard the gentle whir of the machine that was now breathing for Colin. He would be fine. Mary had sent her to this place so he would be cured. Erina knew her faith must be stronger now than ever. Asking for a miracle was one thing; living through one was another entirely.

One of the nurses came over to them. "We're taking him to the Pediatric ICU. You won't be able to see him for a while, so you can wait down here, or—

The bed rolled past her. Erina stepped forward. "Wait!"

She leaned over Colin, who seemed so still, so small and frail on the white sheet. A transparent pipe of some sort went into his mouth, while a tiny one was attached to his arm. Erina had no idea what these devices were, except for the fact that one of them helped him breathe, but at least Colin's color seemed better. She had to trust that these people knew what they were doing.

After all, God had granted this miracle, sending her to this place where doctors could operate on a beating heart.

"I love you," she whispered to her fragile son. She smoothed a hand over his forehead, brushing against his dark, downy hair. His eyes were closed, and she wished she could look into their wide, dark depths one more time. Or that she could see his true smile, just once again. "Holy Mother, watch over him," she whispered.

Then they pushed him away, all the people rushing down the hall, through doors that swung open and then shut, closing her out.

Only then did she bring his blanket to her face to smother a sob, bending at the waist, devastated by the pain she felt. Her son, her only joy, was gone.

"They'll take good care of him."

She'd forgotten the man. Suddenly she realized that his hands held her fast, that his strength helped support her trembling body.

"I've never been separated from him. Not for one minute since his birth," she said softly.

He didn't say anything, just urged her forward with an arm around her shoulders. She felt so weak that she was surprised she could walk. "Where are you takin' me?"

"Someplace quiet. We'll sit down and get some coffee. There's nothing you can do until after they find out what the problem is."

"And how long will that be takin'?"

"Hours, probably. It depends on what they find once they get the results back from the tests."

And what if these tests told them that he needed surgery to fix his heart? Would she even know before they cut into his little chest? Erina stuffed a fist in her mouth, stifling her cries. How could Colin survive such surgery? *Faith,* her inner voice answered. *You must have faith.*

"Come on," the man said gently.

She let him guide her down the wide hallway as she blinked back tears. They went into a small room like the one at his house, one with no windows, that moved downward. In a few seconds a faint bell rang and the doors opened. They were in another part of the hospital.

If she hadn't been so frightened, she realized, she would have been amazed yet again.

He turned her to the right, into a room with large, shiny boxes that had names splashed brightly across them. Coke. Pepsi. The words made no sense. The air smelled like strongly boiled coffee. The odor made her slightly nauseous.

He pulled her down to a chair. "I'll get us some coffee. What do you like in yours?"

She looked up at him, suddenly so tired and sick she couldn't make sense of his words.

"Sugar and cream?"

She nodded.

She hugged her arms, rocking his blanket back and forth as though Colin still rested close to her breast. How many times had she tried to ease his pain and distress by rocking him on their single bed, in the small apartment above Mrs. Abernathy's dress shop? Would she ever hold him again?

"Here you go," the man said, sitting across the table from her.

"Thank you." She held the warm, soft cup with one hand and wiped her eyes with the other. "What is this . . . material?"

"Styrofoam," he said, a puzzled look on his face.

He needed a shave, she thought. Whiskers a few shades darker than his hair covered his jaw and chin. She imagined they would be very coarse and scratchy.

"I know some people don't think it's environmentally sound," he said, "but then, others don't approve of cutting down trees, either."

She looked into his eyes, wondering how he could make so little sense. But these strange cups must be

39

normal to him. She embraced the meager warmth with both hands. Apparently the people in this unusual place didn't like their beverages very hot.

She dipped her head and took a sip—and almost burned her mouth. It was scalding! But the cup was cool.

"Sorry. I should have warned you. Someone just made a fresh pot."

Erina nodded. The coffee tasted a little better than she had expected from the smell of the room. She blew across its surface as they sat at the small table.

The silence stretched as long and tight as her nerves. The man reached over and patted her hand, the gesture comforting and nothing more. Years had passed since anyone except Mrs. Abernathy had offered her affection without expecting something in return. Her da had been happy and affectionate, but he'd passed on three years ago.

"I'm thinkin' that I should apologize for gettin' you involved in my problems. I had no idea . . ."

"Still sticking to your story that you were sent to my condo by the Virgin Mary?"

"Yes. It's the truth I'm tellin' you." She looked into his eyes. They were green, tinged with a bit of blue like the ocean on a calm day. His hair was short and light-colored, like the different shades of yellow and brown on the dried grasses near the beach. His complexion appeared unusually dark for a blond-haired man, as though he spent much time out of doors without a hat. Perhaps he worked at the dock or on one of the shrimp boats. His hands were certainly large and square, not the hands of a man of leisure.

Whatever he did, he didn't look like any man she'd ever seen before.

"I don't even know your name," she said softly.

His features hardened, a muscle jerking in his cheek. "You don't?"

"No. I'm sorry I forgot to ask."

"It's Grant. Grant Austin Kirby."

She felt the room spin around her. "Kirby?"

"Yeah," he said. His voice sounded a thousand miles away.

"But you're not . . . I don't know you."

"And I don't know you either. Which is why I was really surprised when you gave my name to the clerk. Tell me, is your son's father really a Kirby, or did you decide that would make a better story?"

"No," she said, confused. She sat the coffee down on the table, then rubbed her forehead. "His name is Kirby."

"And yours is O'Shea."

"Yes," she said weakly.

"Did you keep your maiden name, or didn't you marry his father?"

She took a deep breath and paused a moment before answering. "It's sad I am to admit that he didn't marry me," Erina said softly. How humiliating to tell your darkest secret to a stranger, even one who shared the same name as Colin's father.

"Which Kirby?"

"Jerrold," she said, looking into the face of this man who had been kind, despite his reluctance to believe her story. He stared at her intently.

He frowned. "I don't remember any Jerrold Kirby.

41

Does he live in Galveston?"

"Yes. In the house on Broadway, when he's not away at school. He's studyin' law at Harvard."

"The only Jerrold Kirby I know of is my great-grandfather. He was a lawyer around the turn of the century in Galveston."

Erina felt a prickle of unease. "What do you mean, the turn of the century?"

"Around 1900. I remember that my great-grandfather's law offices were destroyed in the hurricane in September 1900, but the house wasn't damaged much at all."

"But this isn't . . . What year would this be?"

"It's 1996," he said, his expression one of confusion and irritation. "It's September already, and it's been 1996 all year."

Erina felt her eyes widen as the air seemed to leave her body: 1996? Could it be?

"Erina?"

Holy Mother of God! Her miracle had been granted. She'd been sent forward a hundred years, to a time when doctors could operate on her son. And this man, who had whisked her and Colin to the hospital with such speed, was the great-grandson of the man who had forced his attentions on her—gullible fool that she'd been, falling for his words—then offered her a pittance and never claimed his son.

Of all the people who must live in this strange, future world, why had Mary chosen *him* to help save Colin?

* * *

42

Grant registered immediate alarm at Erina's blanched color and startled expression. Was she going to faint? No; she took a deep breath and the color came back into her pale, high cheeks. She had the most clear, smooth skin he'd ever seen.

"What's wrong?" he said, placing his coffee beside hers on the table.

"The year. It's crazy you'll think I am, but I'm not from your time."

"What do you mean, not from my time? Whose time . . . what are you talking about?"

"When I walked into St. Mary's Cathedral tonight it was October 1896."

"Bull—" Grant stopped himself before he launched into a disbelieving tirade. "There's no way."

"But it's the truth I'm tellin' you! I was born in the year 1875, in County Kildare, and I came to Galveston with my da in 1888."

"Look, showing up in my condo in the middle of the night was a good trick, but I'm not going to believe that you're some sort of time traveler who got zapped into the future. You've been watching too many reruns of 'Quantum Leap.' "

"Now I wouldn't know what you mean by zapped or 'Quantum Leap,' but the Blessed Virgin sent me here to save Colin. And savin' him is what the doctors are doin'!"

"Yes, they are." *I hope*, he added silently. "You don't need to make up some story. I already told the hospital that I'd be responsible for his medical bills if you don't have insurance or money, and I'll keep my word, because of the boy."

"I'm not askin' for your charity, Mr. Kirby. Just because your great-grandda took liberties with my person doesn't mean you're responsible for his son."

"He's not Jerrold Kirby's son!"

"Oh! And I'm thinkin' that I'm in a better position to know the man's nature and what he did to me."

"I'm not going to argue with you about my great-grandfather. I didn't even know the man."

"Well, let me tell you that he was a bonny fine man to look upon. Not too tall, but well made and handsome. He had a fine mustache and thick brown hair."

"You sound like you were in love with him."

"Oh, I was. Or I thought I was. He acted nice to me, and I felt more than a wee bit flattered that he'd notice a servant in his own house. But it wasn't love he was feelin' for me. I found out he was slippery as an eel, and his heart was just as cold."

"Wait a minute!" Grant mentally shook himself. "I'm talking about this like it was real. Forget it!" He pushed himself off the couch and paced the room. For some reason she'd concocted this fantastic story, including just enough family history to keep him intrigued. He didn't understand why . . . but he would.

"Now why would you be angry at me for tellin' the truth?"

"It's not the truth! You *do not* know my great-grandfather."

"Aye, I did know the man, and a bit too well, but no more."

She folded her arms over her chest and sank back into the chair. The baby's blanket, a crazy mix of velvet and satin in a variety of colors, spilled across her chest and the skirt of her gray dress. Spots of pink colored her cheeks, and her eyes flashed with dark fire.

"If you're finished with your coffee, we can go back to the waiting room. They might have some news about your son."

Her demeanor changed immediately, from righteous indignation to worried mother. She bolted from the chair, her long dress swirling around her ankles, revealing black lace-up boots. Damn, but she dressed as though she'd stepped out of another century. She'd planned this little charade right down to the last detail.

They took the elevator back up to the ER, where he escorted her to a row of chairs facing a TV, mounted high on the wall. The channel aired an infomercial about the latest workout machine that promised a miraculous body in just weeks.

Miraculous. That's what she expected him to believe about her mysterious appearance in his life. More like a calculated ploy to get him to take financial responsibility for her baby. Right now she was claiming Colin was the son of a long-dead man. But what about tomorrow? Would she then claim Colin was the son of the heir to the Kirby family, expecting a large payoff for keeping quiet?

He'd fallen into her little scheme quite well, already telling the triage nurse that he'd pay for the surgery. And look at how fast she'd jumped to the conclusion that Colin was his son! If Erina went to the press, he was sure at least one paper would carry the story.

His mother—the socially impeccable Virginia Kramer Kirby—would have a coronary. His attorney would assume the worst and look for someone with whom he could negotiate. His CFO, an extremely practical woman, would launch an all-out plan to liquidate assets in case a settlement was needed.

"What in the name of all that's holy are those people doin'?"

Her agitated voice caused him to whirl and face her again. Huge, startled eyes stared past his head to the television set. Her hands gripped the metal arms of the chair. He glanced up at the TV.

"Exercising," he replied, trying to keep his tone civil.

"But they're not wearin' any clothes! They're in their underthings!"

"Leotards and tank tops," he corrected her.

"And where are those people? They're not in that little box."

"Television," he corrected her. "You know perfectly well that they taped that in a studio somewhere. Don't pull that innocent act on me."

"I'm thinkin' that you're a most infuriatin' man."

"And I'm thinking that you're a very accomplished actress."

"I most certainly am not!" she said in a haughty, offended tone. "I may have a babe and no husband, but it's honest work I do, sewin' and the like. I'm no actress."

"I was referring to your thespian skills, not your profession."

"You think I'm lyin' about where I'm from, and I'm not takin' that lightly."

"I cower at the thought, Miss O'Shea."

She stared at him until her lower lip began to tremble. "I'm no liar," she said in a small voice that broke ever so slightly.

"Damn," he cursed under his breath. Of course he thought she was a liar. What else could he think? That she really was a time traveler? That the baby who had looked up at him so trustingly was his cousin, several times removed?

"It's my son I'm wantin'," she said in a small voice, looking away from him, from the television, from everything in the room, "not a brawl."

In the bright light of the waiting room he could see tears glistening in her eyes. For a moment he'd forgotten that her child was gravely ill and might not survive without major surgery.

"I'm sorry. I shouldn't have upset you."

She said nothing, looking old-fashioned, small, and very young sitting in the dark, thoroughly modern chair. She should be in school somewhere, studying art or Medieval literature or mathematics, not sitting in an emergency waiting room, worried about her child. Despite the lies, despite the deception she might be trying to pull, he wanted to sit beside her, put his arms around her, and tell her everything would be all right.

"Can I get you something else to drink? Something to eat? There's a cafeteria here, but I'm not sure it's open this late."

"I'm fine, thank you, Mr. Kirby."

"Please, call me Grant."

"I'm thinkin' that's too forward."

"I'm an informal kind of guy. And Galveston isn't exactly a metropolitan place."

"Galveston? But it is. It's the largest city in Texas, I'm told, and quite a seaport."

"We're not back to the nineteenth century, are we?"

She sighed, looking at him with a directness that was unnerving. Her eyes were a deep, deep blue, he realized, not black as he'd thought earlier.

"You're not believin' me."

"No. Let's just stay away from that topic, okay?"

"I'll not apologize for speakin' my mind, Mr. Kirby."

"Grant."

She didn't reply, just broke eye contact and looked around the room, dismissing him as an irritating element of the environment. Hell, he'd brought her to the hospital, volunteered to be responsible for the boy, and had every intention of waiting here with her until the surgery was over. Didn't she realize that he cared—for the baby?

"How old are you?" he asked before he could stop the question. It was rude, but he wanted to know.

"I'll be twenty-one in December," she replied, sitting up straighter.

Just as he'd thought, she was way too young to be a mother and such an accomplished actress. He was eleven years older—and probably couldn't concoct nearly as extravagant a story.

With a sigh, he grabbed a couple of magazines and put them on the chair beside her. Then he eased into a seat across from her, crossing his feet and stretching out his legs. It was going to be a long night.

Chapter Three

She knew she should stay awake, but her eyes felt as heavy as wet Turkish carpets. She heard the noise of the hospital, the faint music and murmurs from that magical box called television, and the familiar smell and feel of the blanket she'd made for Colin last spring. The doctors would come soon to tell her about him, but until they did, as much as it hurt, she could do nothing to help him.

She wanted to curl up beside her baby and take a nap, to wake and know that all this had been a dream. He hadn't really been born with a bad heart; she hadn't really asked the Holy Mother for a miracle and been sent a hundred years into the future.

No, when she woke up she would be in her bed above Mrs. Abernathy's dress shop. She'd light a fire in the stove, feed Colin his breakfast, and dress for the day. Then she'd walk down the back stairs and settle her baby into a bassinet beside her chair, and she'd finish the trim on the gown for Miss Bettie Brown. Mrs. Abernathy would bring in a pot of tea and two buttery scones, and they'd talk about Colin and current fashions and upcoming social events that meant new gowns for the island's elite.

Just as soon as she woke up . . .

Grant knew he should be sleeping; there was nothing he could do until the doctors came back with the test results. Then he'd see what decision Erina would make about her son's care. Maybe he'd throw in a few suggestions, since she didn't seem very knowledgeable about modern medicine. He knew he should be furious with her for breaking into his condo and involving him in her life, but somehow he couldn't work up the anger. He found himself making excuses for her weaknesses: She didn't know any better; she had no money; she was desperate to save her child.

She needed a keeper. If she was going to tell stories, they should at least be believable ones. Not some wacky sci-fi fantasy of time travel from the gay nineties in Galveston. Erina O'Shea had a lot to learn about the context of her lies, although he couldn't fault her one bit for delivery.

Now she slept, worry etched across her brow, a frown turning down the corners of her perfectly formed mouth. Her neck rested at an awkward angle, and he knew she'd be stiff when she awoke. Her long gray dress covered her legs and the tops of her black high-top boots. At least they were in fashion. He'd seen a teenager at the Galleria wearing a very similar pair last weekend, only she wore them with black tights, a leather mini skirt, and a cropped sweater that displayed a pierced navel.

Grant was fairly certain Erina O'Shea did not have any pierced body parts.

He wondered if she was telling the truth about how old she was. She didn't appear to be over nineteen. At thirty-one, he felt ancient.

He tried to focus on the magazine he'd picked up, but an article on the ten best fly fishing spots in the western U.S. didn't hold his interest. He'd never been fly fishing, although he had seen that Robert Redford–directed movie about the father and sons who . . .

Damn, he was rambling in his own mind! Blabbering to himself about teenagers with pierced navels and fly fishing. He was going out of his head thinking about everything except the most important two; why was he so drawn to Erina O'Shea, and could her son's failing heart be fixed?

He didn't want to think about those subjects. Not at two-thirty in the morning, he thought, glancing at the wall clock.

The sliding glass doors opened and paramedics pushed a gurney into the triage area.

"Traffic accident on Sea Wall. Drunk as a skunk."

He didn't listen to the rest. The patient, a young man from the sound of his voice, was singing "Ninety-nine Bottles of Beer on the Wall" off-key, obviously not critically injured.

Erina stirred, her eyes opening wide and looking all around her.

"I'm still here," she said, as though the idea baffled her.

"Yes, and so am I."

She focused on him, frowning again. "I thought this was all a dream."

"No, not really. The doctors haven't come back yet with any news."

"How long did I sleep?"

"Not more than ten minutes, I think," Grant answered, glancing at the clock again.

She rubbed her temples. "I had the strangest dream that I was asleep in my own bed above the dress shop with Colin beside me, and my heart just as sad. . . ."

"This would be back in 1896?"

"Of course. It's not a story I told you, Mr. Kirby. It's the truth."

"We'll see."

"I'm thinkin' you give me a headache."

"And I'm thinking that you woke me up in the middle of the night."

"I'm not askin' you to stay," she said bravely, thrusting up her chin in a defiant gesture. "The Holy Mother woke you, not me, so you might be askin' her pardon, if that's your mind. I didn't ask to be sent to your home."

"It's my condo, not my home."

"And what would the difference be?"

"I have an apartment in Houston I call home. It's just off Westheimer, in River Oaks. Maybe you've heard of the area."

"I've never been to Mudville, er, I mean Houston," she said saucily. "Nor can I think of a single reason

53

to waste a dime on the train trip. Galveston is twice the city—"

"You really have your historical perspective down pat, don't you?"

"I'm thinkin' that's another insult."

Grant laughed at her smoldering outrage. "You're good. You're very good."

"I'm not actin'."

"What did you dream?" he asked, changing the subject.

"I dreamed that I was back at Mrs. Abernathy's dress shop, sharing a spot of tea and workin' on my quilt."

"Who's Mrs. Abernathy?"

"The lady I work for. She owns a shop on Post Office Street. I live above the shop."

"By yourself?"

"With Colin, of course," she said indignantly.

"And is there something special about this quilt?"

"It's a piece I'm makin' from scraps of gowns and such. Velvets, brocades, silk. Mrs. Abernathy makes gowns for some of the island's finest ladies, and there's nothin' like the feel of those fine fabrics on a cool winter night. I was almost finished with it when—"

Their conversation was interrupted by the arrival of the doctor who had begun treatment on Colin in the ER. Erina jumped to her feet, her hands clenched together until her knuckles turned white.

Grant stood beside her. She looked as though she was ready to collapse, except for the fever-bright excitement in her eyes.

"Ms. O'Shea. Mr. Kirby." The young doctor nodded at each of them in turn.

Grant read his name from the blue coat as Dr. Jack Cook.

"What news do you have of my Colin?"

The doctor's gaze darted between them. "We've managed to stabilize your son—"

"Her son," Grant said between gritted teeth. He supposed the entire hospital thought Colin was his son. By tomorrow the rumor could be all over town.

"Yes, well, he's resting comfortably at the moment. His vital signs are good and so is his color. We'll continue with the ventilator for now, but hopefully he can be weaned off of that tomorrow."

"I want to see him."

"He's in PDICU—"

"And what is that?"

"The Pediatric Intensive Care Unit. It's for critically ill children. You can see him, but only for a moment."

"But he needs me! You can't have me leavin' my son to the care of strangers."

"Ms. O'Shea, your son is very ill. The X rays showed a possible case of pneumonia, in addition to the heart problem."

"What exactly is wrong with his heart, Dr. Cook?" Grant asked.

The doctor ran a hand through his brown hair. "Why don't we have a seat in the consultation room? I can get you a cup of coffee and we'll talk."

"I just want to know about my son," Erina said with distress.

"I understand. We can sit down and I'll explain everything we know."

"Let's go to the consulting room, Erina. The doctor looks as though he could use a cup of coffee." Grant placed a hand on her elbow and guided her stiff body as they walked behind the doctor back through the doors behind the triage area, down the hallway that led to the examination rooms—or crash rooms, as the nurse had called them—and into a small, windowless office.

"Get some coffee if you'd like, Doctor," Grant said. "We'll wait right here."

"Thanks."

Erina turned to him the minute the doctor cleared the doorway. "And just who do you think you are, Mr. Kirby? Givin' orders and makin' suggestions like you owned the whole hospital?"

"I'm just trying to be polite. The doc is obviously bushed."

"What nonsense would you be talkin' now? The doctor is no bush."

"I didn't say he *was* a bush. He's bushed, as in tired. Look, Erina, I don't want to argue with you."

"Well, I don't want a fight either, but I'll thank you to leave my son's care to me."

Grant felt himself bristle at the suggestion that she'd done a good job so far. "Why? So you can ignore his heart problem another two months, drag him around on a night like this, then depend on the kindness of strangers to pay for his medical bills?"

"I did no such draggin' about! I did everything I could. The doctors would not help me!"

"I find that hard to believe. Any county or city general hospital would have treated your son, even if you didn't have a penny."

"And I'm tellin' you they would not!"

"Am I interrupting?"

Dr. Cook stood in the doorway, holding a cup of coffee and looking just as tired as he did before.

"We're just discussing Colin's previous medical care—or lack of it," Grant explained.

Erina turned to the doctor. "Where I came from, the doctors told me that they could not fix his heart. They said I had to accept that he would not . . ."

She whirled away, covering her face with trembling hands.

"Oh, hell," Grant murmured, recognizing her pain in spite of the fact that she was lying through her teeth. She wasn't from 1896; her claims made no sense. Still, he placed an arm around her and offered her his shoulder to cry on.

Dr. Cook sat down in a chair. "Where are you from, Ms. O'Shea?" the doctor asked.

Grant urged Erina down to the couch, keeping his arm around her for support.

"County Kildare, Ireland," she replied with a sniff, "although now I live—"

"With me," Grant finished, knowing he couldn't have her spouting wild stories. They'd have her in the psychiatric ward while Colin was in PDICU. He couldn't allow that to happen, not until he understood the real reason she was here—and his reaction to her. "At the Galvestonian, on East Beach."

"How long have you been here?"

57

"Here?" Erina said, sweeping her arm wide to indicate the hospital.

"No, in Galveston. Was Colin born here?"

"Not exactly," Grant said, interrupting her.

"So he didn't have any medical care until now?"

"No. The doctors said they couldn't help him, as I've said," Erina answered.

"What difference does it make? I mean, he's here now, and he needs medical care," Grant said, perturbed by the continued inquisition.

"Oh, he'll get the best care we can offer, Mr. Kirby. But you've got to understand that denying a child medical attention is tantamount to child abuse. Unless there's a good reason Ms. O'Shea hasn't had her son treated, then I'm afraid I'll have to notify our social workers to do an evaluation."

"What does that mean?" Erina asked, turning her frightened gaze to Grant.

"That means that they might take Colin away from you." He felt as if he'd just kicked a puppy. She looked so shocked, so afraid. And he also realized that he didn't want Colin taken away, nor put in some foster home or warehoused in a state facility. He was just a little baby.

"No," she whispered. "Not my Colin. He's all I have. I love him with all my heart."

"Ms. O'Shea, I find it hard to believe that any doctor told you there was nothing that could be done for your son's condition."

"Just exactly what is his condition, Doctor?" Grant asked, turning the conversation away from Erina's maternal deficits to a more concrete topic. After all, no one was going to believe her story. There was no sense exposing her to more ridicule or possible confinement as a mental case.

"It's known as Tetralogy of Fallot. There is an obstruction in the right ventricular outflow. This causes hypoxia, or a lack of oxygen, which is why he doesn't have normal color. Hypoxic babies usually have a gray skin tone, with tinges of blue around their fingers, toes, and mouth. When he's in distress the blue color intensifies."

"Can the obstruction be removed?" Grant asked.

"Oh, yes. Surgery is very successful in these cases. After the procedure his heart should be fine."

"You'd be performin' surgery on his heart?" Erina asked, her tone skeptical.

"Yes. As I said, it's a fairly common procedure. Within a week he'll seem like a different child."

"Holy Mother of God," Erina whispered.

Grant felt as though a weight had been lifted from his own heart. He didn't understand why Colin's health and Erina's happiness seemed so important to him. Hell, he'd known them for less than three hours. But the fact was, he felt responsible, for both their physical and emotional well-being. "When can the surgery be performed?"

"I'd like to treat him with antibiotics for his lungs for a few days. He should be off the ventilator tomorrow. If there are no complications, then we should be able to do the surgery in two or three days."

"And he'll be well?"

"Yes. He should be fine. Normally, children recover within a week or two. Of course, he'll need checkups after he leaves the hospital, but there should be no long-term effects of the procedure."

"It *is* a miracle," Erina said softly.

"No, just medicine. Which brings me back to my original question: Why didn't you seek another opinion? You obviously knew something was seriously wrong with your son." Dr. Cook was frowning again, which wasn't a good sign, in Grant's opinion.

He stepped in before Erina could say anything crazy. "I think that as long as there is a question of his previous care, Ms. O'Shea should talk to my attorney before answering any more of your questions. Nothing personal, Dr. Cook, but I think she should be protected from saying anything that may sound a bit . . . well, odd, to you. After all," Grant said, looking at Erina, "Colin is a Kirby. He deserves legal protection as much as he needs medical attention."

"All I want is a truthful explanation," the doctor said, clearly irritated.

"But I already told you—" Erina said.

"Yes, she did, and you said you didn't believe her. Let's just leave it at that for now. We'll be glad to answer any other questions later."

"I'm too tired to argue with you right now. Obviously these other issues will need to be addressed—soon." Dr. Cook finished his coffee in a big gulp. "I'll take you upstairs now to see Colin, Ms. O'Shea. He's been given a sedative to help him relax, so don't be surprised that he's sleeping."

"All right," she said. She looked up at Grant with big, searching eyes. "Will you go with me?"

Something inside him performed a little flip at her raw emotions—fear, confusion, love for her child. The force of her feelings overwhelmed him. "Of course," he said hoarsely.

They followed the doctor down the hall to the elevators, then upstairs to PDICU.

"Erina, you're exhausted. Let's go get some breakfast and sleep for a few hours. Colin is doing fine."

Erina looked up from the bed where her son lay. His little chest rose and fell with the regularity of deep sleep, but she suspected that was caused more by that ventilator, as the doctor called it. Since she'd been sitting beside him, Colin had barely moved.

"What?"

"I said we should get some breakfast."

"What if he wakes up and cries? What if he needs me?"

"The doctor explained that he's sedated. He'll sleep peacefully for quite a while."

"But how will he eat?"

"I'm not sure. Let's ask Dr. Cook."

Mr. Kirby—she couldn't be so familiar as to use his first name, although he'd insisted—helped her up from her chair. She felt very tired, despite the brief nap earlier, and her body ached with weariness. And her breasts hurt terribly. If she didn't get to feed Colin soon, she would be in much more pain, she was afraid.

They walked to the central desk, where nurses and doctors congregated. Dr. Cook bent over some paperwork, writing with one of those pens that didn't need inkwells.

"Dr. Cook," Mr. Kirby said.

The doctor looked up.

"Erina has some questions."

"Yes, Ms. O'Shea?"

"Well, I was wonderin' how you feed a baby with his little mouth filled with the . . . the ventilator."

"I meant to ask you what he's been taking—formula or breast milk."

Erina felt herself blush. "Doctor, could I speak with you privately?" she managed to whisper.

"Of course."

They left Mr. Kirby standing beside the desk, looking slightly irritated. She couldn't worry about him right now; she had more pressing concerns.

She and the doctor stood in a small alcove where supplies seemed to be stored.

"I don't know what you mean by 'formula,' but Colin is being fed the natural way."

"Okay. So I'll get you a breast pump and we'll insert a feeding tube so he can get what he's used to. I suppose your milk agrees with him. He seems a little underweight but generally healthy."

Erina couldn't meet the doctor's eyes. She felt so embarrassed to discuss such issues with a man, especially a young man, even though he was a doctor. "I'm not sure what you mean by a . . . a . . ."

"Feeding tube?"

"No, the other."

"A breast pump?"

"Yes, that one."

"It's a device to relieve you of milk so it can either be fed to the baby later or, as in Colin's case, where he needs a feeding tube."

"Oh." She frowned. "I don't know how to use this . . . thing."

"I'll get one of the nurses to help you."

Erina sighed in relief. "Thank you."

She and the doctor walked back to the desk.

"Well?"

"I'll be seein' a nurse before I leave," Erina announced.

"What's wrong?"

"Nothin' that you need to concern yourself with," she said, looking away from him. Just the idea of explaining her "problem" caused another round of embarrassment.

Dr. Cook smiled. "This won't take long. Why don't you go into the ICU waiting room, Mr. Kirby?"

Erina could tell he was anxious to know what was going on. Well, she wouldn't tell him. The man was entirely too bossy, putting his nose into other people's business way too often. She held her head as high as possible and walked beside the doctor. Even though they walked farther and farther from the desk, she could still feel Mr. Kirby's blue-green eyes burning a hole in her back.

Of course, having him take charge when Colin needed him was wonderful. Mr. Kirby had been wonderful, sweeping her to the hospital in that— what did he call it? A Cherokee?—had been miraculous. At the time she'd been terrified, and she hoped that the Cherokee didn't always travel so fast. She wasn't looking forward to another trip in such a vehicle. She much preferred the slow but predicable electric trolleys on Broadway.

Dr. Cook showed her into a room. She heard him talk softly to a nurse at the doorway; then the nurse was inside the room with a strange device.

"If you'll just unbutton your bodice, Ms. O'Shea, I'll show you how to operate the breast pump. You can take this with you to relieve the pressure whenever you need to. The milk can be stored in the refrigerator and brought to the hospital later."

Erina had no idea what a refrigerator was, but she wasn't going to ask this woman. Besides, she would probably be at the hospital all the time, so that wouldn't be necessary. She had no place to stay, or to work, so perhaps she could just nap in the chairs when she wasn't with Colin. She wasn't sure what she would do for money, but she'd think about that later, she decided as she finished with the buttons on her dress.

The Holy Mother wouldn't have sent her to this time only to abandon her. She would provide. . . .

"Now, the slip."

"The what?"

The woman pointed to the chemise.

Erina blushed and undid the ribbon ties. She'd never been unclothed around another woman except Mrs. Abernathy, who had assisted with Colin's birth, and even then she'd kept on her nightgown.

She jumped when the nurse placed the pump over her naked breast.

"This is what you do," the woman said, and Erina blushed all over again.

Over Erina's objections that she should stay inside with her sleeping son, Grant managed to guide her outside just as the sun came up, peeking through the palm trees along Harborside Drive. The cold front must have pushed through while they were in the hospital, because the clouds were gray and broken, showing the deep rose sky behind them. Grant rubbed his arms against the chill. He knew that Galveston's high humidity made it feel at least ten degrees cooler than the surface temperature, but this morning seemed especially frigid. He should have grabbed a jacket before he left the condo, but he'd been a little occupied with saving Colin's life.

At least Erina had that long, ugly cloak. He wondered where she'd gotten it; maybe in a thrift store.

She stopped and looked around the parking lot, her eyes wide as she stared at each car, at the Ramada Inn across the street, at the power lines. Her shocked glance took in the skyline. "And where would we be goin' to get breakfast?" she asked softly.

"I could use a real breakfast. You know, bacon, eggs, toast, hash browns. How about you?"

"I usually have tea and a scone."

He smiled down at her. "No wonder you're so tiny."

She looked at him as though he'd insulted her. Most women would simply say, "Thank you."

"Are you sayin' we're goin' to a restaurant?"

"Of course. I'm not up for cooking this early in the morning. Besides, I'd have to go to the grocery store first. There's not much in the fridge."

"What is a 'fridge'? "

"A refrigerator."

"Oh. You have one of those?"

He frowned. "Of course. Everyone has at least one refrigerator." His mother had four, if you counted the freezer in the garage. Where in the world had Erina lived that she didn't have such modern conveniences?

Ah, yes: 1896. She was sticking to her story.

He unlocked the door of the Cherokee, which he'd moved to a restricted parking spot earlier. At least he hadn't been blocking the emergency entrance the whole time.

"I'm glad you have a refrigerator."

He raised his eyebrows. "I'll show it to you when we get back to the condo. I didn't realize you'd be so impressed by my appliances."

"I'll not be goin' back to your home, or to your condo, with you alone, Mr. Kirby," she said indignantly.

He helped her into the car and slammed the door. Dammit, he hadn't offered his condo so he could take advantage of her. He hadn't even planned to invite her to stay with him, although he was pretty sure there wasn't anywhere else for her to go.

He eased behind the wheel and started the engine. "Put on your seat-belt," he reminded her.

She fiddled with it. She looked at it. But she didn't slip the end into the latch.

"Here, let me help you," he said finally. He showed

her what to do, how to release the catch, before putting on his.

"Texas has a seat-belt law."

"Oh," she said, staring straight ahead, her hands clenched on the armrests. "I'm hopin' you won't be drivin' this Cherokee quite so fast."

"Of course not. Breakfast isn't an emergency." He put the Jeep into gear. "You're not a backseat driver, are you?"

She looked at him as he backed out of the parking space. "I'm not any kind of driver, except for a pony cart. We had one in Ireland."

"I'm glad to hear that. My mother got her backseat-driver's license at the same time I got a learner's permit."

Erina shook her head, as though he was speaking a foreign language.

"Never mind," he said. "It's not nice to speak ill of one's own mother."

"That's the truth of it," Erina said. "I barely remember my own mum. She died when I was seven, back in County Kildare."

"I'm sorry. It must have been tough growing up without a mother."

"My da was a good parent."

"That's great." Grant felt a shaft of pain at the thought of a "good father." His own had been a drunk, someone who got by on a few sober hours every day before lunch. Then he could do deals like no one else. Everyone in the real estate business knew that Randolph Kirby was a force to be reckoned with—as long as you caught him at the right time. After a three-martini lunch he'd sell you a piece of prime commercial property for the price of a four-rental unit in a depressed neighborhood. Without Brian Abbott around to repair the damage, Kirby Investments would have been bankrupt years ago. Instead, the family business now had holdings worth upward of 400 million dollars. Grant was proud of his own accomplishments in turning the company around, but he never forgot that Brian had been there when the real possibility of disaster had loomed daily.

Grant turned onto Sea Wall and headed west. Few cars were on the road this early. He made good time to one of his favorite breakfast spots.

Erina watched as he unbuckled his seat belt. She did the same, smiling when she was successful. Despite the exhaustion that was etched on her features, she looked beautiful as the soft, pink light of dawn bathed her pale skin.

Their gazes met and held. Grant lost himself in the depths of her eyes, in the emotions she revealed. She seemed so vulnerable. He wanted to wrap his arms around her, protect her from the world, show her that he cared for more than the welfare of her son.

Before he could stop himself he reached toward her, ran a finger along her satiny cheek, and watched her lips part in response.

He was going to kiss her. Despite her lies, despite whatever plan she'd concocted, he wanted her.

He leaned near, watching her eyelids lower, hearing the soft sigh that escaped her parted lips. She smelled of lemons and wool; nothing seductive, yet even her scent aroused him.

Just as his lips were about to touch hers, she let out a shriek and slammed herself against the door.

"Ahh, you're a smooth one too," she said breathlessly, her eyes wide and frightened, "but I'll not be seduced by another Kirby man." She thrust her chin in the air. "I'm not the breakfast you'll be havin'."

Grant blinked, shook his head, and eased back into his seat. He was going mad; there was no other explanation. He'd almost kissed a woman who claimed to be from 1896, who said she was here because of a miracle!

He'd never been tempted to follow in his father's footsteps before, but Erina O'Shea just might drive him to drink.

Chapter Four

She'd never seen so much food assembled for common folks. Only at one of the Kirbys' parties or balls could one find so many meats, different types of bread, fruits, and desserts, all for the choosing. As she stood near the buffet tables, arranged in a rectangle with bright lamps and glass above, she could only stare and wonder where to begin.

"Aren't you hungry?" Grant Kirby asked.

He'd insisted she call him Grant, which seemed entirely too informal. Sweet Mary and Joseph, she didn't need to think of him with any more familiarity than she already did! Then her stomach growled, distracting her from thoughts of the man who stood nearby, an expectant look on his face.

"That I am," she said. The slice of cheese and apple she'd eaten last night after nursing Colin were a distant memory. *A hundred years distant*, she reminded herself.

"Then help yourself. Or I could fill a plate for you, if you're not feeling well."

"I can fill my own plate, thank you, Mr. Kirby." She thrust her chin high and tried to appear in the best of health. To tell the truth, she was dead tired and wished she could sleep as easily as Colin, all snug in that hospital room, with machines that kept him breathing and doctors who knew how to fix his little heart.

"Grant," he said, snapping her back to the present.

"Yes, well, I'm thinkin' that sounds too forward." She looked away from his penetrating gaze and stepped up to the buffet. The smells of breakfast assailed her, making her stomach growl once again. Hoping he hadn't heard her unladylike reaction to the food, she chose a strip of bacon, and then a biscuit.

"Calling me 'Mr. Kirby' makes me feel as if I'm your boss. And we both know you don't want me to tell you what to do."

She looked up at him, standing so close. She felt the heat of his body on her side and back, as warm as the steam rising from the warming pans of the buffet. "I appreciate all you've done for myself and Colin, but I have to remind you that he's my son."

"Believe me, I'm not likely to forget that point," he said. She was sure she heard censure in his voice.

So, he did condemn her for having a child out of wedlock. She sighed as she put some fried potatoes on her plate. She shouldn't be surprised; most people found her guilty of sin, as well they should. She'd encouraged Jerrold Kirby's attentions, although at the time the glances and smiles had seemed so innocent. How was she to know he'd expect so much more? Her mother had died long ago, and her father hadn't told her what men expected from a girl.

The fact that she was only a maid, and he was the son of the house, had seemed romantic to her. Until the night they were alone in the house. . . . She shuddered as she placed some grapes on her plate. What had happened between them had not been romantic. Not in the least.

"Erina?"

She blinked away the memories. "I'm sorry. What did you say?"

"For a moment I thought you'd fallen asleep standing up. Are you sure you're okay?" He looked down at her with such compassionate eyes that she wanted to lean into his strength and warmth. He might think her a sinner, but he was concerned nonetheless.

She tensed, straightened her backbone, and breathed in the air of reason. "I'll be fine. Just a spot of hunger."

She'd have to be more careful around this Mr. Kirby. He seemed to be a truly kind man, deep inside, but that was all the more reason to be a lady in his presence. She'd make sure he didn't mistake any innocent smiles or shy flirting for invitations to assault her person. She'd never repeat the mistakes of her past, even if the despicable act itself had given her Colin.

When they arrived back at their "table," which was really a pub booth similar to ones she remembered from her childhood in Ireland, the tea she'd ordered had arrived, along with coffee for Grant . . . Mr. Kirby.

"You didn't take very much," he observed, looking at her plate.

His own was piled high with small, round pieces of ham, strips of bacon, eggs, biscuits, fried potatoes, and gravy. A smaller plate held an assortment of fruit and pastries. She'd already decided he must labor outdoors for a living; he obviously worked hard at his occupation, else he'd weigh far more. She hadn't detected a bit of fat on him, not in the few times she'd been close. Not that she'd tried to notice, of course.

She turned her attention back to her own plate. "I'll be fine, thank you."

When she opened the small metal pot that held her tea, a string with a piece of paper fluttered against the side. "What's this?" she asked absently.

"You did order tea."

"Yes, but . . ." She bent closer to the little pot and inhaled the steam. Tea, all right. She tugged on the string and retrieved a small, square bag. Apparently the leaves were inside. "This is very handy," she said, looking across the table.

He stared back, a frown line between his eyes.

"You needn't glare at me, Mr. Kirby. I'm enjoyin' the novelty of these new . . . inventions."

He broke off eye contact and shook his head. He pushed a basket of pink and white paper envelopes, each printed with black and red letters, toward her. "If you like tea bags, you'll love sugar packets," he said before returning his attention to his meal.

They ate in silence. Erina enjoyed the food, and the novelty of having someone else wait on her for a change. As she satisfied her hunger, her attention

73

turned to the other diners. All of the women in the restaurant wore either trousers like men or scandalously short skirts and dresses. She supposed she was the one who looked out of place, dressed in her long woolen gown and cloak. No one else's attire resembled hers in the slightest.

The men were dressed similarly to Grant Kirby. Not one of them wore a suit, so she supposed this establishment appealed to working-class people. As she finished her tea, she wondered if there was a wealthy section of town any longer, or if all the people worked at various jobs. Everyone here dressed so casual.

"Feeling a little different?"

She turned her attention back to the man sitting across from her. "Yes, I am. I'm dressed in a different style, but it's more than that. I'm thinkin' that these people aren't servants, but they're not wealthy either. I'm not sure if I belong here, or if I should be havin' breakfast somewhere else."

"Is wealth that important to you?"

"No," she replied automatically. "But how can I tell the difference? How will I know—"

"You sound like a reverse snob. Do you always measure someone by the size of their bank account?"

"No! And you shouldn't be so sensitive about the subject. Not everyone has wealth and power. Many of us need to work—"

"Wait a minute. You think I have no money?"

"I'm thinkin' you work for a livin', like most of us. You're a large, healthy man, Mr. Kirby. You spend a good deal of time out of doors, and I've noticed you don't have the hands of a man of leisure."

"So you've decided I'm a working Joe."

"It's no sin," she said, leaning forward slightly. "The wealthy have the money and the power, here and in Ireland. Always have and probably always will. It's not so easy breakin' into their circle, although I know quite a few merchants who ended up with mansions on Broadway not too many years after gettin' off the boat."

"And what about you? Are you looking for a wealthy man to set you up with a house and money?"

She turned her head away, sinking back into the booth as she felt her energy drain away. Around the restaurant, young women served coffee and tea, diners clinked their spoons and talked to family and friends, but the sounds seemed far away, and the delicious smells of the buffet faded in significance.

Erina remembered the wealthy man who had caught her fancy, then ruined all her illusions about becoming a wife who could entertain in her own parlor, shop with her lady friends, buy the latest bonnets from Paris.

All those silly, girlish notions had vanished on a hard cot in a third-floor bedroom, destroyed by a man whose wealth made him believe he was above the moral principles that the rest of the world were supposed to live by. While imported greenery and red velvet bows adorned the stairs below, Christmas candles lit the mantel in the drawing and music rooms, and unwrapped presents awaited their final destinations in wardrobes and drawers, Jerrold had presented her with a gift of his own. "Merry Christmas, Erina," he'd said with a half-drunken leer as he'd plunged inside her unwilling body.

She couldn't suppress a shudder at the memory.

"Erina?"

"No," she said quickly, glancing back at Grant Kirby's handsome tanned face. "I'm lookin' for no man to care for me or my son."

"But you'll accept my help."

"Only because the Blessed Virgin sent me to you. I'm not sure why she did such a thing, but I'm not one to argue with God in Heaven."

"So you'll take my money?"

"And why would I be needin' your money? Maybe my Colin needs some help, but I'll not be expectin' a thing from you."

"Let me go along with your fantasy for a moment. You say you're from 1896, you arrive in my condo with only the clothes on your back, and yet you say you don't expect anything from me. How do you expect to live, to eat?"

She straightened her spine. "God will provide in his own way, just as he did in gettin' Colin to a hospital that can repair his heart."

"God will provide in the form of *me*," he added.

"I'll work for my livin' if I need to. I'm not afraid of work. I can act as a lady's maid or sew a fine seam. If no one will be needin' me for those jobs, I can cook their meals or clean their houses. I may be a mite on the small side, but I'm strong and hardy. Don't you be worryin' about me, Mr. Kirby. I'll make my way just fine until my Colin is well."

He smiled at her as he finished his coffee. "You're

a spirited, single-minded woman, Erina O'Shea, whatever your story. I must admit that I'm intrigued enough to want to find the truth in all this, even if you do have me marked as a patsy."

"What you mean by a 'patsy' is beyond me, but I'd remind you that I'm not fond of bein' called a liar."

"Fine. Then I think you have a wonderful imagination."

He rose from the booth and pulled out a wallet from the tightly fitting light blue denims he was wearing. Erina watched in outright fascination at the way the pants molded to his body as he moved. Did all men wear their clothes this tight? Perhaps Mr. Grant Kirby had gained a bit of weight and couldn't afford new garments.

He tossed a five-dollar bill on the table.

"And what would that be for?" she asked, amazed that he'd throw money around in such a manner.

"For the tip. What did you think?"

"The tip! Saints preserve us, but that's enough for the week! Have you no sense?"

He smiled again, showing very strong white teeth, but there was no amusement in his eyes. "As I've said before, you have your historical details down pat. Let's cut this foolishness and get out of here. The breakfast crowd is waiting for tables, and I think we've exhausted the subject of my money—or lack of it—for the moment."

He took her elbow, helping her rise from the softly padded cushions of the bench. Erina stared at the five-dollar bill, wondering at the cost of things in this time. Surely not that much. How would she live when she'd be expected to tip a waitress five dollars for bringing her a cup of tea?

But then Grant Kirby retrieved her cloak, folded it over his arm, and guided her toward the restaurant entrance. At a small desk he handed another woman the piece of paper from the waitress, along with a twenty-dollar bill.

"But—"

"Not a word, Erina," he warned in a low voice.

The woman gave him change and thanked him, as well she should for paying such high prices for food. Even if this was an elaborate buffet. Everyone else in the restaurant had seemed to expect the food, hadn't commented on it that she could tell. Perhaps they were accustomed to such excess.

They made their way past many people, standing or sitting on benches near the entrance. All looked at her oddly, lingering on the long dress and cloak. Erina held her chin high and walked out alongside the man who thought she was lying about her background.

Erina doubted that she would become accustomed to this time, these people, even if she stayed here for weeks, months, or years.

Grant drove through the early morning traffic, back up Sea Wall toward the hospital. The sun had risen over the east end of the island, the sky was cloudless and blue, and the wind wasn't blowing like a Blue Norther. The waves to his right weren't covered in whitecaps, as they had been early in the morning. Nature had calmed down considerably since Erina had shown up in his condo. He wished he could say the same.

His hands gripped the wheel tightly, almost of their own accord, probably because he had no other outlet for his frustration. Erina was the best little actress he'd ever seen, ready for an Oscar or an Emmy with her portrayal of a misplaced nineteenth-century domestic. Never had he seen anyone more into a role.

Of course, the other explanation was that some traumatic event had caused her to block or distort her memory. Perhaps her son really was the product of rape. If so, Erina could have constructed a fantasy to explain her son—fill in the gaps in her life she simply couldn't face. She probably needed therapy, but she didn't appear crazy. To her, the world of 1896 would make more sense than 1996.

And if this business of time travel was her fantasy, she'd certainly done her research. From his family's background on the island, his interest in the Galveston Historical Foundation, and his study of Texas history, he knew she was accurate, down to the last detail.

"Where did you get that dress?" he asked casually, willing himself to relax. Getting frustrated about her origins or mental health would do no good.

"I made it," she replied quickly.

He glanced at her, noticing the way the fabric molded to her petite but surprisingly lush body. He suspected she was breast-feeding her baby, which accounted for the roundness pressing against the bodice of the gray wool. If she weren't feeding Colin herself, he supposed her breasts would be small, firm, and high. Just right for—

"Damn," he muttered as he swerved around a car that had slowed to enter the turn lane. In a moment he asked, "Would you like to stop and get something more . . . appropriate? Maybe some jeans and a sweatshirt?"

"I've noticed that I'm the only person dressed this way," she said, running her fingers over the edging on her cloak, "but as you already know, and were so *kind* as to point out, I have no money to buy new clothes. I suppose these will do until I can find myself a job."

"I don't mind buying you a change of clothes."

"I'll not be spendin' your money, Mr. Kirby."

"What if I insist?"

"I doubt you could drag me into a dressmaker's shop and force me to purchase a new dress. Even in your time, I'm thinkin' that would be considered poor manners."

"You're right. I've never seen a woman yet who had to be dragged shopping."

"If you'll just get me back to the hospital, I'll be sayin' good-bye."

He turned onto Harborside, feeling oddly out of place. Erina was going back to her baby, but where, Grant wondered, would he go? Back to his nice, quiet condo? Perhaps catch a football game at noon, call out for pizza, have a few beers?

Somehow, the prospect of relaxing this weekend held no appeal. Not when a baby lay in the Pediatric ICU critically ill, and his mother didn't have a penny to her name. Hell, she couldn't even buy herself a cup of coffee or a snack if she needed one. She knew next to nothing about medicine, so how could she make decisions about her son's care? What if the social worker began asking her questions? If she gave them the same crazy answers she'd given him, would they confine her to a psychiatric ward for evaluation, or report her to child welfare? Colin might be taken away, made a ward of the state. What kind of medical attention would he get then?

No, there was no way he could drive away and leave Erina O'Shea to fend for herself at UTMB. He'd already determined that she needed a keeper; it seemed that the job fell to him.

He pulled into the parking garage, then went up two levels before he found a space. As he turned off the engine, Erina twisted in her seat to look at him.

"Thank you very much for all you've done. I'm sorry I've been such an inconvenience to you, but as I said before, a higher power than me made that decision. I'll be goin' inside now. Colin may be wakin' up soon."

She fumbled with the seat belt, a frown line in her forehead and her mouth moving in what he suspected was a silent litany of Gaelic curses. Grant smiled. She had spunk and, he suspected, a lot of passion locked inside.

The latch finally released, and the belt slid quickly over her chest and shoulders. He had the strongest urge to follow the same path with his hand, to see if her breasts were as firm as they appeared. Instead, he clenched the wheel as she reached for the door handle.

"Wait," he said.

"I need to get inside. I want to see my Colin."

"I'll go with you."

"There's no need, Mr. Kirby. You've done enough."

"Are you trying to get rid of me, by any chance?"

"Of course not! But I'm certain a man such as yourself has more important things to do than follow me around. I'm just goin' inside to sit beside my son and wait for the doctors."

He thought he heard a tiny catch in her voice. "I'll make sure you're settled and see how he's doing."

"There's no need."

"Yes, there is. I care what happens to the little guy. I'm the one who drove him to the hospital, remember? I think he trusted me to take care of him. I can't let him down now."

"That's blarney you're talkin'. Colin's too young to know what's happened to him." She turned away, looking out the car window as though the gray concrete columns fascinated her, and touched the corner of her eye with her fingertip.

"How do you know?" Grant said softly. "He might remember me."

"And what if he does? Will you be here tomorrow, and the day after, and after that?" She shook her head. "No, Mr. Kirby, I think it's best that I go inside now. You've been a bonny fine help, and I appreciate what you've done, but Colin is my responsibility."

Grant felt a moment of pure panic. She was brushing him off! "Look, you may be Colin's mother, but

I've already told the triage nurse that I'd be financially responsible for his medical bills. That is, if you don't have insurance. You don't, do you?"

"No, I have no insurance," she said with another frown. "I didn't know such a thing was possible."

"Then I'll be paying his hospital bills. For that, I want to make sure he has the best care."

"I'll be seein' that his care is fine," she said defensively.

"And do you know a lot about modern medicine? What will you do if the doctors ask you to make a decision between two procedures? How will you know what to say?"

"Well, I'll . . . I'll ask them to explain. Really, Colin is not your responsibility."

"Yes, he is."

"I'll not be arguin' with you over my son, Mr. Kirby."

"Call me Grant."

"I'll do no such thing. Now I'll be sayin' good-bye and thank you."

She managed to get the car door open, then slammed it shut. With a firm step, she walked away from the Jeep. Grant calmly unfastened his seat belt and opened his door. She'd stopped in the middle of the drive, looking around the dimly lit garage.

"Lost?" he said, walking up beside her.

"This is a very confusin' place," she complained. "All these letters and numbers, and those signs just say 'exit.' I want to know where the entrance is to the hospital." Her dark blue eyes looked suspiciously bright and luminous.

"Follow me."

"You're not goin' inside with me, Mr. Kirby."

"Grant."

"Colin is my son." She followed him to the stair-well.

"Funny, but by now I'm sure most of the staff be-lieves he's my son too." Grant opened the metal door and she walked through.

"And why would they be thinkin' such a foolish thing? I've not told them he's yours."

"Maybe the name?" Grant suggested with just a hint of sarcasm as they walked down the short flights.

"Oh. The name. Well, there's no help for it. That's his name, by rights. I'll not change it so you'll look better."

"I'm not worried about it." Not now, anyway. When word reached his mother, his lawyer, and the press, then he'd worry. And backpedal, and run dam-age control. "For now, all that matters is that Colin get well."

"That's very understandin' of you," she said cau-tiously. "I wish his real da were as nice." Erina paused as he opened the door to the ground level.

Grant didn't say anything. He hadn't known his great-grandfather, and had no idea what type of man he'd been. Perhaps he had been more concerned for social position than for his responsibilities. And that left Erina—

"Dammit," he swore, taking her elbow and guiding her toward the hospital entrance.

"What's the matter now?"

"I'm doing it again. I'm believing your story."

She paused as he opened the glass doors, looking up at him with those big, honest dark eyes. "Well, you were bound to sooner or later. After all, it's the truth."

About nine o'clock that night Grant called Brian Abbott, attorney and operating manager of Kirby Investments, at home. He waited as the phone rang once, then twice, rubbing his forehead where a slight headache pounded away like the surf below.

Brian picked up on the fourth ring. "Hello?"

"Hey, Brian. It's Grant."

"What's up, son?"

"Not much. Well, that's not true. Something has come up this weekend, only I don't know how to explain it."

"Just spit it out. You're not in some kind of trouble, are you?"

"No, not me. I met a girl this weekend."

"Dammit, son, I told you to be careful around those beach bums. You weren't smoking any funny stuff on the beach, were you?"

Grant laughed. Brian was hopelessly fixated on the evils of the sixties, from the perspective of someone who worshiped the fifties. "No, nothing like that. This girl showed up inside my condo, in the middle of the night. I have no idea how she got there."

"Sounds kind of kinky."

"Not really. She had a baby with her."

"A baby? You're pulling my leg."

"No, unfortunately, I'm telling you the exact truth.

The baby has a heart problem. I ended up taking him to UTMB, and I've been kind of . . . involved with his care ever since."

"Grant, are you trying to tell me something? Look, if this girl is claiming it's your kid, we'll put the stops to her—"

"She's not," Grant said quickly. "You wouldn't believe me if I told you who she says is the father. Anyway, I just kind of feel responsible. I mean this kid is so little . . . and he's a cute fellow. He needs an operation."

"And I suppose this woman has no money," Brian said with a heavy dose of cynicism.

"Yeah, she doesn't. And no insurance either. I told them at UTMB that I'd be responsible."

"Hell, son, do you know how much heart surgery can cost?" Brian roared.

"I don't think I'll be too surprised. But dammit, Brian, I didn't have any choice. The kid needs the surgery."

"That's what charities and welfare are for. You contribute enough to both to pay for a dozen operations."

"But those are kids I haven't seen. I held this little guy in my arms, and he just seemed so . . . helpless."

"You're a soft touch. I suppose this woman is encouraging you. Is she offering to compensate you for your generosity?"

"She's not like that," Grant said firmly. "As a matter of fact, she's fighting me every step of the way. And she's not really a woman. More of a girl. She says she's twenty."

"Hell, Grant, you sound like you don't even believe how old she is! Why don't you just write her a check and get your butt on back to Houston? I always said your running off to Galveston every weekend was a bad idea. Too much free time. She could even be jail bait. Think about how that would look in the papers, not to mention what it would do to your mother."

"I can't just write a check this time. The kid's having surgery soon. I'm going to stay down here for a few days." He didn't dare tell Brian what the hospital staff already thought—that Colin was his son. Of course, Grant had to admit that he'd done little to dissuade them from the assumption.

"Dammit, Grant, don't start getting involved with this charity case. If you want to make sure the kid's okay, I can have someone take care of it."

"I don't want someone else doing this. Colin is my responsibility."

The phone was silent for just a few seconds. "Not unless you're his daddy," Brian finally said. "Is that what you're saying?"

"I am not the father of this baby," Grant said firmly. "I never saw the mother until yesterday. Well, actually, early this morning." *God, had it only been that long?* "But I'm still going to be here until he's out of danger."

Grant imagined that Brian was pacing his study, running his hand over his receding hairline and frowning.

"Okay. Whatever you say. I can put off that meeting with the Phoenix property management firm, and I'll get the numbers together for the loan payments due on those two shopping centers. I'll fax them to you tomorrow."

"That would be fine. I'll be in and out. I'll take the cel phone in case you need to reach me."

"Grant, are you sure about this?"

"I'm sure, Brian. Hell, I can't explain it, but I've got to be there. Colin needs me. And Erina needs me."

"Erina, huh? Are you sure it's the kid you're concerned about?"

"Good night, Brian. I'll call you tomorrow."

"You do that, son. And keep your perspective on this one. I don't like women who show up out of the blue. They're up to no good."

"Brian, I have yet to figure this one out. But when I do I'll let you know."

"You do that. And don't forget that your place is back here, not frolicking in the sand in Galveston. Damn place is too much like a vacation."

Maybe that's why I like it, Grant thought to himself. "Look, Brian, Mother is going to call you on Monday to discuss that brick warehouse by the Catholic church. You know the one?"

"Yeah, I know it."

"Well, talk it over with Dottie. Unless we're going to lose a ton on it, go ahead and see how much it will cost to turn it over to the diocese."

"Damn, son, you're getting to be a real softy. You'd better get back here fast."

"I'll be back as soon as possible. If there are any complications, I'll call you."

Grant hung up the phone, his thoughts focused on Erina and her motives. How had she gotten into the condo? He'd checked the security system; it was working fine. If she wanted his money, why was she putting up such a fight? And if she wanted more than that, why wasn't she using his obvious attraction to her as an advantage?

Erina O'Shea made no sense whatsoever. But that wouldn't keep him from trying to poke holes in her story about being from the past . . . and making sure her son had a future.

Chapter Five

Grant paused outside the doorway to Colin's room on Monday morning, two paper cups and a bag in one hand, the *Houston Chronicle* under his arm, and a balloon bouquet bobbing over his head. The drapes were still drawn. Erina lay curled on a cot beside Colin's crib, a blanket covering her legs and bottom.

She was still wearing the damned gray dress.

He walked into the room and sat down in the chair next to the cot. "Erina," he whispered.

She barely stirred, partially rolling onto her back.

Grant swallowed the sudden lump in his throat. She looked so young and vulnerable lying there. Long, curly black hair spread out over the pillow and sheet. From this angle, looking down her body from the head of the cot, he could see her black lashes resting against her pale skin, just above the faint pink blush that was entirely natural. He had two strong, equal urges: to protect her and to make love to her.

"Erina," he said again. He took the lid off the tea

90

he'd gotten at the doughnut shop and waved it beside her nose.

She jerked awake. "Colin?" she whispered.

Grant retreated, smiling at her sudden transformation from sleeping beauty to concerned mother. "No, he's still asleep. Beside, he's too young to fix tea for you."

"Good mornin'." She rubbed her eyes. "I was dreamin' again."

"About the dress shop?"

"Aye. I was halfway asleep in my own bed above the shop, with Colin beside me, and my heart was just so sad. . . ." She frowned, as though she couldn't quite grasp the essence of the dream.

"It was just a dream."

She sat up, pushing her hair back with both hands. The thick curls spread out over her shoulders, arms, and chest. "What are you doin' here so early?" she said in a throaty, sleepy voice.

"It's not that early. I wasn't sure how late you'd sleep. Or did you get much sleep last night?" He kept his voice low so he wouldn't wake the baby, and also because it enforced the sense of intimacy he felt, sitting in this hospital room.

"I slept very well, thank you. Colin had a good night."

"He looks so much better."

"The doctor came by last night and said he was doin' very well. He doesn't have pneumonia. His lungs were just a bit congested."

"That's great. Did he say when the surgery was scheduled?"

Erina swung her legs over the side of the cot and accepted the cup of tea. "Tomorrow," she said faintly. "That's so soon."

"I know, but it's best to get it over with."

"My mind knows that, but I'm afraid. He's such a wee babe. I can't believe they're goin' to operate on his heart."

"They do it all the time. Colin will be fine."

"How can you have such faith in the doctors?"

"It's not a question of faith; it's a matter of statistics. The survival rate is very high for this type of surgery. And the doctors here are among the best in the country."

"But to put him in the hands of man . . ."

"As opposed to the hands of God?"

"Yes."

Grant sighed. They really did have a major difference of opinion when it came to beliefs. She trusted in what she couldn't see more than she did in the tangible abilities of trained professionals. He, on the other hand, wasn't even sure that a greater power guided the universe.

He sipped his coffee, glad that it was strong. He hadn't slept well last night, not after leaving Erina alone at the hospital yesterday afternoon. But she'd refused to leave Colin's side after they took him off the ventilator and moved him out of ICU. Grant had been useless after a while, roaming the halls until Erina had insisted he go home to rest. He had—reluctantly—after warning her not to discuss her circumstances to anyone, particularly the social worker.

He'd left her alone at the hospital because he didn't know what else to do, beside making a complete fool of himself.

Since mothers often stayed in the hospital with their infants, they'd set up a cot for her in Colin's room. At least the room was a private one; Grant had seen to that. He was paying the bill, so there was no question of insurance restrictions. And since there was a Kirby wing at the hospital, Erina and Colin had received the best of everything.

Grant was sure everyone assumed Colin was his son. They probably thought they were caring for the Kirby heir, perhaps a future philanthropist who would donate megabucks because his life had been saved at the hospital when he was only an infant.

Okay, let them think it. Grant knew that denying his relationship to Colin would only amuse the staff. They'd still give him knowing looks. The false premise no longer angered him, especially since his mother hadn't found out yet.

"Here, have a doughnut," he said, handing Erina the waxed bag.

"And what's a doughnut?"

"Come on, Erina. Everyone has eaten a doughnut."

"Not me."

"Okay, I'll play along," he said, unwilling to let her continued playacting ruin his mood. "They're good. They're like round pastry, I guess, only fried. Real junk food. I got several different kinds because I wasn't sure what you'd like."

"I'm not sure either," she said, peering into the bag.

"Try the chocolate-covered glazed. They're my favorite."

Erina removed one slightly messy doughnut from the bag and held it with two fingers of one hand. "Are there no plates or forks?"

"No, you have to eat doughnuts with your fingers. It's a tradition."

"If you're sure . . ." she said slowly. She opened her mouth wide, obviously trying to keep the gooey chocolate off her lips. Her small, white teeth bit into the confection and the expression on her face changed from wariness to pure pleasure.

"Oh, this is very good," she said after chewing the first bite. "Very good."

Grant smiled. Tenderness welled up inside him, an emotion he hadn't felt in . . . hell, he didn't know when he'd felt that way. "I'm glad you like it."

Just then Colin let out a little cry. Grant pivoted to watch the infant flail his arms and legs. He looked as if he was ready to let loose with a real bone-chilling wail.

"I need to pick him up. Do you have a napkin?" Erina asked. She held a sticky, half-eaten doughnut in one hand, a cup of tea in the other.

"I'll get him," Grant volunteered, not at all certain why he'd opened his mouth. What did he know about infants? Other than holding his receptionist's daughter a few times and watching a diaper being changed at a company picnic, he'd never been around babies.

Grant set down his coffee, far away from Colin so he wouldn't knock it over and get burned. He tied the balloon bouquet—an impulsive purchase at the gift shop downstairs—onto the crib rail. Then he reached down and scooped the fussing baby into his arms.

Colin quieted immediately. "Spoiled already, aren't you, buster?" Grant said to the infant.

Colin looked up at him and gurgled. Tiny spit bubbles appeared at the corners of his mouth. "Very attractive trick. What else has your mother taught you?"

"She's been teachin' him to sleep a bit longer at night," Erina answered, standing behind Grant.

He felt her breast brush against the back of his arm. The contact lasted less than a second, but he couldn't help his body's involuntary reaction to her nearness. Every nerve seemed to tingle, as though he'd been exposed to a large dose of static electricity. He wanted to put the baby back in his crib, turn to the mother, and kiss her senseless. He imagined that she'd taste better than any doughnut he'd ever eaten.

"You'd better take him," Grant said huskily. "I'm not sure how long I can keep him entertained."

"You're very good with him," Erina said. "I believe you have the touch."

I'd like to show you what kind of touch, Grant said to himself. He wondered if passion had an Irish accent. Instead of alarming Erina with his totally inappropriate case of lust, he eased the infant into her arms, savoring the feel of her firm, round breasts against his forearm.

Perspiration dotted his forehead when he moved away from the crib.

"What's the matter, Mr. Kirby? You're not feelin' ill, are you?"

"No, not at all. It's just a little warm in here. I think I'll . . . I'll just get a breath of fresh air."

He grabbed his coffee and the newspaper, then hurried out of the room before he made a fool of himself over a too-young Irish girl and her cuddly infant son.

"Ms. O'Shea, we're going to take Colin around for his tests. If you'd like to get away for awhile . . ."

The blond nurse looked at Erina, who knew her rumpled gray dress, tangled hair, and scuffed half-boots were far beyond acceptable. She hadn't washed or brushed her hair in over forty-eight hours, and her teeth felt like an old, nappy blanket.

She would appear completely unappealing to anyone. So why had Mr. Kirby looked so closely at her, as though she were not a slovenly mess? When he'd left yesterday she'd thought perhaps she wouldn't see him again. He had no reason to return, having delivered Colin safely to the hospital and the doctors. Perhaps he felt some responsibility for her son; but then, the memory of their near kiss in his Cherokee sprang into her mind, and she felt heat creep into her cheeks.

At the moment when he'd leaned toward her, his intentions had been clear—to press his lips to hers. And just for a second she'd wanted to believe that he hadn't meant to seduce her. That a kiss was all he wanted. That his interest was honorable. But she knew now how wrong she could be about men, and she wasn't going to allow another man to deceive her with enticing looks and sophisticated manners.

So why had he brought her those sinfully delicious pastries called doughnuts and the large group of "Get Well Soon" balloons for Colin? She hadn't even known what to call the shiny, silver objects until the nurse mentioned them.

Erina pushed her unruly hair back with one hand and looked again at her son. He lay in the crib, his attention focused on a colorful, bobbing display of animals. The nurse had called the device a mobile and shown Erina how to wind it up so it played music. She'd never seen such a music box before, but Colin seemed fascinated by the red pig, the blue cow, and the green horse.

"Ms. O'Shea? We need to get Colin to the lab for his tests."

"I can't go with him?"

"Really, it would be best if we take him ourselves. The tests are all routine. They'll take about two hours, so that will give you some time of your own."

Erina spread her heavy, wrinkled skirt with both hands. "I suppose I could do somethin' about my clothes, if you could show me the facilities."

"I can do better than that."

She turned to Mr. Kirby, who'd appeared suddenly in the doorway. Erina had hoped to avoid the man for a while longer. She had too much of a tendency to become flustered around him. And whenever he took charge of a situation, as his tone of voice just now had implied, her life became much more complicated.

"I just need a place to freshen up," she said, lifting her head and looking him straight in the eye. She wasn't about to give in to his bossiness, even if he had been very nice this morning.

"You need a shower and a change of clothes."

"That would probably make you feel much better," the nurse added.

And make me smell a wee bit better. "I didn't bring a change with me," she said defensively.

"That's all right. We can remedy that."

"Mr. Kirby, I'll be remindin' you of my situation," she warned.

"Ms. O'Shea, I'm very well aware of your situation," he countered, placing his hands on his hips. Although they'd gently cradled Colin not so long ago, his hands seemed very large and masculine, his fingers framing the front of his pants an arrogant advertisement.

She tore her eyes away from his . . . hands, and looked again at his eyes. He seemed determined, yet amused by her unwillingness to give in on this point. Did he expect her to challenge him in front of the nurse, a stranger? But then, Mr. Grant Kirby wasn't much more than a stranger himself, and a demanding one at that.

"I'll go somewhere to launder my dress," she said, trying a compromise.

He watched her a moment longer, his brows drawn together. Then his expression lightened, his posture shifted. "Okay. That's a deal." His attention switched to the nurse. "How long did you say we have?"

"About two hours for the tests, but don't worry. When he gets finished we'll give him a bottle, if you'd like to prepare one, Ms. O'Shea, and he can take a nap." The nurse glanced at Colin with true affection, mentioning the task of feeding him as though it were a subject suitable for discussion around a man.

Erina felt her cheeks grow warm at his close scrutiny. "I'll be takin' care of that when Mr. Kirby leaves the room," she announced softly, turning back to the crib. Colin kicked and waved his arms, preparing for a full-fledged fuss. "At the moment I need to feed my son."

"I'll get the car."

She heard his footsteps as he walked toward the door. "Don't be too long, Erina. I don't want to get a ticket."

"A ticket? Would you be goin' to the opera house?"

He laughed. "Very clever. I'll see you downstairs in twenty minutes, okay?"

She had no idea what was so funny, but at the moment she wanted very much to put Colin to her breast. She ached from the fullness. "Very well, Mr. Kirby. Just go along with you now. I have to care for my son."

She waited until both visitors had left the room before unbuttoning her bodice and picking up her son. Erina wrinkled her nose with distaste as she prepared to nurse Colin. Her chemise stuck to her breasts and smelled faintly sour from the leaked milk. She used a damp cloth from the adjoining facilities to wash up.

"Your mother does need a bath, little one," she

crooned to her hungry son as she sat in the chair by the window, "but she doesn't need charity from that particular Kirby."

"Give me whatever you have that will fit a woman this size," Grant said, placing Erina's old, gray dress and black boots on the counter of a trendy boutique on The Strand.

The saleslady picked up the dress with two fingers—looking inside the neck for a size, Grant supposed.

"I don't know what size she wears, but she's real petite. About this tall," he said, gesturing to the center of his chest. "And she's small all over, except . . . well, she's just had a child, and . . ."

"I think I understand," the woman said after a moment of silence. She gave him a tentative smile, held up the dress, and then looked at the bottom of the boots. "Let me see what I can do."

She walked across the store to a rack. Grant shifted from on foot to the other, then leaned his hip against the glass counter. Whatever he brought back to the condo, Erina was bound to look better than she had in that antique-style dress. If she looked more like a twentieth-century woman, maybe she'd quit throwing around lines about being from the past. And maybe if she looked less like a homeless waif, he'd quit feeling so damned protective.

The woman returned with a red leather jacket and miniskirt, then held up a pair of matching knee boots. "This should be her size," she said, smiling.

He eyed the flashy outfit. On any other woman he'd

say definitely; if you could get away with wearing it, you should. But not Erina. She wasn't the red leather type, even if it might make her appear older and more sophisticated.

"I'm sorry. I think she's too modest for that particular outfit."

The saleslady's smile faded.

"It's very nice, but perhaps you could find something a little longer." Lace and flowers came to mind, along with buttery soft wools and cashmere, and silk against her pale skin. "Something soft and feminine. And undergarments."

"Of course." The woman returned to browsing the racks. Grant crossed his legs at the ankle and resumed his pose against the counter.

A few minutes later the saleslady was back, her arms full. She placed the items on the counter.

"I found two skirts—midcalf, a blouse, a two-piece sweater ensemble with a darling ecru lace collar, and a pair of wool slacks. I think a size four petite should fit her. Also, I took the liberty of suggesting some accessories."

Grant glanced at the selections briefly. All of them looked modest enough for Erina. "Fine. Do you have shoes here, or just boots?"

"Yes, both."

"Throw in a couple of pairs, and maybe some brown or black boots. And purses. I don't think she has a purse. Maybe some stockings and things. Just whatever else she'd need. She . . . lost her luggage."

"Yes, of course." The saleslady seemed a bit baffled by his carte blanche attitude, but hurried off again.

When she returned she said, "We don't carry foundation garments here, but the store next door should have a good selection."

Grant stared at her, his mind a blank.

"Undergarments, sir. If she's nursing, she'll need a special bra."

"Oh, right. I forgot about that."

He wondered if Erina's historical accuracy extended as far as going without a modern bra. Probably not. He decided not to take a chance. What size would she wear? He had absolutely no idea, except that her breasts appeared too large for her petite frame.

Grant shook his head, then pulled out his wallet and chose a credit card. Months had passed since he'd bought a gift for a woman. His accountant would no doubt raise his eyebrows at this purchase—and the one next door, at the "foundation" shop.

A few minutes later he walked out of the lingerie store with a total of four shopping bags and two dresses on hangers. One of the bags held Erina's old dress and boots. He probably should have given them to Goodwill, or, better yet, a drama company specializing in period productions, but he didn't know if the old garments meant something special to her. If she'd sewed them herself . . .

What was he thinking? Women didn't sew their own clothes anymore, did they? From what he'd read in economic and business journals, domestic production or even retail fabric couldn't compete with the price of foreign clothing imports. The big discount retailers had the market cornered on low-price merchandise. No, Erina O'Shea hadn't sewed that dress herself, unless it was another part of her elaborate story.

He placed the bags in the back of the Jeep, then drove back to his condo. Erina should be getting out of the tub about now . . . and discovering that she had no clothes.

"Mr. Kirby?" Erina wrapped the thick bathing robe tightly around her, then clutched the lapels together at her neck. Peering through the barely open door, she tried to locate her host, but all she could see was a short hallway and a wall of mirrors in the living room.

"Mr. Kirby?" She pushed open the door into the silence of his home. *Condo*, she corrected herself, whatever that might be. To her, it looked like an apartment.

But she was still amazed by the bathtub and the abundance of warm, fresh water that had flowed from the shiny brass faucet. And toothbrushes and paste that made your mouth feel so clean and fresh. He'd shown her shampoo for her hair and fresh towels that were as thick as ten bathing sheets. After telling her to place her dress and boots outside the door so he could have them cleaned, he left her alone with the amazing inventions.

This world was truly foreign, even more so than when she'd first come to Galveston from Ireland in 1888.

The thick carpet cushioned her footsteps. In the

mirror she saw herself, a dark shadow in the hallway, moving slowly with her hand fisted at her throat.

A frightened shadow, she thought. She didn't want to appear so cowering. She hadn't felt like cringing in a long time, not since Jerrold Kirby had swaggered out of her room in the wee hours of last Christmas morning. As a matter of fact, she did all she could to put on a good show of courage and spunk.

No, she *wasn't* a frightened shadow, even on the inside, when she didn't know what had happened to her host and her clothes. A woman grown, and a mother besides, that's what she was! She smoothed the lapels flat over her upper chest, straightened her spine, and walked into the parlor.

The room was empty.

So was the kitchen, with all those modern white boxes, and the bedroom near the bathing room that she'd used, and the other bedroom, which contained the largest bed she'd ever seen.

His bed. Did he sleep in it alone? She hadn't even asked if he had a wife.

He didn't act as though he had a wife.

She was still staring at the bed, with its unmade cover and sheets so dark a blue that they matched her Colin's eyes, when she heard the door open.

"Erina?"

She hurried from Mr. Kirby's bedroom but didn't get out in time. He stood in the hallway beside the kitchen, holding a number of sacks, as she stepped from his room into the parlor.

"Mr. Kirby. I was just lookin' for you."

He smiled in a way that made her nervous.

"You look good in my robe." Walking toward her, he placed the bags on the sofa. She resisted the urge to back up, to clutch the robe more tightly to her. Surely he wouldn't try to . . .

He walked over to a desk and picked up a few sheets of paper that seemed to come out of a machine that looked something like the telephones they had at the hospital. He seemed to focus on the writing on the paper, but his words were definitely for her. "You don't have to look at me as if I'm going to molest you. That's not my style."

"I don't know what you mean," she said, straightening her spine again. "And I'm only wearin' your robe because it was the only decent garment you left me!" In truth, she'd washed and donned her chemise, but it was wet and clung to her like a second skin.

"I'm well aware that I took your clothes."

"Well, I'll be askin' for my dress back. You had no right to take my property. And I want to go back to the hospital. Colin will be—"

"He's probably still having tests. And he'll be fine. The nurses all love him, or haven't you noticed? They treat him like their own little china doll."

"He's a bonny boy."

"Yes, he is, but it's his mother I want to discuss."

"What do you mean?"

He reached inside a bag and started pulling out garments. "I wasn't sure of your size, so I took your old dress and boots to the shop. The saleslady was very helpful. I hope these fit."

He pulled out beautiful flowing fabrics, soft knitted garments, blouses with lace. Erina felt her eyes go wide, heard the soft sound of the sigh that came from her.

"What have you done, Mr. Kirby? I cannot pay for these clothes!"

"I don't expect you to." He placed two pairs of shiny slippers on the table beside the sofa. "But I'm tired of seeing you in a dress that would be more suited to a museum. So these are for you. If they don't fit, we can exchange them later. And there are some . . . undergarments in this bag. I wasn't sure of your . . . size."

"I'll not be acceptin' clothes from you. That would be most . . . improper."

"Erina," he said, placing his hands on his hips again, "don't argue every point with me, okay? Pick you fights carefully. I'm bigger and more persistent than you, and in the end I'll win."

"I wasn't aware we were havin' a battle, Mr. Kirby."

"And stop calling me 'Mr. Kirby,'" he said, stepping close to her. "That's what people called my father, and he's long gone. I'm Grant, not 'mister.' Just Grant."

She tried to ignore his nearness. The clothes he'd purchased lay about the sofa, draped like a very decadent offering on his own personal altar. Well, she couldn't be bought for a few handfuls of garments.

"I'll not be familiar with you, Mr. Kirby. I'll not—"

His hands gripped her arms, his head tilted to the side, and before she could say another word his lips sealed hers.

Warm. That was the only sensation she felt as all

other thoughts flew from her mind like leaves in an autumn breeze. She closed her eyes in a purely instinctive gesture; she simply couldn't stare at him as his lips moved against hers. He pulled her closer, until their chests met, until she felt the coolness of his leather jacket and the warmth of his large, hard body. The wet chemise pressed even closer to her heated skin, making her shiver. He smelled like sea and salt wind, and clean, strong man. She moaned in response.

Suddenly another memory flashed in her mind, of a strong man kissing her, holding her. There had been no one there to stop him, either. She felt panic rise up like bile. With a strength she wasn't sure she possessed, she broke away from his grip, panting, clutching the robe closed over her heaving chest. "No," she whispered. "I'll fight you. I'll scream—"

"Erina, no," he whispered, reaching out a hand. "I didn't mean . . . Dammit, I wasn't trying to force you."

"No. I won't let you do this." She backed up until she was pressed against the cold glass of the large windows.

He stopped a few feet away. "I'm sorry. I was just angry. And I wanted you to say my name."

"I gave you no rights," she whispered. "I didn't know you thought . . ."

"We're not talking about me now, are we?" he asked softly. He watched her until she hugged her arms around herself, then looked away. Looked into the past.

"No," she finally said. "He came to my room on

Christmas Eve. I . . . I didn't know what he wanted. I thought that he . . . but I was a foolish girl."

"And now you're a much wiser woman?" he asked gently.

"Yes," she said, feeling stronger now. "Yes, I am much wiser. And I know what men like him—like you—really want from a girl or a woman who sews and cleans."

"You know nothing about me."

"All I know is that the Holy Mother sent me here, to your home, so Colin could be saved. I appreciate all you've done for him, and for me, but I'll not be payin' you back with my body."

"Did I ask?"

"You . . . what do you mean?"

"I mean I didn't ask you into my bed. All I did was kiss you when I should have taken a deep breath and cussed a blue streak."

"But you—"

"Miss O'Shea, when and if I ever want you in my bed, you can be sure I'll let you know. Directly, succinctly, and without offering a bribe. Now why don't you take those clothes into the guest bedroom and see if any of them fit? Then we can get our butts over to the hospital and see how your son is doing."

He pivoted and stalked across the room, while Erina stood near the cold glass, the beach far below, and wondered what she'd done to make him so angry.

Chapter Six

"You look . . . great," Grant said, wondering how she could appear any younger or more vulnerable than she did right now. He'd thought the modern clothes would make her somehow different, but he hadn't anticipated his gut reaction to the maroon-flowered, flowing, soft skirt, the sweater that molded itself to her breasts, the lace collar that framed her sweet face. No, he'd hoped to feel differently about her.

Instead, he wanted to put his arms around her, erase that wide-eyed, uncertain look from her face, tell her that everything was going to be fine.

He wanted to kiss her again. This time in passion, not in anger. He wanted to ease his tongue between her lips and—

"Mr. Kirby."

"Grant," he said automatically. His anger had long since vanished, replaced by the damned sense of protectiveness. And tenderness. He recognized the feeling but didn't welcome such a compelling emotion. He'd only known her for two days—much too short a time to develop any real affection. And God, she was so young.

"I cannot be callin' you 'Grant.' That wouldn't be proper."

"Everyone calls me 'Grant.' Just try it. Say, 'Okay, Grant.'"

"I don't think I can do that."

"If you keep calling me 'Mr. Kirby,' I'm just going to have to remind you that's not my name. Maybe by kissing you again, just so you realize who I am." That should convince her. She wouldn't welcome another kiss, not after she'd pushed him away—after he'd frightened her by reminding her of the past. Damn. There he went again, believing her stories. She had *not* been raped by his great-grandfather. She was *not* from the past.

"Look, Erina, why don't you just say it?" he asked in a very reasonable, bland tone. "Just call me Grant. That's all I'm asking."

She narrowed her eyes and crossed her arms over her chest. "I'm thinkin' that you're takin' advantage of me by wantin' me to be familiar with you."

He spread his arms in a gesture of conciliation, then let them drop to his sides. "I haven't asked for a thing, Erina, except this."

She seemed to consider that fact for a long time but, in truth, it must have been only seconds. "Oh, very well. *Grant*. Now, are you happy?"

"No. I'd like to hear you say my name in a sentence. Like, 'I really like my new clothes, Grant.'"

"That's what I wanted to talk to you about. I'm not

sure I can be wearin' these clothes. The skirt's a wee bit short."

He glanced at the hemline, which almost reached her ankles. "Actually, it's a little long."

"I know other women wear their skirts short, but I'm not feelin' comfortable showin' my ankles. I need my boots, at least. These shoes are no help at all."

"You want to blend in, don't you? Why not be practical? You do need to wear hose, probably, or your legs and feet will be cold. The temperature is still pretty cool."

He watched a faint pink blush work into her cheeks. "There's also a bit of a problem with the . . . hose you brought to me. I cannot understand how to wear them. So if you'll just return my boots and stockings, I'll be gettin' dressed."

"Oh, for Pete's sake, Erina, you can stop acting when it's just the two of us. Every woman knows how to get into a pair of panty hose. I think they do it just to irritate men, but that's another story."

"I'm tellin' you, Mr.—"

"Grant."

"Grant. I'm tellin' you that I do not know how to wear that infernal garment. I want my own things back."

"Your dress needs to be cleaned, your boots could use a good polish, and you've been wearing the same stockings for at least two days. Now put on the panty hose and we'll go to the hospital."

"I don't know how to get the blasted things on!"

Grant stalked into the guest bedroom and picked up the offensive hosiery from the bed. He was a thigh-high stockings man himself. He especially liked black ones with wide lacy tops. But he wasn't going to think about that right now. He'd be better off concentrating on the fax Brian had sent earlier, and the one that told him his balance sheet was going to take a serious hit for those balloon loan payments.

"Look," he said to Erina, who'd followed him to the doorway of the bedroom, "you just wad them up like this, all the way down the leg, and put them on, one leg at a time. Don't stick you fingernails through the material. I understand that's a problem. And make sure the tag is in the back."

She folded her arms across her chest. "And where did you learn so much about ladies' undergarments?"

"Commercials. Plus, I've taken off my fair share in the past. Now why don't you try it, unless you'd like me to do it for you."

She unfolded her arms and marched into the room. "I'll try the blasted things, but I cannot imagine why women of your time would wear something that's so difficult, when a simple pair of stockings would work just fine."

"My sentiments exactly," he said with a smile. "Next time I'll buy you some stockings."

"You'll not be buyin' me another thing!"

"I don't know how you're going to stop me."

"I'll just not see you again," she said, thrusting her chin in the air.

"Oh, really? And how are you going to keep me away?"

"I'll tell the hospital not to allow you in the room."

"I'm paying for that room."

"Then I'll move to another one. I'll put Colin in the charity ward, as long as the doctors will save him. But I'll not be ruled by any man, especially one so bent on bein' contrary."

"I'm not contrary. I'm one of the most reasonable, even-tempered people I know." That was the truth. His attorney, accountant, and property managers often told him that he was as businesslike as they come. He'd always thought that was the highest compliment they could give him.

"I doubt you're too fair-minded about your own traits."

"I'm fair-minded about everything."

"Then understand that wearin' these clothes does not feel right to me," she said with passion. "I've never worn a dress so short. I'm not a woman of your society."

"You are now," he said, passing the panty hose to her. "And for as long as you're here you'd better dress and act the part of a woman of this time. I'm not sure of your game, or even if you're completely aware of the story you're telling. But I know that if the authorities think you believe you're from another time, they'll take Colin away. He'd be saved, he'd have the surgery, but you might never see him again."

"No one's takin' my Colin away. I came a hundred years into the future to save him, and I'll be keepin' my son."

He placed his hands on her shoulders and looked into her dark blue eyes. "Then put on the hose. Put on the shoes. Don't worry that people can see your ankles. Most women wear clothes much less modest than these."

In a moment she slumped, the fight gone out of her. "You're right. I must do whatever is necessary to save Colin."

"I'm sorry I've had to tell you what to do. I think maybe we're both just a bit headstrong."

She smiled ever so slightly. "I'm thinkin' maybe you're right."

"I'll try not to tell you everything to do, Erina, but I have to interfere when I feel it's necessary. I've come to care about Colin . . . and about you. I mean, I feel responsible for the two of you. Together. I don't want him to be taken away from you."

"I'll not let anyone take him away. He's my son."

"I know that. I'll do what I can to help, but you've got to cooperate. They could put you in the psychiatric ward and charge you with child abuse if you tell them Colin didn't get medical attention because he's from 1896."

"You're right," she said in a small voice, looking away. "I'll keep my thoughts to myself from now on."

"Good girl," he said, giving her shoulders a pat. He was trying his best to think of her only as a friend-in-need, a too-young mother, an off-limits, out-of-town visitor. Even though he wanted nothing more than to kiss her again and again . . .

"I'll put on the hose now and I'll not say another word about the skirt bein' too short. Then can we go to the hospital?"

"Of course," he said neutrally, giving her a smile. "I'll be ready whenever you are."

She stayed with Colin all night, rocking him back and forth on the cot, just as she did back in her rooms above Mrs. Abernathy's shop. When he slept she watched, leaning over the crib until her eyes misted and she had to turn away before she woke him with her sniffles. Toward dawn she fell asleep in the chair but jerked awake when the nurses came into the room.

"Is it time then?" Time to take him away, to cut open his chest?

"Not yet. I just need to listen to his breathing and his heart," the blond nurse said softly. She placed a metal disk on Colin's chest and the two connecting tubes in her ears.

"How is he?" Erina asked, leaning forward so she could watch her son sleep.

The nurse moved away from the crib. "He's fine. The anesthesiologist should be by in about thirty minutes."

Erina rubbed her temples. "Which doctor is he? There's so many, I forget."

"You really are from the country, aren't you?" the nurse asked with a smile. "The anesthesiologist makes Colin fall asleep and keeps him that way until after the surgery."

Erina walked into the hall with the nurse. "How do you know where I'm from?" she asked warily.

"Mr. Kirby. He explained how you've only been in Galveston a short time, and that you're from the countryside in Ireland. I think it's so romantic. I mean, meeting Mr. Kirby and all. I got the impression he was in Europe last year," the nurse said with a grin and a nudge of her arm. "He's a real hunk."

"A hunk of what?"

The nurse laughed. "Oh, honey, I don't have to tell you, do I? Did you know he was named one of Houston's most eligible bachelors? I wonder if he'll be on that list next year," she said with a smile and a wink. She walked away, shaking her head and chuckling.

Erina frowned, then returned to Colin's room. She wasn't sure what *hunk* meant, but she did get the impression that the nurse believed Grant Kirby was her son's father. And that maybe they'd met in Ireland. Had he planted those ideas in the nurse's mind? Or had she come to those conclusions on her own?

She didn't have time to think of him right now. She wanted her thoughts to be of Colin, and the trauma he would soon undergo. She still had a hard time believing that his heart could be operated on, but all the doctors and nurses told her it was so. And the Blessed Virgin Mary *had* sent them here in a true miracle.

She sat back down in the chair, looping her arms around her knees as she leaned toward the crib. The soft fabric of the new skirt rubbed against her skin, reminding her of the way Mr. Kirby had brought home the bags full of beautiful garments. Even though the styles were foreign to her, she had to admit they were comfortable—especially the special corsetlike device for nursing. How had he known to buy that particular item for her? The thought of him describing her needs to a salesclerk made her blush.

And he had been more than generous with his money. Did he have enough money to buy her such expensive gifts and to pay for Colin's surgery? If a cup of tea cost five dollars, what must this room and the services of all the doctors be worth? Surely more than Mr. Kirby would earn as a laborer.

Somehow she would find a way to pay him back, even if she had to work for years after Colin recovered.

Would she stay in this time? She had no idea. The longer she stayed, the less odd her new surroundings seemed. Only in her dreams of Mrs. Abernathy had she revisited her own time, and then she'd felt like a stranger looking in on the rooms of the dressmaking shop, gliding up the narrow, dark stairs to her own rooms, seeing the place she'd stayed for nearly a year, the place where Colin had been born and had almost died before she took him to St. Mary's Cathedral. She'd seen herself, working on the quilt, which seemed much more finished than when she'd left. Was it a dream or a premonition that she would return to the past?

Or would this be her home? A part of her hoped that she could stay. There were so many wondrous things. The experience was similar to her reaction to arriving in Galveston after living all her life in the Irish countryside. The island had been so . . . alive. So bustling with activity. People working, warehouses under construction, loads of cotton arriving by train, to be processed and shipped around the world. Wagons crowded the streets near the docks and business district, while trolleys made their rounds on Broadway.

She'd loved Galveston from the moment she'd stepped off the boat. Her da had also, jumping into his job landscaping the Kirby estate with such enthusiasm that Erina had laughed each night as he explained the new plants, the variety of flora that could grow in this climate. He'd loved his job, right up until three years ago, when he'd dropped dead between the bushes he was planting in Mrs. Kirby's new rose garden.

She'd like to see more of Galveston in this time. If she did stay, she'd need to know the customs and the town. And if she went back to her own time . . . well, then she'd have the memories of what was to come.

And memories of Mr. Grant Kirby, great-grandson of the man who'd taken her innocence, a cousin, many times removed, to her own son.

Colin moved restlessly, stuffing a little fist in his mouth. Erina sat beside the bed, leaning on the rails of the crib, and smoothed his downy hair.

"How much longer?" Erina asked, fidgeting in her waiting room chair. "He's been in surgery for three hours."

"There's really no way to tell. The doctor said three to five—"

Erina jumped up and began pacing the waiting room floor. "I need to know! I cannot stand the waitin' a minute longer."

Grant watched her as she echoed his own feelings.

118

He'd arrived at the hospital that morning just in time to see the little guy before the anethesthiologist arrived. Erina had drawn within herself, obviously terrified of the surgery her son was about to undergo. Grant had held Colin, put his arm around Erina, and stood with her as they carried the boy away.

He felt as though Colin were his own son. He felt like a little bit of his heart had gone with the boy.

"What can I do, Erina? Do you want me to get you something to eat or drink? Or I can ask the nurse for a sedative for you, if you're too upset."

She whirled back to face him. "I just want my son, whole and healthy, and not cursed for what I—" She cut herself off with a fist stuffed to her mouth. Her face showed the distress of a mother in pain, but not just for her child.

He got up and walked to where she stood, placing his hands on her upper arms. "What are you talking about?

She wouldn't meet his eyes. "It's my fault that Colin was born with a bad heart. He's bein' punished because of my sins."

"Your sins? What could you have possibly done that would be considered a sin?"

She broke away from his hold on her arms and turned toward the window. "I encouraged his father. I thought he . . . I was a foolish girl."

"You've said something like that before, only I got the idea that he took advantage of you. What did you do, smile at this guy? Flirt with him? Ask him to your place and then change your mind?" Grant wondered who Colin's father really was. A high-school sweetheart? A one-night stand? Was he tall, short, dark, light? But what did it matter? No matter who the biological father might be, Erina obviously had received no support from the jerk.

"I . . . I did smile at him. I allowed him to think that I would welcome his attention. I was angry before when I talked about him, and you might have noticed that I have a bit of a temper." She shook her head. "That doesn't matter. I should not have looked at him, or been more than polite. I was a servant in his home."

"Listen, Erina, I don't know where you've been for the last ten years, but let me update you: This is not your fault. You have every right to say 'no' at any time, even if you're both naked and breathing hard. If you were out on a date and he didn't stop, that's called 'date rape.' And if you were an employee . . . well, what he did goes way beyond sexual harassment. Men know the bounds, even if they don't want to admit it."

"No, you don't understand. He didn't know any such thing. He was just takin' what he thought was offered."

"You're making excuses for this jerk."

"He's your own great-grandfather! You should not speak so ill of the man."

"My God, I can't believe this! He *raped* you."

"The truth is that he would not have done so if I hadn't encouraged him."

"Erina, I can't believe you'd defend his actions. What happened to that spunky girl who called him a slippery eel? And quit saying my great-grandfather was the one. We both know that's simply not true."

"It is the truth."

Grant shook his head. Maybe she had been raped. A violation of that sort could certainly cause her to want to forget the facts surrounding Colin's conception. The guy needed to be prosecuted, if he'd gotten away with the crime, and to do that Erina would need to recall the actual events. But perhaps she wasn't able to distinguish the truth at the moment. She might need time or professional help. He could provide both, if only she'd give some indication she was willing to cooperate. At the moment she was sticking to the impossible time-travel story with a frustrating determination.

"Look, let's not argue about that now. How about we go visit Kirby House after Colin has his surgery and gets better? You can show me where all this allegedly occurred."

"The house is still there on Broadway?"

"It's a historic home. People tour it every day. Maybe you've already been . . ." He let his words trail off, hoping she'd admit to visiting the house, coming up with her outrageous story, and seeking him out when she discovered a Kirby heir still resided in Galveston.

"I've not seen the house as it is now. When I last saw it your great-great-grandparents were still livin' there, and Jerrold Kirby was just becomin' a lawyer."

Grant sighed. There was just no shaking her story. "Okay, whatever you say. I'll take you to the house as soon as possible."

"I'd like to see if Mrs. Abernathy's shop is still there on Post Office Street."

"Sure. We can drive by, stop in. I'll even take you to the Galveston Historical Society if you'd like."

"Do they have information on the past?"

"Yes. A lot of it focuses on the hurricane of 1900, though. Much of the island was wiped out. I forget how many thousands of people were killed."

"Oh, that's so sad. I'm sure many of the people I knew lost their lives. I hope Mrs. Abernathy survived. She was a dear, sweet woman. I do miss her so."

"I'm sure you do." No telling who was the model for the fictitious Mrs. Abernathy.

"And what of your family? Did they survive?"

"Yes, they were fine. They moved everything of value upstairs, then stayed on the second floor when the water rose. Almost everything downstairs was ruined."

"Even your granny's beautiful piano, I'd suppose. That piece was too heavy to move."

"My granny's piano? You mean the huge monstrosity with the claw-footed legs?" He'd heard that it had been damaged in the storm surge, but refinishers had done a remarkable job restoring the enormous piece to pre-hurricane splendor.

"Aye, that's the one. I've dusted those keys many times, wishing I knew how to play. Mrs. Kirby was a wonderful talent. She had a voice like a lark."

"She did?"

Erina's face took on a dreamy quality that made her even more appealing. "When they had folks over she'd often play and sing after dinner. I'd listen from upstairs, just thinkin' how grand it would be to have her talent."

"You did?"

"Aye. She was a fine woman to work for. Very fair to us, because her family was from Ireland and she understood how hard it was to come to another country with more dreams than money. That's why I thought her son . . . but never you mind. What's done is done."

"You thought her son would marry you and take you away from your life as a servant."

She blushed and looked away. "I've already admitted that I was a foolish girl, Mr. Kirby. You don't have to be remindin' me."

"There you go, calling me 'Mr. Kirby' again. Shall I kiss you now to remind you of my name?"

"I'm askin' you not to kiss me again. If you're a gentleman, like you said men should be, I'm hopin' you'll honor my request."

He placed his hands against her warm cheeks and tilted her face up. "I'm not sure if I'm a gentleman as much as I am a man, but I'd never harm you," he said softly.

She looked startled for just an instant; then her eyes grew soft and she seemed to melt against him. He felt the tentative brush of her breasts against his chest, the warmth of her body, the womanly smell of her filling his senses. How could he not kiss her, again and again, until she said his name in a sigh of satisfaction?

"Mr. Kirby? Ms. O'Shea?"

He dropped his hands and stepped back, feeling as

though the doctor had thrown a pitcher of ice water over him and Erina.

"Doctor, do you have news of my son?" she asked, her mood changing in an instant.

The surgeon looked tired but not grim-faced. "Yes, I do. Colin's surgery went very well. We were able to repair the obstruction. I'd expect a full recovery."

"Oh, thank you! Thank you." She whirled around between the doctor in front of her and Grant behind her, as though she didn't know what to do.

Grant solved that problem, placing his arms around her and holding her tightly, feeling her joy and energy like electricity, racing from her body to his. And then another feeling, warm and glowing, as joyous as a child's first Christmas, caused him to blink and hide his face in her hair for just a moment.

Colin had survived the surgery. He was going to be okay.

"He'll be in the ICU for the rest of the day and night; then he can probably be transferred back to a regular room."

"Can I see him now?" Erina asked, sniffing, breaking away from Grant's embrace and facing the surgeon again.

"In a little while. He's still in post-op. And don't be surprised that he's still under anesthetic. We keep the little ones sedated and restrained so they don't pull out their IVs and tubes. He'll have some bruising on his chest near the incision. It might look a little scary to you, but he's going to be fine."

"Thank you, Doctor. Thank you so much. This is truly a miracle." Erina clasped the surgeon's hands in what looked to be a very tight grip. He smiled in return.

"I'll be around tomorrow to check on him."

Erina whirled back to Grant as soon as the doctor left. "Did you hear? My Colin is going to be fine. Oh, I'm so happy I could dance with the joy of it!"

"I'm happy too," Grant said, catching Erina's hands in his. "I'm happy for both of you."

"I must thank Mary. She's the reason my Colin is alive today."

"There's a chapel in another part of the hospital. If you'd like to go, I'll take you."

"Yes . . . no, I'd like to go to St. Mary's, if the cathedral is still there. Do you know if it is?"

"Yes, it is. As a matter of fact, there's a legend that as long as the statue of Mary is on top of the spire, the church will be safe. It survived the hurricane intact, with no major damage to even the windows."

"The Holy Mother protects her own, I'm here to say," Erina said joyously. "Oh, can we go to the church? I'd be so grateful to give thanks to her there."

"Sure. Do you want to wait to see Colin?"

"Yes. I want to see my son, and then go to St. Mary's."

"Your wish is my command," Grant said with a smile. At the moment he felt like granting her any favor. Even if she pretended she was from the last century and that a miracle had occurred.

Chapter Seven

Erina enjoyed the drive to St. Mary's Cathedral; the Cherokee didn't travel too fast this time and she got a chance to see more of the changes that had taken place since 1896. When they'd gone to breakfast and to his home before, they'd stayed along the beach, on a road that Mr. Kirby—Grant—called Sea Wall Boulevard. He'd explained that the sea wall had been built after the hurricane of 1900, but Erina still had a difficult time understanding how the island had been raised so many feet in such a massive undertaking.

She looked away from the scenery outside the window and watched him drive. Both of his large, work-roughened hands rested on top of the wheel that steered the Cherokee. He looked straight ahead, his nose straight, his chin solid and strong. She knew from memory that when he smiled—a rare occurrence indeed—a dimple appeared in his cheek.

His hair brushed the collar of his jacket and curled under slightly. She wondered if it felt as soft as it looked. She wished she could reach out and touch the tawny curls, much as she would Colin's hair. But there was nothing childish about the way her imagination seemed to be working. The feelings Grant inspired in her were not motherly, and definitely not appropriate. Not when he'd made it clear that he would accept her affections—and that he wouldn't take them forcefully.

She was simply a guest in his time, and whether she stayed forever or just a few days, she had to think of Colin first and not allow her own nature to lead her astray. She'd done that before with Jerrold Kirby and had more than learned her lesson.

They drove through business and residential areas, passing many buildings that she recognized. The roads looked so very different though, and the cars— she'd learned that was the proper term for these modern carriages—parked along the sides of the road. So many of them! Did no one own a horse and buggy any longer?

"Do the trolleys still run down Broadway?" she asked, craning her neck to see what she could as they crossed that major street. The Kirby mansion was close, along with many other homes she hoped still stood.

"No, just buses."

"What are buses?"

"Come on, Erina," he said in an exasperated tone.

She continued to stare at him. Finally, he explained. "They're like trolleys, but not electric or pulled by mules. They have engines, like my Jeep. I think Galveston does have a trolley of sorts, but it's really a bus that looks like a trolley. There's a historic route and people pay to ride."

"I'd like to ride this new trolley," she said, distracted as she looked ahead for the church. Above the large palm trees and oaks stood the statue of a pale gray Virgin Mary, silhouetted against the bright blue sky, rising behind the cathedral like a protective mother.

"I think the parking lot is on the side of the church," he said as he pulled the Cherokee off the road and steered through an open area in a tall fence. He switched off the engine and turned to her. "Do you want me to come in with you?"

"If you would like." In truth, she didn't know how she'd feel about having him there inside the sanctuary as she gave her personal thanks for the miracle. She didn't even know if he was Catholic, although she suspected he was because all the Kirbys were.

"I'll walk in with you, but I think I'll stay in the back."

"I won't be long."

"Take your time. It's good to be away from the hospital."

"You needn't stay if you'd rather get back to your work," she said. "You've been more than generous with your time and money. I've been meanin' to tell you that I'll be payin' you back, but it might take awhile."

"Erina, I don't want you to pay me back. And I wasn't complaining about being in the hospital so often or so long. I did what I did because I wanted to help Colin—and you. Whatever I gave you was a gift, not a loan."

"But I'm understandin' that things are a lot more expensive now than I'm used to, and I know that you're not a wealthy man, so if—"

He unfastened his seat belt and turned to face her. "What?"

"Your hands. They're big and rough, like a workman. And you don't wear suits, just the denims and cottons of a working man. I'm not complainin', mind you. I think you look grand in them, but I know that you must work for your money, and you needn't spend it on me and my son."

"You can jump to the oddest conclusions of anyone I've ever seen. What are you trying to do, get me to admit how much I'm worth?"

"Mr. Kirby! I'd be doin' no such thing. It's none of my business how much money you have, and it's not even proper to discuss it with you. I'm just informin' you that I'll pay you back when I can."

"Erina, I won't accept a penny of your money. You're making me angry just talking about it."

"I told you it wasn't a proper subject."

"And I told you I have plenty of money to take care of you and Colin," he replied, scowling at her.

She would dearly love to ask him how he'd come by this money, if indeed he had any. Had he inherited it from his family? Surely that must be it. But if he had, he must still work—at something. Good manners forbade her from inquiring, no matter how she longed to know more about him. But how ironic that Jerrold Kirby's money was finally being used to help his son!

"I'll just be goin' into the church then," she said when he remained silent.

He got out of the Cherokee and walked around, opening her door. "You could have looked up my personal or family income in one of the Texas business journals." His eyes flashed, and a muscle in his jaw where that dimple sometimes appeared now jerked in repressed anger.

"I don't know what you mean," she said warily, hoping he didn't become abusive when he was in a temper. She didn't believe he was the type of man who would strike a woman, even if he was more than willing to tell her what to do.

"Don't you? Even though my mother is the primary stockholder, Kirby Investments is still my company. I run it. And we have assets in excess of four hundred million dollars."

With that announcement he took her arm and steered her toward the front doors of the church. She felt numb, her mind refusing to comprehend what he'd just said as her feet automatically moved her forward. As they neared a statue in the middle of a small garden, Erina dug in her heels and stopped.

"Four hundred million *dollars*?"

"Yes," he said before urging her on.

Lord in heaven! How did one man, or even one family, acquire that kind of wealth? Even if tea cost five dollars a cup, four hundred million dollars was too much to comprehend.

Then she entered the vestibule of the church, passed through the heavy oak doors that she knew so well, and slipped inside the darkness of the rear of the church. Finally, something familiar.

"Wait," she said, turning back toward the door. "I need to cover my head."

"You don't need to do that any longer."

"Are you certain?"

"Yes. I remember clearly when my mother gave away an entire closet of hats to charity."

"If you're sure . . ." She turned around and looked in wonder, expecting the cathedral to appear much the same as it had when it was only fifty years old, back in her time. But so much had changed! Instead of pews reaching almost to the doors, a strange sort of display had been erected. Colorful signs and banners, along with pamphlets of different sorts, covered the latticework walls and wooden table tops. There were brightly painted shields of each diocese, but she didn't recognize most of the names.

No, not even her church was familiar any longer. That realization filled her with sadness and a longing for something solid and real in this new world.

The holy water resided in the middle of this new area, so Erina knelt, touched her fingers to the liquid, and made the sign of the cross. At least that tradition had remained the same. As she walked up the aisle toward the altar, more changes became obvious. The beautiful gas lamps were gone, replaced by smaller ones that looked as if they should hold candles but appeared to have the glass bulbs she'd seen before in electric lamps. Gone was the communion rail. The whole area was now raised from the original floor by tiles of white and black marble. Behind the dais was a carved wooden piece that seemed too small for the area. Stained-glass windows faced each other high on the wall, but sunlight did not shine into the church there. She imagined that a wall had been added that blocked the sun.

Most of all, she thought as she approached the Virgin Mary's altar, the statue had changed. The face was different, looking down from a marble table instead of the sturdy oak one she remembered. But this was just an image of Mary, Erina told herself. She could still give thanks, even though nothing about the Holy Mother seemed the same.

What had happened to her statue, the one she'd prayed before with Colin? It must have been replaced long ago by some well-meaning bishop or due to an accident or natural disaster. The fact that she'd transcended time, that she was here when the statue of Mary was long gone, struck her with awe.

Erina knelt at the marble rail that fronted the statue. "Holy Mother, I'm here to give thanks to you for savin' the life of my son Colin. You granted me a miracle, and guided the hands of the doctors as they operated on him. And I want to thank you also for sendin' me to this new time, and lettin' me experience all the wonders of this world."

She stopped her prayer and turned toward the back of the church. Just as she thought, Grant Kirby sat in a back pew, hands folded across his chest, looking at her. Four hundred million dollars. That was unbelievable. Incomprehensible.

She quickly looked away. Resuming her prayer, she closed her eyes and tried to block out the sight of him. "I want to thank you for sendin' me into the care of Mr. Grant Kirby, who has been more than kind to me and Colin. And I ask for your blessin' on him also, because he really is a good man, even if he doesn't believe where I'm from.

"In the name of Christ your son," she ended, crossing herself, "I pray."

Erina stood but still didn't turn back to the rear of the church. She needed to absorb the feeling of peace she'd always found in church, but with his eyes on her, she knew peace would elude her.

As she stood there, uncertain and confused about her feelings for Grant Kirby, a priest entered the church from a door beneath one of the stained-glass windows above the dais. "Can I help you?"

"Yes, Father. If you have time to hear my confession, I'd be very grateful."

"Certainly. Evening mass isn't for another forty-five minutes. Come right this way."

Erina looked at the place he'd indicated with a sweep of his arm toward the front of the church. Nothing more than a table with two chairs and a tiny screen, it looked more like a place to dine than a confessional. Grant would be able to see her there, and she'd feel his eyes on her when she should be concentrating on seeking peace and forgiveness. Then she remembered the velvet-draped confessional she'd seen in the back of the church.

"Father, may I give my confession in the other one? The closed one."

"We don't use that one anymore. It's merely a relic of the past."

"But that's the kind I'm accustomed to. Please, Father. It would mean so much to me."

He hesitated, then nodded. "Just for you. Come."

Erina followed the priest toward the back of the church, glancing just once at Grant. Her heart beat a little faster at his intense look. She slipped inside the confessional, feeling comfortable for the first time in such a long while. Here was something familiar, something from her own era.

"Father, forgive me, for I have sinned," she began. "It has been two weeks since my last confession." *Two weeks and a hundred years*, she amended silently.

The priest said his words, she responded, and then it was time to admit to her sins.

"I doubted the power of the Blessed Virgin on one occasion and lost my temper twice," she admitted. "And I was kissed by a man who is not my husband," she added hurriedly.

"Are you married?"

"No, Father."

"Then that is no sin."

"But Father, I . . . I felt . . . I felt lust for this man."

"Did you act on this lust?"

"No, Father."

"Then you have committed no sin. Go in peace, my child."

"But Father!"

She heard the slide of the velvet curtain, and then the faint footsteps of the priest as he walked away.

She also thought she heard him chuckle.

Erina frowned. Why hadn't the priest told her to say a dozen Hail Marys, or give up something she enjoyed, or attend an extra mass? He didn't seem at all concerned that she'd admitted her feelings for Grant went beyond gratitude.

Shaking her head, she left the confessional. Near the back of the church, she saw Grant place some paper money inside an envelope and slide it into a slot on a wooden box. "Are you ready?" he asked, looking up as though he knew she'd be standing there.

"Aye, I'm ready," she said, still feeling a bit sour over the priest's dismissal of her confession.

"Church must not agree with you. You don't look as if you're in a good mood."

"I'm just not understandin' this time of yours," she said peevishly. "Some people act more than a bit odd."

With that, Grant Kirby burst into laughter—and in church, of all places!

Grant returned Erina to the hospital after buying her lunch on The Strand and listening to her "ooh" and "ahh" over the "changes." Probably since she'd been to Galveston last time, he thought to himself as he drove back to the condo, a year or so ago. And she was so excited by the horse-drawn carriages standing along the streets that she'd spooked one normally placid animal. Grant had slipped the driver a ten and apologized for Erina's exuberance. She was from the country, he said softly so she wouldn't hear, as if that explained her unusual behavior.

She was *not* from 1896, despite her convincing portrayal of a young, innocent, Victorian, Irish-

Catholic . . . what? She wasn't old enough or worldly enough to be a woman, but she was a mother. Grant had no doubt that Colin was her son. She loved that baby too much to be anything else.

She was too damned young, that was for sure. Too young to be a mother, too young for him . . .

He pulled into a parking spot near the elevators and slammed the door of the Cherokee. He couldn't get her out of his head, no matter how hard he tried. No matter how many times he told himself she wasn't his problem. No matter how often he told himself to make sure the baby had what he needed and forget about the mother.

The cold front that had come through on Saturday was rapidly dissipating in the warm breeze off the Gulf. As he opened the door of the condo and stepped inside the air-conditioned comfort, he again wondered how Erina had managed to break in without setting off the alarm system. He knew he'd turned it on before slipping into bed. In many ways he'd become a creature of habit—mostly out of necessity. Being a real estate mogul did not come naturally.

He hadn't wanted to run his father's business. He'd wanted to become a geologist and was well on his way to his undergraduate degree when his father had died.

So he'd transferred to Harvard, after strong alumni recommendations and academic counseling, to study business instead of rocks. Without Brian Abbott's help in getting into Harvard and holding Kirby

Investments together, the company would have folded years ago.

Grant eased into a comfortable chair and dialed Brian's office.

"Where have you been, son? I've been trying to reach you on the cel phone."

"Believe it or not, I've been in church. I had the phone off."

"Church? You?"

Grant chuckled. "Don't sound like the earth is going to split open and swallow me up. I went with a . . . friend."

"It's that woman, isn't it? I knew she'd have a strange effect on you."

"She is different," Grant said, looking around the living room. How did the modern furniture look to her? Too stark and plain?

"How's the kid?"

Grant smiled. "He made it through surgery just great. Erina's at the hospital with him now."

"Good. Now maybe you can get your mind on business. We need to meet with the Phoenix people on Thursday. That's the latest I could make the meeting. We're pushing it at that."

"Okay. I can make Thursday."

"Well, hot damn, son. I'm glad to hear it," Brian said sarcastically, his voice booming over the telephone as though he was right there in the room.

"Don't get on my case. I've had a few things on my mind."

"Grant—"

"What time is the meeting?"

"Ten. I'm having lunch brought in so we can get finished in one day."

"Fax me whatever I need. I'm staying down here until Thursday morning."

"Hell, Grant, come on back to Houston. Your mother's having a dinner party on Wednesday night for one of her pet projects—Friends of the Library, I think. Why don't you—"

"I'm staying down here, Brian. I know you can't accept this, but I'm going to be involved in that baby's recovery."

"It's not the baby I'm concerned with," Brian replied.

Grant ran a hand through his hair. How could he reassure Brian about something he didn't fully understand himself? "I'll be in around nine thirty on Thursday. Just send me what I need before then."

He hung up the phone, concerned that Erina and Colin were coming between him and Brian. He hoped not. Brian was like an uncle, at least. Maybe even a father.

Grant pushed out of the chair and walked around the condo. Funny, he'd always thought of it as peaceful and quiet. Now it seemed empty. Barren. Not at all like Erina, who glowed with warmth and motherly love.

He walked into the guest bedroom. She'd need somewhere to go after Colin was released from the hospital. No one had ever used this extra bedroom except her, when she'd changed clothes after her bath. When was that? Yesterday? It seemed much longer ago than that.

She'd need a crib for Colin, plus some baby clothes and diapers. And other things. He had no idea what a baby needed outside the basics. The guest bedroom contained one double bed, a nightstand, and a dresser. A crib would fit nicely at the end of the bed. And even another chest, to store the baby clothes.

He needed to do something about that soon. The doctor had said that Colin could be released in a week.

Across the room, he heard the fax machine receiving. The information about the Phoenix management firm, no doubt. He had to look at it, just to make sure he had what he needed for the Thursday meeting.

Then he was going back to the hospital to check on Colin. And convince Erina that she should stay at the condo.

Erina learned a lot that afternoon, reading magazines in the Intensive Care waiting room. She didn't understand many of the words that were used, and wanted to know more about some of the historical events that were cited, but she got a good picture of how modern women were supposed to act.

She was shocked to the roots of her hair. Grant had asked her to act more "normal," but there was no way she was going to behave like these women, with their short, revealing clothing, their quest for perfect lovers, and their constant concern over what they ate and drank. She couldn't believe all the articles about the sexual act. Women seemed obsessed with it, for what reason she couldn't imagine. The very idea made her flushed and hot. Despite her attraction to Grant, she didn't believe that the act of coupling could be as wonderful as the writers expressed.

Could it?

She was debating the issue with herself when the object of her speculation appeared in the doorway. She dropped the magazine like a hot pot and tried to calm her racing heart.

"Sorry I've been gone so long. How's Colin?"

"He's fine," she said, sounding somewhat breathless to her own ears. "They let me see him every hour, but only for a few minutes."

"I'm sure he'll be out of ICU soon. I talked to the doctor on my way in."

"You sought him out?"

"No, I saw him in the hall and asked."

"What did he tell you?"

"Basically that Colin was doing great, but he was worried about you."

"And why would the doctor be worryin' about me?"

"Maybe because you look like a strong wind would blow you over."

Erina thought back to the magazines she'd read, and the pictures of tall, curvey models. She supposed she did look underfed and unkempt compared to them. Was Grant Kirby accustomed to those kinds of women? And if so, why was he spending so much time with her?

She raised her chin. "I'm just a bit on the short side, Mr. Kirby."

"Have you eaten anything this afternoon?"

"No, not after the lunch you fed me."

"It's almost dinnertime."

"Then I'll eat a bit soon."

"We'll go out to dinner. Do you like seafood?"

"You mean fish and the like?"

"Yes. Gaido's is what you need. Great food, large portions."

"I'm not leaving Colin again."

"You can't stay here constantly."

"I slept here before. I don't see why I can't stay again."

"You had a cot in his room. Now he's in ICU. You can't stay in these chairs overnight."

"I don't see why not."

"Well, you just can't," he said imperiously. "Let's get some dinner and then we'll come back to the hospital and see Colin again."

She thought of the fresh water, the toothpaste, and sweet-smelling soap at his home, and longed for a moment to refresh herself. But she couldn't put her own needs first.

"Colin is fine. He'll sleep most of the time anyway, so you might as well get some food and rest."

"Why do you want to take me to dinner?" she asked, looking up at him. He wasn't smiling. His arms were crossed over his wide chest in a gesture she'd come to recognize as extreme stubbornness.

"Just because I do. Now why don't we ask if they'll let me see Colin before we go."

"But—"

He walked toward her, stopping in front of her

chair and holding out a hand. "Come on, Erina. I'm starving, even if you aren't."

She gazed up at his handsome face, wondering how he'd become so familiar to her in such a short time. She should tell him to go to dinner alone, that she'd stay with Colin here all night, even if the hospital didn't want her to sleep in these chairs. But he looked so earnest, and seemed to care so for Colin's welfare.

She should tell Grant Kirby that Colin was her child and she'd take care of him. Colin wasn't this man's responsibility.

She held out her hand. "I'm just goin' to dinner with you, Mr. Kirby, and only if Colin is fine."

He quickly pulled her up, catching her against him as she tilted forward. "I asked you to call me Grant."

"I . . . I'm tryin' to remember."

"Remember this." She felt a rush of excitement as his head descended, as she felt his hot breath and then his firm lips lock over hers.

She closed her eyes, allowing herself a brief moment of pleasure. His lips slanted and coaxed a response she couldn't deny. *Just like in the magazines*, she thought. She finally understood what the nurse meant by "hunk." But not even the nurse could know how wonderful he kissed, how he made her feel as though she were floating off the floor in a mist of stars. When she felt his tongue brush against her closed lips she didn't even try to resist his gentle invasion.

"Ms. O'Shea?"

She barely heard her name, but suddenly his lips

were gone and she dropped back to earth in a dizzying fall.

"Yes?" she whispered, still staring into the blazing eyes of Grant Kirby.

"You can see Colin now. Sorry to interrupt."

Erina pushed away from him, but he held her steady when her knees threatened to buckle. The nurse was gone, they were alone again, and yet the spell was broken.

"Do you mind if I go in with you to see him?"

"No," she said, not meeting his eyes.

"I'm not sorry I kissed you, Erina," he said softly.

"I should slap your handsome face," she replied without thinking. As soon as the words left her mouth, she looked at him.

He smiled, the dimple appearing like magic. "I don't think you're into violence, so I'll ignore the threat," he said easily, "but I'm glad to know you find me appealing."

"I didn't say you were appealin'," she said, blushing and looking away. "I just said you had a handsome face. Now I'd like to see my son."

"Whatever you say," he replied with a chuckle.

Colin looked very peaceful, even with all the tubes and bandages across his little chest. Erina knew she was getting used to seeing him attached to machines and things that she'd learned were monitors to check his heart and breathing. She no longer wanted to cry when she saw needles stuck under the skin of her baby. She wished he didn't have to suffer, but she was grateful for the doctors' ability to save Colin's life.

Standing beside her, Grant filled the room with his large body and his warmth. He reached out and stroked his finger down Colin's cheek, brushing against her arm as he bent toward the bed. Erina's heart seemed to flutter at the image of the strong man and the tiny child. How wonderful it would be if Colin had a father like Grant.

What was she thinking? She'd been sent to this time for Colin's surgery, not to find a husband for herself and a father for her baby. And he'd get what he needed to save his life, of that Erina was sure, whether it was in the form of the doctors, the hospital, or a generous man like Grant Kirby. The Holy Mother had not let her down. To ask for more would be both selfish and foolish.

Chapter Eight

They went to dinner at Gaido's on Sea Wall Boulevard. As they walked from the Cherokee to the restaurant, Erina noticed many cars traveling up and down the wide road. The ocean lapped against the sand beyond the sea wall and salt spray tainted the air. The weather had turned balmy, and she was warm in her new clothes.

The restaurant wasn't elaborate on the outside, but inside were carpets and wonderful lighting, along with illuminated cases of cut crystal so beautiful that she had to stop and admire the pieces before being led to the table.

She was surprised that it was nearly dark outside already; she hadn't thought much time had passed since she arrived at the hospital after lunch. Apparently, reading magazines made the hours pass quickly—especially ones with articles on such shocking topics. So different from *Godey's* and *The Saturday Evening Post*.

And, of course, waiting to see Colin gave her a distorted sense of time. She was so happy her baby was going to be well that the world—even this new, unknown time—seemed as bright as the lighted crystal, and so full of hope that her heart was near to bursting.

Over her protests, Grant ordered a large combination of scallops, shrimp, fish, and oysters for her, along with a wonderfully sweet white wine from Germany. She wouldn't be able to eat that much food in days, she told him, but as they talked and sipped the wine, she was surprised at how much of the delicious food simply disappeared.

"I'll not eat another bite all week," she said, wiping her mouth with the cloth napkin. "Thank you for dinner."

"No dessert?" he asked, smiling across the table.

"Not another bite. You can't tempt me with anythin' else." She took a sip of her cooling cup of tea.

"Really? You wound my ego," he said with a half smile that made his eyes sparkle in the candlelight.

She felt a blush warm her cheeks as she remembered the kiss in the waiting room. "I'd best be gettin' back to the hospital now," she said, looking away. The restaurant was full of couples and families. Although she felt a bit disheveled after spending so many hours in her new outfit, she at least knew she was dressed appropriately. She didn't look at all out of place, even though she felt so different on the inside. If she was really a woman of this time, wouldn't she go back to Grant's condo, have sex with him, then "share" the experience with her friends? She could never be that modern. Her religion forbade it;

her experience reinforced the danger of physical attraction. With shaking hands, she refreshed her cup of tea from the hot pot the waiter had brought minutes before.

"I'll take you back to the hospital, but I want you to come home with me later."

"Mr. Kirby!" she said, her spoon clanking loudly as she dropped it against the saucer. The fact that his words echoed her thoughts was too upsetting.

"Calm down, Erina. I have the extra bedroom, and I think it would be a good idea for you to get an uninterrupted night's sleep. You can't stay with Colin in the ICU. I'll take you back to the hospital first thing in the morning."

"I can stay in the waiting room tonight."

"But wouldn't you be more comfortable in a real bed? Besides, you need to change your clothes, and you'd probably like another bath. Since everything I bought for you is still at my place, it makes sense for you to come over tonight."

She leaned forward, resting her forearms on the table. "Why do you want me to come to your condo?"

"Because, as I said, it makes sense. You've got to be exhausted. You need to relax, at least for a little while, and—"

"But why would you be carin' about me and my son?"

"Dammit, Erina, I just do, okay? I don't know why."

"And you don't believe in miracles?"

"No, I don't. I believe I'm attracted to you, despite my best advice to myself that you're way too young and that you've got some secret to hide. I believe that I care about what happens to a baby too small to help himself. I believe I have the money and time to help."

"You don't think that God is guiding us all, and that the Virgin Mary might just be askin' for your faith? She did put us in your condo."

"You broke in. I don't know how or why."

Erina sat up straight against the chair back. "I did no such thing. I went to the cathedral and prayed for a miracle."

Grant leaned forward, resting his elbows on the table and steepling his fingers. "Look, Erina, I think you suffered some trauma. It's easier to believe you're from the past than accept what really happened. Obviously you've studied turn-of-the-century Galveston and my family. Lord knows you've got your historical perspective down solid. But for once just try to tell me where you're really from and what you want from me."

"I want nothing from you for myself. And I've told you what happened to me."

"Did you plan this whole scheme to get your son the medical attention he needs?"

Erina fought the frustration she always felt at Grant's dismissal of the truth. She knew her first reaction was to get angry, but that wouldn't make him believe her. Somehow he had to believe that divine intervention had occurred, but perhaps that would take another miracle. "I didn't plan on meetin' you. I didn't know how the Blessed Virgin would grant a miracle, but I'm grateful she sent me to a man who would care for Colin."

"And after he's well—what then? Surely you want something for yourself: an apartment, a job, an education?"

"I can do just fine. I imagine even in this day ladies need their clothing tended or their houses cleaned. But I'd like a better life for my son. An education for him would be a fine thing. When he grows up he can work with his mind instead of his hands."

Grant glanced at his own hands. Erina noticed again how large they were, how weathered they appeared in contrast to his well-cut hair and clean-shaven jaw. "You want me to provide a college fund for Colin?" he said casually.

"No! I've not asked for a penny of your money."

"You still believe I'm a laborer, don't you?"

"I've no reason to call you a liar, Mr. Kirby."

"Grant. And I really do run our family investment company. That's not what I'd planned to do with my life, but it's what I chose."

"Your job must not be too demandin' then; you don't even go to the office," Erina observed.

"It has its peaks and valleys. Some days I don't even leave the office. I have a corporate attorney, Brian Abbott, who handles the contracts. Dottie Benson is my CFO—Chief Financial Officer—and I have property managers in various cities. In addition, my office staff takes care of the daily operations of the investment firm."

"And this office is in Houston?"

"That's right. I usually just come to Galveston on the weekends to get away from . . . well, to have a change of pace." He paused, looking at her intently.

149

"But I suppose you know that, since you knew where my condo was and when I'd be there."

"I knew no such thing, as I've said before."

He didn't answer, just continued to stare in a most unnerving way.

"Colin and I will be fine if you have to work. I'll remember not to talk to anyone about my past."

"That's good, but that's not the only reason I'm staying in Galveston."

"And what would the other one be?" she asked, feeling a bit breathless from his close perusal.

"A spunky Irish girl who should get an Oscar for the performance of a lifetime."

"I'm not performin'! And I don't know anyone named Oscar."

Grant laughed. "We'll see if you're real, sooner or later."

"I'm here because of a miracle and no words can change that fact."

"As I said, you're certainly consistent."

"And as you've said, you don't believe in miracles."

"That's right."

"Well, I do. And I also believe that the Holy Mother chose you for a reason. I'm not sure why, but maybe it's because Colin was denied his true father, and you are a Kirby who takes responsibility seriously."

"Erina, you did *not* know Jerrold Kirby, in the biblical sense or any other way," Grant said patiently, as though he was speaking to a small child.

"I certainly did, but it's clear you don't believe me, so I won't burden you with the story again."

"Thanks. Now can we go to the hospital, then back

to the condo? I promise I'll be on my best behavior."

"I'm ready," she said, pushing back her chair.

He came around the table and acted the gentleman. "I do trust you," she said as they stood beside the table, "I just don't know how to make you believe. I don't know you very well."

"Brian Abbott, my corporate attorney, is beginning to think the same thing," Grant said with a smile that didn't reach his eyes.

Colin was still sleeping when they arrived at the ICU. Grant leaned against the wall while Erina sat in the chair beside the bed, rubbing her baby's hand and smoothing back his hair. She spoke softly, with that lyrical Irish accent, and he swore she crooned in Gaelic for just a moment.

Erina excused herself for about ten minutes—using the breast pump, no doubt, and blushing as she did so well. He supposed she didn't want him to think of her nursing the baby, but he did. He thought about it a great deal lately, far more than he should.

The nurse ushered them out at nine thirty, telling Erina that Colin was doing fine, and that she should get some sleep. He could tell she wanted to argue, but she yawned instead. Grant smiled as they walked into the corridor.

"I know you hate to leave Colin for the night, but he's going to be fine. I'll have you back as early as you want in the morning."

"You have no work to do tomorrow?"

"No, except to read some papers. I'll probably do

that tonight. On Thursday I have to go back to Houston for a meeting."

"Oh."

She didn't say anything else. As they walked together down the empty hallway, he had a strong urge to take her hand. He didn't—he knew he shouldn't. He'd made a point of telling her how much he could be trusted, that he just wanted her to get a good night's sleep. Well, that wasn't entirely true. He did want her to stay with him, make love with him, sleep with him. And when they woke up together in the morning they would make love once again, take a shower together, then go to the hospital to see Colin.

None of that was going to happen, except the part about seeing Colin in the morning. He was going to keep his word. He wasn't going to give in to his entirely inappropriate urges.

He still didn't understand why he was so obsessed with her. Even if she was suffering some trauma that made her believe she was from the past, she must know how she got into his condo. Grant could not understand why he tolerated such behavior. With anyone else, he would have cut them off immediately. With Erina, he couldn't wait to see what she'd say or do next.

The air was warm and humid as they walked through the corridor to the parking garage. She seemed deep in thought. He wondered what she was thinking about but didn't want to ask. For one thing, she probably wouldn't tell him the truth. She'd make up some story about Galveston in 1896, or her childhood in Ireland, or something that he couldn't be-lieve.

He decided to stay on a fairly safe topic. "Colin looks much better. His color is pink, just like a healthy baby."

"He's never had that good a color before. When I took him to the doctor after he was born the man said that nothin' could be done. I never believed that, though. I kept hopin' that God wouldn't make such a wee baby suffer forever."

Grant opened the door from the second-floor stair-well into the parking garage. "Well, whatever hap-pened, I'm glad he came through the surgery okay. I've grown attached to him. I've been thinking that maybe I should put aside some money for his edu-cation. I can take out an investment policy for him now, and by the time he's eighteen he'll be able to go to the school of his choice."

"If he's still here," Erina said softly.

Their footsteps echoed in the concrete structure, virtually deserted at this time of night. Lonely was the word that came to mind. "What do you mean? Are you planning to move?"

"No, I have no plans myself. But the Blessed Virgin might have different ideas. Perhaps I won't stay in your time forever. I might go back when Colin is well. After all, I don't belong here."

"Don't be ridiculous. You have free will over where you live. And let's have no more talk about miracles. If you want to stay, you can."

"Ah, you don't understand, do you? Sometimes the

world isn't as neat and orderly as you'd like to believe."

"Right. Natural disasters happen. People get sick and die. I'm not talking about that. I'm talking about where you choose to live, where your son will grow up."

They arrived at the Jeep. Grant unlocked the door and walked Erina to the passenger side.

"If I had a choice, I'd stay right here. I'd miss Mrs. Abernathy, but she might already think I'm gone. Maybe somehow I can find out what happened to her."

"Erina, Mrs. Abernathy is a figment of your imagination," Grant said, resting his arm on the door. "Or she's a name you discovered while researching the past. She's not real."

"Aye, she's real. She's a fine, compassionate woman. I'll never forget what she did for me and Colin."

Grant shook his head; she was so far gone in her fantasy that she couldn't consider reality. He wished he'd taken more than one semester of psychology in his college days. "Don't forget to fasten your seat belt."

They drove home in silence. Once they entered the condo Erina seemed especially tense.

"Don't worry. I'll keep my word. I won't make a pass."

"I'm not worried," she said with an upward thrust of her chin.

Grant couldn't resist a smile. "Do you remember where everything is in the bathroom?"

"I believe so. I'll not be bothering you any more tonight."

He dropped his keys on the bar between the kitchen and living area. "It's no bother. If you need anything at all, just call me. I'm a light sleeper."

"So am I, especially since Colin was born. Sometimes it seems as though I hear his every breath, and I always had to listen for . . ."

He saw her eyes fill with tears, saw the strength that seemed to desert her with that admission. In an instant Grant crossed the room and took her in his arms. "Erina, it's okay. Colin is going to be well."

"I know, but I miss him so. I want to go to sleep with him beside me, and wake up knowing he's there. He's all I have."

She felt so good, so right, tucked beneath his chin, next to his heart. "No, don't say that. You love him very much and he loves you. But you're not alone. I'll be here when you need me."

"But you might be gone from my life soon," she said with a watery sob, "and I'd feel so sad if I grew to care for you and never saw you again."

"Is that what's happening? Are you growing to care for me? Because I'll tell you right now, I'm very attracted to you."

She pushed away from his embrace, fighting tears and comfort. "I'd best be gettin' ready for bed. I'm sorry to be a bother."

"You're no bother," he said again, reaching out for her.

But she stepped back, away from his hand, rebuffing his sentiments as certainly as she denied her own. "Good night, Grant. Thank you for dinner and . . . everything."

She slipped into the guest bedroom, as silent as a wraith.

Grant threw himself heavily on the couch. He'd certainly picked a difficult woman to be attracted to, one with secrets and fantasies that he couldn't even imagine. And yet she seemed so much more real that any other woman he'd known.

With a sigh, he flicked on the television and tuned into a financial news channel, then picked up the faxes from Brian. He'd lose himself in his work, at least for a few minutes, and forget that Erina O'Shea was naked behind the door to the guest bathroom.

Erina woke early, just as the sun crept over the east end of the island and gilded the waves with gold and pink. The sky itself was purple and gold, turning to rose as lighter fingers of pink radiated upward. She watched the sun rise from the large windows of what Grant called the living room. She tried to be quiet so she wouldn't wake him too early, but her impatience to see Colin was a tangible thing, pulling her toward the door that led to his bedroom. She actually took a few steps in that direction before stopping herself.

No, she wouldn't venture inside. He'd told her that he'd take her to the hospital whenever she wanted. She was ready now but couldn't bring herself to knock on his door. That was too intimate. She could imagine him in that large bed, looking much like one of the men in the magazines; chest bare and sculpted with muscles, loose pants resting below his waist, a smile on his face. He'd be more temptation than advertisements of those other men.

She hugged her arms around herself and walked into the kitchen. She wished she knew how to operate this stove. She'd make herself a cup of tea—if Grant had any of those tea bags the restaurant used. Of course, the water coming from the pipes was very hot, maybe hot enough to brew her favorite beverage. She began opening cabinets, looking for something familiar.

One of the doors slipped from her fingers and slammed shut. The sudden noise in the still condo surprised her; in an instant, she realized it had awakened Grant also. He stood in the doorway of his bedroom, looking just as she'd imagined him—tall and lean but muscled, and wearing very little. Nothing above the waist and baggy, soft drawstring pants below.

She swallowed, suddenly needing the tea to soothe her parched throat. "I'm sorry I woke you."

"No problem. I was ready to get up."

"I was lookin' for tea bags."

"I think there are some in the canister," he said, walking toward her, running a hand through his sleep-tousled hair.

She scooted back from the counter, giving him plenty of room. In truth, she didn't know what she might do if she stood too close to him. He was too nearly naked, too potently male.

He gave her a sleepy frown. "I'm just going to get you some tea," he said with a touch of irritation. "I wish you wouldn't act like I'm some kind of sex fiend."

"I'm not," she said defensively. She was beginning to think she was the one who had a problem. "I'm just gettin' out of your way."

"Uh-huh," he said absently, turning his back to her and opening one of the ceramic containers that sat next to the refrigerator. That appliance she knew, because she'd used the breast pump and stored the milk in there for Colin. "I hope these aren't too old. I rarely make tea, but my mother insisted I have a well-stocked kitchen."

She couldn't tear her eyes away from his back. Muscles rippled over and around his spine, his shoulders, his arms. His skin was a golden color that reminded her of the sunrise. She'd never realized a man could be so beautiful. "Sounds like she's concerned about you," she said weakly.

"She is," he said, turning and handing her a large cup with a bag already inside. "Actually, she had her chef see that I had a well-stocked kitchen. My mother doesn't know how to cook anything more elaborate than watercress sandwiches."

"She comes from a moneyed family then," Erina said, trying to tear her eyes away from Grant's naked chest to focus on the much less interesting cup.

"That's right. Her family came to Houston when oil was first discovered in East Texas. They made a fortune in refineries."

"What?"

"Large plants that process crude oil."

"Oh." She still had no idea what he was talking about.

He stepped closer. "So, do you want me to heat some water for you?"

"Ah . . . yes, that would be nice."

"Pay attention," he said with a smile. "You can do it yourself the next time."

Erina nodded, wondering if she'd need any appliance to heat water for tea. She could probably just hold it close to her blazing cheeks. She watched him fill the mug with water, then place it in a boxlike device.

"This is a microwave oven. It doesn't get hot, but it heats food or water from within with vibration. It takes about two minutes to boil a cup of water; less if you just want it hot."

His smooth-skinned, muscled arms lifted the mug and placed it inside the black box. He hit some panels with his fingers, but she was so busy watching him that she barely noticed what he was doing.

"I've got to take a shower and get dressed. We can grab a bite to eat on the way to the hospital, or go to the cafeteria later."

"I'd like to see Colin as soon as possible."

"Of course." He reached around her, close enough that she could smell his very masculine scent and feel the golden glow of his sleep-warm body. "Here's the sugar." He pressed a bowl into her hands. "Spoons are in the drawer beside the sink."

He smiled at her again, looking less sleepy and more sexy every moment. "Good morning, Erina," he said, dropping a quick kiss on her lips.

Startled, she stood there as he walked out of the kitchen. When a bell rang on the microwave she jumped and nearly dropped the sugar bowl. Taking a deep breath, she prepared her tea, though she couldn't banish the image of Grant from her mind, or forget the enticing smell and taste of him. Did he know what he did to her?

Chapter Nine

They arrived at the hospital less than an hour later. Grant had showered and shaved, all the while warning his body that Erina was off limits.

She wanted him, but he had a feeling she wasn't aware of her passion. Hadn't she lusted after another man? Maybe not Colin's father, if indeed she'd been raped. But someone? As young as she was, he didn't expect her to be very experienced. However, she had produced a child; didn't that mean something?

When they walked into the PDICU Dr. Cook was standing beside Colin's bed with a woman Grant didn't recognize. From her solemn expression and no-nonsense business suit, he imagined she had some sort of bureaucratic position.

"Dr. Cook," Grant said when they entered the room, "what's going on here?"

"This is Mrs. Henshaw, one of our social workers. She has some questions—"

"About Colin? Is there something wrong with my

baby?" Erina burst into the room, going directly to her son.

"Just the fact that he was denied medical care. He has received no childhood immunizations and has no pediatrician," Mrs. Henshaw said.

Grant stiffened, knowing that the worst thing that could happen would be for someone to threaten Colin's welfare.

"We're concerned for his health, Ms. O'Shea. There are rules that must be followed."

Erina looked up from stroking Colin's hair. "But I did what the doctors told me! I already explained that to Dr. Cook. They said nothin' could be done for his heart."

"Ms. O'Shea, your son has not received even minimal care. It's my job to determine if this lack of care constitutes abuse that should be reported. Or if you could benefit from some counseling."

"No! How can you say that my son is bein' abused? I love him with all my heart."

Mrs. Henshaw said nothing.

"Look, this is ridiculous," Grant said. He was tired of the insinuations, tired of people implying that Erina wasn't a good mother. She might not be telling the truth about a lot of things, but she was an excellent mother. "Erina, please let me handle this," he said to her as she cast a worried gaze from the woman to him. He turned his attention back to the bureaucrat. "There's a simple explanation for what you consider to be child neglect or abuse."

"And what would that be?" Mrs. Henshaw asked.

"Do we have to discuss this here, now?" Grant

asked, playing for time. "I advised Erina not to talk to anyone until she's seen an attorney." And then he'd promptly forgotten that there might be a threat after telling her not to recount her story to the doctors or the social workers. Had she said something they considered suspicious?

"I told Mrs. Henshaw that Colin is receiving the best care possible now," Dr. Cook added. "We expect a full recovery."

"When should Colin be able to leave the hospital?" Grant asked.

"In about four days. He'll be released from ICU today."

"Then why don't we set up a meeting for Friday, Mrs. Henshaw?" Grant suggested. "Erina and I will be there, along with my attorney."

"That's not the way we work, Mr. Kirby."

"Maybe you should. That's the way I work." He crossed the small room to stand beside Erina. "We're not going to have this discussion here. Colin's not going anywhere and neither are we."

"I need Ms. O'Shea to answer some questions."

"With an attorney, in your offices or mine. Not in her child's hospital room."

"I did this as a courtesy, Mr. Kirby. I thought it would be less intrusive than an actual investigation."

"Sounds to me as if this *is* an investigation, Mrs. Henshaw. And Erina has been through enough for the moment."

"Very well. I can't make you talk to me. I just want you to know that we consider each child as an individual. His or her parents' financial situation makes no difference to me." She took a deep breath, raising her eyebrows as if to punctuate her words. "If you have a card, we'll set up an appointment."

Grant reached inside his wallet and pulled out a business card. "Call my office any time, Mrs. Henshaw. We'll get this misunderstanding cleared up."

"I hope it is a misunderstanding, Mr. Kirby. Some people suffer the misconception that social workers want to take children away from their parents. That is not true."

Parents, she said, not mother. So even the stern bureaucrat believed he was Colin's father.

"I'm glad to hear that, Mrs. Henshaw. Now, if you'll excuse us, we'd like to spend some time alone with the baby."

"Of course," she said, picking up a portfolio and walking out the door. "Call me this week, Mr. Kirby, and we'll get the matter settled."

Grant looked down at her business card as he listened to her sturdy heels click across the floor. *Now what?* he thought to himself. *You've gotten yourself into the middle of a social worker's righteous cause.* She didn't care who he was or what he said. *Just the facts.* She was a female Joe Friday.

If Mrs. Henshaw made a negative report about Colin, there was no telling what Child Welfare would do. They'd probably expect some sort of medical documentation on him. Who knew what bureaucrats needed? He'd heard on the news that most agencies could not require a parent to prove that he or she was in the country legally due to the nature of public care provided to immigrants—legal or illegal—but if they asked Erina, what would she say? Would she make up some story about arriving here from Ireland or another century? They could still question her mental competence.

Somehow he knew that Erina had no papers, nothing to prove who she was.

He felt Erina's trembling and placed an arm around her shoulders.

"Why did this happen?" she asked the doctor in a shaking voice. "Did you not believe me?"

"Colin's records indicate several risk factors that child welfare considers crucial. Since you had no answers—"

"I answered your questions! I told you the truth."

"Ms. O'Shea—"

"Let's not get into finger pointing right now," Grant interrupted. "We're just going to have to deal with the situation."

"I don't know what—"

"Let's talk about it later, okay?" he asked gently, hoping Erina wouldn't tell the doctor anything incriminating. "Remember the talk we had?" he whispered into her hair.

She nodded but held herself stiffly, still trembling slightly and obviously upset.

"If you'll excuse us, Dr. Cook?" Grant asked. "Unless you have something else to report about Colin's condition . . ."

"No, he's doing well. I hope you can convince Mrs. Henshaw that he's in good hands. She's new to the department, I understand, and plays everything by the book. That doesn't mean you've done anything wrong. You both apparently love him very much."

The doctor left the room. Erina sagged against him, but when he tried to steer her toward a chair, she pulled away and turned toward Colin. "I won't let them take him away, but I don't even know what they want," she said as she looked down at her son.

Grant watched the baby. The doctor thought he loved Colin, probably as a father loves his son. Dr. Cook didn't know what he was talking about. Oh, Grant knew he cared for the boy, but he didn't love him. Not as a father. He was just doing the boy and his mother a favor.

Colin's eyes were open, his fists flailing as he smiled up at his mother.

"Just in case the authorities get involved," Grant said, "do you have any documentation on coming to the U.S.?"

"Back home, in my apartment."

"And that would be?" Finally, faced with a crisis, she might admit where she'd been living and what she was doing in Galveston.

"I've already told you that I live above Mrs. Abernathy's dress shop," Erina said, distracted by Colin's antics.

"I see."

"I don't believe you do," Erina said, turning to Grant. "That's really where I live. The only other place that might have a record of me entering the country is the office that admitted my da and me when we left the ship."

"So even faced with losing your son you're sticking to this time-travel story."

"It's the truth."

"Well, they're not going to believe it any more than I do."

"I know. How long do you think I might have before they come to take Colin away?"

"They're not taking him anywhere," Grant said, surprised at the surge of emotion he experienced at the thought. Fight or flight; he recognized the reaction, but for him fight was the only option.

"I could take Colin away. . . ."

"No! We're going to come up with an explanation that will satisfy the most stuffy bureaucrat, if it comes to that."

"But I have nothing with me!"

"There are ways to obtain any document," Grant explained, "and with computers, we should be able to produce some sort of history for you."

"I don't know what you mean."

"Don't worry about it. I'll find a way to get you documented."

"Why are you gettin' involved with this new problem?" she asked cautiously.

"I told you; I care about Colin and you. I don't think taking him away from you would be in his best interest."

"Of course not! But I still don't understand why you're makin' this your concern."

"Let's just drop that for now, Erina."

"You don't want to talk about it."

"That's right. Now, let's see Colin for as long as we can."

They stood beside the bed and talked to him, silly

gibberish that he seemed to find amusing. He looked so good that it was hard to believe he'd been gravely ill just days before, that he'd had no chance of a future without the surgery. And Erina seemed so happy, despite her obvious urge to cradle her son close without the wires and tubes.

"I'd like to feed him myself today," she said softly.

Grant looked down at the baby's cupid bow mouth and then realized what she was saying. She wanted to nurse him—right now. "I'll check with the nurse on duty to see if that's okay."

He could clearly imagine how beautiful Erina would look, nursing her son. Her breasts would be full and white, so soft . . .

Taking a deep breath, he stepped up to the PDICU nurses' station. "Ms. O'Shea would like to know if she may breast-feed her baby."

When he secured the approval, and passed on a word of caution to be mindful of the tubes that still connected Colin to the monitors, he returned to the room and watched as she turned her back to him and unbuttoned her blouse. He imagined that she was blushing. She carefully picked up her child. He wanted to stay, he realized. Very badly. He wanted to be part of this mother/child bonding.

"I'll be feedin' him now," Erina said softly.

He thought for a moment of asking her permission to stay in the room. He wanted to. But that would sound too much like begging, and he wasn't a man who begged. "I'll wait for you outside. Then we can go get some breakfast."

"I'll be finished in ten or fifteen minutes," she replied before sitting down in the chair beside the bed.

The last glimpse Grant had before going out the door was Colin's downy hair, his head pressed to Erina's breast, his tiny fist beating happily against her chest.

Erina regarded Grant in the hospital cafeteria over a bowl of oatmeal and a plate of toast. She should feel frightened and nervous—of the social worker saying she wasn't a good mother, of herself being judged to be living in the United States illegally, of a thousand other things. But when she was with Grant, she'd realized upstairs in Colin's hospital room, she felt as though she'd be safe no matter what.

She believed Grant when he said that he'd find a way to document her entry and protect Colin from the social worker. She believed with all her heart that she'd found a true miracle in Grant Kirby.

"Are there no old records of the immigrants who came to Galveston?" she asked after sweetening her cereal.

"I suppose there are. I think there's a database of immigrants at the dock, down by where the *Elisa* is berthed."

"Can you check those records for my da and me?"

"That wouldn't prove much, would it?" Grant said after swallowing a bite of eggs. "I mean, that's just a name. If I were a skeptical man," he said, giving her a searching glance, "I could say that you'd found a name on a manifest or as part of the immigrant files and adopted it so you could convince me of your identity."

"I did no such thing!" How could he be so wonderful one minute and then turn cruel by doubting her once again?

"I'm just saying it's a possibility."

"Maybe, but it's not the truth."

"Erina, there's no way to convince me you're from the past, so give it up. Let's try to think of a way to document you. I assume you have no papers anywhere?"

"Just back at Mrs. Abernathy's—in 1896."

Grant took a deep breath. "Okay. How about Colin? Is there any record of his birth?"

"Of course. I registered his birth at the county offices."

"And that would have been . . ."

"He was born a month early, on August 24, 1896."

"Right. Look, Erina, it would really help if you'd cooperate."

"I'm tellin' you the truth! You'll find no record of me in your time because I'm from the past. If I could produce some documents, I would. Do you not know that I'd move heaven and earth to save my son?"

Grant sighed and looked very serious. "I know that. That's why your story is so hard to believe. I keep thinking that there must be something very serious that keeps you from revealing your identity."

"A miracle is very serious business, but it doesn't keep me from revealin' anything. Check the old records if you'd like."

"Even if I found your name on a manifest and Colin's name in the birth records, that doesn't prove a thing, and I certainly can't use that with Mrs. Henshaw."

"Then what can we do?"

"Come up with a story to satisfy even her hardened heart."

Erina leaned forward, pushing her dish aside. "I'll do anything to keep Colin safe. If I have to lie to Mrs. Henshaw, I'll do it."

"Oh, we'll both have to lie before this is finished," Grant warned her. "Just be certain you can carry it off. I'm not going into the interview alone to face some county or state charges of child abandonment or abuse."

"You didn't abandon Colin! You've done everything possible to save him!"

"Well, I'm not sure I'd place so much importance on my efforts, but you have to understand what the hospital staff and Mrs. Henshaw believes: that I'm Colin's father and that I've kept him a secret for the past two months."

"That's ridiculous!"

"I know, but that's what they believe. If I deny it, they'll just think I'm lying."

Erina sank back into her chair. "I didn't mean for you to be accused of fatherin' a . . . a bastard child." She knew she couldn't keep the catch from her voice as she said the word that branded her baby illegitimate.

"No one's calling Colin a bastard," Grant said forcefully.

"I can face the truth. But I'm going to give him

171

every chance to have a good life anyway."

"Erina, no one cares much for those titles any longer."

"You mean your friends wouldn't ask about Colin's da? Their children wouldn't wonder where his da was when they talked to Colin? I think you're not recallin' how cruel children can be."

Grant shook his head. "You may be right. But he's under no disadvantage legally."

Erina said nothing more on the subject; Grant's mind was made up about Colin and she couldn't discuss the issue without becoming angry. Anyway, she would do whatever was in her power as a mother to keep him happy and safe in whatever world he entered—the nineteenth century or the twentieth.

"What will this story be?"

"Excuse me?"

"The story we're going to tell to Mrs. Henshaw. You said we'd have to lie to the woman."

"Oh, that. I'm going to have to think about it."

"Shouldn't we discuss it together?"

"I want to talk to Brian Abbott. I think I've mentioned his name to you before. I need some advice on what could be considered criminal and what can be proven in court."

"You think we'll have to go to court?"

"I'm not sure. Maybe. Don't worry about it, though. If we do, I'm sure it will just be a technicality."

"What's that?"

"A matter of establishing the proper records."

"Oh. I still think I should help—"

"No. Let me talk to Brian first. Then you and I can discuss strategy."

"You mean you'll be tellin' me what to say."

"That's not what I meant. I have to find out what's possible and what the officials will believe."

"I'll not be goin' along with just any story," Erina said vehemently, "not when my son's future is involved."

"I promise I won't do anything to harm Colin. I told you, I care about him."

"I know you do," Erina said, leaning forward again. "But he's my son and my responsibility."

"We'll get through this together," Grant said gently.

The idea of no longer shouldering all her burdens alone sounded like heaven on earth to Erina. But was she being fair to Grant? He certainly hadn't expected to become involved in the life of a two-month-old baby. Would she be ungrateful if she took Colin from the hospital and disappeared, running away from all the Mrs. Henshaws of the world, away from the commanding presence of Grant Kirby?

She'd be unfair to Colin at least. He needed care, and she had no idea how to provide the nursing he'd need to recover. And after he was recovered? She'd have to wait and see. If life in this new time became too complicated, she might have to leave Grant and elude the bureaucrats.

No one was going to take Colin away from her, but at the same time she couldn't take advantage of Grant Kirby's kindness.

* * *

Grant left Erina at the hospital that afternoon, deciding to do a little investigating on his own. Before he tried to formulate a plan with Brian's help, he needed to know what information Erina might have had access to when she devised her story.

At the Seaport Museum Grant paid his admission and walked immediately to the computer which housed the immigrant database. However, when he began his search he found no records of the year in question.

"What's the problem with researching 1888?" he asked one of the employees of the museum.

"The records from 1871 to 1894 were lost, mostly during the hurricane in 1900. I'm sorry, but there is no way to find out who came over then."

Damn. Had Erina intentionally chosen a year when she couldn't be proven wrong? What was he thinking? Just the idea of time travel was absurd; he didn't need an immigrant database to tell him that.

"Thanks," he said distractedly. When the employee began to walk away, Grant stopped him. "Is there any other place that might have records of that time?"

"The Rosenburg Library has some records, but I'm not sure what. You might check with them."

"I'll do that. Thanks again."

Grant left the dock area, drove to The Strand, and then turned left on Twenty-third down to Post Office Street. Erina claimed Mrs. Abernathy had a dress shop in one of the buildings along this street. Was there an actual building, or had she made that up? He cruised by slowly, watching the Victorian-era buildings for a clue. Several looked old enough, but of course there wasn't a dress shop anymore.

Damn! There had never been a dress shop. For some reason Erina had made up her elaborate story! The fact that he still didn't have a clue as to *why* filled him with frustration. What did he have to do to show Erina he could be trusted?

He pulled up to the curb along the tree-lined street in front of the Rosenburg Library. Two children ran along the sidewalk and up the steps into the building. A mother and child walked by, returning books to the library. An old man using a cane made his way slowly toward the entrance.

Had Erina stood on that sidewalk and observed a similar scene when researching the past? Is this where she got the idea to become a Victorian-era seamstress, a former maid to a well-known family? Maybe there was enough historical detail in the archives to allow her to create a credible past. Erina had the ability to put herself so far inside the character that she'd surprised him on several occasions with her "ignorance" of common, modern conveniences and terms. Would she ever return to the present?

He wouldn't—couldn't—believe she was crazy. She was simply confused. Or in trouble. Or she had experienced something she couldn't face. He wanted to make whatever was wrong, right again. But he couldn't if he didn't know what was bothering Erina.

Slamming the door of the Jeep, he walked quickly into the library. After learning from the reception desk that the reference library was on the third floor, he took the elevator upstairs. Across the hall, the glass-walled historical archives seemed deserted this afternoon.

He signed in and received five books from the reference librarian on Irish immigrants. He learned that there were no records of immigration in Galveston; all documents had been lost in the hurricane of 1900. But he scanned articles, books, and newspapers from 1888 to 1896, hoping for some mention of an Irish gardener named O'Shea, of his daughter, who might have worked for the Kirby family.

He did find a mention of Mrs. Abernathy, who designed a dress for Miss Bettie Brown, one of Galveston's legendary citizens. However, no details existed, and nothing was mentioned of her shop or an apartment above it where a baby named Colin was born.

Of course not. All of that was a figment of Erina's active and vivid imagination. There was no mention of her in the past because she hadn't lived then. She was probably an Irish immigrant, but circa 1996. Just as he'd guessed when he'd first met her, she'd probably created this fantasy to save the life of her son, whom she really did love with all her heart.

Could he fault her for bearing a mother's love for her son? Hardly. If Colin was his son, he'd probably do the same thing given the same set of circumstances. He wouldn't hold her actions against her, and he wouldn't deny Colin the best medical care available.

Grant knew that when he met with Brian Abbott tomorrow he'd upset his old friend, mentor, and attorney even more. He was about to become even more involved in Erina and Colin's lives.

Thrill to the most sensual, adventure-filled Historical Romances on the market today...

FROM  LEISURE BOOKS

As a home subscriber to Leisure Romance Book Club, you'll enjoy the best in today's BRAND-NEW Historical Romance fiction. For over twenty-five years, Leisure Books has brought you the award-winning, high-quality authors you know and love to read. Each Leisure Historical Romance will sweep you away to a world of high adventure...and intimate romance. Discover for yourself all the passion and excitement millions of readers thrill to each and every month.

Save $5.⁰⁰ Each Time You Buy!

Each month, the Leisure Romance Book Club brings you four brand-new titles from Leisure Books, America's foremost publisher of Historical Romances. EACH PACKAGE WILL SAVE YOU $5.00 FROM THE BOOKSTORE PRICE! And you'll never miss a new title with our convenient home delivery service.

Here's how we do it. Each package will carry a FREE 10-DAY EXAMINATION privilege. At the end of that time, if you decide to keep your books, simply pay the low invoice price of $16.96, no shipping or handling charges added. HOME DELIVERY IS ALWAYS FREE. With today's top Historical Romance novels selling for $5.99 and higher, our price SAVES YOU $5.00 with each shipment.

AND YOUR FIRST FOUR-BOOK SHIPMENT IS TOTALLY FREE!
IT'S A BARGAIN YOU CAN'T BEAT! A Super $21.96 Value!

LEISURE BOOKS A Division of Dorchester Publishing Co., Inc.

Get Four Books Totally FREE — A $21.96 Value!

▼ Tear Here and Mail Your FREE Book Card Today! ▼

PLEASE RUSH
MY FOUR FREE
BOOKS TO ME
RIGHT AWAY!

Leisure Romance Book Club
P.O. Box 6613
Edison, NJ 08818-6613

AFFIX
STAMP
HERE

Chapter Ten

After three hours of meeting with the Phoenix management company officials, eating a catered lunch in the executive conference room, and drafting a contract to be completed later, Grant was ready for a few minutes' privacy. Brian would be busy for a while, seeing the rest of the attendees out; Grant slipped into his office and behind his desk.

He hadn't been in for four business days and he hadn't missed the office one bit. He usually sweated the details, right along with Brian and the rest of the staff. But since he'd spent so much time with Erina and had concentrated on Colin's recovery, he hadn't worried about the real estate market in Houston or the other cities where he owned property. He hadn't checked the bond markets and interest rates every morning, and he hadn't wondered what the next quarter's occupancy rate would be.

He picked up a large glass paperweight that his mother had given him last year for his birthday. Blue and lavender swirls caught the strong sunlight coming in through the wall of windows behind his desk. His mother loved to purchase expensive, showy, worthless gifts like this paperweight. He supposed she didn't know what else to buy her son; his only hobby was rock climbing and he didn't need another briefcase.

Erina wouldn't buy a paperweight for Colin, even if he had everything else in the world. She probably do a nice deed, or make something, or whatever "earth mothers" did. When had he and his mother grown so far apart that she resorted to buying him an overpriced chunk of glass?

Brian burst into the office, hitching up his dress slacks over his increasing waistline. "I thought you were going to kick them out the door before they ate the last bite of their strawberry tarts," he said, taking a burgundy leather chair in front of Grant's mahogany desk.

"They didn't look as if they were starving to death. Besides, with what we're going to be paying them, they can afford new desserts."

"You're cruel, son, real cruel," Brian said with a laugh. "So what's the big hurry?"

"I need to talk to you about Colin and Erina."

"I'm not going to like this, am I?"

"No, you're not. As a matter of fact, you may think *I* should be kicked out without finishing dinner."

"What's happened this week? Besides the fact that you're infatuated with a Irish teenager and her illegitimate son?"

Grant frowned, setting the paperweight back on the edge of his desk. "She's not a teenager," he said, uncomfortable with their age difference but aware he couldn't change it. "The UTMB social worker is suspicious of Erina because Colin hasn't had his immunizations and didn't get any previous medical attention. The doctors also mentioned he was slightly underweight." Grant sighed. "I'm also concerned that the social worker might bring the child welfare people in. I don't believe Erina has any documentation on her entry into the country, or even a birth certificate for Colin."

"Good Lord! You mean on top of everything else she's an illegal immigrant?"

"I have no idea. She says she's from 1896."

"What?"

"She thinks she and Colin have traveled forward in time as a result of a miracle at St. Mary's Cathedral."

"You're kidding me, right?"

"No, unfortunately. She's actually very convincing. And she even picked a time from which there are no records."

"Wait just a minute, Grant. The fascination you have for this girl and her baby is getting out of hand."

Grant pushed himself out of his chair and paced the length of his office. "I knew you were going to say that, Brian. And it's going to get worse."

"No, you don't! You just wait—"

"Can't do that, Brian. Now, the way I figure it, what I need right now is a good immigration attorney and a meeting with a private investigator. A really good one."

"Dammit, Grant . . ."

"Think you can arrange something for this afternoon?"

Erina paced Colin's private room, her thoughts more on Grant than on her sleeping son. Night had fallen, but he still wasn't back from Houston. Perhaps something had happened to him. Maybe he'd just grown tired of her problems. He was under no obligation; still, she'd grown to depend on his guidance and . . . his presence.

She'd grown to care for Grant.

The very thought filled her with both excitement and dread. While she'd come to expect his smiles and frowns, his intense looks and heart-pounding kisses, she had no way of knowing how long she'd be in his time. What if she and Colin suddenly disappeared next week, or in two weeks? Oh, Grant would believe her then, no doubt, but his realization would come too late. She'd never see him again—a thought that saddened her terribly.

Once before she'd fantasized about a wealthy young man, and look what had happened! She knew she was safe with Grant; he'd proved himself a gentleman at his condo, leaving her in peace to bathe and dress. But now her heart was in more danger than her person.

She should be focused on Colin, she reminded herself. Although he'd run a degree of fever, the nurse had explained earlier, that was considered normal, and he could still be moved from the intensive care unit. He'd been awake longer today, and she could sit with him for as long as she liked. The hour grew late though, and still there was no sign of Grant.

She had no money for dinner, and although she could help herself to coffee, the brew didn't set well on an empty stomach. A combination of nerves and no food was producing a headache that pounded against her temples with each step.

She stopped pacing and looked out the window. Lights from around the island gave a magical view. She'd remembered—and miss—electric lights if she went back to her own time. Not only were they functional, they were beautiful as well. Grant had explained that at Christmas, homes and businesses were decorated with colored and white electric lights, giving beautiful displays of holiday shapes and messages. She wanted to stay and see such a sight but feared that her time was limited. Her miracle had concerned only Colin's cure, and he was getting better each day.

With a sigh, she walked over and sat in the chair beside the bed. She'd turned off the overhead lights, leaving only a lamp to provide a faint glow in the room. Colin slept peacefully on his back, the bandage from his surgery covered by his little gown.

What would she do if Grant didn't come back? She could sleep here at the hospital for a time, she supposed, but she still had no money, no food. Her new clothes were at Grant's condo. And what about Colin's medical bills? Would Grant pay those now?

"You're workin' yourself into a mean, gloomy mood," she whispered into the darkness, hugging her arms close. How had she become so dependent on a man in such a short period of time?

Minutes passed. A nurse came by and checked Colin, then left with barely a smile. Erina sat in the hard chair, rested her chin on a propped-up hand, and tried to envision life without Grant. The longer she sat there, the more her head pounded and the louder her stomach growled.

Grant stood in the doorway and gazed into the darkened room. The faint light from a low-wattage bulb illuminated Erina as she rested beside Colin's bed. Poor girl. This had been a long day for her.

He stepped into the room, his leather soles making no sound on the flooring. Colin appeared to be sleeping peacefully, his little chest rising and falling regularly, his head turned to the side, away from the light. Grant watched him for a moment, knowing he'd never experienced anything like the feeling of happiness and peace he felt when he looked at this baby. If he didn't know it was impossible, he could almost believe Colin was his son.

But that was impossible, just as Erina's story of being from the past was a fabrication. He had to remember that, especially when she began talking about things she'd done, or questioned him about life today. Sometimes he fell for her wide-eyed vulnerability. Sometimes he had a hard time separating fact from fiction.

He turned to Erina. She was asleep, her neck bent at an awkward angle, her back impossibly slanting toward the small bedside table. If he could, he'd just scoop her up and carry her home. But she'd probably protest, he thought, grinning, and the staff would never understand why it was okay to carry a kicking and screaming woman out of the hospital.

He hunkered down in front of her chair. "Erina?"

Her eyes drifted open. She gazed at him without recognition for just an instant, then launched herself from the chair into his arms.

"I was so worried about you," she said, a death grip around his neck. "Where have you been when all I was doin' was thinkin' the worst?"

"And what was the worst?" he asked with a chuckle.

"That you'd driven that demon Cherokee of yours too fast. Or that . . . Never mind what I was thinkin'."

"Oh, no. What else?" he asked, disengaging her arms from around his neck so he could lean back and see her face.

" 'Tis nothing," she said, blushing.

"Did you think I wasn't coming back?"

"Now what would be givin' you an idea like that?" she asked defensively.

"Because you have the worst poker face I've ever seen."

"What's that supposed to mean?" she asked, her eyes flashing blue fire.

"Just that whatever you're thinking is clearly written on your face."

"I've never been told such a thing before," she said, as though challenging him.

"Maybe no one else was looking closely enough."

Her eyebrows rose and she opened her mouth as though she was going to reply, then shut it and blushed.

"I take it I got the last word in," he said, feeling very carefree for the first time in days.

"I know you enjoy gettin' the last word."

He pushed a strand of hair back behind her ear. "Look at us, bickering and teasing like an old married couple. What do you think that means?"

"I . . . It probably means we've been together too long."

"I think maybe it means something else entirely," Grant said, studying her pale face, her dark eyes, her soft pink lips. Right now they were slightly parted, as though issuing an invitation. When her gaze fell to his mouth he was lost.

He kissed her gently, sweetly, until she responded by parting her lips even more. He teased her with his tongue until she opened for him. Then the kiss changed, turning from a gentle exploration to an explosion of passion. He held her tightly, her breasts firm against his chest, his lower body desperately craving contact with her softness. A part of him wanted to pull her from the chair and lie with her on the floor, the hospital be damned. He wanted Erina, now and with a fierceness he'd never experienced before.

"Visiting hours are over," a stern voice announced, breaking into his fantasy like a bucket of ice water.

They broke apart like naughty schoolchildren. Erina covered her swollen lips with a hand while he stood up, turned to the wall, and tried to tell his body to calm down. Every damn time they kissed at this hospital they got "caught."

"We'll be gone in just a minute," he said, his voice

sounding strained and slightly high. *Great. Just like a teenager.* Not only couldn't he control his raging hormones, now he sounded like he was going through puberty again.

This was no way to impress Erina.

"I suppose you haven't gotten into any trouble," she said, breaking into his thoughts.

"No, but I'm sorry I'm late. I didn't want to call the room and wake up Colin, and I wasn't sure where he was."

"They transferred him to this room late this afternoon. He's doing fine, except that he had just a touch of fever."

"Really?" Grant said, turning to look at the sleeping child. He looked okay, but his cheeks were a bit pink.

"Did the doctor come by?"

"Yes, he did. He told me not to worry."

"Did you worry?"

"Just a bit. The nurse explained that a touch of fever after surgery is not uncommon."

"I've heard that too. Well, if he still has a fever, we can get another opinion tomorrow. I'm not going to risk his health when he's done so well."

"I think the doctor knows what he's doin'," Erina said gently.

"Probably, but I'm not taking any chances with Colin's health."

"You're actin' like you're his da," Erina said, amazement and a trace of resentment in her voice.

"I'm sorry, but it's my nature to take charge. And

I mean it; Colin is going to have the best care possible."

She tilted her head to the side and watched him but said nothing else on the subject. "I suppose I should have a bed brought in."

"Why? You're coming back to the condo with me, aren't you?"

"I wasn't sure," she said, looking him in the eye. "When you didn't come to the hospital I thought perhaps you'd grown tired of . . . Well, I suppose that isn't true."

"No, it's not. I think I was well on my way to proving that until the nurse interrupted." He watched Erina smile slightly and look away. "But if you'd like more proof . . ."

"No! I mean, that's not necessary."

"Darn. I suppose I can wait until the next time I get such an exuberant welcome."

"I . . . You caught me unawares. I was asleep and I'd been thinkin' of you."

He pulled her close, craving contact with her petite body almost as much now as he had earlier. The slight brush of her skirt against his dress slacks, the feel of her breasts against his chest, the near touch of her soft belly against his rapidly hardening body was enough to drive him crazy again. "We'd better get home quickly before someone else interrupts us."

"We'll not be carryin' on like this at your home," she whispered.

"If you say so, although I'd like nothing more than to prove how good we could be together."

"I'd like nothin' more than to stop this madness."

He smiled down at her. "Liar. You want me nearly as much as I want you."

She pushed away from his chest and turned to the bed. "Enough of your seduction, Mr. Kirby."

"So we're back to that. Well, I don't mind. You'll be calling me Grant soon enough. Let's say good night to Colin and get a bite to eat. I haven't had anything since a lunch of wimpy croissant sandwiches about noon. Did you go downstairs and eat?"

"No. . . . I . . . I suppose you know I don't have any money," she said softly.

"Damn, Erina, I'm sorry. I totally forgot to give you some spending money."

"That's not your responsibility. I've taken so much from you already."

"None of that talk. I'll give you some as soon as we get home. That way, if you need dinner or a cab or whatever, you'll have your own money."

"I'll be glad to work for my keep."

"Sorry. I don't need any dresses made," he said, lifting her chin and smiling into her too-serious face. "Besides, we're friends. Shouldn't friends help each other without expecting anything in return?"

"I . . . I suppose."

"Good. Now, kiss Colin good night and I'll take you out to eat."

She placed a kiss on her baby's cheek. Grant leaned over and touched his lips to Colin's forehead. "Sleep tight, tiger," he whispered. Sure enough, the baby's temperature felt normal—at least in his untrained opinion.

Taking Erina's arm, he guided her out the door.

"What do you feel like? Chinese, Italian, steaks, seafood?"

Erina knew something had changed. She didn't know what; she couldn't understand from Grant's odd mood. He seemed happy, yet also introspective and very observant of her. As a matter of fact, she'd felt herself squirm several times under his close perusal as they ate in a small restaurant that sold sandwiches called "hamburgers"—which contained no ham that she could discern.

Grant kept his arm around her shoulders as they walked from the garage to the elevator, then his condo, even though the weather was warm and clear, the breeze fresh and salty. "It's been a long day for both of us," he said as he unlocked the door.

"I suppose I'd sound very ungrateful if I said that I got a bit tired at the hospital today."

"Ungrateful? Not at all. Why would you think that?"

"Because it's a miracle that Colin had the surgery and he's doin' so well. I should just be thankful, but I'm afraid I'm becomin' a bit spoiled."

Grant placed his business case on the small desk near the couch. "I think you should recognize your own needs. You don't have to convince me how devoted you are to Colin."

"I'm not tryin' to convince *you*," she whispered, walking to the large windows and looking out at the dark beach and ocean. She couldn't see much except a little white froth on the waves. In the background she heard Grant push the button on his telephone so it would speak back to him. When he turned on a light she could no longer see outside, only her reflection in the glass.

How different she looked in these new clothes! She would never have believed she'd wear such short skirts, but here she was, her lower legs and ankles exposed. And she could bare her arms without anyone looking at her twice. Her physical appearance made her look like a woman of this century, but was she also changing in her thoughts? Perhaps, about some of the social conventions. But she had to hold fast to her values and beliefs, especially those of the Church. Her blessing as a mother—the health of her child—was a result of her faith in the Blessed Virgin and in God.

She must not think so much of Grant Kirby that she forgot who she was and why she was here. And just because she'd read every magazine in the waiting rooms, advising her of her woman's needs and how to satisfy them, didn't mean that she would take any action.

He finished listening to the messages on his telephone and walked up beside her. "See anything interesting?" he asked, placing his arm around her shoulders and pulling her close.

"No . . . yes," she said, shivering as she came in full contact with the very warm, solid side of his body. He smelled so good, was always so clean and well groomed, unlike the men she'd known in her own time. They'd smelled of hair oil, bay rum cologne, and, sometimes, the odor of stale sweat.

"You sound a little confused tonight," he said,

looking out the window even though he couldn't see a thing.

She suspected he was looking at her. The knowledge made her even more concerned about her appearance, her values, and her desires as a woman. "I feel a bit uncertain. You seem . . . different."

"I think we should sit down and talk," he said. "I do have several things on my mind."

She slipped away from his arm and walked to one of the chairs facing the couch. "What's the matter?"

"Nothing," he said, slipping off his suit coat and placing it over the arm of the couch. He sat down facing her. "But I think things could get bad if we don't take some action."

"The social worker and her threats?"

"Exactly. While I was in Houston today, I talked to an immigration attorney."

"Is that someone who could help get papers for me and Colin?"

Grant shifted on the cushion. "Not exactly. I told him about you and Colin and he gave me some suggestions."

"What did he say?"

"If I can get your papers, he can help."

"But I can't get them! They're in my apartment—in 1896."

"I was afraid you were going to say that."

"What else can I be sayin'?" Why didn't he understand that if she had any way to prove that her entry into the United States was legal, she would? If she could produce Colin's birth certificate, she would. "What about the records that the city or the state keeps? Can I get a copy from them?"

"If there is a birth certificate for Colin, it wouldn't do any good now, would it? I mean, no one is going to believe he's a hundred years old."

Erina crossed her arms over her chest. "Includin' you."

"You have to admit that your story is unbelievable."

The fight went out of her. "I know. If it hadn't happened to me, I wouldn't have believed it either. If I'd been sittin' in my own apartment and you appeared, I wouldn't have believed you were from the future."

He stared at her until she felt uncomfortable. "What can I do?" she asked.

"What can *we* do is more like it. I told you we're in this together." He leaned forward, resting his forearms on his knees. "The attorney's name is Sam Reynolds. He's a good guy. I think he understands the situation."

"What do you mean?"

"That you have no proof whatsoever that you're Erina O'Shea, that Colin is your son, or that you're here legally."

"I cannot believe he'd be that understandin'," she scoffed.

"He's heard a lot of stories in his time."

"This isn't a story!"

"I know; it's the truth. Anyway, Sam said that if we could find your papers, he'd be glad to represent you in case there's a hearing."

"But how can we get something that doesn't exist?"

"We can have some of them re-created."

"What do you mean?"

"We hire someone to make the documents that you should have, like Colin's birth certificate, your birth certificate, and some other type of identity card from Ireland."

"But I haven't lived in Ireland since 1888."

"Erina, please."

"All right! But I'm tellin' the truth. They'll be no record of me in Ireland."

"Would you submit your fingerprints for a check?"

"What do you mean?"

"An investigator will take a print of your fingertips. Each person has a different pattern. That's one way to identify individuals."

"Really?" Erina looked at the swirls and lines on her fingers and marveled that such methods existed. "If it would help, I'd be glad to give you fingerprints."

He seemed surprised by her response but quickly launched into another subject. "And this investigator will probably want to question you, just to make sure you're telling me the same story."

"He's going to see if I'm lyin' to you?"

Grant looked uncomfortable. "Well, in a way. You've got to understand that he needs all the facts he can get to help you."

"And I suppose you told him you didn't believe me?"

"I didn't have to. None of them believed your story, but as you said, who can blame them? It is far-fetched."

"Right you are. And I cannot fault you for that again."

"Thanks. So you'll cooperate with the investigator?"

"I told you I'd do anything to save Colin."

"Even if it means getting married?"

Chapter Eleven

"What?"

She almost shouted the question. Grant was sure his neighbors could hear Erina's startled reply to his bombshell comment.

The idea had been a surprise to him at first too. Now that he'd had time to think about, he could see the merit of such an outrageous proposal.

"Even if Mrs. Henshaw doesn't cause any problems, you still have the ongoing problem of no documentation. What will happen when Colin gets older or if you need some government assistance? Sam mentioned that as the wife of a U.S. citizen, you would have a much better chance of gaining resident status. And if you said that Colin was the son of a U.S. citizen, then—"

"And what man did you have in mind for such a task?"

"You're kidding, right?" He watched the high color of her cheeks, the flash of her dark blue eyes, and changed his opinion of her once again. This wasn't the reaction of a woman—or a girl—trying to trap a rich husband.

"I do not find the holy state of matrimony the subject of jest."

"Look, Erina, I thought this would be clear to you. I'm offering to marry you if necessary to keep Colin out of the hands of the authorities."

She sank back into the chair, her mouth parted in surprise. "Are you daft?" she whispered. "We cannot get married."

"Why not?"

"Because . . . Well, we hardly know each other. We don't love each other. You've already helped me far beyond what any other man would do—"

"And you don't trust my motives."

"I trust you with my son's life, but that's not the point I'm tryin' to make."

"Then tell me why we can't get married to keep him safe."

"First, you said we need documents. And we don't know that the social worker will cause us trouble."

"Believe me, they're like a dog with a bone. If she reports Colin to the child welfare department . . . well, sometimes it takes them a while to decide whether a child is in danger, but once they do they hang on for dear life."

"So you believe that someone in authority will insist on seeing these documents?"

"I don't know, but you've got to be prepared. I'm calling Mrs. Henshaw tomorrow. I'm certain she'll want to set up a meeting immediately with you and me."

Erina closed her eyes and clasped her hands in her lap. "What are you going to tell her?"

"I'm going to say that you'll be glad to meet with her, with me and your attorney. And if she asks about documents, I'll stall her until I can find out how to get counterfeit identification."

"That sounds illegal."

"It is. That's why the attorney doesn't need to know anything about it."

"But I thought you said he suggested it."

"Not in so many words. I just understood what he meant."

"Are you sure you're not just speculatin'? Maybe no one will care about where I'm from or ask for any documents on Colin."

"No, I'm sure this is very serious."

Erina sprang from the chair and paced the width of the room. Her floral skirts swirled around her legs as her long black hair flowed about her shoulders and arms. She seemed agitated, meditative, unapproachable. Grant knew she needed time to think, time to assimilate all the information and options he'd heaped upon her, but they didn't have a lot of time. He needed to finalize a story—a tale almost as outrageous as her claims to be from the past.

He walked to the bar and found a bottle of good cognac from his limited stock. Grabbing two glasses, he poured them each a splash. He returned to the sitting area and stopped in front of Erina. "Here, try this."

She looked at him suspiciously. "What is it?"

"Brandy—cognac. Just sip it."

She did. Her eyes widened and she swallowed hard.

"Not a big drinker, I take it?"

"No."

"Good, neither am I." He sipped his own drink, then put the glass on the coffee table.

"Erina, I have an idea of how we're going to be able to pull this off."

"What do you mean?"

"A story. Come and sit down. I'll tell you my idea."

Erina couldn't sleep. She tossed and turned until her nightgown tangled around her legs. The walls seemed to press in on her; the air was too still, the night too quiet. She couldn't stay in bed a second longer.

Finding the satin robe that matched the night-gown—an extravagant creation Grant had purchased with the other clothing—she slipped her feet into slippers and made her way across the bedroom. She eased open the door. The condo was quiet; Grant was no doubt sound asleep after telling her his preposterous story of how they'd "met."

She tiptoed into the kitchen and looked for a mug that she was sure could be put in the microwave oven. Grant had showed her again how to heat water for hot tea, but she was still unsure of which dishes to use. Some plastic heated okay, he'd said, but she still didn't know what plastic was.

The tall, wide windows beckoned. She took her cup of tea into the living room and looked out into the darkness of night. A full moon had risen high into the night sky, giving the water a blue glow and clearly showing each wave. Erina slid open the latch on the door and pushed it wide, stepping out onto the small balcony.

She was so high up! Twelve floors, Grant had said. No building that high existed in her own time in Galveston. Four stories was the most, she thought. Even though she was so far above the beach, the sound of the waves carried upward, soothing her with their rhythm. She loved the ocean and the beach. Although she hadn't been able to visit it often, she'd treasured each time. Once, she'd accompanied Mrs. Kirby and her two daughters to Murdoch's Bath House for a summer outing. The two girls had dressed in bathing costumes and ventured out into the waves while she and Mrs. Kirby sat above on the veranda built on piers driven into the sand. They'd sipped lemonade and watched the citizens of Galveston mingle, giggle, and generally enjoy the day.

That was one of the times that had made Erina think of marrying well—at least well enough to afford a bathing costume and an occasional day at Murdoch's Bath House. Not long after that summer day, Jerrold Kirby had gone away to college and her father had died. Her dreams had faded, replaced by grief and loneliness.

"A penny for your thoughts."

Grant's voice cut through the softness of the night, making her jump and splash some tea on her hand.

"I didn't mean to frighten you," he said, stepping out beside her on the balcony. "That wasn't hot, was it?" he asked, placing his large hands around her own and cradling the mug.

"No," she said, still shaking from the start he'd given her. Or at least that's what she wanted to believe. His mere presence, his gentle touch, wouldn't make her tremble so.

"What were you thinking so intently?" he asked again.

"Just about the beach. A long time ago I visited a bath house with Mrs. Kirby and her daughters. The day was special to me, but then my life changed. . . ."

"What happened?"

"My da," she said softly.

"I'm sorry."

"I am too. He was a fine man. Colin is named for him."

"Colin Patrick?"

"Patrick was my mother's da's name."

Grant released her hands and went to the railing, staring out into the ocean. "Colin deserves a good life."

"I know. Right after he was born I dreamed of taking him to the beach, teaching him to walk on the wet sand, showing him the waves. When I learned how ill he was I knew I'd never have that chance."

"He'll have that opportunity now."

"But if I don't convince the social worker that he should stay with me, I won't be the one to teach him to walk in the waves." She heard the catch in her voice and tried not to sniffle.

"You will. We're going to make this work." Grant made the statement with such certainty that she could almost believe he was right. He turned to look

199

at her, resting his back against the railing.

"Doesn't the height bother you?" she asked, watching him nervously as he leaned casually against the narrow band of metal.

"No. I've been rock climbing since I was eighteen. I'm used to heights."

"What do you mean, rock climbing?"

"It's a sport, like skiing or surfing or skydiving."

She had no idea what he was talking about.

"You climb almost vertical faces of rock using just a few tools. Sometimes you're dangling from your fingertips hundred of feet above the ground. It's a real rush."

"That sounds horrible! What if you slip and fall?"

"Each climber wears a harness and is attached by chocks wedged into a fissure or driven into the rock. There's a rope that fits through metal rings into the harness and the chocks. You can fall, but you don't fall far."

"But what if the rope breaks, or those chock things pull out of the rock? You could be killed!"

"I'm careful."

She looked at his large, workman's hands. "Is that how you . . . why I thought you worked with your hands?"

"Probably. You don't have to be bulked up to climb, but upper body strength is important. And you depend on your hands to pull you up the face of the mountain or cliff."

She shook her head. "This doesn't sound like a good pastime."

"I enjoy it."

"You enjoy the danger?"

He shrugged. "I enjoy controlling the risk of climbing. It's just you against the rock." He shifted his weight, crossing his legs at the ankles. "Anyway, I learned to climb when I attended the University of Colorado. Some friends already knew how and I went along. I loved it. After living in Houston, and occasionally Galveston, I loved the mountains and the sheer rock faces. It was so different. And I was studying geology, so my interest in rocks fit right in."

"What's geology?"

"The study of rocks, basically."

"You went to college to study rocks?" she asked skeptically. She'd never heard of such a thing.

"Yes. My father wasn't too happy about it either. But that's what I wanted to do. My mother was convinced that I'd come to my senses soon, change my major, and transfer to a 'better' school."

"And did you change your mind? I mean, you're running your da's company."

"No," he said, looking out into the night, "I didn't change my mind. My father died and I didn't have much choice."

"I'm sorry."

"Me too. I was having a hell of a time in Colorado." He looked at her again, smiling in a way that didn't convince her he was telling her much of what he felt. "Have you thought any more about the story?"

"Of course I've thought about it."

"Is that why you couldn't sleep?"

"I'm not sure."

"Do you want to talk some more?"

She shook her head. "I just need to think."

"Do you want me to leave you alone?"

"Yes . . . no. I mean, I'm not sure. I don't want to keep you from your rest."

"I don't need a lot of sleep." He pushed away from the railing and took a step toward her. "I could use a kiss, though," he said softly.

He pressed her up against the cold glass, his body warm and hard. Erina knew she should push him away, should ask him to stop before he even began kissing her, but her resolution faded with the first touch of his lips. When his mouth closed over hers, she could only moan and grasp his shoulders. And when his tongue slipped inside her parted lips, she kissed him back.

She felt as though she were floating above the balcony, high in the breeze that pushed her gown around her legs, far out over the waves that gently pounded against the sand. Yes, she was soaring, and Grant was with her.

His hand was hot against her satin-covered waist, sliding along her ribs . . . and higher. She couldn't believe she would allow such liberties, but her body had awakened and she wanted to feel the touch of his hands on her breasts. And then he gathered the weight into his large hand, rolled the nipple between his fingers, and she thought she might die.

Panting, she broke the kiss. That didn't stop Grant. He trailed his lips down her throat to the sensitive point where her neck joined her shoulder. Her knees buckled. He caught her easily, pressed her more firmly against the glass, and dropped to his knees in front of her.

"What?" she managed to gasp faintly.

And then his mouth closed over her swollen breast.

"No," she moaned as she felt her body respond. A sweet, urgent throbbing began low in her body, a feeling she'd never experienced before. Was this what the magazines meant, passion so strong that a woman could forget where she was, who she was?

"Grant, no," she said again.

He stopped his gentle assault, looking up at her with eyes that seemed to glow in the moonlight. "Why? Just let yourself go. I want to give you pleasure."

"I . . . I can't," she said.

"Is it because of Colin's birth?" he asked. "Is there something wrong?"

"No, I don't think so. But this is wrong. I cannot make love with you."

"Then don't," he said, resting his head against her sensitive breasts. "Let me make love to you, as far as you want to go. I won't demand anything, Erina. I won't force you."

"I know that," she said, her eyes closed as she felt his warm breath against her nipple through the satin. "But being with you this way is against my beliefs, my religion."

"Even if we're engaged? Even if I'm going to be your husband?"

"No. I will not tie you to me in marriage even for Colin's sake."

"You know you will if it's the only way. Erina, let me show you how good it can be."

"Please, don't ask me," she whispered.

He stood up, still touching her but no longer pressed against her. She felt the dampness of his mouth on her breasts, and also the milk that had leaked. What would Grant think of such a blatant reminder of her motherhood?

"Look at me, please."

She opened her eyes, surprised to feel tears escape and spill down her cheeks. She wiped them away, hoping Grant wouldn't notice. But, of course, he did.

"I've made you cry," he said, his voice low and sad.

"No, I'm just confused. I never expected to feel this way."

"You've never wanted a man before?"

"No, never. I read about such things in the magazines at the hospital, but I've never . . . You make me feel so different."

"Is that necessarily bad?"

"I don't know," she said, closing her eyes again as new tears threatened. "I look different in my new clothes. I'm tryin' to act like a woman of your time. But inside I'm still the same person. I cannot go against what my father taught me, what the Church states as doctrine, just because I want to make love with you."

"I appreciate your honesty," he whispered. Then he wrapped his arms around her, holding her close but not trying to kiss or caress her. His face rested against her hair; she felt his steady breathing. He just held her, while the salty breeze blew around them and the waves continued their journey to shore.

It was at that moment that she knew she'd fallen in love with Grant Kirby.

Grant called Sam Reynolds the next morning and set up an appointment for Erina to meet him in Houston on Monday. Then he called Brian.

"We're going ahead with the plan, Brian. Erina and I are meeting Sam on Monday to get the ball rolling. I'd like you to be there too."

"I'll just tell you one more time that I think you've lost your ever lovin' mind."

"I know." Grant rubbed his forehead, where a headache threatened. "Look, I've got to tell Mother something. Our appointment with Sam is for two o'clock. Why don't we have an early dinner at her house around five thirty?"

"Who's we?" Brian asked suspiciously.

"You need to be there too."

"Oh, no I don't. I don't think your mother wants me to see her when she goes ballistic."

"Sure she does. Someone has to be there to commiserate with her. After all, Erina and I will be on one side. You need to hold her hand and agree that she's raised an idiot for a son."

Grant imagined that Brian was shaking his head. "How much are you going to tell her?"

"We're going with the story. Nothing more."

"She's not going to believe it. She'll check back on the calendar. She'll get your travel records. Hell, she'll probably have her own background check done on Erina."

"And what do you think she'll find? When you did your initial check you found nothing, right? Not here or in Ireland."

"That's right, which is just going to tell your mother that Erina is an impostor."

"She'll come around when she sees Colin."

"You're bringing that baby to dinner?" Brian almost shouted.

"No, of course not. He'll probably still be in the hospital on Monday, although he should get to come home on Tuesday. He ran a slight fever, so I'm going to make sure he's well before they release him."

"You've gotten real attached to the boy, haven't you?"

"Yeah. If I didn't know better, I'd swear he was mine, Brian. I mean, he looks like me, and there's this kind of bond I felt the first time I held him."

"That's because he's a little kid and needed help. Don't read more into this than there is."

"I'm trying to retain some objectivity," Grant said, exasperated at himself for the softness and domesticity he was experiencing for the first time. It was Erina's fault too; she inspired that kind of thinking—of warm, cuddly nights sleeping together, making love while the waves crashed to shore. Of eating meals together, snuggling on the couch while they watched television, laughing as they walked along the beach. All those American ideals, those middle-class values that he'd missed so far in his life. He wanted a family—but only if that family was Erina and Colin.

"Okay, I'll call your mother and make plans for dinner on Monday."

"Thanks, Brian. I'll call if anything comes up."

"Think you could squeeze in some contract signing while you're in town attending to your other business?"

"Of course. After we get finished with our appointment at Sam's we can stop by the office. That reminds me: Erina agreed to be fingerprinted for a more intensive background check."

"Really?"

"Yes. It surprised me a little too, how quickly she agreed. But Brian, she'll do anything to protect her baby."

"Sounds like she's thought of everything."

"Or maybe she's just a devoted mother."

"Um-hmm," Brian said. "Do you want me to call the PI we use for security checks?"

"Yes. If possible, he should be at the office when we come by. He could fingerprint Erina and get the information he needs."

"I'll call him. What do you want me to tell him?"

"Just to put a rush on the check. You can say that we're thinking of hiring her for a critical position."

"Okay, but I doubt he'll find anything."

"You may be right." Grant wanted some proof, anything that would tell him who Erina really was, where she was born, where she'd lived. "We'll see you at Sam's office, then. After we get finished at my office we can ride to Mother's together, if you want."

"No way. I'm taking my own car in case she throws me out for aiding and abetting the enemy."

"Hey, I'm not the enemy. I'm her only son, remember?"

"Yeah, I remember. I just hope *she* does when you present your very young Irish love to her."

"She's not my love. I'm just doing the right thing by Colin." Grant ignored the leap in his pulse. He did not love Erina; he did, however, want her. She was so vulnerable, so lovable . . . But he didn't love her.

Really? A little voice inside his head questioned his judgment.

"Whatever you say. I'll see you on Monday."

"Thanks, Brian."

Grant hung up the phone. He couldn't ignore the dichotomy of his logic; he wanted Erina, he was willing to marry and live with her, but he didn't love her.

Of course he didn't. He'd have to trust her to love her, and she still hadn't told him why she'd made up her story. Until she told him the truth about where she was from and how she'd gotten into his condo, he couldn't give his heart to her.

Someday she'd tell him the whole story. She'd admit how and why she had picked him to save the life of her child. And then he'd decide if he could fall in love with her.

Chapter Twelve

Colin looked so much better on Friday morning. Erina and Grant arrived at the hospital just before ten o'clock, due mainly to the fact that she overslept that morning. She wanted nothing more than to sit with her baby, rock him, sing to him, and enjoy his healthy pink color. After Grant watched her with an intense, possessive look on his face, she told him to go back to his work or his condo if he wanted to; she'd stay at the hospital during the day and play with Colin.

She didn't want to think about how Grant had made her feel last night on the balcony.

Grant smiled and said he'd be back to take her to lunch at around twelve thirty. She welcomed the respite but wondered again at his mood. He was very serious about sacrificing his bachelor status for her—or for Colin, actually. But he also wanted her, and she didn't have enough knowledge of men to understand why he wanted her so much and why he was willing to marry her. Was it really to save Colin or did he want her in his bed that badly?

"There's no explainin' some things," she said to Colin as she nursed him in the chair beside the bed. Her baby looked up at her with his clear, dark blue eyes as though he listened to her every word. Perhaps he did. She knew next to nothing about infants; she'd been frightened to death when she learned she was pregnant. Mrs. Abernathy had been a wealth of knowledge, a rock of stability during those trying months. And after Colin was born, early and with his heart problem, Mrs. Abernathy had helped her get to the doctor when all Erina had wanted to do was lie abed and cry.

Colin's eyes drifted shut and he quit nursing. Erina adjusted the nursing bra and rose from the chair. Gently, she lay Colin down for a nap. With little sleep last night, she could use a nap too herself. She didn't want to leave Colin, so with a grimace, she curled up into the chair, tucked her fist underneath her chin, and closed her eyes.

"Erina, wake up."

She heard the words, but it took a moment to register where she was and who was speaking. When she opened her eyes she saw Grant, smiling and holding a . . . rocking chair?

"What's this?" she asked sleepily. He placed the chair, which was adorned with a big blue bow, near the bed.

"It's for you. I noticed the other day how you liked to rock Colin back and forth. I did a little shopping while you were napping."

"What time is it?"

"About twelve thirty."

"Oh." She rubbed her eyes and sat up straight. "That's a lovely chair," she said, reaching out to touch the smooth, dark wood.

"The salesperson said it was comfortable."

"You carried it all the way up here for me?"

"Of course. Well, for you and Colin, actually."

"Thank you." He was doing it again: performing such good deeds that she could swear he was an angel sent to protect her son and provide for her.

But angels didn't kiss like Grant Kirby. She felt her cheeks grow warm at the memory.

"Come and try out the chair," he said, breaking into her thoughts.

She stretched and rose from the hospital chair, noticing for the first time that her neck was stiff and her hand was asleep. When she slid into the big rocker she felt right at home. There was plenty of room to hold Colin, even when he grew too old to rock, and she could rest her elbows on the arms of the chair. She pushed with her foot and set the chair in motion.

"I like it very much," she said, smiling, looking up at Grant.

He bent down and kissed her lips. The touch was brief, the kiss fleeting, but it warmed her as much as his thoughtful gift.

"Let's have some lunch while Colin is sleeping. I've hired a private nurse to look in on him. That way he won't be alone when you're gone."

"Really? I didn't know you could hire private

nurses to work in the hospitals."

"I didn't either, but then I asked what would happen if you couldn't be here during the time when Colin was awake, and the nurse told me that they had to divide their time among several children. She suggested a private nurse, since Colin is in a private room."

"That's very thoughtful, but why wouldn't I be here?"

"In case we went to lunch," he said, steering her toward the door, "or if we have to go to Houston or to meet with Mrs. Henshaw."

"Oh, that." She didn't want to spoil the day thinking about the social worker who thought she was an uncaring mother. And she didn't want to think about what she might have to do if someone decided to investigate her lack of documentation.

They stopped by the nurses' station, and Erina met the private nurse, Mrs. Bea Parker, a very competent-looking woman who reminded her of Mrs. Abernathy. She wore a white uniform with a gray apron and looked very much like a grandmother.

"I'm sure you'll be fine with Colin," Erina said warmly.

"I'm looking forward to meeting the boy," Mrs. Parker said.

"He's sleeping now, but he should waken soon. There are bottles for him in the refrigerator. The nurses know which ones."

"We'll do fine. Have a nice lunch."

Erina smiled as they walked down the corridor toward the elevators. She was proud of her grasp of these new terms, and the fact that she could use them with ease when she hadn't even known them a week ago. She was fitting in very nicely in this century.

"I've set up an appointment for you and me to meet with Sam Reynolds in Houston on Monday," Grant said.

"Are you so sure then that we'll need his help?"

"I'm pretty sure. I also called Mrs. Henshaw this morning. She can't wait to meet with us and find out the 'truth.'"

"She wouldn't recognize the truth," Erina said, mostly to herself.

"I'm not sure *I'd* recognize the truth at the moment. That's why she's going to get our version—the one we can agree on."

"Grant, I don't think that's wise." They stopped at the elevators and waited for the doors to open.

"You know, I really like the way you've begun to use my name," he said with a grin. "How about seafood for lunch? There's a great place where you can sit out over the water and watch the waves. Sometimes even a few surfers."

"Grant, we should talk about this story."

"We will. Before Monday. I promise. After all, you'll need to get all the facts straight before you meet my mother for dinner on Monday."

"Your mother!"

That afternoon the nurse took Colin for a round of tests to see how he was recovering from his surgery. He had no more fever, and that was a good sign.

213

Grant finally convinced Erina to come back to the condo with him for a short time while Colin was out of the room.

Being a father was kind of fun, Grant thought as he unlocked the door to the condo. He had a reason to get out of bed each morning besides just showing up at the office. He looked forward to Colin's smiles more than those of his office or property management staff. And Erina—well, he wanted to make her happy too.

"Now close your eyes. I have a surprise for you."

"What are you doin'?"

He stood behind her and placed his palms over her eyes. "Just walk forward." She took a few tentative steps. "That's it. A few more. Now turn left."

She followed his instructions until they stood at the doorway of the guest bedroom.

"Okay. Now you can look." He took away his hands and moved to stand beside her. "What do you think?"

"Oh, Grant, it's beautiful," she said, awe in her voice. She walked into the room and ran her hand along the carved post of the crib, then traced the length of a rail. "When did you do this?"

"This morning. I decided Colin needed his own baby furniture."

"But there's so much!"

Grant probably *had* gone a bit overboard. But hell, what did he know about babies and their needs? He did know he needed a car seat for Colin, which he'd left in the Jeep so they could bring him home from the hospital safely. The salesperson, a matron who looked as though she'd raised a few of her own, assured him that this furniture was the best. It would last for years, she'd said with a smile, and through several children.

More children with Erina. The thought filled him with longing. If they did need to marry, would she want it to last? Would he? He was beginning to think they could have a good life together—if only she'd tell him the truth. He certainly wanted her, and she wanted him. Her response last night had been endearingly honest. She reacted innocently, even though she'd had a child.

He would teach her about making love, he thought with a fierceness that was foreign to him. The idea of making her his, legally and physically, filled him with a primitive joy. He'd never understood the possessive actions of some men before, but now he did. The attraction he felt for Erina was as elemental as breathing. How had he lived so long without experiencing this emotion?

"You shouldn't have," she said, turning to him with a smile. She seemed completely unaware of his inner turmoil. But the fierce longing must have shown on his face, because she stopped smiling, her eyes widened, and she took a deep breath. Awareness sparked between them.

He took a step into the room. Her bed was there, just waiting for them. He didn't have any protection in the condo, but that wouldn't matter between them. In this room crowded with baby furniture and a chaste double bed, he'd make love to Erina until she cried out her need for him. And she'd have his child—their child.

"Erina," he whispered, wanting her desperately. His body was primed and ready.

"Grant, no," she said, taking a step backward, coming up against the changing table. The sturdy piece tottered against the wall.

But he could make her respond, he thought. He could . . . What was he thinking? He was responding to her like a caveman! This wasn't like him at all. He took a deep, cleansing breath, then wiped his hand across his heated face. "I'm sorry, Erina. I don't know what came over me."

"I'm thinkin' maybe I shouldn't be in your home anymore," she said softly.

"No! I'm not going to harm you. I just . . . damn, I'm not sure what's wrong with me. I admit I want you—very badly, in fact. But I'm not going to force myself on you."

"But you will try to seduce me."

"I know I shouldn't. I tell myself to leave you alone, but you've got to understand that I know how you responded to me last night. That makes me want you so much more."

"That was a mistake. I couldn't sleep and I was thinkin' of other things, and—"

"The reasons don't matter. What happened was real. I wouldn't be much of a man if I didn't want to feel that way again. But I'm not going to put you in that sort of situation."

He closed the gap between them, noticing that she watched him but didn't try to run away. He placed his hands on her shoulders. "Erina, I'll always stop if you say 'no.' "

When she looked up at him, confusion and trust warring in her dark blue eyes, he almost took back his words. Almost. Finally, trust won out and he pushed his physical instincts aside—for the moment.

After they married she'd come to him willingly. She'd be free to make love to him then. She did want him, but she wanted to follow her religious beliefs more.

Just the kind of woman who would make an excellent mother, a wonderful wife. What more could he ask for?

The truth, a voice taunted him. *She may have convictions, but she did show up in your condo with a whopper of a story.* As soon as Colin was well, Grant vowed, he'd get some professional help for Erina. She'd be able to tell him where she was really from, what had really happened in her past.

He pushed his doubts aside for the moment. They needed to get back to the hospital, and besides, nothing could be accomplished by discussing her purported background. Though he hoped that someday soon they'd be able to establish a deeper relationship—one based on trust.

"Now Colin will have a room to come home to," he said with a false cheerfulness. "Maybe we'll find out this afternoon when he can come home."

"Are you sure you want us here? You've gotten very involved in our problems. Each day we cost you more money. Are you absolutely certain that you want us in your home?"

"Erina, I'm certain. I want you—both of you."

* * *

She dreamed that night, the past and the present meshing until she wasn't sure whether she was awake or asleep, or whether she'd returned to her own time.

She was in her room above Mrs. Abernathy's shop, but she sat in the rocking chair Grant had bought for her. Colin rested in the new crib, happy and healthy. Below, she heard Mrs. Abernathy singing in the kitchen. The smell of corned beef and cabbage drifted up the staircase and through her open door.

Looking down in her lap, she noticed the quilt she'd been working on for several months. She was adding more embroidery, strands of silk floss stretched across her hand. The quilt was even more complete than it had been the last time she'd dreamed of it.

Why did she dream of the quilt? It was only a work of scraps "borrowed" from various dresses she'd sewn. Miss Bettie Brown's gold ball gown, a green silk brocade day dress for Mrs. Menard, a silvery-gray velvet coat for the Kempners' daughter. A bit of lace left over from the milliner's shop around the corner.

But whenever she dreamed of the past the unfinished quilt was always there.

She set the rocker in motion, a feeling of sadness washing over her just as the sun broke through the salt-glazed windows and landed on her lap. What was wrong? She couldn't quite put her finger on the problem, but whatever it was, she felt a deep sense of loss. It wasn't Colin; he was fine and healthy.

The feeling intensified until she got up from the rocker and, holding the quilt to her chest, walked to the window. She looked outside. Suddenly a cloud passed over the sun. Daylight turned to dark; Post Office Street turned into the beach below Grant's window. The waves pounded against the brick of his building as she looked down, way down, twelve floors. But she lived on the second floor!

She opened the window and leaned out. Dizziness assailed her. She tried to draw back inside but felt drawn even farther over the railing. Railing? There was no balcony in her apartment. But the wind called to her, the waves urged her on, and then she was falling, falling, all the way to the sandy shore.

She awoke with a gasp, her heart pounding, her body covered in sweat. The sense of tumbling through space was so fresh in her mind that she had to hold on to the mattress to stop the spinning sensation. Finally her heartbeat slowed and her breathing returned to normal.

Moonlight filtered through the drapes at the window, illuminating the guest bedroom in Grant's condo. The new furniture lined the walls, the crib standing at the foot of the bed in which she slept.

She hadn't gone back in time, but the dream had been so real. Why was she mixing the past and the present, and why now? She'd never placed much significance on dreams, although she'd known others who experienced everything from night terrors to silly fantasies they swore would come true.

Somehow, these dreams of the past seemed different. Maybe that was how she would return—just go to sleep one night and wake up in the past. But would she know she'd returned, or would she think it was only a dream?

Chapter Thirteen

"Are you sure I look all right?" Erina asked, fidgeting in the Cherokee as they drove on Broadway out of Galveston.

Grant was certain she'd asked the question twice before. Ever since buying a new outfit specifically for the trip to Houston, she'd fretted over how she would appear to the attorney and to Grant's mother.

"You look great," he said. The blue, tiny-flowered dress she'd chosen was modest but clung to her curves in all the right places. Her long black hair was pulled back with a lacy bow, but a few tendrils escaped around her temples and in front of her ears. It wouldn't take Sam Reynolds, Brian Abbott, or his mother any great stretch of their imagination to believe he'd fallen for Erina O'Shea at first sight.

"As a matter of fact, if you looked any better, I don't think I'd want you to leave the condo."

"What do you mean? Is there something wrong? Am I dressed inappropriately to meet your mother?"

"No, not at all. And she's not the one I'm concerned

about. It's Sam and Brian who'll probably be a bit too charmed by your appearance." As the words left his mouth, he recognized the possessive, protective attitude he'd developed about Erina. She was charming, beautiful, and projected an innocent sexuality that had turned him into a lusty fool. Would she have the same effect on Sam and Brian?

If she did, they'd better have the good sense to keep their thoughts to themselves. Erina was his.

Damn, he *did* sound like a caveman. He'd never been that way around a woman before. As a matter of fact, if a woman got possessive with him, it had always been time to leave the relationship. He'd never wanted to be "tied down" until now.

Erina seemed to be pondering his words; then she said, "Are you sayin' I'm sexy?"

She sounded so surprised and confused that Grant burst out laughing before he could stop himself. "Darling, you are definitely sexy. Where did you come up with that, though?"

"From the magazines. They claim that women are supposed to be sexy, but I didn't know . . . that is, I never thought of myself that way."

"Well, you are, but just for me."

"Why is that?"

"Because Sam and Brian are too old for you."

"I thought you believed you were too old for me too."

"I am, but I'm not as old as those two."

"My da was fifteen years older than my mother, yet she died when I was just a babe. I don't think age has much to do with . . . things."

"Older men are usually attracted to younger women, but you're younger than most."

"In my time I'm considered quite mature."

"Well, in the 1800s, I think the average lifespan was about fifty years. So if you'd lived back then, you'd be almost middle-aged at twenty. But you don't live then, you live now. And twenty is very young."

"Will your mother and the attorneys think poorly of me because I've had a child?"

"No." They'd better not. Not when he'd claimed the child as his own.

"I'm havin' a hard time believin' you," she said, looking out the window. "What's this?" she asked, her tone indicating she was quite startled. She edged forward on the seat—as much as the seat belt would allow—and looked with wide eyes out the windshield.

"The bridge over the bay," Grant answered, wondering what kind of story she'd come up with next. "Surely you noticed it when you drove to the island the first time. Or did you fly into the local airport?"

"No, I got off the ship. I haven't been off the island before, but I know that a railroad bridge was built from Houston to transport cotton to Galveston. But nothing like this!" Her hands had a death grip on the dashboard.

"It's perfectly safe. We're not that high."

"I think maybe we're higher than your condo."

"I doubt that. Just sit back and relax. If you're going to get this frightened over a bridge, then you're going to have a heart attack when you see the traffic in Houston."

"Traffic?"

"On the interstates and highways that go around and through town. They're notoriously crowded."

"Oh."

He could tell she wasn't too concerned about traffic. Maybe she'd been in Houston traffic before. *Or maybe she doesn't know what you mean,* a little voice said. He pushed aside the notion that she really hadn't crossed a large bridge or driven in traffic. At least her air of conviction would help with their story, both with Sam and his mother.

"How long does it take to drive to Mr. Reynolds's office?"

"About forty-five minutes. Just sit back and relax. We're driving through the salt marshes now, but soon we'll be on solid ground."

"This road seems very solid," she said, glancing out the window at the tall grasses and water on either side of the highway.

"It is. I meant the rest of the ground. Not much is built out here because of the land. Kind of like around my condo. There are salt marshes there too."

"Yes, I've seen them. I like the beach, though."

"If it gets a little warmer we should start exercising along the beach. We can take Colin for walks."

"I'd like that." She was quiet for a moment, then added, "But I'm not sure how long Colin and I will be here."

"Let's not get into this right now, okay? You know I want you to stay. Unless there's somewhere else you need to be, I don't see why you can't stay in Galveston."

"Oh, I think we'll be stayin' in Galveston," she said softly, "but I'm not sure in what time."

He ignored that remark. Traffic picked up as they passed the outlet mall. He didn't need to think about Erina's fantasy right now; he needed to concentrate on getting them to Sam's office—and convincing everyone that Erina was Grant's fiancée and Colin was his son.

Erina sat on the edge of the chair in Sam Reynolds's office, wondering if she would be able to get through this meeting without bursting out with the truth. But as she listened to Grant tell the story so convincingly, she began to believe it herself. He sounded so sincere! If she hadn't known he was spinning a yarn, she would have wept from the depth of the emotion he evoked.

She glanced at Brian Abbott, Grant's friend and attorney, and wondered what the man was thinking. He displayed little on his face—at least to her. She suspected he was much more open to Grant. He probably thought all this was her idea, a way to get Grant to marry her so she could take his money. As though he felt her eyes on him, Mr. Abbott looked at her. His eyes narrowed even as he smiled slightly. She imagined he was assessing her, trying to decide who and what she was.

Well, she didn't blame the man. If her friend had suddenly decided to marry an unknown person and declare himself the parent of a child, she would be suspicious too. She smiled at Mr. Abbott and scooted back into her chair as Grant began to explain how she'd arrived in the United States.

"On a private plane," Sam Reynolds said.

"That's right. She didn't go through Customs because she didn't realize she needed to."

"Grant, that's a bit hard to believe. Surely the pilot or your friend knew that she needed to enter the United States legally."

"Yes, I think they mentioned it. They would have mentioned it, wouldn't they, Erina?" he asked, turning to her.

"Yes, I suppose so," she answered carefully.

"But then Colin became ill suddenly. All Erina could think of was finding me fast and getting Colin to the emergency room."

"I can understand how that crisis would preclude any formalities, but what about later?" Mr. Reynolds asked, looking between Grant and her.

She looked to Grant.

"Since Colin was admitted to the hospital Erina has been with him constantly, and I've been there quite a bit too. We haven't had time to contact INS."

"What is INS?" Erina asked.

"The Immigration and Naturalization Service."

"And these are the people I need to see?"

"Yes," Mr. Reynolds answered, "but when you do see them, I'll be with you. You don't need to contact them now."

"So you'll represent Erina?" Grant asked.

"Yes, and you knew darn well I would," Mr. Reynolds said, shaking his head. "I still don't know the whole story, but I'm convinced that with Colin's critical medical condition, we can successfully represent this case to INS. The worst thing that could happen is that Erina might need to go back to Ireland for a short period and re-apply—"

"No," Grant stated. "She's staying here. If necessary, we'll marry immediately. They won't deport the wife and son of an American citizen."

"Now Grant, don't jump the gun," Mr. Abbot said in a cautious voice.

"Don't worry about this, Brian. We'll do what's necessary."

"That's what I'm afraid of," Erina heard him murmur.

She'd been right about Mr. Abbott's disapproval of her, but apparently he was also unhappy with Grant. She prayed that she hadn't come between the two men. Surely Grant wouldn't do anything to jeopardize their friendship. She had a feeling Mr. Abbott was like a second father to Grant.

"As soon as we receive Erina's documents from Ireland, I'll courier them to you," Grant was saying to Mr. Reynolds.

"You do that. And make sure that everything—I mean *everything*—is in order."

"It will be," Grant assured him.

Erina had no idea how he could make such an outrageous claim. Everything they gave to the attorney would be a lie. She'd need to attend mass and confession after this one, and she'd have to take Grant with her. She just hoped she would be forgiven for telling such a story.

Grant got up from the chair beside her, then reached down and helped her to her feet. She felt a bit shaky. All these lies . . . But she didn't have a choice, she told herself. She had to do this to save Colin because no one, including Grant, would believe the truth.

Brian Abbott walked with them past Mr. Reynolds's secretary and out the door of his law office, which was located in the tallest building Erina had ever seen. She'd been terrified to get into the elevator to ride to the twenty-seventh floor, although Grant had assured her that the trip was perfectly safe. Now they had to ride back down to the ground. Erina didn't want to think about the chances that the elevator could fall.

"I think that went pretty well," Grant said as they stood waiting for the doors to open.

"I think you're full of—"

"Watch your language in front of a lady," Grant warned Brian quickly.

Mr. Abbott looked at her. "I just hope that these documents you're getting will be authentic enough to get past INS and child welfare."

"I've been told they will be," Grant said. "I mean, why wouldn't they be?"

"Yes, why indeed?" Mr. Abbott asked sarcastically.

"Brian, you need to be with me on this. Either that, or just back out now. You don't have to be involved if you're not comfortable, because I'm going to help Erina and Colin whether you like it or not."

"Hell, Grant, you don't know what you might be getting into. What if there's something criminal involved? Have you thought about that?"

"No. What I'm thinking is that I'm helping Erina

and her son, a baby who needed medical attention or he was going to die. There's nothing criminal about that."

"Yes, but—"

The elevator doors opened and Erina walked in first, her cheeks blazing. She wanted to tell Mr. Abbott what she thought, but did she dare? Not if her outburst would hurt Grant. For him, she'd hold her tongue and let him vent his suspicions. As long as Grant didn't listen to him. As long as he didn't desert her . . . and Colin.

"Brian, I need to know if you're going to support me on this," Grant said, pushing a button that would send them plummeting down to the ground floor. Erina placed her palm against the wall to provide some stability while the elevator descended.

"I think you're a damn fool," Mr. Abbott growled in a low voice. "There had to be another way to help her and the kid."

"What other way?"

"Did you try money?"

"Okay, that's it," Grant said, reaching for his friend and grabbing a handful of shirt and tie.

"Grant, no!" Erina cried out, tearing herself away from the wall to hold on to Grant's other arm. "You mustn't fight with Mr. Abbott. He's your dear friend. I won't have you fightin' him, do you hear me?"

Grant looked at her as though she'd suddenly sprouted another head. His eyes blazed and his cheeks were flushed. His brows, darker than his sun-streaked hair, drew together over his eyes. She looked at him, pleading silently with him. Soon his

229

expression calmed and he let go of Mr. Abbott's shirt.

She turned to the older man. "Now Mr. Abbott, you can think what you will of me. I'm a poor Irish girl and I know I'm not the kind that you'd have Grant marry, but I'm not deaf and I'm not stupid. I didn't ask for his money or his name. All I ever asked for is help for Colin."

She turned to Grant. "And you . . . well, you need to remember that I have a mind and a voice. I'd thank you not to speak about me as though I were a child. I'm a woman grown.

"Now I'm not goin' to be the cause of an argument between the two of you. So settle your differences right now. I'm none too fond of meetin' Grant's mother with both of you bickerin' in the background."

Grant stared at her for a long time. He smiled, and then he laughed. After reaching over and holding her hand he turned to Mr. Abbott. "Any more questions? I think Erina is in charge now."

"Damnation. I'm convinced that you can pull off any story you want," he said with a bit of admiration and a shake of his head. His expression sobered. "But do you think your mother's going to be as easy?"

"Leave Mother to me," Grant said, "and Erina. You're there for Mother's moral support and a possible shoulder to cry on."

"Whatever you say, son. I just hope you have a miracle up your sleeve in case she decides to have you investigated," Mr. Abbott murmured as the elevator doors opened.

A miracle. Erina was afraid one miracle in a lifetime was all she was going to get.

They stopped at Grant's office so he could sign some important papers. Erina was impressed again; she didn't know much about businesses, but this one looked prosperous. The desks were dark wood, but there were many windows and glass partitions, some etched with designs of flowers and birds. She could tell the people who worked for Grant were curious about her, but they smiled shyly, their gazes darting between herself and Grant.

She sat on the edge of a leather chair in his office. The decor seemed almost too bare. There were no photographs of family like the ones Sam Reynolds had on his desk and shelves. Several works of art hung on the wall, but Erina couldn't understand what they represented. To her, they were just the pretty colors of a sunset in slashes across a pale lavender background.

But she could watch Grant while he bent over some contracts Brian Abbott was explaining to him. The men talked so quietly that Erina couldn't understand what they were saying, but she was sure this was the business that Grant's company did and not a personal issue. His face appeared different when he discussed business. She'd seen the same expression when he talked on the telephone. Did he dislike what he did, or did he need to concentrate fully on the documents?

She couldn't tell because he seldom talked about his business. One thing she knew was that he wasn't in any hurry to rush back to this office, despite the pleasant people and surroundings. He had stayed in his condo in Galveston, taking her back and forth to the hospital and buying baby furniture for Colin when he could have been working.

With a sigh, she shifted on the chair. Grant made her feel in a way she'd never imagined: hot and achy, lost to his kisses and craving his touch. She was also drawn to the kindness in him, but there were many things about him she didn't know. Perhaps after dinner tonight she'd understand more. Surely when she saw him with his mother she'd get a better idea of the kind of family he'd grown up in.

Because if she stayed in this time, she knew she'd think of Grant and family often. She'd think of them walking along the beach with Colin . . . and perhaps other children. Children with blond hair and dimples. She gripped the arms of the chair and suppressed a sigh.

"Erina?" Grant said, looking up from his desk. "Are you getting tired? I'll be finished in just a few minutes."

"I'm fine. I'm just thinkin' about . . . Colin."

"Why don't you ask my secretary to help you phone the hospital? You can talk to Colin's nurse and make sure he's okay."

"She can do that?"

"Of course. You can call anywhere you'd like."

"Excuse me then," she said to both Grant and Mr. Abbott.

She watched Grant's secretary, a charmingly efficient woman named Margaret, dial the telephone and connect with the hospital. Within a few seconds she handed the phone to Erina. "Mrs. Bea Parker is on the line," she said, smiling.

"Mrs. Parker?"

"Hello, Ms. O'Shea. Little Colin is fine. He's lying in his bed, trying to reach the mobile above his bed."

"He does love to look at the colors and shapes."

They talked for just a little longer about Colin's health; then Erina said good-bye. As she hung up the phone, Grant and Mr. Abbott came out of the office.

"Erina, I'd like you to talk to someone."

"Of course," she said, surprised that he had something else planned at the office. She supposed that anything to prolong her ordeal with his mother would be welcome, but the waiting was beginning to set her nerves on edge.

She walked beside Grant down a row of offices, stopping in front of one that read CONFERENCE ROOM on the door.

"Do you remember when I asked if you would give your fingerprints to a private investigator?"

"Yes."

"Brian managed to get in touch with him. He's waiting inside. If you would, give him some information and he'll take your prints."

"And what will he be doin' with my fingerprints?"

"He'll check police and government databases to see if you match anyone on file."

"I won't, you know," she said, looking up into his blue-green eyes. "I'm not from your time."

"That's why I want him to check you out. If he doesn't find anything, then INS won't either. We'll be in much better shape to face whatever questions they have for us—"

233

"You will be, you mean. I know perfectly well where I'm from."

"If you don't want to do this, just say so." Grant paused with his hand on the doorknob.

"I don't mind," she replied, but a lump formed in her chest when she thought that Grant didn't believe her—and probably never would.

The private investigator took only a few minutes to "print" her. He used a special kind of ink that seemed invisible, but then turned black on the paper. And he asked only a few basic questions about her place of birth and other numbers and identifications, which she didn't have. Grant told him to forget using her date of birth. The man looked at him strangely but nodded. Throughout the whole ordeal, Erina kept thinking about how many lies they'd told, and how many they had yet to tell to his mother.

A few minutes later he was gone. Grant said, "We're finished here. Are you ready for dinner?" He opened the door for her.

"I'm not sure I can eat a thing," she answered honestly, queasy at the thought of the way they were deceiving the people most important to him. He hadn't talked about his mother, about what kind of woman she was. Erina had no idea what to expect, but she would have been nervous even without the lies.

"Don't worry. We won't eat right away. Mother will want to put us on the grill for a while and watch us sizzle."

"She's not that bad," Mr. Abbott said, joining them in the hallway.

"I think you're prejudiced," Grant said with a smile.

"Hmm."

"Perhaps dinner would be more pleasant if you went without me," Erina volunteered.

"No way," Grant said. "We're in this together. Don't forget that."

Grant's mother was as intimidating as every other society matron Erina had ever met. Tall, slim, and with a regal bearing, she stood in the foyer of her home like a queen receiving her subjects. Her eyes were wide and deep set, looking down at Erina as if she were a thief come to steal the silver—or the son.

"Mother, may I present Erina O'Shea, recently of Ireland?" Grant said formally, yet with a bit of a smile.

"Erina, this is my mother, Virginia Kramer Kirby."

"Pleased to meet you, ma'am," Erina replied, resisting the urge to curtsy to the tall, blond woman. Instead, she stood a little straighter.

Mrs. Kirby extended her hand and Erina shook it tentatively. There was no warmth in the handshake; it was polite at best. She reminded herself to be as gracious as possible; this was Grant's mother and he must love her, even if he didn't talk about her.

"Welcome to Houston," Mrs. Kirby said, crossing her arms in front of her.

"Thank you." Erina looked around the entryway of the large brick home. A decorative gilt paper covered the bottom half of the walls, with cream paint above it, and light, almost golden stained wood around the tall window and along the floor. A large mirror hung above an ornate white-and-gold credenza, its doors painted with twining vines and flowers. Overhead, a gold and crystal chandelier glistened in the afternoon sun.

Jerrold Kirby's mother would have loved this entry hall.

"How about something to drink before dinner, Mother?" Grant finally asked when the silence stretched too long.

"Of course. Where are my manners? But Erina seemed so interested in the decor," Mrs. Kirby said with a smile that didn't reach her eyes. "Please, come into the library and we'll have some wine. I received an excellent vintage just the other day."

Grant reached for Erina's hand again, this time holding on as they walked down a short hallway past an impressive staircase.

"I hope dinner didn't ruin any of your plans," Grant said as they took a seat in a dark, masculine-looking room. Bookcases lined a fireplace. The walls were a dark red, matching the red, black, and gold-patterned rug laid over the hardwood floor.

Erina sat next to Grant on a cane-backed leather settee. She resisted the urge to slide closer to him on the uncomfortable piece of furniture, sitting up straight and trying to appear confident when that was the last thing in the world she felt.

"Just a tennis game at the club," Mrs. Kirby replied. "We're getting ready for the tournament."

"My mother is a great tennis player," Grant told Erina. "She took the trophy last year in the senior division at the country club."

Mrs. Kirby twirled around, a white-knuckled grip on a bottle of wine in one hand, a cork extractor in the other. "Grant, why don't you do the honors while Erina and I have a chance to talk?"

"Of course," he said, rising from the settee.

Mrs. Kirby settled in a wing-backed chair that resembled a throne. "Have you been in the country long, Erina?"

"No, not really." *At least, not in this time,* she added to herself to justify the lie. She'd been in Galveston for eight years in 1896.

"And are you here visiting friends or on business?"

"Well, actually—"

"Mother, why don't you save the inquisition so I can join in the fun," Grant said, walking up with two glasses of white wine.

"Really, Grant, there's no reason to be defensive," she said, taking a sip of wine. "Is there?"

He handed a glass to Erina. "Not at all. But Erina is my guest. I didn't expect her to face one of your chats alone."

"Honestly, Grant—"

"You know I'm not exaggerating, Mother. You love to intimidate the common folk."

"I do no such thing!"

"Grant, please," Erina said softly, "don't argue over me."

"This isn't about you, sweetheart," he said, bringing over his own glass of wine and sitting beside her. "This is a long-standing disagreement we have."

"That's not true. I can't imagine where you get

these ideas. I'm just making conversation." Mrs. Kirby took a sip of her wine, her gaze on them both.

Erina felt a blush creeping into her cheeks at the endearment Grant had used. Although she knew the reason they were there—to explain her and Colin's relationship to Grant—she still wasn't used to thinking of herself as his "sweetheart."

"Brian should be here soon," Grant said. "He wanted to bring his own car."

"Yes, he told me he was coming," Mrs. Kirby said. "By the way, Erina, how long will you be staying in the United States?"

"Mother!"

"Well, what do you want me to say? I'm trying to find an acceptable topic of conversation."

"Why don't you just wait for me to explain everything when Brian gets here?" Grant said, leaning back and placing his arm across the settee. Erina felt the brush of his fingers, against her hair. Chills chased heat down her spine.

A chime sounded. Erina jumped, but Grant placed his hand on her shoulder. "That must be Brian."

"Maria will get it," Mrs. Kirby said.

Silence descended for just a few moments before Mr. Abbott's large, bearlike frame filled the doorway of the library.

"Sorry I'm late," he said. "Traffic along Westheimer was a . . . awful."

Erina watched Mrs. Kirby as she tracked Mr. Abbott with her gaze. Her face softened and she looked much less regal than when she'd greeted them. Odd, how the woman would appear warmer to a friend than to her own son.

"Let me get you a glass of wine, Brian," Mrs. Kirby offered. "Or would you like something stronger?"

"Scotch would be nice," he said, walking over to stand beside her. "I've got a feeling I might need it," he said in a low voice.

"I may join you," Erina heard Mrs. Kirby whisper.

As soon as they took their seats, Grant said, "So, is everyone ready to hear about Erina? I could wait until after dinner if you'd like."

"No! That is, I'm sure we're all anxious to hear why Erina is here."

Grant smiled. "I thought so. Well, it all started last fall when I went to Europe."

Mrs. Kirby's brow drew together in a frown. "I don't remember a trip you made to Europe last year."

"For climbing," Grant explained. "I'm not sure I even mentioned it. It was a very quick trip between Thanksgiving and Christmas. I'm sure you were busy with your charities and the holiday season."

"Perhaps," she replied, not quite convinced.

"It was a spur-of-the-moment thing. I heard about a good place to climb in Ireland."

"I thought you went to Europe."

"Ireland is in Europe."

"Did you go with one of your friends from around here?"

"No, I didn't go with anyone you know, Mother. Just a climbing instructor from Colorado."

"Oh, I see," she said. Erina got the impression Colorado was a sore spot between mother and son. "And that is where you met Grant?" she asked Erina.

"Yes," she replied, crossing her fingers in the folds of her skirt. *Please forgive me for lying*, she prayed silently. *I'm doing this for Colin.*

Grant looked deeply into her eyes. "I forgot all about climbing when I saw Erina."

"And where was that?"

"Just in the village."

"Um hmm," she heard Brian Abbott murmur.

"And what did you do there?" Mrs. Kirby asked her.

"Do?"

"Yes. Did you live there? Work there?"

"I lived in the village with my da," Erina answered carefully. That was true. Before 1888 she'd never left their small village.

"Her father was a landscape architect," Grant said.

"He was a gardener," Erina whispered as she turned her head toward Grant.

"Yes, I know," he whispered back, his breath hot against her ear. She shivered at the pleasurable chills that raced through her.

He smiled and faced his mother again. "I'm afraid I swept her off her feet," he said, playing with a strand of Erina's hair. "She'd never met anyone as determined as I was."

"You mean you took advantage of an innocent child," his mother said, censure in her voice.

"No! He didn't take advantage of me," Erina said quickly, angry that Grant would make himself seem so callous in front of his mother and his friend.

"She's just saying that to make me look better," Grant added.

"Um hmm," Mr. Abbott murmured again, his lips against the glass of scotch.

"That's a very touching story, but what does it have to do with why Erina is visiting us in Houston?"

"Actually she's visiting me in Galveston," Grant corrected. "You see, I had to leave Ireland after less than a week. Something came up and I couldn't stay any longer."

Um hmm," Mr. Abbott murmured.

"I tried to contact Erina but couldn't get through. I called the embassy, but that was during the budget crisis last year and the offices were closed. You remember that funding problem the government had last year?"

Apparently Grant was weaving fact and fiction together. Erina watched as Mrs. Kirby nodded, her eyes narrowed in speculation. "I take it you couldn't contact Erina for some time."

"That's right. Then her father died and she had to move."

Heavenly Father, forgive us, Erina silently prayed again, *for our lies to this woman.*

"I'm sorry about your father, dear, but again, I wonder why you're here now."

"I wasn't sure I could find your son, Mrs. Kirby," Erina said, glancing at Grant for moral support. He nodded. "I probably wouldn't have tried to find him, but you see, I . . . we . . ."

"What Erina is trying to tell you is that my time in Ireland was very fruitful. We have a son."

"Aye, a son named Colin," Erina continued quickly as color drained from Mrs. Kirby's face. "And he's a sweet child, just two months old, but he has a heart problem that needed an operation, and—"

"In any case, congratulations. You're a grandmother," Grant announced with a smile as Mrs. Kirby slumped back against her chair.

Chapter Fourteen

"I thought you should hear it from me first," Grant said as his mother regained her composure.

"Grant, are you absolutely certain?" she asked, her voice sounding weak for the first time in years.

"Yes, Mother."

"How did this happen?" she asked, a bit of panic in her voice.

"The usual way, I suppose. The heat of passion and all that. Do you really want the details?"

"Of course not! That was a rhetorical question."

"Aren't you at least curious about your grandson?"

"Grant, give me a moment, please. This is a shock."

"Yes, Grant," Brian said, draining his scotch, "this whole story is a shock."

Grant doubted much of anything would surprise Brian at this moment. He'd known the basic idea all along; he'd already expressed his displeasure.

"What's this about a heart condition?" Grant's mother asked finally.

"Colin was born with a hole in his heart," Erina

explained. "He always looked blue around his mouth, his fingers, and toes. The doctors . . . where I was said that they couldn't help him. That's why I needed Grant's help. I had to find a way to save my baby."

"But if you couldn't find him before, how did you locate him? And why wait until after the baby's birth?"

"I . . ."

Maria entered the library. "Dinner is ready, Mrs. Kirby."

"Of course. We'll be right there." She turned her attention back to Erina. "We can finish this later."

Brian set down his empty glass on the butler's table and escorted Grant's mother out of the room.

Grant took Erina's hand when she rose. "You're doing great," he said. "Just keep with the story and we'll be fine."

"Your mother thinks I made all this up to take your money."

"Mothers always think that. Don't worry about it."

"I won't be comin' between you and your family. Even Mr. Abbot is vexed with you. I feel like a cheat."

"Don't." He traced a finger along the curve of Erina's cheek. The skin was as soft as Colin's. "The problem between my mother and me didn't happen because of you."

"What then?"

"I'm afraid I've never been the son she thought I should be. I didn't try hard enough when I was younger. I didn't go to the right college. I'm just not what she wanted in a child."

"That's a horrible thing to say! How can you know what's in her heart? Surely she loves you just the same."

"Let's drop it, okay? My mother and I just don't want the same things from life and probably never will."

"Grant, I . . . I feel bad that I'm makin' you look even worse in front of the people you love."

"Are you sure that's what you're doing?" he asked, resisting the urge to kiss her soft lips.

"I believe so," she whispered, leaning close.

"Grant? Are you coming?" His mother's voice from the open doorway cut through the heavily charged room.

"Yes, of course," he replied, taking Erina's arm and steering her toward the door. He pushed all thoughts of kissing Erina from his mind—at least for now.

After they walked down the hall and into the dining room Grant took a seat beside Erina. His mother already sat at the head of the table, with Brian on her left. As Grant watched Brian across the polished expanse of mahogany, he wondered what his old friend was thinking. The conversation in the library had no doubt reinforced his opinion that Grant was certifiable.

His mother rang for dinner to be served.

"This is your great-great-grandmother's table," Erina whispered to him in an excited tone.

"How do you know?" he asked, amused by the change in topic.

"I'll have you know that I've polished it enough to know it by sight," she replied in a hushed tone.

"When your great-grandfather was a boy he carved his initials inside one of the legs, way up high so it couldn't be seen."

"I'm sorry, dear. What did you say?" his mother asked.

"Erina was just commenting that she believes your table is an antique."

"Yes, it is. It was brought to Galveston by Grant's great-great-grandparents when they settled there from England."

"I'm so glad it survived the hurricane," Erina said. "Grant told me about the storm and how the downstairs of the house flooded."

Grant felt his stomach do a little flop. He'd never inquired about his mother's furniture. Although he knew Galveston's history and contributed to the historical society, he'd never felt any personal interest in the past except in a very general way. But that didn't mean there were initials carved on one of the legs. Erina's observation that the table had been in his family for generations could have been a lucky guess.

Erina smiled at him. Her eyes said, *I told you so.*

Only the presence of his mother and Brian kept Grant from getting down on his knees and looking under the table for the initials Erina was so sure existed. Perhaps being confronted with the truth would help her deal with what she had to. There was no way she could guess about something like initials.

"Do you have an interest in antiques, Erina?"

"Yes, I suppose I do, ma'am." She looked around the room. Grant wondered what she thought of the heavy mahogany pieces set against the gold walls and light wainscoting. Did she have any other stories about specific pieces of furniture? He'd always liked this room, but it was only used for formal occasions—like dinner with the mother of the next generation of Kirbys: the soon-to-be daughter-in-law.

Except his mother didn't know that yet. He hadn't dropped that bombshell.

Maria served a puréed soup with some kind of toasted bread. Grant noticed that Erina seemed nervous again. She waited until he took his first spoonful of soup before tasting hers.

"Grant just signed the contracts for the new management firm in Phoenix," Brian announced.

"I didn't know you were changing companies." Grant's mother turned to him.

"Occupancy rates were down," he explained.

"But the company is doing well, isn't it?" she asked.

"Very well, Mother. Brian and I are meeting with my people next week to discuss the Dallas properties. Their rates are up, but Dallas is having another building boom. We'll have to be positioned to take advantage of existing properties."

"I'm sure you'll do what is necessary," she said, dismissing the subject of business as she always did when she realized that the company and her income were not in danger.

They finished the first course and the plates were removed. While Maria was gone, Grant said, "I want you to meet Colin as soon as possible, Mother. He's in UTMB at the moment but should be released to-morrow."

"Well, of course. I just . . . this has caught me by surprise."

Grant imagined the idea of being a grandmother was as upsetting as the thought of him fathering a child. Of course, he hadn't fathered this child, but that was a minor point. Colin would still be *his* son, no matter who the biological father was. "Why don't you come down on Wednesday?"

"To your condo?"

"Yes."

"I'm surprised again. I didn't know you invited anyone to your weekend hideaway."

"I don't," he said emphatically. He'd never invited anyone from work or any family member to Galves-ton. That was his private place; now it was his and Erina's. Since her arrival the condo had become hers . . . and Colin's as well, with the addition of the baby furniture. "But this is a special occasion, isn't it? Would Wednesday be convenient for you?"

"I suppose. What time?"

He turned to Erina. "What would be best for Colin?"

"He takes a nap after lunch, but he's usually awake by two o'clock. Or you could come in the morning, before lunch."

"Morning would be best for me. How about ten o'clock? That way I won't interfere with his sched-ule."

"That would be fine. We'll be expecting you. Brian, you're invited also, of course."

"I may just take you up on that," he said, looking at Grant's mother.

Maria served the next course, some type of chicken dish. His mother watched her weight and cholesterol very carefully, every meal. She'd once told him that an extra two pounds looked like ten in a photo. And Virginia Kramer Kirby had her picture in the society pages very often.

"Good. It's settled then." He turned to Erina. "Our first guests, sweetheart."

He watched a wealth of emotions flash across her expressive face. Dread, excitement, fear, hope. As always, Erina was a surprise. He felt exhilarated by her presence, ready for each new day with an anticipation that he had never experienced before except during a challenging climb. And then the feeling was fleeting. With Erina, he thought perhaps it could last a lifetime, if only she'd tell him the real story.

All in all, he thought as they finished dinner, the evening had gone pretty well. His mother hadn't fainted or thrown a fit at the idea of a grandchild. Of course, he hadn't informed her that he and Erina might get married. One thing at a time. Perhaps he'd break the news on Wednesday. By then he should have Erina's documents.

He hoped the ink would be dry.

While everyone else relaxed, as much as possible, in the living room, Grant excused himself for a minute. He was sure they thought he was going to the bathroom, but he slipped into the empty dining room instead.

When he was sure that no one was around he bent

down on one knee and looked at the leg of the table. No initials there. He tried another one, feeling increasingly stupid. He didn't believe Erina's claims, she'd never been in his mother's house before. She'd probably never expected him to verify whether the initials were there. This was just an exercise to satisfy his curiosity.

But as he knelt by the third leg and looked up high, two age-darkened initials were obvious. J.K. stared back at him, a message from the past.

How in the hell had Erina known? Could she really have seen those initials when they were freshly carved, over a hundred years ago? Of course not. What was he thinking? She might have a good reason for making up her story, but if *he* bought into the fantasy, he'd be crazy.

Erina didn't know what to say on the way back to Galveston. Grant was quiet, steering the Jeep with one hand as he rubbed his chin with the other. He'd placed a round silver object into a slot, filling the interior with music the likes of which she'd never heard before. At first she hadn't liked the mixture of sounds and voices, but soon she grew accustomed to the music and tried to understand the lyrics of the songs.

Before she knew it, they were driving over the bridge. Lights from along the bay reflected in the water, creating a beautiful picture that made her forget how afraid she was of heights.

"Would you like to stop by the hospital?"

"Yes, I would," she said, startled to hear Grant's

voice after such a long silence.

He drove down Broadway, past the Kirby home, closed now to the public but lit so people could see the architecture and the sign out front. She had mixed feelings about her three years there; she'd enjoyed Mrs. Kirby and the girls, but Jerrold Kirby had destroyed her dreams in the servants' quarters upstairs. She'd never expected to go back, but maybe she could visit it in this time. Perhaps now, when it was bound to look different, she could put her own ghosts to rest.

Grant remained silent as they drove into the parking garage of UTMB.

"Are you angry with me for tonight?" she finally asked. "Did I say or do something wrong?"

"No!" he said quickly. "You were great. I'm sorry. I've just had a lot of things to think about."

"If you're havin' second thoughts, I understand," she said, placing her hand on his arm.

"I'm not having second thoughts about getting involved with you or with Colin. But I am a little confused."

"About what?"

"Things like the initials under the table leg. I know you couldn't have had time to look for those ahead of time because you were with me before dinner."

"Of course I didn't look. I just remember seeing the initials and asking Jerrold Kirby about them when I first went to work for Mrs. Kirby . . . your great-great-grandmother, that is."

He was silent for quite some time, turning off the music and the engine. "Erina, you know I can't be-

251

lieve your story. Time travel isn't possible."

"I know you refuse to let yourself believe."

"Whatever. The fact is, I don't believe in miracles."

"Oh, but you should," she said softly. "The world is a much better place because of them."

"I've read stories about paranormal happenings. I've enjoyed movies where something fantastic occurs. But I've never known anyone who experienced an actual miracle."

"Of course you do," she said.

"Who?" he asked, turning toward her.

"You know Colin and me."

Grant shook his head and smiled. "You never give up, do you?"

"I'll never deny my faith. If you could believe in the power of God, you could believe in miracles."

"I can't believe in miracles," he stated again.

"I cannot make you believe. Perhaps someday you will."

"I believe that you're here, and that you're real, and that I want you very much," he whispered as he leaned toward her.

She should have pulled away, pushed him back, done something to make him stop. But his eyes held her fast, and his clean masculine scent entranced her until she could only welcome his warm, firm lips. As always, his kiss was like visiting heaven. She allowed herself to float and swirl in the passion he created, forgetting everything but his touch. His hand stole to her breast and she whimpered, part in longing and part in pain.

"What's wrong?" he asked, pulling back slightly.

"I'm . . . I need to . . ." She couldn't finish the sentence. The reason was too embarrassing.

"You need to nurse Colin," he said for her.

"Yes," she whispered.

"Let's get you inside then. I didn't mean to hurt you."

"You didn't," she said, unable to look at him. "I'm just not used to . . . you know what I mean."

"You're not used to a man's touch."

"Of course not."

"Erina," he said, leaning closer so his lips hovered close to hers, "I'm glad. I want to be the only one who makes you hot. I want to teach you about passion."

"Grant, please, don't," she said.

"If you want to wait until we're married, I understand. But I'm beginning to think that whether we need to marry for INS or child welfare, we should just because I'll lose my mind if I can't make love to you soon."

"Perhaps it's not me. You might feel this way about another woman," she answered weakly.

"No, I've never felt this way about any other woman. The closest thing I've ever experienced was being a teenager with a car, a girlfriend, and no place to go. But that was just hormones. This is . . . something else."

"What do you think it is?" she asked tentatively, afraid of asking but wanting to know the answer more than anything.

"I don't know," he said, brushing his fingers across

her cheek and through her hair. "But I don't want it to stop."

She leaned forward, closing the gap between them, and for the first time she initiated the kiss. He allowed her the time to mold her lips to his, to taste him, to stroke him with her tongue. Then he encouraged her, parting his lips, letting her kiss him as he'd kissed her. The feeling of excitement and power was overwhelming. She wanted to sink inside, to lose herself in him until they became one.

She eased away from the kiss before she gave in to her own desires. Now was not the time; this was not the place. Besides, she truly believed in the sanctity of marriage, not in fleeting passion.

Was this love? She knew she'd fallen in love with him, but how did he feel about her? Did he feel the same passion, hope, and joy?

"We'd better go inside before we fog up the windows," he said.

"What do you mean?"

"A heavy makeout session in a car often produces fog on the windows. It's another one of those teenage memories that you're bringing back in me."

"Oh. Then I suppose we should go inside."

"Okay," he said, still not releasing her. Although the car was dark, Erina imagined that he could see her clearly, that he was memorizing her features, her smell, her very essence.

He closed his eyes, took a deep breath, and sat back in his own seat. "I'm going to need a cold shower when we get back to the condo."

"Why would you take a cold shower? Do you have

no more hot water?" she asked, unfastening her seat belt.

"Another expression," he said, opening the door of the Jeep. He walked around to her side of the car and opened her door. "It means that I need to cool down a specific part of my body." He lifted her from the seat with his large hands under her arms, then slid her down his body. Her tight breasts brushed against his chest, sending tingles throughout her body. He eased her lower, until she brushed against the hardness that pressed against his slacks.

Erina had the totally inappropriate and shocking urge to wrap her legs around his waist and hold tight. Just the idea made her hot, but not just her cheeks. This heat was all over, throbbing low in her body, where she wanted to be joined with Grant.

Her toes touched the ground and she sagged against him. Breathing hard, she looked up into his gleaming eyes. "I think I need one of those cold showers too," she whispered.

He smiled, then laughed, hugging her close. "Maybe we'd better get inside the hospital before we embarrass ourselves and a lot of other people."

"Yes, I think that's a good idea." She stepped back, smoothing her clothes and pressing her flaming cheeks. At the moment she needed to nurse Colin, calm her racing pulse, and forget that Grant Kirby was more temptation than any woman should have to face.

While Erina was at the hospital the next morning, the documents arrived in a plain brown envelope via an equally plain courier. Grant passed the man an enveloped filled with hundred dollar bills after checking the quality. He was no expert, but the Irish birth certificate for Erina and Colin looked authentic.

He hoped they were good enough for Sam Reynolds.

The birthdate they'd chosen was her own, December 6. The year he'd selected based on her claims that she'd be twenty-one on that date. She said she'd been born in 1875, which he changed to 1975. Just looking at the date made him shudder. She really was too young for him, but dammit, she didn't feel like a girl when he held her in his arms. She didn't seem immature when they talked. Whatever her true background, he was sure she'd worked and been on her own, giving her experience with life that most teenagers never experienced. And she was a mother already, aged beyond her years by that experience.

He slipped the birth certificates back into the envelope and placed it on his desk. They'd still have some explaining to do when they met with INS. Their hands would no doubt be slapped for Erina entering the U.S. illegally. But if they could just show the bureaucrats how serious Colin's condition had been, how wonderfully he'd recovered, then they had a good chance.

Perhaps they should have Dr. Cook attend the meeting. No, that was too much too soon. First they needed to get an idea of how much trouble they were in.

And, he thought, picking up the phone, he'd better

check what the procedures were for getting married. He assumed they'd need a blood test and a license from one of the county offices, but beyond that, he hadn't a clue.

Erina had Grant take her to St. Mary's Cathedral for the noon mass on Tuesday, although he hadn't been excited about coming himself. He'd shown her the documents that had arrived that morning, which gave her even more reason to go to church. She chided him for his lies and made him feel guilty, and he sat with her as the priest said the holy words.

She wished that she could give her confession then, but the priest was busy. She vowed to herself to come back and confess everything so she'd be forgiven. Urging Grant to do the same had no effect, however. He said he would think about it, which meant that he had no intention of telling all they'd done to a priest.

After mass, she felt better. She and Grant ate a quick sandwich at a restaurant by the pier. A ship named the *Elissa* was docked nearby. Grant called it a tourist attraction, and while they ate, Erina saw people walk across the polished decks, go below, and emerge to stare up at the tall masts.

"Have you been there before?" Grant asked, looking at her intently.

"No, of course not."

"That's where they have the database of immigrants."

"Really?" she said, excited. "That's the listing of all the people who came to Galveston, isn't it?" At his nod, she asked, "Do you think my da and I are in this database?"

"I already checked there and at the Rosenburg library. Most of the records were destroyed in the hurricane."

"Oh." She felt a little sad that there was no documentation of her arrival in Galveston. So many immigrants had come in those years, and now no one could discover who they were.

"I just thought perhaps you'd gone to the *Elissa* or the museum."

"No. It wasn't here in the last century," she said automatically, used to Grant's attempts to expose her as a fraud.

She'd arrived on a steamer, not a schooner, so the ship didn't evoke any memories in her. However, she had to smile at the public's fascination with old things. In her time, unless an item had true value, there was no sentimentality. The Victorian society embraced the modern, as long as items conformed to rules of taste. The vulgarity of the previous periods was quickly discarded. Now people seemed to love anything from the past.

She realized that she would be considered an "expert" by some of these people. She knew how items worked, how homes were decorated, how Victorians dressed. Was there a use for this information? She'd have to ask Grant—if she stayed in this time.

After lunch they returned to the hospital to meet with Dr. Cook. He was going to tell them if Colin could come home today.

"Well, Doctor," Grant asked as they stood beside Colin's bed, "has he recovered?"

"He's done very well. I'm going to release him as long as you don't take him away from the area. If he has any abnormal responses at all—rapid pulse, trouble breathing, or loss of appetite, for example—I want him back at the hospital immediately."

"I can really take him out of the hospital?" Erina asked, a sense of excitement welling up inside her.

"Yes. Just be cautious of his incision and watch his fluid intake. I'll give you a prescription for some antibiotics he'll take for ten days. I'll want to see him then."

"I'll do whatever you say. Oh, Doctor, I'm so happy to be takin' my baby home!"

"Our baby," Grant said, smiling down at her. "We're going to take our baby home."

Chapter Fifteen

Late Tuesday night, Erina slipped out of bed at Colin's whimper. She'd barely slept, anticipating every heartbeat, listening to his breathing as he slept in his new crib. The night-light that Grant had purchased, an oddly dressed mouse with large eyes and a smiling face, glowed in the darkness so she could see Colin clearly. Sitting atop the mattress on the corner of the bed was a soft, furry toy that Grant called a stuffed animal, similar to the night-light.

She smiled down at Colin, who opened his eyes and blinked several times. Then he screwed up his mouth in anticipation of a full-bodied cry.

She picked him up quickly, mindful of his incision but anxious to keep him from waking Grant. As much as he seemed to enjoy Colin, she'd been told by both Mrs. Abernathy and Mrs. Kirby that men did not want to be bothered by a baby's demands. That would be especially true since Colin wasn't Grant's child.

Opening the bodice of her nightgown and settling

into the rocking chair, she put Colin to her breast before he could do any more than give a few weak cries. He latched on, thankfully hungry since she was full with milk. With a push of her foot, she set the chair in motion and leaned back her head.

Life couldn't be much better than this, she thought as she rocked slowly. Her baby was home, his heart healed; she had a warm, secure place to live; she was with a wonderful man who seemed to truly care for her and her child.

If only he would believe that she was from the past. If only he had faith in miracles. And if only she'd be allowed to stay in this wonderful time.

She opened her eyes when Colin stopped nursing so strongly, ready to put him back to bed so she could get a little rest. Grant's mother was coming in the morning, and Erina had no idea what the woman would say or do. She'd been surprised yesterday, to be sure, but she'd been polite when Grant had told her about Colin. Erina felt a bit sorry for the lady, because Colin wasn't really her grandchild, even if Erina wished it were so with all her heart.

Colin looked around the room, no longer interested in her breast. "What can you see, my little one?" Erina whispered. "Do you like your new room? Grant bought you some fine furniture, I'll have you know."

"He'll need his own room soon."

Erina jumped, clutching Colin against her breast. Her heartbeat leaped when she saw Grant, standing in the doorway with those loose pants, barely tied

261

low beneath his waist, his arms crossed over his wide, muscled chest.

"You startled me," she said softly.

"I'm sorry. I just wanted to watch you nurse Colin. The sight is beautiful."

"You . . . you shouldn't have gotten up."

"I told you I was a light sleeper. I heard Colin whimper."

"I tried to keep him quiet."

"I don't mind," Grant said, pushing away from the door and walking toward the rocking chair. "Here, let me take him while you . . . well, I suppose you need to pull your gown together. Not that I mind the view."

She blushed from her forehead to her breasts. How could Grant be so nice, then so outrageous? She didn't know whether she should hug him or scold him.

He reached down and lifted Colin in those big hands—which brushed against her breast and caused a flurry of tingles through her body. Her eyes met his hooded gaze. He smiled slowly. "Sorry," he said, but his expression said just the opposite.

She jerked her gown together and clamped her lips shut. She wouldn't say a thing; any words that came out of her mouth right now would be nonsensical babble.

Grant strolled across the room with Colin against his chest, talking in hushed tones.

"So you like your new room, hmm? I thought you'd like Mickey. He was always my favorite too. When you get older we'll take you to Walt Disney World.

Your mother and I will have a great time and we'll tell you all about the trip later, because you won't remember. But that's okay, because we'll go back."

Erina smiled at the two of them and Grant's silly talk to the baby. She had no idea what the Walt Disney World place might be, but suddenly she wanted to see it. She wanted to know who Mickey was and why Grant liked him as a child. She wanted to have a life that included Grant holding Colin, treating him like a real son.

She blinked away tears of happiness and yearning as Grant paced the floor. Within minutes, Colin fell asleep, nestled snugly against Grant's wide, warm chest. Erina felt a twinge of envy; she wished she had the right to snuggle against Grant and fall asleep in his arms.

He lay the baby back in the crib and covered him with the quilt. Grant was smiling as he tiptoed away from the crib.

"He's sound asleep," Grant whispered. Reaching down, he pulled Erina from the rocking chair. "Now it's your turn."

"You're wonderful with him."

"I'm not sure why. I've never been around babies much."

"I think it's a natural talent."

"How about my talent with women? You in particular. What do you think of that?"

"I think you're used to gettin' what you want," she said as he pulled her closer. "And I think you have some real natural ability there too."

"Oh? What kind of ability?" he asked playfully,

holding her loosely in his arms. His hands rubbed up and down her back.

She closed her eyes and just enjoyed his touch. This was wrong; she knew she shouldn't be in a bedroom with a man, especially all alone, at night, with someone like Grant. He could tempt a saint. He'd certainly tempted her so she struggled to be virtuous.

His lips brushed against her forehead as she leaned closer to him. If they truly were married, he'd have the right to be in her bedroom. To hold her, kiss her. To make love to her. The act itself wouldn't be like before; Grant was tender and thoughtful, not given to violence or drunkenness. He would provide for her and Colin, and they would be a family. She'd have everything she'd ever wanted.

She lay her cheek against his naked skin and breathed in his scent. Beneath her hand, which had crept up to his chest of its own accord, she felt his strong heartbeat and the crisp hair of his chest. He was a large, strong man, but not one who would use that strength against her. She and Colin would be safe in Grant's care.

But to give in to her own desires would be wrong. Grant thought that he wanted to marry her because he desired her, and also because he needed to keep Colin safe. That wasn't the reason Grant should marry. He should find someone he loved, because Erina knew that now people married for love, not for fortunes. He didn't need the money of a dowry, if a thing like that even existed anymore. He needed a home, a wife who loved him, children he could love in return.

She could not be that woman. She didn't even know if she'd stay in this time. What if they married and then she went back to her own time? Grant would be tied by holy bonds but would have no wife, no child. He would need to petition the church for an annulment to marry again. And that didn't even consider the legal problems her disappearance might cause.

He probably hadn't considered these problems; he was thinking of the present, and besides, he didn't believe that she was from the past. If only he could believe . . .

"Marry me, Erina," he whispered against her hair. "Then we can be together like this always. You wouldn't be violating your principles. And I know you want me."

She tried to shake her head, but she was too close to his chest. She only managed to rub against his warm skin. "I can't," she whispered so softly she wondered if he could hear her.

"Why?"

"Because you don't believe I could be sent back to my own time. Because you want to marry me out of a sense of duty and kindness, and I don't want to bind you in marriage to save us from Mrs. Henshaw and the INS."

"Does it matter so much why I want to marry you, as long as it's right? I know you want to be with me too. I can see it in your eyes, feel it in the way your heart beats fast when I hold you."

She didn't know how to reply. She didn't know at

this moment if the reasons mattered. "But what if I do go back in time?"

"What if you don't?"

She had no answer to that. "I need to think about what you're askin'. In my heart, I know you'd be sacrificin' yourself for me and Colin, and that's not right."

"If holding you and Colin close to my heart is a sacrifice, it's one I'm more than willing to make."

"Oh, Grant." She closed her eyes again and let him hold her. How would it feel to lie on the bed beside him, warm and secure? If they married, she could be with him every night. Every night . . .

"I can't," she said, pushing away from him with a hand against his chest. "I need to think, and that's impossible with you so close."

He drew in a deep breath. When he stood straighter his loose pants fell even lower below his waist. She looked away quickly before she learned more about a man's body than she was ready to see.

He tightened the string of his pants so they didn't threaten to fall off his body. "I'll give you all the time I can," he said, "but I want you to know that I've never asked a woman to marry me before. This isn't just a good deed. I really want you, Erina. I know I shouldn't. I know you're too young for me, but I can't help how I feel."

"But what if I must return to my own time?"

"You don't have to go anywhere."

"If I'm called back—"

"Just say that you can't go. No one will come between us."

"No person, but . . . but the Holy Mother may want me to return to my own time."

"Erina, that's a fantasy."

"No, it's not."

"Let's not discuss it. Just think about what I said, okay?"

She nodded.

He dropped his hands and stepped back toward the doorway. "I could lie beside you in the bed," he offered, smiling so that his dimple showed.

She smiled back, unable to resist his humor. "I don't think that would be a good idea."

"I think it would be a very good idea," he said softly, raising his eyebrow.

She placed a hand over her mouth to keep from giggling like a schoolgirl. "Good night, Grant."

"Good night, Erina."

She checked on Colin once more, then curled up in her bed. If only she could think of a way to marry Grant without feeling as though she'd taken advantage of him. If only she believed he was truly happy with the bargain.

He'd asked her to think about his offer. How could she not?

At the last moment Grant realized that Colin had no clothes. How had that happened? Grant had thought of everything—furniture, mattress, sheets, a soft Mickey Mouse—but no clothes. He felt like slapping himself in the forehead. Instead, he grabbed his keys and ran for the door.

"If Mother comes before I get back, just entertain

her. Maybe Colin will cooperate and play in his crib."

"Entertain her! How would I be doin' that?"

"I don't know. Make her some tea." With that, he dashed out the door.

He wasn't sure where to buy baby clothes. He should have checked the Yellow Pages, he supposed, but all he could think of was that his mother was going to believe his baby had no clothes. That no one had thought enough of Colin to buy him a decent outfit.

There was a maternity shop in a strip shopping center not too far away. They might know where to go.

At ten minutes until ten o'clock, he remembered Brian's car phone number.

"Brian, this is Grant. Is Mother with you?"

"Yes."

"Where are you?"

"Just pulling into the parking lot."

"Damn."

"Well, hell, it's nice to see you too."

"I don't mean it that way. It's just that I had to run out and get something."

"So you're not upstairs?"

"No, I'm on my way back. Can you stall Mother?"

He heard a sound like the phone being dropped, then muttered curses. In a second, a voice said, "Grant, what's going on here?"

"Nothing, Mother," he said.

"Where are you?"

"I'm on Sea Wall. I'll be there soon."

"Well, I should hope so. You did invite us, after all."

"Mother, just wait for me downstairs, okay?"

"Where is . . . she?"

"Erina is in the condo with Colin."

"Then I'll see you there." She hung up the phone.

"Damn," Grant muttered. He stepped on the gas but didn't go far before seeing blue lights flashing behind him. Great. The morning was starting off just great.

Erina lay Colin down in his crib and answered the telephone. This was only her second time using the modern device and she felt a bit nervous. "Hello?"

"There's a Mrs. Kirby and Mr. Abbott to see Mr. Kirby," the man at the front desk announced.

"They're here?" Erina knew she hadn't kept the panic out of her voice. How was she supposed to face Grant's mother alone?

"Yes, ma'am. May I send them up?"

"No! I mean, yes." She couldn't leave Mrs. Kirby sitting downstairs in the lobby. She took a deep breath. "Please ask them to come up."

She dashed into the bedroom to check her blouse and skirt. There was no need to pinch color into her cheeks; she was already flushed. Tucking a strand of hair behind her ear, she walked quickly into the parlor—or the living room, as Grant called it—and looked around once more. Everything was in place—except Grant.

Where was he? She didn't want to face these people alone. They might ask her something she couldn't answer, or comment on a modern custom that she wasn't familiar with.

Fix tea! That's what she was supposed to do. She rushed into the kitchen and looked for a formal tea pot. Before she could find one, Colin began to cry. She forgot the tea as she hurried into the bedroom. She'd nursed him just a half hour ago, so that couldn't be the reason for his tears. The idea that something could go wrong with his heart was always on her mind.

She scooped him into her arms. "Hush, darlin'. Your mother's here now."

Colin continued to fuss. Erina checked his diaper, but it wasn't wet. She lay him back on the mattress and lifted the bandage covering his incision. The scar was even and pink, with no sign there was a problem.

"Oh, darlin', what's the problem?"

The doorbell rang. Torn between caring for her son and making a good impression on Grant's mother, she chose her son. Picking him up, she hurried to the door.

"Mrs. Kirby, please come in," Erina said over Colin's whimpering cries. "I don't know what's wrong with him. Just a minute ago he began to fuss."

"Well, I . . ." She turned to Mr. Abbott. "Brian, see if you can do something."

"Ginny, I don't know anything about babies."

Colin drooled on Erina's blouse, leaving a large wet stain on the front. "Oh!"

"For heaven's sake," Mrs. Kirby said, reaching for the baby. "Let me hold him while you change." With a flourish, she grabbed a kitchen towel and placed it over the shoulder of her pale pink suit.

"Please be careful of his surgery," Erina said when Mrs. Kirby lifted him gently from her arms.

"Of course I'll be careful. I know how to handle a child."

The door opened then, letting in a burst of warm air and Grant, holding two bags in his arms. There was no place for him to go, however, since three other adults were standing in the tiny entry area by the kitchen.

"What's going on?"

"Colin is fussin'," Erina explained with a catch in her voice, "and I don't know what's wrong with him."

At that moment, he let out a very loud burp.

"That's what's wrong with him," Mrs. Kirby said, patting him on the back with her perfectly manicured hand. She turned to Grant. "Now just exactly what was so important that you went off and let Erina meet us alone?"

"Colin needed some . . . things," he said with a shrug.

"And Erina needs you here," his mother said. She walked into the living room, still lightly patting Colin's back. "A father should be there for his son," she said softly, gazing out the windows, "and for his . . ." She turned back around. "But then you know that."

"Yes, I know that," Grant said, walking up to his mother.

"He looks like you," she said, looking at Colin. The baby smiled back, reaching for her perfectly styled hair.

"Yes, but he has Erina's eyes," Grant said.

"I don't know. Your eyes were blue when you were his age."

Colin grinned and cooed, making both adults laugh together. Then they looked at each other, longing in both their eyes.

Erina crossed her arms, leaned against the wall, and blinked back tears. She had a feeling that Grant and his mother hadn't been this close in years. He'd said that he was a disappointment to his mother, but Erina didn't see that. She suspected that he was just very different than what Mrs. Kirby was accustomed to. Perhaps she didn't know him well.

"Quite a scene," Mr. Abbott whispered to Erina.

She'd forgotten he was there. Turning, she expected to see censure in his face, but that wasn't the expression he wore. Instead, he seemed contemplative.

"I think it's a beautiful thing we're seein'."

"I think you're right." He turned away and looking inside the kitchen. "So, how about some coffee? I've got a feeling we're going to be here for a while."

Erina collapsed on the couch beside Grant after his mother and Brian left and Colin, dressed in one of his new outfits, was taking a nap.

"Tired?" he asked, holding her hand. Her skin was soft, her fingers fine-boned and delicate.

"I'm exhausted. I didn't know visitin' could be so hard."

"I guess we weren't as prepared as we thought."

She nodded. "I'm not good at that sort of thing. I've never had company come to visit before."

"Really? Not even when you lived with your father in Ireland?"

"We lived in a very small village. Any visitin' to be done was taken care of over the half-door of the kitchen or at the town market."

"How about friends your own age? Did you go shopping in the city or whatever else teenage girls do?" Maybe she'd admit something that would give him a clue as to her real origins.

"We had no way into the city, and besides, what would we have done there? Shopping and the like takes money, somethin' we were all without back in Ireland. That's the reason my da decided to come to America. There was no way to make a decent livin'. Mr. Kirby knew of my da's work through a friend in Ireland and asked him to create gardens for their new home on Broadway."

Grant couldn't suppress a sigh as she talked about her fictitious life in the 1890s. "And what did you do in Galveston once you arrived?"

"We lived above the carriage house. Mrs. Kirby allowed me to sit in with the children's tutor, so I continued my education from the parish school I'd attended in Ireland."

"And what about when your father . . ."

"I continued to live and work for Mrs. Kirby. She was very kind."

"Your life sounds lonely to me. Didn't you miss doing what other girls your age were doing?"

She tilted her head. "I was doin' what other girls did, only I had a better time of it. Some worked in

273

far worse places or had harsh employers. I was very lucky."

"Child labor doesn't seem like a lucky condition to me."

"You might think I was a child, but I wasn't. True, I was only thirteen when my da and I came to America, but I was seventeen when he died. I could have married before that if I'd found a man who caught my eye, but I enjoyed livin' with my da and working for Mrs. Kirby."

Grant shook his head. "You shouldn't have had to work."

"Haven't you been readin' your Bible? There's nothin' wrong with honest work."

"Children should have time to play, not work for a living."

"Workin' did no harm to me."

"You were lucky to have a family, I suppose, even though you lost your father."

"Aye, I was."

"So you never found a young man you wanted to marry?" he asked, bringing her attention back to her earlier statement.

He watched a slight blush creep into her cheeks. "No, not then. I'm afraid I was a bit spoiled by Mrs. Kirby. I didn't want to live in a tiny room with six or seven babes clinging to my skirts and only cabbage and potatoes for the pot."

"There's nothing wrong with wanting a good life . . . unless you violate your principles to get what you think you deserve."

"I'm only admittin' that I aspired a *bit* above my station."

"Above your station? Don't be silly."

"I used to dream of having my own house and friends to come visit, but . . . well, I've never been more than a maid or a seamstress. Now I'm livin' in a fine place with a man and entertainin' his mother. The Fates have a fine sense of humor, I'm thinkin'."

"Maybe you're just getting what you deserve. Perhaps you were meant to have what you dreamed about."

"I'm not sure that dreams come true."

"That sounds pretty cynical for someone who believes in miracles."

"Oh, I think you can make your dreams come true with hard work and a bit of luck, but I don't think everyone gets their heart's desire just because they want it."

"I'd agree to that. But sometimes luck—good or bad—plays a larger role in life."

"Like the bad luck of your da dyin' young," she said gently.

"That wasn't luck," Grant scoffed. "He did that to himself. No one poured those drinks down his throat."

"Ah, but he was unlucky to be born cravin' the bottle."

"And he was too weak to stop."

"Perhaps. It's not easy to know what's in another's heart."

That was certainly true. He was sure Erina's heart

275

was good and pure, but he still had no idea who she really was.

Before they could pursue the discussion the telephone rang. Grant picked it up quickly so the ringing wouldn't waken Colin.

"Hello?"

"Mr. Kirby?"

"Yes?"

"This is Mrs. Henshaw. I'd like to schedule a meeting with you and Ms. O'Shea for tomorrow afternoon at three o'clock."

"Tomorrow? Isn't that a little quick?"

"I don't believe so. I'm concerned about the welfare of that child. To be quite frank, you seem to be hiding something. I'm not sure what, but—"

"I'll contact our attorney and see if he's available."

"Having a high-priced lawyer enter into our conversations isn't going to benefit our investigation of Colin's condition."

"I'll agree that lawyers don't always help, but look at it from my perspective; you're insulting Erina's character by insinuating that she's not a good mother. I'm simply trying to protect her from that kind of thinking."

"I haven't filed any report on Ms. O'Shea."

"Good. But I'd feel more comfortable with my attorney present, just in case."

"This is a preliminary meeting to gather information. This is not an inquisition."

"Whatever you say. I'll still need to see if my attorney is available."

"I certainly hope he is. I wouldn't want to get a

protective order for the child just because his parents are being uncooperative."

"Don't threaten me with court orders, Mrs. Henshaw."

"Don't impede this investigation, Mr. Kirby. If Colin is your child, then you are equally liable for his condition."

"There is no condition. His heart has been repaired and he's doing great."

"The condition is lack of vaccinations and emergency medical attention, combined with his low weight. Ms. O'Shea was unable to answer even the most basic questions and seemed completely unaware of her responsibilities as a parent. That's not the kind of person who should have primary care of a seriously ill infant. She obviously needs training in parenting skills."

"Erina is a great mother." Grant discounted his own suspicions regarding her abilities when she'd first shown up at his condo. He hadn't known her then. He hadn't realized how deeply she loved her son. "And she's not alone. We'll be at your office tomorrow afternoon, Mrs. Henshaw, and I'll expect an apology from you for your suspicions about Erina."

He hung up the phone, his hand shaking from the anger he'd tried to hold inside. Wrapped up in his own thoughts, he hadn't considered how the conversation would frighten Erina until he heard a faint sound from her. She sat beside him, a hand over her mouth, her eyes wide.

"I'm sorry," he said, slipping his arms around her. "I suppose our idyllic world was bound to collide with reality sometime soon. But we'll be okay. Sam Reynolds is on our side. That social worker isn't going to do anything to separate you and Colin."

"I wish I had your faith in people," she said against his shoulder.

"You'd be surprised how much faith money can buy," he said automatically. And it was true; money talked, even if Mrs. Henshaw claimed it had no influence on the process. One had only to look in any jail or courthouse across the country to validate that assumption. When she realized that he was going to claim Colin as his son, marry Erina, and hire as many lawyers as necessary to fight these outrageous suspicions, she'd back down.

"Erina, I'll admit that there was a time when I dreaded the idea of other people thinking that I'd fathered an illegitimate child with a young Irish girl. But no more. I'm proud of you and Colin, and I'm not going to let anyone separate us."

"We can place our faith in others to save us from the laws of man, but what about the laws of God? I'm tellin' lies and we're deceivin' your own mother. That's not right. I'm afraid God might not be as easy to convince as Mrs. Henshaw."

"I'll tell you what: Let me take care of the bureaucrats of the world and I'll leave the religion to you."

"I wish life was that simple," she said, "but I'm thinkin' I'll need your prayers."

"I'll give you what I can, Erina, but I don't have the same kind of faith as you."

"I know," she said softly, sighing against his shoulder. "I'll pray for us all and hope that's enough."

Chapter Sixteen

Erina woke in a cold sweat near dawn on Thursday morning. Heart pounding, she struggled to remember what had caused such terror. On shaking legs, she stumbled across the floor to stare into Colin's crib. He slept peacefully, his fist resting against his parted lips.

She held on to the rails of the crib and fought the sense of panic that still held her in its grasp. What had caused her to feel this way?

Then the dream—or the night terror—filtered into her consciousness. She slipped into the rocking chair, unable to stand any longer.

She was in her room over Mrs. Abernathy's shop, sewing her quilt. Today she was embroidering a chain stitch in red silk on a piece of silver velvet. Concentrating on the needle and thread, on their precise placement in the fabric, she hadn't at first noticed the silence. When she lifted her head and looked around, Colin's crib was gone. She threw the quilt to the floor and ran across the room, calling him, crying.

When she couldn't find him upstairs she ran below, calling "Colin!" over and over again. Mrs. Abernathy came out of the shop and looked at her curiously.

"Colin! Where is my baby?" Erina asked.

"Who?" Mrs. Abernathy said. "You don't have a baby."

"Yes I do! Where is he? Where is my Colin?"

She ran through the dress shop, scattering bolts of fabric and trim in her wake. She rushed outside, blinking against the brightness as she cried for her son. Where was he? Everyone looked at her as though she was ready for Bedlam.

"You don't have a son," they all chanted as she ran through the street.

She fell to her knees on the rough wood blocks of the Strand.

That's when she awoke, the terror so real she could smell it, touch it, taste it. Just re-living the dream made her feel the same panic.

Erina concentrated on calming herself. She set the rocker in motion and told herself that no one was going to take her baby away. She was just reacting to Mrs. Henshaw's telephone call. Grant had promised that no one would take Colin away, and she trusted Grant as much as she loved him. The emotion she felt for him grew each day until it had become a part of her. To lose either Colin or Grant would make her feel as though her heart were missing.

Grant would find a way to allow her to stay, both legally and in this time. She had faith that she would be here forever, together with Colin and Grant.

After the meeting with Mrs. Henshaw on Thursday afternoon Erina was ready to do whatever was necessary to save Colin from the clutches of the county officials. Although she was sure that many children benefitted from such efforts, Colin wasn't one of them. He hadn't been abandoned or abused; he hadn't been denied medical care on a whim or because she was lazy. Yet Mrs. Henshaw had her rules, the hospital had protocol, and now Erina was being investigated.

Mr. Reynolds had been a great help with the legal matters, and Grant had been so supportive, but as soon as Erina sat down in his Cherokee, she knew the time had come to take action. She'd told him once that she'd do whatever was necessary to save her child. Now she was going to have to compromise her principles by sacrificing the man she'd grown to love.

She was going to have to marry Grant.

She glanced across the jeep at him. He was angry, she knew, at the "system," as he called it, and at Mrs. Henshaw in particular for pursuing the investigation. He'd once said that the officials were like a dog with a bone, and now she knew what he'd meant.

"Grant?"

He took a deep breath and rubbed his forehead. "Yes?"

"If you'd still be willin' . . . that is, I think perhaps

281

it would be best if we married."

He was silent for so long she thought he'd changed his mind. Or that she'd misunderstood his intentions all along. But then he smiled, revealing the dimple in his cheek. "It's about time," he said softly.

"I'm bein' selfish in acceptin' your offer," she said, looking into his eyes. They flashed with life even in the dim light of the parking garage. "But I'm worried about Colin. That woman—"

"She's not going to be able to do a thing once Colin is legally mine."

"What do you mean?"

"Once I legally claim him and we're married, he'll have two parents, not just one. They're focusing on you at the moment because you had custody of him when he needed surgery. But now they'll have to fight us both. And they know they can't win that battle."

"Are you sayin' that Colin will be under your care and no longer under mine?" The idea that Grant could take her child away was almost as devastating as that of a stranger snatching him from her arms.

"No," he said, reaching across the Cherokee and running a hand through her hair. "No, sweetheart, that's not what I meant. We'll be a couple. You know, fifty-fifty. I'm not trying to take your baby away from you."

"It's not that I'm doubtin' you, you understand, but who can protect my right to raise my child? What if you decide I'm not a fit mother?"

"I don't think that."

"What if you did? You don't believe I'm from the

past. Someday you might decide I'm daft—too daft to be a mother."

"Erina, you're borrowing trouble. Just because I don't believe your story doesn't mean I think you're crazy. Oh, I might have thought that at first, when you showed up in my condo and I had to rush Colin to the hospital, but I don't anymore. I know you're as sane as I am."

"But what do you believe about me, Grant?" She had never asked him such a question before, but now she needed to know—before they became tied to each other for all eternity.

"Do you really want to talk about this in the car, sitting in a parking garage?"

"No, but I'm thinkin' we need to discuss the subject."

"Okay," he said, taking a deep breath and placing both his hands on the steering wheel. "Tonight, after dinner, we'll have a long talk."

She nodded, looking away. Did she really want to know what he thought about her? Who he believed she was? Because if he didn't think she was from the past, where did he think she'd come from?

Mrs. Parker was walking the floor with Colin when they arrived home from the meeting. Grant was in no mood to chat but smiled at the nurse before checking his messages and the fax machine. Everything seemed to be running smoothly at Kirby Investments. He hoped Brian and Dottie weren't too busy without him there, but he knew he couldn't concentrate on business with so much going on in his personal life.

After all, it wasn't every day that a woman agreed to marry him.

He turned back just as Erina took Colin into the bedroom. Dinnertime, he supposed.

"When you need me again just give a call," Mrs. Parker said, picking up her purse.

"As a matter of fact, something has come up and we'll need to be in Houston tomorrow. Would you be available then?"

"Yes. Just let me know what time."

"I'll call you later. Thank you, Mrs. Parker."

The nurse let herself out. Grant followed her and turned the lock, then kicked off his shoes and walked through the living room and down the short hall, and stopped at the guest bedroom doorway.

Erina sat in the rocker, nursing Colin. Late afternoon sunlight came through the high windows of her room, casting blue highlights in her hair. She talked softly to her baby, but Grant couldn't make out the words.

Who was Colin's real father? Did she know his name, or had an anonymous man attacked her? Grant could understand why she'd make up a story about Jerrold Kirby if the truth was too hard to face. But Grant knew that someday, Colin would want to know the truth. What would Erina tell her son then? He hoped she'd be able to face reality before that happened.

Grant told himself again that the identity of Colin's real father didn't matter. Colin would be raised as his son, no matter who his biological father was. But a part of him wanted to know the truth. He wanted Erina to trust him enough to confide in him, no matter how horrible or embarrassing the story was.

She looked up, as though she'd listened to his thoughts and heard his doubts. Her face serious, she rocked in the chair without her usual discomfort at being caught nursing. She was so modest that he had no idea what she would really look like naked. But he could dream. Oh, he could dream . . .

He felt his body stir at the image of Erina walking toward him, natural and uninhibited. When they married would she do that? Or would she be as modest as ever?

He couldn't wait to find out. His body definitely wanted to know the answer.

"I think I'll go out and get us some dinner," he said. "What would you like?"

"Anything is fine with me."

"Seafood, steaks, Italian?"

"I liked those wee shrimp we had the other day," she said.

"Good. I'll get those."

"I can cook, you know," she said as he was about to turn away. "You'll not be gettin' a woman without skills."

He smiled. "I'm not worried about whether you can cook. I want you to be a wife, not a maid or a chef."

"I've no experience bein' a wife."

"That's okay. I don't have any experience being a husband."

She smiled back. "I suppose we'll both be learnin'."

"I suppose so." A stray thought crept into his mind. "Erina, you do know I expect us to be really married, don't you?"

"Yes, I suppose so," she said, even though she looked a bit confused.

"And that means we'll be sharing a bed and . . . everything."

That comment earned a blush. "Yes, I know."

He took a deep breath. "Okay. I just wanted to make sure we were clear about that."

She nodded. "I mean to be a good wife to you, Grant Kirby."

"And I promise to be a good husband and father."

Erina shifted Colin on her lap. "Grant, I've got a powerful yearnin'—"

"For me?"

"For those wee shrimp."

He laughed at one of her first attempts at humor. "I won't be gone long."

After they bathed Colin and put him to bed Erina followed Grant into the living room and sat beside him on the couch.

"Do you want to talk now?" he asked.

She nodded. "I need to know what you believe." Although she'd been busy this evening, uncertainty continued to plague her. How could Grant want to marry her and not believe her?

"I admit I was pretty confused when you first showed up. I mean, I go through securing the condo for the night as a ritual; I have business and financial

286

documents here from time to time. I know that I locked the condo and turned on the alarm system before I went to bed. And I know that you didn't climb the side of the building and enter through the balcony."

"Heavens, no! I could not stand the height."

"I figured that. I suppose that means you don't want to learn to climb with me."

"I don't think I could even watch from the ground," she stated, shivering at the thought of Grant hanging from a rock ledge, hundreds of feet about the earth.

"So anyway, I decided you must have gotten in before I locked up. You must have hid until later."

"You think I hid in this place with a sick baby? Do you not think he'd cry?"

"He was asleep, I'm sure, or he would have."

"Colin was dyin'! Do you think I'd hide in a closet while his heart stopped beatin'?" Grant's story was more ridiculous than her own. At least hers made sense—if you believed in miracles.

He shrugged. "That's the only explanation that makes sense."

"Or you could just believe that the Virgin Mary sent me to the future."

"I'm sorry, Erina, but I *can't* believe that."

"So you think I'm lyin' to you," she stated, her heart breaking at the thought.

"No, I don't. I think you absolutely believe your story."

"I don't know what you mean. Of course I believe my story; it's the truth!"

"As your mind knows it. Look, let's say something

traumatic happened to you. Maybe you really were raped and your mind just couldn't deal with the emotional pain. You read a book about Galveston's past and unconsciously created this fantasy about Jerrold Kirby. That's much easier to deal with because Colin's father has a face and a name."

"That's absurd! I know exactly what happened to me."

"Erina, think about what you're claiming. You say you're from 1896. No one has ever documented a case of time travel. It doesn't really exist."

"It does because Mary willed it to happen."

He ran a hand over his face. "Your religion has become part of the fantasy. You chose me to save Colin because you believe Jerrold Kirby is the father of your baby."

"I didn't choose you, the Holy Mother did. I didn't even know who you were."

"I'm sure it seemed that way to you. I remember that you appeared confused about my identity. But that just means it's part of the fantasy."

"Grant, do you know how crazy you sound?" She was beginning to believe that he was the one creating stories in his head.

"What I'm proposing is based on psychological fact, not on miracles. I know it sounds far-fetched, but not as weird as traveling in time."

"To me it sounds even more odd. But then, the time travel actually happened to me. I can understand how you'd have a hard time believin' me since you didn't experience it yourself."

He touched her cheek, his eyes tender. "I know

that you believe you're from the past, and that's all right with me. I hope that someday you'll remember what really happened, but if you don't, I'm willing to live with that."

"Well, that's very understandin' of you, but you happen to be wrong," she said, still a bit upset that he thought she'd made up a story, even if he thought she wasn't aware it was a story.

"I think I'm right, and that someday we'll find out the truth."

The idea that they might find out the truth because she went back to the past filled her with dread. What could be more horrible than proving she was telling the truth only to lose Grant forever?

Arguing about who was right wouldn't solve any problems. If he was willing to accept her, thinking she'd created a fantasy inside her head, then she could accept him with his skeptical view of miracles.

"I understand," she said at last. "Once you said we should agree to disagree. I think that's a good idea."

He smiled. "Good. I don't want your past coming between us."

"Neither do I," she said, closing her eyes and resting her face against his hand. "Neither do I."

Chapter Seventeen

Grant's newly discovered closeness to his mother was a tenuous thing that needed to be carefully nurtured. Instead, he was about to shock her with a rush wedding. She'd taken to the idea of having a grandchild remarkably well, but how would she react to acquiring a daughter-in-law?

On Friday morning Mrs. Parker came to the condo to stay with Colin so Grant and Erina could go to Houston. He needed to tell his mother in person, with Brian in attendance, he hoped. Then, after all the discussions and explanations were over, they needed to plan a wedding.

"I don't suppose you'd agree to a civil ceremony," he said to Erina as they walked toward the Jeep.

"What's a civil ceremony?"

"Where you go before a civil authority, like a Justice of the Peace or a judge, to get married."

"And not be married in the eyes of the Church? No, I couldn't do that."

"I was afraid you'd say that."

"And why would you be afraid?"

"Because I'm not sure how long it takes to get married in the Catholic Church. I'm sure we'll need some kind of approval. I remember when one of my property managers got married, he and his wife went through required pre-wedding counseling sessions and had to sign all kinds of documents. We don't have time for that."

"I'm sure we can make a priest understand that."

"I hope so. If we can't, then we can get married in a civil ceremony and have a church wedding later."

She stopped him before they got into the Jeep. "I'll not consider myself truly married until our union is blessed by the Church."

"But mainly we'll need the marital status for Mrs. Henshaw and the INS."

"Yes, but I just wanted you to know that I can't be your wife . . . in every way . . . until we're truly married."

What she was saying finally penetrated. "You mean we can't sleep together?"

"Sleep or anything else," she stated with a nod of her head.

"Oh."

"And you'll not be talkin' me out of this, Grant Kirby."

"I wouldn't even try," he said, unlocking the door for her. "I know how important religion is to you."

"To us all," she corrected him.

He didn't say anything more; Erina had the kind of faith that went deep and spread wide. She didn't go around trying to convert others, but she did have a way of reminding him of the abstract philosophies he'd learned as a child.

They drove to Houston in light traffic, chatting about the sights, the music, and the weather. But as soon as they neared his mother's house, Grant felt himself pull away. He wasn't looking forward to informing her of the hasty wedding, but, he kept reminding himself, his mother had taken to the idea of Colin remarkably well. Brian would be more resistant; but then, he'd made himself clear about his doubts from the first.

Brian just didn't understand the overwhelming attraction Grant felt for Erina. The way she made him feel protective of her and Colin.

"I'm a bit fearful of tellin' your mother," Erina said as they sat in the oval driveway.

"So am I." He took a deep breath. "Are you ready?"

Erina nodded.

His mother met them at the door instead of letting Maria answer the doorbell. And she seemed more relaxed, maybe even a little friendlier as they took seats in the living room.

"You didn't bring Colin?" she said chidingly.

"No, the doctors said to keep him in Galveston for now. Mrs. Parker is with him."

"She's a retired registered nurse," Grant explained. "I hired her while Colin was still in the hospital."

"Then she's not a stranger."

"No, she's a fine woman," Erina said. "She reminds me of . . . someone I once knew."

"Someone in Ireland?"

"No . . ."

Grant knew what Erina was thinking: She couldn't tell his mother about the fictitious Mrs. Abernathy, Having this fantasy inside Erina's head must be a real problem for her; she had to constantly think about what she was going to say. If she said something about the past that seemed perfectly normal to her, others would react negatively, just as he had. He hadn't really thought about her story from that angle before. At first he'd thought she was trying to remember or assemble a background as she went. Now he knew that wasn't the case.

Brian followed Maria into the room, helping with coffee and tea. "What's up, Grant?"

"Erina and I have some news," he said, reaching for her hand. "We've decided to get married."

"Married?"

"Yes, Mother. We think it's the right thing to do."

"Well, I can't say that I'm too surprised."

"Really? I would have thought you'd at least give us a little token opposition."

"Grant, you make me sound like an ogre! I never give you grief just for the fun of it."

Grant smiled. "I didn't mean that. It's just that Brian has been trying to talk me out of rushing into my . . . involvement with Erina and Colin from the beginning. I guess I expected the same."

"Well, Colin is your son. You should take responsibility for him. And if you cared enough for Erina to . . . get involved with her when she was obviously young and inexperienced, you should do the right thing."

"It wasn't Grant's fault," Erina said, defending him.

"I'm not sure we should say it was anyone's fault, dear," his mother replied patiently. "But the fact is that you're here now and so is Colin. As Brian is fond of telling me regarding real estate matters, this is not a problem, it's an opportunity."

"Mother, I'm so glad you feel that way. We're going to need your help in getting the wedding set up. Due to the investigation of Erina by the UTMB social worker and the need to establish her legally with the INS, we need to get married quickly. With my name and influence, I hope to deflect some of the questions they might have about Colin's background and Erina's entry into the U.S."

"I'll call the parish priest right away. But I wish you'd give me time to plan a proper wedding. Even a few months would be enough time to—"

"Mother, we're talking about a few days here."

"Days! Grant, I doubt that anything can be arranged that quickly."

"One thing I've come to realize lately is that anything's possible," he said, looking at Erina. "So I think we can arrange something, don't you?"

"I . . . I suppose," his mother said, putting down her coffee cup and pacing the floor. "Yes, I'm sure we can." She turned back to Grant. "By the way, did you make a decision on that property by the church?"

Grant smiled. "Funny you should ask. I've decided that would make a great outreach center."

"Excellent. I'll get on the phone immediately."

Brian raised his eyebrows and watched her retreating figure. "I haven't seen her this excited about a project in years."

"This isn't a project," Grant said. "It's our wedding. Let's keep that in perspective."

Armed with Grant and Erina's birth certificates, they arrived at the Harris County Clerk's office at noon, just in time for the lunch crowd rush. Erina looked around the large room, amazed at all the people who were here to get married. All kinds of people mingled together, something she wouldn't have seen in 1896.

And most of the women were much older than she, lending credence to Grant's statement that she was too young for him. For the first time in years she did feel young. Since her father's death, and especially since Colin's birth, she'd been mature and responsible to the best of her ability. The idea that she had someone beside herself with whom to share the joys and burdens filled her with hope for the future.

Surely Mary wouldn't send her back in time if she and Grant married in the Church. God's judgments sometimes seemed harsh, but Erina refused to believe He was cruel and unfeeling. He wouldn't separate a family, joined in holy matrimony, would he?

Finally they arrived at the counter where they would acquire their marriage license. Grant had called earlier and received a paper through the telephone, a process he called a "fax." They'd completed the form and had it witnessed and notarized at his office. Now he presented it to the clerk, along with their birth certificates.

"There is a three-day, seventy-two-hour waiting period," she said in a singsong voice. Stamping another form, she looked up and said, "That will be thirty-one dollars."

Grant paid the money and received the license.

"Now all we have to do is talk to the priest," he said.

"I'm hopin' your mother had good luck talkin' to the man."

"Trust me; if anyone can get the Church to agree to a speedy wedding, it's my mother."

Erina hoped he was right. "I wish we could have been married at St. Mary's Cathedral, but I understand that your own parish church would be important to you and your mother."

"It's really her church," Grant explained. "I don't attend regularly and haven't for years."

"Shame on you, Grant Kirby," Erina said, taking his arm. "I'll expect you to mend your ways. Colin needs a good example."

Grant smiled. "I suppose you're right. I guess being a father is more complicated than I imagined."

"No, bein' a father is very simple," she said, remembering her own da. "Just do what's right and your children will follow in your footsteps."

"You make it sound so simple. Life isn't necessarily like that, Erina. Not anymore."

"I think life is as simple as you make it," she said as they walked out the door into the bright sunshine. "And I know you're going to be a good father to

Colin. You're a good man."

"And that's the only criteria?"

"Aye, I think so. What else is important?"

Grant seemed deep in thought as they drove away from the downtown offices. Erina forgot about his mood as she looked out the windows at the tall buildings. They amazed and frightened her. How could they stand upright, so tall and yet so thin? Someday she'd find out.

They drove back toward Grant's mother's house but turned onto another street.

"Where would we be goin'?"

"Back to my place. I should have taken you by before, but I didn't think about it."

"This is the apartment where you live most of the time?"

"Yes. It's close to my office." He pulled into a parking garage and inserted a thin card into a machine that opened the gate. "I'll introduce you and get you signed up so you won't have any problem coming or going."

"Is every place so guarded?"

Grant pulled into a parking place and turned off the engine. "High-rise buildings like my condo and this apartment are safer. Otherwise, criminals could walk right up to the door."

Like I walked right into your condo in Galveston, Erina thought to herself. The fact that he refused to believe her story still stung, but she was trying to be understanding of his feelings.

She signed a card and met a very nice man who sat near the elevators and seemed to know everyone by name. "You won't have any problem now. Use this card to get in and out the door when the security guard isn't here. I'll get a key made for the apartment."

"All right." She placed the card in her purse, which was mostly empty. She wondered what most women carried about with them.

They rode upstairs to the sixth floor in a beautiful mirrored elevator with brass doors. Grant walked her down the hall, which was richly carpeted and had brass and crystal sconces on the walls.

When she walked into Grant's apartment she was amazed by the wealth displayed. This was the type of home she'd expect a wealthy man to have. It was far, far different from his condo.

The walls were covered with deep green paint and a printed paper. The floors were covered in thick, richly colored Turkish carpets over wood. The furniture was a combination of fabrics and styles, much like she'd seen in magazines at the hospital. It looked very rich, but it didn't look much like Grant.

"I know it's ostentatious," he said, leading her into the parlor. "My mother had her decorator do it." He shrugged. "All she told her decorator was that I was a bachelor and the place needed to look good for entertaining. I didn't really care, so if you'd like to change anything, feel free."

"You'd want me to change your apartment?"

"Our apartment," he corrected. "You're going to live here too, and I want you to be comfortable. Of course, we'll have to redecorate the guest bedroom as a nursery for Colin anyway, so you might as well do the whole place."

"But I . . . I wouldn't know where to start!" Just the thought of buying new furniture in 1996 filled her with dread. She really didn't know where to start. If she went by her own skills and knowledge, they'd end up with a Victorian-era home.

"There's no hurry. My mother will help you."

"Oh." She'd forgotten that she wasn't alone. And Grant's mother did seem to be very willing to help with the wedding.

"As a matter of fact, I can call her and ask her to come over. The two of you can discuss the wedding and decorating and whatever else while I'm gone."

"Where would you be goin'?"

"I've got to run by the office, but I'll call Mother first."

Erina sank down on one of the chairs, an uncomfortable piece covered in a leopard-skin print. This was what Grant's wife was expected to do, she realized. She had a lot to learn about life—more than she'd expected when she'd lived in her own time.

His mother would help, she realized. Erina took a deep breath. The idea of being a wife seemed overwhelming at the moment. She wished Mrs. Abernathy was here. She could ask her about the more personal aspects of being a wife. That's something she could never do with Grant's mother, especially when they'd deceived the poor woman into thinking that they'd already . . . acted like a married couple.

"Make yourself at home. There should be drinks in the refrigerator or in the bar," Grant said.

He walked up to the chair, placed his hands on the arms, and leaned over her. "I won't be long," he said; then he kissed her.

They'd been so busy that they hadn't kissed recently. She'd missed it; oh, how she'd missed his kisses. She closed her eyes and parted her lips so he could deepen the contact, and he didn't disappoint her. Within seconds she wished he could stay and teach her more about the passion she was just discovering.

He broke the kiss, his eyes clouded with desire. He rested his forehead against hers, his breathing uneven. "I hope we don't have to wait long for the wedding—or, more specifically, the wedding night."

"I'm just as anxious to be your wife," she whispered. "I hope I don't disappoint you. I know most women have a bit more experience than I do."

"I don't care about experience. I know we're going to be great together."

She smiled, believing the same thing. "I'll be waitin' for you to return."

"Have a good visit with my mother. She's already talked to the parish priest and she'll fill you in."

"I'm sure we'll have a fine time."

"You don't sound too convincing," Grant teased.

"I like your mother, Grant, but she is a bit intimidatin'."

"Yes, but I think she honestly likes you. And I know she adores Colin. I've never seen her like that before."

"I'm so glad. I think she loves you very much."

Grant seemed embarrassed by her observation.

"I've got to get to the office. I'll see you in a couple of hours."

She watched him go with such love inside her. Grant was a good man. He would be a good father.

And besides, he was a hunk, she thought with a smile.

Grant arrived at Brian's office just as some of the staff were leaving for the weekend. Unless they were busy he'd always encouraged a short day on Friday. Today, Grant was glad for the semiprivacy. He wasn't sure if news of his upcoming marriage had leaked out, but he didn't want to spend the afternoon getting an equal measure of congratulatory slaps and curious looks.

He was equally glad that the hospital staff had been discreet. He'd half expected to see his name splashed across some tabloid with a photo of a startled Erina and a crying Colin.

"Hey, son, come on in," Brian said from behind his large, cluttered desk, the phone to his ear. "I'll be with you in just a minute."

Grant took a seat and looked around the office. Brian was a true Texan, with the requisite Western paintings on the walls and the bronze cowboy and horse statue on the credenza. Two uncomfortable leather chairs faced the desk; the seats were hard and straight so guests wouldn't want to linger and chat. Brian got down to business fast and concluded promptly.

He might look and sound like just another good ol' boy, but Brian was no fool. He'd graduated near the top of his class at Harvard and had a mind like a steel trap and instincts that were astounding.

He hung up the phone. "Is everything arranged for that wedding?"

"I didn't ask Mother yet. She's coming over to the apartment to talk to Erina. I'm sure they'll get the plans finalized."

"I hope you know what you're doing."

Grant nodded. "I feel good about this."

"No doubts?"

"Not one."

"What about your bride's story of being from the past? Has she 'fessed up?"

"No, she still claims a miracle occurred. I have a theory that something bad happened to her and she created that story to help her cope. But whatever the truth, I'm not worried. Erina is as good as they come. She's a great mother and . . . well, hell, she just makes me feel good."

"I know that it's hard to reason clearly when you're not thinking with your brain, but marriage is for a long, long time. And divorces last even longer."

"I'm not worried, Brian. I know that sounds as if I've flipped, but I can't help thinking that this is going to be the best thing I've ever done."

"I hope you're right. Is that what you came to tell me?

"Not really." Grant shifted in the uncomfortable chair. "I've come to a decision about Kirby Investments. You've known since the beginning that my heart wasn't in the real estate business. The problem was that if I didn't manage the company, what would

I do? So I told myself that I should stay and just do it. Hell, almost anyone in America would have felt blessed to inherit such a position."

"You've taken to real estate real well, even if it wasn't your first choice. Are you sure this isn't just some kind of reaction to getting married?"

"No, but being around Erina and Colin has made me re-evaluate my priorities. I'm going to have a family now, Brian, and I want to spend more time with them."

"What are you thinking?"

"A real estate investment trust. I think it's the answer for all of us."

"You're ready to give up the family business, sell it off to a bunch of investors?"

"I'm ready to settle up, that's for sure. I think Mother will agree. We'd be viable as an investment trust. I don't think the public offering would be a problem. But I want you to know one thing; you're family too."

Brian shook his head. "I'm not family. I'm part of the hired help."

"Bull. For years, you *were* Kirby Investments. When—if—we go public, you'll be taken care of. If you want to continue representing the firm, you can. I'll set it up. I'll probably be around for at least a year. If you want out, then we can arrange that too."

"What are you going to do?"

"I'm not sure. I've been thinking about a few things. You know how much I love to climb. I've got some ideas for new equipment. I'd like to explore that, maybe in partnership with a couple of guides I know."

"You haven't talked this over with your mother?"

"No. I thought I'd dropped enough bombshells for a week or so."

"When are you going to talk to her?"

"After the wedding. She'll have enough to do until then. Erina doesn't seem to know much about wedding customs and . . . hell, whatever it is that needs to be done."

"Your mother is the woman to get this wedding on track."

"That's for sure." Grant looked down at the standard beige office carpet. Not working with Brian would be like losing a family member, but setting up a REIT would give them all financial and personal freedom.

"If the trust goes through and you end up with some extra time on your hands, can you think of anything you'd like to do?"

Brian shrugged. "Go fishing, I guess."

Grant laughed. "I have a better idea. I think you should learn a little more about tennis. Maybe make a few more appearances at the country club. Get involved in some charities."

"Hell, then I'd be doing what your mo—oh, no you don't. Don't start matchmaking. Just because you're infatuated doesn't mean the rest of us have lost our minds."

"Don't give me that. You know you're attracted to her. Why not go for it?"

"We're about as alike as night and day."

"You're no more different from Mother than Erina is from me."

"Exactly my point."

"Well, we're getting married on Wednesday. What does that say about you and Mother?"

"Not a damn thing. Now get on back to your girl and leave my love life alone."

"I wasn't aware that you had one," Grant said, laughing at the mock ferocity of Brian's response.

"Out!"

"You'll talk with a brokerage representative?"

"I know just the one to call. Believe it or not, this isn't a total surprise."

"Really?"

"You've always been a little restless. I'm not too surprised."

"As usual, you're one step ahead of me." Grant pushed himself out of the chair. "I'll get back to the apartment. I'll call you if anything comes up this weekend."

"If you need me . . ."

"I know. Thanks, Brian." Grant paused in the doorway. "This is going to work out, you know."

"The investment trust or the wedding?"

"Both."

Chapter Eighteen

"The priest doesn't want to marry us," Erina told Grant as soon as he came through the door.

"What do you mean?" he asked, walking over to the refrigerator beneath the bar. He took out a soft drink and opened the can.

"You mother said that he doesn't believe we should marry so quickly," Erina explained, clasping her hands together. She'd felt extremely nervous ever since Grant's mother had arrived with the news.

"He's resistant," Mrs. Kirby explained with a patience Erina found exasperating.

"What's the problem?" Grant asked.

"If you'd remember your teachings as a boy, or even attend mass occasionally, I'm sure you'd realize that marriage is considered a solemn occasion. The Church believes you should enter into the union with a bit of forethought," his mother explained.

"I'm entering into this with lots of thought," Grant said defensively.

"But you want to get married in five days," she said.

"I'd like to take a few months and plan a big wedding, if that's what Erina wants." He looked at her, and her heart skipped a beat. She'd never imagined having a large wedding with a white gown, not since Jerrold Kirby had changed her life. "Unfortunately, we don't have the time, with the social worker and the INS problems. I want to make sure that no one can take Colin and Erina away."

"I understand, but the church is more cautious. They expect baptismal certificates and an Affidavit of Free Status, along with your attendance at pre-wedding counseling."

"We can't do that. What other options do we have?" he asked.

"What we need to do is convince the father that we are serious," Erina answered. "We should go to see him and explain the truth."

"The truth that we have very little documentation on you and Colin?" Grant asked as he walked toward her.

She sat down in one of the chairs beside the sofa. "I'm thinkin' we shouldn't lie to a priest," she said, before recalling that Grant's mother didn't know the truth—the truth he wouldn't believe.

"Erina, I don't want you to have to lie."

"What are you two talking about?"

"Erina thinks we should tell the whole story of how she came to the U.S. and why she has nothing except birth certificates for herself and Colin."

"Surely you could just allow some time to obtain

307

the proper documentation. You could even take the wedding counseling on a weekend."

"Mother, I know we won't be able to get those certificates."

"Why not?"

"I'm from a very small village in Ireland. I don't think the church is there anymore," Erina hedged. In fact, she was fairly certain the small chapel had long since crumbled away. When she and her da had attended the thatched roof had leaked and the wind had whistled between the stones. Outside, the cemetery where her mother was buried was in better condition than the church itself.

"But if you attended mass somewhere else recently . . . Surely someone knows you and can vouch for you," Mrs. Kirby said.

"No," Erina said, "there's no one. Not anymore. They're all . . . gone." That was the truth. Mrs. Abernathy would be the closest person to a relative, and she'd surely been dead now for at least fifty years.

"You've certainly gotten yourself into a mess this time, Grant," his mother said.

"I don't want to cause problems for you and your family," Erina said, looking up at him. "Maybe it would be best if—"

"Maybe we should make an appointment to see the priest tomorrow. Erina needs to get back to Colin before tonight."

"I don't like to leave him for so long," she explained.

"You should just move in here. That would be much more convenient."

"Colin's doctor wants him to stay in Galveston until he has his checkup on Thursday morning. He's still on antibiotics. Besides, his nurse is in Galveston."

Erina didn't want to bring up the subject at the moment, but she dreaded moving into this apartment. She'd much rather stay in Galveston, even though she realized now that the condo wasn't as grand as what the Kirbys were accustomed to. She'd miss the sound of the surf and the smell of the ocean. As a matter of fact, at the moment she'd like nothing better than to run back to Grant's condo, lock the door, and stay there forever.

But she couldn't run away from her problems that easily. And she couldn't ignore the teachings of the Church. If she stayed too long with Grant, she'd want to be his wife in every way. She needed the blessing of a priest before that happened.

"Do you have the church's phone number? I'll call and make an appointment for tomorrow. We'll get this straightened out."

Grant's mother gave him the number. When he'd gone into the other room to make the telephone call Erina turned to Mrs. Kirby. "I'm sorry that this is such a problem. I wish it could be otherwise."

"My dear, nothing is easy. Don't worry. I've never seen anyone whom Grant couldn't turn around. He doesn't realize it, but he's so much like his father in that way." Her face took on a wistful look before settling into a more reserved expression. "That is, when he wasn't drinking. But thankfully, between Brian and Grant, Kirby Investments is on solid footing once again."

"Grant doesn't discuss his business with me," Erina said weakly. She didn't want to discuss family matters or business with Mrs. Kirby at the moment.

Grant came back into the room. "We've got an appointment for eleven tomorrow morning," he announced. "Father Flannigan is anxious to meet Erina."

"Father Flannigan? He's Irish, then?"

"By family, not by birth. But perhaps he has a bit of sympathy for a fellow Irishman—or Irishwoman, as the case may be," Grant said with a smile.

Grant walked into the priest's dark, quiet office prepared to defend Erina and his relationship with her. She didn't need his help. From the minute she perched on the edge of one of the leather chairs facing the desk, her tentative smile won over the cherubic-looking father.

"And what's the rush with you two young people?" Father Flannigan had asked right out, a smile in place even as he looked at Erina's very young face.

"We have a bit of a problem with Colin," Erina answered quickly.

"Ah, yes. Mrs. Kirby explained the whole story to me earlier. I'm sorry the baby had such a serious heart problem, but I'm glad he's doing so well." The priest's smile faded as he stepled his fingers and looked at them above his reading glasses. "Now, I must say that you two have gone about this all wrong."

"What do you mean?" Grant asked, moving forward in the chair and resting his hands on his knees. If this man thought he'd give Erina a hard time for—

"Courting, marriage, then babies, Mr. Kirby," the priest answered. "I know your mother didn't raise you to disregard the laws of God and man."

"Of course not," Erina said, jumping in quickly. "This wasn't Grant's fault."

"I'm not blaming just him," the man said, looking at Erina over his half glasses. "You should have thought of the church's teachings before leaping into . . . a situation with this young man."

"Yes, Father," Erina said, bowing her head.

"And you, Mr. Kirby, should have gone back to Ireland to make things right with this young woman."

"I realize that now, Father. That's what I'm trying to do—make things right."

The priest turned his attention to Erina. "You're the problem, young lady. Mrs. Kirby said you have no Church records."

"That's true, Father. Our village church burned when I was twelve. My baptismal certificate was destroyed, and I have no idea where the priests went afterwards. My da and I moved . . . away the next year."

"Do you have no one from the village who could vouch for your baptism?"

"No, Father. I don't even know how to contact anyone there. It was a very small village."

Father Flannigan sighed. "Would you be willing to sign a Supplitory Oath stating that you were baptized in the Catholic Church?"

"Of course! I've attended the church my whole life, Father."

"And what do you say, Mr. Kirby? Can you give me a good reason to disregard our pre-wedding counseling?"

Grant paused before answering, knowing that what he was about to say could sway the priest's decision. "I'm not entering into this marriage with my eyes closed, Father Flannigan," he said slowly. "I know our need to marry seems rushed, but Colin is our major concern. He was born without the benefit of a ceremony in the Church, and we can make that up to him now. As for Erina and me, well, we both know what we want. I would have asked her to marry me earlier if only I'd known . . ."

He let his sentence trail off, leaving the good father with the implication that he hadn't known about her pregnancy. That might have been true; he would have married Erina if she was pregnant—with his or another man's child—although at the thought of consummating their marriage he was glad she'd already had the baby. His body reacted strongly to the image of the two of them entwined in his big bed in just a few nights.

"And you, Ms. O'Shea—are you entering into this marriage with realistic expectations?"

"Yes, Father. I intend to be a good wife and mother, keeping my family in the Church."

"Very well. I can suspend the requirements if I agree that the circumstances are beyond the scope of our regular counseling and certification. I believe this case qualifies."

"Oh, thank you, Father!" Erina cried, reaching for Grant's hand. She squeezed him with surprising strength, happiness radiating from her like the sunshine on a sandy beach. "The father has given us permission!"

"I know," Grant said, smiling at her beautiful face, her features alight with hope and joy.

"Where's that oath, Father?" Grant asked, still smiling, reluctantly breaking his gaze away from Erina. "We have a lot of plans to make."

The wedding took place at two o'clock Wednesday afternoon in a small chapel. Mr. Abbott and Grant's mother were the witnesses, with Colin held in the arms of Mrs. Parker in the second row of pews.

Grant had called Dr. Cook and received permission to bring Colin to Houston with Mrs. Parker. He was going to stay the night with her at Mrs. Kirby's home. Erina knew that meant she and Grant would be alone in his apartment. The thought made her flush all over and tingle in the most unexpected places.

Erina couldn't believe all that had happened since last Friday, when they'd told Mrs. Kirby and Mr. Abbot of the intended wedding. The appointment with Father Flannigan had gone better than she could have expected, far better than she'd dared to hope. And the look on Grant's face had made all her doubts vanish. He didn't appear to be a man who was being forced to marry.

313

After leaving the parish, Mrs. Kirby had taken Erina shopping to buy a wedding gown. Erina rubbed a hand over the beautiful ivory lace and seed pearls. The skirt ended in something called a handkerchief hem, with *v*'s of lace falling between her knees and ankles. Fine ivory silk hose, held in place by satin garters, covered her legs, and on her feet were ivory satin shoes with low, curved heels.

Before the wedding Mrs. Kirby had given her a family heirloom, a choker of pearls that had belonged to Grant's great-great-grandmother. When she'd put them around Erina's neck she'd burst into tears, hugging the older woman. How could she explain that she'd seen those pearls on the throat of *her* Mrs. Kirby, a hundred years ago?

Now, as Erina stood beside Grant in the quiet little chapel, she felt her eyes fill with tears again. In a few minutes she would be Mrs. Kirby, although she wasn't marrying the man she'd been infatuated with as a girl. She was a woman now, and in love with Grant, not some immature, dashing young man who took what he wanted without a thought for others. Grant had given up his freedom to save her and Colin. Could the luck of the Irish be with her more than it was today?

"With this ring, I thee wed," Grant said, watching her eyes as he slipped a heavy band on her finger. He smiled, and when she looked down she almost gasped as the emerald and diamond ring sparkled even in the dim lights of the chapel. She'd never expected such an extravagant wedding band.

"Emeralds to remind you of Ireland," he whispered.

With shaking hands she slipped a plain gold band on Grant's finger, a ring his mother had helped her select. Because Erina didn't know what to buy and had no money of her own, she'd opted for simplicity. Besides, Mrs. Kirby had said that Grant led an active life and a gold band could always be polished. Given his hobby of climbing cliffs, that had seemed a good idea.

After the rings had been exchanged Erina glanced back at Colin, catching a wink and a misty-eyed smile from Mrs. Parker. Grant squeezed her hand and smiled, as though he understood Erina's joy. Even Mrs. Kirby and Mr. Abbott seemed pleased to be at the wedding. Truly, this was the happiest day of her life.

They knelt and received the blessing, and then Father Flannigan pronounced them man and wife and Grant was kissing her. She closed her eyes and allowed herself a moment of pure bliss before reality intruded in the form of sniffles and sobs.

Erina pushed back from Grant's smiling face and turned to the people watching them. Mrs. Kirby dabbed her eyes, her arm linked through Mr. Abbott's. Mrs. Parker wiped her nose with a tissue as she clutched Colin close to her bosom.

The bride smiled, tears running down her cheeks, then began to laugh. Grant spun her toward him, grinning, so handsome in his dark suit, white shirt, and tie. She'd never seen him dressed this way. The idea that he was hers—all hers—made her want to hug the whole world on this fine day.

As soon as the priest stepped down, everyone came forward to congratulate them. Even if Grant didn't love her, he and his family cared enough to make this day special. And at that moment Erina felt truly loved.

Grant tried to relax on the way from the small reception at his mother's house back to his apartment. A glorious sunset illuminated the western sky. The night was mild and clear, yet the only thing he could think about was getting Erina back home—all to himself.

Married.

The thought should have brought chills to him, made him think of chains and shackles, but he could envision Erina lying on his king-size bed, gloriously naked with her long black hair spread around her. The arousal that image provoked made him shift on the white leather seat. *Think of the other benefits of marriage*, he told himself. Someone to come home to each night, to talk with and plan their future with. Quiet dinners together, long walks on the beach. A house with a noisy den and a driveway filled with bicycles. He wanted all of that with Erina.

But at the moment he wanted to get her safely inside his apartment.

"Are you tired?" he asked. He needed conversation to keep him from seducing her right there in the limo.

"Not really," she replied in a dreamy voice. "This day has been so special. I cannot tell you how wonderful . . . and yet I think you know what you've done for me."

"I'm just as happy as you are," he replied easily, then realized how true that statement was. He'd conceived of the idea of marriage as a way to protect Colin and Erina, but he knew now that he wanted them to be a couple, sharing life and someday, hopefully, love. He felt that she could come to love him in time, and he already cared very deeply for her.

The limo stopped at the entrance to the apartment building. In a few moments the driver came to open Erina's door. When she started to get out Grant said, "Wait a minute."

He exited first, then assisted her from the car. Before she could take a step he swung her into his arms and carried her past the smiling driver.

"Add twenty percent and send me the bill," Grant said to the man.

"Grant, you cannot carry me all the way inside," Erina said, protesting despite the way her arms clenched his neck.

"Of course I can." He carried her past George, the grinning night security guard, and into the elevator. "I see no reason to put you down."

"But I must be heavy."

"You don't weigh as much as a backpack," he said, determined to see—very, very soon—just how his bride looked without her wedding gown.

They got off on his floor and made it to his door without incident. However, his key was in his front pant's pocket. "Reach in the left pocket of my pants and get my key, please."

She looked a bit scandalized at his suggestion. "I can't."

"Sure you can. I'm not about to let you go."

She blushed, then reached tentatively into the pocket. He felt her small, firm fingers search for the elusive key. "Lower," he urged, thinking she just might get a big surprise if she searched a bit to the right.

"I have it," she announced a second later.

"Unlock the door quick before we embarrass the neighbors by starting the honeymoon in the hall."

Erina giggled, a sound he found charming. She didn't laugh often enough; he'd have to make sure she had a reason to smile and laugh from now on.

Pushing the door shut with his foot, he strode quickly to the bedroom. His mother's decorator had done a splendid job, he realized, looking around at the many candles, the fresh flowers, the lace-edged sheets. The scents were as rich and seductive as Erina's long black hair.

"It's like a fairy tale," she said breathlessly as she surveyed the room.

"Just as long as it isn't *Beauty and the Beast*," he replied, letting her slide down his body so she could become familiar with his bedroom—before she became familiar with him.

"No, that's not the one," she said, trailing her hand along the soft comforter of the bed. She walked to the antique mirrored armoire. "I think it's called *Cinderella*. I feel as though I've found my prince."

"No, I've just found my princess in hiding," he said, walking up behind her. He placed his hands on her delicate shoulders. He did have large, rough hands. But tonight, he hoped they'd give her pleasure.

He kissed the side of her neck as he watched her face in the mirror. She closed her eyes and moaned. In the background candles flickered inside crystal bowls and brass hurricane lamps. The scent of vanilla drifted through the air, along with the faint smell of the cream-colored roses in tall vases.

But what he sensed most was the growing heat and awareness of Erina, warm and soft in her wedding gown. *Married.* The idea that he was about to make love to his wife filled him with desire.

"I want you so much," he whispered into her ear. "I promised myself that I'd go slowly, that I wouldn't rush you, but all I can think about is taking that beautiful dress off you."

"I . . . I don't know what to say or do," she whispered, looking into his eyes in the mirror.

"Then don't do anything but feel." He slid his hands to her back and began unfastening the many small buttons down the back of the dress. His fingers brushed against her skin and she trembled, closing her eyes and biting her bottom lip with those small, white teeth. He wanted to feel her mouth on him that way, gently nipping. But he'd save that pleasure for later. Right now he wanted to concentrate on her.

He peeled the dress apart, looking down at Erina's ivory slip. So many layers. This seduction was slow, he realized, but he didn't mind. He could take hours undressing her, as long as he knew what was waiting for him at the end. Her softness and warmth. A welcome home. A joining of bodies and minds.

With a sweep of his hands the dress slid down her arms, hung momentarily on her full breasts, then pooled on the floor. He took her hands and urged her to step out of the lacy puddle. That brought her closer to him, flush against his aroused body.

"You're beautiful," he murmured against her shoulder before placing a kiss there. His lips brushed against the strands of pearls circling her throat. His mother had remembered the heirloom, he thought with pride. What a perfect gift for Erina's wedding day.

"I'm a plain one," she said softly.

"No, you're not. There's not a plain inch of skin on your body. Not a plain strand of hair on your head. Don't you know how special you are? To me, you look as though you stepped from the pages of a fairy tale. A princess, come to me from long ago."

He trailed kisses up the slope of her shoulder to her neck. "No, you're not plain, Erina O'Shea Kirby. You're magic."

He tugged the straps of her slip off her shoulders, down her arms, over her hips. She stood trembling in her lacy bra and panties and, below, satin garters that held up creamy stockings. Her breasts were full and white, her waist small and her stomach gently curved.

"You're perfect," he whispered, watching his hands skim her arms, hug her waist, then inch higher to cup her breasts. Her nipples instantly hardened and she moaned.

"Are you sore?"

"No, but you make me feel . . . as I did on the balcony that night. I've never felt that way before."

"Tight and aching?" he asked, lightly caressing her through the lace.

"Yes," she whispered, closing her eyes and leaning back against him.

"I think it's time to lay down, don't you?" As much as he enjoyed watching Erina's response in the mirror, he wasn't sure how long he could stand there. Sooner or later he'd collapse from need. Right now he wanted nothing more than to rid himself of his own clothes and feel her against his body.

She turned and looped her arms around his neck. "Yes, but you need to undress too. I feel odd wearin' so little when you're still in your suit."

"Whatever you want, princess." He hugged her closer, burying his face in her hair. When he opened his eyes he saw the back of her, so pale against the darkness of his clothes. Her bottom was round and barely covered by lacy panties that matched her bra. The thought of what she would feel like made him even harder.

He slid his hands to her buttocks, making her gasp. Then he lifted her, urging her thighs apart so she could straddle his waist. "Hold on," he said, speaking to himself as much as to her.

She tentatively tightened her legs around him, then clutched him harder. "I had a fantasy of holdin' on to you like this," she admitted, her face buried in his neck. "I didn't know if such things were done."

"You can do anything you want to me," he said, settling her on the high bed. "Anything."

With a yank of his tie, he loosened it, then began

unbuttoning his shirt. The soft cotton failed to co-operate. He was about to yank it apart when Erina's hands replaced his.

"Let me," she said, and she deftly slid each button from the hole with far more finesse than he possessed at the moment. He wanted her so badly that he ached. She was sitting on the bed, her legs straddling his thighs, and all he could think about was making her cry out in passion.

She pushed his shirt and suit coat off his shoulders and down his arms, just as he'd removed her dress. With a look of wonder on her face she touched his chest.

"I wondered what it would be like to be free to touch you," she admitted. "You are so strong, so big."

"I don't feel very strong at the moment. Right now, I feel as weak as a kitten."

"Then perhaps you should lie down," she said with a slight smile that made his heart beat faster.

"Not until you get me out of these pants," he challenged.

Her fingers weren't as sure on his belt buckle and buttons. She fumbled when it came to his zipper; he was forced to help her tug it down along the ridge of his arousal. He moaned when she exerted the least amount of pressure on his already rigid flesh, which was still covered by his briefs.

"Does it hurt?" she asked innocently.

"Not the way you mean," he whispered against her lips, then kissed her, hard and openmouthed. She seemed startled at first, then relaxed as he slid his tongue into her mouth. At the first touch of her tongue to his, he deepened the kiss even more, urging her to let her passion go.

She seemed to sense what he wanted, because she came up full against him, her breasts teasing his bare chest. She held him tightly, grasping his shoulders, his arms. He slipped his hands lower, cupping her bottom and rubbing her against his arousal.

He broke off the kiss, panting, trying to control his body. He was hotter than he'd ever been before. Burning up with need. "Oh, God, Erina," he whispered against the top of her head. "You have no idea how much I want you."

With shaking hands he pulled himself away from her and sat on the bed. He jerked off his shoes and socks, then yanked his pants down his legs. His shirt, tie, and suit coat ended up on the floor across the room.

He noticed she was struggling with her hose. "Let me," he said. His own hands trembling, he unfastened the garters and slid the silky stockings down her legs, kissing her knee, her shin, her calf. When he got to her ankle he noticed a tiny cut.

"You hurt yourself," he said softly, kissing the damaged area.

"I had to learn to shave my legs," she admitted breathlessly. "I'm afraid I'm not very good at it yet."

He smiled against her soft skin and removed the stocking from the other leg.

He settled her legs on either side of his thighs and reached around her back to unhook her bra. He felt her tremble beneath his fingers. "Nervous?"

"Terribly," she whispered, the words a soft caress

on his neck. "I've never removed my clothes in front of another person before."

"Never?" he said, smiling when the catch came loose. He eased away the lacy garment.

"No, never."

"I've never wanted to remove another person's clothes more," he said, hoping to put her at ease, "so this will be a first for both of us."

"But you've made love to other women."

"Yes, but never to my wife," he said softly as he leaned down and kissed her gently, deeply, until she again responded with all the buried passion she had yet to explore. As he continued the kiss, he coaxed her back on the bed, sweeping his hand down her body until he caught the waist of her panties.

He paused before removing this last piece of clothing. "This is just between us, Erina. Two people who care for each other, making love, giving and receiving pleasure. No one else. Okay?"

She looked up at him with large, dark, trusting eyes. "Yes. I'm not afraid of you. I know you'd never hurt me."

He felt empowered by her trust. With a quick sweep of his hands, he removed her panties. Before she could have second thoughts he skimmed off his briefs and stretched out beside her, his erection pressed against her thigh.

She shivered, although he knew she couldn't be cold. The room seemed unusually warm with the candles glowing and their scents mingling in the air. His own skin was burning hot, especially that part of him that begged for release.

Not yet, he told himself. Not until she's really ready.

He kissed her lips, her cheek, her neck. Lying beside him in nothing but the heirloom pearls and her wedding band, she smelled fresh and pure, with no artificial fragrance to mar the perfection of skin. His mouth trailed lower, to trace her collarbone, then lower still, to the slope of her breast. He could feel her heart pounding, her lungs straining for breath. When he touched her nipple with his tongue she jumped as if he'd shocked her. A bead of milk appeared, and he licked it away.

His hands swept her stomach, her hips, down to her thighs. She shifted on the bed as if she couldn't decide what she wanted. Then he cupped her, stroked her, and she gasped his name.

"That's right, my princess." She was damp and swollen. "You do want me," he whispered against her neck.

He stroked her until she began moving against him, her moans the sweetest sound he'd ever heard. And then he moved between her thighs, pressing against her, stroking her as he eased inside.

Heaven must feel like this, he thought. She was tight and warm, closing around him before he could thrust fully.

"Relax, sweetheart. It's okay. Just relax and let it happen."

He felt the muscles of her thighs loosen a little, so he urged her to wrap her legs around his waist again. He kissed her as he began to move, slowly at first, then deeper as she opened to him. He wasn't sure how long he could last, so he reached between them and touched her where they were joined.

She screamed his name, convulsing around him so hard that it drove him over the edge. With a cry, he surged one last time, his body gloriously complete for the first time. "Erina," he rasped as he tightened his grip around her and fell into oblivion.

Erina awoke to the heavy weight of Grant lying across her, the smell of vanilla and roses in the air, and the feeling that she'd experienced another miracle.

She reached up and touched Grant's hair, lying soft against her breast. His breath teased her with memories of his kisses. She'd known before that she loved him; if they'd never experienced what they'd shared this night, she would have been happy. But now . . . she could never have imagined such passion, not even after reading about it in the magazines at the hospital.

Nothing, not even his kisses and caresses on the balcony, had prepared her for the reality of making love with Grant.

He settled closer, his arm tightening around her. How long had they both slept after . . . afterwards? The candles still burned brightly, lighting the room in a lovely yellow glow that reminded her of her own time. No sounds intruded, and the drapes were tightly drawn. The hour could be early still, or very late. But what did it matter? This night she had no obligations, no worries except pleasing her husband . . . and herself.

She ran her fingers through his hair, hugged him closer, and smiled into the night. Grant had been right that what happened was between only them. No memories had intruded to ruin the moment. She didn't resent the other women for sharing their bodies with Grant, and he didn't seem to mind that she wasn't a virgin. All that was in the past, where it belonged. They'd never need to talk about it again.

She soon realized that the air conditioner—a wonderful invention in most cases—was fanning cool air over their bodies. She shivered, the warm glow of their lovemaking deserting her. With a sigh, she eased from beneath Grant and reached for the sheet and comforter.

He mumbled a protest at her movement, and she smiled. She'd never imagined that men could be so endearing, so entertaining. As she covered him with the sheet and draped the comforter across his legs, she realized she needed to make a trip to the bathroom. Making love was certainly enjoyable, but it had some new and embarrassing consequences.

And at that moment she realized what one of the consequences could be. The wetness between her legs . . . she could have Grant's child! She sagged against the side of the bed as the idea formed in her mind. With trembling fingers she touched her stomach, which was still slightly soft from Colin's birth. She wasn't ready to have another baby, as much as she would love to carry Grant's child.

You're being selfish, she told herself. If conceiving a child was God's will, she would have another baby. But the very human, weak part of her wanted to keep

Grant to herself. She wanted time to watch Colin grow and prosper. She wanted to learn more about this time in which she now lived.

Dear God, please let me live my life in this time—in Grant's time, she silently prayed. Surely now that she was married in the eyes of the Church she'd be able to stay forever.

Yes, she would stay forever. With a renewed sense of hope, she pushed herself away from the bed and walked silently into the bathroom. She closed the door, then searched the wall for a light switch.

When the lights over the sink came on she gasped. Mirrors reflected the fixtures over the twin sinks—and her very naked, flushed-pink body. She pivoted in the center of the room. The bath was as extravagant and lush as the rest of the apartment, from the gold fixtures to the huge, soft towels. Both a tub and a shower, much like those she'd seen in a decorating magazine, nestled between two closets.

Well, she'd just have to get accustomed to such luxury. Grant obviously enjoyed such things, so it was her duty to do the same. One thing that she wasn't used to yet was the expensive jewelry. She wouldn't dare remove her wedding ring, but the pearls . . . When she tried to work the clasp they refused to cooperate. She'd have to wear them to bed and have Grant remove them in the morning.

She washed as quietly as possible so she wouldn't disturb him, then turned out the light and eased open the door—walking right into the very solid, warm body of her husband.

"Grant! You frightened me."

His eyes gleamed in the candlelight. "Did I? Is that why your heart is beating so fast?" he asked as he placed a hand on her naked chest.

She looked at his large, tanned hand against her skin. She was naked! She'd forgotten that small detail as he'd surprised her in the doorway, but now the realization that she stood before Grant wearing only the strand of pearls filled her with a strange mixture of excitement and fear. Would he find her attractive now that his lust had been satisfied?

She shouldn't care—vanity was a sin—but she couldn't help wondering. She looked up into his eyes and found them glowing with a desire as strong as before.

"Grant," she whispered, leaning toward him as his hand moved lower, circling her back, pulling her against his warm, aroused body.

"I missed you," he said simply before he lowered his mouth.

She met his kiss, her lips parted, hungry for the taste and feel of him. He wore no clothes, just the musky scent of their lovemaking. She found the essence stimulating in the extreme. The part of her that had been so gloriously satisfied not very long ago leaped to life again, craving Grant's touch.

This time he took his time when he carried her to the huge bed. He kissed his way down her body, over her milk-swollen breasts to her navel. And when he ventured lower she tugged on his shoulders and urged him to stop. But he didn't. He did things to her that made her crazy with need. She'd never imagined that a man would do that. But oh, he kissed her so privately, so shamefully, that she cried out, begging him for release.

He surged inside her, moving slickly and strongly as she held him tightly with her arms and legs and listened to his whispered words of encouragement. This time he didn't need to touch her intimately to take her over that high ledge and let her soar. She cried out his name as she fell through a special night sky filled with thousands of stars. And Grant was with her on that extraordinary journey, calling her name, bringing her gently to rest on a bed of lace and roses.

Chapter Nineteen

Facing Grant in the light of day, knowing that he was watching her, was one of the hardest things Erina had ever done. Every time she looked at him she remembered what he'd done to her—and what he'd taught her to do to him—in the wee hours of the morning. She was in a constant state of flushed cheeks and suppressed smiles as they drove toward Galveston.

Colin cooed and played in his car seat. He'd been a little angel, Mrs. Parker had said this morning when they picked him up from Grant's mother's house. And Mrs. Kirby . . . she looked at the two of them as though she knew what they'd done in the dark hours of the night.

Now, as they crossed the high bridge over the bay, Erina no longer felt a sense of panic at the height. Maybe it was just because she'd ridden in the Cherokee several times before, or maybe it was because she felt relaxed and confident for the first time in years.

They pulled into the parking garage of UTMB minutes later.

"I talked to Sam Reynolds and told him about the wedding. I'll be sending over a copy of the marriage certificate later today. I'm sure that will go a long way toward getting your status settled."

"I couldn't bear the thought of havin' to leave you . . . now."

Grant smiled, his eyes hooded in a very sexy way. "I may never let you out of my sight—at least not for forty or fifty years."

She wanted to lean toward him, to kiss him just one more time, but Colin let out an angry wail at sitting so long in the Jeep.

"He's making his wishes known this morning," Grant observed, the dimple still in his cheek. "I guess he's jealous that I took his mommy away for so long yesterday."

"Under most conditions, I'd agree with him that I'd stayed away too long. But I just can't be agreein' with him this fine day."

"It is a fine day, isn't it?" Grant asked as he reached into the back seat and unfastened Colin from his car seat. "Just the first of a lifetime of fine days."

Colin's checkup didn't take over an hour. Dr. Cook pronounced him well, healing with no problems. The doctor wanted to see him again in a month, but that was just routine, he explained. Colin didn't even need any more medicine.

Erina left the hospital feeling as though another part of her life was falling into place.

"What would you like to do with the rest of the

day?" Grant asked as they walked toward the Jeep.

"I'm not sure," she said, thinking of the many sights she hadn't seen yet. She'd wanted to ride the new trolley, walk on the beach, visit the homes that had survived the hurricane and the years. "Wait, I know!" she said, suddenly excited. "Can we visit Kirby House? I'd love to see how it looks now."

Grant looked at her a little strangely but nodded. "Of course. They're probably having tours all day."

"Good. I so want to see the place again. I'd forgotten how much in the past few days, with all the excitement of the wedding, but when I saw your mother's table I remembered how it used to look."

"You know what I'm going to say, don't you?"

"That you don't believe I'm from the past. I know. But please take me to Kirby House. I promise I won't do or say anything odd in front of others."

"I'm not worried about that, sweetheart. You can say or do anything you want—as long as you don't start removing your clothes in public. I'm afraid I'd have to put my foot down there," he said in a teasing way.

"As if I would be takin' my clothes off anywhere," she replied with a smile.

"Oh, I remember your clothes coming off last night. Very clearly, in fact. If the memory gets any better, we're going to have to detour to the condo and put Colin down for a nap."

Erina placed a hand over her mouth and giggled like a schoolgirl. "Maybe after visitin' Kirby House," she said between bursts of laughter.

"I'll hold you to that," he said with a wink as he started the engine.

Kirby House was built in New Orleans style of red brick, with high steps out front and lots of iron grill-work around the porch and windows. Erina had always loved the house, which looked much as it had a hundred years before. The main difference was in the landscaping; now palm trees clustered in the front where an oak had once stood, and oleanders lined the wall leading from the main house to the coach house.

Grant had called ahead from his car telephone and made arrangements for a private tour. Being married to a respected, wealthy man did have some advantages, she thought with a smile. Of course, she would have loved him anyway. Inside, Grant was as kind as they come. Outside . . . well, he did make her heart flutter every time she looked at him.

They parked along the side and walked up the front steps like any other tourist family. *Family.* That's what they were now. The idea that within two weeks she had acquired the husband of her dreams and a healthy baby made Erina want to laugh out loud, to hug the world, and tell everyone of her good fortune.

"Marriage seems to agree with you. You're certainly in a good mood today," Grant observed as he opened one of the double, leaded-glass front doors.

"Oh, and I wouldn't know why that would be," she said, grinning as she carried Colin inside the dark foyer.

As soon as she entered the mansion, however, her smile faded and a sense of déjà vu assailed her. Even Colin became quiet, looking around at the red-patterned walls and gilt accents with wide blue eyes.

"It looks so different," Erina said softly. "Like there is no family here; like the house has no soul."

"Houses don't have souls," Grant said, walking a few steps forward on the creaking wood floor.

"I don't know. I think maybe they do, if they're lived in and loved." Someday she'd like to have a house that comforted her family, a place of warmth and happiness.

He shrugged. "A house has always been just a place to sleep, eat, and entertain to me."

"Even your condo?"

"That's different."

"I know," Erina said, walking toward a red velvet settee centered on one wall of the hallway. "I think the condo is how you'd like your life to be, far away from your family's world, and your apartment is just part of that world."

"That's pretty deep for this early in the day," Grant observed lightly as he studied a painting on the opposite wall.

"I'm not sayin' anything ill of your apartment or your mother's home, mind you, but somehow they don't seem like *you*."

He walked toward her, standing so close she was forced to look up into his eyes. "You're right. And I've been giving my life a lot of thought lately. I haven't mentioned this before, but I've decided to get out of the real estate business."

"How can you be doin' that?" From what Erina understood, Kirby Investments was the family business. Surely Grant wouldn't turn his back on his mother and his friends.

"I'm going to offer Kirby Investments on the stock market as an investment. It's called a Real Estate Investment Trust. Shares will be sold to many people, who will get a dividend and a chance to make money when the stock goes up in price. I'll retain a voting share, as will Mother and Brian. But over the next year, I'm going to get out of the management end. Brian is considering whether he'll retire or stay. It's up to him."

"That's such a big decision. Are you certain?"

"Yes. I never wanted to be in the business. This way I'll have time to spend with you and Colin, and hopefully other children in the future." He smiled and touched her cheek. "You're blushing. Are you thinking about last night?" he asked softly.

"How could I not think of it?" she said, looking away. "We could be blessed with another child from . . . what we did."

"Yes, and if I'd been thinking more clearly I would have asked if you wanted me to use protection. But I wasn't thinking clearly at all. All I wanted was to—well, let's not go into that right here. I'd have to carry you upstairs and find a comfortable, private place."

She blushed all the more at the idea of making love to Grant again, but her smile faded as she remembered where she was. She'd made a fool of herself over Jerrold Kirby in this house; she'd lost her virginity as a result of his drunken attack.

And if she'd never worked for Mrs. Kirby, never smiled shyly at Jerrold, she wouldn't have had Colin. And she would never have needed a miracle or been sent to Grant's time.

Now was not the time to think about that, though. Later, when they were alone, she'd tell Grant how she felt. Instead she said, "What else will you do, besides stay home with me and watch Colin grow up?"

"I'm thinking about designing some new climbing gear, maybe go into business with some instructor friends of mine. We've talked about improvements that could be made. That way, you and I could live wherever we wanted. I have no ties to Houston, but if you want to stay there, we can."

"Can we live in Galveston?"

"If you want. Or we can travel. You may like Colorado or California. Or anywhere else. We could split our time between a few different locations if you want, maybe Colorado in the summer and Galveston the rest of the year. I'm pretty open."

"I've never been to any of those other places."

"We can go anywhere you'd like."

The freedom his money allowed was as foreign to Erina as the idea of engines that propelled cars at sixty miles an hour or airplanes that flew through the sky. But, she had to admit, she'd love to travel.

"Could we go back to Ireland some day?"

"Whenever you want. It's less than ten hours away by plane."

"Ten hours! It took us four weeks from Dublin to Galveston."

Just as Grant was about to comment, a short, stout

337

woman in Victorian dress bustled into the hallway.

"Hello! Welcome to Kirby House."

"I'm Grant Kirby, and this my wife, Erina." His eyes rested on a still-curious Colin. "And our son."

"Yes, yes, Mr. Kirby. Thank you for calling ahead. And such a beautiful wife and child," the woman said, grinning at Colin. "How old is he?"

"Two months," Erina answered.

"What a wonderful age! Well, if you're ready for your tour, we can begin in the music room."

She and Grant followed the tour guide through the rooms of the first floor. Surprisingly, much of the original furniture was here, including the huge piano that she and Grant had talked about before. The ivory keys were yellow with age, but the finish had been restored to its original shine.

Each room was roped off with heavy velvet so people wouldn't walk on the old carpets or touch delicate items like Mrs. Kirby's silver tea service. In the dining room another table, similar to the one at Grant's mother's house, sat beneath twin crystal chandeliers and hosted a large gilt and crystal epergne. The family's china rested in a cabinet that matched the table.

"This furniture is new," Erina said before the tour guide began to speak. "But the china and the chandeliers are old."

The woman verified Erina's observations. Grant looked at her oddly, but she continued to follow the woman through the butler's pantry and into the kitchen.

They walked up the servant's stairs to the second

floor, a route Erina knew well. Grant took Colin from Erina's arms as she started up the narrow steps. As a girl, she'd carried a tall stack of sunshine-smelling linens upstairs many, many times. She'd taken tea to the ladies' parlor at the top of the main staircase, and brushed Mrs. Kirby's long brown hair when her maid was indisposed.

So many memories. They were as clear to her as if they'd happened yesterday, yet she hadn't been in the Kirby's house for over a year. *And a hundred years.* She was part of this time now, and had to start thinking in those terms. She'd never forget her past, but the future called to her with promises of love and joy.

They went into the master bedroom upstairs, which looked much as it had in the 1800s. Mrs. Kirby's silver brush and comb set rested on her cherry vanity as it always had. Lace panels covered the windows and blue brocade drapes blocked out the sun during the hottest part of the day. The wallpaper and border was new, but similar to the blue and gold pattern Mrs. Kirby had ordered from France in the 1880s.

When it came time to enter Jerrold Kirby's bedroom Erina hung back, feigning interest in a landscape painting in the wide hallway. Within seconds Grant walked back to where she stood.

"What's wrong?"

"I have no need to see that room."

"Do you think that's where he—"

"No! It was upstairs on the third floor. I just don't

want to remember . . . him. I'd rather see the rest of the house."

"It's just a fantasy, Erina. Don't let your imagination cause you any pain."

"It's not my imagination. Jerrold Kirby lived in that room until he went away to college. He used to climb out his window onto the balcony and throw apples at the other children. Once he climbed down the ironwork and fell into his mother's rosebush. Don't tell me those things didn't happen!"

"How did you know all that?" their tour guide asked, peering from behind Grant in the doorway.

"I . . . perhaps I heard it somewhere."

"But that's not part of the tour. Some of those stories are in our background information on the family, though. Have you ever been a tour guide?"

"No." But perhaps she should be. Who could be a more authentic orator of the past? If she hadn't been so upset at Grant's continued denial of her background, she would have laughed at the irony.

"Why don't we go on to another room?" Grant suggested.

"It's just so odd," the woman mumbled.

"My wife studies history, especially Galveston's past."

Thankfully, everyone let the subject drop as they walked into the next bedroom, which had been occupied by Jerrold's sister Kathleen.

"This chest-on-chest was imported from Ireland and withstood the hurricane of 1900. Records indicate that the Kirbys used it to store fresh fruit and vegetables from the kitchen when everyone moved upstairs. There are still stains in the bottom of the drawers." The guide pulled out the middle drawer to show the dark, round spots.

When Erina looked up her breath caught in her throat. She could barely hear the woman's words as her heart began to pound.

"The bed is authentic to the period and was made on the mainland in Galveston county," the guide explained, smiling as she walked across the room. "The quilt was made right here in Galveston in the 1890s and was donated to the historical society by a dressmaker."

"Mrs. Abernathy," Erina whispered, feeling the blood drain from her face.

"Why, yes, it was! How did you know that?"

Grant hurried over, Colin clutched in his arms. "Erina, are you okay?"

She couldn't answer. All she could do was stand and stare at her own quilt, lying so innocently across Kathleen Kirby's bed.

"Would you excuse us for just a minute? My wife's not feeling well," Grant said to the woman. "Maybe if you could get her a glass of water from downstairs . . ."

"Of course. Sit down, dear; I'll be right back."

The woman's footsteps echoed down the hallway. Erina walked slowly toward the bed.

"Sweetheart, why don't you sit down? You're as white as a sheet. You look like you've seen a ghost."

"I have," she whispered.

Grant caught her arm. "Erina, you've got me worried."

341

"I . . ." Colin began to fuss and reached out his little arms. "Let me hold my son," she said softly. "I need to hold Colin."

The nightmare she'd experienced at Grant's condo came back to haunt her. Suddenly holding on to her son seemed the most important thing in her life. She mustn't let him go. She mustn't lose her son.

"Erina, talk to me. What's going on?"

"This is my quilt," she said softly, moving closer to the bed. "I made this quilt after I left Kirby House— after Jerrold . . . I used the scraps from different gowns I worked on."

She stopped near the foot of the bed. "But when I left it wasn't finished. I'd never embroidered any of this," she said, pointing to the pieces that contained the tiny stitches she'd learned as a child. "See here? It's the rockin' chair you bought for me. And our initials inside the heart." Tears filled her eyes.

Grant stood beside her, worry and a growing sense of panic reflected in his handsome features. "Erina, let's get out of here. You're really scaring me."

"Don't you see? Don't you know what this means?" Tears streamed down her face as Colin began to squirm and cry. "I'm goin' back. All along I've been fooling myself into thinkin' that I could stay with you when . . ."

"Erina, no. That's not what this means. This is some kind of joke, some—"

"Oh, Grant, if only you could believe." She wanted to touch him, to feel his warmth and share her love one more time. But even as she swayed toward him she felt the pull of the past. Looking back at the quilt, her fingers reached out and traced the pattern of the heart.

"I love you, Grant," she whispered.

"Erina!"

And then there was nothing but the blinding white light.

"Erina!"

Grant screamed her name, thrust his hand toward the blinding flash of light. Too late! Like the flash powder in a magician's act, she'd disappeared into the brightness.

"Erina!" he cried again, staring around the room, looking for some explanation, some trapdoor. Something to prove that what he'd just witnessed hadn't really happened. But the floor beneath the bed was solid, with no sign that anything unusual had just happened here.

He reached out and touched the quilt. Just as she'd said, a rocking chair was embroidered on velvet, bordered by intricate stitches in soft gray. And on another square was a heart, made of tiny loops of red with their initials inside: E.O. and G.K.

"Oh, my God!"

"What's wrong, Mr. Kirby?"

The tour guide came into the room with a glass of water and a wet towel. "Where's Mrs. Kirby?"

Grant stood there staring at her, his heart pounding, unable to answer her. What could he say? That one minute Erina and Colin had been standing there by the bed and the next she'd vanished in a blinding flash of light?

It was impossible; it was unbelievable. . . .

If only you could believe. She'd said those words to him before she'd disappeared. And she'd said that she loved him. She'd never said that before. Why would she say it now, then vanish?

Why?

"Mr. Kirby?"

"She's gone," he whispered into the stillness of the room.

"What do you mean? Did she and the baby leave the house?"

"She's gone," was all he could whisper as he walked through the doorway.

"Mr. Kirby!"

He ran down the stairs, but when he got to the bottom he had no idea where to go, what to do. When he heard the footsteps of the tour guide behind him he ran out the front door of Kirby House.

"Erina!" Looking right and left, he ran toward the Jeep. Where was she? She hadn't left him. She hadn't.

When he reached the car and she wasn't there he felt like collapsing in defeat. At the same time he wanted to run through the streets, calling out her name. He wanted to throw himself on the ground and pound his fists against the earth. He wanted to rant to the heavens.

"Oh, God." It was true. It was all true, all her stories, all her claims to be from the past. There was no record of Erina O'Shea in the present because she'd never been here before she'd appeared in his condo. There was nothing wrong with his security system.

She hadn't sneaked inside and hidden for hours with Colin.

She really was from the past and he'd lost her. Just when he . . .

Grant dropped to his knees on the hard asphalt, tears filling his eyes. "I love you, Erina," he said aloud, looking into the clear blue sky. "I love you. I believe you."

Only silence greeted his labored breathing and his tears. The silence of his lonely years, the void of his life without his wife, his love, his Erina.

Chapter Twenty

"Erina?"

She spun around at the voice. Standing in the doorway was Mrs. Abernathy, dressed in her night-clothes, a muslin cap on her gray hair. She held an oil lamp in her hand, filling the room with soft light. "Where have you been, girl? And what was that noise?"

"Noise?"

"Sounded like the pop of a fire, it did."

"I . . . I don't know."

Mrs. Abernathy walked over to her and placed her hand on Erina's forehead. "You feel warm. Are you coming down with a cold?"

"No, I don't . . . Mrs. Abernathy, what day is this?"

"What kind of question is that? Why, it's Thursday!"

"What's the date?"

"You are running a fever. Let's get you to bed. I have no idea why you're up and dressed at this hour of the night."

"Please, what's the date?"

"Let's see," Mrs. Abernathy said, rubbing her chin. "It's October the eighth, near midnight." She hooked her arm through Erina's and led her toward the bed. "Where in the world did you get those clothes? Why, the skirt's a scandal! Have you been out like that?"

"Yes, I've been to the church." And she'd come back in time to her own home, just minutes after she'd left.

Oh, Grant. Where are you? What's going on inside your head? Do you believe me now? All she wanted to do was sink down on the bed and cry.

"At this time of night? What were you thinking?"

"Colin was so ill," she said automatically, her voice sounding flat and lifeless. When she looked down at her son, who was yawning, she noticed that his color was still pink, and he was dressed in some of his new clothes.

"Poor little lad. He's so quiet."

Erina sat on the bed and grasped Mrs. Abernathy's hand, pulling her down beside her. "Do you believe in miracles?" Erina asked, looking intently at the older woman.

"Why, I suppose. The Church says that miracles occur."

"Yes, they do. Mrs. Abernathy, I need to show you something."

"What—"

"Just look." Erina lay Colin on the bed and unzipped his romper, as she'd learned to call the one-piece garment.

347

"Where did you get those strange clothes? I've never seen the like!"

Erina didn't answer, just peeled apart the fabric over Colin's chest.

"Good Lord!" Mrs. Abernathy exclaimed. "What has happened to your baby?"

"He's been cured. Oh, Mrs. Abernathy, I know this will be hard for you to believe, but I went to the church tonight to pray for a miracle to save Colin's life. He was so blue, havin' such a hard time with his poor little heart. I prayed to the Blessed Virgin to save my son and she . . ."

"She what? Tell me!"

"She sent me a hundred years into the future, into the hands of a good, kind man who took Colin to the hospital. And they operated on his heart."

The older woman reached out and touched the pink scar. "Surgery on his heart? But how?"

Erina shrugged. "I don't know the exact way they do it. All I know is that his heart is fixed. This mornin'—" She had to stop; she couldn't talk past the lump in her throat. "I'm sorry. I'm just so surprised to be back here. I thought we'd live our lives in 1996, with . . . with Grant."

"He's the man who helped Colin?"

"Yes. He's the man . . . the man I love." Erina collapsed against Mrs. Abernathy's shoulder, letting the older woman hold her as she'd held Colin so many times. "What am I going to do?"

"Oh, my poor lamb, I don't know. I just don't know."

* * *

Somehow Grant dragged himself back to the condo. He had no idea how he got there, or whether he'd run down a score of pedestrians on his way. All he knew was that Erina and Colin were gone to a place where even he, with all his money and contacts, couldn't find them.

Had they gone back safely? Could Colin survive without postsurgical checkups and modern medicine? Had Erina eventually married someone else who could be a good husband to her and a father to Colin? There were no records before the hurricane, so he couldn't know if they'd even gone back to her time—October 1896.

He opened the doors to the balcony and went outside, leaning against the rail and watching the waves come in from the Gulf. How long ago had they kissed on this very spot, letting their desire run free for a few brief moments? A week? So much had happened since then. His life had been changed forever by Erina and Colin, but it was too late. Too late.

He sank against the sliding glass doors, letting himself cry for the second time since childhood. Even when his father died he hadn't cried. Now he couldn't stop. He sobbed like a baby as the steady southerly wind dried the tears on his cheeks.

He wasn't sure how long he sat out there, but eventually he realized that the wind had changed. It was cooler now, and a hint of rain drifted on the breeze. Perhaps another cold front, like the one that had come through the weekend Erina had arrived, he thought with a shaft of pain. Oh, Erina, what has happened to you? Where are you, love?

He pushed himself up from the concrete floor, feeling a hundred years old at least as he limped inside the condo. Everywhere he looked he could see her. Standing in the kitchen, trying to learn how to make hot tea. Walking across the living room carrying Colin. Emerging from his bedroom doorway swallowed up in his bathrobe, a startled look on her face.

Would he really never see her again? He simply couldn't imagine not finding her, somehow, somewhere, even though he believed that she'd gone back to her own time. He believed her now, when it was too late.

But was it too late to find out if she'd lived past the hurricane? Since she knew it was coming, perhaps she would leave the island for safer ground. She wouldn't risk Colin's life. She'd resettle somewhere else. There should be a record of her sometime after 1900. He just needed to know where.

But that won't bring her back, whispered a voice inside his head. But if he at least knew she was safe . . . And what if she didn't show up anywhere? How should he interpret that? That she hadn't gone back in time? That she hadn't survived?

He picked up the phone with shaking hands and called the private investigator Brian had used before. The man had Erina's fingerprints, her name. He could search for her in the computer databases. If she'd lived in the past, surely there was a record.

But what if she married someone else? The house and their possessions would be in the man's name. Erina was only twenty years old in 1896, so she should have lived until the 1950s or 1960s, at least.

But she'd still be dead today. And what about Colin? He'd been born in 1896, so he could have lived until the 1970s, '80s, or even longer. He would have been one hundred years old this past August—not totally inconceivable.

Grant fought back a wave of panic as the investigator answered the phone.

Within minutes he told the man to search for Erina O'Shea and Erina Kirby, and Colin Patrick Kirby, not in the present, but in the past. Back to 1900, Grant told the surprised man. Find some record of her and her child. He knew he sounded crazy to the investigator—as crazy as Erina had sounded to him at first. How had she endured his skepticism?

When he hung up the phone he paced the floor. He'd told the man to drop everything else on his calendar, charge anything he wanted. Grant had to know immediately. He had to find Erina, to tell her that he was wrong, that he was sorry. To ask her forgiveness for ever doubting her.

Exhausted, he dropped down on the couch, resting his elbows on his knees and cradling his head. "Oh, God, I've got to know."

Later, when the phone didn't ring, he walked into her bedroom and curled up on her bed. A beautiful, long, black hair rested on her pillow. Grant held it, curled it around his ring finger, and cried again for his loss. When all his tears were gone he lay dry-eyed through the night, breathing in her scent and trying to reach out to her somehow, across the years, to tell her how much he loved her.

The next morning he received a call from the investigator: No record existed anywhere in the United States or in Ireland of an Erina O'Shea or an Erina Kirby from 1900 on. Nor was there anything on a Colin Patrick Kirby, born in 1896. Grant hung up the phone realizing that he might never know what had happened to them.

He made a decision then. All the efforts he could expend wouldn't bring Erina back; only one thing would. He had to find a way to cause another miracle. She'd disappeared at Kirby House. He'd go back there, he'd pray, he'd petition her God for intervention. She was his wife; he thought of Colin as his son. Didn't the Church consider matrimony a holy state? Why would they be separated after they'd been married by a priest?

He shaved and showered, threw on fresh clothes, and drove to Kirby House. It was closed, so he sat in the car until ten o'clock, when the tour guides arrived. He waited, remembering how happy she'd been just yesterday after Colin's checkup, with the marriage, with life in general. She'd giggled and laughed, making him smile more than he had in ages.

She'd been everything he could have imagined and more on their wedding night. For all practical purposes, she had been a virgin, but she'd responded to him with an honest passion that had turned into a realization of her own desire by night's end. If they had a hundred years together, he'd never learn everything about her. Yet he was more than willing to try.

He rubbed his scratchy eyes. The doors to Kirby House opened and he jumped out of the Jeep, running up the steps two at a time.

"I'm Grant Kirby," he told the startled tour guide. "I was here yesterday with my wife and baby. A different lady was here. Older, with gray hair."

"Yes, we alternate days. What can I do for you?"

"Something happened upstairs in one of the bedrooms. Something . . . bizarre." He ran a hand through his hair. "I've got to get back up there and find a way to get them back."

"Your wife and child are missing?"

"Yes. Not in the usual sense. One minute we were standing there together and the next, she was gone. Gone, just like that," he said, snapping his fingers. "I've got to find her."

The guide looked at him as though he were mentally deficient. "Mr. Kirby, your wife is not here," she explained patiently. "I've just opened up the house and no one was here."

"I know they're not here now," he said. "They were here yesterday. They vanished. I've got to go up there. I've got to find a way to get them back."

"Where did they go?"

"Back. Back to the past." He didn't wait for the tour guide to ask him any more questions. He simply bounded up the stairs and down the hall, looking for the right bedroom.

There it was: Kathleen Kirby's bedroom, with Erina's quilt on top of the bed. All the glorious colors, all the tiny stitches, all the work she'd put into piecing it together. A labor of love, that's what the quilt was. Could he find her through it?

He knelt on the floor beside the bed and placed his

hand over the embroidered heart. "Erina, come back to me please. Come back. I love you. I need you and Colin."

He stayed on the floor, trying to talk to Erina, thinking about everything she'd said and done while she was with him. He stayed beside the bed until the tour guide became concerned and asked him to leave, and even longer, until she called the police to talk to him.

As the afternoon wore on, they left him alone. Everyone thought he was crazy, but he was still a Kirby and a multimillionaire. They closed the door to the room and left him alone to talk to Erina, to plead with her to come back. He became angry at fate, at whatever force guided their lives. When nothing happened he cursed God for taking her away.

There was no response, but Erina's words kept echoing in his head. *If only you could believe.* Had she meant in her, or in something else altogether? And if she meant in God, in the power of miracles, what would his answer be?

Erina knew she shouldn't feel so betrayed, but she couldn't help the desolation that constantly overpowered her. How could Mary be so wonderful as to grant a miracle to save Colin only to separate a husband and wife joined by the Church?

But Grant lied to the priest, a little voice reminded her. *You should have told the father the truth and asked for his mercy. You should have been honest in your intentions, but you had more belief in Grant than you did in your faith.*

"Stop it!" she cried, putting her hands over her ears. She didn't want to hear the truth, now that it was too late. Now that it only tormented her further.

She was also tormented by imagining what Grant thought, what he'd experienced when she vanished before his eyes. Did he drive back to Houston or stay in Galveston? Was he angry? Sad? Had he cried for her?

She needed a project to keep her mind off Grant and everything they'd lost in one blinding flash of light, so when she wasn't caring for Colin she worked on her quilt, her eyes filled with tears most of the time. Mrs. Abernathy came up to check on her several times a day, bringing tea and a meat pie at lunch, and tea and scones later in the day. By the time the sun began to set, the quilt was finished, and Erina felt emotionally and physically exhausted.

She would never be able to live with herself until she confessed her sins. But Colin was fussy, no doubt missing Grant just as she did. Tomorrow she'd go to the church and tell the priest everything that had happened. If the good father thought her crazy, so be it. She simply couldn't go on like this, torn between the two times, between her love of the Church and her love for Grant.

As the sun dipped low in the sky, Colin napped and so did Erina. She dreamed of a house by the beach, with sunshine and windows that gave a glorious view of the ocean. All the furniture was light, soft, and comfortable. Standing outside on the sand was Grant, holding Colin in his arms while the seagulls drifted in the breeze overhead and a large dog, his fur almost the color of Grant's sun-bleached hair, bounded toward the surf.

She walked toward the windows, holding out her hand. Grant turned and smiled, reaching out to her, beckoning her to join them. She put her hand against the cool glass and looked for a door, but there was none. She ran along the barrier, searching, leaving smudged prints in her wake, but could not find the way outside. Grant turned away and walked toward the water, but she couldn't follow. She beat against the glass, but it didn't break. She yelled until her throat was raw, but to no avail.

Erina woke with a start, her heart racing as she looked around the dark room. The candle she'd lit earlier had burned down. Colin stirred, so she reached down and lifted him into her arms. She felt so weak that her hands shook. The dream was so real; the house was just what she would have wanted had she stayed with Grant.

But she wasn't with him. The door to the future was just as real as the glass barrier in her dream.

After she nursed Colin and changed his diaper— missing the paper ones from the future as she secured the soft fabric around his waist—she paced her small room. Restlessness set in, leaving her edgy and her mind racing. She'd prayed for a miracle once; was it possible to pray for one again? But the miracle had been for Colin, not for herself. She doubted if Mary would be inclined to bestow another one for such a selfish reason.

But what about Grant? He loved her, even if he'd never said the words. He had shown it every time he looked at her, in each kiss, in all his actions. Now Grant might even realize the depth of his feelings. The fact that he was suffering alone added to her own anguish.

If only she could help him, reassure him through all the years. *You've done that through the quilt,* she told herself. But was that all she could do?

No. She could use the power of prayer to help Grant. If the Blessed Virgin would allow her one more wish, she'd send strength and faith to him across the years.

"We need to go out," she told Colin. "Back to St. Mary's Cathedral." Suddenly she felt energized, her restlessness turned to purpose.

She grabbed a shawl and Colin's blanket, wrapping him securely against the evening breeze. At the last minute she turned back to the quilt. A sense of unease tickled the back of her neck, as though she didn't want to be parted from her labor of love. But she couldn't drag the heavy quilt with her to the church. Carrying Colin was enough of a burden.

Besides the quilt must end up in Kirby House. The knowledge made her aware of how vulnerable they all were to time. What if the quilt was ruined in the hurricane? What if it wasn't donated to the Galveston Historical Society?

She unwrapped Colin and placed him on the bed. Grabbing her lap desk, she sat beside him and wrote a note to Mrs. Abernathy, telling her of the hurricane and the importance of donating the quilt. She added that if anything happened to Erina, she should make sure to leave Galveston before September 1900, and take the quilt with her. So many people had died in that awful storm. Erina knew she couldn't be one of them, and she couldn't let Mrs. Abernathy perish either.

After looking around the room one more time, she bundled up Colin and walked out the door, leaving the folded quilt and note on top of her bed.

A half hour later she knelt at the altar of St. Mary's and lit a candle. The night reminded her so much of when she'd presented Colin to the Holy Mother for a miracle. To her it was weeks ago. In the reality of 1896, it was yesterday.

Colin began to fuss, so she rocked him in her arms while she knelt. "Blessed Virgin, please hear my prayers. I come to you tonight to ask for help for my husband, Grant Kirby. I told you he was a good man, a kind man. But his faith has been sorely tested and he doesn't believe. I ask you to help him find faith, to comfort him during his time of need."

Erina bowed her head over Colin, tears coming to her eyes. "I love him so much," she whispered. "I'll bear whatever burdens I must because of the deceptions about my marriage, but in my heart he is my husband. He needs me, and if I cannot be there, please give him the comfort of faith. Please, Blessed Virgin, guide him during these dark days. Guide him back to God, Mary, please. I pray."

Grant stayed at Kirby House until it closed for the day at six o'clock. He had failed to bring Erina and Colin back. Was there no hope then? As he stood on the front steps and heard the lock click behind him, he felt even more desolate than before.

If only you could believe. Erina's words came back to haunt him again. She was the kindest, most giving person he'd ever known. A woman of faith and virtue, the kind of person who represented everything good about the Church.

And as he looked out at the twilight sky, he knew what he had to do.

He ran to the Jeep, jumped in and started the engine. With an excitement that he hadn't felt since Erina's disappearance he drove to St. Mary's Cathedral. The parking lot was empty, and when he ran to the doors he found them locked.

"No," he whispered. He ran down the side of the building but found no other entry. He changed directions, searching the side near the parking lot. There! He went through a gate and bounded up the stairs.

A priest answered the door, dabbing his mouth with a napkin. He'd obviously been eating dinner.

"Please, Father, I need to get inside the church. It's . . . important. I have to—"

"Calm down, son," the father said. "Come inside and take a breath."

Grant realized then that he was breathing hard, that he probably appeared to be a wild man to the priest. He entered through the open door, standing inside a sunroom filled with plants.

"I can see you're troubled. Can I help?"

"I'm not sure. I . . . I think I need to confess what I've done, and then I need to pray."

"We usually do confessions on Saturday, but I

think you have a more serious need." The priest took his arm and steered him through the kitchen, past the dining room where two other priests sat around the table, and down a long hallway. "Come with me."

Grant followed the man through a room that had obviously been enclosed at some earlier time. The original brick could still be seen. They entered the church above the altars, through a door Grant had noticed when he'd visited St. Mary's with Erina.

"Have a seat at the confessional. I'll be with you in just a moment."

Grant did as he was told, his heart still pounding. A sense of rightness assailed him here in the church, as though he'd been called here. He couldn't explain the feeling, but he knew that in this place he would feel closer to Erina.

He gave his confession to the priest, telling him of the miracle that had occurred, of his doubts about Erina, about how he'd grown to love her even when he thought she was deluding herself about her background. He confessed the lies he'd told to INS, Sam Reynolds, Mrs. Henshaw, and everyone else. He admitted that he'd lied to his mother and to the priest in Houston so he and Erina could marry in the Church.

When he was finished he dropped his head to his hands and wept silently.

The priest spoke quietly to him for a long time. If the man thought Grant was crazy to believe that someone had traveled in time, he never said a word. Grant felt a weight lifting from his shoulders as he listened to the absolution. He'd sinned, but he could be forgiven.

He'd do whatever was necessary to make himself the man he should be, he vowed as the confession ended. He'd strayed, but mostly from neglect. Erina had showed him the importance of faith, and he'd never forget that lesson.

The priest left him alone to pray in the quiet, dim church. Following Erina's example, he walked softly to the statue of the Virgin Mary and knelt. Again, he felt closer to Erina in this holy place.

"Holy Mary, Mother of God," he began, then prayed with all his heart for the first time since he was a boy. He closed his eyes and thought of nothing else but asking forgiveness for the wrongs he'd done, for lacking faith in Erina.

"She's the kindest, the best person I've ever known. She asked for a miracle to save her son and you granted it. She would never ask for anything for herself, but please, protect and watch over Erina. I know she's hurting. She has so much love to give, so much that I never realized what we shared when she was here with me. If only I could see her one more time, to tell her how much I love her. Please, if there is any way, tell Erina of my love. Tell her what I never got to say, tell her—"

Behind his closed eyes he sensed a brightness, as though the priest had suddenly switched on the overhead lights. He opened his eyes, expecting to find the father standing above him near the doorway behind the altar. But there was no one there.

"Grant?"

He pivoted at the sound of the voice he'd never expected to hear again. Standing before him, holding Colin tightly in her arms, was Erina.

"Oh, God," he whispered, reaching for her with trembling arms. "Is it really you? Are you really back?"

"Yes! Oh, yes," she cried, melting into his embrace. "I was in the church, praying for you, and then I got up to leave and . . . Oh, Grant, it is a miracle."

"I love you," he said, tilting up her face so he could see her through the tears filling his eyes. "I love you and I believe you and I want you forever."

She smiled, touching his face as though she couldn't believe he was really here. Her eyes were also brimming with tears of happiness. "I know," she whispered. "I always had faith in you."

He hugged her again, then took Colin from her arms. "We're a family, Erina, and we'll be together always."

There was a sound of someone coughing discreetly behind them. They turned to see the priest standing there, a baffled look on his face. "What's going on here?" he asked.

"It's a miracle, Father," Erina said joyfully. "A miracle of love."

BITTERROOT

VICTORIA CHANCELLOR

Bestselling Author Of *Forever & A Day*

In the Wyoming Territory—a land both breathtaking and brutal—bitterroots grow every summer for a brief time. Therapist Rebecca Hartford has never seen such a plant—until she is swept back to the days of Indian medicine men, feuding ranchers, and her pioneer forebears. Nor has she ever known a man as dark, menacing, and devastatingly handsome as Sloan Travers. Sloan hides a tormented past, and Rebecca vows to use her professional skills to help the former Union soldier, even though she longs to succumb to personal desire. But when a mysterious shaman warns Rebecca that her sojourn in the Old West will last only as long as the bitterroot blooms, she can only pray that her love for Sloan is strong enough to span the ages....

_52087-7 $5.50 US/$7.50 CAN

FOREVER & A DAY

VICTORIA CHANCELLOR

When Linda O'Rourke returns to her grandmother's South Carolina beach house, it is for a quiet summer of tying up loose ends. And although the lovely dwelling charms her, she can't help but remember the evil presence that threatened her there so many years ago. Plagued by her fear, and tormented by visions of a virile Englishman tempting her with his every caress, she is unprepared for reality in the form of the mysterious and handsome Gifford Knight. His kisses evoke memories of the man in her dreams, but his sensual demands are all too real. Linda longs to surrender to Giff's masterful touch, but is it a safe haven she finds in his arms, or the beginning of her worst nightmare?

_52063-X $5.50 US/$7.50 CAN

TIMESWEPT

Don't miss these passionate time-travel romances, in which modern-day heroines fulfill their hearts' desires with men from different eras.

Reflections In Time by Elizabeth Crane. When practical-minded Renata O'Neal submits to hypnosis to cure her insomnia, she never expects to wake up in 1880s Louisiana—or in love with fiery Nathan Blue. But vicious secrets and Victorian sensibilities threaten to keep Renata and Nathan apart...until Renata vows that nothing will separate her from the most deliciously alluring man of any century.
_52089-3 $4.99 US/$6.99 CAN

Apollo's Fault by Miriam Raftery. Taylor James's wrinkled Shar-Pei puppy, Apollo, will lead her on the romantic adventure of a lifetime. One minute Taylor and Apollo are in modern-day San Francisco, and the next thing she knows, the lovely historian finds herself facing the terror of California's most infamous earthquake—and a love so monumental it threatens to shake the foundations of her world.
_52084-2 $4.99 US/$6.99 CAN

Dorchester Publishing Co., Inc.
65 Commerce Road
Stamford, CT 06902

Please add $1.75 for shipping and handling for the first book and $.50 for each book thereafter. NY, NYC, PA and CT residents, please add appropriate sales tax. No cash, stamps, or C.O.D.s. All orders shipped within 6 weeks via postal service book rate. Canadian orders require $2.00 extra postage and must be paid in U.S. dollars through a U.S. banking facility.

Name _____
Address _____
City _____ State _____ Zip _____
I have enclosed $_____ in payment for the checked book(s).
Payment <u>must</u> accompany all orders. ☐ Please send a free catalog.

Desperado's Gold
Linda Jones

Jilted at the altar and stranded in the Arizona desert by a blown gasket in her Mustang convertible, Catalina Lane hopes only for a tow truck and a lift to the nearest gas station. She certainly doesn't expect a real live desperado. But suddenly, catapulted back in time to the days of the Old West, Catalina is transported into a world of blazing six-guns and ladies of the evening.

When Jackson Cady, the infamous gunslinger known as "Kid Creede," returns to Baxter, it's to kill a man and earn a reward, not to use his gold to rescue a naive librarian from the clutches of a greedy madam. He never would have dreamed that the beauty who babbled so incoherently about the twentieth century would have such an impact on him. But the longer he spends time with her, the more he finds himself captivated by her tender touch and luscious body— and when he looks deep into her amber eyes, he knows that the passion that smolders between them is a treasure more precious than any desperado's gold.

_52140-7 $5.50 US/$6.50 CAN

DON'T MISS THESE DAZZLING
TIME-TRAVEL ROMANCES BY

MARTI JONES

A Love Through Time. Although tree surgeon Libby Pfifer can explain root rot and Japanese beetles, she can't understand how a fall from the oldest oak in Fort Pickens, Florida, lands her in another century. Yet there she is, face-to-face with the great medicine man Geronimo, and an army captain whose devastating good looks tempt her even while his brusque manner makes her want to wring his neck.
_51991-7 $4.99 US/$5.99 CAN

Time's Healing Heart. No man has ever swept Madeline St. Thomas off her feet, and after she buries herself in her career, she loses hope of finding one. But when a freak accident propels her to the Old South, Maddie is rescued by Devon Crowe, a stranger with the face of an angel and the body of an Adonis. Only his burning touch and smoldering kisses will awaken the forgotten longings in her heart.
_51954-2 $4.99 US/$5.99 CAN

Dorchester Publishing Co., Inc.
65 Commerce Road
Stamford, CT 06902

Please add $1.75 for shipping and handling for the first book and $.50 for each book thereafter. NY, NYC, PA and CT residents, please add appropriate sales tax. No cash, stamps, or C.O.D.s. All orders shipped within 6 weeks via postal service book rate. Canadian orders require $2.00 extra postage and must be paid in U.S. dollars through a U.S. banking facility.

Name _____
Address _____
City _____ State _____ Zip _____
I have enclosed $_____ in payment for the checked book(s).
Payment <u>must</u> accompany all orders.☐ Please send a free catalog.

A va

Jewels gone missing...

Artifacts declared forgeries...

Romance blooms among

Clouds of Suspicion
CLOUDS OF SUSPICION

by Request™

Three novels of romantic suspense
by one of your favorite authors

Books by Lynn Erickson

LYNN ERICKSON

CLOUDS OF SUSPICION

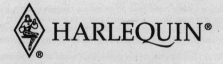

HARLEQUIN®

TORONTO • NEW YORK • LONDON
AMSTERDAM • PARIS • SYDNEY • HAMBURG
STOCKHOLM • ATHENS • TOKYO • MILAN • MADRID
PRAGUE • WARSAW • BUDAPEST • AUCKLAND

HARLEQUIN BOOKS

by Request—CLOUDS OF SUSPICION

Copyright © 2000 by Harlequin Books S.A.

ISBN 0-373-20179-6

The publisher acknowledges the copyright holders of the individual works as follows:

ARENA OF FEAR
Copyright © 1986 by Carla Peltonen and Molly Swanton
A PERFECT GEM
Copyright © 1987 by Molly Swanton and Carla Peltonen
FIRECLOUD
Copyright © 1988 by Molly Swanton and Carla Peltonen

This edition published by arrangement with Harlequin Books S.A.

Visit us at www.eHarlequin.com

Printed in U.S.A.

CONTENTS

Had Melanie aligned herself with the man responsible for her sister's disappearance?

Arena of Fear

Chapter One

He was there again on Thursday.

Melanie Royce rolled over onto her stomach and felt the hot Spanish sun pounding on her back. She turned her head very slightly, hoping her sunglasses hid the direction of her gaze.

Yes. There was no doubt about it. The man, unobtrusively sunning himself some fifteen yards down the sandy beach of Torremolinos, was watching her.

Or us, Melanie thought. He might be watching her sister, Cecily, too. Yet somehow Melanie didn't think so. She had the curious feeling that his presence there was solely for her benefit but she didn't know why. It seemed as though they were two leading actors on the crowded beach, as though everyone else was merely an extra. She wondered just what role she was supposed to be playing.

Why would some stranger be that interested in her?

"I'm thirsty..." Cecily groaned and rolled over, too, squinting her gold-flecked eyes against the fierce summer sun. "Let's get a Coke."

"Go ahead," Melanie said distractedly.

"You're lazy today." Cecily stood up and stretched

luxuriously as she searched the beach in front of the Los Jazmines hotel for a waiter.

She really was lovely, Melanie thought, noticing the many appreciative eyes turned in her sister's direction. Cecily, at nineteen, still possessed that air of unbridled adolescent pride, that smooth-skinned perfection celebrated by a youth-oriented culture. Her long slender limbs were flawlessly tanned, her auburn hair shone richly in the sun, and she had the tilted golden eyes unique to Oscar Royce's two daughters.

Cecily sparkled like a well-cut gem; Melanie, nine years older than her sister, seemed reserved and withdrawn by comparison. At least, that was the impression people often had of her.

"You know, with the kind of money you're spending here," remarked Cecily, as she continued to scan the beach, "you'd think they could have *one* waiter around."

"Never mind." Melanie pushed herself up from the bright towel and adjusted her dark green suit. "I'll go get us both a drink. Watch my camera, though."

Cecily shrugged and immediately resumed her prone position, intent on soaking up every last ray of sun.

The sand was blisteringly hot under Melanie's bare feet as she forged her way between the sunbathers toward the outdoor bar of the swank hotel.

The beach was only moderately crowded that hot afternoon. Everyone else must have been at the turquoise pools that dotted the grounds of the hotels. The tourists were mostly English and Scandinavian, those notorious sun worshipers from their misty northern isles. In the States, Melanie would have expected to hear a hundred radios blaring, but here the noise was subdued, as if the tourists respected one anothers' privacy.

She glanced around at the bodies that gave clear evidence of the lengths of their owners' vacations: fish-belly white to pink to tan. Even the swimsuits were unique to Europeans. The men all wore the tight-fitting stretch bikinis that outlined their private parts. Among the women there were few old-lady cover-ups. Regardless of a woman's age or shape, she wore a colorful, revealing suit. Some even had on bikinis, their stomachs bulging and heavy breasts billowing.

The atmosphere seemed to say, "Anything goes."

And it was hotter and drier on the Spanish coast than the beaches Melanie remembered in Cape Cod and New Jersey, where she had often gone as a child. Torremolinos was a little like California in the summer. The difference was, of course, the scenery. The rolling, green-clad hills of southern Spain swept down nearly to the Mediterranean shore and were specked with modern one-story white-washed villas and high-rise luxury hotels with pools and palm trees.

Melanie picked up her feet quickly, gasping once or twice from the burning sand, and sought the cooler cement of the pad surrounding Los Jazmines' bar.

Like her sister, she had every male head on the beach swiveling toward her, but she had long since learned to disregard the unwanted attention. That way, they left her alone. Besides, she thought, with her pale skin, she never looked her best in a bathing suit. While Cecily tanned, Melanie merely sprouted more freckles.

It *was* hot. She leaned against the smooth tiled counter and felt the heat of the day close around her. Her dark red hair hung half in and half out of a loosely wound knot, the long strands stuck to her burning back.

"Can I get two Cokes?" she asked.

"*Sí,*" said the bartender with a grin, "for the pretty *americana.*"

Melanie turned toward the water again, looking for Cecily. There she was with two beautifully tanned young Europeans standing over her, practically panting like puppy dogs. Melanie could so easily imagine the scenario: one of the men reaching down and snatching her valuable camera while Cecily flirted with the other.

She waited for the Cokes. In Spain, she'd learned, nothing was done with great haste. Automatically, her gaze strayed down the beach to the stranger and she saw that now he was staring directly at her; she hadn't expected to catch him at it. Inexplicably, Melanie felt a shock of adrenaline rush through her body. In the two days that he had been there, not once had she actually caught him looking straight at her.

She turned away quickly, unaccountably confused. Her Cokes were ready and she signed the check, then began heading back toward Cecily. The unforgiving sun was pressing on her shoulders and the sand still scorched her feet. She took great care, even while hurrying, not to spill the drinks, but her mind was on those two Continental types ogling her sister, and she wondered just how to get rid of them.

"Here's yours." She handed Cecily a glass.

"Thanks." Cecily looked pleadingly at Melanie, then rolled her eyes. "I was just telling these nice men that we're expecting friends. Right, Mel…?"

"Oh, yes. We *are* waiting for someone. Do you mind?" She took up the game. One might have thought from their groans and protests that the two men were mortally wounded but they did finally leave, promising in very good English to return the following day.

"That's not like you," Melanie said, settling herself on the towel.

"What isn't?"

"Ditching those guys."

"I'm not interested." Cecily flopped onto her back and shaded her eyes from the sun.

"You've got someone else, I bet."

"Maybe." Cecily's voice was carefully nonchalant.

"Someone from the university?" Melanie probed.

Her sister had been attending the University of Madrid for a year, studying Spanish history and language. Melanie had a sneaking suspicion that Cecily had chosen Madrid rather than London or Edinburgh or the Sorbonne just to spite their parents. In the view of the elder Royces' social circle, Madrid didn't have the same respectability or prestige as the other places.

"Why do you want to know about my private life?" Cecily demanded. "What is this, the third degree?"

"Is he married or something?" Melanie asked cautiously. "I mean, what's the big secret?"

"No, he's not *married* or something," her sister said, pouting a little.

"Sorry, I'm just curious."

Silence from Cecily. This man must be different, Melanie thought. Usually her sister bubbled over with descriptions: neat, gorgeous, a hunk, cool. Those were her favorite words. But this chilly silence was unlike Cecily.

Melanie turned her head to study her sister. Cecily's eyes were closed, the sun gilding the tips of her long lashes. Her expression was sulky, yet her face seemed terribly young and vulnerable. Or was it just that Melanie had become bitter and dried up and spinsterish?

Yet her sister *was* different somehow. Perhaps this was simply the sign of a new maturity, unfamiliar to Melanie. Though there seemed to be a kind of anger in Cecily's sullen responses. Growing pains? Adolescent problems? Shouldn't Cecily be past that sort of thing by now?

"Here we are, lying on a beach. The lap of luxury," Cecily said abruptly, rolling over to face her older sister.

"Nice, isn't it?"

"Well…" Cecily hesitated, as if debating something. "But the whole world is still going on around us. Famines. Disasters. Injustice. Don't you ever feel a little… guilty?"

"I got over it," Melanie said lightly.

"Mel!" Cecily sounded outraged.

"I mean I try not to dwell on it. I can't apologize forever because of my family's good fortune in owning a steel mill. I give to charity. I do the best I can at my work.

I keep up on the world's problems. I vote responsibly."
She shrugged. "What else can I do?"

"Get involved," Cecily said seriously.

"I'm involved in lots of things."

"You know what I mean."

"Not really. Do you mean I should wear camouflage
gear and join some underground group? Or should I stuff
envelopes for my favorite senator?"

"I do *not* mean that. I mean...well, find a cause you
believe in and *do* something about it."

Melanie shut her eyes for a moment in reflection. "I
think what I do is important."

"Photography?"

"Yes. My work lets people see the world. I just finished
a layout on Ethiopia, if you'll recall."

"I know, but taking pictures isn't like filling their stomachs or bandaging wounds or educating—"

"No, it isn't. But what it does do, Cecily, is let people
really see the conditions others live in. Sure," she said,
"they read about it and see a few minutes of film shot for
the nightly news, but a layout like the one I just finished
really tells the story. Believe me."

"I suppose it's just not my kind of thing. I feel as if I
need to get more involved. You know, maybe live in a
place like that for a year or two. Really do something."
Cecily's brow knitted. "It's more than just famine, Mel.
It's politics and warehouses sitting loaded with grain on
the docks and dirty old men lounging behind big desks
selling guns and planes to kill innocent people."

That was idealistic youth speaking. Who exactly was
this new man in Cecily's life? For that was where these
ideas came from—Melanie was sure of it.

"I went to Washington once and demonstrated for
women's rights."

"You did?" Cecily was wide-eyed.

"I felt slightly foolish but I was glad I'd gone. There
was a certain feeling...comradeship, commitment—it's

hard to describe.'' She paused. ''Bob walked out on me the next day.''

''The bum.''

''True,'' Melanie said wryly.

''Not all men are like Bob.''

''Also true.''

Cecily turned onto her back again. ''I want to do something really important. I refuse just to sit around on my behind and go to school, get married, have kids...you know.''

''You can do whatever you like, Cecily. Nothing's stopping you.''

''Only Mother and Dad.''

''They never stopped you from doing anything,'' Melanie said with a laugh. ''I was always the one who had to do that!''

''Mel...'' Cecily's voice was very serious, very young. ''I don't want to go home to Cleveland.''

''Why not? You'll be back in Madrid in six weeks.''

''I just don't want to. I can't face being shut up in the mill all summer, doing some job that doesn't mean anything to me. I'd rather die!''

''You have to go home now. They've planned to be there. They're even cutting short their trip to China, for goodness' sake.''

Cecily rolled her eyes. ''Wow! Terrible calamity!''

''Come on, Cecily, you know you have to go home.''

''Why, damn it? They don't care about me—or you. What they care about is their social life and their cocktail parties and dinners and golf and tennis. They only had kids because it was the expected thing to do and you know it!''

''They care. I know Mother and Dad often seem... distracted, but they're looking forward so much to seeing you. Really. Try to understand.''

''I don't want to understand their way of life. It's disgusting. They don't *do* anything. They're useless.''

"The world needs people like them. People who can run the economy, manage others. Everyone can't be a crusader."

Cecily made a face. "This world needs lots of crusaders. It's a rotten place and it's going to get worse. Somebody needs to do something."

"Like what?" Melanie pressed.

Cecily didn't answer. A small bubble of alarm swelled in Melanie's chest. But that was ridiculous. She probably wouldn't be worrying if Cecily were going to school in the good ol' U.S. of A. but a Spanish University was a different matter and one about which she knew nothing. Good thing Cecily was going home for a little while.

"Do you ever hear from Bob?" Cecily asked unexpectedly.

"No. Not for many years."

"You know, I had a crush on him. A terrible one. I felt so guilty."

"How old were you? Twelve? Perfectly natural."

"To have a crush on your older sister's husband?"

"Sure. Although what you saw in him…" Melanie shook her head.

"Same thing you did. Handsome and charming—that was Bob."

"Yes."

"Does it still hurt?"

Melanie ducked her head as if to avoid the question. "Sometimes," she finally answered.

"Bob, the two-month wonder. All my friends felt sorry for you. Married two months and he splits."

Melanie grimaced. "Pity from teeny-boppers. Ugh."

"Bob was a gold digger. Big deal. I brush three of them off a day."

"Good for you," Melanie said. "I didn't have the sense to see it then and I wonder if I could spot one today."

"You could, all right, if you weren't so naive." Then

suddenly Cecily's face was suffused with shame. "I'm really sorry. What a jerk I can be."

"It's okay."

"No, it isn't. Rubbing salt in the wounds. Forgive me?"

The lines in Melanie's face softened. "Only if you get us two more sodas and *only* if you let me photograph you."

It had been two years since Melanie had last seen her sister. They had both been home in Ohio from time to time over the past years, but somehow always missed each other by days.

Melanie put aside her anxiety over her sister's unsettling new ideals—weren't college kids allowed a little anger at the world?—and began shooting a few pictures of Cecily, trying to catch the fluid grace of her movements. Then she swung the camera toward the water's edge, looking, as always, for that perfect, natural shot.

She took two pictures of a toddler but the light wasn't quite right. Later in the afternoon, everything would be bathed in that soft gilded Mediterranean light, as if the atmosphere were filled with gold dust. If she could capture that light...

Click. This one might be okay. Click. An old man and his wife laughing, letting a cold wave break over their sunburned backs. Click, click.

She scanned the blue water through the long telephoto lens. Out past the softly breaking waves was a man... Beautiful. She brought him into focus. Better than beautiful. His black hair was glinting in the bright sun as he swam, and his head turned easily from side to side, as one long arm reached out to pull the water behind him and then the other arm was swinging forward. She saw the arm muscles working, the cords bunching in his shoulders, the body sliding smoothly, lithely through the sea.

Yet...familiar somehow.

Slowly, carefully, as if she might shatter the moment,

Melanie moved her camera away from the man, back to the shore and down the beach.

His towel had been vacated.

Swiftly, she swung the camera out to sea again; there he was, still moving gracefully through the water. The stranger.

Then he stopped. He trod water for a prolonged time and he looked across the blue sea and across the expanse of sand and directly into her golden stare behind the lens. She didn't dare breathe. She took a picture and willed her hand to hold the camera steady, for she didn't want to risk losing this unpredictable game.

Only when he tired of treading water and his powerful stroke began to carry him back to shore did she let the camera hang at her neck once again. She took a deep breath.

"Your ice is melting," Cecily suddenly piped up from her place next to Melanie.

"My…ice?" For long minutes now, Melanie had not been conscious of anything else on the beach, had not even noticed Cecily returning.

"In your drink, Mel." Cecily rolled over again and closed her eyes.

He finally emerged from the water like a glistening god, a god of myth, certainly not a mortal man. He was all long limb and lean muscle and tapered waist. Tan from head to foot, except for a thin line around the waistline of his bathing suit when he moved.

His facial expression was impassive but he didn't look at her as he made his way to his towel and stretched out under the sun once more.

She wondered if he was a Spaniard. Could be. But with that distinctive bone structure—the very dark shadowed eyes, the thin nose, the high cheeks and strong jaw—he was definitely not from the southern provinces of Spain. Where, then? Curiosity gnawed at her, making his presence there on the beach even more overwhelming.

Her eyes tried to leave him, then with great reluctance returned to stay. It seemed that she saw each droplet of water on his chest evaporate, saw the rivulets of seawater dry to salt on the long bulge of thigh, saw the thick dark hair stiffen into unruly waves.

He appeared to be relaxed. Melanie told herself that he was just a man on holiday, obviously enjoying the beach in the south of Spain, as well as the sun, the sea, the wine. Of course. Did it matter that he looked at her so often, that she could *feel* his eyes on her? Wasn't it normal? Man stares at woman, she glances over, he looks away.

What's so mysterious about that, she wondered.

And yet he was somehow too alert in his apparent repose. The mere angle and immobility of his handsome head seemed to suggest that he was there for a single purpose: to observe her.

Ridiculous. The whole thing was in her mind. A fantasy. It had been too long since she'd looked at a man in that way; she'd deliberately kept herself from noticing.

When had she first begun to hide from the pain of the real world—or, more accurately, from the painful possibilities of emotional commitment? After Bob, or even before that, when she'd taken up a camera in her sophomore year at college? And now her life had settled into a kind of routine. Plenty of travel, enough assignments to keep her busy, an occasional date with a reporter she met on location.

Oh, they were easy sorts to have dinner with. An assignment, especially in a crisis area, only lasted so long, then everyone flew out to the next site. New places, new faces. She would lift her camera and snap away, seeing the world through the safe barrier of a camera lens.

Sure, she'd had a couple of flings in the past seven years. There had been that absolutely stunningly gorgeous blond Swede she'd met in Stockholm when she'd been covering a marathon. And the dapper Englishman in Nicaragua. But they'd both disappointed her; they'd treated her so casually and coldly and temporarily that she'd withdrawn behind her camera completely. As she thought about her life, she began to feel a little sorry for herself. Drab old Melanie Royce, twenty-eight, unmarried and un-involved, heading to the ends of the earth. Heading nowhere.

It suddenly occurred to her why this stranger on the beach struck her so forcefully. He seemed almost to know something about her. She had the feeling that he was not only looking at her but through her, as though he saw past the facade of cool competence and recognized the void that was there.

A tiny thread of anxiety continued to coil and uncoil in her belly, annoying but impossible to ignore.

The afternoon waned. Cecily napped comfortably; Melanie dozed off once, then rose and went for a swim. When she returned to her towel he was still at his post, never turning his head in her direction, yet ever aware.

She considered standing up, shoulders set, and marching over to confront him. But what would that prove?

She began to imagine all kinds of things. He was Madrid's James Bond, yes, come to the beach because she'd been mistakenly identified as a Soviet spy. Or Oscar, their father, had sent him to watch over his daughters. No way. No matter how lovable, Oscar and Muriel Royce were the most unlikely candidates in the world for Parents of the Year. Maybe the strange man liked tall females with wide mouths and freckled skin? And if he *did* simply like her looks, why not approach her? Married? Was he married with ten kids? When did that ever stop a man, especially a Continental type, from at least offering to buy Melanie a glass of wine?

Stop watching me! Melanie's brain cried out. Yet when she looked through the throng on the beach once more, she saw that his eyes were closed. But couldn't she see a muscle ticking in that finely chiseled jawline? Not from fifteen yards away.

Eventually she noticed that the afternoon sun had sunk low in the sky. Everything shimmered as if dusted with gold by the magic Mediterranean light.

She dropped her magazine with a sigh and rested her chin on a fist as she watched the beach empty. The man was still there, lying on his back with one knee up, completely relaxed. She even thought she could see the calm rise and fall of his smooth brown chest. In the splendid light of late afternoon, he had a truly godlike beauty, she thought. And it only enhanced the mystery.

She rolled onto her back and stared at the palm-fringed shoreline and the row of tall white hotels lining the beach. Soft, mellow, burnished gold against gently sloping deep green hills. An exotic setting for her mysterious stranger. Or maybe Melanie was being ridiculously fanciful. Maybe there was nothing more to him than to any other man on the beach. She'd ask her sister what she thought. Cecily would tell her if she was crazy or not.

"Cecily," she said suddenly, "see that man over there?" She turned to point out the stranger.

But he was gone.

IT WAS TO BE their last night in Torremolinos and Cecily wanted to celebrate.

"Let's paint the town red." She dressed in baggy wrinkled cotton slacks and an oversize T-shirt—no bra—then stood looking at herself in the hotel's full-length mirror. "Not bad," she said. "At least I managed to get a decent tan before I have to lock myself up in an office for the rest of the summer."

"Maybe you'll enjoy the work," said Melanie as she stepped from the bathroom into the suite and stopped short, taking in her sister's dinner outfit.

"Not bloody likely, as my last boyfriend used to say."

"English?"

Cecily nodded. "But that's over."

"So you just have this one guy you're dating now?"

Cecily nodded.

"But you still don't want to talk about him." Melanie tossed her bath towel onto the bed and slipped on her panties and bra.

"I don't know if you'd understand him."

"So…am I going to be allowed to meet him back in Madrid?"

"Maybe. But you'll probably run to Mother and Dad and say he's weird or something."

"Why do you say that?"

"Oh, I don't know," she said, shrugging. "No reason, I guess. He's just a little different."

And that was the end of that, thought Melanie.

Cecily began to push aside hangers in Melanie's closet. "Nice dresses, Mel. But terribly American."

"Really? Should I try to dress like a Frenchwoman?"

"Wouldn't hurt. Wow!" she breathed. "Now *this* number is perfect." Cecily pulled out a summer-weight melon-and-rust-colored print that had no back but sported a loose plunging neckline and promised to cling to every contour of Melanie's lean figure. "This is *you*." Cecily held up the dress expectantly.

"I feel like I'm back in college with a roommate trying to help me choose a dress for some big date." But it was sort of fun—the companionship of a sister all grown up and caring.

"Oh, wear it. We're going to that great seafood place. You promised. And we can eat mountains of lobster and butter and have every man in the place drooling after us."

"Is that the purpose of painting the town?"

"Sure. Food and men."

"What about your boyfriend?"

"He's in Madrid."

"Oh. Then it's not all that serious."

"Of course it is. Now come on, get dressed. I'm totally famished."

Cecily wore her auburn hair down, swinging casually

at her shoulders. Melanie twisted her even longer dark red hair into a knot and fastened it with a bamboo catch.

Of course Cecily had a comment. "That's too old-fashioned. You should get a good cut and let it hang. Your hair is much thicker than mine and would look fabulous."

"Maybe I will," Melanie said, "someday."

She did borrow some of Cecily's eye shadow, stroking on three blending shades of blue and green. Melanie had never considered herself a beauty, but she did have great eyes and an acceptable nose, nice and straight even if it was a touch too long. Her mouth was wide, but that was okay, too. At least according to that fortune hunter husband of hers, who had told her men were attracted to women with wide, sensual mouths.

"Think you'll ever remarry?" Cecily asked as they stepped out of the hotel and began to stroll slowly along the promenade.

"Maybe," Melanie admitted. "I've met a couple of guys here and there but they all seem to know about Royce Steel."

"That's just in your head. And even if it isn't, not all men are gold diggers."

"It's hard to weed them out, though. I realize how this sounds, Cecily, but it's easier to travel around by myself and take pictures and play it safe."

"You'll never meet anyone special until you get out from behind that camera."

"You're getting awfully wise in your old age, little sister."

"Aren't I, though?" Cecily agreed smugly.

Melanie made one more casual attempt to find out about Cecily's new boyfriend, then gave up. Why the secret, she wondered. Was he someone that Cecily knew their parents would disapprove of? Someone Melanie herself might find a reason to distrust? After all, she was almost a parent to her sister. Even though they rarely saw each other nowadays, they were in frequent touch with phone calls and letters. And until Cecily had come to Spain and the university, the communication between the two of them had been special.

Melanie guessed that her sister was growing up, and becoming independent at last. That was good. But this somewhat radical talk intimidated Melanie more than a little. It brought to mind what had happened two decades ago in the sixties, when so many of the naively idealistic young had failed to come to grips with reality.

Where had Cecily picked up these ideas? Were they simply the influence of her new boyfriend, as Melanie suspected?

They walked by several fine tourist boutiques and some restaurants with outdoor seating under colorful umbrellas and palm trees. The special atmosphere of southern Spain surrounded them: the combination of medieval tradition and modern resort, liberally sprinkled with signs of the Moorish past. *El Andalus*, the conquering Moors had named southern Spain, or Andalusia, as it later came to be called. A land of milk and honey with a benign climate and fertile soil and ample rainfall. A land where the sweet scent of orange blossoms filled the air.

The contrast with Madrid's hectic big-city pace was amazing. To the Andalusians, the Madrileños, or natives of Madrid, were hard and brash, and the Castilians of the capital thought the southerners lazy and self-indulgent. A bit like New Englanders and southern plantation-owners in nineteenth-century America, mused Melanie.

The shops were tasteful, offering elegant leather goods from Madrid, silk blouses and dresses and lingerie, gorgeous shoes, paintings by local artists. Picasso had been Spanish, she recalled, even though he'd lived in France. She should have looked in the galleries. Maybe there was a young unknown talent, a new Picasso, languishing around here somewhere.

They passed a poster shop and Cecily stopped to look in the window. "I love that one." She pointed at the picture of a black bull charging a gracefully poised matador. The tableau held a certain amount of tension, Melanie had to admit. Across the top of the poster was announced: *Corrida de Torros. 10 Julio 1980. Pamplona.* Cecily translated automatically: Bullfight. July 10, 1980. Pamplona.

They turned away from the window and continued walking. Their final destination was still farther down the long well-appointed promenade known as the Carihuela to the locals. They were dining on seafood—the best in Torremolinos—at a restaurant called El Cangrejo, which meant "the crab," Cecily had explained.

The evening air was warm and dry. On the hills behind the beaches the villas glowed serenely in the last of the sunlight. Melanie thought it was a pity they couldn't stay longer in Torremolinos but they were heading back to Madrid the next day, then to New York and Ohio. She supposed she was fortunate to have been in Africa finishing a magazine assignment at the time that Cecily was due to fly home. They had at least been able to spend a few days together.

"There's the place," Cecily said, breaking into Melanie's thoughts. "Looks perfect. I can even smell the shrimp."

They entered the restaurant and Cecily spoke to the maître d'. Melanie spoke very little Spanish but her sister was completely fluent now. It came in handy, even though most of the people in Torremolinos spoke some English. The maître d' immediately flashed the two sisters a very special, very appreciative Andalusian smile, more eloquent than an entire conversation, and bowed them into his domain. Cecily winked at Melanie over his head, then adjusted her triumphant smile to one of politeness as he straightened up and, with a flourish, began to lead them toward a table.

As they followed him, Melanie looked around her at the attractive dining room. There was a small tiled fountain in the center and myriad shells and pieces of coral adorning the beams and walls. She noticed the softly candle-lit tables, the fine shell-pink linen and sparkling silver. The stucco walls were punctuated by windows, all wide open, and the atmosphere was heavy with the aroma of fresh fish cooking and salty sea air. Very nice, very appealing. And quite crowded.

They were nearly at their seats when Cecily stopped abruptly, gazing across the fountain toward a table against the opposite wall. "Why...why that looks like..." And she took Melanie's arm and began to steer her toward the distant table. "I can't believe it! But it is!" She turned to Melanie. "Come on, I want you to meet this really great guy."

Melanie was behind Cecily and until the women were directly in front of the table, she couldn't see this man her sister was so delighted to have run into.

Then she was standing there and he was smiling at Cecily and getting to his feet, shaking her sister's hand warmly. It was all too dreamlike. That handsome finely chiseled face, the casual white shirt and trousers, the long lean body, the very dark eyes that came slowly and inevitably to rest on Melanie.

Cecily was talking. Melanie forced herself to concentrate on her sister's words. "And we're just here until tomorrow," she was saying pleasantly. Then, "Professor Sanlucar, this is Melanie Royce, my sister."

He reached out his hand and took Melanie's. His grip was firm but gentle; his smile seemed charming and quite genuine. Melanie shook his hand but the words stuck in her throat.

"Your sister mentioned that she was going on holiday with you," he said in practically perfect Oxford English. "It's so nice to meet you, Miss Royce."

And Melanie could only murmur something trite and meaningless in reply while her mind spun away in chaos, crying, *it can't be him, my stranger...*

Chapter Two

Cecily seemed to assume, as a matter of course, that they would join Professor Sanlucar for dinner. Melanie wanted to grab her sister's arm and bolt. She wanted to make some excuse to leave his table, but Cecily was chatting away as if it had already been settled that they were having dinner with him. There was nothing, absolutely nothing, Melanie could do.

And inevitably, he asked, "You will join me, won't you?"

"Why, sure, we'd love too," Cecily said gaily. "Wouldn't we, Mel?"

There was a terrible moment of strained silence as the man's dark eyes swung around to her, then Melanie forced herself to smile. "Why, yes, thank you, Professor."

The waiter scurried for chairs and place settings, grinning and nodding at them as if he had personally engineered the fortuitous meeting. Finally they were seated and wine was poured into their glasses. Melanie felt a vortex of intolerable confusion and embarrassment whirling within her. She fought for her equilibrium.

"You must not call me Professor, Miss Royce. My

name is Teo.'' He pronounced it ''Tay-oh'' in the Spanish style.

She nodded inanely, knowing she would never, never call him Teo. Nor would she offer him her own Christian name.

Up close he looked a little older than she'd imagined, with strong lines on his face and a few gray hairs among the jet-black curls. It seemed to her that the mysterious watchful stranger on the beach had receded. Physically, he now looked more subdued, less imposing than that man whose body had glimmered with energy and danger.

It was all so awkward. Did he know she had seen him observing her on the beach? Did he know she had watched him through her lens, studied him as if he were a specimen under a microscope? Melanie shut her eyes in humiliation.

''Cecily tells me you are a free-lance photojournalist,'' Teo Sanlucar was saying to her in his smoothly modulated voice. A lovely voice, full of warmth and interest and sincerity. Yet full of secrets, too. Or was that only Melanie's wild imagination again?

''Yes,'' she answered shortly, sipping her wine.

''And you've just flown here from Africa?'' he prompted.

''I was working in Ethiopia at one of the relocation camps.''

''It must have been very sad,'' he said gravely.

Mutely, Melanie nodded. It had been terrible. The proud fine people reduced to dust-covered skeletons. The suffering, the inexcusable dying.

Teo spoke in a low gentle voice. ''I must confess that I am fascinated by a woman who can do such things and go to such places and yet remain so beautiful and untouched by it all.''

''Really,'' Melanie murmured, flustered. She twirled her wineglass between her fingers and refused to meet his gaze. ''Are all Spanish men so bold?''

"I would not know, not being Spanish, Miss Royce," he replied.

She looked at him in confusion.

Cecily was grinning. "That's a mortal insult, Mel. The professor here is a Basque."

"Yes, Miss Royce. I come from an ancient race that has lived in the Pyrenees mountains since pre-Roman times. We have our own language, our own laws and our own rather different way of looking at life."

"How interesting," Melanie said coolly. "What way is that?"

Teo smiled at her in challenge. "You must visit my part of the country and find out."

"It's kind of you, but Cecily and I are leaving for home in a few days and I doubt we'd have time."

"What a pity. I think you would enjoy our cool green mountains. The opportunities for photography are endless." He smiled at her as if they were old friends and repeated his invitation to visit his family someday. "We Basques are a very warm people. We live passionately, savoring each day, never hiding our emotions, for they are life itself to us."

Then what had he been doing on the beach, watching her through those unreadable dark eyes of his, so secretive?

And yet she saw the smile that curved his chiseled lips now, the frankness in his eyes, the *warmth*. Could this conceivably be the same man who'd behaved so mysteriously on the beach?

"Yes," he was saying, "I feel I should try to persuade you to visit the Basques someday. Truly."

What kind of game was he playing? Did he seriously expect her to take him up on his offer? Or was his manner just another variation on the typical Continental approach? He made her uncomfortable and Melanie felt again, as she had on the beach, that he seemed to see right through her, to know her most private thoughts and emotions. Yet how could he? They had just met.

"How did you learn such excellent English?" Melanie asked, parrying his suggestion.

"I attended Oxford University as an undergraduate and read history there."

"I see."

"I should have gone to the United States and studied, you are thinking, and then I would have learned my English with an American accent," he said lightly.

"Oh, no!" put in Cecily. "I *love* your English accent. It's so elegant."

"Thank you," Teo said, nodding soberly.

It was on the tip of Melanie's tongue to agree, but she wouldn't give him the satisfaction. He did have a wonderfully well-bred Oxford accent, though.

Cecily seized the conversation at that point, asking Teo about a course she had taken from him. Teo and her sister slipped into Spanish and Melanie felt, paradoxically, both relieved and left out.

The menus arrived—large and glossy, with gold tassels. Cecily would have to translate for her.

"Your sister's Spanish has become quite fluent," Teo said to her.

Cecily flushed and thanked him.

"I'm glad to hear that," Melanie replied.

"Her Basque, however," he said, smiling drolly, "is nonexistent."

"Nobody learns Basque," Cecily said, laughing, "unless they were born Basque."

"Alas, all too true," Teo admitted. He reached into his breast pocket and pulled out a pair of horn-rimmed glasses and put them on to read the menu.

Melanie couldn't help staring, studying with fascination the metamorphosis brought about by the glasses. The intense dark eyes became studious, the face lost its mystery and became mild, the sense of sparking energy became dimmed. The change was so stunning and so unexpected that Melanie practically gaped. Her mind kept trying to mesh the disparate images of Teo Sanlucar: the friendly dinner partner, the polite, bespectacled history professor and the enigmatic stranger on the beach.

Cecily jabbered on about Madrid and Torremolinos and the university, her usual carefree, high-spirited self. Melanie was grateful for her sister's effusiveness as it covered her own rather distracted silence. She almost squirmed in her seat, discomfited by Teo's probing, knowledgeable eyes.

It suddenly struck her. Had this meeting been coincidental? Had she imagined his vigilance on the beach? But how could he possibly have known where she and Cecily would be? And why would he have cared? He *had* mentioned Cecily telling him about the trip they were making to Torremolinos. But what reason could he possibly have for showing up in the same place?

It was coincidence, of course. The Costa del Sol, the sun coast, was a very popular resort area. And El Cangrejo, this posh restaurant, was just as popular, a natural place for a vacationer to choose.

Pure accident.

"Isn't that so, Miss Royce?" Teo Sanlucar was asking her.

She jumped, startled, and her hand accidentally brushed her wineglass, tipping it. A few drops of blood-red wine stained the linen tablecloth in the split second before Teo's lean brown hand reached out, cat-quick, to right the glass.

"Oh, I'm sorry," Melanie said, dabbing at the crimson spot with her napkin, her cheeks burning.

"I asked if you agreed," Teo repeated.

"I'm sorry, I wasn't following the conversation."

"We were talking about the contrasts between the provinces of Spain, Mel," Cecily said patronizingly. "Like how different it is here from Madrid and Barcelona."

"Well, yes, it is different but I couldn't venture an opinion. I haven't seen enough of Spain," she responded uncertainly.

"Have you seen a bullfight yet?" Teo asked.

"Goodness, no—we haven't had time."

"It's the season. You should try to catch one. Perhaps when you get back to Madrid. You are going back shortly?" he asked, one dark brow quirked.

"Too soon for me," Cecily said. "I'd rather stay here for a while."

"But surely your parents are most anxious to see you. How could you disappoint them?" Teo said gravely, taking off his glasses and putting them in his pocket.

"They don't care," replied Cecily, pouting. "They're in *China*!"

"On their way home by now," Melanie chided gently.

Cecily pursed her lips and rolled her eyes. She was still terribly immature, despite her veneer of sophistication, thought Melanie. Nineteen. A late-life child of Oscar and Muriel Royce. The nine years between the two sisters made quite a difference—practically a generation. The world's at everyone's feet when they're nineteen, Melanie reflected, and they know more than everyone else on any subject that comes up. They're so absolutely sure of right and wrong. Everything was black and white at nineteen. It was only as a person matured that the shades of gray emerged. Melanie knew all about those shades of gray.

She sipped her wine again and met Teo's eyes over her glass. His were sparkling with a kind of humor, as if he were reading her thoughts and agreeing with Melanie's assessment of her younger sister.

They ordered. Or rather, Cecily and Teo ordered for her. The meal was delicious: steaming saffron rice and butter-drenched Mediterranean prawns. Melanie tried to enjoy it but her appetite had fled. Teo Sanlucar's presence seemed to overshadow everything.

Why? she demanded of herself. Why should this

stranger, this college professor, fascinate her so much? What was it about him that appeared so ominous to her? Once dinner was over, they'd go their separate ways and never see each other again. And yet she could not erase from her brain the image of him on the beach, watching her—or Cecily—or both of them. Why?

He insisted on paying the bill, covering Melanie's hand when she reached for it to pay her share and Cecily's.

"No, no," he said, "allow me."

"We couldn't..." And she continued to argue—a trait learned from her generous father—but Melanie hadn't the slightest idea of what she was saying. All she knew was that his hand was resting on hers, warm and firm and compelling, and her pulse began to hammer in her neck. It always did when she was unnerved or confused.

In the end she agreed, but only, she told herself, to make him remove his hand, to be free of his unsettling touch.

After the bill was paid they threaded their way through the rows of tables. The maître d' bowed them out with a flourish and said something gracious in Spanish to Teo and Cecily.

Then they were standing on the promenade in front of El Cangrejo and Teo was offering to walk them to their hotel.

"Really, it's not necessary," Melanie protested, wanting desperately to get away from the man. She felt, somehow, that she couldn't take a full breath in his presence. Her chest was constricted, squeezing her heart, making that pulse leap.

"I couldn't let two such lovely ladies walk alone," he persisted, "at night, in a strange town."

"But our hotel is just down the Carihuela."

"So is mine. Good. Then you have no excuse to rid yourself of my company. I shall walk with you."

Why didn't Melanie appreciate his concern for them? Did he truly care? Yes, she thought, he did, but there was another edge to his concern, a tension of some kind. His offer was not quite as casual as it seemed.

What was he after?

He was an attractive man, polite but not stiffly so, dynamic, intelligent, well educated. She should have welcomed his attentions.

The sea breeze that brushed Melanie's face was tangy and warm. It ruffled the fabric of her skirt and lifted Teo's black curls from his forehead. His face was all shadows and dark hollows in the subtropical night.

"You are leaving tomorrow, you say?" he asked then.

"I didn't say," replied Melanie.

"I'm sure Cecily must have mentioned it."

"Yes, we're starting back tomorrow," Cecily sighed. "But I'm going to stretch it out as long as possible. I'm going to show my sister every tourist spot on the way. It may take us days. Granada, Toledo, the works."

"Of course she must see them."

Teo walked between them, tall and lean in the sultry darkness, his white shirt glowing. People passed them, wearing brightly colored resort clothes, talking, laughing, chattering in several different languages. Melanie remained silent. She listened to the night sounds, to the palm fronds overhead that rattled in the offshore breeze and the sea that soughed at the sandy verge beyond the lighted promenade.

They reached their hotel. Strategically placed spotlights illuminated the beautifully arranged foliage; the large plate-glass doors gleamed and winked, reflecting the light, as people pushed through them.

"Thank you for walking us back," Melanie said carefully. She wanted the man gone. Gone from her side, gone from her life. In some way, he frightened her, though she couldn't have said exactly why.

"I'm so glad we met you in the restaurant," Cecily gushed. "Actually it's been quite boring here."

"My pleasure entirely, *Señoritas*," Teo said.

"Well, I'll see you back at the university in the fall," Cecily said.

"Certainly. Let me know when you return." He turned to Melanie. "I am so pleased to have met you, Miss Royce." He bowed slightly, then straightened. His eyes were dark holes in his shadowed face. She had a sudden compulsion to see his expression but he stood with his back to the hotel lights.

She murmured something polite, then realized he was holding out his hand. She had to return the gesture, to clasp his hand in hers. Her heart gave a lurch as she felt his touch. He held her hand a second too long, his lean brown fingers almost caressing her skin.

"*Buenos noches.* Good night," he said. Then, in an undertone, he added something very odd. "Take care of your sister, Miss Royce. She's so very young."

He turned quickly and vanished into the soft Spanish night.

Chapter Three

Saturday, July 3

Cecily angrily threw some underwear into her suitcase. "I still don't see why I have to go back with you. You can make up some kind of excuse for me." She paced around her tiny apartment.

"You have to go back and you know it," Melanie said sharply. "Look, if it's this new guy, well, he'll still be here when you get back to Madrid. Just think of how happy you'll be to see each other."

"Oh, you just don't understand."

"Did he give you a hard time last night or something?" Melanie hoped her sister wouldn't regard her question as prying, but Cecily had turned singularly sullen after they'd arrived in Madrid and she'd gone to see him.

"His name is Carlos," Cecily grumbled, "and he didn't give me a hard time. He's not like that. He's really wonderful. He isn't one of those useless, frivolous *boys* Mother always shoves at me. And he isn't an uptight, cold Castilian. He's a Basque. He's serious. He believes in serious, important things."

What things, Melanie wondered.

"Basque men are so...so complex, so profound. Don't you think that's true?" Cecily was saying.

"I couldn't say. I don't really know any Basque men."

"Yes you do. Professor Sanlucar. He introduced me to Carlos, in fact."

"I hardly know your professor," Melanie said, thrust abruptly back to that evening, to El Cangrejo, to her mysterious and beautiful stranger...

No. She shook her head as if to dispel the wayward fantasy. Nothing mysterious about Professor Teo Sanlucar. He was just a teacher who had been on vacation, too.

"He *is* attractive, isn't he? With those soulful black eyes and that gorgeous hair," she heard Cecily saying. "And he's a supernice man, too. All the girls at the university are crazy about him."

"I can imagine."

"Of course he's not the least bit interested in any of them," Cecily shrugged. "He's too old."

"Old?"

"Thirty-five, at least."

"Oh, yes, that's ancient," Melanie said dryly.

"Well, you know what I mean."

Melanie raised an eyebrow. "I'm not so sure." Then, casually, "I'm certain your professor has a family, anyway."

"No, he doesn't. Carlos told me. He's footloose and fancy-free. Odd."

"Why odd?"

"Well, he's so good-looking and sexy."

"Mmm."

"And an excellent teacher."

Melanie sat on the bed, watching her sister go about her perfunctory packing. Suddenly she remembered the pictures she'd taken in Torremolinos. She'd just been having fun, she had to admit; even when she wasn't on assignment, she couldn't stop herself from shooting roll after roll of film. Was it simply because she no longer felt comfortable without her camera, as Cecily had implied? Or because you never knew when the perfect picture might appear in your viewfinder? Her black-and-white work she usually developed and printed herself, but these she'd just handed over to a local photography lab as soon as she and Cecily had returned to Madrid. She considered them summer holiday snapshots, she told herself, no more and no less. Some of them were dreadful and some quite good, especially a couple of Cecily that their parents would love to have.

She reached into her ever-handy camera bag and pulled them out. "This is a great picture of you, if I do say so myself." She tipped it in Cecily's direction.

"Ugh! Look at my thighs."

"It's my angle. I was sitting when I took it. It's still a good picture, though."

She leafed through the photographs. There he was. Melanie must have taken ten pictures of him—at the time, she hadn't realized it was so many—and the best were the ones in which he was lying on his towel, one arm behind his head, one knee bent. There was nothing left to the imagination in her shots. She'd used a zoom lens to get in all those details: the dark, salt-stiff hair, the chiseled arch of his nose, the smooth-skinned chest with the crisp dark hairs that grew downward in a line to disappear beneath his trunks. The flat belly, even the masculine bulge in his white swimsuit. The thighs, glistening in the sun. Their long muscles suggested that perhaps he'd been a runner at one time. He even had nicely shaped feet.

She sifted through several more photographs. There were two of him swimming—not so good. Her hand must have been shaking a little…

"You took a picture of the professor?" Cecily asked from over Melanie's shoulder.

"Well, I didn't know who he was. He was just a subject," she replied, putting the pictures away in her bag, unaccountably embarrassed.

Cecily yanked some wrinkled clothes out of a drawer

then stopped, staring at them, unfocused. "I could fly home next week," she finally said, her voice hopeful.

"Cecily, we're going tomorrow morning and that's that." Melanie readied herself for an argument but when she looked at her sister, Cecily's face was wiped clean of her previous irritation. Somehow that worried her; Cecily was not one to hide her feelings. Nor did she give up that easily.

"I'm going back to my hotel to pack now. I'll pick you up at nine. Is that too early for the Spanish dinner hour?"

"A little," Cecily said, "but it's okay. They've learned to forgive tourists."

"Swell of them. Now you finish packing. We have to leave early and turn in the rental car at the airport, remember? I'll see you later, okay?"

"Sure. I've got a great place I want to take you. Real flamenco dancers. I mean, not the tourist stuff, the real thing."

"Sounds great," Melanie said, preoccupied with gathering up her camera equipment and her purse. She wasn't paying much attention to her sister, who moved around the room in a jerky, nervous manner. She did notice that Cecily wouldn't meet her gaze or hug her goodbye. So she was going to sulk, after all, Melanie thought.

She drove back toward the center of Madrid, where her hotel was situated. The traffic was heavy, as usual, but because it was Saturday, she was at least spared the rush-hour hysteria. The day had been hot and Cecily's apartment even hotter. Melanie's thick hair stuck uncomfortably to her neck. But the cool breath of wind coming in the open car window was soothing, even though the Spanish sun hung high and still in the western sky. The quality of the light up here on the central plateau was entirely different from that in southern Spain. It was crystal clear and sharp, not the least bit golden, Melanie noted.

She had her street map laid out on the passenger seat and stopped several times to check it. Without Cecily, she was lost in the sprawling capital, especially when she reached the rabbit-warren of old winding cobblestone streets around the Plaza Mayor. Now if only she could recall exactly where to turn…

She was staying in a small, elegant private hotel in the old part of town, a place Cecily had found for her. Full of atmosphere and real Spanish hospitality. But a little hard to find. As for parking…well, she guessed Madrid was like any other big city.

She was straining to locate and read the street signs when she inadvertently strayed into the wrong lane. There was a sudden screech of brakes from behind. She, too, quickly slammed on her brakes, realizing what she'd done. A middle-aged man pulled his car beside hers, holding up traffic as he leaned across his seat and gave Melanie a good tongue-lashing to the tune of a dozen horns.

Then he did the craziest thing; his eyes widened, as if he'd only just seen her, and his face split in a huge smile. He winked and then he was gone in a symphony of horn blowing.

She really needn't have driven all the way from the campus back into the heart of Madrid, but she'd wanted to give Cecily a couple of hours alone with Carlos. Their last night and all. But now it seemed a really dumb idea. She should have stayed around to meet Carlos. Or, better yet, she should have made Cecily come back with her and stay in her hotel room. Why hadn't she thought of that? Perhaps she'd suggest it tonight.

Twenty minutes later, as she finally entered her room and kicked off her shoes, Melanie hoped Cecily would have stopped sulking by the time they got back to Ohio. Surely her sister wasn't that immature. It wasn't as if she were being dragged away forever from her life here in Madrid. It was only for six weeks.…

The shower was refreshing; afterward the air conditioning chilled her wet skin. She dressed, then threw a few last things into her suitcase and checked her purse, a habit she'd developed since she'd started traveling so much. Passport, traveler's checks, credit cards, international driver's license, airplane tickets. All set.

The doorman handed her into the gray car she'd rented, smiling and nodding as he wished her a good evening.

The sun was setting behind the Guadarrama mountains as Melanie drove out Calle Princesa to university city. There was an orange glow behind the rough-edged black hills. The colors were as clear as the air—brilliant, too perfect to last, almost tragic in their brief glory.

She pulled to the side of the road and took her camera out of its case. Then she walked across the street, dodging a car or two. She carefully chose her angle and composed her shot, focusing on a small stone church, stark against the vivid sunset colors. A dramatic picture.

A dramatic city. No wonder her sister had fallen in love with Madrid. The highest capital in Europe. Its undulating plateau of sand and clay had once been the site of a Moorish fort, Cecily had told her. Yet for Melanie the city conjured up images of medieval Europe; it was in the air, down a winding alley, across a sun-beaten hill. It caught her senses and caressed them pleasantly.

The Old World was compelling, Melanie thought once again. Its ancient cities and timeless villages had a kind of serenity, a calm beauty that she was able to capture in a series of perfect images.

For a moment she regretted having no one with whom to share her vision. But she always traveled alone. She was used to it and had developed automatic defenses against uncomfortable situations. She was quite capable of withdrawing into herself completely or reading with utter concentration. Still, it could be lonely, she admitted to herself. Safe but lonely.

This evening, however, she would have her sister's companionship. Melanie was looking forward to a pleasant night out, not quite the usual tourist's view of Madrid. And perhaps Cecily would tell her a bit more about this

Carlos. Then, the next day, she and Cecily would fly home
and her sister would get a good dose of midwestern America. Life would look a little less romantic in Ohio than it
did in Spain. A little less romantic and a lot more realistic.

It was a good thing Melanie had come to Madrid.

She pushed open one of the double doors leading into
the courtyard of Cecily's building and walked up the wide
elaborate staircase. It was all for show—the apartments
were tiny and plain. She knocked on Cecily's door once,
then opened it and walked in. "Cecily? Ready yet?"

The room was silent and too empty. Melanie knew instantly, instinctively, that it had been vacant for hours.

Her first thought was that Cecily had run away, gone
into hiding—with Carlos most likely—to avoid going
home. Cecily had always been a willful child who got
what she wanted, and she'd made it only too clear that
she hadn't wanted to go home to Cleveland.

Anger welled up in Melanie's chest. How could Cecily
do this? How could she leave Melanie in the lurch and
disappoint their parents? How dared she indulge herself
in this childish way?

Melanie stood in the small apartment and looked
around. There were two half-empty cups of tea on the
kitchen counter and dirty dishes in the sink. Someone had
been there with Cecily. Carlos? Had he convinced her to
go away with him? Young passion could be powerfully
persuasive.

She went into the bedroom and stopped short, her heart
flying into her throat. The covers had been pulled off the
bed, a chair lay overturned on its side and papers from a
small table had fluttered to the floor. It looked as though
a struggle had taken place there. What had happened?

Melanie's brain raced with possibilities. Carlos and Cecily had had an argument and Carlos had become violent.
Or Cecily herself had flown into a rage of some kind. But
then, where *was* Cecily?

Or—the thought struck her sickeningly—with all the

violence going on in large cities, and Cecily coming from a wealthy background, could she have been…abducted?

Melanie sucked in a terrified breath. She tried to calm herself, to think. She examined the room, desperately searching for clues, not knowing what she was looking for. The two suitcases Cecily had packed that afternoon sat in the corner. Her sister's purse was gone. Drawers were mostly empty, but she had no way of knowing whether Cecily had taken anything with her or not. A knot of fear twisted in Melanie's stomach.

A lone sandal lay by the bedroom door. One sandal. Had Cecily been dragged out? No, there were neighbors. Wouldn't someone have heard?

Quickly, her heart pounding, Melanie went out into the hall, chose a door and knocked on it. No answer. Another door. An elderly lady opened it but couldn't understand what Melanie was asking.

"Cecily?" the old woman quavered. *"Sí, la americana."* The American.

Eventually Melanie gathered that Cecily had left earlier that evening with a young man. *Un novio.* A boyfriend. His name? The lady didn't know.

Other neighbors knew nothing, hadn't seen Cecily or refused to comprehend Melanie's minimal Spanish.

She went back to Cecily's place and threw herself down in a chair. It had to be Carlos. She had no other leads, not a clue, not a note. Only the awful emptiness of the apartment and one lonely sandal.

Could Cecily be late returning from somewhere? Should she wait? She checked the time: almost ten. And Cecily had expected her at nine. Could her sister have deliberately messed up the bedroom to mislead her? Could she have?

She had to look for Cecily. Carlos was a start but she didn't know his last name. She had to find out.

Quickly she scribbled a note, on the remote chance that Cecily might return to the apartment. All the while, she searched for reasons, possibilities, explanations. Was Cecily pulling some sort of sick stunt? Were she and Carlos conspiring together to make this look like a kidnapping? No, that was too farfetched. Or was it? Cecily had been acting strange lately, talking of causes and crusades. Or was she, perhaps unwittingly, involved in some kind of crime? She had to find out.

What should she do?

The first thing was to find someone Cecily had known, someone who spoke English. Someone who might know something. Carlos's last name, at least.

She rifled every drawer in the apartment and finally found an untidy pile of paper scraps with names and addresses scribbled on them. Most of Cecily's friends and acquaintances had Spanish names and Melanie was afraid they wouldn't speak English. Then she found one: Joan Tattenham, Residencia de Mujeres, 505 Calle Isobel. No phone, but then Cecily's apartment had no phone anyway.

She left the tiny apartment, hurtling down the stairs to her car. It was almost dark by now. She tried to read her map by the car's interior light but the street names were so tiny. Thankfully, the *sereno* came by with his flashlight. The *sereno*, that medieval character, an anachronism somehow carried over into the twentieth century. The man who saw to the safety of the neighborhood after dark, who had on his iron ring the key to every courtyard on his beat and unlocked one's door if one clapped loudly in the dark, echoing street to attract his attention.

"Señorita." He nodded politely.

"Could you tell me where Isobel Street is, please? *Por favor, la Calle Isobel.*" Melanie asked. But his answer was too rapid for her to understand. Eventually he put his finger on a spot on the map—a dirty finger, with a thick blackened nail. *"Aquí,"* he rasped, "Here." The street was not far away. Melanie thanked him profusely, tipped him and waved goodbye out her window.

Calle Isobel. She found it after a few unsuccessful tries.

The address turned out to be a dormitory. The matron, disgruntled, went up to get Señorita Tattenham for her. Melanie waited, heart pounding, fingers nervously tapping the arm of her chair. Perhaps Joan Tattenham wouldn't know anything....

"Hi!" A young, rather stocky girl with a bright smile was walking across the room. "I'll bet you're Cecily's sister. The hair..."

"Joan Tattenham?"

"Yes. Not too many of us Tattenhams around here."

"I'm Melanie Royce. I do appreciate your talking to me so late." She tried to keep the panic from her voice.

"Late? It's early in Madrid. I was bored, anyway. Is there something wrong? I mean, I wonder why you looked me up."

"Well, not exactly wrong. I just wondered how well you knew my sister."

"Pretty well. I mean, we Americans seem to naturally gravitate together. But lately, Cecily's been hanging out with a new group. Some guys. For a while there, I thought she'd forgotten how to speak English."

"What group is this? You see, I'm trying to locate her. A family crisis," she lied.

"She's not in her apartment?"

"No."

"Well, I hate to give her away. I mean, I don't want her getting in trouble or anything..."

"Oh, she won't, really. This is kind of an emergency."

"She's probably with Carlos, then, Carlos Echeverria."

"But where is this Carlos?"

Joan shrugged. "He's probably gone home for the *feria*. The fiesta. It starts on the sixth. All the Basques go home for that week. It's a big deal."

"Where is his home?"

"Somewhere up in Basque country. Near Pamplona, I think."

"Pamplona? You mean that town where they have the running of the bulls?"

"Yeah. You know, Hemingway and bullfights and lotsa vino. It's this week."

"And you think Carlos and Cecily have gone there?"

"Probably. If Carlos isn't still here, that's where he's gone. But I'll tell you how to find out." She paused a moment. "Professor Sanlucar. He'll know. He's sort of a mentor to Carlos. They come from the same neck of the woods and they're pretty chummy. Those Basques stick together."

Professor Sanlucar! Melanie felt as if someone had punched her in the stomach. So he was involved in this somehow. It wasn't a coincidence, then, that he'd been on the beach in Torremolinos watching them. And that he'd shown up at the same restaurant. The sense of foreboding she'd felt had been accurate enough, after all. He'd been following them! He knew Carlos—it just couldn't be a coincidence. And what had he said that night? "Take care of your sister." She hadn't given it much thought then, but now...

What had Cecily got herself into?

She forced herself to sound calm; her voice quavered only a little when she spoke again.

"How can I find Professor Sanlucar, Joan?"

"Well, I have no idea where he lives but he'll be in his office tomorrow morning, I'm sure. He's generally around on weekends in case a student needs him or anything," she added helpfully.

Melanie left the *residencia* with the directions to Teo Sanlucar's office on a scrap of paper in her pocket. A grim feeling of futility gripped her—and of apprehension. The mysterious professor was the link. She was sure of it. Somehow he tied everything together; somehow he was involved in Cecily's disappearance. But how? And why?

She stopped by her sister's apartment again. There was a light on when she pushed the door open. She burst inside. "Cecily? Cecily!" But the apartment was empty. The light was the one she'd turned on herself and forgotten to click off.

She felt wretchedly near tears. It was too late to do anything that night. She briefly considered calling the police, but that would be a serious mistake if it turned out Cecily was merely having a fling with her lover. The Spanish police—the notorious Guardia Civil—were touchy and unforgiving, especially with foreigners. No, she couldn't go to them, not yet.

Slowly, tiredly, she drove back to her hotel through the heavy dinner-hour traffic. The streets teemed with people—walking, laughing, smoking, gesturing. The restaurants were crowded, the lights bright, the air warm and filled with the smell of olive oil and garlic and old cobblestones and dust.

Melanie went back to her hotel room and sat on the edge of her bed, thinking. She felt that something was terribly wrong, something was out of place. A large piece of the puzzle was missing.

And it was very likely that Professor Sanlucar could give her that missing piece—if he wanted to.

THE NEXT MORNING, Melanie was up early. She had her coffee and roll alone in the hotel dining room. The residents of Madrid rose late and breakfasted even later, about ten, and foreigners usually took on the custom when they visited. She was nervous and edgy, afraid that she wouldn't be able to track down the professor. Perhaps he hadn't even returned from the south of Spain yet.

She sent a telegram to her parents. She and Cecily wouldn't be home that day. Not for a few days. Something vague about Cecily missing an examination... She hated to lie but she couldn't bring herself to tell them the truth. Why should they worry until she was sure there was really something to worry about?

The drive out Calle Princesa to the university was becoming familiar; she didn't even need her map. The hills were illuminated with the morning sunlight but the streets were nearly empty, except for the ubiquitous elderly ladies dressed in black, carrying their string bags full of the day's groceries. The cafés were vacant, too, save for the proud, white-aproned owners standing behind their bars polishing glasses, and the young sweeper boys busy with their brooms.

The university was still asleep this Sunday morning. It was hard to believe she'd find anyone there at all. Melanie chewed her lip—her mission might have to wait. She even stopped by her sister's apartment, not really expecting Cecily to be there, but just in case... Then she carefully followed Joan's directions. She got confused once in a labyrinth of narrow streets but eventually found herself in front of the building that matched the address. It was ordinary and fairly new, one of those generic European buildings devoid of character, constructed of cement blocks, plain and utilitarian in design.

She parked the rental car and stared up at the windows. It was an uncivilized hour for the Spanish—not even nine o'clock. She wondered whether anyone would be at work in these offices so early in the morning. But the glass panes only reflected the morning sunlight, telling her nothing.

Taking a deep breath, Melanie pushed tentatively at the front door. It opened. So someone, a janitor perhaps, had already arrived. The musty, familiar smell of classrooms and chalk and paper assailed her as she stood in the dim corridor, listening. There was no sound. She checked the professor's office number on a directory board—twenty-one. Upstairs? She'd wait forever if she had to. Her footsteps echoed as she walked down the hallway and climbed the stairs. She tried to soften her steps. Ridiculous. There was obviously no one around to notice. No one at all.

Number twenty-one. A blank brown door. Timidly, Melanie knocked. The sound was shockingly loud in the hollow silence. She reminded herself that there was no one to hear her knock and she rapped at the smooth brown wood again, gathering courage. She'd just have to wait, then. Perhaps there was a café nearby.

The door swung inward as if in defiance of her very thought. She stood there, stupefied for a moment while her heart gave a great lurch.

"*Sí?*" a voice asked, a voice she remembered well. A deep mellow voice, now edged with a hint of annoyance.

Then he was standing before her, his expression quizzical behind his glasses. "Ah, Miss Royce, excuse me for sounding a bit put out. I try to work early, when the rest of Spain is still abed or in church. Do come in."

There was no surprise in his voice, Melanie observed. It almost seemed as though he'd expected her.

"I'm sorry to disturb you, but I'm having a bit of trouble locating Cecily." She knew she must have sounded ridiculously juvenile, and alarmist, to boot.

"Cecily? Ah." He gestured to a chair, then sat behind his desk, leaning forward in his seat and clasping his hands together in front of him, elbows resting on the desk. He wore a short-sleeved shirt, white against his tan. Melanie could see the muscles in his forearms tighten under the brown skin.

"Actually, she disappeared last night. She didn't leave any kind of note or message. We were to have flown home this morning. Naturally I'm worried."

His dark eyes met hers impassively over the folded hands. "What exactly do you mean, 'disappeared'?"

"I mean just that—disappeared," Melanie said curtly.

"Why do you come to me, Miss Royce? I haven't seen Cecily since Torremolinos."

"One of my sister's friends told me you know Carlos." She met his eyes levelly and was surprisingly upset by the frown that creased his brow.

"Carlos?"

"Carlos Echeverria, her boyfriend. You *do* know him?"

"Yes," Teo said slowly, "I know him."

She waited but nothing more was forthcoming. What was going on here? Teo Sanlucar didn't even seem very surprised by her visit. She had a sudden horrible feeling that he knew precisely what had happened to Cecily.

"Well, do you know where my sister is?" Her voice rang shrilly in her own ears.

The man looked at her carefully, his eyes narrowed in deliberation. "No," he said after a long moment, "or I would tell you."

He was lying, she thought instantly, irrationally. She felt stifled by the miasma of confusion and deceit that seemed to fill the small room. Why wasn't he telling the truth? She tried to calm herself, to think logically, but her mind raged with questions.

"Well," he said finally, "I would hazard a guess that your sister ran off with Carlos Echeverria. But I'm sure there's nothing to worry about."

"Nothing to worry about? When we're supposed to be on a plane right now? When she's disappeared without leaving word and there are signs of a struggle in her apartment? If it were your sister, wouldn't you be worried, Professor Sanlucar?" Melanie stopped abruptly, fighting panic, then cleared her throat. "I'm really terribly upset. If you don't know where she is, do you think I should go to the police?"

His dark eyebrows drew together and Melanie thought she saw his hands tighten. "The *policía*? No, Miss Royce. This is merely a summer fling."

"I don't think so, begging your pardon, Professor Sanlucar. There *is* something going on here. Something concerning Carlos."

"You have not met Carlos?" he asked.

"No, but Cecily told me a little about him."

"A handsome young man. Very bright. A touch wild perhaps. Like your sister."

He was telling her nothing, evading the issue entirely. Did he think this was some kind of joke? "Where are they?" Melanie demanded. "You know where they've gone, don't you? I have to talk to Cecily."

"I think perhaps you'd best leave them alone. Your sister will hardly thank you for chasing her down. You are not, after all, her mother. Why don't you go home, Miss Royce, as you planned?"

"I'm not going anywhere without at least talking to her!" Melanie got up and leaned over the professor's desk.

"Please, don't upset yourself so. They've probably gone to Pamplona, to the *feria.* Everyone goes there this week. It's a grand event. The young people adore it." He met her gaze openly, his dark eyes probing hers deeply. Then he shrugged in a very Spanish gesture. "Carlos is a Basque. He could not miss the *feria.*"

"Then I'll go to Pamplona and find her!"

"An impossible task. The city is so full of people this week that without help, it is simply not possible to find someone among all the crowds. Especially for a stranger like yourself. Truly, you should go home and your sister will call you. Then think how foolish you'll feel that you went to all this trouble."

He rose and walked around his desk to stand over her. "Trust me, Miss Royce. I know these young people. They are thoughtless, but they mean no harm. Go home, Miss Royce," he said in a concerned voice.

Melanie stood up and straightened her shoulders. His nearness made her uncomfortable, but she forced herself to look him squarely in the eye. "I guess I'll just have to go to this Basque country of yours by myself. Without anyone's help. I'll find her. Believe me, I'll find her." She swung the strap of her purse firmly onto her shoulder. "And I think, *Professor*, that you are not telling me as much as you know. There's something strange here, I know there is, and I'm going to find out exactly what's going on!"

"I'm terribly sorry you would think such a thing of me. What could I possibly have to hide?" He spoke softly, spreading his hands in a gesture of innocence.

"I have no idea. But I'll find out. Thank you *so* much for your help," she said sarcastically. She turned to leave, then impulsively whirled around to face him again. "By the way, why were you watching us on the beach at Torremolinos?"

He removed his glasses; instantly Melanie sensed the uncanny energy, the power he discharged. She instinctively backed off a step.

He watched her closely for a moment, then said, "Why, protecting you, Miss Royce. What else?"

Chapter Four

Monday, July 5

Melanie drove north out of Madrid very early the next morning. She'd had to hire the car for an indefinite length of time and locate a map—a good one, as she was traveling alone and couldn't afford to get lost in the vast central region of Spain.

The Feria de Pamplona. A week-long festival—a fete— honoring San Fermín. Melanie had already learned from a travel agency in Madrid that there were no rooms to be had anywhere in the Pamplona area, just as Teo Sanlucar had warned her.

First it had taken her most of the previous afternoon to even find a travel agent working on Sunday. Then he'd had no success at reserving accommodation for her. "Lock your car and sleep in it," had been his final suggestion. *Swell.*

The sere rounded hills of the interior Iberian Peninsula fell away behind her as she drove. It was harsh unforgiving country. Every so often she passed through a small village nestled on a hillside, but the populated areas of the plateau were few and sparse.

To the north and east, the landscape began to alter subtly. There were more villages and the rolling hills grew greener; they were dotted with brush now. When she stopped for fuel and lunch at Soria, she could see the mountainous terrain in the distance, misted to a bluish hue. She took several pictures and delighted her hosts at the restaurant by including them in her photographs.

Very gradually the road began to rise after Soria. The hills gave way to green, steep-sided mountains covered with deciduous trees. Melanie drove through ancient villages of small stone houses whose walls were smooth and worn with age. She felt as though she were suspended in timelessness; these places, she thought, looked much the same as they had for the past hundred years. Old stone wells still sat in the village squares although they were no longer used. The faces of the women were seamed and their black, proud eyes followed Melanie as she drove slowly through their towns, making her feel an oddity among them: a woman traveling alone to some faceless destiny.

These Spanish women rarely traveled. Even in this day and age they were tied to their villages, their homes, their church. And Melanie felt their scornful black eyes on her as she drove into their vision, then past, then beyond.

She saw her first sign for Pamplona and sighed in relief. Her back ached and she was hungry again. She already knew about the lodging; would it be difficult to find a restaurant, as well?

From far off she could see the plateau of Pamplona. The great dark cathedral was outlined against the mountains that rose behind the city, each successive layer of hills mistier than the one before.

Pamplona. The capital city of Navarre, made famous by Hemingway's novel *The Sun Also Rises*. Melanie had read the book in high school but couldn't remember it very clearly. Something about bulls and wine—lots of wine—and Jake Barnes's hopeless love affair.

The moment she hit the outskirts of the city, she could feel the excitement, an explosion of emotion that swept everything before it even though the *feria* didn't actually begin until the next day. Yet the people were already gathering from everywhere. It was impossible to drive farther than the outlying streets, for the roads were thronged. Melanie finally found a place to park near the soccer stadium and locked her car, taking her camera and her heavy purse.

She began to walk toward the old city, jostled all the way by the *feria*-goers who were gearing up for the first day of the fiesta. The houses here were nestled close together. Above her, she saw flags of red, white and green— the Basque flag—draped from narrow windows. Anticipation hung in the air, as palpable as the heat.

And it was hot in Pamplona, all right. Perhaps the crowds made it seem hotter than it was, but even in the late afternoon, Melanie was covered in a fine sheen of perspiration.

She almost forgot why she had come. The folk dancing in the streets, the singing and the haunting rhythms of the hollow drums and the Basque flute were hypnotic enticements to let herself go. She felt a kindred thrill in spite of herself.

Hemingway. She was beginning to understand his zeal for this untamed place, for these proud, independent people. On the sides of buildings were posters of the bullfights: the handsomely clad matadors, the snorting wild-eyed beasts. There was one just like the poster they'd seen in the shop window in Torremolinos. It struck her that, in a strange way, she had come full circle. She remembered standing on the Carihuela, studying the poster, and it almost seemed that if she turned, Cecily would be there beside her saying, ''I love that one.'' But she was a world away; Cecily was missing and now Melanie stood alone on a street in Pamplona, blasted by sound and heat and people. She recalled the utter dissipation of Hemingway's Jake Barnes as she watched the crowds dancing and drinking and shouting with hysterical fervor. Despite her anxiety, her heart beat with the rhythm of the hollow drums.

"Vino! Señorita?" A bota bag was raised above her head and she drank, the warm red wine hissing into the back of her throat, dribbling down her chin and staining her white blouse. Melanie laughed, caught hopelessly in the lusty moment. The fiesta was truly a time apart, with no past and no future.

Occasionally a strange language caught her ear. Once she stopped and asked an English-speaking tourist what it was.

"Euskara," the young woman told her. "It's the Basques' word for their own language."

"I don't recognize a word of it," Melanie said.

"No one does, except them," the woman said simply. "As far as anyone knows, the language has no relation to any other. It's a real mystery."

"Someone should solve it," Melanie mused.

The central plaza, which was surrounded by dozens of hotels and cafés, was so crowded that she was forced to let the throng carry her in its flow. She could see a bandstand in the center of the plaza where men in white shirts and loose white trousers were playing a frenzied tune on guitars, to the overpowering encouragement of the people. She tried to take a picture but it was impossible, for she was wedged in the crowd, shoulder to shoulder, trapped. Finally she managed to break free and, spun off to one side, wound up nearly in the laps of some people sitting around a table at an outdoor restaurant.

"Excuse me!" Melanie gasped, but they only laughed and offered her a glass of wine. Eventually she disengaged herself and sought a safe—if still crammed—hotel lobby.

There were definitely no rooms to be had. *"Nada, señorita.* Nothing."

"A telephone?" Melanie inquired.

He pointed to a quieter corner of the narrow lobby. *"Teléfono."*

Of course she had to wait even to use the telephone book, and then when she finally had it in her hands she was crushed to see the list of Echeverrias in the book. There were hundreds of them. It was like looking up a Smith in the New York directory without knowing a first name or an address.

Apprehension gnawed at her, but Melanie pushed her fears to the back of her mind. Cecily was out there somewhere. She knew it. And if she waited, if she sat in one of the cafés long enough, surely Cecily would eventually come by.

She began to look for an empty seat. Finding a table by herself was out. There obviously were no private tables to be had, but a group of Australian students who saw her casting about graciously asked her to join them.

"It's great, isn't it?" asked one girl whose features were distinctive and generous, her smile bubbling with life.

"It's breathtaking," Melanie agreed.

She bought the group a carafe of wine and ordered some food: cheeses and fruits and lamb tidbits in oil and garlic. The students were grateful and eyed her traveler's checks longingly.

"*You* must have a room here," one of the young men said.

Melanie shook her head. "All the money in the world couldn't buy a room this week."

"So sleep in the soccer field," he suggested. "We're going to."

It was a grim prospect, but Melanie was starting to think she might not have any choice.

"You all alone?" the girl asked.

"Sort of. My sister is here but I've lost her."

"No wonder," threw in a handsome towhead.

Melanie sat there for what seemed like hours. Dusk began to settle over the plateau of Pamplona, moving in from the mountains and resting lightly on the festive city.

Young boys, dressed in the ubiquitous white, stood on brawnier shoulders and lit the street lamps.

"At least it's cooling off," Melanie observed. "It's much more humid here than in Madrid."

Her eyes began to ache from scanning the ever-moving throng in the plaza for a possible sight of Cecily. The din grew louder—impossible, but it did—and the drinking more ferocious. In spite of the meal, Melanie was definitely feeling lightheaded from the strong wine. Finally she couldn't stomach another drop and managed to get herself a soda and lime. It didn't help the throbbing in her temples in the least.

No wonder Hemingway had such an earthy reputation, she thought, and no wonder he wrote so convincingly about physical excess. He used to do this for an entire week!

"You know," said the towhead, "you'll never find your sister in this. Not unless she's looking for you."

"Well…" Melanie said, disheartened, "I just have to keep trying, don't I?"

The music from the bandstand was almost obscured now by the ever-increasing clamor from the hordes of milling revelers. Melanie's head was pounding. It seemed to her as if some invisible hand had pushed everyone's self-destruct button. Wild!

Her sister was out there somewhere in that crazed throng, perhaps only a few feet away. But it was becoming painfully clear to Melanie that her chances of finding Cecily in this madness were scant.

She was never sure, afterward, exactly what it was that caught her eye, that prompted recognition. The familiar outline of cheek and hair? Or perhaps it was the carriage, relaxed yet ever aware. In any case, he was there, moving along with the flow, passing in front of the café, his head appearing once, then again, among the masses.

She knew only one thing: there was the man who was her link to Cecily.

Melanie jumped to her feet, ignoring the surprised faces of her young companions. "Bye," she cried, snatching up her purse and her camera. She looked frantically through the throng, standing on tiptoe. Where was he? She pushed into the eddying crowd. "Pardon me. *Perdóname*," she kept saying, shoving through the tightly packed bodies, tapping the shoulders of a dozen men until they turned and looked at her quizzically or expectantly. It was always the wrong man. Oh, no! She'd lost him.

Melanie moved on, pushing by the slow-moving, sated carousers, edging around the groups that were standing still, forcing her way past the lines of dancers and drinkers. On and on.

It was like a dream in which she was rushing and everything else was in slow motion.

Where had he gone?

"*Vino!*" came a booming voice in her ear, "*Trinken! Beber*. Drink!"

Melanie felt a hand on her arm and turned, startled. "Let go of me!" she cried. "Please!"

He only threw back his big head and laughed lustily, drunkenly clutching her sleeve.

An inexplicable, claustrophobic panic engulfed her. And then suddenly there was a hand on her other arm and she pulled away desperately. Music crashed in her ears; the odor of wine and sweaty bodies assailed her sickeningly.

"Let *go* of me!" She managed to yank herself free from one of her captors.

"Melanie…"

She spun around to gape at the man still gripping her other arm. "It's *you*," she gasped.

"Come on," he said tugging gently at her wrist, "let's get out of this crowd."

As he led her from the central plaza, she felt fresh moist air caressing her skin. She began to breathe normally again, no longer so intimidated by the crush.

She finally stopped and disengaged her arm from his hand. It felt, strangely, as if she'd severed herself from a lifeline.

"Professor Sanlucar," she said, "why are you here? How did you find me?"

"It's Teo," he stated evenly. "So many questions, Melanie."

"But why?" she pressed, searching his face.

Teo Sanlucar shrugged eloquently. "There is nothing mysterious. I always come to the Feria de Pamplona."

"Okay. Fine," she breathed, "let's say I believe you…" He regarded her closely. "Then do you mind explaining how you just happened to walk directly in front of me like that?"

His finely sculpted lips parted in a wide, amused smile. "Mere coincidence."

There was no doubt in her mind that he was lying. She looked at him keenly, noting the way he stood there, the easy relaxed set of his shoulders, the self-assurance of his bearing. He was a man totally in control, a man who could look her directly in the eye and lie through his teeth.

She backed away from him slightly. "You were following me."

He laughed and the deep masculine timbre sent shock waves through her limbs. "We Basques are always looking for a lovely woman, Melanie. I am only too human."

She felt hot waves of embarrassment washing up her neck. What was he doing to her? What kind of game was he playing? "That's…a lie," she shot back. "That has nothing to do with why you followed me."

The laughter left his dark eyes abruptly. "Think what you will. But might I be so bold as to suggest that you should appreciate a sincere compliment for what it is?"

European men certainly had a way of jumping right in. Their unsubtle flattery and straightforward propositions discomfited Melanie right down to her toes.

"I have said too much." Teo cocked his head slightly

o one side. "You must forgive me. I will let you go on your way now. I have detained you long enough." He bowed, a mere nod of his head, but did not turn away to leave.

Sudden panic seized Melanie. "Wait," she whispered uncertainly. "Please, wait…"

She could see his dark raised brow and the thin, uncompromising set of his lips. It was all so ironic. She *couldn't* let him go. He was her link to Cecily and Carlos.

"Yes, Melanie?"

"I…well, couldn't I buy you a drink or something?"

"A drink, Melanie?"

Her reluctance to let him leave was painfully obvious. Humiliating. He probably figured she was trying to pick him up—the brazen *americana*. This was so awkward. Oh, why couldn't he make it easier for her? But then, Melanie suspected that he'd never intended to simply walk away.

"I really couldn't stand another drink," she admitted, breaking the silence. "Perhaps you would walk with me for a while?"

"Of course."

He took her arm gently—but possessively, she thought—and they walked the narrow, cobbled streets of Pamplona.

"What do you think of the Basque country?" Teo asked her.

"I haven't seen much. Just this…this…"

"Insanity?" he asked and she could hear the laughter in his voice. "The Basques play as hard as they work. We have a saying: 'To know how to live is to know enough.' Do you not think that is the best way?"

Melanie looked at him to see if he were teasing. "No, actually I prefer the golden mean prescribed by the ancient Greeks."

"A woman of her own mind."

"I hope so," she replied coolly.

"It has been said of us Basques that we are crusty in
dividualists, hard and independent. But the truth is we
only seek the leisure to enjoy ourselves," Teo said.

"Are you speaking for yourself?"

"Not entirely. You see, I am educated and my crust
has worn smooth. My father tells me I have grown soft.'

"Soft," Melanie repeated, recalling his lean brown
body on the beach.

"He also says I must prove my manhood by having
sons." And Teo smiled deliberately, tauntingly.

"Well, what's stopping you?" Melanie asked.

He shrugged, adroitly sidestepping a young man, who
staggered into their path. "The small question of morality
I have no wife."

"That should be easy enough to remedy."

"Not as easy as you might imagine, Melanie." His
voice was low and he bent his head so that she could hear
him above the din. She wondered why he was saying
these things to her. And all the while, as they walked
through the crowded streets, she searched for a glimpse
of Cecily.

He finally asked the question which had formed, unspoken, between them. "Where are you staying?"

She stopped and looked up into his eyes. "Well, I've
got a purse full of traveler's checks but no one seems to
want my money."

"I thought as much."

"Any suggestions?"

"Several. You could, naturally, sleep in your car."

"So I've been told."

"Thousands sleep in the soccer field."

She nodded wearily.

"Then there is a place... No. I would offend you by
suggesting it."

"Try me, Teo."

"My uncle, Esteban, has a lovely home some ten kil
ometers from the city."

"I couldn't."

"You most certainly could. In fact, if I were to tell him I left an *amiga*, a lady, on the streets at night and alone…" He spread his hands in mock shame.

"I really…"

"Allow me to persuade you, Melanie."

"I simply can't impose on your uncle. Imagine how mortified I would feel if I let you take me there and dump me on his doorstep…."

"I would be alongside you, Melanie. And my uncle is a very hospitable gentleman."

"And you?" she asked curiously. "Where will you stay?"

"At Esteban's, also. You see, my parents reside in Bilbao, close to the family business, and my sister lives with her husband up on the coast. And I myself, naturally, reside primarily in Madrid."

"You usually stay at your uncle's, then?"

"Always, when I am in the area." He studied her quietly for a moment. "You would, of course, have a room to yourself."

"Of course." Melanie looked away hastily.

"Then it is settled."

She suspected then that he had planned the whole thing—probably when she'd left his office in Madrid—but right now it didn't matter. He was absolutely correct. She'd be foolhardy to remain on the streets at night alone.

He'd said quite pointedly, a room of her own. Still, she hardly knew him…

Melanie searched his expressionless face for a moment. She decided that she could trust him not to lure her to this Esteban's house and then turn his hospitable offer into a sick little proposition. He considered himself too much of a gentleman, and he took his honor too seriously.

"Where is your car?" he asked.

"Out somewhere near the soccer field."

He smiled charmingly, "So you *had* thought of sleeping quarters."

"Sort of," Melanie admitted.

"We shall go get mine, then," he said, "and I'll drive you to yours and you can follow."

She was so exhausted that it sounded fine; at this point, she'd have settled for almost anything. And the next day she would be rested and could start the search for her sister all over again.

Teo Sanlucar. She ran his name through her mind. An enigmatic man. The link, Melanie still believed, to Cecily and her curious disappearance.

Melanie had been wondering whether to press him on the subject as they threaded their way toward the outlying streets. He had answers; she was sure of it. And yet he remained so politely closed, replying to whatever she said with very correct, one-line answers. "It is always hot during the *feria*." "Yes, the tourists come from many parts of Europe." And when she carefully, obliquely, mentioned her sister, he said only, "No, I have not had the pleasure of running into Cecily."

So smooth, so casual. Even the way he walked beside her, always allowing her to go first, his long-fingered hand at her back, on her elbow, was so—she searched her mind for the word—so intimate.

There was something nightmarish and yet alluring about the whole situation. This man inspired strangely contradictory emotions in her: she feared him, yet she was unaccountably attracted to him. How could she feel unnerved by his presence at the same moment as she felt warmed by the touch of his hand?

Melanie followed the lights of Teo's car away from the city. As they drove, fewer and fewer vehicles passed them. It was pitch-black, and patches of fog hung in the gullies and ravines along the winding road.

She had an impression of lush mountains on either side of the roadway—old mountains that were softly contoured by centuries of rain and wind. There were trees, gloomy, indistinct shapes, by the roadside. The unfamiliar landscape was eerie in the darkness and Melanie was thankful to see Teo's lights ahead of her. Strange, she reflected, going so quickly from the crush of Pamplona to the dark, deserted mountains.

Who was this uncle, Esteban Sanlucar? Where exactly was this lovely house of his? Was he acquainted with Carlos, too? Were they all somehow involved in Cecily's disappearance?

It was bewildering. Yet the facts stood clearly in Melanie's mind. Teo *had* been watching them on the beach, he knew this Carlos and he had "coincidentally" run into Melanie in Pamplona. He was watching her, all right, and he was somehow linked to Cecily's peculiar behavior. But was he merely Melanie's acquaintance and would-be protector, as he seemed to want her to believe, or was he there to keep her from uncovering a secret?

He would say, "So many questions, Melanie," then smile that infuriatingly charming smile of his.

Esteban's home turned out to be a large stone-and-stucco structure roofed with red tile and built against a magnificent hillside. It was impressive looking even at night, with its long, steep cobblestone drive ending at a circular lawn. There were granite steps leading up to a small veranda and the front door, which was guarded by a pair of stone lions.

Teo rapped on the door, then said to Melanie, "You will enjoy Esteban. He is very informal and well educated. His English is not quite as good as mine, but it is passable. He'll expect you not to stand on ceremony with him. Feel free to speak your mind."

"Oh, I will, I'm sure," she said.

Uncle Esteban was hardly the avuncular type. Only a few years Teo's senior—a late-life child, Melanie supposed—he epitomized European dignity and manners.

His silvering hair and finely chiseled features gave him

a distinguished appearance. He stood an inch or so taller than Teo's six-foot height and was dressed in a studiously casual manner: a pale blue dress shirt rolled twice at the cuffs, loose-fitting gray summer slacks wrinkled in just the right way, expensive Italian sandals.

When he shook Melanie's hand she saw first the manicure, then the family gold-seal ring. *Impeccable* described Esteban, from his personal grooming to his tasteful, gracious home.

"Allow a *dama* to wander the streets at night?" he gasped at Teo's explanation, "*señorita*, chivalry is not yet dead."

"I'm sure this is a terrible imposition…" Melanie began.

"Nonsense. Come in, come in." He turned to Teo. "Lucia is in Pamplona, so be a good boy and carry the *señorita*'s belongings to the south room." Then he said to Melanie, "I call him my little nephew, but he is not so little, is he? You follow him upstairs and have a nice, long bath. A nap, if you wish. Then we shall have supper—" He stopped himself. "I am so sorry. I have, how do you say it? a mental block. I always forget that the *americanos* dine early and retire early. If you prefer," he added courteously, "you may retire for the night."

"Oh, no," Melanie said, "a bath would be perfect. But I'll certainly be down again. Supper sounds like a wonderful idea."

"*Muy bien*—very good. Now go along and do relax. The *feria* is most exhausting."

Teo ushered Melanie into her room and opened the French doors to the balcony, letting in the cool and refreshing night air. "If you have need of anything, there is a rope over there—" he nodded to the corner of the spacious guest room "—just pull it and a bell will ring in the kitchen."

"Thank you," Melanie said, but somehow she couldn't

envision Teo or his gracious uncle rushing up the stairs
with buckets of hot water or silver trays of food.

"I shall see you below, then." He left the room and
disappeared down the long, dim hall.

I'm impressed, Melanie thought. Sure, her parents had
money—new money—but Esteban exuded that special
Old World wealth. And it was more than just money. The
house itself was hundreds of years old and so were the
elegant furnishings. As for his demeanor, it took centuries
of breeding and tradition to produce a man like Esteban
Sanlucar. Teo, too. Although Teo, she decided, lived in
the twentieth century. Esteban, she suspected, was more
traditional.

What had he said? "Chivalry is not dead."

She lazed in the blue-tiled bath adjoining her room for
what seemed an indecent length of time but kept reassuring herself that here, things were done at a slower pace.
Her hosts expected her to have a leisurely bath, so it
would have been inappropriate to shower quickly and rush
down the stairs.

She swept her hair into a neat chignon and fastened it
with a silver clasp that had belonged to her grandmother.
She wore the dress Cecily had so liked, the dress she'd
worn to the restaurant that last evening in Torremolinos,
the melon and rust crepe that displayed her back.

She wandered out onto the balcony off her bedroom
and breathed the sweet scent of the misty night. Her headache was gone and she felt oddly relaxed. Reluctantly she
walked back in and checked her camera—habit—put her
purse in a bottom dresser drawer—also habit—then closed
the bedroom door behind her.

Both men rose to greet her as Melanie entered the large
living room that was decorated with tiles and rugs in
muted earth tones. The furniture was modern and comfortable, blending well with the carefully chosen antiques
scattered among sofas and chairs and polished tables.

"This is a beautiful room," Melanie said, glancing around her.

"Thank you," Esteban replied, taking her arm and showing her to an elegant couch, "I arranged it myself."

Melanie raised a brow. "You obviously have a flair for this kind of thing."

"Ah, yes. I enjoy it enormously. But sadly, I lack the time to refurbish the entire house. Always I am too busy."

"It's lovely like this," Melanie said with an honest smile.

"Can I get you a wine or a brandy?" Teo asked.

"A brandy, please."

Esteban seated himself beside her on the couch. "I very rarely go into town during the week of the *feria* any longer," he explained. "I find that it's an experience best savored by the young and, of course," he added with a light laugh, "your marvelous Hemingway."

"I was thinking that myself today."

"Ah, but you're still young enough…"

Teo brought the snifter and placed it on the table before Melanie. She could see that he had just showered, because his hair was damp and curling slightly above the collar of his fresh white shirt. He had shaved, too, she noticed, as she allowed the aroma of his shaving cream to drift into her senses.

"I'm terribly sorry to have to ask, Señor Sanlucar," Melanie said to Teo's uncle, "but I really must call my parents. They'll be worried. Of course, I'll charge the call to my credit card."

"You are welcome to use the telephone in my library. Teo, show her, please."

The library was small and cozy, obviously well used. A pile of papers sat on the desk next to an old-fashioned telephone. "Here you are. Take your time, Melanie," Teo said, "and here is your brandy. You forgot it." Then, discreetly, he left her there alone with the snifter in her hand. She could feel the satiny warmth of the glass where he had held it.

For a few moments she sat in the dim light, breathing deeply and trying to relax before she called her parents. Teo's and Esteban's voices drifted lazily toward her from the other room. Very distinguished, very male. Melanie again had the sensation she'd felt on the beach: that she'd become an actress in a drama she didn't understand. The lines were already written for her, but she didn't know how the story ended.

What had Teo told her in Madrid? He was her protector. She felt suddenly helpless, as if she'd lost control of the situation and was being led down blind alleys, one after the other.

The voices continued to float into the library, sometimes in simple conversation, sometimes lowered and hushed. Always in Basque. What were they saying?

Then, in her mind's eye, Melanie envisioned Teo, his finely chiseled face, those eyes, often warm and friendly, alluring yet sometimes unfathomable. What did Teo want of her; why had he invited her to his uncle's house? What was there about this man that attracted her yet at the same moment caused fear to lurch from the corners of her mind?

She shook off her uneasiness and looked at her watch. Eleven o'clock local time. That meant it would be late afternoon in Ohio. A good time to catch someone at home. While she waited for the call to go through, she sipped her brandy, grateful that Teo had remembered to bring it, and tried to translate the titles of the books on Esteban's shelves.

When the phone finally rang in her parents' home, it was Denise who answered—her mother's maid. "Denise? Is Mother or Dad there? What? Can you hear me now? Yes, I'm in Spain. Yes, still in Spain. No, I don't know. Denise, can you put Dad on? Thanks."

"Mel, what the hell is going on?"

"Dad, oh, it's good to hear you. Everyone okay?" She had to fight the impulse to blurt out the whole story. She had to bite her lip to hold it back.

"Sure, honey. Now your mother had a nice dinner planned, a few old friends, and you two didn't show up. And after the long flight back from Hong Kong, that wire almost prostrated her. What's up?"

"Dad, it's hard to explain. Cecily has this new boy-friend and he wanted her to see this special festival in Pamplona—that's where I am. And, well, it was all very sudden. You know Cecily."

"Where is that girl? I want to talk to her!"

"She's staying with a…a friend. She's not here right now."

"Where are you?"

"I'm with a…another friend of her boyfriend. Esteban Sanlucar. Spell it?" She spelled the name, gave the phone number. "That's where I'll be for a few days. He speaks English. No, Dad, I'm not sure—I'll call. Tell Mother not to plan any of her 'little' parties, okay?"

She hung up and swallowed hard. Then she downed a good stiff shot of the brandy. Lies, lies. She wondered abruptly if Teo had been listening. If he had, he must have been a bit surprised by her end of the conversation.

Returning to the living room was like entering a different world. From Cleveland to the Basque country, from her father's gruff, familiar Midwest twang to the cultured British English of Teo and Esteban.

"You reached them?" Teo asked.

"Yes, thank you."

"Good, good," Esteban said, beaming.

After that, they talked of everyday things—the role of King Carlos in Spain, worldwide inflation, finally her career as a free-lance photographer. Esteban spoke knowledgeably about photography and called it a form of artistry, which delighted Melanie. He made her promise to send him the layout of Ethiopia that she'd sold to *Life*.

Then they strolled into the dining room. Melanie was embarrassed to realize that Esteban had prepared a light supper for them while they'd bathed. He'd even set a handsome table, lit candles and turned on some soft classical music in the background.

"You've gone to so much trouble," Melanie said. "It's very kind of you."

"Ah," said Esteban as he helped Melanie into her chair, "I delight in playing the host. I enjoy cooking and, sadly, there are too few visitors with whom to share my meals."

Between the gazpacho and the salad, Teo caught Melanie's eye. "Would it be rude to explain your sudden visit to Pamplona to Esteban?"

Melanie shook her head but she suspected that Teo's uncle already knew.

"Melanie and her sister were scheduled to fly to the United States yesterday morning but Cecily—who was one of my students, Esteban—decided to change the plans—"

"What Teo means," Melanie broke in, "is that my sister has run off with a young Basque named Carlos Echeverria. And I'm afraid this Carlos is some sort of a crusader..."

"A crusader?" mused Esteban.

"Yes," Melanie clarified, "meaning that he's filled my sister's head full of horror stories—injustice, starving people, all the burdens of the world, Esteban. She kept talking about doing something worthwhile."

"It is merely youth speaking. Growing pains, my dear Melanie. Did we not have our own such worries in our early years?" He waved a hand in the air as if dismissing Melanie's fears.

"It was more than talk, Esteban," she added. "I'm certain Cecily has run off with this Carlos to plan something—"

"Plan something?" Teo interrupted.

"I don't know," Melanie admitted, almost saying *but I'll bet you do...*

"I think you should enjoy the *feria*," Teo said, "then, as I suggested in Madrid, fly home. Your sister will call you and all will be well."

Melanie sighed deeply. "I can't believe that everything is all right. I know my sister. I just wish I knew Carlos." She looked directly at Esteban. "Do you know Carlos Echeverria?"

Esteban's dark brows knitted together. It seemed to Melanie that he took too long to answer. "Perhaps. I cannot recall. There are so many Echeverrias in the Basque country."

"But Teo knows him," Melanie said, pinning Teo with a hard gaze. "Don't you?"

"You know that I do, Melanie."

"And are you acquainted with his family?"

For only an instant—or did she imagine it?—Teo's eyes met his uncle's in a meaningful glance. "I do not believe I know his family, Melanie."

They ate thinly sliced cold beef with béarnaise sauce and sautéed baby carrots, then for dessert, chilled raspberries. Melanie didn't mention the subject of Cecily's whereabouts again, as it was only too obvious that neither man was going to help her.

Why? she kept wondering. What did they know that was too secret or too dangerous to tell her? Or were the Sanlucars involved in Cecily's peculiar disappearance?

Somewhere a clock struck midnight. The candles burned low, and the dimming light veiled Esteban's and Teo's faces in flickering shadows. Outside the open French doors a fog rolled in, low to the earth, obscuring the mountainside. The room seemed moist and close. But as Melanie looked from one shadowed face to the other, she felt a singular chill.

Teo's eyes found hers and held them for a prolonged moment. She had the disquieting impression that he was reaching into her very soul, probing, willing her into submission. And yet he merely sat there, across the well-appointed table, the dim light dancing in those dark, worldly eyes.

She looked down at her hands but she could still feel his gaze on her, more poignant than a touch. Her heart pounded heavily and she tried in desperation to focus this strange, shadowed fear.

What were they hiding from her, these handsome distinguished men, these mysterious Basques?

Chapter Five

Tuesday, July 6

Melanie lay in the big, carved Spanish bed and felt sleep drain slowly and reluctantly from her body. Somewhere in the house a door opened and then closed. She rolled over and looked at her watch: six-thirty. Still early. Too early to do anything about Cecily.

Anxiety gnawed at her once more. Where was Cecily? How thoughtless and cruel of her to do this to her family! Or had she been taken somewhere against her will? Melanie rose and stretched, then padded across the big room to the French doors and opened them. Mist curled around the stone balustrade of the balcony. Low on the horizon, diffused sunlight attempted to penetrate the morning fog. As she watched, a bright spot of blue appeared and then widened into a patch of sunlit sky.

The humidity caressed her, causing her dark red hair to spring into curls. She stood there in her sheer nightgown and felt the cool moisture and watched the brilliant green hills emerge damply from the mist. It was the kind of place where fairy tales were born, where princesses were hidden and heroes came forth from fog-shrouded mountain paths, where dragons had their lairs and elves dug caves. Lovely and verdant and a little bit mysterious…

The sun was just striking her balcony, slanting through the treetops, touching the greenery with brightness. Melanie got her camera and checked the light meter. The haze would be hard to capture, but exquisite if she could manage it. She quickly took several pictures, aware that the light was already beginning to change and the enchantment would soon be lost. The blue hole in the sky was steadily enlarging. Then, suddenly, the mist was completely gone; day had arrived. The scene was no longer mythical, merely beautiful. Melanie turned back to her room.

Shaking off her whimsy, she began to get dressed. Something practical: white slacks, a cool cotton blouse in pale green. Today she would have to take some positive steps in the search for her sister. Teo seemed to want her to leave the whole problem of Cecily's disappearance alone. Why? Did he have something to hide? And why wouldn't he tell her everything he knew? Did he have some personal stake in this drama? Or was it merely his reticence that she misunderstood, mistrusted?

She pulled her hair into a ponytail and tied a green scarf around it, placed her camera in its case, hefted her big shoulder bag and stepped out into the hallway. It was very quiet; she suddenly felt a little uncertain. Like an intruder. She barely knew Teo. As for Esteban, he was a total stranger. Another dark-eyed Basque with the unmistakable stamp of the Sanlucar family on him. He and Teo could have been brothers.

The dining room was empty, but there was soft singing coming from the kitchen, an odd, plaintive song in a language that sounded totally alien to Melanie. Basque. She tentatively entered the enormous kitchen. At the far end, in front of the sink, was a woman, the singer. She was busy washing dishes, her song filling the room with a deep, mellow contralto.

"Perdóname," began Melanie. "Pardon me."

The woman turned. She smiled at Melanie. *"Buenos*

días, señorita.'' Then there was a string of Spanish that
Melanie could not follow. Eventually she learned that the
woman's name was Lucia, the Señores Sanlucar were
afuera—outside—and that *café* was ready if she wanted
any.

She walked out onto the lawn and saw a patio off the
dining room, to one side of the house. There it was quiet
and secluded, shaded by locust trees so that dappled fairy
light fell over the table and over the two dark-headed men
who sat in deep conversation, their heads close together.
As Melanie walked across the flagstoned patio, she heard
them speaking the same odd language as Lucia's song.
The same language she'd heard spoken, from time to time,
at the *feria*. Basque. To her, it sounded like a series of
clicks and *s*'s and *x*'s, as if the user were tapping his
tongue on the roof of his mouth.

"Good morning," she said. They both looked up and
glanced at each other in what seemed to her a private
manner. Then Esteban Sanlucar's face split into a wide
smile. He rose quickly and came to her.

"You have found us," he said. "Come, sit down. A
lovely morning, is it not?"

"Yes, lovely." Melanie sat in the chair that Esteban
held out for her.

"Buenos días, Melanie," Teo said softly. "Did you
sleep well?"

"Yes, thank you," she replied.

"I wondered… I happened to step out onto my balcony
this morning and saw you."

She looked down at the flagstones, placing her purse
and her camera bag at her feet. "I was taking pictures."
But she should have put on her robe first, she thought.

"It escapes me," he said, "the word for such a morning as this."

"Evocative," she said aloud.

"Perhaps. Or perhaps merely lovely."

Lucia came out of the kitchen then, coffeepot in hand. Esteban spoke to his maid in that same strange tongue.

"Teo, that's Basque, isn't it?" Melanie could not resist asking.

"Yes, my dear Melanie, that is our native language. An ancient tongue, unrelated to any other known language. It has baffled language buffs for hundreds of years, being like Hebrew in its pronouns and like some American Indian languages in its verbs."

"How odd."

"Yes, sometimes I think the archetypal Basque individualist concocted it thousands of years ago just to frustrate the modern philologists."

Esteban chuckled. "Is that what you teach your students?" he chided.

"Ah, no. I teach them that Basques are the core of the Iberian character, and that they are the best administrators in Spain and the most vigorous among Spaniards."

"Without prejudice," Melanie said, straight-faced despite her amusement.

"But of course," Teo said, his eyebrows raised mockingly.

He was charming when he wanted to be, Melanie thought. And so handsome in the golden morning light. The planes of his cheeks glistened a little from his morning shave. His eyes were so dark—almost black—that they reflected tiny points of light. Reflected much more than they revealed.

His smile was sincere, yet it held a certain tension. What was Teo Sanlucar hiding? And why, she asked herself, why? Why had he been in Torremolinos? Had he really been there to "protect" her, as he'd stated so enigmatically? And protect her from what?

But, somehow, she knew she'd get no answer if she asked.

Lucia was pouring hot, fragrant coffee into Melanie's cup, all the while chattering away in Basque.

"What would you like to eat, Lucia wishes to know," Esteban broke in. "She speaks Spanish, of course, but since you did not seem to understand her..." He shrugged.

"I'm terribly sorry. My French is better," Melanie said. "But please," she continued, smiling at Lucia, "tell her something simple—a roll, toast. I never eat much in the morning."

Lucia seemed to disapprove very strongly of light breakfasts. Even Melanie could translate her frown and admonishing finger.

"She repeats an old Basque saying: if the belly does not eat, the belly itself will fail," Teo explained. "And she goes on to tell us that you are much too skinny and therefore you will never have healthy babies." His expression was completely serious, though Melanie could have sworn there was a teasing hint of irony in his voice. "But never mind—Lucia has many old-fashioned ideas. I myself am a modern man. I expect you are eminently capable of bearing a dozen fine children. If you should want to." Then he did smile, an open, boyish grin that lit up his face.

Esteban rattled off something in Basque and they both chuckled. "How rude of us," Teo said, "not including you in on our private jokes. But, you realize, Basque is an odd language, impossible to translate. Its meanings are inherent in innuendo and oblique references. What my uncle just said was, literally, 'a fine wine can come in a dusty bottle' but I assure you we do not equate you with a dusty bottle."

"I would prefer to discuss my sister, if you don't mind," Melanie said brusquely. "I really do appreciate your hospitality, but I'm terribly worried. I'd like to go into Pamplona this morning for the running of the bulls. I understand it's an important event and I thought... Well, if, as you said, Carlos is such an avid fan of the *feria*, perhaps they'll be there."

Teo was silent for a moment. "It *is* quite a spectacle, but the crowds are terrible, worse than yesterday. I doubt you'd ever be able to find your sister."

"I must try. I have to do something. At least it's a starting point." She was aware, again, of the two men exchanging glances. "If you'll just give me directions back to Pamplona. It was dark last night—"

"I couldn't possibly allow you to go alone," Teo said curtly.

"I don't need a baby-sitter, Teo. I'm sure I can manage on my own."

Esteban asked something in Basque. Teo answered quickly. Esteban laughed. "Baby-sitter," he repeated. "I was not familiar with the word. But, Teo, you must accompany Señorita Royce. I could not permit her to wander around with those *locos*, those crazies, all by herself. The Fiesta de San Fermín is, how shall I say, *feroz*, wild."

"I lived through a bombing in Beirut and famine in Ethiopia, Señor Sanlucar. I doubt if Pamplona can touch me," Melanie said quietly.

"Nevertheless, I offer my services," said Teo, raising a hand to forestall her objections. "I insist. Although I pray that we run into nothing more than a few drunken revelers," he said with a thin smile. "I am too much the coward to face war and famine. I admire your courage greatly, Melanie."

He was deliberately baiting her. She was sure of it. Not to mention the fact that he was being patronizing. And thoroughly aggravating. Melanie closed her mouth tightly and felt the hot color rise to her cheeks. She finished her coffee and nibbled on the roll Lucia had brought her. Esteban excused himself. Teo remained seated, elbows on the arms of his chair, hands folded, his dark eyes fixed on her. Eventually he said, "I apologize. That was unnecessary. But you had just insulted my role as your host. Basque men are notoriously touchy, you know."

"I didn't know."

"Come, let us not quarrel. You are worried about your sister. I am worried about you. We have something in common."

"You're worried about me? That's ridiculous. Look, you wouldn't be my host if I hadn't practically thrown myself on you. I mean, you were forced to take me in. So there's no reason for you to worry about me and my problems, is there?"

"One is never forced to offer hospitality to a damsel in distress. It comes naturally." He was teasing again.

Melanie stood. "I'm going to Pamplona now. I appreciate your kindness. I'll try to find a hotel room today."

He still sat there, his chin resting on his clasped hands. "You'll find no room in Pamplona this week, Melanie. And I *am* going with you."

Melanie did not like this feeling that Teo was manipulating her. She stood there weighing his offer—no, she thought, he'd issued a directive. On the one hand, her emotional response was to walk out on him, away from this lovely hidden home, to strike out once again on her own. On the other hand, she could view her predicament as an opportunity in several ways. He was providing lodging where there was none. He *did* know this Basque country, whereas she was a stranger. And he was somehow linked to Cecily's disappearance; Melanie would wager plenty on that.

She made an effort to give in gracefully. "I would be a fool to say no to such a kind offer," she said smoothly. "Shall we go?"

He nodded; one dark brow was raised very slightly.

Teo drove them in his white Mercedes convertible. He skillfully negotiated the winding, twisting roads through the hills to Pamplona, and Melanie found herself relaxing, asking a dozen questions out of sheer curiosity.

"Your uncle. Is he married?"

"No," Teo said, laughing. "He is far too fond of his life of luxury. Women adore him. He is a lawyer, you know, the legal counsel for my family's business in Bilbao. He travels between my parents' apartment there and his country home.''

"What is your family's business?"

"Parts for ships. Heavy machinery. I am the black sheep of the family, scorning the exciting world of business for the ivory tower of academe.''

"The Basques. Haven't I read about problems here? Unrest. I'm not sure…''

"Ah, yes, the eternal problem. The first thing you must know is that a Basque does not see himself as a Spaniard. We are a different race, if you will. Other Basques live across the border in the French Pyrenees. We consider it an insult to lump us in with the Spanish.'' He glanced at Melanie, noticing her intent expression. "The Basques are a stiff-necked and stubborn people. They want autonomy from the government in Madrid. Frankly, I try to stay out of politics. From time to time, however, there is violence. It all stems from the Civil War back in '36 when the Basques fought against Franco. They lost and were punished. It is said a Basque never forgets and perhaps that is correct. But things are improving these days. Shall we not speak of something more interesting?''

"The running of the bulls. Tell me about it.''

"An ancient custom dating from 1591. The fiesta is actually a religious festival honoring San Fermín, the patron saint of Pamplona, who was a martyr. Nowhere in the world will you see quite the same spectacle. One main street is barricaded off down its entire length, from pens at the edge of town to the bullring. The six bulls who will fight in the afternoon's *corrida* are run from their corrals to the bullring, accompanied by steers to keep them calm. The men who wish to run in front of them must arrive on the scene very early—''

"Have you ever done it?'' Melanie interrupted.

"When I was young. Many times. Now there are so many tourists that come for the thrill—one hundred thousand, they say—that very few Spanish, I think, are included in the running anymore. The men run in front of the bulls along the street. When they reach the bullring, the *toros* are put into pens, but then the fun begins. Young heifers that are brought into the arena at night are set loose in the ring. They are not so terribly dangerous because their horns are padded, but they are in a fine panic with the noise and the crowds.''

''I don't really understand why anyone would do it,'' Melanie said pensively. ''It's dangerous, isn't it?''

He shrugged eloquently, his eyes never leaving the unpredictable curves. ''Sometimes. The bull will only attack you if he is forced to. He is frightened himself. You see that scar?'' He held up his forearm, and Melanie saw the ropy white line running from elbow to wrist.

''A bull did that?'' she breathed.

''Yes. I was careless once. But it was merely a scratch. I was lucky.''

''*Lucky.*''

''Last year some were killed, many were hurt. Bruises and broken bones and so on. It only makes more come the following year. To test themselves.''

''Crazy.''

''Yes, I agree. But there is an attraction that has *fuerza*, force. You will see.''

Just then, as they rounded a curve, they came upon a shepherd with his flock of sheep milling right in the middle of the road. Teo jammed on his brakes, automatically putting out an arm to keep Melanie from lurching forward.

''Good Lord!'' Melanie gasped.

''Sorry,'' Teo said. ''A frequent hazard on these back roads.''

He withdrew his arm, but she could still feel its phantom touch across her chest.

She glanced at his profile as he drove. A strong nose, the beautifully modeled curve of his lips, a firm jawline. And those lovely slim brown hands on the steering wheel.

Hands that could belong to an artist, a lover... She stopped her thoughts abruptly and snapped her attention back to the winding road.

It was becoming hot as Teo drove through the outskirts of Pamplona, a depressing area of ugly factories and dirty smoke stacks. It seemed hard to believe that a valiant and exciting tradition took place in such a grimy, nondescript town. Then suddenly they were in the old city, among the narrow cobbled streets, overhanging balconies and dim, smoky cafés she remembered from the day before.

Teo certainly knew his way around. The previous afternoon, Melanie had not had any choice but to leave her car on the outskirts of Pamplona. Now she watched amazed as Teo simply darted down an alley close to the central plaza, pulled his Mercedes into a tiny opening between some trash cans and turned off the key.

"Will your car be safe here?" she couldn't help asking.

"Safer here than on a street."

They walked down the dank alley and out onto a street. Someone immediately bumped into her.

"*Vino?*" slurred a freckle-faced, obviously American young man.

"A little early, isn't it?" Melanie said dryly.

"Hey, an American! Hey, honey, come on, let's go watch the bulls! Hey, wait up, Johnny!" And he ran off, following his friend.

"You see?" Teo came to her side. "They've all got their noses bent with wine, as the Basques would say. You *do* need my protection."

"From the likes of him?" Melanie smiled. "He was ready to pass out. He only needed a little push."

"Come, then—it will start soon. We must find a place to watch. Luckily I know someone who has a balcony right over the street where the bulls run."

They pushed their way through the crowds, Melanie clutching her camera while Teo ran interference. Actually she was glad of his presence. She'd thought it crowded the day before, but as Teo had warned, it didn't compare to this, the first official day of the *feria* and the running of the bulls. All the shoving, cheering, howling young people were crammed in one area, everyone vying for a spot from which to view the spectacle. Young people from every nation on earth had gathered here, all with their bota bags and rucksacks, all looking for adventure, excitement, memories. And Melanie automatically searched every sunburned, sweating face, in case it was Cecily's.

The noise was mindless, the heat and press of the crowd relentless. Melanie wanted to take some pictures, but like the day before in the plaza, she couldn't even raise her arms.

"Are you all right?" Teo shouted once. She could only smile and nod, holding on to his hand for dear life, trudging along behind him. Finally he pulled her into a doorway and the crowd surged by them in all its elemental energy, like a river in flood leaving behind a couple of sticks.

"Wow!" Melanie said.

"Do you see what Esteban and I meant?"

"Do I ever! Yesterday was calm compared to this."

"Come, you must meet Jaime, then we will go up to his balcony."

They were in a long narrow bar. One wall was lined with bottles; a few empty tables were scattered along the other. Jaime came out of the dimness and greeted Teo effusively, in Basque. They spoke for a time, then he turned to Melanie. "*Señorita, bienvenido*, welcome." He shook her hand, grinning, the sweat oily on his dark face. "You unnerstan'?"

"Yes, *sí, gracias*." She nodded and smiled. "Thank you."

"*Que bonita*," Jaime said in an aside to Teo.

She understood that much. "Pretty," he'd called her. Did all Spanish—or Basque—men need to comment on a woman's looks?

Teo led her to the back of the long room, to a flight of rickety steps. She looked at him questioningly. He nodded. Upstairs was obviously Jaime's living room, very neat and formal, with doilies on every chair and a crucifix on one wall. The room was heavily curtained, dim and cool. A muted roar filled the air—the crowd outside—then came a cannon blast.

''Quick, they're starting.'' The bellow rose, reaching a crescendo, a communal howling, a fever pitch of joy and excitement. Teo pushed aside the curtains and opened the doors onto a narrow balcony.

The hot air hit Melanie's face like a blow. The noise pounded in her ears. The crowd clustered along the high wooden barricades that lined the street below. People spilled off balconies and rooftops, hung onto signs, crouched on posts, clung by fingers to walls. Everywhere there were bodies wedged together, screaming, mouths open, faces alight, tense with expectation.

Her camera! Quickly Melanie pulled it out, checked the light meter, focused. There! That dark, slim man with his mouth open. Over there! A threesome, perched like birds on the top of the barricade, handing their bota bag around, their faces red with sunburn, their throats working to swallow the stream of wine.

Then the roar escalated. It didn't seem possible, but still the clamor swelled and throbbed and beat at the air. Faces turned. Melanie thought she felt the floor tremble, vibrate. Then, from the head of the long street they came—the men, the runners, all of them dressed in white with red sashes and red kerchiefs. They ran, jammed together in the narrow, walled-off street, panting, sweating. Hundreds of them, looking over their shoulders to see how close the bulls were.

They ran as the crowd shrieked its pleasure, its fear, its adoration. They fled their deadly enemy, their lover, their best friend, the bull. They ran because they had to feel it, once in their lives at least, to face real, pulsating, snorting

physical danger, to prove themselves. And they ran because there were a hundred men—five hundred—behind
them, panting, grunting, scrambling, shot through with the
same terror and frenzy and thrill.

They were past in a rush of white and red and flying
feet. Then the bulls: huge black and brown backs, heaving, shining with sweat, flashing slim legs and ugly
hooked horns with tips honed to wicked points. Thrusting,
tossing heads on thick muscular necks, the staccato of
galloping feet, the smell of animal flesh and hot angry
bull breath, the glint of a wicked red eye.

They were gone in a whirlwind of dust and sweat smell
and the receding thunder of their passing. Melanie found
herself taking a deep breath; she was sure she had not
breathed while they were below her. But she had taken
pictures, dozens of pictures. She let her camera hang on
its strap and felt her hands tremble in reaction.

Now she knew what they were talking about. Now she
knew why men came from all over for this insanity, why
they gathered and drank and danced and caroused and
donned their pure white and their crimson sashes, why
they ran before the bulls.

"You see?" Teo was whispering in her ear and the
touch of his warm breath on her hair made her shudder
with a thrill of exquisite delight. Something about the raw
force of the spectacle she'd just seen made Melanie
acutely sensitive to sensation. Her belly flip-flopped and
the hairs on her neck rose at Teo's closeness. She was
suddenly aware that his hand rested lightly on her waist,
and she moved uneasily away, trying to put some distance
between them.

"Now we must go to the bullring and watch the fun,"
Teo was saying, his voice intimate and disturbing in her
ear, "for there must be a release after all that intensity."

Everyone was going to the bullring. Teo and Melanie
were swept along with the crowd, more and more tightly
packed together, until they burst through the entranceway

and found seats in the huge circular amphitheater. The sun was higher, burning in a pellucid Spanish sky, reflecting off the bright red barrier wall that encircled the floor of the arena. Red, Melanie wondered, to distract the bull? But the bulls were gone now, replaced by several small heifers with padded horns. The men were there, dirtier and sweatier now, grinning broadly. They ran and dodged the cows and jumped out of the way while the crowd screamed its approval.

"What are they doing that for?" Melanie asked.

"To let everyone get a chance at the game, I suppose. An opportunity to prove one's valor without the danger of serious harm. Comic relief, I guess one might say."

"They're not the same as the steers that ran with the bulls, are they?"

"No, these are young cows, *novillas*. Actually they're more excitable than steers."

"And where did they come from?" Melanie asked.

"They keep them in a pen at night. See, over there?" He pointed to a slatted gate across the arena. "They are removed in the afternoon, of course, before the bullfight. It would make them too nervous, you see."

Melanie scanned the crowd through her lens, taking pictures. And looking for Cecily's face. There were so many young girls—thousands, tens of thousands. It seemed hopeless, but still she searched.

"Enough?" asked Teo finally.

"Yes," Melanie said with a laugh, "I've had enough. And you say this goes on every day?"

"Every day this week."

"I'm not sure I could handle it again." She rose and followed him from the stands.

They walked back through the emptied streets, shaded by the graceful old buildings.

"If you are really determined to experience local color you must stay for the *corrida* this afternoon."

"The bullfight?"

"Yes, I believe there are some good men today."

"I couldn't presume upon you…"

"But Esteban made me promise, you recall. You are my guest."

"I would love to see one. Is it terribly gory?" She shuddered a little.

"I will not lie. Yes, gory and brave and wonderful and sad."

"I suppose I should. And perhaps Cecily…"

"Perhaps…"

She had run out of film by the time they stopped for a cool drink in one of the cafés on the central plaza. The place was called the Iruña, Teo told her. The same café where Hemingway had sat and drunk absinthe. As she expected, every seat was filled and they shared a table with a young German couple who sat entwined, totally immersed in each other. They made Melanie unaccountably nervous.

Teo was attentive, a perfect gentleman. She wondered if she were wrong to distrust him so intensely; she even admitted to herself that she'd needed him to get around this crazy, crowded carnival. And yet…there remained that tension about him, something beneath the surface, secretive and shadowed. His eyes were always on her, studying, watching. She felt the power of his maleness, the attraction of his self-containment, the lure of his dark beauty.

And then her worry would surface again, and she would see him only as a means of searching for Cecily.

"We'll get some film after we relax a minute. You Americans…" He smiled and took her hand in his. "You must learn to relax."

Relax! Every muscle in her body snapped taut, every nerve tingled. She wanted to snatch her hand away but couldn't.

"Let's go get my film," she suggested quickly, "before I forget."

"If you insist," he said.

It was better to be moving, to be doing something. She took an inordinately long time to choose her film, even though she knew exactly what she wanted. Then she looked over the souvenirs and chose some postcards. Teo stood by patiently, his arms folded, his expression blank. She wondered if he were bored but she didn't care—he'd asked for guard duty, hadn't he?

Later in the afternoon Teo took her to Los Tres Reyes for a meal. It was an elegant place specializing in Basque seafood dishes—fish and shellfish cooked in garlic and spices and oil. Strong, heady fare accompanied by harsh red wine and fresh crusty bread. Hungry and exhausted, she ate ravenously.

Teo watched her, apparently enjoying her pleasure. "Lucia would be proud of you."

"So would my mother. Oh, I do feel better, though." It was cool in the restaurant; the service was excellent and unobtrusive. "And please, let me pay for this meal. I'm accepting your hospitality, after all; please let me do this in return."

He waved a hand in dismissal. "There will be no bill. A cousin of mine owns this restaurant. Otherwise, believe me, I would allow you to." He grinned, an eyebrow tilting rakishly. "It costs a small fortune."

MELANIE'S FIRST LOOK at a matador in all his gilded glory dashed her false notions of a bloodthirsty, arrogant Spaniard who fought only for the notoriety.

He stood in the center of the ring, proud and composed, bowing to the crowd. He was dressed in his *traje de luces*, the traditional "suit of lights." She focused her lens on him and saw his dark eyes and was amazed at the sad tranquillity emanating from them.

"Is he afraid?" she asked Teo.

"Of course, but his fear is mingled with compassion. For the bull, as huge and terrifying as he seems, is also afraid. The matador has great love and respect ·for his adversary.''

''Beauty and the beast,'' Melanie murmured to herself.

The actual bullfight was a carefully orchestrated dance. An undeniable power and excitement clung to every movement of matador and bull. The sadness was there— and the splendor. The mass of humanity jammed in the bullring cheered, roaring their pleasure and their love for the man and the bull, glorying in the courage and the death.

It was cruel, yes, Melanie thought, but there was also something splendid about it, appealing to some primitive human need to sacrifice the most beautiful and the best.

There were three bulls, Teo told her, one to each magnificently arrayed matador; this was followed by a break, then three more bulls. Melanie was surprised; she'd always thought a bullfight consisted of one man and one bull.

Teo pointed out the matador's moves; the crowd sighed and groaned and shouted ''Olé'' with each close sweep of the deadly horns, so she knew how often the bright, graceful figure was in danger.

''Are you enjoying yourself?'' he asked her after the first bull, bending close so that she could hear him.

She turned toward him and saw his eyes fastened on her face. Just then the crowd roared its bold praise; the sound held Melanie breathless and rocked her. Deep in Teo's dark, sober gaze she sensed a question, a question that lured her, enthralled her. The hot Spanish sun beat on her head as she swayed in the fathomless ocean of sound. His eyes, his deep compelling voice. The scent of dust and red wine and sweat.

Answer. She must answer. Tearing her eyes from his, she said, inanely, ''Oh, yes. Exciting, isn't it?'' and felt her heart begin to beat again, heavy and turgid in her breast.

The second bull thundered into the ring, leaving his

hoofprints in the pale sand. He stood there, full of power, his big head swinging around, searching. Again Melanie thought: how could a puny man face *that*?

Teo told her about watching the bull, not the horse, when the bull charged the picador. He told her what to watch for as the picador thrust his lance, placing it with accuracy and precision. She began to understand the rit-ualized actions. He explained it all to her so that the thing became less a show with random, incomprehensible hor-rors and more a planned series of events leading to a definite end.

She began to see how a good matador controlled the bull smoothly, effortlessly, and how the bulls differed in temperament, some difficult, some easy. She realized that there was a purity of line to the good matadors' move-ments, with no wasted motion, no needless gesture.

The fourth bull was the best. He was fierce and ugly, a piebald color, mottled black and white. He had courage and pride and Melanie could see that the matador loved him, even spoke to him quietly, intimately, like a lover.

The bull charged and crooked his horns again and again, never tiring. He was a noble creature. Every move he made was perfect. The crowd screamed its apprecia-tion, adoring the man, the bull, the pair of them.

"Ah," Teo said, "this one is special. A Murcia bull. The best."

The matador's short cape swirled, drawing the piebald bull into its power. The crowd screamed at a particularly close miss. The matador deliberately turned his back on the bull and strutted away, but the bull merely waited, like a gentleman, for his opponent to turn once more.

The duel began anew.

The time for the killing came. The matador had his sword hidden in his cape, ready to plunge it deep into the animal's thick neck. The bull pawed the ground, un-daunted. The crowd shrieked as one voice, splitting the air, torn between their reverence for the bull and their admiration for the man. Melanie had never heard anything like it.

The matador walked to the center of the ring and raised his sword, asking the crowd. They screamed in answer, the stands vibrating to the volume. "I don't believe it," Teo breathed. "They will save this bull. He is too noble to die. I have not seen this—ever."

"You mean the matador won't kill this bull?"

"The crowd requires his life," Teo said, shaking his head in amazement.

And this time, instead of being dragged out a carcass, the bull trotted out proudly, his head high, his ropelike tail flicking.

Melanie was utterly drained as they left the *corrida*, carried along by the thousands who poured out of the bullring as water drains when a plug is pulled.

Still she scanned the faces, always watching for Cecily. She wanted to ask Teo, to demand the truth that she was positive he knew, but she was somehow afraid. They rounded the corner into the central plaza. People were taking up their café seats again, to sip a late-afternoon aperitif, to discuss their astonishment at the unexpected outcome of the *corrida*, and to watch the teeming hordes of humanity, a show in itself. Then, much later, they would dine in the warm darkness, drink too much wine, begin the party all over again. And in the morning there was the running of the bulls once more.... An endless cycle of pleasure and thrill and the primitive purging of emotion.

Melanie's head snapped up. Her hand instinctively touched Teo's arm; immediately he halted. "There!" she cried. "Do you see her?" She strained to see through the crowd. Yes! It was Cecily's dark red hair.

"What is it?" Teo asked.

"Cecily!" And she left him, running, pushing past people, her camera bag and purse flapping and banging against her side.

"Cecily!" she cried, following the apparition, but it was like moving underwater, slowed down and horribly frustrating. She thought the auburn head turned once; there was a flash of her sister's profile. But then it was gone, swallowed up in the enormous maw of the crowd.

She stopped finally, panting and drenched in sweat. A group of young people, arms linked, singing and dancing some silly dance of their own, jostled her as they came by. She felt foolish, bereft, near tears. A sense of futility washed over her.

And then Teo was at her side, his hand on her arm.

"Oh, Teo, it was Cecily! But I lost her. How am I ever going to find her? What's going on?" Her voice was strained and desperate.

He said nothing but gently pushed her loosened hair back from her face. After a while, he spoke, his voice low and soft. "Come, Melanie, you need to rest a bit. This whole thing has been too much for you."

He led her to a café. Miraculously, there was a table and instantly a glass was set before her.

"Try some. It's Izarra, a Basque drink," he said. "Made from mountain flowers."

She wanted to put her head down on the table and cry, but her pride stopped her. Instead she swallowed some of the Izarra; it tasted strong, not at all like flowers, but it slid easily down her throat. Soon a warm glow tingled in her stomach.

"I'll take you home," Teo said.

"Then you won't help me find my sister."

"I can't, Melanie. Truly I can't. I don't know where she is."

"Do you believe I saw her just now?"

He shrugged. "Perhaps you did."

"Why would she run off like that? She knows I'd worry."

"Love—or passion—sometimes twists a person's mind," he suggested.

"You mean Carlos? But still, she could have told me. There's something terribly wrong, I know it."

"There's no more you can do tonight, Melanie. Perhaps tomorrow…"

"I'm going to keep looking," she said fiercely. "Everyone seems to want me to leave it alone, but I won't! I'll find her!"

Teo said nothing, but gave her an odd, worried look. Did he think she was insane to be so stubborn? Maybe she was. Maybe Cecily was only enjoying herself, stealing a moment of pleasure in the turbulent thrill of the *feria*.

The evening shadows grew weak and thin across the plaza. Lights winked on. Once again, young boys stood on the toughened shoulders of older men and lighted the street lamps. People staggered by, arm in arm, laughing, dancing. And always, everywhere, bota bags were upraised, squirting the warm red wine down a thousand parched throats. Somewhere a flute played, a winsome trilling from the shadows.

"*Hola*, Teo," she heard a man say.

"Sevé." Teo nodded at a short, burly man who stood by the table. He wore the white and red of the bull runners, a black beret on his head.

She expected Teo to introduce her, but he didn't; she might not have been there at all. The men spoke Basque. There was a kind of intensity about the narrow-eyed stranger that made Melanie sit up straight. He spoke quickly, quietly, with an urgency that seemed out of keeping with the festivities surrounding them.

Teo answered coolly, his eyes hard and brilliant, and the man seemed to become argumentative. Once, Melanie was sure she heard the name Carlos.

The barrel-chested man—this Sevé—said something staccato and final—a curse?—and disappeared back into the mob as suddenly as he'd appeared.

"Who was that?" Melanie asked.

"An acquaintance."

"He knows something about my sister," she said quietly.

Teo looked at her sharply. "Why would you say that?"

"I heard the name Carlos. Look, Teo, I'm not stupid. There's something dangerous going on—I can *feel* it— and I'm afraid. Where's my sister?"

His inscrutable gaze held hers for a tense moment, then fell away. A muscle ticked in his smooth-shaven cheek. "As God is my witness, Melanie, I would tell you if I could."

Chapter Six

Wednesday, July 7

Melanie drifted slowly out of a deep sleep to the insistent noise of someone knocking at her door.

"Just a minute," she called groggily.

It was barely dawn and the room was still dark as she pulled on a loose kimono and went to the door.

"Excuse the intrusion, Melanie," said Estaban, who was also clad in a robe. "There is an overseas telephone call for you. Your father."

He'd switched on the hall lights and she could see his sleep-tousled hair and his eyes, heavy lidded and solemn looking.

"My father?" she repeated, following him down the long corridor.

"I took the call in my bedroom," he explained, "but you may use the telephone in the library."

She hastened down the long staircase, her bare feet sticky on the cold, polished floor.

Why would her father be calling? He knew it was early morning in Spain. A terrible apprehension gripped her.

She located the telephone and picked up the receiver. "Dad? It's Melanie."

The line crackled. "Melanie—" his voice emerged as

if from a tunnel "—something dreadful has happened. I hope this is a joke…"

The apprehension bloomed into full-blown fear and she sank weakly onto the leather couch. "What's happened? Is it Mother?"

"No, it's about a call I had from Spain a few minutes ago. It was a man and he said… Hell, Melanie, he said your sister is being held… He wants me to wire half a million dollars to Pamplona!"

"Oh, my Lord," Melanie breathed. "Oh, no!"

"Is this some sort of sick joke?"

She tried desperately to collect her thoughts. "A joke? No. I don't…think so, Dad."

"How in hell… I can't…"

"Let me think, please, Dad." She was faintly aware of Esteban and Teo entering the room, switching on lamps. And then Teo walked over and sat on the edge of the couch, close beside her. "Dad," she managed, "what else did this man say?"

"He had me write down instructions and told me if I called the police, Cecily… Dear God in Heaven, he threatened to kill her!"

A great sob welled up in Melanie's chest. Teo must have seen her reaction because he put a gentle hand on her shoulder.

"Melanie?" her father said. "The man also knew *you* were there."

"How…" she began but then she knew. Carlos must have seen her in the plaza yesterday when she had tried to follow Cecily.

"Are you sure this isn't some crazy prank? I mean…"

"It's no prank." She paused. "What in heaven's name are we going to do?"

There was silence on the hissing line for a minute. "I'm going to pay it," he said gravely, his voice tense with fear. "I have to."

"Dad, I need to think."

"There's no time. Listen, I'll wire the money to this bank in Pamplona. You'd better get a pencil…"

Melanie took a deep, quavering breath and looked over at Teo. "Can you get me a pencil and paper?"

He rose swiftly to his feet and walked to the desk, opening a drawer, taking out a notepad and pen. Somewhere in Melanie's mind, she registered that Teo was half dressed, wearing only a pair of white slacks—no shirt. She had an impression of his broad, naked back, of the muscles across his shoulders. "Here," he said quietly, handing her the items.

Melanie wrote down the name of the bank and the location of a telephone booth in Pamplona where she was to be at 5:00 P.M. on Friday evening, July 9. Unconsciously, she underlined the date over and over while her father talked.

"The man expects you to have the money when he calls you at that phone booth," he explained. "It's only two days, Melanie. I'm going to have a hell of a time…"

"Can you get that much money, Dad?"

"Yes. But it'll be hard."

"My Lord," Melanie whispered. "I'm so sorry."

"Your mother and I are terribly worried about you, too, honey. You've got to do *exactly* what this man tells you. I'd fly over immediately to help you, Mel, but I can't leave your mother alone like this and she couldn't collect that much money without my help, anyway. I'm stuck here."

"I understand. Is Mother all right?"

"Neither of us is all right," he replied in a strained voice. "I'm dreadfully worried and I'm sorry you have to be the one to face this…"

"I'll be okay," she said miserably, feeling alone and far from home as the fear tightened in her stomach.

"You just make darn good and sure you're careful, Mel. This Esteban—is he trustworthy? How well do you know him?" Her father's voice was taut with worry.

Oh, how she wanted to blurt the whole thing out, her fear, her suspicions, the awful spot she was in. But she couldn't; she knew Esteban and Teo were listening. Cecily's life depended on her.

"He's fine, Dad. Yes, very trustworthy. I'm in good hands."

"And let me tell you something else. If there's even a *hint* that this isn't going as planned, I'll call Interpol and the CIA and King Juan Carlos, if I have to!"

"It'll work out, I know it, Dad. Just don't do anything yet, until I have the money," she said hastily. "I can handle everything at this end."

"That's our girl. And, Melanie, I'll keep you informed about the money transfer."

"Okay."

"I wish I was there with you."

"I know."

"Just keep your head, and for the love of God, honey, don't do anything foolish."

"I won't."

"And remember it's only money. We'll all pray for Cecily."

"Yes...pray."

"Goodbye, Melanie. I'll be in touch as soon as I've arranged the transfer."

"Goodbye, Dad. Tell Mother everything is going to be all right. And...I love you both."

When she'd hung up, Melanie sat for a long while, holding back tears and staring blindly into the distance. How had Cecily got herself involved with this...this kidnapper? Oh, there was no doubt that Carlos was involved in the kidnapping; he might even have been the caller. Her stupid, *stupid* sister!

A painful sob escaped Melanie's throat and then the tears came. She finally hid her face in her hands and cried miserably, without restraint. She was vaguely aware that

Teo and Esteban were trying to comfort her, but she could barely understand what they were saying.

"I was afraid of something..." Teo said before his words trailed away.

"My dear, sweet woman." Esteban placed a warm hand on her other shoulder.

She suddenly wanted to scream. They were both too close, touching her, crowding her, offering her words of comfort. How dared they!

Feeling claustrophobic, Melanie jumped to her feet. "I'm all right," she said quickly. "Please...I'm all right." She paced the library floor, back and forth, back and forth. The room was silent except for the ticking of the clock and the muffled sound of Melanie's footsteps; no one spoke.

Melanie stopped pacing suddenly and turned, looking carefully from Esteban to Teo. On their faces she saw lines of deep concern, but neither of the men seemed truly surprised.

What had Teo said a few minutes earlier? "I was afraid of something..." She stared at him.

Eventually they moved to the kitchen, while Esteban brewed a pot of coffee. Melanie was calmer but still unable to focus her thoughts. What a mess Cecily had created! And now, all Melanie had was a scribbled note with a time and a place to receive a telephone call and her father's assurance that he would have the money at the Banco de Navarra as fast as possible.

What if he didn't?

But Melanie would face that grim prospect if and when it happened.

She looked up from her place at the polished table. Teo was speaking to his uncle in a low voice while taking coffee cups down from a cupboard. It struck her again and again: they weren't in the least bit surprised by the news of Cecily's kidnapping. They'd known...

She studied the men. Tall and distinguished Esteban

with his silvering hair and his expensive, burgundy satin robe. Teo, the portrait of masculinity, his naked sun-dark back toward her, his white trousers, loosely fitting over his lean hips, the long taper of his legs. They had both known. She was convinced of it, though how they'd known, or why, Melanie could not say. But that didn't matter. The only important thing was that these dashing Basques were at the root of Cecily's horrible situation.

She recalled with complete and sudden clarity Teo talking harshly to the stranger in the café yesterday. Sevé. That was his name. She'd bet he was involved in this. Maybe it had even been Sevé and not Carlos on the phone to her father. How many were involved? Half a million dollars was a lot of money....

Teo handed her a cup of coffee and sat down on the other side of the table.

"It's shocking," he began.

"Yes," Melanie said, her golden-flecked eyes watching him cautiously. Her brain was beginning to function, grudgingly. She could not put the suspicions out of her head. She tried to keep her wits about her, tried not to spit out the accusations that were on her tongue. But she could test him. Of course she could. "Teo," she said, her voice still breaking slightly, "I think I should call in the police."

She could see a dark shadow cross his handsome features. He turned his head, met his uncle's intent gaze for a moment, then looked back at Melanie. "No. You must not call the police."

"Why, Teo?" she pressed.

He regarded her closely for a long moment, his liquid brown eyes traveling her face; uneasily, she pulled the loose folds of her rosy silk kimono together at the throat. "I believe you told us that your father was instructed to keep the authorities out of this matter."

"He was," she said in a controlled voice. "But of course the kidnappers would say that."

"Naturally."

"I simply think the Guardia Civil could handle this better than I."

"Perhaps. But you would be taking a great risk with your sister's life, Melanie."

"How? I can even give them Carlos Echeverria's name."

"You are so very certain Carlos is involved?"

"Quite certain. And I think—" she started to say, but prudently she cut herself off.

Teo's dark brow was drawn into a deep frown. His eyes never left her, and Melanie felt a spurt of fear. She'd said too much.

"What do you think?" Teo asked with deliberate calm.

Melanie stared down at her folded hands. "Nothing."

"I see." He sat silently for a time. Finally he said, "If you believe Carlos is involved, you obviously assume that Cecily is being held by Basques. In that case, to contact the police would be very dangerous, indeed." He paused, then reached across the table as if to place his hand over hers. But Melanie quickly picked up her coffee cup, avoiding his touch. Teo shrugged eloquently. "So be it," he said. "The issue is this. The Guardia Civil and the Basques have long been enemies. Trust me in this. And believe me, the Basques have ears everywhere. Call it an intelligence network, if you will. Whatever. But rest assured, if you should contact the police, word will spread throughout the city as if on wings. It is clear that this man means business. I would not cross him, Melanie Royce."

"Teo is correct," Esteban put in. "Be this man terrorist or a member of a known violent faction or even if he is working on his own, such a move on your part would be too great a risk."

Melanie sat very still. "I understand what you're saying." She glanced from one to the other. "Only too well."

"Then you will not contact the authorities," Teo said.

"No, I won't." Melanie lied. She knew that she would not call them at present, but as for the future… She would just have to wait and see.

She finally disengaged herself from their observation and returned to the solitude of her bedroom. Nevertheless, she suspected that Teo would not let her stray too far from his watchful eye.

She was a prisoner in a strange land. She was completely out of her element, yet she couldn't leave, no matter how much she wanted to. The day before, she'd been hypnotized by the magic of the *feria*, the running of the bulls, the powerful and eloquently beautiful bullfights, the moments with Teo under the cloudless Spanish sky. She'd submitted, half willingly, to the thrill of primitive emotions, to the strange enchantment she felt in Teo's presence. Now she was a captive of that same lure, but the mood had turned sinister and ugly. How could she have let herself be touched by Teo, be charmed by his soft words, be held spellbound by the fascination of his dark eyes? *How?*

She took a shower, unnecessarily; she'd showered the night before. She walked out onto her balcony and gulped deep breaths of air, then strode angrily back into her bedroom. Her cell. She sat on her bed and tried to comb her damp hair but tears, hot and stinging, came to her eyes. She cried until she was exhausted with it, then slowly she got up, and slowly began to dress.

Wearing tan slacks and a loose, dark green shirt, Melanie finally reappeared downstairs. She needed to get away, to think by herself. It was unbearable to be constantly under guard, so to speak. She'd drive into Pamplona, anywhere, and think out this whole confused mess on her own.

"You're going where?" Teo exclaimed when Melanie defiantly announced her intention.

"For a drive. Perhaps to Pamplona. I'm not sure."

He came to his feet. "Well, I am sure, Melanie. It is enough that Cecily is in danger."

"Am I your prisoner?" she demanded outright.

"Certainly not." His tone was wounded and tinged with anger.

"Then let me go without an argument."

"I cannot."

Melanie drew in a breath of frustration. "I'm going for a walk, Teo. I've got to be by myself."

He strode over to where Melanie stood. "You must be careful." And she could almost believe the concern in his deep voice. Almost.

"Just don't crowd me, Teo," Melanie said deliberately, then turned and walked away from him, like a child rebelliously disobeying a too-strict parent.

She went in no particular direction. It didn't matter. But she did stay away from the winding road and walked instead along the ridge of a sloping meadow far above the valley's basin.

Beyond her on the slanting lea, goats and sheep were grazing, but she could see no shepherd. Somewhere in the distance, however, a dog barked occasionally.

It was lovely, serene country. There were stands of tall fir, their prickly needles thickly covering the ground, and intermingled with the firs, Melanie saw oaks and some kind of ash tree. It was damp and cool in the meadow; a light morning mist still hung in the ravines and twisted under trees.

From the hillside she could look out over a series of mountains that climbed away from her, one overlapping the other. Far off, on the crest of a hill, stood an old castle with turrets and towers. An enchanted castle. Melanie thought of ancient times, when the Spanish of Navarra fought the invading Moors from Africa. Perhaps, long ago, an armor-clad knight had come out of that castle on his great steed to ride among the hills, to make war on his enemies. She could almost envision the warrior, the sun glinting off his helmet and shield.

And then centuries later, these hills had seen the Spanish Civil War. Hemingway's Robert Jordan in *For Whom the Bell Tolls* had roamed these Basque forests, rifle in hand, his young face windburned, his feet moving noiselessly in his rope sandals.

Robert Jordan had made love to the beautiful shaven-headed girl, Maria, in a place like this, under a blanket. Her mind stopped dead at the inadvertent thought. Why had she thought of that? But she could almost see them in her mind's eye—the American guerrilla and the girl, Maria. They'd been so happy during their brief idyll.

But Robert Jordan had given up his life on the prickly floor of a forest like the one right over there, trying to save this land for its people.

A proud and secretive land.

And to Melanie, a land now filled with shadows and faceless fears.

Cecily. She had to think about her sister's predicament. Should she go to the police? Of course the kidnappers had instructed Oscar Royce to do no such thing. Of course Teo and Esteban backed them up. But Melanie *could* give the police the name of Carlos Echeverria.

She stood at the point where the meadow touched the forest. She looked down into the valley below and saw a narrow, twisting river, the summer sun white on the rushing water. She took a few pictures.

Where was Cecily? In Pamplona, roped to a chair in some dingy, dark room? Or in the mountains somewhere? Were her abductors feeding her, allowing her to go to the bathroom?

And then Teo Sanlucar's face superimposed itself upon the ghastly images. A darkly handsome face with those beautifully sculpted features and the strong, square jaw. It was difficult to believe the worst of him, but more and more she felt that she had no choice. It hurt, because

Melanie had to admit that Teo Sanlucar was beginning to obsess her.

Eventually Melanie turned, her exploration finished, and began heading back toward Esteban's. Back to her jail.

It was as if the valley narrowed as she walked, as if the house summoned her against her will. She couldn't bear it. Everything was too close, pressing on her mind and her body. It had to stop. She would confront Teo and Esteban. Both of them. Oh, she'd be careful for she couldn't let them know how much she suspected. But they had to stop…guarding her.

Her legs were tired from the downhill hike by the time she reached the house. Yet she did feel slightly better. Getting away for a couple of hours had been the right thing to do. And she knew that, somehow or other, she was going to rescue Cecily. She would dance their dance, do whatever it took, but Melanie was not going to let anything happen to her sister.

She saw that Teo was breakfasting on the patio. She walked directly to him.

He stood up in one fluid movement. "Melanie," he said, "I'm glad you are back. We were becoming worried."

"You needn't have concerned yourself."

"Where did you go for so long a time?"

"Teo, look," she began.

"Sit down, please, Melanie. I did not mean to pressure you."

Melanie sighed and sank wearily into the wrought-iron chair that Teo held for her. "I took a walk up into the hills. It was lovely."

"Yes. The quiet forests. They are lovely." He passed her a basket of rolls. "Do you feel better now?"

"How can I feel better when Cecily is being held somewhere? Probably starving…" She eyed the basket warily. "I don't even feel like eating."

"Of course not. But you must."

He was being so infuriatingly reasonable. His attitude only served to heighten Melanie's already aroused temper. "Will you stop doing that?"

"What, Melanie?" Teo sat forward, leaning his elbows on the table, and in his habitual manner he clasped his hands and rested his chin on them.

"Stop...stop patronizing me!"

"I apologize—"

"And stop apologizing!" She knew her behavior was hardly that of a grateful guest, *But let's face it,* Melanie reminded herself, she was more prisoner than guest.

"Would you prefer," he said slowly then, "that I be blunt with you?"

"Yes." Her gaze snapped around to his.

"All right. My uncle and I have decided that you must leave the Basque country and go back to Madrid. From there you can fly to the States—"

"You and Esteban have decided! You're joking, of course." She smiled at him disdainfully.

He looked at her with somber eyes. "I make no jest of this, Melanie. Every minute you remain here is dangerous for you. These men—"

"Men," she fired back at him. "How would you know that there's more than one?"

"I make the assumption only. This man, if you will, must be desperate to have kidnapped your sister. What if he thought two hostages better than one?"

"You forget one thing. Who would take him his money?"

Teo shook his head. "Melanie...Melanie," he whispered gently, "you are so blind. Don't you think he already knows that you stay here with us? Can't you see that he merely has to instruct me or my uncle to make delivery of the ransom?"

"Anything is possible," Melanie said carefully.

"Then fly back to your family where it is safe."

And get out of your way, she thought. "No. I'm staying. And frankly, Teo, if I could find a room anywhere in Pamplona, I would leave this house instantly."

He looked as if she had physically slapped him. "Are we such ogres. Do you really believe we mean you harm?"

She didn't answer, didn't meet his eyes, but her lips closed in a firm line.

"Yes? Well then, Señorita Royce, you are a fool."

Melanie rose to her feet. "Now that we each know where the other stands, Professor Sanlucar, I think I'll take my leave." She began walking across the verdant lawn. Then, as if his stare were a hand pressing at her back, she turned to look at him, to catch the expression of fury she expected to find on his face.

Yet he merely sat, quiet and unmoving. He was watching her, yes, but there was no malice or anger in his eyes. Instead, he looked at her with a kind of wistful regret.

Chapter Seven

Wednesday, July 7

He found her later that afternoon on a nearby hillside, taking pictures of a flock of sheep and the young Basque shepherd boy who guarded them.

"Melanie," she heard him say, and as she turned her head toward his voice, she saw that he was walking up the hill toward her—a stranger really, a straight slim dark man with a handsome face and unreadable eyes.

"Checking up on me?" she asked sarcastically, putting the lens cap on her camera, her concentration gone.

He ignored her question. "I want to apologize for speaking so harshly to you earlier. I was worried about you. I still am."

"Don't start in on me again. There's nothing to discuss. I'm staying."

"*Bueno*...good, so that is settled then. But you cannot be left alone to worry so much. There is nothing you can do until Friday evening. Please, let me make amends for my bad temper."

Slowly and deliberately, Melanie put the camera in its case without answering. When she'd finally finished, she looked up at him and said sarcastically, "And just how do you propose to do that? I'm not exactly in the mood for dining and dancing."

"I thought I would take you into Pamplona. There are many diversions there, things that might cause you to for-get—for a time."

"That's hardly likely," she said with studied coolness.

"But there is nothing you can do. Waiting is a hard thing," he said gently, "and sometimes a friend can help."

She stared at him. "A friend? Are you my friend, Teo? I hardly know you."

There was not a flicker of change in his face; the black eyes were calm, the mouth unsmiling. "Yes, Melanie, I am your friend. Believe me, please."

His voice was convincing and Melanie felt torn be-tween her desire to believe him and her decision to dis-trust him. He seemed sincerely concerned and yet...there was so much he wasn't telling her, so much hidden behind the facade of gentility and good manners.

"Well, do you give your consent?" he asked.

She turned away from him and began to walk down the hill, angry at her own weakness, her impulsive attraction to this man. Angry at his insistence. "To what?" she asked. "Another tour of Pamplona? Another friend's bal-cony and cousin's restaurant? Should I be impressed?"

She was aware of him falling into step with her. She walked faster. His hand touched her arm then, bringing her to a stop. She refused to face him, however, and stood there with her head down, her shoulders tense.

"You are angry with me. A very American anger. Very open. A Spanish woman would hide her temper," he said pensively.

"I am not in any mood to hide my temper, Teo. Why don't you level with me?"

"Level with you. I like that. Do not the cowboys say that?"

"Amusing," she said dryly, still not looking up.

''Come into Pamplona with me,'' he urged softly. ''I will show you our cathedral. Fifteenth-century. You might find some marvelous pictures.''

At last she looked up into his face. He was smiling down at her, like a doting parent amused by his child's temper tantrum.

''Teo,'' she sighed, ''I'm really not in the mood.''

His lean dark hand cupped her chin and tilted her face up to his. ''Moods can change.''

''Please...'' She didn't know what she meant exactly, what she was asking, but his face was so close, his hand so warm and strong on her skin. She could smell the faint aroma of his after-shave. His eyelashes were black as ink and very long. The sun glinted off one smoothly shaved, finely molded cheek. She tried to pull away but his touch left her in a kind of paralysis. For one sudden, dizzy, horrifying moment she thought he was going to kiss her. Panic and wonder burst within her. It struck Melanie shamefully—she wanted Teo to take her in his arms, to hold her and kiss her and make love to her. She wanted to feel those long-fingered hands on her flesh, stroking her hips and molding her breasts, preparing her in every way for love.

Yes, she was aching for this man. And she knew that he could tell. Her gaze was still locked with his: her breathing was shallow, as if a fist were squeezing her lungs, constricting them. He wasn't the dark, shadow-filled man she had thought him to be. No, Teo was kind and sincere and caring. Warm. Hadn't he shown that side to her many times already?

But he didn't kiss her. He released her and she stepped back, shaken.

''You will come to Pamplona, then?'' he asked.

''Yes,'' she said breathlessly. ''I'll come.''

He drove expertly, taking the curves with perfect timing. She could not help but notice the sinews in his arm tightening as he shifted, or the bulge of his thigh muscle under his pearl-gray slacks as he pressed the accelerator and the brake. Her awareness of his beauty and her re-action to his nearness made her feel furious with herself again. He was a stranger, a Basque, somehow involved in Cecily's kidnapping. She must keep her distance from him. Yet she had the impression that he was deliberately forcing his presence on her. She wondered why he was being so kind, so attentive. What did he want from her?

As usual, the streets were filled with crowds. The same people, their faces slack with wine, still grinning, shout-ing, laughing. But now it seemed like a sleazy carnival to Melanie, a city of sideshows, grotesque and almost re-pulsive. Her constant, gnawing worry about Cecily was too strong a counterpoint to the joviality she saw around her. The bota bags were repeatedly raised to greedy mouths. The dancers moved with wild, lewd gestures, their faces distorted as the sun beat on them mercilessly. Yet somewhere, Cecily was being held, perhaps tortured or hurt...

"Try to forget," Teo said.

She merely looked at him and shook her head silently. They walked down a narrow street; deftly he shielded her from the worst of the revelers, as if he understood her pain. She felt stifled and panicky, her whole world stum-bling toward destruction. What to do? Where to go? Whom to trust?

It suddenly seemed to Melanie that there were police-men everywhere, on every corner and walking down the streets in pairs, ever vigilant during this week of craziness. The Guardia Civil. Everyone had heard of them—a para-military police force, controlled from Madrid, uniformed in green with black patent-leather hats and tall boots. The ultimate symbol of strict law and order.

Did she dare go up to one and tell her story? Could they help? Somehow she sensed that Teo would never allow it—but what if she managed to steal away? Then she recalled his warning. If Cecily's kidnappers found out, if there was one slip, her sister would be dead. No, she couldn't take the chance. Another pair of policemen came by just then, so close she could have touched them as they passed her in the narrow, ancient street. She only had to put out a hand or call to them. But they were already gone, their boots thumping away from her, out of reach.

"The cathedral," Teo said.

She looked up at it, a huge brown mass, thick and solid in the Spanish style. Not graceful like French cathedrals or stately like English ones, but with the strength of piety in its very walls. She automatically readied her camera, automatically chose angles and composed her shots. She took a few pictures; Teo seemed to expect her to. But her heart wasn't in it.

Inside it was dark and the pillars seemed to ascend endlessly. People knelt before candles in the cool hush. Incense wafted in the air, reminding her that San Fermín was a religious festival, too.

Teo pointed out the huge leaded-glass windows. Silently, she prayed for Cecily's safety. Somehow the atmosphere allowed her to do that, even though she wasn't Catholic.

And then Teo knelt down for a few minutes and bowed his head in prayer. Melanie waited in the rear of the church, studying him, thinking about him. She acknowledged to herself that he was a very complex being, an intelligent man, sensitive and gentle. There was no denying it. Whatever his involvement in this mess, whatever his reasons for keeping the truth from Melanie, he was nevertheless filled with concern for her and Cecily. But the contradiction between what Melanie assumed about Teo's actions and the impressions she had of his character and his feelings, refused to give her peace.

Finally he was beside her once more, his compelling eyes soft in the dimness, his mouth curving into a friendly smile. "I hope I did not keep you waiting too long?"

She shook her head. "No. The cathedral is lovely. I feel peaceful in here."

"I do, too." Then he took her hand for a moment and squeezed it tenderly. "I am certain peace will be yours again, Melanie," he said, "when your sister's ordeal is over."

"When it's over," Melanie whispered, desperately longing to believe Teo. Longing to believe that it would soon be over. Her thoughts were with Cecily, when Teo raised her hand to his lips, catching her by surprise. Suddenly she was in the grip of pure sensation, alone in the dim sanctuary with Teo, his mouth touching her hand, sending tingling waves up her arm. For a moment, she wished she could simply give herself up to his strength. For a moment, she let herself believe that this man could become her lover, that she could find love and peace and trust with him.

He lowered her hand but did not release it. She felt his warmth surging through her and yet his touch conveyed something else now, a reluctance, a hesitancy not present before. His mind was pulling away from her; she could see it in his eyes. And then, for an instant, she saw pain there but he covered it quickly, smiling down at Melanie, squeezing her hand once more.

"Shall we go?" he asked quietly.

"I think we should," was all she could reply, and then he released her and she felt almost as though a safety line had been severed.

When they emerged into the bright sunlight and heat, the atmosphere took Melanie's breath away. The noise was overwhelming, the music harsh and relentless.

"Something to drink?" Teo suggested.

"Is there someplace quiet?" she asked ruefully.

"Quiet is only relative in Pamplona this week," he said with a laugh. He took her back to Jaime's bar. They sat toward the rear, in the dimness, and she sipped on soda water while Teo had a beer. Jaime spoke to him across the nearly empty bar. "It is quiet at this hour," Teo said, "but later Jaime will be very busy."

They were served tiny plates of *tapas*, Spanish hors d'oeuvres. Normally one ate them standing up at the bar, but Jaime honored his old friend. There were a dozen delicacies: squid and octopus, tiny smoked shrimp, cheese and bread cubes, olives and marinated vegetables.

"You must have a decent meal," Teo said. "This is not enough."

"No, please, I'm fine. I couldn't eat—really, I couldn't."

He ordered something for himself and Jaime served him, then sat down and helped himself to the bread, talking and chewing. He murmured something close to Teo's ear, all the while grinning at Melanie. And then some other comment, this time in Basque.

"He says you are as pretty as a star," Teo translated. "I can only agree."

"What else did he say?"

"It is untranslatable." Teo smiled maddeningly.

The bar began to fill up. A group of American girls were herded in by two young Spaniards. The girls were being plied with wine and the *feria* week's specialty—a sheep's head, roasted whole. The girls shrieked and laughed and delicately picked meat off the skull. Melanie shrank back in her corner; she couldn't bear to talk to them.

"Please, can we go?" Melanie whispered. "Can we go back to Esteban's?"

"But of course."

Jaime bowed them out, grinning and chattering. Teo guided her through the streets quickly; she was glad for the strength of his hand on her back. The streets were like a nightmare to her: too hot, too crowded, too wild with self-indulgent debauchery. The cries and music and laughter tore at her; the colors and faces streamed together into

a terrible blur. She realized abruptly that her eyes were
filled with tears.

They finally reached Teo's car, and as he held the door
open for her she ducked thankfully inside. To be cool and
quiet once more, to be able to think...

"Are you all right?" he asked with concern, sliding
into the driver's seat.

She was digging in her purse for a tissue, embarrassed,
unable to speak. Hysteria welled up inside her. She could
do nothing but shake her head.

"Here." Quietly he handed her a clean handkerchief.

She pressed it to her eyes and wiped her sweat-
dampened neck and blew her nose. "Thanks," she managed.

"My poor little lost American. I'm so sorry you had to
become involved in this thing. You should be safe at
home in, where did you say? Ohio." He took the handkerchief from her hand and with a clean, dry corner
dabbed at her forehead and upper lip. "You need to rest.
I was wrong to bring you to the city. I thought perhaps it
would help." He leaned over her, so close that she could
see the whorls his whiskers made on his smooth tanned
cheek.

"I'm okay now. It was just the heat, really."

He put the top down on his sporty car and drove slowly,
so that the wind cooled her cheeks and fanned her hair.
She leaned her head back and closed her eyes, feeling the
hysteria fade. The money would arrive, she would deliver
it and Cecily would be freed. Very simple. She could do
it. And when Cecily was safe she would walk boldly into
the headquarters of the Guardia Civil and tell them everything. Even about Teo and Esteban Sanlucar. Until
then, she would bide her time and wait and not arouse
their suspicions. She could do it if she had to.

Esteban was gone for the evening, Lucia told Teo. She
had prepared dinner and would return at nine to serve
them. Esteban had insisted.

"But I feel like I'm causing so much trouble," Melanie protested.

"Not at all," Teo replied gravely.

She sank into a chair on the cool patio and accepted a brandy from Teo. It made her feel relaxed and a bit disjointed.

"Better?" he asked.

"Yes, thank you."

"Try not to worry about your sister. She will be fine. Your father will send the money and then they will release her."

"Do you know the story of the Lindbergh baby's kidnapping?" Melanie asked, leaning her chin on one hand. "They found him dead after they'd paid the ransom. I keep thinking about that. Don't kidnappers usually kill their victims? Even when they're paid?"

"Melanie, you must not think such things."

She continued stubbornly. "I seem to remember some statistics I read somewhere. Most kidnap victims—I can't recall the exact number—are killed. No matter what you do."

"That will not happen, Melanie, believe me. The men who have your sister want money, not blood."

"How do you know?" Melanie's eyes swung around to meet his; her tone sharpened. "Do you know who has her?"

"Of course not. I am merely guessing. I am attempting to relieve your anxiety."

But she looked at him searchingly. Was he lying?

The sun slipped deep into a valley beyond them. Long golden strands of light filtered through the tall mossy trees lining Esteban's patio; crickets chirped in the freshly mown grass and the earth smelled damp and fertile. Everywhere Melanie looked she saw serenity; in spite of her anxiety and depression, she saw the profound beauty, the enchantment of this land. How differently she might have viewed it if…if what? If she were sitting on the patio that evening with a close friend, a lover perhaps?

She stared down into her brandy glass, absently twisting it in her fingers, lightly sloshing the amber liquid against the curved crystal sides. The brandy, the glass tabletop, the walls of Esteban's house all glowed with the gold of the setting sun. She looked up into Teo's eyes. They too were gilded. And as always, he was watching her.

She took a long bath that evening, trying to soak away the desperation and the fear that hounded her. She dozed off in the bathtub, then jerked awake to the image of someone, some indistinct figure, pointing a gun at Cecily's head. Melanie thrust the picture of a cowering Cecily from her mind and quickly stepped out of the cooling water.

She dressed in a white skirt and turquoise blouse and wound her hair up into a knot. Her face in the mirror was pale, washed out by the bright blouse, shadowed under the eyes. Her freckles stood out sickly against the whiteness of her skin. But what did it matter?

She found Teo in the living room, reading a magazine. He wore his glasses, which somehow made him seem milder, less dangerous. She remembered having the same reaction that last night in Torremolinos, at the restaurant.

He removed the glasses and stood up. "You look lovely."

"I look like a hag," she replied scornfully.

"Never."

He was elegantly dressed in pleated white linen pants, a white shirt open at the throat and a beige nubby silk sports coat. She was forcefully reminded that he belonged to an ancient culture, one that was at its peak when America was a wilderness. A man who was utterly foreign to her yet in a curious way, familiar. She couldn't explain it, but she felt that something bound them together.

The table was set perfectly, even to the candles that

flickered and touched the silver and glass and china with points of light.

"All this just for us?" she asked. "We could eat in the kitchen, for goodness' sake."

"Esteban would be scandalized," Teo said, smiling.

There was soup, then *calamare en su tinta*, squid in its own ink. Lucia's specialty, he told her. It was served with saffron rice and followed by flan, a creamy custard. Melanie's sincere and effusive appreciation delighted Lucia, who cleared the dishes, then quietly slipped away.

Teo poured a brandy for each of them. "Tell me about your family," he said. "I'm curious."

"Oh, we're very ordinary. My grandfather made a lot of money in steel during the war—World War II, that is. And we live in a comfortable Georgian house that isn't the least bit ancient. In a suburb of Cleveland. An ordinary city."

"You are somewhat older than Cecily. Are you close?"

"I practically raised her. My parents are very social, very busy. There were always live-in baby-sitters, but I guess I felt responsible for Cecily. Then I got married—"

"You are married?" he interrupted quickly. "But I thought…Señorita Royce…"

She was curiously embarrassed by his sudden reaction. "It is Miss Royce. The marriage didn't work out. I was very young. Oh, you don't want to hear that stuff."

"Ah, but I do. It may help me to understand you a little."

"It was eight years ago and we were only married for two months. My father had it annulled."

"Did you love this man?"

"I thought I did. I decided afterward that I had no idea what love was." She shrugged.

"And nobody has taught you since?"

"I haven't let anyone near enough." She wondered, distantly, whether her unwonted frankness was due to the several glasses of brandy she'd had. Or was it the intimacy of the situation? Or perhaps just her exhaustion, her emotional vulnerability.

He sat forward, silent, his hands clasped together in his habitual manner.

She had no idea what he was thinking and whether the fact of her brief marriage left any impression on him. Why should he care, this strange, dark man who made her so uncomfortable, who attracted her so much against her will?

"What about you? I thought Spanish families arranged their sons' marriages—at a young age," she dared.

"I'm Basque, not Spanish," he reminded her gently. "The simple truth is I refused to be pushed. And somehow time ran away and here I am, still single. There was a girl in England when I was at school. But she refused to consider living in my country, so nothing came of it. I expect by now she's fat and motherly. Of course, I could be wrong." And he smiled, as if mocking his own judgment. "My mother still nags me about it constantly even though she has several grandchildren already."

"My mother does the same thing. Luckily she's got Cecily—" Then the horror came back to her, bursting with immediacy, and she could feel the color drain from her face.

Teo rose and hurried toward her, pulling an empty chair next to hers. "No, *querida*, do not think of it." He put his hand over hers comfortingly.

Who was this man sitting so close to her, touching her? His expression was one of concern, his voice gentle. The candlelight flickered on his dark eyes, on the soft fabric of his jacket strained by his broad shoulders, on the mouth that was made to give a woman pleasure.

Who was he really? Friend or foe? Criminal or protector? Scholarly professor or proud Basque? How could a man dance with so many shadows?

She turned her head and looked into his eyes for the

answers. She saw none. She pulled her hand away from his, on the pretext of smoothing back her hair.

They were both silent for a time, silent in the eloquently hushed dining room that seemed to be growing smaller by the second. Teo was utterly relaxed, so close to her that she was sure he could hear her heart beating, could sense the tension writhing in her stomach. She took a breath; it quivered in her chest, and she reached for her brandy glass, accidentally knocking it over.

"Oh, no," she said, mopping the linen with her napkin. "I've done it again. I'm so clumsy."

Once more he covered her hand with his. "Lucia will get it," he said, his breath brushing her neck. "You are nervous this evening. Is it something I have done?" He sounded so sincere.

"No," Melanie replied too quickly. "I mean yes. You do make me a little edgy."

"I am sorry for that. I have seen you happy and laughing. Worry does not suit you."

"It doesn't suit anyone, Teo."

"And do you worry about being alone in this house with me?"

There was that constricted feeling in her chest again. She tried not to look at him. He was so close, so very close. "Should I worry?" she managed.

He didn't answer, not immediately. In his eyes she could see indecision; she also thought she saw desire. Finally he said, "You are safe with me," and she was a little disappointed in spite of herself. But Teo wasn't finished talking, not yet. "I think you have a certain—what shall I say—fear of men, Melanie."

"That's absurd," she began.

"And you are so young," he went on, undaunted. "It is a tragedy. Wounds of the heart must be allowed to heal."

"There are always scars," she threw out defensively.

"Scars, yes, but something tells me you view these scars as more significant than they really are."

"That is none of your concern." Her voice shook. Her stomach knotted. In her heart she knew he was right; it was just that no one had ever put it so bluntly. No one else had ever bothered to look beyond her defenses. She wasn't used to this kind of probing. She added more words to her description of this complex man—exasperatingly honest.

"I feel somehow," he was saying, "that you are my concern, Melanie. You must realize that I would like to…"

Instantly Melanie pushed back her chair, making a terrible scraping sound on the polished tiles. "I'm going to bed now," she said shakily.

He turned in his seat to look up at her but all he said was, "Good night, Melanie. Rest well."

Sleep eluded her. She was too overwrought, too tired to sleep, her nerves jangling, her body trembling with exhaustion. Eventually she rose and slipped out through the curtains, onto the stone balcony. The night breeze lifted her hair and molded her nightgown to her body. She stood, as if on the prow of a ship, her hands on the railing, her eyes closed, feeling the fresh damp soothing air. A lopsided moon, a day or so from fullness, silvered the mountaintops, glimmering on the mist crawling in the hollows.

Now, perhaps, she could sleep. As Melanie turned toward the doorway, she heard a sound below her, the quiet shuffle of a footstep. Was it Esteban returning?

A ghostly shadow detached itself from the blackness. She saw that it was a man, dressed in white with a black Basque beret on his head. He moved stealthily toward the cars, obviously trying not to awaken anyone.

Instinctively, Melanie shrank back into a dark corner of the balcony. Was it a thief? Should she alert someone?

The man looked up just then, as if to search her out in her dark corner, as if he knew she was there.

It was Teo.

She stifled her gasp of shock. He turned and moved on, away from her, and soon she heard the quiet *chunk* of a car door closing and the crunching of wheels on the gravel driveway.

Long moments later Melanie realized she was still standing there, her fingernails digging into her palms, her knuckles white.

Where was he going secretly in the night? Where? Her heart raced in agonized confusion. What should she do?

Then, as if a voice had spoken aloud in her brain, she knew. She made her way into her room, found her kimono and threw it over her shoulders. She walked resolutely down the deserted hallway, her bare feet clammy against the cold smoothness of the marble floor, halting outside his room. She boldly pushed open the door and entered, then sat down in a chair and settled herself for a long wait. Her eyes scanned the room in a cursory inspection, but something kept her from searching his dresser drawers or looking through the books and letters piled beside the bed. Something stopped her from violating his privacy in so complete and final a way. Yet she couldn't have said exactly what it was, or why she flinched from such an open expression of her distrust. Was she still harboring hopes—or illusions—about Teo Sanlucar, despite what she'd just seen?

Somewhere in the darkness a clock intruded upon the silence. A beam creaked. As Melanie sat waiting, she suddenly remembered what Teo had called her earlier that evening.

Querida, he had said. *Querida*. Melanie knew what that word meant. It meant "beloved."

Chapter Eight

His voice nudged her into wakefulness.

At first she was disoriented and sat up too quickly, her back and neck aching from her fitful sleep in his hard chair.

"Melanie..." he was saying in a soft and caressing tone. "What on earth are you...?" He crouched in front of her on his haunches, and his hands rested on either arm of the chair, imprisoning her. "Are you all right?" he asked.

"Yes...I just..." How to put it? She had planned to confront him, not to fall asleep in his bedroom.

"I wanted to talk to you, Teo. I fell asleep," she explained lamely.

"So I see." He was so close she could detect an odor on his clothes; it was a familiar smell, conjuring up some vague, pleasant association from her past. She finally grasped the elusive memory; it was wood smoke that she smelled.

"Couldn't whatever you wanted to talk to me about have waited until morning?" he asked.

"No," she said quickly. "I mean, yes, of course it could have." She looked at his face in the semidarkness, at the long shadows that cut grooves in his cheeks, at his dark eyes glinting in the lamplight. His hair was unruly, as if stirred by the night wind, his lean body, although outwardly relaxed, was nevertheless poised in readiness. She was acutely aware of him and knew then what a foolish mistake it had been to come to his room.

"If you'll move," she said carefully, "I'll leave now."

"And our talk?"

"In the morning, Teo." She could see those intelligent, long-lashed eyes studying her, boring into her, probing her hidden fears. Inadvertently, Melanie pulled the folds of her robe together.

"You are here now," he said. "Perhaps in the morning you will have changed your mind."

"Changed my mind?"

"About telling me what was so important that you felt you had to come to a man's room, in the middle of the night, in a state of..."

It was what he hadn't said that caused the tension to coil in her stomach. "It's not what you're thinking."

"Then pray enlighten me."

She edged back in the chair as if the few inches more she put between them would protect her. "All right, Teo. I came in here to wait and find out exactly where you'd gone at so late an hour."

"I see." A slow smile gathered at the corners of his mouth. "Would you believe that I went to visit a village maid?"

"I find that unlikely."

"Ah...then perhaps I merely went for a long walk in the moonlight?"

"You smell of wood smoke, Teo," she observed dispassionately. "Did you build a fire for warmth?"

He came smoothly to his feet and backed a step or two away from her. He stood as if in thought, his head cocked, his hands resting on his hips. "Should I tell you? Do you trust me at all, Melanie?"

"Yes." But she was answering his first question, not the one about trust, she thought.

"I was visiting friends in the hills. I was simply trying to pursue information about Cecily."

Melanie rose too, but veered away from him and walked to a window. "Let's say I believe you. Why couldn't you have visited these friends of yours at a more suitable hour?"

"For the obvious reasons, Melanie. Had I been seen at their houses by anyone who held sympathy for Cecily's abductors, I could have placed my friends in a compromising position."

"Is everything everyone does around here so well-known? My," she said sarcastically, whirling around to face him, "but you Basques are a suspicious lot."

"You are exactly correct. I told you once before that the Basques are an insular race. They feel it necessary to have an excellent network of information."

"They are not the CIA, Teo."

"No. They are more skilled, in some ways. More cunning, Melanie."

"Nice country…" she reflected, a hint of bitterness in her voice.

"My people have been forced to be wary and therefore close-knit."

"Maybe… And did you find out anything?"

Teo's face was impassive. He walked slowly in her direction until he stood only inches away. "First you must answer a question for me, Melanie," he said, speaking so quietly that she was forced to lean toward him.

"What?" she asked, trying with all her strength to resist his compelling voice.

"Tell me what it is you think I have done."

"Done?" Her heart was in her throat, and her knees felt suddenly weak.

"Yes. Why is it you have no trust for me, Melanie?"

"I…do trust you." Her gaze fell away from his. "I

guess I'm so worried about Cecily that I must seem suspicious of everyone.''

''You do.''

''Well, I'm not.'' Even to her own ears the lie sounded unconvincing. ''Tell me what you found out.''

He watched her for a moment, then shrugged. ''It could be that your sister is being held by the Cax Carot.'' He put a silencing finger to her lips. ''Allow me to finish. I do not know this for a certainty, but there is reason to suspect it.''

''Who are they?''

''I must consider how to describe these youths.'' He searched for words. ''They believe that one must protect oneself from a dangerous world, in which the bomb may be exploded at any moment. A world where greedy nations and men take whatever they wish from one another. The Cax Carot ready themselves for the worst...''

''Survivalists.''

''That, I assume, is what you would label them.''

''They're not...terrorists, are they?''

He shook his head. ''They do not believe in such things. Only, as you put it, survival.''

''Why would they want so much money?''

''Who can say? Perhaps they buy food and weapons.''

''Half a million American dollars can buy a lot of food and guns, Teo.''

''One might say these boys have grown too big for their trousers...''

''Their britches,'' she corrected automatically.

''Yes. Whatever.''

''And Carlos Echeverria? Is he a survivalist? In the Cax Carot?''

''Perhaps.''

She turned away and gazed out over the moon-bathed hills. ''You haven't told me much.''

''There is little more to tell.''

"Do you have any idea if this Cax Carot has a head-quarters or something?"

"Again, I can be of little help. I can only assume, as do you, that they hide out in the mountains. Is that not where a survivalist would feel most safe?"

"Perhaps," she agreed warily. Yet what Teo had said did make sense. Certainly the theory of survivalism described in part her sister's current outlook. Was it possible Teo was telling her the truth? Was he just an innocent bystander, like herself? Could she be so mistaken about him? After all, a man who was so obviously wealthy did not need to kidnap someone for a ransom. If he were guilty, it must be for some other reason. Idealism? Thrills? A history professor grown bored with the classroom, perhaps. What *was* his motive?

And Cecily. Melanie wondered again whether her sister was entirely innocent. Certainly she'd been kidnapped, but had she knowingly involved herself with the very man—or men—who were now holding her captive?

Questions flew around in Melanie's head. She felt that she was getting closer to some truth but its core still eluded her. And yet, if what Teo said was true, shouldn't she feel hopeful? Young, idealistic survivalists did not kill naive American girls.

But then there was Sevé. He was neither young nor, Melanie was sure, an idealist.

Teo took a step toward her and caught her hands in his, clasping them with a gentle strength. "I hope you can find it in your heart to believe me," he said softly, his breath warm on her forehead.

She couldn't answer. Instead she was held immobile with indecision and the exquisite agony of his touch.

"It was a mistake to have come to my room, Melanie," he said slowly. "It was also a mistake to have come to Pamplona."

"You're wrong on both counts," she said. "It was very

right for me to have come to Pamplona, and as for your room—''

"As for my room," he broke in harshly, "I am only too human. You cannot be so blind as to think I do not desire you. My bed is but a few feet away, and all you need do is walk there with me, Melanie. But you won't. I know that. You are too afraid of me and too afraid of your own responses."

Her eyes flew up to meet his, and she saw a kind of pain and warning there and felt weakened by the evidence of his undisguised torment. She wanted suddenly to draw him toward her. To be surrounded by those beautifully formed arms. And yet all her instincts told her to flee from him, to run for her life.

She pulled back from his closeness but paradoxically tightened the clasp of their hands.

"I have to...go, Teo," she whispered.

He held her a moment longer, and his quiet strength seemed to flow into her body. Then he let her go. "Leave me," he said, the lines in his face suddenly stern. "Leave me and go back to your room before I forget what a poor liar you are or that you are a guest in this house and I am a gentleman."

Somehow she managed to cross to the door, to pull it open and walk down the dim hallway to her own room. She even managed to sleep but she couldn't escape Teo. Even in her sleep, in the privacy of her dreams, he was there.

THE NEXT DAY, Thursday, seemed to drag. Once again, she'd been awakened early by Esteban with a call from her father—an unsettling call telling her that he was wiring the money through New York to Madrid that afternoon.

"There'll be a rush order put on it, Mel," he'd said, "so it should be in Pamplona on Friday."

"Should be?"

"I've pulled every string I know to hurry this up, honey. You sound as if you think we're not worried sick over here."

"I'm sorry," she'd said, "I know how upset you are." Then she'd reassured him that she was safe and being watched over every minute. What Melanie could not tell her father was that her bodyguards might very well be involved in the kidnapping. Esteban had been standing over her the whole time.

She breakfasted with Esteban. Teo was nowhere to be seen. Afterward, Esteban offered to take her into Pamplona, but Melanie had no heart for the fiesta that day. She simply moped around the huge house, taking an occasional photograph, tormented continually by a single thought. What if the money didn't arrive?

It rained lightly in the valley that afternoon. She sat in the living room, mutely staring out of the windows at the quiet drizzle. Was it raining in Pamplona? She could imagine the thousands upon thousands of tourists all jamming into the shops and restaurants. An ugly vision.

She tapped a finger absently against her chin. What if the money didn't arrive by tomorrow? The police. She'd have to think about getting in touch with them somehow. She remembered all the reasons Teo had told her not to, but those reasons might be utterly invalid. She wished she knew. And then, even if the money arrived on time, Cecily's life might be forfeited anyway. The Lindbergh baby pattern...

She watched the gray mist cloak the mountains and her stomach twisted in anguished indecision: what should she do?

She heard Teo finally return to the house in the early evening. Melanie was in the library, leafing through books and magazines, feeling edgy and irritable and bored, almost as if she were crawling out of her skin.

She could hear Esteban's low voice coming from the living room, but he and Teo were speaking in Basque.

She walked purposefully into their midst. "Good evening, Teo," she interrupted.

He looked over to where she stood, and Melanie was surprised at the weariness she saw in his face. "Good evening, Melanie."

The men continued their conversation as if she weren't there at all. It infuriated her. She began to pace the room, feeling like an outsider, feeling like...a prisoner. Yes, she felt a resurgence of that earlier emotion, that sense of being imprisoned. She fingered an ashtray, looked at a photograph, sat down, then stood up. She walked to the French doors that led out onto the lawn and turned around to face Teo and Esteban, still engrossed in conversation, still ignoring her presence.

"It's stopped raining," she said and they looked over at her, surprised, as though they'd forgotten she was there. "Lovely evening, isn't it?" Melanie said firmly.

"Beautiful," Esteban replied. He glanced at Teo. "You are tired."

"*Sí.*" And Teo rested his gaze on Melanie. "Please excuse my appearance." He was wearing white cotton trousers and a white shirt. Both had dried, muddy smudges on them as did one of his unshaven cheeks. "I will go clean up now, if you do not mind." He gave a slight bow in Melanie's direction.

"Of course," she said loftily.

He was singularly quiet at dinner. His eyes would meet Esteban's, then he would stare off into the distance. He seemed preoccupied, his brow creased by a deep frown.

Melanie picked at her food. She had little interest in dinner. But it was a perfect opportunity to study Teo, and she took full advantage of his curious lack of interest in his surroundings. He'd washed and shaved and donned a clean white shirt and trousers. His shaving lotion clung to him softly, tantalizing her senses. The silver at his temples seemed to stand out that evening, and the lines of concentration on his face somehow aged him. He would al-

ways be a handsome man, she guessed, but the loss of
tenderness in his expression made her annoyingly anxious.

Who was he? How many different faces did he show
the world? There was the tender, caring side of him. The
intellect, too. She'd heard him speak sarcastically, though
never cruelly; she'd seen him pray. He was a gentleman,
through and through. Hadn't last night proved that much?
And he could show pain, could bare his soul to her, could
risk her rejection and withstand her distrust.

And now who was this Teo sitting silently at the table?
Something was troubling him—that showed plainly on his
face, in those dark, long-lashed eyes. But what?

What was he thinking? Where had he been all day?

"Teo," she said, "were you at the fiesta?"

He shook his head. "I was visiting some people."

"Was it about Cecily?"

"Yes."

"Did you find out anything?"

He glanced at Esteban, then at her. "Nothing more."

Melanie leaned back in her chair and fell silent.

Over brandy, he said to his uncle, "I'll be going out
again tonight." That was all. No explanation whatsoever.
Melanie guessed that Esteban already knew Teo's destination. If only she could...

A thought struck her. Of course she could! But how?

She remembered watching Teo the previous night from
her balcony. It wouldn't be so difficult to follow, would
it?

Melanie waited a few minutes then yawned. "I am
dreadfully sleepy tonight."

Both men turned their dark heads toward her.
"Please," Esteban said, "if you are tired, take your rest,
Melanie."

"Maybe I should," she agreed smoothly.

It seemed so easy. She walked up the stairs as if weary
to the bone and closed her bedroom door gently. Then she
began to rush. First she stripped off her dress and threw

it on top of her suitcase. Then she put on chocolate-brown slacks and her dark green shirt. Camouflage. She even pulled down the covers on her bed and shoved some bunched-up clothes underneath to make it look as if she were asleep—just in case. She tied her hair back in a practical ponytail and even considered blackening her face, the only part of her that might reflect light. What could she use? Mascara? It would take forever. No, she'd just have to chance it. No one would get that close to her, anyway, not if she could help it.

She was ready.

Melanie turned off the lights and stepped onto the balcony to wait in the shadows.

She had it all planned. At the far end of the hall was a set of narrow stairs leading to the kitchen. From there, she could get to the back door. Of course, Lucia might still be about, but dinner was long over. Surely the cook had retired by now.

Her car! Would Esteban or Lucia hear her start the engine? Most likely not. She'd parked at the far end of the circle; surely the lawn and the trees and the stone walls would muffle the sound. Besides, Esteban would have no reason to be listening for her. She was certain it wouldn't occur to either of the men that she might follow Teo.

She was pleased with her cleverness. Let Teo sneak off to his "friend." Soon enough, she would know exactly what he was up to.

The mist eddied around her, causing her hair to spring into curls. She was pressed back against the stone wall and could feel the cool dampness seeping into her clothes, chilling her skin. She wished he would hurry.... Then finally, she saw a rectangle of light on the lawn below— light spilling from his bedroom window. Shortly after, it was dark on the lawn once more. She listened but could hear nothing. So she imagined his progress, down the hall, down the front stairs, to the door.

She crossed her fingers, took a deep breath, then made her move.

Peering out of a crack in her bedroom door, Melanie saw that there was no one in the hallway. She rushed as silently as she could toward the back staircase. The floor creaked beneath her sneakers once, and her heart sank.

Hurry! she thought. Or she might miss him...

The kitchen was dark and empty. Thank God! Gingerly, she closed the back door, careful not to lock it. Then she paused. What if Esteban checked it before he went to bed?

But she couldn't worry about that now. That was a problem she'd just have to deal with if and when it came her way.

She peeked out across the lawn from around the corner of the house. Teo's car was still there. Then she heard the front door of the house, its sound echoing off the hillside as it was firmly closed.

Yes! There he was!

She waited as he stepped into his car and turned on the motor. He began to pull away and she ran quickly across the lawn toward her car, crouching, using the trees and the night shadows to hide herself.

Oh, clever, clever!

She started her car, the quiet little engine sounding to her like a Concorde jet.

Oh, my Lord, she thought, cringing inwardly, her knuckles white on the steering wheel, what if Esteban discovered her ruse? But what could he do now? Drag her out of the car and lock her in her room?

She pulled away from the curve of the lawn, leaving her lights off, and steered down the long drive. Which way had he gone—left or right?

Yes! There were his lights bouncing off the trees a couple of hundred yards down the road to the right. Then his car disappeared around a bend.

She switched on her own headlights and followed. Then, when she came to the same bend in the road, she turned them off, slowed down and strained to see in the pale moonlight.

His taillights showed in the distance; at least they were something to follow, a moving beacon in the night. Then they disappeared. She turned her lights back on. Over and over again, Melanie followed the same routine, finding it amazingly easy. The roads were not all that dark, especially with no other cars to blind her and a liquid moon to brighten the way.

The road led in the opposite direction from Pamplona— or so she assumed. It twisted through the tall hills and once over a bridge. Always, she could find his lights in the distance, however, and frequently she was able to turn hers on.

It was deserted country. Deserted and a bit frightening with the mottled moonlight on the twisted road, forming eerie shadows.

Very seldom did Melanie pass a house, and only once did she drive through a tiny village, where she deemed it safe to turn on her parking lights, the accepted European custom for driving in cities at night.

She had driven a little over eight kilometers when she saw Teo's brake lights illuminate a straight stretch of road ahead of her. She pulled to the soft, muddy side of the road and came to a stop a few hundred yards behind him. Then she could make out his interior lights switching on and off as he opened the door to step out of his car. Silently, she opened and closed her own door and began walking swiftly in his direction. He couldn't conceivably see her in her dark clothes from that distance, but still she clung closer to the trees than to the road.

As he was once again dressed in the familiar white of the Basques, Melanie could easily see his pale form moving ahead of her. She saw that he'd turned off the road and entered a meadow.

Where was he going? She could see no houses anywhere; there were only sloping meadows and steep hills on either side of the road. Very curious indeed.

She made her way into the meadow and discovered that there was a rocky path to follow. She stayed at least a hundred yards behind him, losing his shadow every so often but always finding him again, still ahead of her.

The low, sweeping meadows ended abruptly and the path began to climb sharply along the ridge of a mountain. She grew tired and drew deep breaths into her lungs. If only she could rest a bit.

Above her was a forest; below, a slope fell away gradually. Then the path switched back, rounding onto the hidden side of the mountain where it continued to climb. Once, she missed Teo's figure for a few interminable minutes and fear swept over her. What if she had lost him? Or worse, what if he'd stopped and she bumped right into him? But then finally, mercifully, she saw Teo again, coming out of the thick pines and beginning to cross a wide expanse of meadow.

There were other pale shapes in the clearing—sheep—but more important, there was a cabin on its far side. Light spilled out from two tiny windows. She stood still at the edge of the forest for a moment, speculating. Smoke rose from a stone chimney into the night sky. Of course, the wood smoke on Teo's clothing.

She saw him enter the cabin and close the door. Melanie began to move again across the grassy meadow, startling a sheep once and frightening herself out of her own wits as the ewe jumped across a ditch, giving Melanie a wide berth.

She was terrified that someone might see her approach. There was no cover whatsoever. And the moon kept emerging from the patchy blanket of clouds. She saw a boulder near the cabin and crouched as she came up behind it.

She was so close now. The light from one of the sooty windows fell softly onto the meadow in front of Melanie, laying a small, hazy square on the ground. Then she could see a figure—a man's figure—through the window, his white-clad back leaning against the pane, blocking her vision.

Was it Teo?

No matter. This was a perfect moment for Melanie to sneak up to the side of the cabin undetected. She took the opportunity, ducking low, finally pressing herself up against the rough stones of the wall.

She caught her breath and suddenly wished she were back at Esteban's safe and sound.

But you're not, she told herself and she knew she had to summon the courage to peek into that window. She could do it. She could!

Holding her breath, Melanie tried to see if the man's back was still partially blocking the window.

Yes.

She took advantage of the inadvertent shield he provided and moved slightly so that she could see a portion of the cabin's interior. Her heart was in her throat.

Then she could see three men sitting around a peasant table, a kerosene lamp in its center.

She almost gasped aloud; one of the men was the one who'd argued with Teo at the café. Sevé. She didn't recognize the other men or the one whose back hid the rest of the room from her vision, but she had an impression of youth. Then her eyes were drawn to the opposite wall and the hair rose on her arms. There were two rifles leaning against the stones. *My God...*

The man at the window moved suddenly into the room and Melanie quickly ducked her head. It was long minutes before she braved another look. The entire room was visible now. There was Teo, standing in the dimness on the far side of the cabin, across from Sevé and the youths.

He was looking down at a cot...

He shifted his weight.

And there, lying on the cot, looking pale and exhausted, was Cecily.

Chapter Nine

Melanie only became aware of her surroundings when she tripped on a rock and fell to her knees. She stayed there for a minute on all fours, gasping for breath, sobbing with fear and horror and a terrible certainty. Slowly she stood, brushed the dirt off her knees and the grit and gravel from her hands. One of her palms stung; she must have cut it in falling. It didn't matter.

Teo Sanlucar had lied to her from the beginning. Suspecting him had put her on edge, but knowing he was involved twisted like a knife in her heart. All those lies, those caring looks. *Querida.* It meant nothing; it was just part of his role—and he'd played his role well. Of all the men in the world, how had he got past her ironbound caution and touched her heart?

She began walking down the path again, feeling her way. She had a desperate urge to run, but it was too dark and the mountainside was too rough. She had to be gone before Teo returned to his car. If he discovered that she'd followed him...

She must never let him know what she'd done or that she knew he was involved. To do so would put Cecily, not to mention herself, in even greater danger. Melanie knew she had to remain free in order to plan, to get the money, to call the police if need be. Somehow she had to make sure those men did not kill Cecily. How?

Once, she was afraid she was lost; a huge gnarled tree with twisted branches like grasping arms suddenly stood in her path. Had it been there before? Or had she been too intent on following Teo to notice it? She wished she had a flashlight but where could she have got one? The entire time she'd been in that house, she'd been watched. Oh, how conveniently she'd fallen into his hands!

She could, of course, get in her car and simply leave, leave the Basque country behind and fly home. Which was what Teo had told her to do. But that wasn't even a remote choice, not with her sister all alone in that awful hut... Who were those men? Which one was Carlos? What exactly did they want the money for?

She stumbled on through the shadowed night, down, down. Her car was there, just out of sight, some hundred yards behind Teo's. She'd been deathly afraid it would be gone and she'd be left alone in the night where those men with their wicked-looking guns would find her.

She stopped and listened for a few minutes in case Teo had left the cabin after her. But there was only the rustling of the trees and the sound of a stream somewhere. A night bird called softly and in the underbrush a small animal disturbed some branches. It was quiet, and utterly peaceful, with the scent of green growing things and the damp night air.

Starting her car, she winced as the noise broke the silence, but then she was away, driving back along the twisted road, praying she remembered how to get to Esteban's, praying no one noticed the unlocked door or her missing car.

It was nearly three in the morning by the time she turned her lights off and pulled up into the driveway. She slumped over the steering wheel, resting her head on her hands, too tired to think or plan anymore. She dragged herself to the back door. What if someone had awakened and locked it?

It was still open. But Melanie was too drained to rejoice in the fact. She crept wearily up the back staircase and to her room, closing and locking the door behind her. Then, carefully, she closed and locked the patio door and drew the curtains together. When she turned on the light, she saw that her one hand was raw with a slash of dried blood on the palm. The knees of her pants were muddy, grass-stained, torn. Her sneakers were muddy, too. She scraped off the mud and flushed it down the toilet. She cleaned up as well as she could in the bathroom and hid her muddy, blood-stained clothes in the bottom of her suit-case.

Then sleep, blessed forgetfulness. Not even the sound of Teo's car, slipping quietly up the drive, wakened her.

By ten the next morning she was downstairs, trying to ask Lucia when the banks in Pamplona opened.

There were many, Lucia told her, misunderstanding her Spanish.

In her limited Spanish, Melanie tried again, impatiently.

And finally, Lucia understood; she grinned widely, using the kitchen clock to indicate what time *el banco* opened.

"Nine-thirty. Tell *los señores* I go *banco*," Melanie said, gesturing in the vague direction of Pamplona.

Her father had wired the money yesterday; perhaps it was already there. She doubted it, because overseas money transfers usually took several days. But her father had specified a rush order.

Lucia asked whether she wanted coffee, but Melanie politely declined. "No, *gracias*, no coffee. Later."

To her relief no one was about. Teo undoubtedly was sleeping late, if indeed he had returned. But his car was there, pulled up near the house; its tires were muddy.

Her heart clutched in fear. She glanced quickly at her own car. Its tires, too, were muddy. Had he noticed them last night? She bit her lip and hoped not. She'd get into Pamplona and wash them off somehow.

"Going somewhere so early?"

She whirled around at the sound of his voice, dropping her car keys. "Oh, you startled me!"

He stood before her, looking as fresh as if he'd been in bed asleep all night. His white sport shirt was crisp and clean, his khaki pants pressed and immaculate.

"Sorry. But I repeat, are you leaving us at this early hour?" Were his eyes more hooded than usual? Did he see the mud on her tires?

"Yes, I'm going to the bank to see if the money has arrived."

"Let me drive you. The fiesta is still going on, you know. You'll never be able to park."

"I'll take my chances."

"I insist," he said quietly.

He couldn't know, could he? Her skin crawled with fear. She bent down to pick up her keys, trying to hide her face, wondering if he saw the truth in it. But he moved faster than she did, scooping up the keys and handing them to her, his eyes dark and unreadable, his touch electric. Then he took her hand in his and turned its palm up.

"What is this? A nasty cut. But, Melanie, how did this happen?"

She shrank inside her skin. "Oh, that? Oh, it's nothing. I cut it on a broken mirror in my makeup case."

"Why on earth didn't you ask for a bandage?"

She shrugged. "They never stay on your hand, do they?"

His acute gaze seemed to reach inside her as they stood there silently, her hand still held in his. Again, his glance fell to the cut, then swung sharply back to her face. His touch was cautious. She thought inanely that he might hold an injured bird in the same manner as he did her hand: gently, carefully…reverently.

Melanie's heart felt squeezed. She tried to smile, to

show her gratitude for his concern. Wasn't that what he would expect?

"You can let me go now," she said quietly.

He looked at the scrapes on her hand once more, saying as if to himself, "A cut from a mirror..." before he freed her. For a moment neither of them spoke. Uncontrollable panic rose in Melanie's breast. Any second he was going to tell her that the game was up and that he knew she had followed him.

"Have you eaten?" he asked suddenly, his voice shattering the tense quiet.

She swallowed hard. "No, really, I'm too nervous. I'd like to get to the bank."

"Of course. Come then. I'll buy you breakfast in town."

Did he notice that she pressed against the car door, as far from him as possible? Did he see her hands tremble with nervousness? Did he believe her lie about the cut on her hand?

On the drive to Pamplona, Teo was his usual, open self. He made casual conversation, pointing out things on the way—a fourteenth-century castle on a distant hill, a sheep herder driving his flock to greener pastures.

"Over there, near the river—" he nodded "—is an old wool mill. It's still in use."

"Interesting," Melanie murmured distractedly.

He went on to regale her with local Basque legends concerning the surrounding countryside; he seemed to be trying especially hard to entertain Melanie, or was he really the kind, generous man he seemed to be? From time to time, she asked herself if she could have been mistaken about Teo. And then she would remember him standing in the cabin with those men, dressed as one of them, and she would feel a surge of fear. If Teo Sanlucar knew she'd followed him—what would he do?

Still, his conversation kept her mind occupied, kept her

from thinking too much, from imagining unknown horrors.

She watched him out of the corner of her eye, as she held her whipping hair out of her face with one hand. Teo seemed almost to be enjoying the drive; the Mercedes' top was down, and his black hair was blowing wildly in the wind. He looked young and carefree and innocent. But what had Cecily thought when her brilliant Professor Sanlucar had turned out to be a common criminal?

As she'd expected, the streets were already swarming. It was excruciatingly slow going and Teo had to practically push his way through the crowds. He pulled up right in front of the bank, double parked, and stepped out of the car.

"You're going to leave it here?" she asked in amazement.

"Of course. We won't be long."

He ushered her into the bank, his hand on the small of her back. "Please wait here. I will be just a moment."

He returned with a short, distinguished-looking man whose formal black suit and small brush mustache proclaimed him a banker.

"Señorita Royce," Teo was saying to the man, "is expecting a wire. Quite a large sum, as I was telling you,"

"*Señorita*, it is my pleasure," the man said. "Please allow me to introduce myself. I am Diego Pacheco." He spread his hands in a Latin gesture. "However, I am sorry to inform you, Señorita Royce, that there is no wire for you."

Melanie's heart sank. Señor Pacheco was saying something to Teo in Spanish. Teo answered and the man's face registered astonishment, then consternation. He spoke rapidly.

"Señor Pacheco says that such a large sum will take time to collect, if you want cash," Teo told her. "His bank does not have such amounts on hand."

"I doubt the...people I'm doing business with will accept a check,'' Melanie said dryly. ''How long will it take?''

''A few days, *señorita*,'' the banker answered. ''Monday, Tuesday, I do not know.''

''I see.'' She fought to keep the panic from her voice.

''I will watch for this wire myself,'' Señor Pacheco assured her. ''I will expedite the collection of cash.''

''Thank you,'' Melanie said faintly. ''I appreciate your help.''

''There is something else,'' Señor Pacheco explained, his brow creased in a frown. ''A sum this large will attract attention in Madrid when it comes through. Our government, you understand, may be interested—for tax purposes.'' He spread his hands to express his helplessness and shook his head apologetically. How much did he suspect?

''If anyone asks,'' she said firmly, ''this money is meant to buy a house, a summer home.''

''Ah, *sí*, I understand. A property. Of course.''

He didn't believe her, but never mind. By the time anyone could start to look too closely, this whole nightmare would be over.

As they left the bank, Teo's hand was at her back again. She wanted to knock his arm away, to scream at him: *''Let my sister go!''*

''We will check with Señor Pacheco this afternoon,'' he said quietly. ''And then you will know what to tell them when they call you at five.''

''It's not my father's fault,'' she insisted breathlessly. ''It's not. You know that. He wired the money yesterday. Surely those men will understand. They have to.''

''Of course they will. Don't worry.''

''Don't worry! With my sister held prisoner up there—'' She clamped her mouth shut instantly, cutting off her sentence.

He seemed not to notice. She watched his face carefully, but he looked as worried as she felt. Sincerely worried. He took her to a café near the outskirts of town, which was not quite so crowded as those in the plaza, and they sat under a vine-covered trellis. The tables were spread with checkered oilcloth and the floor tiles were cracked. A working man's place. She refused his offer of breakfast, but agreed to a cup of coffee. It was hot and sweet and she immediately felt somewhat revived.

"They will wait, won't they?" she asked again. "I mean, if the money isn't here, what can they do?"

"Nothing, I expect."

"By the way, did you find out anything more last night?" He'd made no secret of his nocturnal journey; why not ask?

"No, nothing more. Except that Cecily is well."

"Did you see her?" she burst out.

"No, Melanie, I merely heard that. How could I see her?"

Lies! How dare he sit there and lie to her like that? How dare he dirty himself with such low deception? What kind of man was he?

Teo deftly steered the conversation away from Cecily. He began talking about the factory district of Pamplona and the modernization being carried out there. There didn't seem to be much that the professor didn't know something about—he was a veritable book of knowledge, she thought sarcastically to herself.

How did he manage to continually put up that congenial facade of his in the face of Cecily's predicament? What did he really feel, Melanie wondered. Did he care what happened to Cecily—and to her?

After reading the menu, he asked again if Melanie was hungry. When she again told him no, he removed his glasses and smiled. "You do not eat enough. Through such an ordeal you would be wise to keep up your strength," he said.

"I don't have much of an appetite these days," she replied.

Still smiling slightly, he shook his head and studied her openly. There it was again, she realized uncomfortably, that charm, that look in his eyes that told her he was thinking of her in more than a casual way. Desire. He didn't even bother to hide it.

She squirmed in her hard chair, avoiding his gaze, trying to quell the tingling in her stomach.

It's not fair, she thought. Teo had no right to be so damned appealing, to turn on his charm, to try to lure her. And what could she do to stop him—tell him she knew he was involved in the Cax Carot? She had to sit there and fight the attraction. It simply wasn't fair.

They left the small café and Teo, as always, handed her into his car. His Mercedes. Once more, she asked herself why a man as obviously well-off as Teo would need money? But then, perhaps neither he nor Esteban was really all that well-off. Perhaps their creditors were breathing down their necks at this very minute. What kind of factory had Teo told her his family owned? Machinery, parts for ships? Was the Sanlucar family in dire financial straits? It was possible...

On the drive to Esteban's, he parked in a small shopping area near the factory district.

"I will only be a moment," he said, stepping out of the car.

She watched his ease of movement as he entered a store. Then he was back, sliding into his seat, turning toward her. He produced a box of Band-Aids and a small bottle of iodine, then took her hand in his to doctor her scrapes. But all she could think was that he had obviously not forgotten her cut. Did he suspect something? Or had she convinced him with her story about the broken mirror? Was he merely being the ever-conscientious host and protector?

At three, just before the Banco de Navarra closed for siesta, Teo phoned Señor Pacheco. When he hung up and slowly turned to Melanie, she could tell by his expression. "It's not there," she said flatly.

"No. Señor Pacheco even phoned the main office in Madrid. Nothing yet. It may take until Monday."

She covered her face with her hands. "Will they believe me? Will they kill Cecily?"

"No," he soothed. "They must believe you. It is the truth."

Pulling her face from her hands, she cried bitterly, "The truth! Since when has the truth meant anything!" But he only stood there, a look of sympathy on his face, his eyes clouded with anxiety.

When they arrived back at Esteban's house, she phoned her parents again.

"Hell, Melanie, I wired that money yesterday, like they said! It has to go through New York and Madrid. And there's a weekend coming up. What do they want? I'm not a magician!"

"I'll explain it. I'll make them believe me, Dad. They'll wait."

"Hang in there, Mel. Thank God you're there."

"Right, Dad."

Hang in there. Well, she was trying.

She went to her room and attempted to sleep after the phone call, but she kept remembering the interior of that ugly little cabin. She had a clear image of its few shabby furnishings and the terrible bilious light that had made everyone there look drained and sickly. And the guns... Would those men really harm Cecily? What about Carlos, her sister's erstwhile lover? Even if he had deliberately lured Cecily into this thing, surely he would not let them hurt her.

In her mind's eye, she kept seeing clocks, all different sizes and shapes, each one, however, reading the same: 5:00 P.M. She went over again and again what she would say to this man when he called her at the phone booth.

She must make the caller believe her sincerity. It wasn't her fault the money wasn't there. It wasn't her fault!

Then she would see Cecily, her sister's pinched, pale face, the suntan gone, the freckles standing out as if she were ill. And her own pallid face, Melanie thought, must look the same as Cecily's—worried, sickly and white. How long could she keep up this facade for Teo and his uncle? How long before she broke down and the accusations poured from her lips?

Punctually at four-thirty, Teo knocked on her door. "Melanie? Are you ready?"

Naturally, he insisted on driving her into the city for the phone call. She was not allowed to go anywhere alone. And how convenient an excuse it was to say she must be protected! Yet, she thought, what would she do if he'd let her go alone? Nothing.

The phone booth, an old-fashioned wood-and-glass one, was on a corner near the central plaza. How would she hear? The noise all around her was deafening. The hollow drums thumped, the flutes wailed, the dancers' heads went up and down, up and down above the crowd. A young man lay rolling on the ground in the plaza, laughing hysterically, his shirt stained with wine.

She could do nothing but stand there, waiting, with the crowd jolting and shoving her. The minutes crawled slowly by. And then the phone rang. Melanie leaped for it.

"*Pronto,*" a voice called. "*¿Pronto?*"

"Hello? This is Melanie Royce…"

The voice said something, then the line went dead.

"Who was it?" Teo asked.

"I don't know. A wrong number maybe." She fought a growing hysteria.

They waited. Three minutes past five, four minutes, five. At eight minutes after five the phone rang again. Melanie stared at it, afraid for a moment. Then she snatched it up. "Hello? Don't hang up, please. This is

Melanie Royce.'' She held her breath, aching inside with fear.

''Señorita Royce?'' A harsh, heavily accented voice. Sevé? ''You have my money?''

''No, not yet. But it's coming. My father wired it yesterday. It'll be here very soon.'' Her words tripped over themselves, rushing to get out.

There was silence on the line.

''Hello? Hello?'' cried Melanie. ''Please!''

''It better be here. *Mañana.* Tomorrow. Or your sister may get hurt.''

''No, please! Don't hurt her! The money will come. And…and how do I know you really have Cecily? How do I know she's still alive?''

''You must take my word on that. The word of a gentleman.'' He laughed hoarsely.

''Let me talk to her, please.''

''Tomorrow at five at this same *teléfono.* No more time.'' The line went dead.

''Hello, hello! Oh, please!'' But there was no one at the other end.

She hung up the phone and turned to leave the booth, swaying as if drugged.

''Melanie, what happened?'' Teo asked anxiously.

''I have till tomorrow at five. He'll call again.'' She shuddered. ''I guess I should be relieved.''

He put a hand on her arm. ''You are very brave, Melanie.''

She withdrew from his touch. ''Me? I'm scared to death, Teo.''

''That is nothing. Like the matador. He is afraid, but still he does it. He faces his worst fear. That is true courage.''

Dinner at Esteban's that night was a sad charade. As always, the table was beautifully laid, and the candlelight winked cheerfully off the crystal. To Melanie, the whole scene was a bitter parody of ease and well-being. Esteban spoke gravely, trying to draw her into the conversation, but she found it difficult to respond graciously. The food stuck in her throat while Teo offered the best morsels off the serving platter or another glass of wine or a particularly ripe peach. She wanted to scream "Stop it!" She wanted to run from the room, to knock the exquisite lamps off their tables.

She looked up once to find Teo's eyes on her. "Your sister will not be harmed," he said softly.

"Can you promise me that?" she pressed.

He smiled sadly. "Would that I could. But nevertheless, I am sure. Alas, poor Melanie, this is hard on you."

"A brandy," suggested Esteban. "That such a thing should happen to a guest of mine! A brandy, and you will sleep."

Her room was a kind of haven, a place where she could let out the sobs of frustration and pummel her mattress in impotent fury. A place where she could sink down onto her bed and cry and feel herself safe from prying eyes.

Then she rose, her fists clenched at her sides. She would have to keep her wits about her. Neither Teo nor his uncle must ever know her fear and her loneliness; she would have to conceal the strain she felt at deceiving them, the tearing worry over her sister. She must stay strong for a few more days—until the money came. She must lie and hide her true feelings and let them see nothing, *nothing* of the truth.

The curtains were billowing at the balcony doors. Melanie was drawn to the cool moist air, scented with the fragrance of the overhanging trees. A breeze, almost a wind, blew from over the hills, from the ocean, fresh and bracing. She took a deep breath and leaned on the balustrade, looking up at the starry night sky. The moon hung like a huge blank eye, faintly veined. Its light would be bright enough to reveal anyone leaving the house that night. Was Teo going out again? And why did he go? Did he need to reassure Sevé that the money was truly on its way?

There was a noise behind her, footsteps, a low voice calling her name. "Melanie?"

Her breath caught in her throat.

"Melanie, are you there?"

Oh, God, please let him leave her alone.

Then he was behind her on the balcony, the familiar, faint smell of after-shave reaching her nostrils. "I was worried. You weren't in your room." He paused. "I knocked."

"I was out here."

"Yes."

He was standing too close, and suddenly the night was sultry. Melanie's breath came too quickly and a pulse beat strongly in her neck, jumping against her hot skin. She could sense him moving even closer; if she didn't turn around maybe he'd leave, maybe—

"Are you all right?" he asked quietly.

She laughed then, a short, nervous sound. "All right? No, I'm not all right. I'm worried sick, I'm half out of my mind—" Her strained torrent stopped short and she drew in her breath with a gasp as he stepped even nearer. She felt trapped, like an animal, her heart leaping in fear, her breath coming fast, her body taut with adrenaline. She had to run, to escape; her muscles tensed involuntarily.

But his hand was on her shoulder and he was turning her toward him, slowly, slowly. His dark head bent and his eyes, glittering like black coals in the night, were fixed on hers and his mouth descended. Melanie was frantic. Where did the game end? His lips were on hers, warm and firm. She could taste him, smell him. Her head whirled with the explosion of sensation: the touch of his mouth, his hands hard on her shoulders, the heat of him.

She closed her eyes and let him kiss her, let him open her mouth and find the honey inside, let him knead her shoulders with his strong brown hands. She could only close her mind to the sweet torment and endure it while her arms hung limply at her sides.

But her resolve waned, and slowly and inevitably her arms slid around his back. How could she! her mind screamed even as his mouth moved from her lips to her throat and waves of raw pleasure coursed through her veins.

Teo took his time, as if they had all night to stand on the misty balcony, embracing. If he had pressed her, she might have summoned the strength to repel him. As it was, her response grew until her mouth opened willingly to receive his and her hands began to massage the long muscles of his back.

She wanted him. And yet the wild notion of fully submitting to his caresses was abhorrent to her sense of right and wrong. She couldn't believe she was standing there in her scant silk nightgown, allowing him to pull her against his chest, to feel his male hardness pressing into her leg.

He moved his hands from her shoulders and touched the swell of her breast, feather soft, reverently. The pulse in the hollow of her throat leaped compulsively, and she gasped as his mouth moved over hers with more demand. Then suddenly his lips left hers, and his head bent and he was kissing the curve of one breast through the smooth peach-colored silk. Her nipples grew taut. He kissed each slowly, with infinite patience. She tried a thousand times to say no. But his careful ministrations, his gentle, giving caresses made her heart cry, *yes, take me. Teo. Let me take you.*

He kissed her earlobe and whispered, ''I want you,'' and her stomach rolled over and the agony of indecision held her silent. ''Let me love you, Melanie.''

She said yes. She told herself that it was all part of the game—Teo mustn't suspect. But she knew it was a lie. God help her, she wanted him, as much as he wanted her.

She ached to feel his warmth, to rise to his passion, to welcome sweet oblivion.

His nakedness in the sultry night was beautiful, making her feel lovely herself as the thin silk gown slipped from her body and dropped in a circle at her feet by the bedside.

He kissed her everywhere, in sensitive places she'd never realized she possessed. Her spine, the white curve of her hip, behind her knees, even her ankles. Every inch of her flesh was ripe, ready to be plucked by his mouth, to be savored by his tongue. Gasp after gasp escaped Melanie unashamedly. Once she breathed, "I never knew it could be this way."

Still he did not poise himself above her. He waited. He drew her out until she was pulling at his shoulders with her hands, dizzy with urgency.

Finally he entered her, ending her suspense. Melanie instinctively moved to his rhythm, responded to his quickening thrusts. Almost immediately she felt a deep physical release, a sensation so unexpected, so exquisite that she cried out, her head thrashing from side to side, her mouth moving as if in prayer.

His soft laugh reached her consciousness. She froze.

"Melanie," he said, "do not pull away. That was but the first pleasure. Let me show you, please," and he began caressing her again, slowly, slowly, until she relaxed beneath him and at last, amazed, she felt desire rekindling.

It was impossible, but he brought her to a fever pitch once more. Her flesh began to burn, her movements matched his, faster, faster, and then she was moaning and gasping and kneading his back with her hands and the fire raged until it exploded in brilliant flashes in and around her. It had been so beautiful, so wonderful, that her tears mingled with their sweat.

She'd thought, she'd hoped, he would stay with her in the big bed, but after kissing and stroking her lovingly he shifted away from her and groaned.

"We'd be doing this all night," he said softly, "and you must rest."

"You're right, of course," she said, just as softly, and he turned once more and kissed her.

"Are you afraid I might lock you up and keep you my prisoner?" he said against her lips.

"Am I your prisoner?"

"Only if you want to be." He rose then and dressed in the darkness. His words rang in her head: only if she wanted to be. And when he was gone she cried into the pillow and wondered how it had all happened, how she had let herself go like that. And she wondered if she did want to be his lover, his prisoner. If somehow he had just removed her shackles, and the choice, now, was hers.

Chapter Ten

Saturday, July 10

Melanie was puffy eyed when she descended the stairs the next morning. It had been a long, image-filled night in which sleep had come only in brief, restless spurts. She'd lain in the bed and cursed her weakness, cursed the flaw in her character that had allowed her to yearn for a man who had betrayed her. And not only had she yearned for him, she thought in shame, she'd willingly surrendered her body to his.

She looked into the living room. No Teo or Esteban. Then she glanced through the French doors onto the patio. They weren't there, either.

Why did Teo have to be a traitor? Couldn't she have awakened that morning and found it had all been a dreadful mistake and Teo was innocent? And yet she'd seen him in that cabin, standing watch over her sister. A sinister and devious man—and her lover, she thought, heartsick.

Teo Sanlucar. He was like an itch under her skin, a roar in her head, a knife thrust in her breast. He'd become the nucleus of her existence. And she'd let it happen.

No, Melanie thought, she hadn't just let it happen. She had wanted him all along, secretly gloried in his dark watchfulness on the beach even while she'd been afraid. She had asked for it.

Of course she knew that when she did find Teo and Esteban their faces and their words would be solicitous— poor dear Melanie. She suddenly felt she couldn't bear it, couldn't enact the disgusting farce for even one more minute.

Much to her surprise, neither man was at home.

Lucia smiled warmly and handed Melanie a note from Teo. It read: "Esteban has gone to Bilbao for the day and I have gone out on business." *Business,* she sneered. "Please wait with Lucia and I shall return and drive you to the bank this afternoon. Teo."

Melanie sat in the kitchen and sipped coffee and envisioned him with her sister and those awful men. How had Cecily got herself into this fix? Had her sister actually been so blind where Carlos was concerned that she hadn't seen what he was doing or where he was leading her? How else could it have happened? Cecily wasn't selected at random to be kidnapped. Her foolish, naive sister...

Nine o'clock came and went. Melanie telephoned Diego Pacheco at the bank, for the second time in an hour.

"It is Saturday," he tried to explain, "and even though we remain open this day until one, the banks in New York, I fear, are closed." But a wire transfer could come in from Madrid, he told her in a kind voice. She must, of course, try again later.

It won't come, Melanie thought as she hung up. What would the Cax Carot do to her sister? How could Melanie make them understand that the transfer was complicated by a weekend now? But any reasonable person knew that.

Reasonable? A kidnapper?

There was a hope. Teo. Surely he would explain the situation to his comrades. Teo would not let them harm Cecily. He might be greedy and deceitful, but a killer? And he was still a man of learning and culture, a professor of history...he could not be a murderer!

By ten the waiting had become intolerable. How could she just sit in this elegant house and do nothing?

It came to Melanie suddenly. The money most likely was not going to arrive on a weekend. She had to accept that. And there was no guarantee that Teo could keep Cecily from harm. But perhaps the police could.

She dashed up the stairs to her bedroom two at a time and collected her purse and camera. Then she turned and stared mutely at the unmade bed. A shiver crawled up her spine. Had she really made love there with Teo only a few short hours ago? Could it have been as wonderful as she remembered? A disturbing thought insinuated itself into her mind. Was it possible that, in spite of the guilt she was feeling, she had come to care for her treacherous Basque? That she felt not only an intense attraction but something deeper? She couldn't think about it now.

She turned from the bed and walked quickly to a small inlaid desk in a corner of the room, where she scratched out a note for Teo. "I have gone shopping. The waiting is driving me crazy. Melanie." Downstairs she handed the note to Lucia.

"*Por Señor Teo.*"

"*Sí, señorita,*" Lucia said, nodding and smiling.

Then Melanie hurried out to her car. The drive was becoming familiar. She took the curves along the winding road smoothly, if a little too fast, but at least this time there were no animals to bar her path.

On the outskirts of Pamplona she found a parking place near an ironworks factory and locked her car. The police station, she recalled, was close to the older part of town, perhaps three or four blocks west of the square. She didn't know its exact location, but that didn't matter. She began heading in the direction of the plaza. There would be a policeman on every corner and all she needed to do was ask directions.

Melanie had plenty to tell the Guardia Civil. She knew the kidnappers, and she even knew where they were holding Cecily. Why hadn't she gone and done this before? Could it be that she dreaded giving the police Teo's name?

She stopped short. What if these Basque kidnappers really did have a pipeline to the police? What if the very policeman she spoke to was a Basque infiltrator?

She began to walk again. But if the police acted quickly, surely no one could get word to Teo or Sevé in time for them to react.

The element of surprise would be on the side of the Guardia Civil.

As she approached the plaza the crowds were frenzied, shoving and elbowing her, making it impossible to hurry. She spotted one of the ever-present policemen in his formal, polished attire and walked toward him. If anyone were following—which was always a possibility—she'd pretend to photograph the officer.

She received the directions, and just in case, she took his picture.

Clever, she was so clever!

Then she headed in the direction he had indicated but stopped once or twice to take a few more pictures. *Act normal,* she told herself.

There it was, the station house. Just down the street now, so near. And yet, would she be seen by someone as she entered? If she hadn't been followed, did the kidnappers perhaps have someone watching the station?

She stood at the corner and took a picture of the cathedral's steeple, which emerged between the buildings. Then she moved her camera up and down the crowded street as if looking for another shot. She scanned the many faces. She did the same thing two more times, viewing the entire block to her satisfaction. There were no strange men watching her. She saw only *feria*-goers and tourists.

She took a deep breath and crossed to the other side of the street, two buildings away from the station house. Someone offered her wine and Melanie took it, smiling,

trying to appear as if she were joining the gaiety of the
crowd.

She moved on down the block, stopping to look in a
shop window. She was nearly there.

A moment before she was going to turn and head up
the steps of the police station, she caught a reflection in
the windowpane. Her heart jumped in fear.

There, on the other side of the street, was a young man
in a black beret. He was standing still, out of time with
the flux, facing in her direction.

Melanie kept her back to him, pretending to window-
shop. The hordes of people moved past the man in both
directions but he remained rooted to his spot.

He was watching her.

Melanie made a quick decision and began strolling very
slowly in the opposite direction from the police station;
her hands were fumbling with her camera.

She stopped, keeping her head turned away from the
man in the beret. She lifted her camera and shot a picture
of God knew what, then very slowly she swung it around,
aiming in his direction. She swept the camera slowly past
him, as if looking for something photogenic; she saw his
dark head turn quickly. Her heart leaped wildly and her
hands began to tremble.

Dumb! She had been so stupid! She should have known
they'd either have someone tailing her or someone watching the police station. Now she was a prisoner of her own
audacity.

What was she going to do?

She was so painfully conspicuous, standing one building away from the police station. If she walked in, would
the young man rush to tell Sevé? Then they would kill
Cecily and disappear into the hills, as Basques had done
for centuries.

Move, think!

She spotted a group of student types nearby, drunk as

lords. She made an elaborate production of taking their picture.

Not good enough. She was standing there like a criminal caught in the act, next to the police station!

She began walking again. To head in the direction opposite the station was so open a ruse that surely he would spot it and report to Teo or Sevé that Melanie had seen him, then fled.

She turned around again and pretended to be searching the street for something specific. Then she set off with a purposeful stride to the corner directly in front of the station. She stepped off the curb and walked diagonally across the road, weaving through traffic, bumping into people.

Then she stood in front of the shop—a shoe shop—and looked in the window. She couldn't see him because the glass was facing the wrong way, but Melanie sensed he was still there. She could almost feel his dark eyes following her every move.

She entered the shop.

Shoes. She didn't need any, but she knew she had better walk out with a package and a contented look on her face.

Melanie spent a long time selecting a pair of Italian pumps. Finally she paid the clerk with a traveler's check, at a terrible rate of exchange, and left with her package.

There he was. Studiously nonchalant, positioned across the street from her, his head turned away. All he needed was a newspaper to hide behind, she thought.

Melanie began walking in the general direction of her car. There was nothing more she could do to allay his suspicions. It had been foolish of her to consider going to the police in the first place. And God help Cecily if the young Basque reported Melanie's suspicious movements to his superiors. But he had no reason to, did he? She had played it wisely. So what if he'd seen her on the same street as the police station?

Melanie drove out of Pamplona barely aware that she

was operating a vehicle. She was thinking of Teo, trying
to imagine his reaction to her note. Shopping. He'd never
believe it! He'd put one and one together and know that
she was up to something.

Foolish!

Perhaps she could beat him back to Esteban's and destroy the note.

She drove too quickly along the narrow road; once, she
nearly collided with a goat. Her blouse was sticking to
her back with nervous perspiration.

When she pulled up the long drive her heart sank—
Teo's car was already there.

She entered the house, feeling both guilty and frightened. As she passed the two stone lions, she took a deep
breath and told herself to act normal, to calm down. Whatever Teo might suspect, he couldn't prove a thing.

Peeking into the living room, she saw that he wasn't
there. She looked out the French doors onto the lawn. Not
there, either. Finally she spotted him in the library, deep
in concentration. He hadn't noticed her yet. She stood
motionless, gripping her shopping bag, watching him. He
looked like the professor again, with his reading glasses
on and the papers scattered across the desk. The house
seemed suddenly too hushed, and she felt as if she should
go back to the front door, bang it open and shout, "Hi!
I'm home!"

But she had to face him. Melanie squared her shoulders,
walked to the library door and cleared her throat.
"Hello." She forced a smile to her lips. "What are you
doing—correcting papers?"

He looked up finally, his train of thought broken.
"Hello," he said, "and yes, that is exactly what I am
doing. Summer students, Melanie."

"Don't you find it hard to concentrate with everything
that's happened?"

"Yes. But that does not excuse neglecting my work."

"I see." She wondered, inanely, if Cecily had a paper in that stack.

He removed his glasses then, rubbing his eyes before he looked back up to Melanie. "Where did you go?"

A chill crawled across her flesh. "You got my note, didn't you?" she asked levelly.

"Yes. But I found it difficult to believe you could shop under such pressure, Melanie. You amaze me." His dark eyes rested on her.

She looked away and shrugged. "I called the bank several times and the money had still not arrived. I was so nervous..." She smiled weakly.

"Of course."

"So I had to go somewhere, do something, anything..."

"Shopping."

"Yes." She looked back at him and held up the plastic bag that was sticky and warm in her hand. "Shoes."

"Shoes. I see."

"I killed some time." She tried to smile again but her face felt as though it might crack with the effort.

He was silent for too long a time. Finally he said, "You did not do anything...foolish, did you, Melanie?"

"Foolish?"

"Yes. Such as contact someone...say, the *policía*?"

Melanie did her utmost to appear surprised, adding a touch of wounded pride to her expression. "I would never do anything to compromise Cecily. How could you even think such a thing?"

He was not very quick to answer. "I merely asked." Then he placed his elbows on the desk, hands folded under his chin in that familiar pose, and he sat there silently, studying her. The moment stretched out agonizingly.

Deliberately she changed the subject. "Is Esteban home yet?"

He shook his head. "Still in Bilbao, I assume."

"Oh..."

"And," he added, "Lucia is also gone for the afternoon."

He was letting her know how alone they were, and a picture flashed into her mind: Teo standing behind her last night on the balcony, turning her to face him, his mouth descending...

"Have you eaten?"

"What?" she asked breathlessly.

"Eaten?"

She shook her head.

"Well, then, we must be in Pamplona at five. Perhaps I could take you for the afternoon meal..."

"No, thank you. I'm really not..."

"I insist. You see, I am a poor cook and without Esteban or Lucia, I am afraid we will both starve."

Melanie shook her head again. "Please, not Pamplona. The crowds..."

"I understand." He sat for a minute more, thinking. Then he looked at his watch. "Could you prepare a basket of food? Things that are left from before?"

"Leftovers."

"Yes. Then perhaps we might drive somewhere. I have a place in mind."

"But the bank?"

"We shall telephone Señor Pacheco first. The money will come when it comes. We cannot make it arrive any sooner. I will not allow you to sit here, worrying so."

"I'm not sure..."

He got to his feet, pushing papers together, leaving neat stacks for later. "I shall telephone the bank now. Could you attend to the basket?"

"I guess so," she said listlessly, "but where are we going?"

He looked up from the desk. "Allow me to surprise you, Melanie."

She found a basket covered in cobwebs in the laundry room and cleaned it carefully. Then she wrapped cheese and bread and placed them inside, together with several bunches of plump green grapes. Teo walked into the kitchen with two wine glasses and a dusty bottle.

"I am no cook, but I would make an excellent wine steward." He smiled charmingly.

A picnic, Melanie thought, feeling suddenly restless. "Maybe we should just eat here. I'm not in the mood…"

"Nonsense. We will steal a few hours from your worries. I absolutely insist."

She was a prisoner, a prisoner of his deceit, his lies and his overbearing charm. She hadn't the heart to fight him.

"Come, change your clothing and perhaps this afternoon will be a pleasant surprise for you."

For a moment as their eyes met and their gazes locked, Melanie thought that he might take a step toward her, pull her into his arms, bring his mouth down on hers. It all came flooding back, his embrace, his artful hands, the thrust of his powerful male body against hers.

"Aren't you going to change?" Teo asked then, his mouth curved in a small knowledgeable smile.

"Change," she breathed. "Of course." She tore her stare away in embarrassed confusion.

She changed into slacks. Then they were off on a mysterious jaunt, Teo's so-called pleasant surprise.

They took his Mercedes and he put the top down as they headed north on a winding mountain road that Melanie didn't recognize.

"Where are we going?" she asked curiously.

"Back to the past," was all he would tell her, but his voice was teasing.

"Well, that's fine," Melanie said, "but don't forget, I have to be at that phone booth in Pamplona at five."

"You will be at the telephone on time. Now relax."

"Relax…" she mumbled to herself.

Any other time, it would have been a beautiful drive up through the foothills of the Pyrenees. Teo was charming and Melanie repeatedly had to remind herself that he was the enemy—he was *not* a handsome, debonair Basque taking her for a romantic drive in his sporty convertible.

It was very difficult for her to hate him.

The road began to rise into the higher mountains. As they ascended, Melanie noticed a kind of mist covering the countryside, lying low in the ravines and sneaking up into the forests. It was by no means a cold fog, but it was heavy, blotting out the sun, muffling all sound. They came to a stop at a crossroads in the dense forest once, and Melanie could hear the twittering of birds from deep within the misty woods.

They drove on. As the fog thickened, the valley seemed to grow darker and the foliage greener. It was breathtakingly lovely. Haunting, Melanie thought.

"You could at least tell me where we are," she said over the soft purr of the engine. She was a little nervous. Did this trip have anything to do with the kidnapping? Some rendezvous?

"Roncesvalles Pass," Teo said. "Does that sound familiar?"

It did, indeed, but Melanie had to search her memory. "I know," she said, a bit irked that he was testing her. "The song of Roland," she put in smugly.

"Yes. Very good," said the professor as he pulled off the road at the crest of a lofty hill. He turned the car off. *"Le Chanson de Roland."* He stepped out of the car and came around to open her door. "From here we must walk."

Melanie swung her legs out and hesitated a moment, finally taking his proffered hand. "I don't remember a thing about Roland," she admitted. "There's an old legend, isn't there?"

Teo shrugged as he began to lead her along a mossy path heading into the shrouded forest, away from the roadside. "Myth? Fact? It really does not matter."

"That's a very strange thing for a history professor to say."

"Perhaps I am a romantic at heart." His smile was tender, yet she could not believe this was merely an innocent jaunt into the past. Why had he really brought her there? To keep her off guard, to lull her suspicions? Or did he have a different motive in mind? Was he trying to seduce her in yet another way?

Melanie could almost imagine their lovemaking, the tidy picnic basket beside them, a mossy bed beneath, the mist soft and dewy on their naked flesh.

Stop this, her mind commanded. She must not think of him in that way. It was too dangerous; he made it too easy for her to let go, to forget. Hadn't she found that out already?

She glanced at their surroundings, so alien, so unearthly, on that fog-shrouded mountainside.

She moved away from his side as they walked and watched him carefully from the corner of her eye. The hills seemed to encroach upon them, so thick with tall mossy trees and the clouds of mist that she could see only a few yards in any direction. She looked nervously around. Were the kidnappers hidden in the fog somewhere?

The path finally brought them out into a small clearing. Below was the spectacular view of a deep valley, half-hidden now in fog. Surrounding them were dark forests, the trees vague shapes in the mist. There was utter silence and Melanie had the disconcerting feeling that they were the only two living creatures on the mountainside. What did the mist hide?

Teo stopped and stood still, his hands on his hips, as he turned to look in all directions. "Roncesvalles Pass," he said quietly, reverently. He kneeled down on the moist grass and looked up at her. "It's damp and I forgot a blanket, but we'll survive. And we have food."

She knelt down alongside him and opened the picnic basket. Wine, grapes, cheese and bread. Even Esteban's crystal glasses. So very charming...

"Hungry?" He looked at her with concern.

"A little. What was the legend of Roland, by the way?" she asked.

"It is difficult to pry the truth from lore." He smiled and cut her pieces of bread and cheese. "Legend has it that thousands of Moorish Saracens attacked Charlemagne and that one of his many knights, the fairest knight of all, Roland, blew his horn on this hill to warn his uncle who was riding far ahead on the point. The infamous mists of Roncesvalles, however, swallowed the sound of Roland's horn and the knight, who turned his face to the south so that his uncle, Charlemagne, would know of his brave confrontation with the Saracens, perished boldly."

"It's a very heroic tale," Melanie said, sipping wine.

"Very," Teo agreed. "It was even written that when Charlemagne returned safely to France and told Roland's fiancée, she dropped dead on the spot."

Melanie grimaced. "A dreadful ending."

"Quite." He laughed lightly. "But then there is the story, probably far more historically accurate, that Roland did not perish at all."

"I see. And no doubt Charlemagne was not in Spain to rid Europe of the dastardly Saracens, either."

"No," said Teo, "it is believed that he was not. He apparently rode to Spain to make a pilgrimage to Santiago de Compostela and encountered a handful of Basques on his way back into France. There was, of course, a skirmish here, but to what extent it was important, who knows?"

"I like Roland blowing his horn with thousands of bloodthirsty Saracens at his heels."

"So do I,"

Melanie took some more bread and glanced around. It was so lovely and quiet in this unearthly forest with the cool, damp air caressing her skin. She could almost see the knights on their great horses, their heavy armor dull in the hazy light, and hear the ring of their swords before the sound was lost in the mists.

She glanced at Teo; he sat close to her on the damp grass, beads of moisture on his dark curling hair. What did he want with her? Why were they here on this deserted pass? Uncomfortably she shifted her position a little farther away from him.

"You do not eat much," he said gently.

"I'm worried, you know that, Teo. I've been worried for days now. It's sort of hard for me to enjoy myself..."

"Of course, I understand."

She looked at him narrowly. He sounded sympathetic, but she didn't believe a word of it. With her own eyes she'd seen him standing in that hut, talking to the kidnappers.

He ate a grape, his pensive gaze resting on her. Then he seemed to give a slight shrug. "Still, it is an interesting spot, is it not? Esteban is far more familiar than I with the many romantic legends of the Pyrenees. I wish you had the time..." Then he paused. "But, no. Once your sister is safe, you will, of course, leave this land of mine."

"Of course," she said boldly. "What would keep me here? This place will never hold fond memories for me, you know."

He looked suddenly wounded, suddenly boyish and alone and hurt. And an unaccountable feeling of guilt swept over her.

"I could not hope that you might remain for a time?" he asked.

"I don't think so," she began.

"Even after...last night?"

Melanie's eyes dropped to her lap abruptly. "I think we should...forget about last night." Her heart thudded heavily; she wanted never to forget, never.

"It will stay with me always." Teo's voice was gentle and sorrowful. He reached out a hand and tilted her chin and she could no longer avoid his gaze. *Oh, God,* she cried inwardly. *I still want him.* And then his hand was behind her head, his long fingers moving through the knot of her coppery hair, loosening it, tenderly urging her toward him.

She responded to his touch, and even as she damned herself she let his lips move over hers and her mouth parted. But there were tears burning in her eyes this time. They spilled finally and Teo tasted them.

He drew back. "You're crying."

"Yes," she whispered.

"Why?"

"Because I'm hurting, Teo. Because I want you to kiss me, but I'm afraid."

"I don't understand…"

Melanie could say nothing. What could she have told him—that she knew he was involved with Cecily's kidnappers?

"You have shut me away," Teo said long moments later.

She nodded, wiping at a stubborn tear.

"And so you will find your sister and merely leave the Basque country. Forever?"

"Yes," Melanie said, "once Cecily is safe…"

"I wish you could have seen another side of life here. It can be very wonderful."

"I'm sure you're right," she said stiffly, as the fog crept silently around them, wrapping Melanie and Teo in an eerie embrace.

They left the magical mountains, driving down toward Pamplona, which lay to the south. Suddenly the sun was on Melanie's shoulders once more, and perspiration dampened her neck. She took a deep breath of relief, put on her sunglasses and repinned the knot in her hair.

She looked at her watch. It was four o'clock. Had the money arrived in Pamplona? Well, if it hadn't, then Teo could just go tell his comrades that she had done everything humanly possible. Was it her fault that wire transfers could not be made on a moment's notice? Perhaps if they hadn't been so greedy…

Teo was quiet as he drove smoothly and expertly along the twisting road. She could see the plateau of Pamplona ahead, baking beneath the Spanish sun.

She looked again at Teo, at his slightly graying hair, at the strong, chiseled profile and the sun-darkened forearms flexing as he steered. They should be driving in to celebrate the *feria*—to drink and dance and cheer the bull and the matador. But that was impossible.

Teo drove as near to the bank as possible and parked, wedging his car between two very old, beat-up Volkswagens.

"Your car will be destroyed," Melanie said, and she felt a perverse sort of satisfaction.

He shrugged. "This will only take a minute. Señor Pacheco is waiting for us."

Melanie knew that in Spain banks closed at 1:00 P.M. on Saturdays. She was grateful to Señor Pacheco for remaining there, just for her. Still, when he unlocked the door and let them both in, his expression told her the worst.

"As I explained," he said with deep concern, "I placed a telephone call to Madrid but my…tracer, you say? has gone nowhere." He spread his hands helplessly. "Perhaps Monday, your American money arrives. *¿Sí?*"

Melanie sank into a chair in the lobby. It would take until Monday. Dear God, how was she going to explain it to this Sevé? He'd never believe her. He would think that she was just stalling.

But then—and she glanced up from her folded hands— there was always Teo to explain on her behalf. He could sneak off from Esteban's tonight and tell Sevé what had happened.

Oh, wasn't she lucky, Melanie thought sarcastically, to have Teo on her side?

They left the bank with Señor Pacheco's assurance that he had already spoken to several other banks in Navarre and that as soon as the wire did come in, the large amount of cash would be made available.

At least it was one less thing to worry about, she supposed.

She dreaded the telephone call. It wasn't fair that she had to be the one to tear out her hair worrying. Why couldn't her father have flown over? So what if her mother, the delicate and ever-social Muriel, couldn't possibly stay alone during the ordeal. So what!

How about me, Melanie railed inwardly as they walked. What about her ordeal?

She was deep in thought when Teo placed a hand on her arm; surprised, she came to a halt. "What is the matter?"

"It's not fair," Melanie said sharply.

"I see." His dark brow creased in a frown. "Seldom is life fair," he said pensively.

"Is that so?" Melanie fired back. "It seems to me that everyone around me has control of his life. Everyone else has choices. Everyone but me. I'm the prisoner of all this." And she made an angry sweeping gesture with her hand. Even Cecily had made her own choices—she'd chosen to take up with Carlos, hadn't she? And it seemed safe to assume that was why both she and Cecily were in this mess now.

He softly touched her arm. "I know, but it will come out all right, Melanie, We will find a way."

She only shook him off and walked ahead swiftly, pushing through the happy, laughing, heedless mass of people.

The telephone booth sat ominously at the end of the block. Someone was using it. The time was now four forty-five. Surely the man wouldn't talk all night.

At five o'clock however, he still had not hung up.

Melanie panicked. "Tell him to hang up, Teo!" she pleaded.

Teo walked to the booth and rapped on the glass door,

speaking to the occupant in Spanish. She caught a few words; Teo was telling him that they were awaiting an important call, *vida y muerte*. Life and death.

The man looked at them both, shook his head, said *adios* or some such thing, and hung up.

Melanie sighed with relief.

Still, it was three minutes after five by her watch. Had she missed the call? My God.

At ten after, she was twisting her hands nervously, her dark red hair wringing wet at the nape of her neck.

"Why doesn't he call?" she said over and over.

Teo had no explanation. "He must call, Melanie, if he wants his money," he reassured her. "Please do not worry."

"Worry?" she hissed, half out of her mind. "Why would I *worry*?"

It was twelve after five. The street was crowded and noisy with hordes of fiesta lovers, pushing and bumping into one another, offering their bota bags, laughing and cheering, arms around shoulders, dancing and bobbing up and down, up and down.

There were always cars jamming the narrow street. It would momentarily clear to the tune of many horns, then jam up once again.

Melanie never saw the nondescript auto that pulled up near them, blocking traffic. She was looking at Teo, trying to avoid the crush of the throng, when suddenly Teo's face darkened at something he saw over her shoulder.

Melanie turned around quickly. Two men in white shirts and black berets had disengaged themselves from the crowd and before she had time to react, they were standing on either side of her, each taking an arm.

"What do you think you're—?" she gasped, then felt a cold, hard object shoved into her ribs. Disbelieving, she looked down. Half-hidden in one of the men's hands was a gun. "No," she breathed, too terrified to move.

"*Vayate,*" one of the men said. "Go. The car." He flicked his head toward the curb.

"I…" Melanie tried to turn her head. Where was Teo? Why didn't he stop them?

"Go," came the other man's curt command and suddenly they were pulling her toward a car.

She was shoved into the back seat before she could think, and in the madness of the fiesta, no one had noticed, not a soul.

"What are you doing!" she demanded.

The driver turned around. It was Sevé. "Keep quiet," he said in a low, threatening voice, and Melanie's heart flew into her throat. She looked at them, panic-stricken, helpless.

Teo? *Where is he?*

She twisted in her seat to stare out the window, ignoring the young Basque who sat tensely beside her. The car was already moving, but she could still see Teo standing there, utterly motionless, buffeted by the revelers, his hands shoved in his pockets and his face totally devoid of expression.

She turned around again. Damn him to hell, she thought. How very proud of himself he must be—he'd delivered her straight into this madman's hands.

And then Sevé moved his head slightly, his dark eyes catching hers in the mirror. "You have played games with us, Señorita Royce." He grinned slowly. "Now it will cost you greatly."

Chapter Eleven

The car swerved around a corner too fast and threw Melanie against the man on her left. Her mind was spinning in futility and confusion, unable to absorb what had happened. It seemed so unreal that she was sitting there, in this car, being driven out of Pamplona. She was aware of faces flashing by the window, of Sevé pressing on the horn again and again, scattering people before him, jerkily stopping and starting the car.

The men on either side of her smelled of sweat and wood smoke. They were dressed in dirty white with the inevitable black berets giving them an air of rakishness. She looked again, closer. Why, they truly were boys! Not even twenty. One watched her as a rodent would watch a snake about to strike, in paralyzed fascination. The other had turned his head away—unable to meet her eyes? They each carried ugly black handguns stuck in their red sashes. The one in the front passenger seat turned and smiled sickly at her, as if in apology. He was so young he had pimples on his face. What was going on? These kidnappers were practically children. Except Sevé.

And Teo.

Had he known this was planned? Had he led her to the

phone booth, as a lamb is led to slaughter, and calmly handed her over to these men? Or had he, too, been surprised by Sevé's coup?

What were they going to do with her? She was afraid to speak, but she forced herself to lean forward and ask Sevé, "Where are we going? What do you want from me? If anything happens to either me or my sister, you will not get the money."

But Sevé never turned his head. He laughed, a low harsh chortle that made Melanie shiver. He was evil, pure evil.

She fell back against the car seat, weak with fear, her heart pounding drumbeats inside her head. Her parents would call... They would be frantic with worry. And there was no one now to help either her or Cecily. No one. They were alone, prisoners of this insane Sevé and his protégés. It was only too obvious that he was their leader, that the boys were afraid of him. But where did Teo fit in to this mess? And what, exactly, had he and Sevé argued about that night in the café?

Melanie could only sit there and endure the bumpy ride, the proximity of the boys with their guns, the evil aura of Sevé. She clung to the belief that they were taking her to Cecily and that they could not harm her—or Cecily—until they got the money.

But what would happen then?

Eventually she leaned forward and tried once more. "My father wired the money two days ago. You must believe that. It had to go through New York and Madrid. I've checked with the bank many times. The money has not arrived yet."

Sevé said nothing. The boy in the front seat turned, though, and stared at her gravely. Did he understand?

"Please, we've tried to do what you said. But it takes several days for a money transfer. Believe me, I would give it to you if I had it."

The boy with the bad complexion said something to Sevé in Basque. There was a grunt in answer. Then silence.

It suddenly occurred to Melanie to pay attention to their route. Most likely they were taking her to that cabin where she'd seen Cecily. But Melanie couldn't be certain, so she tried to mark her surroundings, just in case the information came in handy at some point. Sevé was driving up into the hills, along a road that twisted and turned. What direction from Pamplona? She craned her neck around to look at the sun. It was behind them. They were going east then, perhaps northeast. How long had they been driving? She glanced surreptitiously at her watch. Five forty-three. They'd abducted her a few minutes after five. She estimated that they'd gone maybe thirty kilometers—twenty miles or so. She'd keep track.

Sevé followed the rough road until it ended, then pulled up and parked at the edge of a path that led up the mountainside. It seemed vaguely familiar to Melanie. Of course, this was where she'd followed Teo; the path led to the hut. But it had been dark then, and everything had looked different.

When she got out of the car, Sevé snatched her camera bag; he removed the camera, clumsily yanking off its case. He pried open the back with uncaring fingers and pulled out the film, deliberately exposing it. He tossed the ruined film aside and removed the unopened rolls, grinning as he flattened them with a boot heel. Then he threw the empty camera into the bag and handed it to Melanie with a mocking flourish. After that he searched her shoulder bag. Her traveler's checks he leafed through and put back. The same with her car keys and some pesetas.

What was he looking for?

Finally, he seemed satisfied and returned the purse to her. There was much talking then, as if Melanie's four kidnappers now felt safe. Pointing toward the path, the pimply boy said, "You walk." The other two nodded, their hands on their guns.

"And do not try to run," said Sevé harshly. "There are bullets in these guns."

They walked. The hike seemed much shorter in the sunlight than it had at night. The gnarled tree was there, but it no longer looked so ominous. The meadows alternated with evergreen forests; Melanie recalled the smell of pine in her nostrils that night.

The hut looked smaller and more insignificant by daylight. A shepherd's cabin. It was made of stone and wood and its roof was thatched. Sheep grazed beyond it, their plump white forms like dirty powder puffs dotting the green field. Smoke rose in a lazy spiral from the stone chimney.

Sevé shouted across the meadow. The plank door opened inward and a man stepped out and waved, then shouted something back.

Cecily must be in there, Melanie thought. Was she all right? She'd been held prisoner in that place for days—it must have been close to a week. Did they feed her? Let her sleep?

Sevé pushed Melanie unnecessarily, so that she stumbled through the low doorway.

"Melanie!" she heard, "Oh, Mel!" And then Cecily was hugging her fiercely, crying, sobbing hysterically with fright and relief.

She shook her sister sharply. "Stop it, Cecily." Then, holding her at arm's length, she asked, "Are you okay? Did they hurt you?"

"No, I mean yes, I'm okay."

"Did they…" Melanie hesitated to put her fear into words, but Cecily caught on.

"They're not into rape," she said disdainfully, "only kidnapping."

"Well, I guess that's something. Oh, Cecily, how did you ever get yourself into this?"

"Oh, don't, *don't* be superior. I couldn't stand it, Mel. I've been so bored and scared and I was so worried..." And she burst into tears again. "I was afraid... They threatened to get you, too. The money... What did Dad say? Oh, Mel, I'm so sorry..."

"What's going on, Cecily? You disappeared in Madrid. I was half out of my mind... What is going on?" Then she looked around at the dirty, unkempt cabin, at the young boys who stared at them as if they were strange beasts of some sort, at Sevé who smiled gloatingly and stood leaning on a long black, wicked-looking rifle.

"Can we go outside?" she asked.

Cecily shook her head, wiping away tears with one grimy hand. She was dirty and pale, her jeans were wrinkled and spotted, her T-shirt stained. "They won't let us." She gulped back tears. "Except to go to the outhouse. Under guard."

Melanie closed her eyes and swallowed hard. They were truly prisoners.

"Come on, let's sit down on your bed, at least. Tell me, from the beginning. I have to know what's going on, Cecily."

"Oh, Mel, it's such a mess." She sniffed. "You know, in Madrid, how I didn't want to go home with you?"

Melanie nodded.

"It was because Carlos and I and his friends... They call themselves the Cax Carot. That's Basque for some kind of dance. Anyway, this group...I thought...oh, gee, Mel, they sounded so wonderful, so, so idealistic, I thought..."

"Go on. What were you going to do?"

"You see, they believe you have to have someplace to go, all ready with food and weapons and medicine and books and stuff. For when the bomb falls and destroys civilization. A place like this, up in the mountains where it'll be safe. That's what they wanted to do, to supply this cottage and build another. They needed money."

Melanie sat very still, listening.

"And Sevé taught them all kinds of things, like hunting and tracking and fishing and survival. So we decided, Carlos and I, that we should pretend I was kidnapped and Mother and Dad would send some money and then I'd pretend to be freed but the Cax would have the money. It was only pretend, Mel, and Mother and Dad can afford it. They have so much..."

"Sort of instant socialism," Melanie said pensively. "So what happened?"

"Oh, God, it all went wrong." She looked around and lowered her voice. "It was Sevé. He went along at first. He said what a good idea it was. That they'd buy guns and a generator and dried food and stuff. Then at the beginning of the *feria*, he turned all hard and...and vicious. And he made them...Melanie, they didn't want to, but he threatened... Oh, I don't know, they spoke Basque, then Carlos was afraid to talk to me. Sevé threatened them, said they were already in so much trouble and he'd kill them—and me—if they didn't do as he said." Cecily hid her face in her hands. "And then he called Dad and asked for five hundred thousand dollars! Mel, I swear, I didn't know! The guys, Carlos, they were only going to ask for two or three thousand. Melanie, I swear, they didn't know, they didn't mean...!"

"Shh! I believe you." She thought for a minute. "So the boys knew Sevé before?"

"Yes, see, they're all from around here. They've known each other for ages. Sevé was, well, sort of their idol." She lowered her voice. "He's a mercenary. He fought in Africa and South America. He's scary, Mel, real scary. But at first he was fun and he knew so much about survival and weapons and stuff. They were like Boy Scouts, you know. At first—"

"How did Sevé know our family could afford such a big ransom, Cecily?"

"Well," she said, shamefaced, "it was because I

bragged to Carlos. It was when we first had the idea and I thought the money was just going to be a small amount. And then Sevé found out.''

''I see. So he realized he could use you to get a lot more. And you walked right into it, made it real easy for him,'' Melanie mused, shaking her head.

''We didn't *know*!'' Cecily wailed. ''And then it was too late. Oh, I'm so sorry! It's turned out to be a horrible nightmare. Oh, Mel…''

''Carlos. Which one is he?''

Cecily answered sullenly. ''He's outside. The good-looking blondish one. I thought he loved me. I loved him…'' She sounded bitter. ''But he's so scared of Sevé he'd wet his pants if Sevé told him to!''

Everything made sense now—her own foreboding in Torremolinos, Cecily's abrupt disappearance… And Teo's attempt to convince her to go back home. Of course he'd wanted her out of the way. Then he could have picked up the money and there would have been no complications. Nobody would have been looking for Cecily, nobody would have suspected him, nobody would have been around to call in the Guardia Civil. Oh, Lord, no wonder he'd been so adamantly against her calling the police. Melanie sat for a minute, staring off into the distance, thinking. Gullible. There was no other word for it. She'd been utterly taken in by Teo. She'd known all along that he was involved in this—with her own eyes she'd even seen him in this very cabin. And yet she'd blinded herself and hoped like a fool. A decision of the heart, certainly not the brain. Her skin felt hot and feverish, burning with shame and humiliation.

She'd slept with him, acquiescing fully to his every whim. Dear Lord in heaven, she'd even come up with a few whims of her own during their lovemaking!

Stupid, she thought, naive and stupid. Well, she was paying for it now.

"What is it, Mel?" Cecily asked, putting a tentative hand on her sister's arm.

"Nothing." Melanie shook her head irritably.

"I know something's bugging you. Come on."

"Don't you think being kidnapped is enough?"

"Yes," Cecily admitted in a small, chagrined voice.

Melanie looked at her sister for a long moment. She shrugged. "Something *is* bothering me. It's Teo. I want to know what he's got to do with all this. Did you have any idea he was involved in this group?"

"Well, yes, I knew he was part of the Cax, sort of an intellectual leader. He knows Carlos very well. I think their families are old friends."

"Isn't that cozy," Melanie muttered darkly. "Did you and Carlos tell him your plans back in Madrid?"

"Well, you see, he used to invite us over to his apartment, you know, on Saturday nights. We'd all go there and—"

"All?" Melanie interrupted.

"Most of the Cax Carot are students, Mel. Anyway, we would go over there and drink wine and talk about things."

"And he filled your heads with all this survivalist stuff…"

"Well, no, he didn't. That was Sevé. We all went to Teo's because everyone thought he was such a great guy and besides that, he's a Basque and they really stick together. Carlos said it was the only place he felt comfortable in Madrid. There's some hard feeling between the Basques and the rest of Spain, you know."

"But he went along with this Sevé. He used you students," Melanie insisted angrily.

"I don't know. He may have heard what we were planning. I'm not sure. We knew he would have disagreed, so we didn't tell him but he may have caught on," Cecily explained.

"Don't be silly. He set it up. He knew from the beginning. He knew Sevé. They probably grew up together."

"Teo wouldn't—"

"Then why was he here, Cecily? I followed him the other night and saw him right here, dressed like one of them!" she stated scornfully. "Your brilliant nice-guy professor!"

"He is nice!" Then she looked down at her hands. "He was," she said more softly. "Oh, I don't know…"

"Well, I do. He took a bunch of easily influenced students and used them."

"I really liked him…"

Melanie said nothing, afraid she might betray her own strong feelings, her own blind spot where he was concerned. She had been no better than those students of his… She looked at Cecily. "Did you kids know Sevé well in Madrid?"

Cecily shook her head. "I didn't. But Carlos would tell me once in a while that Sevé was around. He talked like he was a hero or something."

"Of course. A great man, a mercenary. For God's sake, Cecily, he's a killer! Hanging around a campus—it's sick!"

"But the professor wasn't like that. Honestly."

"Oh, no? Have you forgotten that he was in Torremolinos?"

"Well, yes… But I don't understand…"

"Simple. He was there to watch us. To make darn good and sure you didn't hop on a plane and leave Spain. He either did it on his own, or maybe it was Sevé's brilliant idea. Who cares?" Melanie suddenly felt like crying. "You do understand now that these men are evil, don't you, Cecily?"

Cecily nodded slowly. "I really thought Teo was wonderful, a really great guy, a good teacher. I'm so scared. I'll never be able to trust my judgment again, Mel. I've been making mistakes all along."

So Cecily thought they were going to get out of there. Melanie wished she herself felt so sure. Kidnappers could be caught afterward if there were witnesses who could identify them. These boys—and Sevé—had no masks on. Melanie and her sister would be those witnesses—if the Cax Carot released them. The thought chilled Melanie to the bone. No masks. Then they didn't care! Or rather Sevé didn't care that they knew his name and his face. And then Melanie knew, as surely as she knew her own name, that Sevé meant to kill them both as soon as he got the money. The boys, perhaps, weren't part of the murder scheme; but Sevé—what had he to lose?

And Teo Sanlucar? Did he know what the future held for the two sisters? Had he planned with Sevé? Or maybe that had been the real issue of their argument that night…

"What are we going to do, Mel? I heard them saying the money wasn't here yet and I got so scared. The way Sevé looked at me. And then you—they got you, too. Why? What happened? Oh, I've been going crazy up here. How did you even know I was going to Pamplona?"

Melanie thought for a minute before answering. "First of all—" she lowered her voice "—we're going to see if we can escape. If we can't, we'll wait for the money. The bank won't give the money to anyone but me."

"Hey, gee, that's right." Cecily brightened.

"As for why I'm here, I don't really know. Maybe they were afraid I'd go to the police."

Cecily shuddered. "Sevé told me what they'd do if you went to the police, or if Dad did. He's a terrible man. I think," Cecily whispered, "I think he'd kill someone without blinking an eye. He's killed hundreds of men— he brags about it."

"Did you know I've been staying with the Sanlucars?" Melanie asked.

"Sevé told me you were in Pamplona, but not that. I knew Professor Sanlucar was from here and had family— but how did you find him?"

"Oh, it wasn't hard. He followed me from Madrid. I went to see him there—at the university. And then in Pamplona, well, there wasn't a hotel room and he conveniently came along and offered me his uncle's house. It was all a setup. Do you know his uncle, Esteban?''

"No. I knew he had someone here, that's all."

"How well do you know Teo? I mean, could he have been a mercenary at one time, too?" Melanie asked. "Maybe he was in the Spanish military once..."

"Hey, he was just my professor. As to that, Mel, I have a feeling you'd know better. You've been staying in the same house for—how many days?" Cecily remarked dryly.

"Well, I don't have a clue. He's not exactly easy to know," she replied sharply, then asked, "Would Carlos help you secretly, if you asked him?"

"No, I tried. Oh, how I tried. I even tried, well, you know..." Cecily looked away, embarrassed.

"I can guess. No go, huh?"

"He's too scared. I think Sevé really would kill someone who helped us." She shook her head miserably.

"How many are there?"

"Six including Sevé. Two are always on guard—with guns. The door is locked. The windows are locked. I thought of breaking them, but the noise would alert the guards. The walls are stone. The roof is too high. Mel, I've been studying this place for days!"

"The outhouse, then."

Cecily shook her head. "How?"

"A loose board? A window?"

"The window's tiny and up high. Loose boards, I don't know. And anyway, there's always a guard."

Melanie stood. Boldly she turned and went toward the door. She called to Sevé, "I have to go to the ladies' room, please. The Damas, you understand?"

"*Sí.*" He said something brusque to the pimply boy

who stood just outside. "Follow him," Sevé said, "and no forget he has a gun and he know how to use it."

The foul-smelling little building was about a hundred feet behind the cabin. Her heart sank; it was made of stone. She went inside, horribly aware of the boy just a few feet away. Quickly she stood on the seat and felt around the roof. Thatch. It could be pushed aside. She could probably crawl out. But the noise she'd make… And how would she be able to free Cecily? Perhaps if she came up with some excuse for them to be in the outhouse together? How? She'd have to think. It was a possibility.

Then, on the way back to the cabin, Melanie thought of another possibility. She could try to escape when they took her into town to get the money. In the city she could run and get lost among the crowds. But Cecily would be left behind. No, that wouldn't do. But she still had time. The next day was Sunday and the banks would be closed. She had at least until Monday. She'd think of something by then.

She'd have to.

On the way into the cabin she looked carefully at the youths who lounged around the door. There was one who was tall and slim as a reed; his hair was dark blond, thick and wavy. His eyes were green.

"You're Carlos, aren't you?" she said, standing right in front of him. "Aren't you ashamed of yourself?" She paused. "Will you help us?"

He didn't answer; his eyes slid away. Did he understand English?

"Listen, Carlos, if you help us, my parents will pay you for it. We won't tell the police. Do you understand? You can't get away with this. You're ruining your life. Your parents…" She was sure she saw a painful shadow cross his face. She put a hand on his arm, and lowered her voice. "He'll kill us, you know. That Sevé. He'll shoot us like he'd shoot rats. And you'll be guilty, too."

No response.

"You're all cowards!" she shouted then, turning to the others. "Don't do this! There's only one of him and—" she held up her hand, fingers spread "—five of you!"

They shuffled nervously, fingering their guns. Afraid.

Sevé burst out of the cabin and grabbed her arm, dragging her over to the rough wall and slamming her against it. His face was contorted in rage. "What? You try something? Stupid! They no listen!"

The stones hurt her back. Sevé's grip numbed her arm. She felt her stomach clutch with fear. He was going to kill her right then!

But he only spat on the ground at her feet and grated out something in Basque to the others. Then he pulled her inside, flinging her onto the cot where Cecily sat. She lost her balance, half falling on her sister. Tears of fear and anger and humiliation welled up inside her.

"Melanie, I heard you," Cecily was saying. "Wow, I'd never have had the nerve! What did they do?"

Painfully, Melanie pulled herself upright and rubbed her sore arm. She was shaking all over. "Nothing," she said woodenly. "They did nothing."

They could hear Sevé talking to the men outside, haranguing them. Cecily ran to the window and tried to see what was going on. Suddenly they heard two gunshots. Cecily jumped back from the window with a cry; Melanie felt every muscle in her body go rigid.

"What?" she rasped to her sister.

"I...I don't know." Cecily's face was as white as snow.

The door flew open and Sevé swaggered in, banging it shut behind him. He laughed coldly. "Don't worry. I no shoot anybody. Not yet. Only to warn them. And you, too."

He approached Melanie, thrusting his face close to hers. She could smell the odor of his sweat and the sour wine on his breath. He was unshaven and the red kerchief about his weathered neck was twisted and filthy. She shrank back.

"*Señorita,*" he said hoarsely. "Tomorrow you will call your rich parents and tell them I want twice the money! For two daughters! One million I want now because I do not get it soon enough. You hear? And I want it all by *el fin de la feria*. In four days, *señorita*. By the end of the Fiesta de San Fermín."

Chapter Twelve

Sunday, July 11

Melanie was wakened sometime after midnight by the sound of two men speaking outside the cabin door. They seemed to be arguing, their voices alternately raised and lowered. She propped herself up on an elbow, shifting in her cramped space on the narrow bed next to Cecily, and strained to hear.

They were speaking Basque.

What was going on? she wondered, feeling apprehensive. Who was it? Was Sevé tongue-lashing one of the young boys, berating him for some error?

It was cold in the cabin. She looked toward the fireplace; the logs had burned down to a few glowing embers. There was wood next to the hearth, but for some unaccountable reason, Melanie hesitated to rise and rekindle the fire. It was because of those men outside, because there was something intimidating in their tones and she felt it safer to shrink back into her corner with Cecily.

The arguing halted abruptly. Melanie looked at the door through the darkness and wished that whoever had been quarreling would start again. It suddenly seemed entirely too quiet.

She lay there, cold and shaking, watching the door. She

could feel the harsh roughness of the filthy wool blanket
that covered her and smell the stale odor that permeated
it. Her skin crawled from its touch, and she wondered if
they'd both get vermin from the bedding. It was awful,
she told herself, that she could think of such inconse-
quential things when her very life was in danger.

Her eyes fastened on the door again. The latch rattled
a little. Was Sevé coming to kill them in their sleep? Or
had one of the boys decided that he needed a little amo-
rous diversion? Her muscles tensed and she looked around
desperately for a weapon—a stick, or a heavy pot, a
chair—anything she could grab. She willed the door to
stay closed. But she saw the latch slowly move, raised as
if by an invisible hand. The door creaked, then swung
inward. Her heart quickened and she gently nudged Cecily. Her sister was asleep.

What did this intruder want?

A lone man, a tall shadow filling the portal, stood silhouetted in the moonlight for a long time. Then the figure
began to walk toward the cot.

"Get out of here," Melanie hissed.

He stopped and stood over her, large in the night.

"Get out!" she whispered harshly.

"Do not be afraid, Melanie."

"You…" Her voice was very quiet, disbelieving.
"What nerve…showing up here."

"Melanie, I—"

"No. Don't say anything. One more word and I'll
scratch your eyes out."

"I see that you are unharmed. I will leave you, then,"
Teo said, but he hesitated, and Melanie could feel the
tension emanating from his body, could see the rigid set
of his shoulders against the diffused light from outside.

She felt brittle and close to tears, caught between outrage that he would have the nerve to let her recognize him
and a pathetic relief that he had come at last.

"You are unharmed," he'd said. And she despised herself for the fatal weakness that let her still care—and still look for signs that he cared.

"Wait!" she cried softly.

He turned, pausing, a tall shadow in the musty cabin.

"Can you get us out of here? Will you help us? Teo—" Her voice choked and stopped.

His silence was oppressive. Finally he spoke and his voice was harsh. "I cannot. The men outside have guns and will use them."

"You could, I know you could!" she whispered, heartbroken. "You won't do it. Teo, how can you be part of this? How can you?"

"I must go," Teo said in a strained whisper. "But when I am gone, ask yourself, didn't I tell you to leave Spain? Did I not warn you over and over?"

Her lips compressed into an unforgiving line.

"So be it."

She could not see his face, but she wondered if it was pain she'd heard in his voice. He stood unmoving, a dark, shadowy form in the moonlight. "For your own sake," he said, "do not anger Sevé, Melanie."

"So good of you to worry about us."

"Just remember. That is all." He turned on his heel and left, closing the cabin door softly, and the latch fell back into place with a quiet click.

"It was Teo, wasn't it?" Cecily spoke in the darkness. "I'm so scared," she whimpered.

"So am I," Melanie said softly, "so am I."

She lay awake for a long time, listening to the night. Somewhere, far off in the deep timber, an owl hooted. There was the sound of trickling water that she hadn't noticed during the day. The silence seemed unearthly without the noise of a passing car once in a while. She felt more alone than she ever had since coming to this country of the Basques.

She grimaced, knowing why she had felt more secure before her own kidnapping. Teo. He had kept her his prisoner, yes, but his hand had always been at her back and the strength of his dark eyes had watched over her. He'd been her protector, just as he'd said. And now she had no one.

Cecily had fallen back to sleep and was taking up most of the narrow cot they were forced to share. Melanie shifted her carefully and tried every technique she could think of to get to sleep. It was exhaustion that finally won out.

At dawn she and her sister were roughly awakened by one of the young Basques. "Food," he said, nodding toward the cabin door.

Melanie looked at him curiously.

"He wants us to cook," Cecily explained, sighing wearily.

"*Us?*"

"Yes. It was Sevé's idea. A few days ago. I guess he thinks women should be slaves."

"Not this one," Melanie murmured.

But in the end, after the young guard had reported that Melanie refused to do the cooking, Sevé entered the cabin and dragged her out, shoving her toward a fire, pointing at the greasy tin plates and crusty pans.

Under great protest, Melanie cooked.

Teo was nowhere to be seen. Melanie supposed he had returned to Esteban's, to his creature comforts, his comfortable bed and elegant meals. Or perhaps he had been an apparition, dark and ghostly in the night; perhaps he had not been there at all.

She scrambled eggs in a charred iron pan and looked around the campsite in the light of day. There were sleeping bags hanging out on branches to air. A couple of army-style pup tents sat in the woods and the familiar outhouse was behind the cabin. She glanced at the thatched roof of the latrine and once again thought of escape.

Everything seemed sharper, purer, more defined, in the

clear mountain air. It was fresher in the woods. A ridiculous thought, Melanie decided, and quite irrelevant, considering their situation. And yet her senses were keen with the smell of burning wood and brewing coffee, the sound of squirrels chattering, the warble of a bird nearby, the touch of the hot iron pan in her hand.

She thought of taking a few pictures then almost laughed. Take a picture of her kidnappers? Besides, Sevé had ruined her film.

She was busy slicing ham when she felt her skin begin to crawl, as if she were being watched. She straightened from her crouched position, spinning around to look behind her. Teo was leaning against a tree near the camp, his eyes fastened on her.

A gasp caught in Melanie's throat. She'd thought him gone. Where had he been earlier? Standing there, watching while Sevé dragged her out of the cabin?

Her eyes narrowed. Teo, her self-proclaimed protector. What a laugh!

He moved then, striding over to one of the guards, saying something she couldn't hear to the boy, who seemed to be listening respectfully. Even as he spoke, Teo's pensive gaze still rested on Melanie. Then when he was done talking, he headed away from the camp, along the path Melanie knew so well.

He was leaving. Going, undoubtedly, for a decent meal or a bath or whatever. Leaving them in Sevé's hands.

Damn him, she swore under her breath even as her heart was squeezed by a terrible anguish.

When he was gone from her sight, a white form disappearing into the depths of the trees, Melanie turned back to cutting the meat, hacking at it, wiping the treacherous tears from her eyes.

The men ate piles of eggs and ham and stale bread. They all still wore their grimy clothes and dusty black berets. Two of them—Carlos was one—sat on rocks near the cabin, sharpening hunting knives. Another was sitting close to the fire, cleaning a rifle, polishing its stock with an oily rag, over and over again.

These kids were so stupid and blind, Melanie thought. She felt sorry for them, but her pity was vastly overshadowed by her own anxiety.

And where had Sevé gone?

As if in response to her question, he emerged moments later from the dusky forest, carrying a dead rabbit in one hand, brandishing a long knife in the other.

He grinned widely, revealing his ugly, broken teeth. "Supper!" he shouted gleefully.

Melanie turned to her sister. "The big man," she sneered, "the Great White Hunter."

Sevé approached the women and tossed the pathetic little carcass at their feet. "Clean it."

"You must be—"

But Cecily interrupted Melanie quickly. "Here, I'll do it." She gave Melanie a warning glance.

Maybe it was wrong of her to harbor such vengeful feelings, Melanie reflected, but she swore to herself that if and when they got out of this ordeal, she was going to see Sevé pay.

It was midmorning when he barged into the cabin. "Come," he ordered, looking directly at Melanie, "we call your father now."

"Go on," pleaded Cecily, "don't make him mad. He's crazy," she whispered fervently.

Grudgingly, Melanie picked up her purse and her camera bag and followed Sevé out. The hike down the mountain was growing familiar—the meadows and forests, even her giant old tree. She would have delighted in the splendid country had Sevé not been right at her heel, his hot breath on her neck.

"Must you walk so close?" Melanie asked once.

He merely grinned, his dark eyes traveling leisurely over her body.

She turned and began walking again, more quickly, vowing to keep her opinions to herself.

"Remember," Sevé said from behind her, "twice the money." They trekked to a village some four kilometers from where Sevé had parked the car. It took over an hour to make the overseas connection, and when Melanie was finally on the line to Ohio, she was horrified to find out her father wasn't home.

"A million dollars!" Muriel cried, aghast. "Are these men insane?"

Melanie felt like crying. "Mother," she said, "didn't you hear me? This is no joke, for God's sake! They're holding me now, too! *Please*, just tell Dad. Tell him to wire the same amount as before. Tell him to do it as fast as possible. *Please*."

The line went silent for a minute. "What if he doesn't have it?"

"He'd better have it," Melanie choked out. "Believe me, Mother, Dad can get his hands on it somehow." She could almost see Muriel biting her lower lip, hand pressed to her heart.

"All right, darling. Your dad will handle everything. Is Cecily okay?"

"Yes. We're okay, for now. But, Mother, these men mean business. You must get the money sent as fast as possible."

"Are those men...bothering you?"

"No, Mother—all they want is money."

"I'm so afraid..." Her mother's voice trailed off.

"Tell Dad. He'll handle everything. And don't...worry, Mother."

When Melanie finally hung up, Sevé pulled her out of the phone booth and held her arm in a vicelike grip. "Problem? There is a problem?"

"No," Melanie said wearily. "My mother is just very upset."

"What?"

"Nothing."

The hike back up to the cabin tired Melanie. Sevé, as always, stayed right on her heel, prodding her, rudely laughing when she stumbled once, not even offering to help her to her feet.

Melanie shot him a hateful glance. "You're a vicious man."

"Veeshus," he mispronounced it. "What is the meaning?"

"Look it up," Melanie retorted, hastening her footsteps.

Carlos and the others were sitting outside when they returned. She might have happened on a student outing, Melanie thought, but when the young faces looked up and saw Sevé, their expressions became blank and guarded.

The fools! Hadn't they realized yet where Sevé was leading them? There were five of them. Sevé was only a man, one single man!

But it was useless. Admittedly, he possessed a certain power, a charisma of some sort. His mere presence seemed to quell any thoughts of disobedience or rebellion.

Melanie walked inside the cabin, threw herself down on the cot and fought back tears of frustration.

It must have been several hours before she opened her eyes again. Pale light slanted through the cabin's sooty window, and dust motes danced in the panel of brightness.

Melanie looked at her watch. Six o'clock. How had she managed to fall asleep? She sat up and felt a little dizzy. Was she getting sick? But no, she always felt lightheaded after a nap in the afternoon.

An idea came to her. Maybe she should get sick... Where was Cecily?

She walked to the door and pulled it open. Cecily was cooking something over the small camp stove. She looked up and smiled. "You're awake."

"Yes," Melanie said. "Could you come here? I feel kind of...ill."

"What's wrong?" Cecily asked as she closed the door behind her.

Melanie put a finger to her lips. "Shh...nothing's wrong."

"But you said..."

"I know what I said, Cecily. Look, I've got an idea. Now hear me out before you go off in a panic. Okay?"

Cecily nodded. "Sure."

Melanie explained her plan to her sister.

"That's nuts, Mel. I mean, you'll get us...killed," she whispered.

"They won't kill anybody until they have the money," Melanie hissed, "and then it may be too late."

"I think you're crazy. The money will come and they'll let us go."

"Maybe," Melanie said darkly, "but I refuse to let that criminal get away with a million dollars!"

"But won't the police catch him someday?"

"Maybe, and then again, maybe not. He could hide in these hills forever."

Cecily was silent for a long minute. "Okay, let's go for it. I've been sitting on my butt long enough."

"Good girl. It's a deal." Melanie stuck out her hand for Cecily to shake.

"Oh, wow..." She grasped Melanie's hand. "This better work."

They waited until dusk. Melanie made it look good by staying in the cabin while Cecily cooked outside. She refused to eat any of the meal, and she even made sure Cecily told Sevé in Spanish that her sister was not feeling well. And then after the sun had disappeared behind a ridge and it grew dark in the east, Melanie stuffed her passport and some pesetas in her pocket, glanced wistfully at her camera and let out a huge moan. "Cecily! Oh, Cecily, come here quick! Ohhh!"

Cecily helped a staggering Melanie out of the cabin and into the outhouse. The men stood mutely watching; what was wrong with the *americana*, their faces warily asked. Even Sevé stayed away after he'd heard Cecily call over her shoulder in Spanish that her sister had female troubles.

No man on earth knew how to cope with that circumstance.

Behind the closed door, Melanie whispered, "If I have to stay in here, I *am* going to be sick."

Cecily went to work on the roof, tugging away thatch, while Melanie made all sorts of moans and groans to her sister's signals. And then finally there was room for them to crawl out.

Darkness fell over the camp. The fire would help, too, Melanie hoped, as the men standing around its warmth would be partially blinded by the bright flames. Cecily, younger and more agile, had no difficulty pulling herself up through the roof and letting herself down behind the outhouse.

It was Melanie's turn. She made a few more retching sounds and tried to pull herself up. No way. She tried again. Dear God, she wasn't going to make it. It was like trying to chin herself. Melanie hadn't chinned herself since high school!

"Come on," she heard Cecily's whisper. "Think of Sevé catching us…"

Catching and killing us, Melanie thought. She tried again, finally able to get a foothold on a loose stone. A little more! Yes! She was up, pulling her legs through the hole, sucking in fresh air.

"Ooh," she groaned from behind the outhouse. "Ooh, Cecily…I'm so sick," and they both crouched, lying low, then rushing for the cover of the trees.

They had only minutes before the men would notice that there was silence from the outhouse. "Hurry," Melanie gasped, pushing Cecily along, putting distance between them and the fire's glow.

Melanie's plan was simple: skirt the meadow by using the forest to conceal themselves, find the path, run as fast

as possible down to the road. If Sevé and his men chased
them, surely she and Cecily would hear the noise and
could duck into the woods until they passed.

They did stumble onto the path, but it took them twice
as long as she'd expected to get there. Melanie tried to
peer across the grassy field toward the fire, but she
couldn't hear anything. She listened hard for voices or
cries of discovery, but the wind was blowing away from
them and the trees were rustling all around her.

"They must know by now," Cecily said breathlessly.

Melanie nodded. "But I don't know where they are.
Maybe on the path ahead of us? I don't know."

"What do we do?"

"Follow the trail down as quietly as we can. We ought
to be able to hear six men, no matter where they are.
Right?"

The path was bathed in moonlight where it crossed the
clearing but in the depths of the forest it was completely
dark. The trees were eerie shapes against the sky and their
roots seemed to twist grotesquely on the path, reaching
out for Melanie's legs.

"Where are they?" Cecily panted when they stopped
before dashing across yet another clearing.

"I don't know. Behind us, maybe."

"What if they reach the road first, though?"

"We'll leave the path before the road, then. We can
find our way out somehow." She gave Cecily's arm a
reassuring pat in the darkness. "Come on. The coast looks
clear."

The question of the men's whereabouts beat at Melanie
relentlessly. It was like being chased as a kid and almost
wanting to be caught, just to end the agony of the suspense. Melanie had never been very good at those games.
Neither, she remembered, had Cecily.

Her legs were tired and her lungs ached. Even when
they stopped to catch their breath and listen, Melanie's

heart pumped furiously. They had to be getting close to the road, they had to be!

There was that giant gnarled tree. Oh, yes! They were going to make it!

Melanie held her sister back for a moment and listened again. She could hear nothing, only an owl hooting in the night somewhere. As she recalled, ahead of the tree there was one small clearing, then forest again, then the road. If they made it across this last meadow lying before them, and into the cover of the forest, they could leave the path at that point and wind their way through the timber until they came out onto the road somewhere below where Sevé kept his car.

They started across the clearing, crouched low, rushing, feeling exposed. They were so close now...

Ahead were the trees where they could safely leave the path without getting lost. She could see that it was dark and tunnellike, spooky, where the trail entered the forest again. But Melanie reminded herself that there was more protection among the trees.

Stepping from the moonlit path into the darkness, Melanie let out a tentative sigh of relief. Almost there...

She turned to Cecily. "A few more yards and we'll get off the path," she whispered, then forged ahead once again.

It was very, very dark. She tripped over a rock, caught herself and kept going. Up ahead was a bend in the trail. They'd leave it there. She could feel Cecily's hand groping at her back, then her sister's sharp intake of breath. "I hear something!" she whispered desperately.

Melanie froze. There was a cracking sound just ahead of them, a twig snapping under a foot, the beam of a flashlight spearing through the trees. She spun around to reach for Cecily but it was too late. The light touched her and she froze in horror.

"*¿Qué diablo?*" came a voice she knew too well. He

grabbed her arm, steadying her, and Melanie struggled in fright. "Melanie? What on earth…?"

"Let us go!" she gasped. "Oh, God, let us go!"

Then there were voices on the trail behind them.

"Teo! *Please*…" But already it was too late. She could hear the men's feet, crunching through the undergrowth, rushing toward them. "No…" Melanie sobbed, sinking to her knees. "No…"

Sevé was violently angry, raging at his men, at Teo, then standing over Melanie and Cecily and hollering in their faces, shaking his rifle at them. Cecily clung in terror to her sister.

"Stop it!" she was crying. "Make him leave us alone!"

Something in Melanie finally gave way. She raised herself to her full five feet seven inches and faced Sevé.

"Leave us alone!" she shrieked. It was the wrong thing to have done. Sevé grabbed both her arms and began shaking her and then Teo was there, pulling him away, shouting at Sevé in Basque.

Finally Sevé let her go and stood glaring at Teo. They exchanged a few more heated words, then Teo turned to Melanie.

"Get going back up the trail," he ordered. *"Now."*

She would have confronted him, too, but what would it get her? More bruises on her arm?

Feeling utterly defeated, Melanie helped Cecily to her feet and began to walk. One foot in front of the other. Her strength was depleted, her head pounding with rage and frustration.

The men pushed them hard. A sick little punishment, Melanie observed with a strange sense of detachment. She just kept going, trying to hold her head up, trying to ignore the ache in her muscles.

They passed her twisted tree. She looked into the moon-lit sky and felt a hand at her back, helping her gently along.

She turned around. It was Teo. "Get your hands off me," she said in a deadened voice.

She could feel him stiffen as he pulled his hand away. "Have it your way," he said simply.

The incident was not lost on Sevé. He said something obviously crude to Teo in Basque and laughed. "*La señorita* no like you, either, eh, *mi amigo*? Cold, she is, like ice. And even if you are so fine she no like you to touch!" And he kept laughing, a bloodcurdling cackle that filled the night.

"I warn you, Melanie, do as you are told," Teo said quietly. "It is all I can tell you."

"And what if I don't?" she shot back in challenge.

"The price will be greater than you can afford."

Later, after they had finally reached camp, and she lay on the hard, narrow bed, staring into the blackness, Melanie could still hear Sevé's laughter as it echoed through the secretive mountains of the Basques.

Chapter Thirteen

Monday, July 12

The morning was overcast and gray, as somber as Melanie's mood. The fog rolled in from the ocean and hung on the hillsides, tattered when the wind blew, solid when it was still. Everything seemed to close in on her: the walls of the cabin, the sky itself. A damp chill made her shiver incessantly.

If they had planned their escape for today, the fog might have hidden them. But now it was too late. And Teo, not Melanie, was to phone the bank that morning, so there would be no chance to escape in the village.

Teo appeared from out of the mist at midmorning but did not immediately enter the hut. He spoke to Sevé first. Their voices went on for a long time, Sevé's shouting and frenzied, Teo's calm and even. Melanie's heart clutched with fear. What was wrong?

Finally Teo came inside. His face was drawn and tired looking. "The money is here," he said flatly.

"Thank goodness," Cecily breathed.

How innocent she was, thought Melanie. Once Sevé had the money, their lives were forfeited. And Teo knew it as well as she did. But did he even care?

"There is a small problem, however," he went on.

"Oh, Lord, no!" Cecily wailed.

Melanie merely sat, staring at her dirty fingernails.

"It will take another day for Señor Pacheco to gather enough cash."

One more day. Then what?

Cecily buried her face in her hands. "I can't stand another day! I can't!"

Better another day in here—alive—than what tomorrow might bring, thought Melanie. Teo was looking at her, wondering at her singular lack of response. "Are you all right?" he asked. "He did you no harm yesterday…?"

"Nothing that matters," she bit out coldly.

"Melanie—" he started to say then cut himself off. "Only half the money is here, of course. I have tried very hard to convince him that a bird in the fist…"

"A bird in the hand," Melanie corrected tiredly.

"But Sevé, I am afraid, wants as much as he can get. He is torn between greed and prudence."

"And you? What makes you tick, Teo?" she asked.

But he only scrutinized her darkly once again.

The door burst open. Sevé. His bullet-round head was sunk between his shoulders as if he were an enraged bull. "One day more!" he shouted. "Always one day more!"

"Señor Pacheco at the bank promises it will be ready tomorrow," Melanie said. "Didn't Teo tell you? The money's here."

He lurched around, his rifle bumping carelessly against a chair. Teo lashed out a warning in Basque. Sevé growled back. A rabid animal, a cold-blooded killer. Then he whirled to face Melanie. "*You!* So smart! Always one day more! This is your trick! And tomorrow it will be there. If not—" He shook his fist threateningly.

"If not what, Señor Sevé?" Melanie asked coolly. She sat motionless, looking squarely at him, her gold-flecked eyes narrowed and flashing with defiance. There was a core of strength in Melanie that she had never suspected.

It seemed to grow inside her, taking on a will of its own. A recklessness.

Sevé glared at her hotly, then his eyes fell and he paced the floor. A perverse satisfaction surged through Melanie—she'd stared him down, the great dangerous mercenary. At her shoulder, she could feel Cecily shrinking away from the tension between Melanie and her adversary.

Finally Sevé turned on her. He shouted in Basque. Spittle gathered at the corners of his mouth in his fury. Teo tried to say something but Sevé ignored him.

Then, abruptly, Sevé stopped ranting. He smiled evilly and Melanie thought that was worse than his anger.

"Ay, the *señorita* is very brave. Yes, very brave." He strode over and jerked her to her feet and pushed his face close to hers, holding her arm with one iron-hard hand. "Do you know what I do with a woman like you? I *tame* her. Yes. I will enjoy to tame you. So rich, so clean, so cold. Yes."

Melanie's nerve fled and she was paralyzed with horror in his grasp. The room turned black in front of her eyes. She never even heard Teo shout at Sevé. She only knew she would die if this animal touched her. But she would not beg. No, she would never lower herself to beg him. She closed her eyes and gritted her teeth.

He was shoving her into the wall with both hands, his gun slung on his shoulder now, his thick body grinding against hers. She turned her face away. "So, *señorita*, you no like Sevé? Eh? Maybe I will keep you until I get more money. Maybe you will learn to be more polite, *sí*?"

She was aware of Cecily leaping to her feet, her face white and scared, her hands reaching for Sevé. But he knocked her aside without a backward glance.

Thrusting his head forward, he tried to kiss Melanie on the mouth, but she turned her head away again. Then his brutal fingers were clutching her chin and he was pressing his rough, unshaven face to hers. The sour wine smell from his breath was nauseating and a scream of hysteria bubbled up inside her.

"No!" Cecily cried, "Please leave her alone!"

Then, abruptly, Sevé was yanked off her, his hold torn away. Melanie collapsed onto the floor, sobbing, wiping her mouth.

Sevé crouched, his arms in front of him, facing Teo. There was an unearthly, dangerous silence between them. It took a second for her numbed brain to register what had happened: Teo had pulled him off her.

With a roar of rage Sevé threw aside his gun and launched himself at Teo, his hands reaching for the taller man's neck. He was screaming curses and panting as they fell to the floor, locked together. They broke apart; Sevé kicked out at Teo. They rolled on the ground, slamming into the table, knocking over chairs. The thuds of blows hitting home, grunts, the terrible ferocity of two powerful men clashing.

Melanie watched, frozen, then her eyes flew up to the door, which had burst open. Two of the young men were staring in, their faces pale and frightened. They backed off and the door slammed shut; they would not dare to interrupt such a battle.

When she looked again, Teo was dragging Sevé up by his shirt. Teo was breathing hard and one sleeve was torn off, showing the lean brown strength of his arm as he held Sevé up against the wall. Teo's lip was split and bleeding, his chest heaving, his eyes storm dark.

Sevé glared at him through a swollen eye. The anger and challenge on their faces terrified Melanie. The words poured from Sevé's twisted mouth—an explosion of savagery. He shouted and Carlos and two others sprang in through the door, their guns raised.

Slowly, Teo backed off, his hands upraised, his voice cold and low. She wished she could understand what they were saying. She felt limp with relief, confused, still weak

with horror. She could only think: he had saved her from
that beast! He had fought for her!

They went outside, all of them, leaving the women
alone in the hut. Cecily collapsed on her cot, pale and
trembling. "Oh, Mel, what are we going to do?"

Melanie straightened slowly, inching her way up, using
the wall for support. She felt bruised all over. "Hang in
there." She tried a smile; it felt crooked and stiff.

"He's so horrible. I thought… Thank God Teo was
here."

"Yes."

"It's only until tomorrow, isn't it? Then he'll let us go.
The money's here, isn't it?"

"Yes, tomorrow," Melanie said. "I'm sure he'll let us
go tomorrow."

The men's voices outside the hut were low, droning on
and on, occasionally raised in anger. They could hear
Sevé, spitting viciousness. Then Teo's voice, calm and
cold.

"What are they saying?" cried Cecily. "If only they'd
speak Spanish!"

The door opened once more. Both sisters watched it
with dread and fascination. Had Sevé won this round?
Would he now be able to do as he pleased with them?

But it was Teo. "Sevé has agreed—I think—to take the
money that is here. He says he will release both of you.
But if he does not receive the money tomorrow he threatens to…do you some harm." Inadvertently he touched the
cut on his lip. "I only tell you this that you may realize
the gravity of your situation. Do not goad Sevé again."

"You mean like I just did?" Melanie asked. "I'm
sorry. I didn't think… I want to thank you…"

He turned his gaze on her almost angrily. "What did
you expect me to do? Let the man maul you? Do you
think I am enjoying this? Please—" he sounded tired "—
just do as I say. Don't push your fortune."

"Don't push your luck," Melanie said automatically, then added, "I'm sorry, it doesn't matter."

"I think he will leave you alone now."

"Does your lip hurt?" Cecily asked. "Maybe you need stitches."

He almost laughed. "I think that can wait, Cecily. I seem to have a few other things on my mind now." He went on. "Tomorrow I will phone Diego Pacheco. As soon as he has collected the money I will return here. Melanie, you will be taken to the bank, then escorted back here. Do not push, Melanie. This man is dangerous. Now I must leave. Is there anything I can do for you before I go?"

Cecily gave a little cry. "Oh, yes! Could I take a bath somewhere, or a shower? I've been here almost a week. I'm filthy! If I don't wash my hair, I'll die!" Then she thought a minute. "And some chocolate. I'm craving some gooey chocolate."

"Gooey chocolate and a bath," Teo repeated dully. "I'll see what I can do." He stood in the middle of the room a few moments longer. It seemed to Melanie that he was hesitant; perhaps he didn't want to leave them. Her heart began that familiar, uncomfortable aching again, as if her blood had suddenly become too heavy.

She looked at Teo carefully, saw his finely chiseled features, his elegant bearing and the drying cut on his lip. He'd got that because of her; he'd fought his comrade on her behalf. Did it hurt him that she was no longer interested? Did he care about what they'd shared the beautiful night that could never happen between them again?

There was a sadness in his eyes. A look of regret, she thought. What was he thinking? She wished he would leave. The longer he stayed, the more painful it was for Melanie; he might be her betrayer, yes, but only a few nights ago, she had given herself to him willingly.

"I must go now," he said finally, and his gaze met hers for one last moment before he turned and left.

The bath turned out to be a dip in a nearby river, under guard. Carlos and three of the other young men walked the women down to the riverbank and insisted that they stay within sight of the guards at all times. An angry conversation ensued between Carlos and Cecily.

"Goddamn it! Those creeps!" Cecily complained. "Can you believe it?"

"Unfortunately, yes," Melanie said.

"Well, let 'em look then! I need a bath!" Deliberately Cecily took off her clothes and, shivering, walked down into the river. The sky was still gray, the air chilly.

"Brr! It's freezing!" she yelled. But she ducked her head and began washing her hair with the bar of soap that was all Carlos had been able to find.

The four boys looked everywhere but at Cecily. They were horribly embarrassed. Carlos blushed like a girl but held his gun unwaveringly.

Melanie shrugged and turned her back to undress. She needn't have, because the boys studiously ignored them both. The water was cold but clear. She borrowed the bar of soap from Cecily and washed her own hair, remembering fondly, ruefully, her long luxurious baths at Esteban's.

In the water Melanie took the opportunity to whisper to Cecily, "Do you think Carlos would let us go? I mean, now that they're away from Sevé's influence? Do you think it's worth trying him?"

Cecily shrugged. "I can try. But we already know what to expect—I know now that he's a coward!"

There were only the rough wool blankets for towels. Cecily marched out of the river and wrung out her hair. Water ran off her skin in sparkling rivulets and her tan line was like a stark white bikini. Eventually she picked up the blanket and draped it over herself.

"Carlos," she called, then said something in Spanish. He walked over and answered, unsmiling. Cecily bent her head close to him and spoke earnestly, quietly, for a long time.

Melanie wrapped the other blanket tightly around herself and watched. Carlos couldn't take his eyes off Cecily's damp, half-nude body. But he shook his head and said something in a vehement tone of voice.

Cecily was begging, putting a hand on Carlos's arm. He shook it off and raised his gun. Cecily stood there and glared at him, then said something angrily, turned on her heel and walked away.

"I tried," she grated out. "Now it's your turn. Think of something."

They dressed in the same grubby clothes they'd been wearing for the past days. Cecily complained about it loudly in both Spanish and English. Her suitcase had been left in the cheap hotel room in Pamplona she and Carlos had shared when they arrived. Sevé had forbidden Carlos or anyone to return to fetch it. She was sure it had long since been stolen.

"And I had one pair of really worn jeans that I loved," Cecily recalled. "All they let me keep was my passport." Then she launched into another diatribe in Spanish. One of the guards laughed behind his hand at something she said and Carlos turned on him furiously.

In the early afternoon the sun began to burn off the layer of clouds. The sisters sat on their blankets in front of the cabin, drying their hair and brushing it with the brush from Melanie's purse. How fortunate they were to be allowed to stay outside, she thought bitterly.

She wished she could have photographed the rustic scene: the green sloping meadow, the darker trees, the mountains, the cotton-ball sheep, the old stone shepherd's hut. But if she did, she would have to include the boys with their berets and guns, Sevé with his black eye, the ugly green army tents. It was truly like some kind of perverted Boy Scout camp, without the smiles and fun and comradeship. These boys were tense and afraid and utterly miserable. Melanie felt sorry for them and their misguided ideals, but she pushed the feeling aside. The most important thing was her survival and Cecily's.

If she somehow got hold of one of their guns, she wondered, could she actually shoot someone with it? She told herself that she could use a weapon on Sevé, all right, but the young boys…?

And Teo. Could she shoot Teo if he stood between her and freedom? Could she pull a trigger and see bullets smash into his smooth, tanned skin, his dark handsome face? She shivered. But what if it came to a choice between her and Cecily's lives and his?

But of course it was most unlikely she could get her hands on a gun. The boys were careful. Sevé had trained them well. They all slept outside the house, one right in front of the heavy plank door. There was no way to sneak out and take a gun; besides, there were always two of them awake.

There must be a way to escape, there must be!

Cecily was chasing a late-born lamb across the grass, laughing, looking so young, so innocent. Carlos watched her, his face full of pain and regret. She finally caught the little thing and carried it back to its mother. "Isn't it cute?" she called to Melanie.

Melanie smiled and nodded and waved. If there was more time, they'd be able to work on the sympathy of the boys. She knew Carlos and the others could eventually be persuaded to let them go.

But Sevé—and Teo. Those were the two strong ones, the leaders.

Sevé left for a while that afternoon and the atmosphere lightened. Carlos made some sort of excuse to talk to Cecily. Melanie approached the pimply-faced boy casually and, pointing to the sun, asked him the Spanish word for it.

"Sol," he answered. *"El sol."*

"Do you speak English?" she asked then.

"Leetle." He gave a weak apologetic grin.

"I am Melanie," she said, smiling. "What is your name?"

"*Me llama* Antonio."

"Ah, Antonio. Do they call you Tony?"

"To-nee," he said and laughed.

No harm making a friend. It might come in handy. "How do you say hungry?" asked Melanie, rubbing her stomach.

He placed a finger on his own narrow chest. *"Tengo hambre,"* he said triumphantly.

"Well then, Tony, *tengo hambre*," Melanie replied.

He thought that was very funny and told all the others.

"Clever," Cecily said dryly. "Now we get to cook."

But this time the boys brought out a round loaf of bread and a chunk of cheese. Laughing and talking, they laid down their guns and sliced thick slabs and handed them around. Dark red strong wine washed down the repast. It could have been a picnic.

Then Sevé came back. He carried a dead chicken by the legs. Stolen, no doubt. He scowled and the boys jumped, grabbing their guns, their faces suddenly hard and frightened.

"The prodigal returns," Melanie whispered to her sister.

"He could use a bath, too," muttered Cecily. "Enough is enough."

The mist reappeared in the evening, necessitating a fire in the hut. Cecily struggled to kindle it, but the damp wood didn't light easily and the small room filled with smoke.

Melanie wondered if Teo was going to come back that night. Had his lip healed yet? She couldn't help remembering the vicious fight, seeing it over and over in her head. It had been a revelation to her, a terrifying revelation. Did it take so little to reduce a man, even a man as

cultured and intelligent as Teo Sanlucar, to a primitive,
bestial state? Was civilization, then, so superficial?

She couldn't sleep. She couldn't stop brooding on what
the next day—their last?—would hold for them. How
would Sevé kill them? Bullets, knives, strangling? Would
Teo help or would he stand by, disinterested?

She must get away! She and Cecily must manage to
escape! Tomorrow she would be escorted into Pamplona.
Once she had the money, it was as good as over.

Or was it?

An idea came to her then, in the darkest hour of that
night.

Chapter Fourteen

Tuesday, July 13

It wasn't going exactly as Melanie had expected. She'd hoped they would all leave the camp and make the trip to the bank together.

But Sevé was too smart for that. "No, *señorita*," he told her, "the sister stays. First, I have the money. Second, the girl is free. *Entiende?*"

Melanie glared at him; she understood only too well. Once she'd picked up the money, he would tell her that they were going back to the camp and she and Cecily would be set free. Of course, Sevé thought he held the trump card—Cecily—but Melanie was going to change the rules of his game.

Sevé stood in the cabin, telling her they would leave in five minutes, tossing a paper sack at Melanie's feet.

"You wear clothes in there," he stated, then stood watching as she picked up the bag and opened it curiously.

Inside were slacks and a blouse, clean. Her own clothes from her suitcase in Esteban's house. Naturally, Melanie thought, they wouldn't want her looking disreputable and attracting too much attention. She could just see Teo rummaging through her suitcase, finding the dirt- and blood-stained clothes she had worn the night she'd followed him to the cabin.

What had he thought when he found them?

"Put clothes on!" Sevé said impatiently.

Melanie looked at him hard. "Get out of here, then."

He hesitated, grinning. Finally he chortled, the ugly laugh rolling around his throat, grating on Melanie's nerves. He left.

"I want to go, too," Cecily said. "I can't bear another moment here! Oh, Mel..."

"We'll be safe soon. You'll see."

"But what if they won't let us go?" she asked.

Melanie avoided her sister's apprehensive glance. So Cecily was finally putting two and two together. When she spoke, she tried to sound sincere. "Of course they'll let us go. They'll be happy as larks to see us get on a plane and leave."

"But what if—"

"Shh." Melanie tousled Cecily's hair playfully. "There's no problem; they only want the money. You'll see."

Cecily hugged her. "I hope you're right."

"I'd better be going." Melanie couldn't stand the imploring look in her sister's eyes another second. She brusquely gathered up her purse and camera bag and took a deep breath before she marched out the cabin door. When she emerged, the heads of the men turned in her direction. Hadn't they ever seen clean clothes before?

They were waiting for her, ready to leave. Even Teo. He stood some distance from the rest of the group, his eyes always following her. She tried to decipher his expression. Was that regret she saw on his face?

There were the three men, Sevé, Teo and Antonio, and then Melanie. Teo sat next to her in the back seat of Sevé's car, but she shrank as far away from him as she could. She kept catching Sevé's eyes on her in the rearview mirror as he negotiated the narrow, winding road.

He was watching her very carefully, his dark gaze prying away the cloak of her pretended indifference. Dear God, she hoped he couldn't read her mind.

No one spoke much during the drive. Melanie found that unsettling. She wondered what each man was thinking. No doubt Sevé was planning his very prosperous future, or perhaps wondering how to dispose of two female bodies. And Antonio, To-nee, what was going on in his young, impressionable head? Was he envisioning himself with all those expensive new toys he would have, the guns and knives and bombs? Or perhaps he had begun to suspect that he and his *compañeros* were in too deep with Sevé. In their early, idealistic days, had any of these young Cax Carot members realized they would end up criminals?

Teo. He was the most silent of the three. He sat in that relaxed pose she knew so well but as always, there was a watchfulness about him, an air of detached observation. It was evident in the way he held his head and the alert look in his eyes, even while he stared out of the window at the passing scenery.

She was too aware of Teo. Too aware of the scabbed cut on his lip. Too keenly attentive to his smallest movements, to each nuance of emotion on his face, the pitch of his body, the way he would upon occasion look at the back of Sevé's head and then at the scenery once again.

He never looked at her, though.

Teo Sanlucar, she thought, professor of history, was going to be in for a big surprise. Perhaps he *should* have been watching her.

It was almost the last day of the Fiesta de San Fermín. Even though they were still several kilometers from the city's outskirts, the road was already crowded with cars and motorcycles and bicycles. Pamplona, Melanie knew, would be a madhouse. Perfect. And even better than that, the bank was situated near a corner...

It took them almost an hour to drive the last two kilometers. Sweat poured from Sevé's body, staining his dirty white shirt. His face was set in rigid lines. Melanie could see him reach for the horn many times but then draw his hand back, clenching it into a white-knuckled fist. With the weapons they carried, it obviously wouldn't do to call attention to themselves.

The hot morning sun pounded on the car, on the stretch of road ahead, on the dark roofs of the factories. It glinted off windows, beat on uncovered heads, melted the ice cream that vendors hawked on corners. The merciless Spanish sun.

Melanie squirmed uncomfortably in the heat. Her hair clung to the nape of her neck, her hands were sticky and she could feel a trickle of perspiration between her breasts. The car was stuck in an endless line of cars, all trying to park as close as possible to the central plaza.

She looked beside her, at Teo. He was leaning forward a little in his seat, glancing out of the window at the crowds. His shirt was dry. Did nothing perturb him?

He turned his head and for a moment their eyes met and held. She thought he was going to say something but he didn't. He simply sat watching her, his expression unreadable. Melanie forced herself to look away. Would it always hurt so terribly?

It took Sevé another half hour to drive from the factory district through a maze of apartment complexes and into the old section of the city.

There was noise all around them. Droves of shouting, laughing, singing fiesta-goers blocked the streets. The din of the traffic and the crowds filled every block, every alley, every shadowy corner of the city.

Sevé steered into the block where the bank was located and finally managed to double-park. Ordinarily, letting his car sit in the middle of the narrow street, blocking traffic, would have caused a commotion. But as it was, there were dozens of stopped cars jamming the street, their occupants hanging out of rolled-down windows, laughing, sharing their pleasure with passersby. It was a scene of complete bedlam.

Sevé turned in his seat and threw an Iberia airlines bag into Melanie's lap. "Go and fill it." He grinned widely.

Melanie stared at him for a moment and then looked at Teo. "You can still call this off," she said.

"You had better go." Teo's voice was very quiet.

"Go!" commanded Sevé.

When Melanie stepped out onto the street, Antonio and Teo did the same, tailing her to the door of the bank.

At the entrance, she turned to Teo. "Aren't you coming in?" she asked sarcastically.

He shook his head.

"No? Then I'll have to say hello to Señor Pacheco for you. He'll be so disappointed." She was well aware that her voice quavered.

"Go on, Melanie. Finish the task."

She nodded sadly, then said, "I had hoped that you, of all people, would stop this madness."

"I cannot." And for once, his eyes refused to meet hers.

Señor Pacheco had everything ready. He spotted Melanie among the crowds in his lobby and ushered her into his office with a flourish.

"You have told me very little about this very curious transaction," he said as he opened a huge, sealed sack of money brought in by two cashiers. "It is none of my affair…" He began to pull out dozens of neatly banded stacks of pesetas. "But is there anything I might do?"

"Thank you, but no." Melanie shook her head.

"I know that you said the money was for a property, *señorita,* but I have wondered. Would I be indiscreet if I alerted the *policía* when you left?"

The man obviously suspected something. No one paid for real estate with half a million dollars worth of pesetas—in cash. "Please, *señor,* there is no need. This matter will be taken care of tonight." She tried to give him a confident smile. "You have been very kind through all this. I appreciate your help."

He bowed his head with dignity.

She signed the bank draft, which was drawn on the Banco de Madrid, and began to pack the bundles of money into the Iberia bag.

"Are you not going to count the money?" He looked at her in disbelief.

"No," Melanie replied.

He had a grave expression on his dark face. "This is not wise."

"It won't matter," she remarked.

Teo and Antonio stood watch outside. Melanie peered through the glass doors, took a deep breath, then pushed them open. She knew she had to move quickly. She glanced at the corner. Yes, the policeman was there.

Teo was standing on the street just outside the bank, waiting for her. So was Antonio. Sevé was still in the car.

She walked purposefully in the direction of the policeman, then stopped near enough so that the officer could see everything she did and hear her if she raised her voice. She turned then and stared deliberately and boldly at Teo.

"Melanie..." he said, beginning to move toward her.

"Stop right there," she ordered, clutching the bag to her chest. She could see Sevé in the car, craning his neck to watch. He spun around in his seat and threw open the car door, then instantly he was out on the street heading toward her, a murderous look on his face.

Fiesta-goers were shouldering and jostling Melanie. Their ceaseless din pulsed in her ears as she stood staring at the three men, the bag held tight against her body, only a few yards from the policeman.

For a moment, they all stood silent and unmoving like a tableau frozen in time. Then Melanie broke the strange spell.

"Don't come any closer," she told them. "If I scream from here, every policeman in this city will be down your throats in a minute." She looked at Sevé. He was crouched low, like an animal, ready to pounce.

"No," Teo ground out, putting a restraining arm in front of Sevé's body. Then he said something in Basque and Sevé glared at Melanie in rage.

She moved another step away from them. "I am going to walk away from you now," she said in a brittle voice. "I want you to bring my sister to the bullring when the fights are over, at ten tonight. You'll get this bag then and I'll get Cecily."

"I'll kill her!" Sevé's teeth were bared.

"Then you won't get your money, will you, Sevé?"

Teo was still trying to hold him back, but Antonio merely stood there, dumbfounded.

"One more thing," Melanie said, her mouth cotton dry with fear. "Tell Antonio to approach me very slowly and look into the bag. He mustn't touch me, though. Now tell him, Teo."

Teo hesitated, staring at Melanie incredulously. Finally he spoke to Antonio in Basque and the young man nodded. Melanie realized this part of her desperate scheme was risky, but it was vital that Sevé know the money was really there, in the bag.

Antonio took several steps in her direction, then looked past her once toward the policeman.

When he was close enough, Melanie said, "Stop!" He did, and she unzipped the bag and tipped it in his direction just long enough for him to view the neat stacks of money.

He turned his head and nodded to his comrades.

"The bullring at ten," Melanie said hoarsely. "You understand?"

"Yes." Teo's voice was barely audible, his lean body stiff and tensed for action.

She backed away a few more steps, then turned and hurried to the corner, rounding it, disappearing past the policeman and into the evermoving surge of bodies.

For now, she was safe. Yet her mental picture of Sevé,

crouched and cornered like a wolf, his dark eyes hooded in fury, followed her relentlessly.

ANTONIO HAD TRAILED HER. Melanie, however, had expected someone to do precisely that. What she had not counted on was another of the Cax Carot joining him. She'd been sitting at a crowded table, quietly drinking her soda and lime, periodically glancing up to keep track of her pursuer. And then, suddenly, there were two of them.

Sevé must have sent someone out immediately after returning to the camp. It occurred to Melanie that she'd been unwise to come to the plaza, the most obvious of all places, and to sit at a corner café with an ever-present policeman nearby. How easy she had made it for the other man to find Antonio and join him! Stupid!

They were good—she had to give them that, at least.

She must rethink her plans, then. She had already taken into account the necessity of losing one tail but now, with the two of them...

Melanie stood near a corner, close to a policeman, and checked her watch. It was five o'clock. She had hours to kill. Hours in which to perfect her plan and make it foolproof, but she needed to lose the two men first.

She pushed her way through the frenzied crowd to another café, all the while working out an idea that had come to her. It could succeed. She studied the hotel that stood behind the café: the location of the front door, the size of the building—not too big, not too small, four stories. The crush of people could be to her advantage if she used it wisely.

She needed a cover, though, to confuse her pursuers— and for protection. Eyeing the people jammed around the tables of the outdoor café, she decided on one particular foursome.

It wasn't her ordinary kind of behavior to do the sort of thing she had in mind, but these were extraordinary circumstances. It was a question of absolute necessity, and she couldn't afford to be squeamish.

It was funny, she thought later, how easy it was—just then—for her to turn into a brashly presumptuous person. She'd chosen a table of Californians. She didn't question for a second that they were from the Golden State. Their sun-bleached hair and perfect tans and their air of youthful enthusiasm told her that. They were exactly what she needed to carry out her plan.

"Hey, you guys," she said breezily, "mind if I join you?" She leaned down to them conspiratorially. "There's this creepy Spaniard following me."

"Hey, sure, I know what you mean," said the slim blond girl. "Thank goodness I've got these three to run interference for me." She rolled her eyes. "Those Spanish guys are randy to the max."

"My name's Melanie. You having fun?"

"Wow! Fun? This place is the most!" said one of the boys. "I'm Ted. This is Buzz and Toro and Franny."

"You know we all ran with the bulls yesterday?" said Buzz. "And this guy next to me got flattened, like *that*!" He gestured with his palm. "Then I'll be a son of a gun if he didn't get right up after the bull passed and keep running!" He shook his head wonderingly and fingered his dirty red kerchief.

Melanie saw To-nee waiting for her to get up and leave the café. She was safe with her new friends, but she was impatient to lose her two young pursuers.

"Where're you from?" Franny was asking.

"Ohio."

"Oh, wow, I've got an uncle in Toledo. Dick Ledbetter—you know him?"

"Ledbetter?" Melanie thought a moment. "No, can't say I do." Where was the second spy? She had an irresistible urge to look behind her.

The group was sharing a meal of marinated mussels

and olives and tidbits of octopus. Melanie ordered a bottle of five-hundred-peseta wine.

"Gosh, you can get it for a hundred and fifty," Toro exclaimed.

"Never mind, nothing but the best." Melanie smiled graciously, feeling rather like a bountiful grandmother.

Was she going to be able to lose To-nee and friend—just for those precious minutes she needed? She laughed at some asinine remark of Ted's and glanced toward the street. There they both were, standing motionless and close together, unmindful of the jostling throng, watching her carefully. Then she saw a figure approaching Antonio—a familiar figure—Teo. He had obviously been sent by Sevé to help find her. Three men after her, three men to evade and fool and deceive with nothing but her wits. She had to succeed or Cecily's life wouldn't be worth two cents.

And Teo, the traitor, the beautiful dark stranger to whom she'd given herself, willingly and lovingly. Now he was hunting her down, a hound on her trail.

To-nee was pointing her out, and Teo was looking across the crowded plaza, straight toward her. Studiously she avoided glancing in his direction and laughed gaily at something Franny said.

How was she going to get out of their sight?

Ted moved his chair noticeably closer. "So you're from Ohio," he said. "Going to Ohio State?"

She almost choked on her wine. "Well, actually I'm out of school."

"What'd you major in?" His arm was on the back of her chair.

"Oh…photography."

Ted nodded sagely.

It came to her suddenly, that proverbial light bulb switching on in her head. It might work!

"Do you know if there's a bathroom in that hotel behind us?" she asked.

"I guess so."

"Would you mind walking me to the lobby? I mean, these Spanish men!" She rolled her eyes.

"I'd be glad to," he said sincerely.

They both walked toward the hotel; Melanie took his arm and looked around, as if she felt anxious about being followed. Only it wasn't an act. But her pursuers couldn't do a thing, not with Ted so close—and he was close. Melanie let him guide her through the crowds, even let him press snugly against her.

Ted must have noticed her anxiety. When they stopped to allow a large group of Spaniards to go by, he said, "Boy, you really are nervous. You're as stiff as a board."

"I am?"

He nodded and smiled. "But don't worry, you're with me now. They won't bother you."

"It's just all this madness, I guess." She tried to return his smile, but her face felt brittle.

She glanced over her shoulder. There were the three men, very near, yet obviously afraid to try anything with so many tourists around. Still, Melanie was not comforted. Not with Teo so close. His face was carved in unforgiving lines, his dark eyes menacing. He looked slowly from Melanie to Ted and back, and she could almost see the muscle in his jaw grow taut and begin to twitch.

Good, she thought, let Teo think she really had picked someone up. Let him see how easy it was and that she didn't care if he saw or not.

The notion buoyed her momentarily, but her satisfaction didn't last long. It hurt terribly to see Teo looking at her with threat in his eyes.

Ted began to walk again, leading Melanie, threading his way in and out of the masses toward the hotel. Finally they were entering the lobby, and the cooler air fanned Melanie's hot cheeks.

"Thank you, Ted," she said just inside the door. "I'm fine now. Go on back to the table."

"I'll wait," he replied meaningfully.

"Oh, no, really—I'll be perfectly all right here."

"Okay," he said reluctantly, "but the next bottle's on me."

"That'll be great," she managed to reply.

He left. Melanie took a deep breath and started toward the front desk. When she was certain Ted was gone, she turned and walked quickly to one of the big windows that looked out onto the street. She wanted to make sure that Teo and his sidekicks were still there.

They were. And as she expected, Antonio was looking perplexed, gesturing to the other two, staring at the hotel, then at the alley, and back to the front door.

Teo, too, was casting about, but he didn't look nearly as disconcerted as Antonio. He appeared to be taking charge, telling the youths to calm down, assuring them that Melanie couldn't have escaped.

He nodded toward the front entrance and spoke to Antonio as if to say, You watch the front. Then Teo and the other young man began to head in the direction of the alley, no doubt to guard the rear exit.

Now, she thought, let Antonio's curiosity overcome him. Let him get itchy and begin to wonder what she was up to. Let him leave his post and follow her inside. Come on, Antonio.

Melanie left her place at the window, crossed the lobby and climbed the narrow steps. Would her plan work? There were people everywhere, bumping into her on the stairs, talking in the hallways, milling around in the corridors on the way to their rooms.

On the second landing she stopped and glanced around the hallway. Yes, there was a door marked Damas. Ladies. She pushed it—locked. Damn! *Hurry up,* Melanie prayed, *get out of there before Antonio climbs those stairs.* She rattled the door handle several times. *Hurry up!*

Finally the door was unlatched and swung open. Melanie ducked in quickly past the scowling woman, thinking furiously, trying to recall every ploy in every mystery book she had ever read. How would Agatha Christie have done it?

The light in her head flared again. Of course!

She left the door unlocked—oh, how clever she was— then went into the toilet stall and stepped up onto the seat; the stall would appear to be empty if Antonio were to peer into the bathroom, looking for a pair of feet. She could imagine him entering the lobby, desperately searching for her, then noticing the staircase. He would eventually deduce that she hadn't slipped out the back because his partners were there and she couldn't have got past them. He would know that she'd gone up the stairs.

Come on, she thought.

He'd go to the first landing, push open the doors to the broom closet, to the bathroom. He might even have to wait to see who came out of the bathroom if it was occupied. And then, still looking watchfully around him, he would assume that Melanie had gone up another flight of stairs.

The minutes ticked by. It struck Melanie that someone might come in to use the toilet. She listened and kept her fingers crossed. No one came.

More minutes passed. Had she underestimated his curiosity? Surely he wouldn't stand out in front of the hotel forever…

She felt claustrophobic in the small cubicle. Sweat burst out on her forehead and neck and under her arms. She could feel it roll down her skin beneath her clothes. The faint odor of urine, mixed with a strong disinfectant, made her stomach lurch. It seemed she was always hiding in small, smelly bathrooms!

Hurry, Antonio!

Her legs felt weak; if only she could sit down. Shifting her position, she wiped at the sweat ineffectually. She stared down at the floor. It was made of small white tiles, many of them broken. There was a pattern of cracks radiating like a star out from the toilet. The lines between the tiles were perfectly straight rows, except for one corner where they went all crooked. Melanie wondered why. Had the workman lost patience with his task? Or got lazy? Gone mad?

Hurry, hurry, Antonio. Don't you want to know where the lady went?

Suddenly she could hear voices in the hallway, men and women. Someone opened the door to the bathroom, a woman who was still talking to someone in heavily accented Spanish while she held the door ajar. Melanie sucked in her breath. The woman finally pushed on the door to the stall and found it locked.

"*Ocupado*. It's occupied," Melanie said. "I'll be a while, sorry." Then she repeated it as best she could in her poor Spanish.

The woman grumbled something in French and left.

Another minute went by, agonizingly slow.

Why didn't he come? He couldn't wait out front all day...

And then she sensed he was there. Melanie thought her heart was going to burst. She heard the outside door carefully pushed open, and there was an awful moment of silence. She imagined him crouching, looking for that telltale pair of feet. Frightening things flew into her head: Antonio had read the same book, he would wait outside the bathroom, he wouldn't check the third floor...

The muscles in her thighs were quivering; the sweat popping out on her brow was salty and blinding. But she didn't dare breathe or move to wipe it away. If he didn't leave in a moment, she thought desperately, she was going to give the game up, throw herself at his mercy.

It seemed deathly quiet in the bathroom, in the hotel. It was earshatteringly still. Until she heard the harsh whisper of a man's voice. He whispered in Basque, something short and hard and questioning—Antonio. She recognized his voice. He must have been asking if the ladies' room was empty. Then she heard his footsteps as he entered, uncertain, hesitant footsteps.

Oh, God. She stood there, trembling, sweating, praying. *Don't look in the toilet, To-nee—don't look!*

Another cautious step. He was probably embarrassed to be invading the Damas, the ladies' room, a young man like that. Would he dare look in the stall?

Melanie wanted to close her eyes but she couldn't. She kept staring at the door of the stall, waiting for him to rattle it, waiting, heart pounding, legs shaking from tension. Would she be able to run or scream or hit him? She took quick, shallow, silent breaths—she was beginning to feel weak and dizzy from lack of oxygen. She couldn't take a deep breath; he'd hear her. *Please,* she prayed, *please, let him leave!*

Then, abruptly, the outer door opened and she heard quick, firm footsteps. A man's voice, speaking Basque. Dear Lord, she knew that voice! It was Teo! He said something to Antonio in an urgent tone, commanding, loud. Tony answered submissively; he sounded a little scared. She wished, more than anything, that she could understand them.

Then Teo was talking again, talking angrily. After that, she heard footsteps pattering on the tile, the creak of the outer door, and a few seconds later, the bang of the door slamming shut.

Then utter silence.

Melanie took a deep breath. Her knees felt as though they were giving out. She wondered how long she had to stay there to make sure they were gone. What if she walked out of the ladies' room to find them lying in wait for her? And then, if she waited too long, they'd have time to check the other floors and descend to the lobby again to catch her. She was torn with indecision.

Finally she couldn't bear to procrastinate another second. She straightened painfully and slowly, still standing on the rim, and risked a peek over the top of the stall.

Empty. Gingerly, she stepped down, pushed open the first door, then carefully eased the other open just a crack. She could see no one, certainly not Antonio or Teo. She pushed it open farther. They must have mounted the stairs to the third floor.

Her heart beating wildly, Melanie raced down the hall, down the two flights of stairs and into the crowded lobby.

Antonio was not there. Neither was Teo.

Sweat still beaded her brow and upper lip. Automatically she wiped at it with one hand, her other still clutching the Iberia airlines bag to her chest.

She stuck her head outside. There was no sign of them there, either, nor was the other young Basque in sight. He still had to be out back, then. Thank God…

There was no Ted in sight and droves of tourists crammed the plaza. She hurried down the steps and merged with them. She thought fleetingly of the danger Cecily was in. Her plan had to work!

She headed purposefully away from the plaza, the late-afternoon sun pressing on her shoulders like a hot hand, the heavy crush of dancers and drinkers swallowing her up until her auburn head was only one of a thousand anonymous bobbing heads that filled the ancient, twisted streets of Pamplona.

Chapter Fifteen

Tuesday, July 13

Her timing was perfect. It was the hour that the *corrida*, the bullfight, started. Everything was so easy. All she had to do was let herself be swept along with the crowd that surged like a gigantic tidal wave toward the bullring. It was almost the end of the *feria* and people were gathering for the second-last bullfight of this enchanted week, a week that was suspended in time. A week quite apart from the concerns of the real world.

She took a moment to duck into a shop and buy a gray patterned silk scarf and white blouse. Lucky that Sevé hadn't taken her traveler's checks. The blouse covered her clothes and the scarf hid her unusually colored hair, in case Teo was still searching for her.

A man next to her offered her his wine bottle while they waited at the entrance to the bullring. She shook her head but smiled her gratitude.

She had no ticket, of course. The doormen were yelling *"Billetes!"* on either side of the entrance and snatching the slips of paper people held out. Melanie just stayed in the middle of the crowd and was carried into the stadium on its tide. Even if she'd had a ticket, she would never have been able to hand it to anyone.

The bands were playing and the stadium was nearly full. The hot afternoon sun beat down. Melanie looked around and tried to get her bearings. It would be best, she thought, to reconnoiter while the place was full. Then, if anyone challenged her, she had an excuse: she was just another *turista*—a tourist—who was lost.

It didn't seem to matter that Melanie was laden with an airline bag and her purse and camera bag. Most of the young people had bags of some description over their shoulders; they had to tote their belongings around, as they slept in the open soccer field and had nowhere to leave their things. She fitted right in.

Making her way around the tiers of seats, she looked for the entrance to the interior of the bullring. Teo had pointed out the corrals where they kept the bulls and the stables for the picadors' horses. There must be rooms for the *toreros*. And corridors leading to the doors in the outside walls. She had to find out.

She had to smile a lot and act carefree and hang around the very bottom row of seats in the hope of figuring out how the amphitheater was designed. But there were barricades everywhere—not a chance of getting into the ring itself and that's where she needed to be. The doorways all opened out of the ring itself. But she studied them, just in case.

She had to sit through the whole bullfight, wishing she could have enjoyed its stark, formalized beauty. Time crept by in odd, jerky snatches. Her watch seemed to crawl and then suddenly a whole hour would be gone.

Each bull was loosed into the ring as the matador stood waiting. They circled each other warily, the massive beast pawing the sandy earth. Melanie could almost see the hot breath puffing from the bull's nostrils. The red capes flashed, the bulls charged, once, twice, three times. *Olé!*

It was brave and beautiful and hypnotic.

The fallen beasts were dragged from the ring. Once, it was the matador who was carried out on a stretcher, and the cheers of the crowd caught Melanie totally by surprise. They were cheering and saluting the bull. Of course. The beast had fought valiantly and won.

The afternoon waned, becoming a blur of richly clad matadors in black-and-gold jackets and of great-humped beasts with murderous horns and massively muscled bodies glistening under the sun.

Melanie was hot and tired and hungry. A vendor came by yelling *"Naranja! Naranja fresca!"* Orange drink. She bought a bottle and drank the excessively sweet stuff. She got some peanuts from another vendor.

She didn't dare drink any of the wine offered her by the laughing, inebriated people who packed the stands around her. She was afraid she'd fall asleep or burst into tears or do something ridiculous.

The last bull was dragged out of the ring through the cavernous, double-doored opening. The *torero* bowed and accepted the cheers and whistles, the flowers and hats and even T-shirts thrown at his feet as accolades. Then the people began to leave, filing out slowly, body pressing against body. Melanie went with them, dragging her heavy bags, mingling, her scarf pulled over her hair. She was swept with the others around the curve of the bullring. But instead of following the crowd back into town, she fought her way out of the traffic and walked around the bullring to the far side.

Yes, there was the truck that had come to collect the bull carcasses. Several men were lifting a bull onto the truck, unharnessing the donkeys. They talked and laughed in a familiar routine. The big week was almost over for them. She saw immediately that there was a wide door gaping open, a door that led into the bullring.

"Perdóname," Melanie said, stepping up to one of the men—an official-looking sort. *"Por favor, yo soy*…photographer. I am photographer. *Time* magazine." As she spoke, she busily pulled her camera out of the bag and made a show of checking the light meter and the lens.

Then she smiled and held up the empty camera. "Please, can I take pictures for the magazine?"

"*Periódico*," translated one of the men.

"*Sí*," she said, nodding, "*periódico. Fotografías.* Okay?"

They grinned hugely. She focused, then pretended to take several pictures of them and the dead bulls and the donkeys. They acted like small children at a birthday party.

"Can I go inside? More *fotografías*?"

The official-looking one nodded, pointing to himself. He strutted proudly.

Oh, lord, she thought, he wanted to go with her.

"*No, no, por favor.* You are working. I can go alone." She gave them each some of the last remaining pesetas in her purse, thinking of the half million in ransom money.

They finally let her go. She walked in through the broad tunnel that opened out into the ring. The white sand had already been smoothed over; it glistened dully in the twilight. She stood in the empty ring, and the wall encircling the arena was blood-red in the fading light. The rows and rows of seats climbed in a circle around her and she heard in her head the echo of cheering, the noise, the music. Right here the bull had thundered toward a tiny magenta scrap of material and the *torero* had spun away, his gold-encrusted suit flashing sparks in the gilded light.

And here Sevé would come to collect his money. Did he plan for her and Cecily to die in the ring like the huge, powerful, hump-necked bulls? Or was that to happen later? And Teo—would he be there to watch?

She looked toward the corral that housed the heifers that were loosed into the ring after the running of the bulls. They had not yet been brought back to the bullring. What time was that going to happen? It had better happen soon, she thought.

She pretended to take pictures in case anyone was watching. Click, click. Too bad she had no film. There were interesting angles where the dusk's long shadows reached across the circular tiers of seats. A hushed feeling of expectancy hovered in the ring. Or was that merely the reflection of her own tension?

The empty heifer corral lay right behind one of the barricades. Past it a long narrow corridor reached blackly toward the outside wall of the bullring. Looking around to see if anyone noticed, Melanie opened the corral gate and slipped through. There was another gate, then the corridor. It smelled damp, of cow dung and mold. But at the end she found a smooth, heavy metal door. She felt around in the dimness for the latch; it was open. Thank God—she'd been afraid that it might lock from the other side. But what lay beyond? She pushed the massive door; a crack of light showed, and she saw that it did indeed open to the outside. Good. She had their escape route. Still, she wondered when they would return the heifers to that empty corral.

Regardless, Melanie needed a place to hide until Sevé arrived with Cecily. She knew he'd come armed and with his five youthful bodyguards. And she suspected he'd come early, hoping to surprise her as she walked into the ring—alone—with the Iberia airlines bag full of money.

She passed an old man with a broom. Nodding and smiling and holding up her camera, she got by him. Somewhere there had to be a room, a closet, something. Yes, there, down another corridor. Several doors. She tried one after another. Locked. Finally one was open. She peeked inside, ready with an excuse if anyone was there.

It was empty. Obviously a dressing room, with capes and shoes flung on the benches, a dirty shirt and some rags. It smelled of blood, male sweat and grimy clothes. It was perfect. Locking the door, Melanie sank down on the bench and closed her eyes in relief.

Now, if only the cheerful fellows working outside the back door didn't notice her disappearance and start looking for her...

She must have dozed. She was jerked awake by a muffled explosion. A heavy thud, then another, then a whole volley, like gunshots. Sevé! She looked around frantically. The unfamiliar walls of the room stared blankly back at her and it took a moment to reorient herself.

She glanced at her watch: 9:37. Her heart thumped wildly. Sevé would come soon—or perhaps he was already there, waiting. Those explosions…she must be very careful. He had guns and men and strength. She had nothing but the Iberia airlines bag and her wits.

She crept out of the changing room. It was fully dark now in the corridor. The bullring seemed deserted but she stayed in the shadows, stopping every few feet to listen. There was only silent velvety darkness and the palest glimmer of sand in the ring.

Suddenly the sky lit up in an explosion of color. Boom! Boom!

Fireworks! Of course! That was what she'd heard—part of the *feria* celebrations. The sky split with another resounding crack, and Melanie could see the red and white and gold sparks blossom above her.

Beautiful. The flower spread, popping, into appendages that sagged downward, exploding into more blossoms at their extremities. She shuddered at the violent beauty of it and the frightening similarity of its sound to gunfire. Sevé…

Hugging the wall, Melanie hid behind a barricade in the inky shadows. She could see all the entrances and the tiers rising around her, row upon row. Empty, hushed. Or were they hiding Sevé and Teo and the five boys? The Cax Carot. A dance, she had been told. A dance of violence and terror and madness. A shadow dance.

A sound intruded upon her thoughts. A stamping, a shuffling, the low whoof of an animal's breath. Her eyes shifted instantly, searching for the source of the noise. There, in the corral. It was filled now with dark forms. Her eyes had grown accustomed to the darkness and she could make out the milling shapes. Then a deep lowing sound confirmed it.

The heifers were there in their pen, awaiting the next morning when the men in white and red would stream into the ring, followed by the bulls. It would be the last morning, the last running of the bulls, the last day of the Fiesta de San Fermín.

She could hear cheers and screams and music coming from the city outside the circular walls that contained her. The penultimate eve of mad celebration.

Was Sevé already in the bullring somewhere, waiting for her?

The heifers stamped nervously in their pen and snorted as another brilliant blossom exploded in the black sky. She'd seen these cows bowl over a lot of strong men in the bullring that first morning. But then there had been noise and chaotic excitement and men running everywhere. Would the heifers be as edgy at this time of night? Melanie could have filled a book with what she didn't know about cows.

She thought fleetingly about the door at the end of the tunnel. The latch. She'd checked it. What she hadn't checked, though, was whether there was a lock on the other side. She'd assumed—

A noise, something, a movement, snatched her attention. It was coming from across the arena. Yes! There was a shadow, moving along the wall. And another. Her heart lurched in apprehension.

She stood perfectly still, watching and listening.

Another explosion of fireworks lit the night sky, briefly illuminating the arena. Then there was darkness again.

A minute passed. Then another. Finally she heard a voice.

"Where are you, *señorita*? Are you here yet?" Sevé. His tone was taunting, sarcastic, too loud in the echoing, empty stands. "Where is my money?"

Melanie crouched by the cattle pen, afraid he would

shoot when she spoke up. She tried to make herself as small a target as possible. "Where is my sister?"

"I'm here!" Cecily cried, sounding terrified.

Melanie swallowed hard. This was the time, her only chance. It had to work. "I'm here! Over here! I have the money."

She could see the dark forms moving again, rounding the curved side of the arena. Closer, closer. They were there, in front of her, dim shadows against the pale sand of the ring. Would they shoot? But if they did the noise would attract attention and the police would come. Or would the shots merely sound like fireworks? Her heart thudded like a drum in her chest.

Sevé was there and three other boys. She thought Carlos was one. Cecily. And Teo. He stood there, tall and slim, his features blots of darkness, his expression impenetrable, slightly diabolical in the night.

Slowly Melanie held out the airline bag toward Sevé. He must come to her. "Bring my sister here."

Cecily was pushed forward, stumbling to her side. "Oh, Mel! Boy, was I—"

"Shh!" Melanie hissed. Quickly now, only a few moments. If they were going to shoot—

Now, now was the time... She felt for the latch on the gate, praying her movements went unnoticed in the dark. "I'm going to throw it, Sevé, out into the ring, then we are going."

"*Sí, señorita,*" came Sevé's rough voice. "You have your sister. The money, *por favor.*"

Then, all at once, Melanie threw the bag as far as she could, swung open the corral gate, grabbed Cecily's hand and ran into the midst of the heifers. She shouted, slapped the nearest bony, dusty rump, kicked at them, swung her heavy purse at their heads. There were startled snorts and moos and the clatter of hooves and horns on wooden walls. She dodged, dragging Cecily with her. Then the heifers began to stream out into the ring, snuffling and pawing and shoving at one another.

A man cried out in surprise, then fear. The shadowed forms moved faster, swinging their horns, panicking in the dark, unfamiliar place, unable to recognize their enemy.

Melanie was pulling Cecily into the back of the corral, feeling along the wooden walls for the other gate. Her breath came in tearing gasps. "What?" Cecily kept asking. "Where are we going? What's going on?" Melanie could hear the heifers stampeding among the men, careering around the ring in a nightmarish dance. There were thuds, curses, a gunshot, the terrified snorting of the creatures as they raced, bumping and crashing into the men.

She could hear Sevé shouting furiously in Basque. By now he must have seen the contents of the airline bag.

The gate. Fumbling, hurting her fingers, she unlatched it and pulled Cecily through, shoving the gate shut behind them. "This way!" she panted. "Come on!"

She tried to hurry through the pitch-black tunnel, the corridor to the outside, to freedom and safety. One hand felt against the dank wall, the other held on to Cecily for dear life. Cobwebs stuck to her face; she felt as if nameless, slimy things were crawling over her body. As if bullets would flame out of the blackness behind to mow them down.

Had anyone seen where they went? Or were Sevé and his cohorts too busy with the heifers?

Cecily was behind her, panting, too, and sobbing in fear.

"There's a door," Melanie gasped. "Right up here."

The corridor seemed endless. She stumbled on the uneven dirt floor, utterly blind in the unrelieved darkness. Cecily tripped once and cried out, falling to her knees. Melanie dragged her up, feeling for the door. It was there, nearby—she knew it was! It had been there a few hours before!

Behind her, the voices were cut off but she could hear muted gunshots from the bullring. Were they shooting at one another or at the heifers—poor, terrifed beasts? And what would happen when Sevé realized that his men were chasing shadows? She tried to imagine what he would do then, but her head was pounding with fright.

At last her outstretched hand bumped into the smooth cold metal of the door. She felt feverishly around for the latch. Which side had it been on? Yes, there it was. She tugged on it; it didn't give. She rattled it, pulled harder.

It was locked from the outside.

There was no time to think or regret or even cry out in frustration.

"What is it?" Cecily panted.

But Melanie didn't answer. She was frozen, paralyzed with horror.

Another shot echoed down the long corridor. Had it come from the arena or was someone shooting blindly into the tunnel's blackness? Maybe Sevé wouldn't find her and Cecily. Or maybe he would flee before people outside realized that there were shots coming from within the bullring.

"Oh, God," Cecily moaned, her sweat-damp body pressed to Melanie's.

Melanie pulled on the door, again and again. It merely rattled implacably. A sob welled in her breast.

A moment later they both heard it. A footstep. Another footstep. Someone was in the tunnel!

The hollow steps echoed in the musty corridor. Melanie's hands groped around her as if a door would appear by some miracle. Nothing…

There was no escape! Only the locked door, the solid walls, the hard-packed dirt floor…

The footfalls grew louder, louder. It was as if all the air had been sucked out of the narrow, claustrophobic passageway. Melanie tried to draw in a breath but couldn't. Her heartbeat pounded in her ears.

Then he was there, a presence in the inky blackness. Melanie heard her sister's sharp intake of breath and clutched Cecily's arm, as they tried to shrink into the cold wall.

Who was it? What would he do? She waited, tense, her muscles rigid and tight, as if that would protect her from the bullets she expected would smash into her at any second.

"Do not do anything foolish," came a deep voice and Melanie desperately searched her mind for knowledge of its owner.

She knew that voice! They were lost, then, trapped, condemned to death in a dark hole while crowds celebrated exuberantly a few feet away.

It was Esteban Sanlucar.

Chapter Sixteen

Wednesday, July 14

"So, after you lost Teo and Antonio in the hotel, you returned the money to the bank." Esteban chuckled. "What a trick."

The setting sun thrust long shadows onto the patio at Esteban's house. Melanie sat with her hands in her lap, feeling drained and relieved and a bit light-headed from the abrupt release of tension. "I was sure Sevé was planning to kill us, anyway. After all, we knew who he was and could identify him. I was determined that he wouldn't benefit from his crimes."

"Now tell me once more how you planned to get away from those two who followed you. And with Teo there, also."

Again she described hiding in the hotel's bathroom. Esteban laughed, throwing back his handsome dark head.

Melanie smiled a little self-consciously and sipped her brandy.

"I certainly wish I'd known that you were on my side," she finally said. "It would have made things a lot more comfortable for me."

"Ah, but I could not risk it. We could not," Esteban replied. "My nephew feared a slip. Knowledge on your part might have made you act suspiciously and Sevé might have caught on. So you had to hate and fear us.''

She turned to study Teo, who sat silently in one of the patio chairs, hands clasped together in his habitual manner. His dark eyes returned her gaze without emotion. Quickly she snatched her glance away.

"Most clever of all was to walk away from Sevé, right in front of the bank, carrying the money."

"I had no choice," Melanie said quietly.

"And the *novillas*, the heifers," Esteban went on. "A stroke, a coup of great perfection."

"Yes," Teo put in dryly, "it almost ruined my own little surprise."

"The *policía*," Esteban said, nodding. "They were nearly as surprised as Sevé to enter into the ring and find a true *corrida* happening."

"Nobody was as surprised as I was," Melanie said. "I mean, to think I was going to be killed in a second and then…to find you had come to *save* us and the Guardia Civil had the Cax Carot surrounded in the ring."

"I apologize again for putting you through such an ordeal," Teo said quietly, "but I was afraid to call the police until the last moment. And then I was almost unable to reach a telephone to call Esteban. I think perhaps Sevé did not quite trust me."

"And in the hotel when Antonio was looking for me?" Melanie asked. "Did you know I was there?"

"I knew you were somewhere in the hotel. I assumed you planned to evade us somehow, so I told Antonio that I'd seen you running out of the kitchen door. I called him all sorts of rude names of stupidity." Teo shook his head ruefully. "I had no idea we were so close to you. I only wanted him out of the hotel."

"You'll never know what I was going through in there," she breathed.

"I am sorry. There was nothing else I could do. Sevé

watched me like a hawk. He is not such a bad judge of men. He knew he could not trust me.''

''I can't imagine why not. You certainly had *me* convinced,'' Melanie said.

''Well, he knew I disapproved of violence. We had already argued. You see, I had hoped to get Cecily away from them without involving the police.''

''And without me complicating things,'' she put in.

A thin smile curved Teo's mouth. ''Yes. But you were too much for me.'' The smile left his lips. ''Those boys— Carlos and the rest—they are good boys. I've known them all since they were children. It was Sevé's influence. He was their idol. The man wanted his own little kingdom and he needed followers, slaves, if you will. I tried very hard to see that their kidnap plan did not succeed.''

''So that was why you were at Torremolinos,'' Melanie mused.

''I was trying to prevent them from going through with the plan, hoping you would both fly home to Ohio as soon as possible. But unfortunately...'' And he shrugged his shoulders.

''And then I found you in your office and accused you of...all those things. I'm sorry, Teo, terribly sorry.''

''There is no need for apologies. You have suffered. I think perhaps I should have gone to the police immediately, as soon as you told me Cecily was gone. I knew what was going to happen then.''

''But Sevé might have killed her.''

Teo nodded gravely. ''That was my fear.''

''And the night we would have escaped—''

''Except for my most unpropitious appearance,'' he said wryly.

''How is our little Cecily?'' interrupted Esteban.

''Asleep, I hope,'' Melanie replied. ''Your doctor gave her some pills.''

''The poor child,'' Esteban said, shaking his head.

"She's not too young to realize her own responsibility in all this," said Melanie.

"But all young ones make mistakes. Did you not?" Esteban went on and Melanie thought of her too-quick, futile marriage. "These boys were misguided. Truly, they are victims, too. Victims of Sevé."

"What will happen to them?" asked Melanie.

"They will go to trial," said Teo. "Our system can be very severe. I will do my best with the authorities."

"I hope they've learned something," she said quietly. "And Cecily, too."

"You are worried about your sister." Teo's eyes reached across the patio to hers. His features were sun-dark and handsome in the gilded Spanish evening.

She held his gaze. "Yes. She's going to need help to forget this. She feels so guilty and ashamed."

"And what will you do now?" he asked softly.

"Excuse me," Esteban broke in, "but I must discuss supper with Lucia." He rose and smiled benignly down at them, holding out a restraining hand. "You two stay here, relax and talk. It is over now."

To Melanie, his absence seemed a thing of heavy significance because it left her alone with Teo for the first time that evening. For the first time since their picnic on the magical, misted Roncesvalles Pass. She shifted nervously in her chair and played with her brandy snifter, turning it around and around in her hands, watching the sun's last rays glow on the amber liquid.

"Well?" Teo insisted gently.

"Well, what?"

"What are your plans?"

"Oh. As soon as the police are through questioning Cecily, I'll take her home. My parents are wrecks—you can imagine."

"But of course. So you go back to Cleveland, Ohio."

"For a while, anyway. Then I'll probably go somewhere on an assignment."

"Where?"

"Oh, who knows? I was thinking about Bangladesh to see how they're recovering from the flooding last year. Or China. I'd like to see the new China." She looked off into the distance, to the green mountains of the Basques. "Maybe some magazine will send me somewhere."

"So you keep traveling, Melanie. Running from whatever it is that bedevils you."

She looked up, startled, into his somber gaze. "I hadn't exactly thought I was running. I do my job."

"Ah, yes, but nevertheless you are running away."

"From what?" she asked coolly.

"From love, from commitment."

She stirred uneasily in her seat once again. "I thought you were a history professor, not a psychologist."

"What is history but the study of mankind's behavior?" he asked, smiling.

"I hardly think my behavior is worthy of anyone's study."

The sky was turning lavender and purple behind the mountains. Crickets chirped beyond the patio, and the first star hung low in the east. Mist began curling up from the hollows.

"There is much good in my people and my country," Teo said. "I would like you to see that side of us. I wish you would allow me to show it to you."

Melanie looked down at her hands. What was he asking her? Was he merely being the professor? The proud Basque? The perfect host? "I...I really have to go home. It's very nice of you but..."

"I see." He smiled and reached out to cover her hands, still held in her lap, with his own lean brown fingers. "You must keep running, then?"

"I'm only going home, Teo." Her skin burned under his touch. She could not meet his gaze, afraid that she'd say—or do—something stupid, something irrevocable. To stay with Teo, to let her heart fly free, to strike off its shackles. To learn about him and his beloved Basque country, to know him...

He withdrew his hand and left her feeling strangely forsaken. "Home? Melanie, somehow I cannot see you in your Ohio. Can you be happy there?"

"As happy as I can be anywhere," she replied, knowing it was a lie.

THE DRIVE BACK TO MADRID was a dismal one. Cecily was uncharacteristically listless and quiet, thinking, no doubt, of her guilt and her lost Carlos, of her kidnapping, of her loss of innocence. They wound down out of the green hills into the sere brown ones, then to the dry plateau of Madrid. The city teemed with traffic, but unlike Pamplona's masses, Madrid's were sober, intent Castilians.

Melanie and her sister went to the elegant private hotel that Melanie had stayed in before. Cecily had not even suggested that she return to her apartment, and Melanie had no intention of letting the girl out of her sight. If Cecily returned to school in Madrid, her things would be there. If not, someone could box them and send it all back to Ohio.

Esteban had phoned and arranged everything for them: the hotel room, the airplane tickets. He'd sent Lucia into Pamplona to pick up some clothes for Cecily, as her suitcase had not been located. The woman had returned with stockings and a slip and a print dress that somehow did not suit Cecily. She'd put it on, however, without a word and her apathy had Melanie worried.

Esteban had done everything he could to make things easy for them. He'd kissed them both goodbye and invited them back to stay with him. But Teo had not been there the morning of their departure. "He is gone back to his classes," Esteban had said offhandedly.

Was Teo in Madrid then? Was he in his featureless

office, working, reading, wearing his horn-rimmed glasses? Or had that merely been a polite lie?

Neither Melanie nor Cecily had the heart to go out to dinner. They ate quietly in the hotel's small dining room. *Paella*, the saffron-flavored rice, chicken and seafood concoction, and fresh bread. No wine. Neither of them could bear the thought of wine.

Melanie phoned their parents late that night, knowing it was early evening in Ohio. "Yes, we're in Madrid. We'll be home tomorrow, Dad. You already have the flight number. We're fine, really."

"I'm flying to New York to meet you," her father said.

"Oh, for goodness' sake, you don't have to do that."

"I'm going to, anyway," replied Oscar adamantly. "Kennedy, tomorrow."

"Dad—"

"See you, Mel. Let me talk to your sister."

Reluctantly, Cecily took the phone from Melanie's hand. "Dad?" she ventured brokenly.

Melanie found it painful to hear her sister's side of the conversation, painful to see Cecily's misery and guilt.

"Yes, I'm fine," Cecily said. "Dad, I'm so sorry. I never thought this would happen. You must be furious. You must hate me." She broke into tears at something Oscar said. "Daddy," she wept, as she had when she was a child. Then wordlessly she handed the phone to Melanie and the tears were still making shiny paths down her face.

"Mel, try to calm her down. I'm not mad, just relieved. Tell her. I tried to."

"I will, Dad. See you tomorrow."

She hung up and turned to see Cecily huddled on the bed, crying hysterically. "Oh, look what I've done!" she wailed. "I can't stand it. Everyone will hate me and talk about me behind my back. I'm horrible, hateful!"

Melanie went to sit by her sister, awkwardly putting a hand on her shoulder. "No one will ever think that, Ce-

cily. You had a big adventure. Thank heavens it turned
out all right."

"But...but Carlos and the boys, in so much trouble!"
She lifted her tear-streaked face. "I told the police they
were good to us, I tried to help them, Mel—truly I did.
Will it help, do you think?"

"I'm sure it will," Melanie soothed. "I said the same
thing."

"And Esteban—oh, he must think I'm a terrible, ridiculous person. And Teo and you—"

"Everyone was worried about you, that's all. It was not
your fault."

"You may say so, but I'll never forgive myself." Cecily sniffed miserably.

In the morning Cecily looked a bit puffy around the
eyes but she obviously felt better. She put on the print
dress and made a face at her reflection in the mirror. The
stockings and slip went into the wastebasket.

They drove to the airport in the dense Madrid traffic
and returned the gray Seat. Melanie felt a curious tightness in her throat and behind her eyes. They were leaving
Spain, leaving the light-hearted Mediterranean beaches of
Andalusia, the sober, cosmopolitan streets of Madrid, the
isolated green hills of the Basques.

She was leaving Esteban and his serene retreat. Leaving
the frenzied streets of Pamplona during the *feria*.

And Teo. His face would appear in her mind's eye at
odd times, jolting her, sending her heart racing. His features would flash before her as if on a movie screen;
sometimes he would be smiling, sometimes angry. Or serious, his hands folded under his chin, his dark eyes scrutinizing her. Or she would see the unruly, curling dark
hair with its sprinkle of gray. His hands lean and tanned
and capable, his strong neck as he turned his head, perhaps. Or the glint of the sun, golden on his cheek and
jawline.

At times she would turn, hearing his voice in her ear,

hearing him call her name, but he was never there. A man in a crowd would suddenly look familiar, but then she would glance at him a second time and see that he was a stranger, with only the remotest resemblance to Teo.

The Madrid airport was very crowded; this was a weekend during the busiest time of the year, the tourist season. There were more Americans than Spaniards, Melanie thought. She was sure some of the faces she saw looked familiar; they had been on the streets of Pamplona or in the bullring during a *corrida*.

Her luggage was checked through. Cecily had none, only her passport. The police in Pamplona had promised to send her luggage when and if they found it.

The sisters wandered over to the airport departure lounge, which was noisy but cool. They were settling down to wait for their flight, when Cecily asked, "Should I buy Dad a bottle of duty-free Scotch?"

"With what?" Melanie retorted, smiling.

"Oh, that's right. I don't have a cent. I could borrow some from you."

"Sure, I guess it's the least we can do. And some perfume for Mother. Something exotic. I'm just going to sit here."

"Okay, I'll be right back."

Good, Cecily was thinking of someone besides herself. It was a start, anyway.

Melanie tried to relax in the hard molded-plastic seat. The air conditioning was so cool that it was almost uncomfortable. Hard to believe it was about a hundred degrees outside. She closed her eyes, leaning back, one hand on her camera bag. Teo's face appeared in the dancing blackness, smiling at her. He was saying her name, "Melanie," in that way he had, British but with a touch of elegant, rolling Spanish, too. "Melanie." She heard it in her head, echoing, but if she opened her eyes he wouldn't be there.

"Melanie." So clear, so familiar.

A hand touched her arm, her eyes blinked open. "Cec…" she started to say, but the word faded on her lips. She gasped and felt her heart give a wild surge.

"Melanie?" he said softly again.

"Teo?" she breathed.

"I thought you were asleep," he said, smiling. "You wouldn't open your eyes."

"Teo?" Slowly she stood, facing him, the roar of the airport receding. She put out a hand to touch him, to see if he was real. He caught her hand, imprisoning it in both of his, turning it over and kissing it.

"Melanie, I couldn't let you go without seeing you once more. I was a coward at Esteban's. I couldn't bear—"

"Teo?"

"Is that all you can say?" His eyes met hers questioningly.

"Yes," she whispered.

"Well, then. I will say it for you. Come back with me. Stay here. I love you; you must know that."

"I…I can't…Cecily. My luggage…" She was stunned, unable to think; he still held her hand.

"Cecily can go home by herself. And as for your clothes—unimportant. You have your camera, don't you?"

"Yes," she murmured.

"Well?"

"But…but…" She was flooded with confusion and delight and an odd kind of release.

"The only reason for you not to come is if you do not love me, Melanie," he said gravely.

She stood there, buffeted by artificial coldness, by children crying and people speaking a dozen different languages, by the roar of a jet taking off outside, and she decided. Her face split into a smile, her heart burst open, her soul flew into her eyes. "Yes!" she said firmly, "I'll come."

"Hey, Teo, what are you doing here?" Cecily cried, returning with her plastic bag of presents.

"I'm going to marry your sister," he replied.

Cecily stared at Teo, then turned to Melanie, and finally stared at both of them, open-mouthed. "Is this for real?" she asked, astounded.

"You bet it is," Melanie said with a soft laugh.

"What'll I tell Mother and Dad?" Cecily cried.

"Tell them...tell them...I'll send them a picture!"

Jane sensed that Graham was up to something...
something hazardous to their happiness!

A Perfect Gem

CHAPTER ONE

*This book is dedicated to the memory of Smedley But-
ler, of whom it must be said his truth was even stranger
than my fiction, and to Bob Duggan, the real-life Rob
Dearborn and head of Executive Security International
of Aspen, Colorado. I ask his forgiveness for any liberties taken with his character and thank him for his
invaluable assistance.*

JANE MANNING'S HANDS GRIPPED THE WHEEL competently
as she steered into a skid that brought her dangerously
close to the edge of the road. The car she drove was an
old state-trooper cruiser with a beefed-up suspension and
a throaty-sounding engine; in the back seat sat her passenger, a silent blond man who was bounced around as
she evaded her pursuers.

"Hang on," Jane called over her shoulder to her
charge, "I'm going to try something."

She downshifted, pulled out of the skid skillfully and
glanced once again into her rearview mirror. One of the
drivers chasing her had overcorrected his skid and slid off
the road into a sagebrush-lined ditch. Good.

The ribbon of pavement lay in front of her, curving
away across the dry Colorado plateau. The July sun glared
into her eyes and made her back stick to the plastic seat
of the car. Jane watched carefully, her eyes darting back
and forth across her field of vision and then to the rearview mirror again. What else would they pull? Two cars

had started out chasing her but were there more waiting in ambush behind that pile of old tires? Or would men with machine guns pop up from that ditch and shoot at her and her passenger? Would there be a barricade ahead?

There was no time to consider that, Jane thought as she weaved expertly across the roadway in order to present a difficult target. Venturing another quick glance in the mirror, she saw that the remaining car was speeding up, nudging her bumper. Jane stepped on the gas, forcing the pedal to the floor as the sound of machine-gun fire reached her ears. She drove like a demon, just on the edge of control, while sweat trickled from her brow into her eyes. Adrenaline pumped through her veins furiously and she fought the instinct to duck her head.

Okay, this was it. She jammed on the brakes, heard the squeal of tires, smelled hot rubber. The driver behind her braked violently to avoid a collision and Jane spun the wheel, screeching into a 180-degree turn, then hit the gas, leaving the other car smoking and stalled, in a ditch, half off the road.

She'd done it! Jane pulled up at the starting line of the track and got out of her car. She opened the back door and grinned widely at the tall blond man who emerged unperturbed from the back seat.

"Good work," said Rob Dearborn quietly, shaking her hand.

"I passed?" Jane asked.

Dearborn nodded in his usual unemotional way. Not a hint of the hair-raising ride he'd just been subjected to showed on his coolly placid features. He gave away nothing beyond his always carefully selected words. "You pass," was all he said.

Jane pumped his hand even harder. The other students, all men, crowded around, congratulating her. "Good driving…helluva maneuver…great control…smart move."

Jane turned to them and smiled, feeling triumph and

relief and satisfaction. "Wow, what a way to pass a final exam!" she exclaimed.

Graduation was a week later. The International Security Academy of Aspen, Colorado, the most renowned body-guard training school in the United States, always held its graduation party in the Steak Pit, an unpretentious restaurant that catered to local Aspenites. After finishing the salad, the juicy steaks, the steaming baked potatoes, everybody sat back and relaxed as Rob Dearborn, the head of the ISA, stood and gave a short speech.

Jane Manning sat with the nineteen other students and listened carefully to her teacher's words. She had been studying for almost two years: weaponry, martial arts, bomb detection, evasive driving, first aid, electronic surveillance, the psychology of criminals, followed by an intensive, two-week practical session in Aspen. This evening was the culmination of it all.

"You've learned how to use certain methods to protect yourselves and your clients," Rob Dearborn was saying. "But the use of violence is only a last resort. If you have to use your physical skills or a gun you've already failed in the principal lesson, which is staying out of trouble. When a weapon is drawn, you are committed to using it, perhaps eliminating more favorable options."

Jane listened in rapt attention. There wasn't much Rob Dearborn said that was not to the point, significant and well reasoned. Despite his laconic manner, he was a man who appeared to know something no one else was privileged to know and Jane respected him enormously. She sat straighter in her chair, proud of what she'd accomplished under his tutelage, ready to put into practice her hard-earned skills.

"The world is entering a chaotic time," Dearborn continued. His high cheekbones and air of perfect control and containment reminded one of a blond samurai warrior. "There will be crises. You *will* be needed."

Then the other teachers gave their speeches. They all had something to say: the burly ex-Secret Service agent who dealt with the field of security; the well-built, sun-tanned former FBI man who taught undercover skills; the Indianapolis 500 racer who was in charge of evasive driving; the bearded paramedic who instructed students in first aid; and the powerful, stocky teacher of evasion techniques and client protection, who liked to play terrorist against his students.

There were awards: best marksman, best driver, best reflexes. Jane gasped in surprise when she got an award for her achievement in Hwa Rang Do, the exacting form of Korean karate the students all had to learn from Rob himself. She went up to collect her certificate from him while the nearly all-male audience clapped and hooted. Jane felt herself blushing with pleasure and on-the-spot embarrassment.

When she sat down again her father shook his head in baffled consternation. One of her older brothers, James, punched her in the biceps gently and mouthed, "Congratulations, squirt."

After the presentations there was much bantering, good-natured teasing, high spirits and a few damp eyes. Jane introduced her father, Tom Manning, and her brothers, James and Jared, to Rob Dearborn.

"You've raised quite a girl there," said Rob with his calm smile.

"I certainly have," replied Tom Manning in his characteristically straightforward fashion. Nevertheless he was still shaking his head in bewilderment. For all his pride in her, Jane knew precisely what he was thinking: *my little girl, a bodyguard*?

"She'll do well," Rob commented. "I've got some people interested in her already."

"For a job?" queried Jared.

"*Of course*," said Jane, mortified. "Women make the best bodyguards."

The three male Mannings appeared skeptical.

"It's true in many cases," explained Rob, rescuing her. "Female bodyguards help a client keep a low profile. They don't *look* like bodyguards. It can be very effective."

"But she's not, you know, strong," protested James. "Not like a man."

"She's learned ways of disabling an attacker by using his own weight against him. She's quick and wiry and knows her karate. She'll manage very well," Rob assured him.

"That remains to be seen," said her father, still shaking his head.

When the evening came to a close and it was time to say goodbye, Jane felt a bit teary-eyed. Who knew when the students' paths might cross again? They had all grown so close, as people do when they are subjected to difficult, demanding times together. There had been the terrible moments of doubt when Ned, the overweight young man from Florida, nearly killed himself in the driving school; there had been the sadness and confusion of all the students when three had dropped out of the course after only two days of intense training; there had been the time when Jane herself had frozen during a well-staged terrorist attack involving two young women wheeling baby carriages.

But there had been the good times as well: the night the other students, all men, had invited Jane to go for a beer; the day they had received their black sweatshirts with the Korean karate symbol on the front and International Security Academy stenciled on the back; the time they'd all hit the bull's-eye in target practice.

And for Jane, especially, there had been Rob, who'd

encouraged her when everything and everyone seemed to be against her goal of completing the bodyguard course.

"Why do you want to become a bodyguard?" Rob Dearborn had asked during her initial interview two years before.

Jane had considered the question carefully before answering. "I want something more than staying on our ranch. I want more than marriage and a family. I want to do something exciting and maybe a little dangerous. I want to *prove* myself."

Rob had nodded, understanding, and Jane had known then that she could do it. She could do anything if she set her mind to it. Maybe she felt that way because she'd been raised by her widowed father and four older brothers. There'd never been any slack for little Janey. She'd been expected to take the rough-and-tumble existence of growing up on a ranch, the wild horseback rides, the stubborn calves to rope, trees to climb, haylofts to jump out of, dares and challenges to accept. It had made her tough physically and stubborn mentally.

And yet there was nothing unfeminine about Jane. Five feet eight inches tall, she was slim in build with small breasts, a narrow waist and a compact rear end. Her nose was too small, turned up and freckled; one front tooth was not even with the other and her gaze was alarmingly level. She had green eyes, dark brows and heavy brown hair cut in an easy-to-keep pageboy style. She knew she was often described as down-to-earth, wholesome, refreshing, at best "cute." Never beautiful, sexy or glamorous. And even though Jane was twenty-six years old, she only looked eighteen.

"That's good," Rob had told her when she complained. "No one would ever suspect you of being a bodyguard. Use it to your advantage, Jane."

Two long years of hope and frustration and doubt had passed and now the course was over. Rob had said the graduates were ready to face the real world. She sure hoped he was right as she exchanged addresses and final goodbyes. With her father and brothers Jane walked out of the restaurant into the cool summer night of Aspen and drew in a breath of crystal-clear mountain air.

"So now you're a bodyguard," said Jared. "You gonna *guard* our stock?"

She ignored him pointedly and climbed into the dusty station wagon for the hour and a half ride home to Rifle, Colorado, where the Manning ranch was located.

"Now, really, squirt, what're you gonna do?" asked James.

"I'll wait until Rob places me. He's always got people calling him. You heard what he said. Someone's already interested."

"What if you get a client who's *too* interested in lady bodyguards?" Jared teased.

"I'd probably punch him out," she said coolly, "and then quit."

"You'll have to leave home," said her father sadly. "No one wants a bodyguard in Rifle, I reckon. It'll be some big city feller, some sheikh or the likes."

"Maybe. But, Daddy, you knew I was going to leave sooner or later."

Her father kept driving, his strong craggy profile shadowed, his Stetson drawn down low over his brow. "I guess. But not so far away." His large work-worn hands grasped the steering wheel as if it were a tractor. "If your mother knew..."

"You know she'd want me to do what I had to, Daddy," Jane said softly. "And I have to do this."

"You can always come home, Janey, whenever..."

"I know."

She'd heard the same thing from all five members of her family for years now. Not one of them could understand her restlessness or her need to pit herself against the world. However, it was to their collective credit that they never actually tried to stop her from doing anything. They might argue, grouse, tease, even swear, but the final decision had always been Jane's and she'd never shied from making them.

Originally, she had decided to go to veterinary school in Fort Collins when she'd graduated from the University of Colorado in Boulder. Her father had grumbled half-heartedly about marriage and a home but Jane was determined, and he took it in stride, even coming to like the idea of a homegrown vet to care for the valuable rodeo stock he raised.

Then, after two years and a lot of soul-searching, she'd realized veterinary school was not for her. She needed wider vistas and more excitement. Returning home, she'd helped out with the stock, broken a few mustangs, raced quarter horses at the local fairgrounds, dated casually and had been bored silly.

One day the *Denver Post*'s front page had featured Rob Dearborn and his International Security Academy, and Jane had been hooked. "Women have edge as hired shadows," a headline had shouted. Jane had read the article then reread it. "Holy cow," she'd whispered to herself, a great hope growing in her chest and a surging excitement. She'd run out to the barn where her father had been holding his prize quarter horse stallion for the blacksmith.

"Daddy, read this!" she'd cried, waving the paper in his face. "This is for me!"

"Take it easy, Janey, you'll scare Indigo."

The yelling and arguing had begun at the dinner table that evening. "Go ahead and do it, squirt," said James, the youngest male. "Plumb insane," scoffed Jared, the joker. "You sure you want to do this?" asked Joe, the oldest and most serious of the group. Married with a young son, he'd come over for a family conference.

"I'm as sure as I'll ever be," answered Jane with assurance.

"You just need a man," said John, the second oldest. He was engaged and tended to be chauvinistic about women of late.

Jane stood up and leaned over the table. "That's about the dumbest remark anybody's made!"

"Sit down, Jane," said her father. "Now, tell me again—what do you have to do and how much will it cost?"

Jane sank down into her seat, glowering at John, and began to explain everything to her father.

Six weeks later she had been interviewed by Rob Dearborn and then enrolled in the course. Texts were mailed to her: manuals on weaponry and surveillance, the history of terrorism, criminal psychology, emergency first aid. She'd studied hard every day. Her brothers had strutted around looking smug and superior, waiting for her to give it up. Her father had watched her thoughtfully but said nothing. She knew they all wanted her to change her mind about being a bodyguard but something intractable and resolute in her wouldn't give in.

Once a week she'd driven the hour and a half up the Roaring Fork River to Aspen to take Rob's Hwa Rang Do class, which Jane found grueling yet fascinating. It was hard physically but graceful, much like the discipline of ballet. It encompassed the mind, too, for concentration was a powerful aspect of Oriental martial arts. And respect for the teacher; a bow over folded hands was required at the start and end of class.

Jane learned that Hwa Rang Do began in Korea in A.D. 540 as a form of court entertainment. *By women.* Only later was the art form taken over by men and turned to warlike use. The study of the discipline consisted of innumerable "forms"—moves, joint locks, holds and kicks in combination that could disable, immobilize, even kill an opponent. They were repeated over and over until they became instinctive. Anyone attacking a Hwa Rang Do practitioner would find himself in an instant, reflexive whirl of hands or feet that could do great damage.

A year after Jane had begun her karate training, a year in which her brothers teased her without mercy, she finally got in a stew one day and tossed James to the floor of the barn with little more than a turn of her wrist. The jeers and taunting stopped miraculously.

Rob, however, always warned against the indiscriminate use of violence—of any sort. "I haven't used Hwa Rang Do in anger in fifteen years," he told his students. Rob was a fourth-degree black belt and just watching him move was exciting. While the rest of the class struggled, grunted and sweated, Rob flicked, feinted, and struck snakelike, totally in control, moving *with* his body instead of against it.

"Your hands and feet are deadly weapons," Rob would say and when Jane watched him demonstrate a kick or a hold she knew his words were true.

Jane had passed all the tests on guns with flying colors: she would assemble and reassemble the weapons, and practice her shooting over and over until her arms were tired and then start again. She knew the feel of weapons and their capabilities but was much more comfortable without one. Rob assured her that a bodyguard did not need to carry a gun; if her client were indeed attacked, chances were things would move so quickly there would be no opportunity to use a weapon, anyway. Up close, her hands were just as effective.

Now the months and months of work were over, Jane thought, as her father drove along the dark road home to Rifle. Would she really get a job as a bodyguard? Sudden doubts assailed her. What if her client were hurt, kidnapped, or even killed? Her training had been rigorous, her dedication complete, but the responsibility now seemed awesome.

The lights of Glenwood Springs appeared in the distance, and her father turned west on Interstate 70 and followed the Colorado River toward Rifle. She wondered where she would end up working. A foreign country maybe? Someplace exotic? Would she be a nanny for some top executive's children or a guard for a political figure? Probably she'd never see a moment of action in her life; Rob had told all of his students that it was more likely that a client would break a bone, get stung by a bee or have a coronary than get kidnapped. Jane wasn't sure whether she'd prefer an uneventful career or an action-packed one.

"So, you've done it," her father said finally. "I have to admit I sure was proud of you tonight. A little puzzled maybe but proud. And scared, Janey."

"Me, too," Jane said fervently.

IT WAS VERY HOT in Rifle, Colorado, the second Sunday in July but the heat didn't stop the ranchers from gathering at the Garfield County Fairgrounds for a day of quarter horse racing. Anywhere else where the thermometer hit ninety-nine degrees, people would have worn shorts, T-shirts, maybe a sundress and sandals. Not in Rifle. From toddlers to grandparents, everyone in the shaded stands wore Levi's, Western shirts, straw cowboy hats and boots.

Jane was dressed exactly the same save for the number twenty tied over her shirt. She was riding four horses in various races that day—two young ones for neighboring ranchers, a promising mare for her father and good old Indigo, who was bound to win the half-mile open event.

She loved the excitement of racing, the thunder of the horses' hooves as they pounded at top speed around the track. Quarter horses raced short distances but they "went

like hell,'' as the old-timers said. Two-dollar bets could
be placed before each of the eight races.

"Get that girth tight,'' came a humor-filled voice from
over Jane's shoulder as she struggled with the leather strap
holding the lightweight racing saddle on.

She turned, pushed her cowboy hat back and squinted
up at a suntanned, handsome man on a powerful bay
horse; he was one of the race marshals. "Branch Taggart,'' she said, smiling. "Haven't seen you in ages.''

"Too long, Jane. I hear you been learnin' to be a bodyguard. Is that crazy rumor true?'' His grin widened.

"Sure is, Branch. I just graduated. I'm waiting for a
job right now.''

Branch leaned forward in his saddle, his smile fading.
The big bay sidestepped nervously. "Jane, you are kiddin'
me.''

She deliberately turned her back on him and continued
pulling her horse's girth tight. "I'm dead serious,
Branch.''

"You think we could go out tonight and talk about it
over a beer or two?''

She cocked her head up at him and wiped the sweat
off her upper lip with a finger before answering. "Sure,
why not? But don't think I'm going to listen to you haranguing me about my career.''

Branch straightened, held a hand up and chuckled. "I'll
try my damnedest not to,'' he said then kicked his horse
and trotted off toward the track.

Jane leaned against the horse she was saddling and
watched him go. His broad shoulders filled his denim shirt
and his big brimmed straw hat was set at the correct,
rakish angle. She and Branch had been seeing each other
on and off ever since she'd graduated from college. He
was older, about thirty-five, and very much a local. He
wanted a wife, Jane knew. She liked Branch. But he was
a little too predictable, too much like her father and her

brothers, too much like all the men she'd met. She shrugged and turned back to her horse, gave his belly a slap to make sure he wasn't puffed up, then tightened the girth another notch.

The bugle was sounding for the first race. "That's us," Jane said to the three other riders nearby. She switched her cowboy hat for a hard hat, swung up on her horse and let her father lead her out to the track. And all the way she kept thinking: *Branch Taggart is a good catch, a good man. Why can't I be like other girls and just get married?*

Jane won her first race with ease, lost the second to a rangy gray gelding, then won again with Hazel, her father's new mare. The thrill of the race itself always filled her, moved her, but it was a fleeting thrill. After only a few moments it was over and Jane felt the heat and breathed in the dust.

The afternoon's big race was the open event in which she was riding Indigo. Branch trotted his horse over to wish her luck. Her brother, Joe, and his wife, Trish, came by with little Joey. Her father grew increasingly silent—a sign of nervousness, Jane knew.

Indigo stomped and wet patches of sweat appeared on his neck. He knew what was coming.

The bugle blew once more and Jane's heart, as always, skipped a beat. Four other riders were competing against her. The distance was just over a half mile, a long race for quarter horses.

"Ain't your horse there gettin' too old?" asked the young boy who was starting in the gate next to her.

"Not yet," Jane said and the boy laughed, unbelieving.

The gun went off, the gates sprang open and Jane crouched forward in the stirrups as Indigo burst out onto the track. His muscles gathered powerfully under her as he got into stride. "Come on, Indigo!" she shouted but he knew what to do and Jane didn't even need the crop.

They rounded the curve, all the horses bunched up and

leaning into the rail. The dust spurted up under their hooves, while lather flew in specks off the horses' straining necks. Jane urged Indigo on with her hands and feet and voice, and he began to pull ahead. The horse on the inside, with the young boy astride, suddenly swerved toward Jane—deliberately? her mind flashed. But Indigo kept his stride and moved past and then there was nothing but the empty track ahead and the finish line.

Her father came running up the minute the race was over. "That kid hurt either of you?" he asked.

Jane took her hat off and swung a leg over the horse's withers, then slid to the ground. "I don't think so but we'll check Indigo out later."

"Scared me silly, that kid," said her father, taking the horse's reins.

"Me, too," breathed Jane, "but I loved it. What a thrill!"

Tom Manning looked at his daughter sourly.

"Well, I'll bet you wagered plenty on old Indigo here. Would you rather I'd pulled him up and lost?" Jane teased.

"Maybe I do."

But Jane only laughed and put an arm around her father's shoulders.

Later that evening they pulled up at the barn to unload their horses; hot, tired and dusty. Jared came out of the ranch house to help them.

"God, I need a shower," said Jane as they walked toward the house.

"Oh, I forgot to tell you," her brother began. "Rob Dearborn called earlier. He says call him at home. I wrote the number down—"

"Why didn't you *tell* me!" cried Jane.

"I just did."

She began to run. "It's about a job, I know it is!"

She dialed the number without even taking off her hat. "Oh boy, oh boy," she whispered to herself.

Rob's wife answered. "Sure, just a minute," she said to Jane's query.

"Hello, Jane," came Rob's familiar, uninflected voice. "I think we've got you a prospect."

"What? Where? When?"

"Hold on," said Rob. "It's for a courier service in New York."

"Courier service?" Jane was picturing a delivery boy on a bicycle, a Federal Express van, mailbags.

"They deliver art, gems, valuable securities, anything and everything worth stealing. Anywhere in the world."

"Oh, wow."

"They like the idea of women bodyguards and want to interview you."

"Where? When?" Jane was hopping up and down with excitement.

"They have a man who'll be in the area next Friday. He'll come to your place. I've given them all the particulars. They're very interested, Jane."

"Here? Next Friday?"

"Yes. And good luck, Jane. This is a great opportunity for you."

"Oh, thank you, Rob. Boy, am I excited! Thanks again!"

She hung up and turned to her father and brothers who had—very casually—gathered around to listen.

"I've got a job interview, you guys! For a job in New York! Oh boy! And he's coming *here* next Friday!"

"Way to go, squirt," said James and he gave her a none-too-gentle punch in the arm.

CHAPTER TWO

THE SMALL, UNOBTRUSIVE SIGN reading Norcom marked the entrance to the sprawling complex. Graham Smith pulled his sporty rental car into the drive and noted the perfectly manicured lawns; the low, trimmed bushes that butted up against the cement block plant; the blue tinted glass and sloping skylights that faced the visitors' parking lot. He pulled into a vacant spot, climbed out of the Audi and surveyed his surroundings. Silicon Valley. Aptly named, Graham thought, comparing the place with the ancient, teeming cities and silent hills of Japan from where he had just returned. Norcom was situated in the ultramodern metropolis that covered the floor of the valley, spreading like a surrealistic set for some sci-fi flick.

Crossing the parking lot, Graham glanced around once more. Nothing was out of place. No cars had followed him too closely from the airport, no one had seemed too nervous or too studiously casual. Automatically he patted the inside pocket of his European-cut, steel-blue sport coat of slubbed silk and assured himself that the microchip was still there.

Ten grand, he mused. A lot of money. More than a year's salary for some people yet it had taken Graham less than twenty-four hours to earn it. All he'd done was visit Norcom's Tokyo production office, pick up the prototype of the chip, fly to San Francisco and make the short drive south to Silicon Valley. It meant nothing to him that the chip was top secret, revolutionary, the so-called breakthrough of the decade in computer science. His job was merely to deliver it. And he was nearly finished; he almost had the ten thousand earned. Everything had gone smoothly, like clockwork.

He identified himself to the security guard at Norcom and waited for clearance to enter the plant. A familiar, mild disappointment settled over him. Too many of his courier jobs went without incident and, Graham admitted to himself, an occasional hitch did add a certain interest to his work. Not that he would welcome a theft, of course, but a foiled attempt every so often…

"You may go in, Mr. Smith," said the guard, and the man handed him a badge that Graham pinned to the breast pocket of his silk jacket.

His mother, Renée, a French Canadian from Montreal, often told Graham that someday he was going to grow too cocky and outsmart himself. "You're one of those thrill seekers, *mon cher*," she'd say in her slightly accented voice. "Someone who can't sit still for a moment. You should have stayed in the foreign service, like your father. At least *he* had the common sense to know when he was well off."

But Graham hadn't wanted the life afforded him by working for the U.S. government. It had been too narrow and confining. Sure, he'd graduated from Georgetown University—like his half American, half English father, Smedley, before him—and at first he'd liked the idea of working in the foreign service.

Graham had even found his own special niche when he was transferred into security and he'd learned all the new electronic techniques used to protect Americans working for the government at home and abroad. He'd even studied martial arts under a Chinese master when he'd been stationed with the embassy in Hong Kong for two years. He'd gleaned a lot from the foreign service, done some courier work for diplomats and liked that end of it even more. Then, when he'd found there was a real need for trained couriers in the private sector, he'd gotten the notion to quit the service and strike out on his own as a free-lance courier.

It was lucrative work, not to mention the opportunity it provided for travel and adventure. So he'd given notice to the government, advertised his skills in national newspapers and fallen into his present work effortlessly, with that deft touch and winning smile, which as Renée Smith once put it, "Could charm the money from a Scot."

If asked where he saw his life heading, Graham would have answered lightly. "Who knows? I hope it's a surprise and I sure don't agonize over it." And in that statement there was more than a little truth. He was easygoing, a charmer, a man who did not consciously seek involvement. His life-style produced misconceptions about his true self, at least where women were concerned. They seemed to view him as flighty, not the type to settle down at all. But Graham saw himself as one who had not yet found the right mate, that one person who would share his life and his need for adventure, who would neither tie him down nor make impossible demands of him.

She was out there somewhere, he knew, waiting for him, ready to accept him exactly as he was.

He was thirty-three years old, Graham thought as he greeted the receptionist at Norcom, and already he could almost retire on what he'd earned in the last three years. But he couldn't retire. What would he do for kicks then?

"Mr. Smith," the smartly dressed young woman said, "we've been expecting you. I'll buzz Dr. Laurence." She smiled. "If you'll just have a seat, I'm sure she'll be right along."

He sat in the comfortable, pastel-colored reception area and looked up idly at the skylight. It was a beautiful July day outside, sunny and pleasantly warm. At home, in New York, it would be hot and muggy, the steam rising from subway vents in the streets, hot metallic air pumping out of myriad dripping air-conditioners that studded every building, the white summer sky close and burdened with moisture.

Perhaps, he ventured to himself, there would be a message on his answering machine when he got home to his brownstone, a new job awaiting him. It was amazing how fast his reputation for integrity and speed had spread in the corporate world, how quickly one courier assignment had led to another. And all in the space of a few years.

He glanced over at the young, auburn-haired receptionist and her gaze snapped away from his instantly. Graham enjoyed her attention. He loved women, all kinds, all shapes. He adored their mannerisms, their strengths, their foibles. He liked the way their minds worked with immutable, realistic logic. He appreciated their clothes, their curves, their jewelry, their makeup, their intelligence and nurturing abilities. And, recognizing his admiration, women liked him in return.

Graham was also cognizant of the effect his uncommon good looks had on most women. He accepted it without conceit or vanity. At thirty-three he'd kept his trim, six-foot-two frame in excellent shape by practicing his martial arts and working out at a gym when he was in New York. But it wasn't just his physique that drew the interested perusal of women. It was also his unusual coloring. His hair was thick and somewhat unruly and strawberry-blond. His complexion was ruddy and healthy and his eyes very blue, a startling China-blue like his father's. He also had Smedley Smith's mouth, wide and humor-filled, and the family's hollow cheeks above a lean, narrow jaw. His nose jutted out in masculine generosity.

All in all, Graham possessed the look of an adventurer, of a man born out of his time perhaps, someone who should have been commanding a sixteenth-century galleon. As it was, he was never certain if his appearance was a gift or a hindrance. Women, although initially attracted, tended to become wary of him.

Dr. Laurence, whom Graham had never met, finally

rounded a corner from behind the receptionist. She was tall—strikingly so—at least five foot ten, he guessed, and stunning, with jet-black hair falling softly to her shoulders and wide-set brown eyes that perused him confidently.

"Mr. Smith," she began, "so nice to meet you at last. It's always difficult to do business by phone, don't you think?"

"Absolutely," he replied, shaking her hand, observing the firm breasts beneath the loose white lab jacket. She was wearing heels. He drew himself up to his full height. Striking, he thought once more, and obviously smart as well. Dr. Laurence, Graham recalled, was Norcom's top research technician, a woman who had, at thirty-five, been written up in *Time* and *Scientific American* and God knew how many professional journals.

"You have our precious little baby, of course?" she asked.

"I do. Safe and sound."

"Would you follow me, please?"

She led him down a long, sterile corridor past many closed doors. Then she stopped and produced a key and opened a door that had Dr. Jeanette Laurence stenciled on it. Inside was a tidy office and on the far side of the room was another door, leading, he imagined, into the lab area of the giant plant.

Jeanette Laurence indicated a chair for Graham to sit in. "I have to admit," she said, smiling a little self-consciously, "I didn't sleep a wink last night."

"Worried about the microchip?"

She nodded. "You must understand, it's been seven years in production. And it's been in my head for ten years."

"So you developed it yourself? Impressive."

"Thank you. It's been my life's work. The chip will make computing possible for anyone. It will be easier to operate our new computer than it will be to run the simplest of typewriters." She went on to explain to Graham some of the technical breakthroughs provided by the microchip's existence but he found his interest waning. What did hold his attention was Dr. Laurence.

"And you see," she was saying, "a child of four will be able… Oh, listen to me, will you? You probably couldn't care less."

"Would you be angry if I said I didn't?" he admitted, his blue eyes twinkling. "In my line of work, it doesn't really matter what I carry. Just as long as I complete the job successfully."

Graham reached into his inside pocket and produced the sealed courier envelope that held the chip.

"Oh, am I glad to see this!" She smiled and breathed a sigh of relief. "Any number of computer companies would give anything to get hold of it."

"I can imagine."

"I hope you didn't have any trouble," she said.

"None. In fact, I rather expected there might be an incident. At least in Hawaii, where we stopped to refuel."

"I'll tell you, Mr. Smith, your fee was worth every penny. Within the next four years Norcom is going to lead the world market in sales with this chip."

"I'm glad to hear that. And," he added, "I'm very glad you're satisfied with my service."

"Oh, we are." She pulled open a desk drawer and produced a cashier's check made out to Graham Smith for the sum of ten thousand dollars. "I got your name through a friend in San Francisco," she remarked, handing him the check. "He works at Delmar Labs, pharmaceuticals."

"Yes, I did a job for them last year," Graham recalled.

"That's right. My friend said you were tops, too."

"Do thank him for me." Graham put the check into his coat pocket and stood. "It's been a pleasure doing business with Norcom." He held out his hand and when she shook it, Graham felt a certain reluctance on her part to let the touch end. So the good doctor had felt the attraction as well.

''You're staying in San Francisco?'' she asked, her tone considerably lighter than it had been up to now.

''Actually,'' replied Graham, ''I'd like to but I'm off on another job. Flying out tonight, in fact.''

''Oh, I see.''

''You live in the city?''

She shook her head. ''No. Just south of it, though.''

''Umm. Well,'' he said, opening the door and turning to give her one of his devil-may-care smiles, ''if you're ever in New York...''

''I'll make a point of calling you.''

''Goodbye, Dr. Laurence.'' He closed the door and strode down the hall, all the while toying with the idea of spending the night in California although he had another obligation. He lifted his hand to the security guard, shut the door to Norcom and Dr. Laurence behind him and felt a twinge of regret.

DAMN LEW RAPP, thought Graham without true malice as his flight touched down that night in Grand Junction, Colorado. How had he let Lew talk him into doing this favor? He didn't even work for Mercury officially; he'd merely taken on two or three odd jobs for Lew since last spring. He *could* have been turning down the sheets for Jeanette Laurence at that very moment. Instead, he was in some rinky-dink Western Slope city in the middle of the Rockies, having to search out a lonely motel because tomorrow he'd promised Lew that he'd conduct an interview.

Lew could have done it himself, Graham decided, as he tossed his bag onto the bed at the Holiday Inn. But Lew, the owner of Mercury Courier and Smedley Smith's old pal from the foreign service, had felt Graham's expertise was invaluable in this area whereas Lew's experience with bodyguards and security was scant.

Ordinarily, Graham would not have minded this favor. From his days in security with the foreign service he was quite familiar with the credentials necessary for a bodyguard. He would certainly look this prospect over on Lew's behalf and admittedly Rifle, Colorado, was on his way back to New York—sort of—but tonight he was tired due to a bad case of jet lag. And it *was* difficult to get Jeanette Laurence, all glorious five feet ten of her, out of his head.

The following morning sunlight streamed through the opening in the green-patterned curtains of Graham's motel room. He looked at his watch. Eight-thirty. The interview was scheduled for noon. Rifle—an appropriate name for a Western town—was, what, sixty miles or so from Grand Junction?

He picked up a rental car and ate at a roadside inn, a real cowboy joint, with wagon wheels on the rough wooden walls, oil lamps hanging from the ceiling, sawdust on the floor and waitresses in jeans, boots and Stetsons. After two cups of coffee and a man-sized breakfast, he was feeling amazingly well considering he'd been in Japan only a day and a half before.

He paid his check and rose to leave.

"You come back now, mister, real soon." The waitress smiled brightly and winked at him.

"Might just do that," replied Graham easily, affecting her accent, his blue eyes alight with devilish charm.

Swinging open the saloon-style doors and striding back into the bright sunlight, Graham patted his full stomach, hitched up his belt and, fully awake now, surveyed the sweeping country of western Colorado.

It was big and breathtakingly empty. His route to Rifle followed the gently curving Colorado River. Funny, he mused, but he'd always thought of the Colorado as a mighty white-water scenic wonder, deadly and challenging, as it thundered down deep canyons and crashed across massive boulders.

Not this section, he saw. Instead, the slow, wide river carved muddy turns in the broad valley floor. And on either side of the water, grazing land spread, rising in the far distance to mesas with their amazingly chopped-off pinnacles. Above these steep-sided and striated natural elevations was the bluest sky Graham had ever seen.

An image struck him: a knife in God's sure hand, slicing off the peaks of ancient mountains and leaving behind these huge, squat, utterly flat-topped mesas for man to wonder over eons later.

The light here had a remarkable clarity and the air was so dry that the scenery looked as if it were painted onto a blue backdrop, the shadows too precise, the colors too pure, the lines too perfect. He decided that he'd like to climb those mountains someday to see if they were real.

Graham drove, enjoying the scenery, marveling over the wild, untamed western lands. He stopped twice along the roadside and checked the map. It wouldn't be too hard to miss a town the size of Rifle. And then he thought about Lew Rapp back in New York on this hot July day, stuck in the Mercury office, pushing paper around his desk. And instead of cussing Lew for asking this favor of him, Graham laughed out loud. This was no favor, it was a bonus!

Besides, Lew had his hands full anyway. Mercury's couriers had been hit by robbers three times in the past few months and Lew was beginning to gnash his teeth. The police were getting nowhere with solving the thefts and the bonding agent and the insurance company, Lloyd's of London, were breathing hard down Lew Rapp's neck. Either the thefts ended or they'd cancel Lew's bond and his policy next year when they were up for renewal.

No wonder Lew had hired a bodyguard for his couriers last month. And since the two-year-old business was growing by the week, he needed a second guard. It was quite a responsibility for Graham to judge this prospective bodyguard's suitability. Lew, of course, would make the final decision should Graham give a thumbs-up.

He had to wonder though if a young, inexperienced

woman would even fit the bill. Could she handle herself in a pinch?

Rifle was everything Graham had expected and less. A few years back, during all the hype about oil shale development, Rifle property had been the hottest real estate in western Colorado but now the small, rural community sat slumbering beside the Colorado River. Oil had proven to be too expensive to extract from the shale. Rifle had boomed and then collapsed overnight. And yet, despite its rundown look, Graham liked the homey atmosphere of Rifle. It still retained a flavor of the Old West, a charm left over from the days when cattlemen had driven their herds there to the busiest stockyards west of Chicago.

At a gas station he asked directions to the Manning ranch.

"You cross the river up that road," pointed out the man, "then head east a piece."

"A piece?"

"Two, maybe three miles. Watch fer the cattle crossin' and a dirt road off to the left."

Ten minutes later Graham thought he had it all down pat. A half hour later he was hopelessly lost on a muddy, pitted washboard of a road. He stopped the rental car, got out, glanced around and scratched his head. To the north was a precariously steep mountainside, heavily wooded with tall dark spruce. To the east and west was open rangeland and to the south nothing but aspen trees, more grazing land, more aspens. Not a house was in sight. Not even the river was visible.

Swell.

He got back in the car, not knowing that it had rained the previous night and certainly not realizing that his rear-wheel-drive Chevy didn't have a prayer of getting out of the muddy rut he'd stopped in. Fifteen minutes later, tired of spinning the tires, sloshing up mud and rocking back and forth, Graham climbed back out and stood shaking his head.

"Well," he said aloud, "if I have to get stuck like some stupid city dude, it may as well be in paradise."

"Got that right, pardner," came a voice from behind him.

Graham spun around. Sitting astride a big horse was a real live cowboy. "Good morning," Graham said, "glad to see you. Glad to see *anyone*."

"Bet you are." The cowpoke had been sitting casually in his saddle, arms folded over the horn, reins dangling loosely from one work-hardened hand. He straightened lazily, tipped the brim of his hat and grinned. "Need some help?"

"Sure. And I'll tell you what—if you'll climb in the car I'll do the pushing." There now, wasn't that the gentlemanly thing to offer?

"In those duds?" The cowboy eyed Graham speculatively, a taunting grin curving thin lips.

Graham looked down at his silk slacks and hundred-dollar Italian loafers. "You're absolutely right. *I'll* drive, *you* push." His blue eyes met green ones and danced in challenge.

The man laughed and dismounted, leaving his horse ground tied. "Where're you headed anyway, mister?"

From inside the car Graham called, "The Manning ranch. Know where it is?"

"Just might at that." The cowboy put a strong shoulder to the trunk of the car and braced himself.

"How far off the path am I?"

"Half mile or so." He grunted with effort as he shoved. "Back the way you came. Off to the left."

Finally the car lurched forward and Graham was able to turn it around without getting stuck again. "Thanks," he said. "I better be heading to the ranch."

"Yeah," said the cowboy, "Jane gets real angry when people aren't on time."

"Jane Manning?"

"My sister. I'm John. John Manning. Pleased to know

you, Mr. Smith.'' He put a booted foot in the stirrup, lifted himself back into the saddle and tipped his hat again. ''Be seein' you.'' He pulled gently on the reins and his horse loped easily over a hill and out of sight.

''I'll be damned,'' said Graham, grinning as he put the car into gear and headed back the way he'd come.

It was a good half-mile drive along the dirt road John Manning had told him about before Graham spotted the ranch house. The sprawling wooden structure sat in the open, surrounded by cattle-dotted rangeland. To the north of the barn and corral was wooded mountainside, thick with deep green spruce trees that rose to delineate the clear blue Colorado sky.

Now this was what he'd call heaven, Graham thought. The scene was straight out of an old John Wayne movie, promising the good life laced with adventure. He had to wonder why someone would want to leave all this, to trade in a life of real Western ranching for a job in the city.

He parked the mud-spattered Chevy near the corral and got out. A moment later he heard a screen door bang and he looked in the direction of the house. A woman was crossing the wide porch and covering the intervening ground in long-legged strides, approaching him. And in that gait of hers Graham read a number of things. Her sway, her body language, told him of purpose and confidence and strength. This was no willy-nilly farm girl out to play games.

She wore working boots and jeans and a loose green tank top tucked in beneath a wide leather belt. There was a lot of limb to her—strong yet beautifully curved arms, long nicely shaped legs, a woman's hips and buttocks— and small firm breasts, a lovely throat and an open, friendly smile.

''Hi,'' came a husky, feminine voice and her hand was thrust out for him to clasp. Clear green eyes—the color of emerald precisely—met his. "I'm Jane Manning and you must be Graham Smith. Please call me Jane."

Somehow he found his voice. "Graham…ah, you can call me Graham." He took her hand and felt the strength in her grasp.

"Come on inside where it's cool," she offered and he followed her across the dirt-packed ground toward the ranch house, realizing that something about this woman had just left him stammering.

She fixed them coffee in a spacious kitchen that was decades old but still cozy and serviceable. And as they were conversing—small talk, things about his flight and the drive to Rifle—all that filled Graham's head was the unexpected vision of this woman, this Jane Manning, whom he'd come to interview. She was not exactly beautiful, but her features added up to a total look that, to Graham's eyes, was *right*. He couldn't stop staring at her, studying her face, learning its secrets. She had an adorable bridge of freckles across her small, upturned nose, sparkling green eyes fringed by dark lashes, a wide curving mouth and strong teeth. Her oval face was framed by dark brown glossy hair, blunt-cut to her shoulders, bangs over her brow. She wore only a touch of makeup but it was enough.

Jane led him into a den. The dark-paneled room smelled of old leather and was furnished with Victorian antiques, mostly oak pieces. On one wall was an antelope head; on another was a snarling bear.

"You hunt?" asked Graham, putting his coffee mug down on a table.

"Not since I was a kid." Jane sat in a chair across from him. "But my brothers do."

"How many brothers?" He knew about one. Should he mention his rescuer? No, his mind answered him firmly.

"Four," she replied. "All older. Joe, the oldest," she went on, "is married now and built a place down on the south hundred. I thought you could use his old room to-night...."

"I really wasn't planning on staying."

"Suit yourself," answered Jane in a straightforward manner. Was that what he liked—her openness, the frank tilt of her chin? "If you change your mind," she added, "the offer stands."

"I'll remember that."

She rose and picked up a stack of papers from the desk, handing them to Graham. "I knew you'd want to look over my credentials," she said.

"Of course." He glanced down and began to leaf through the papers. Suddenly he looked up. "You went through the ISA?"

Jane nodded. "I sure did. I was hoping you'd heard of it."

"Everyone," he said levelly, "who's connected with any sort of security has heard of it—and of Rob Dearborn."

"Yes, I know," she said, as if reading his thoughts. "Rob has quite a reputation. He intimidates a lot of his students because of it."

"But not you?"

Jane shrugged her smooth, sun-browned shoulders. "I got along fine with him. He inspired me. In fact, we became good friends."

How *good*, Graham wondered, experiencing an unaccountable, indefinable surge of emotion.

"Oh, he was tough on me," she was saying, "but then he's tough on everyone."

"Your certificate from the academy states you passed everything with flying colors."

"I worked very hard," she said steadfastly.

"Umm," mumbled Graham, glancing back down at the papers in his hand and wondering suddenly if Jane Manning could throw him. It would be most interesting, he mused with a glint in his blue eyes, to find out. He looked up. "I'm not bad myself in the martial arts."

"I studied Korean Hwa Rang Do," she explained. "Are you familiar with it?"

"Hwa Rang Do," he said, then coughed behind a hand to gain time. "Oh, sure."

"Would you like more coffee?"

"Thanks."

She left him momentarily and Graham took the opportunity to gather his thoughts. Jane was certainly qualified as a bodyguard even if she only looked eighteen. And Lew specifically wanted another woman because they were so difficult to spot in a crowd....

"Here's your coffee." Jane sat down. "I should tell you, I'm trained in weapons but I prefer my hands. I never liked guns."

"Nasty things, aren't they?"

"And I can do evasive driving, work with electronic surveillance…"

"You are definitely a most impressive woman, Jane," Graham said.

She hesitated and gave him an anxious look. "I'm being pushy," she admitted. "I'm sorry. But I really do want this job, Mr…Graham, and I'll do whatever it takes to convince you I'm your person."

"Of course." There it was again, that self-confidence, the open manner, the honesty. How refreshing! "You have to understand, though, I'm only conducting a preliminary interview. Mr. Rapp will be making the final decision."

"Oh." She sounded disappointed.

"I don't actually work for Mercury Courier." He felt he ought to explain. "I'm a free-lance courier. Lew Rapp is a very old friend of my family and I'm doing him a favor."

"I assume, though, that you're familiar with bodyguarding and security?"

Aha! She was challenging *him* now. "Very much so," replied Graham. "I was with the foreign service for a few years, attached to security. I did some bodyguarding myself."

"Oh," she said, obviously relieved that he was qualified to judge her capabilities.

It was Graham's turn to go on the offensive; this was an unusual game to be playing with a woman and he was finding it quite enjoyable. "I have a few more questions," he began. "For instance, I'd like to know what made you decide on this particular profession."

"Well," said Jane, "I was looking for something special to do, something exciting and different. I graduated from the University of Colorado, then I went to veterinary school in Fort Collins. But I found out that it wasn't for me. Then I came home for a while and helped out around here. I was, you know, sort of waiting, biding my time. I knew there was something out there for me to do. When I heard about the ISA I knew what it was."

Graham cleared his throat. "It is a bit odd for a woman—"

She laughed charmingly. "Well, at least you're polite about it." She leaned forward and spoke earnestly. "Rob explained it. Psychologically, all of his students are thrill seekers. But I want to channel my need for excitement productively."

"Most commendable," murmured Graham, watching her mouth and the way her lips curved. How could a woman who'd done everything she'd done look so damn young and innocent? "You realize," he continued, catching her gaze, "it will mean leaving Colorado for a long time."

"You mean seeing the world?" Her eyes sparkled. "I can hardly wait. I've got an itch to see things, to go places."

"To have some adventures."

"Oh, you bet. Lots of them."

"I understand." A woman of his own mind.

"There you are, Jane," came a gruff voice from the doorway. "Am I interrupting?"

On the threshold stood a white-haired man of about sixty. He was tall and a bit stooped, wiry, his face browned and weathered from years on the range. He had to be Jane's father.

She stood. "Daddy, this is Graham Smith. Graham, my father, Tom Manning."

"How do you do?" said Graham, rising, shaking the man's hand.

"I do just fine, young man. Question is, what sort of employment are you offering my girl here?"

"Daddy!"

Graham's visit was growing more interesting by the minute. And he couldn't help himself, he liked Tom Manning's approach. Hell, if Graham ever had a daughter he'd be just as concerned about her welfare. The truth was— and he should tell her father—that if it were up to Graham, he'd say Jane could have a shot at the job. Of course, the final decision was not up to him but Lew.

"I like knowing the people my children associate themselves with," Tom was explaining in that same frank manner as Jane's. "I trust you're staying the night?"

"Well, I..."

"Daddy," Jane said, "Mr. Smith has to be on his way."

"Of course," interrupted Graham, "I *could* take an extra night." He'd been planning to fly straight to Norfolk to spend the weekend at his dad's place on the beach in North Carolina, do some work on their thirty-five-year-old sailboat, the *Renée*, but the invitation to stay at the Manning ranch was extremely tempting. He'd been traveling a lot this past week. It was a Friday, after all. The country here was certainly captivating. And so, he admitted to himself, was Jane Manning.

"Now sit back down there, Mr. Smith," said Tom

Manning, "and tell me how you got so confounded lost and stuck so bad my boy had to push your car out of the mud."

"What?" asked Jane, her dark brow arched.

"Well, you see," Graham began, "it was like this...."

CHAPTER THREE

JANE MADE HIM A SANDWICH from the leftover pot roast for lunch. It had lots of mayonnaise and horseradish, the way he liked it. And an ice-cold beer. She sat at the kitchen table with him while he ate, her chin resting on her hand, letting Graham get a delectable view of her emerald-green eyes and soft lips.

The sight almost took his appetite away. Almost.

"You drove from Grand Junction this morning?" she was asking and he had to force himself to concentrate on her words.

"Uh, yes. I've never been there before. To tell you the truth, I never *heard* of Grand Junction before."

She shrugged. "I'm not surprised. Did you come from New York for this interview?"

"No. I was on the West Coast after doing a job in Japan, so it was almost on my way."

"Japan." She said it breathlessly in that throaty voice of hers, longingly. "What kind of job?"

He should have been wary or irritated at her frank curiosity but he wasn't; it was too genuine.

"I had to pick up an electronic component and deliver it to a Silicon Valley firm."

"For Mercury Courier?"

"No, it was a free-lance job."

She seemed disappointed. "Does Mercury do jobs like that?" she asked hopefully.

"Sure, Mercury does anything they're asked. Once, Lew told me, a courier had to deliver a very valuable parrot. It squawked curses all the way across the country in the airplane.''

She threw her head back and laughed, so that her long graceful throat showed, her eyes crinkled and he could see that she had one crooked tooth in front that was much more attractive than the perfection of a movie star's smile. It was absolutely endearing. Graham decided he was going to tell her a lot more funny stories.

''I *love* it,'' she said.

''Well—'' Graham stopped munching on the sandwich and looked her right in the eye, serious suddenly ''—there's danger in this line of work, you know. It isn't all squawking parrots.''

Her eyes met his in total understanding. No fear, no naive bravado, no nutty self-destructive urge peered from their emerald depths. ''I know,'' she said calmly. ''I hope you didn't get the impression I'm only out for thrills. I've been taught to avoid danger at all costs.'' She hesitated, as if weighing something in her mind, but obviously decided to go ahead and say it. ''I *want* this job. I know I can do it. I just want a chance to prove myself.''

Perfect. She was perfect. Every reaction was precisely right. Graham would have hired her on the spot but, of course, it was not up to him. Nevertheless, he'd recommend her as highly as he could. And then he wondered if his desire to see more of Jane Manning was coloring his judgment. Because he *did* want to see more of her and he'd sure hate to make the trek out to Rifle, Colorado, for a date every Saturday night.

He changed the subject to one that was safer. ''I really didn't thank your brother John properly for pushing me out of the mud.''

''Was he insufferable?'' she asked with a grin. ''John loves to put dudes on.'' She looked startled then added hastily, ''I mean, not that you're a dude, exactly.''

It was Graham's turn to laugh. ''But that's what I am!''

She eyed him carefully. ''You don't look like a dude,

except for your clothes, that is. But I'll bet Jared's your size and I'm sure you could borrow a pair of his jeans, that is…if you're staying.''

Did she want him to stay? An odd, melting warmth suffused Graham's midsection. ''Stay? Well, I just might at that.''

''Good,'' she said firmly, as if it were all settled.

FIVE BIG STRONG MEN filed into the dining room at 6:00 p.m. sharp, each of them scrutinizing Graham with decided suspicion and curiosity.

Jane introduced them. John grinned widely as he took Graham's hand. ''See you made it,'' he quipped.

Joe, the oldest, shook Graham's hand, too. ''Just on my way home,'' he explained, ''but I wanted to meet you before I went.''

James, the youngest, full of fun and easygoing, greeted him next. He was followed by Jared. Yes, he was about Graham's size. Thirty-three waist, thirty-four inseam, forty-two chest, Graham guessed. Well-worn jeans and scuffed, low-heeled boots and a line on his forehead dividing the white skin above from the suntan below.

Tom Manning gave Graham a sharp look. ''So, you're staying,'' he remarked.

It took all of Graham's considerable charm and courage to smile and act unconcerned. He felt like a mouse under the paws of a family of cats. Would they eat him for dinner or let him go?

''Hot out, isn't it?'' he asked, resolutely cheerful. He had the distinct feeling that Jane Manning would view with disparagement any man who could not stand up to her menfolk.

''Normal,'' said Tom. ''Can't air-condition the range.''

''Daddy,'' admonished Jane.

There was a middle-aged woman who came in to do the cooking, a gaunt, sour-looking lady who appeared tough enough to handle the Manning clan with one hand busy stirring the chili pot.

Joe left, tipping his hat to Graham. The rest sat down at the heavy, claw-footed oak table. Jane led Graham to a seat next to hers and whispered to him, "Don't mind Daddy. He's overprotective."

"Hey, no problem," Graham whispered back. Overprotective, he thought. Did that mean emotionally or physically?

The meal began with chili. Scorching and spicy. Then a thick beefsteak, a mound of salad and biscuits still hot from the oven. Apple pie for dessert. Jane ate a respectable amount of food but nothing like her brothers, and Graham had to admit he did justice to the meal, too.

A chipped enamel pot of very strong coffee was placed in the center of the table and everyone sipped the brew from heavy mugs. No decaf for the Mannings!

"So," Tom Manning began, "you're interviewing my daughter here for a bodyguard job in a company called Mercury Courier. Is that correct?"

"Yes, sir." Good Lord, Graham hadn't called anyone "sir" since Boy Scout camp!

"Tell me something about this company."

So Graham told them all about Lew Rapp, what the company did and what Jane's duties would be. At one point he wondered who was interviewing whom here.

"Why do these couriers need bodyguards?" asked Tom.

"Mercury Courier is a licensed, bonded and insured company. In order to keep the insurance and the bond, bodyguards are being required as of this year. You know about the insurance crisis, I suppose."

"We aren't that ignorant," said Jared.

"Of course not," Graham amended hastily.

"So there's danger of these couriers actually being waylaid," Tom concluded with narrowed eyes.

"It's a precaution, Mr. Manning, like carrying an extra

gallon of gas in your car. You'd probably never need it.''
He wondered what kind of a look Tom Manning would
shoot him from those faded eyes if Graham told him about
the holdups the Mercury couriers had experienced lately.

''Come on, Daddy, let's not badger poor Graham,'' interjected Jane. She turned to Jared. ''I wondered if Graham could borrow your jeans and boots for the evening.
You look to be the same size.''

''Sure. You gonna ride, Smith?''

''I have ridden...'' Graham started to say.

''We got this gentle ol' pony,'' James said, a devilish
grin on his face, ''that'd be perfect for you.''

Graham groaned inwardly. Setup. The gentle ol' pony
would turn out to be a raging stallion with fire coming
out of its nostrils and a notorious dislike for Eastern
dudes. How did he get himself into these situations?

Jane was looking at him, waiting for his answer, trying
to hide a smile.

''Hell,'' said Graham unflinchingly, ''I'd love to ride
your nice old pony.''

He changed into a clean pair of Jared's jeans and
donned the pointy-toed, fancy-stitched boots. His hand-
sewn French shirt looked a bit out of place but he rolled
up the sleeves and unbuttoned the collar. Glancing into
the mirror, he undid another button for that sporty look.
Not bad. Jared's well-worn pants fit him just fine. All he
lacked was a Stetson with a sweat-stained band but, he
supposed, he'd have to earn that.

He emerged from Joe's room, the guest room now, feeling somewhat foolish and out of place, but how could he
have known what he was getting himself into when he'd
told Lew he'd interview Jane Manning? No one had mentioned the gentle ol' pony or all these rather *large* Western
fellas....

And, as if the Manning men weren't enough to intimidate just about anyone, there was yet another male in the
crowd that greeted Graham. This one was blondish, tall,

very tall, maybe weighing two hundred pounds—about thirty-five or so and all solid, range-riding muscle. He was a good-looking guy with a big white smile and laughing blue eyes that were as clear as the sky. Who was he? And where had Jane gone? The sound of running water and the rattle of dishes in the kitchen told him she'd temporarily abandoned him.

"This is Branch Taggart," Jane's father said, striding across the living room to make the introductions. "Branch here is a friend of Jane's…from way back. How long has it been, Jane?" he called out.

First the challenge of the ride on the horse and now this: Jane's *friend*. Tom Manning seemed to be throwing every curve he could at Graham. Was it to divert Graham's attention from Jane? The jealous-overprotective-father routine? Or was Graham merely supersensitive at present, too aware of Jane, too anxious to be one of the guys, to impress the very pretty lady?

"Pleased to meet you, Smith," said Taggart, clamping Graham's hand with the relentless pressure of a bulldog's jaws.

"My pleasure," replied Graham in a silky voice as his knuckles turned white.

"Hear you've come to interview Jane for a job in New York."

"That's right."

Jane emerged from the kitchen and handed Taggart a can of beer, then stood looking up at the two men, her head cocked slightly, her thumbs hooked in her jean pockets. Was she enjoying this? A million questions batted around in Graham's head. Was this big blond hulking cowboy really Jane's boyfriend—her lover? Of course a woman as attractive as Jane *should* have a lover, shouldn't she? After all, thought Graham darkly, why *wouldn't* she have someone tall and strong and cocky who'd come over to meet the dude from New York? Especially since that dude might take his lady away to the city. It was only to be expected, but blast it, Graham was getting darn tired of Branch Taggart and he'd only just met the man!

"The boys tell me you're a courier," Taggart was saying. "Odd job, isn't it?"

"Branch," began Jane in her husky voice.

"No, that's all right," Graham interjected with a whole lot more charm than he was feeling. "A lot of people are curious about my line of work."

"What does a courier do?"

"Oh, this and that."

"They deliver parrots," said Jane as her cheeks dimpled with a smile.

"Parrots?"

Graham grinned. "An inside joke."

"I see." Branch popped the top of his beer and took a long swig, his blue eyes meeting Graham's over the top of the can. "You going for a ride or something?" He eyed Graham's outfit long and speculatively, his lip curling at one corner.

"He's gonna give Pard a workout, right, Smith?" said James from where he sat straddling a wooden chair, twirling his Stetson on one finger.

"Pard, eh? Thought you fellas put him out to pasture a long while back. Sure you can handle the old boy, Smith?"

"Why, sure I can, Branch. At least I can give it a try, can't I?"

"Don't see why not."

And wouldn't you just love it, Taggart, if I end up on my butt in the dust. He tried his best not to, but Graham glanced at Jane in spite of himself, to catch her reactions. Now, in the movies, anyway, the gal would stand up for the poor, unsuspecting Eastern dude who'd been roped into this situation by a bunch of slaphappy cowpokes. But evidently not Miss Manning here. She stood not three feet from him, rocking back on her boot heels, smiling, not in the least troubled. Of course, the Westerns Graham had seen took place in an age long past, when women stayed home, cooked and had babies. Somehow he could not see Jane landing the part.

"It's gonna get dark soon," John said, rising from his chair. "You staying for the ride, Branch, or did you just come over to drink a beer and sweet-talk my sister?"

"Hey, John." Jane narrowed her eyes at her brother but Branch merely laughed good-naturedly.

"Always did like your cold brew, John. And now that you mention it, I wouldn't miss Smith's ride for anything."

"Go and have your fun," said Jane then. "I think I'll finish up in the kitchen." She did, however, walk Graham to the door ahead of the others. "You know you don't have to go through with this."

"Why, Miss Manning," Graham murmured, leaning toward her, "I didn't know you cared."

"It's your funeral." She smiled and pushed open the door for him and the men, all six of them now, filed out and sauntered toward the corral.

Graham wondered, as the evening sun struck distant peaks and gold touched the tips of dark spruce trees, if Jane had stayed behind in the kitchen out of necessity or because she was embarrassed to see Graham make a fool of himself. At any rate, even though he missed her already, even though he'd much rather watch Branch Taggart bite the dust as opposed to himself, he was just as glad she wasn't going to see him fail Bronco Busting 101. *Especially* in front of her friend here.

Pard stood in the corral, head hanging down. He was a thick-necked, pale-colored Appaloosa who looked as harmless as a lamb. It was only when John bridled and saddled Pard that he came alive. His ears perked forward, his eyes grew bright, his neck arched, his big body seemed to radiate excitement.

"You get on the left side," Taggart said helpfully.

"Why, thanks for the tip," Graham answered. He gathered the reins and swung up into the deep-seated Western saddle. Pard stood stock-still for a moment and Graham just had time to notice that the Mannings and Taggart all ducked under the corral fence—*oh hell*—when he felt Pard gather himself, take the bit in his teeth, put his head down and go on a rampage.

The horse jumped stiff-legged, landed hard, twisted, and leaped again. Dust rose in a choking cloud and somewhere Graham heard a voice yell, "Ride 'em, cowboy!"

Then the ground came up very hard and he was sitting in the middle of the corral, shaken to the core, while Pard stood eyeing him.

Graham slowly got to his feet and slapped dust off Jared's jeans.

"Guess Pard is feelin' his oats," said James, mock-apologetically. "You want to try another horse?"

"No way. I'll stick with Pard here. That was the most fun I've had since I did a belly flop from the twelve-meter diving board, fellas."

Limping slightly, Graham approached the now docile horse and mounted again. This time he kept a tight rein and a hold on the pommel. Pard humped his back and gave a jolting jump or two; then he kicked out his hind legs but this time his bucking lacked its original enthusiasm. Graham was beginning to enjoy himself.

And then Jane was there, an arm hooked over the corral rail, Taggart by her side. "Did they really give you *Pard*?" she called to him. "Those creeps!"

"Oh, he's a great piece of horseflesh," Graham called back. "There's more to him than meets the eye!"

By then Pard had settled down to a bone-rattling gallop around the corral and Graham was feeling much better. He was glad Jane hadn't seen him bite the dust. He pulled Pard up into a trot then a walk, then kicked him into a lope, neck-reined him into a figure-eight loop around the enclosure, stopped him, backed him up, and spun him around on his hind feet.

"Well-trained horse you got here," he said casually to the men's carefully expressionless faces.

"Thanks," choked out John finally.

"Well, I'll be damned," he heard Branch Taggart say.

Jane looked triumphant, as if she were responsible for Graham's skill. She slapped John on the shoulder and bubbled over with laughter. John looked shamefaced, then a grin split his lips and he was laughing, too, and soon all four of the Manning men were guffawing and pounding one another on the back. Only one of the group was still unsmiling—Branch. Of course, Graham knew, he'd just won a round in front of Taggart's lady—a very uncool thing to have done. Nevertheless, Graham was feeling as pleased with himself as a high school kid who'd just scored a touchdown in front of the prettiest cheerleader in the squad—the girl who was going steady with the quarterback.

"I gotta hand it to you," Branch said as he strode over to Graham, "that was a nice ride."

"Lucky," put in Graham—the true gentleman.

"Skilled." And he put his hand out and shook Graham's; this time there were no white knuckles. "Well, glad to have met you, Smith. I gotta be getting along here, early call tomorrow. You know how us ranchers are."

"Sure."

"Walk me to the pickup?" he asked, turning to Jane, and Graham tried to look busy with Pard's reins.

They were gone a long time. Five minutes, at least. It seemed like an hour to Graham as he stood alongside the men talking horseflesh and the like. And he really hadn't the slightest notion what they were chatting about because all he could see from across the corral was Jane standing near the mud-spattered pickup and Branch, leaning casually against the driver's door, his head bent close to her shell-pink ear. What were they saying, exactly? Making a date for next Saturday night? Getting engaged? A knot twisted in Graham's stomach and he felt hot and dizzy suddenly. Must have been the hair-raising ride.

"And when you hit the dust there, pardner," John was saying, "I thought for sure it was all over!"

Somehow Jane was beside him. Graham didn't have to look; he could simply feel her presence there, smell her scent—fragrant, clean, as fresh as a mountain meadow full of bluebells and primroses.

"Taggart leave?" asked Jared.

Jane nodded and looked down at her hands for a moment.

"Haven't seen him around for a while," John put in artlessly.

"We haven't been going out for ages, if it's any of your business."

"You don't have to go and get all huffy like that. I only asked—"

"Kids," Tom Manning warned, "that'll do."

"Come on." Jane turned to Graham and smiled.

"Let's leave these guys to their practical jokes and go for a ride. I'll show you some of the rodeo stock."

"Sounds great," he said, relishing in the knowledge that Jane and Branch had not been seeing each other in some time. He waited while she saddled up a fine-looking black stallion she called Indigo and they set out across the wide irrigated fields toward the distant rise of gray-brown buttes. The sun was dipping to the west, the air was dry and warm and scented with sagebrush, the shadows were growing long.

"You *can* ride," she said after a while. "Those guys are going to hurt someone one day with their stunts."

"I have to confess I've never ridden a horse like Pard. I've just done some fox hunting in Virginia when I was stationed in Washington."

"Pard's an ugly old thing but he was a champion cow horse in his day. I think he enjoys his times in the spotlight more than my brothers do."

"Do all male visitors undergo the same test?" asked Graham, enjoying the easy rhythm of the horse, the scenery, the woman riding by his side, especially the woman. Slim, lithe, strong, she was a natural rider, an athlete whose body always moved in balance, without wasted movement. A woman whose eyes met his forthrightly, with no coy games, who seemed totally in command of her life, who knew what she wanted.

"Only the ones they think can take it."

"I'm flattered."

"And they're impressed. What else do you do well, Graham Smith?"

"I'm an excellent cook," he said. "I speak fluent French. I'm good at my job."

She waited.

"Actually, I swam in school and ran track. I did a four-and-a-half-minute mile once. Oh, and I sail a bit."

"A bit?"

"Well, I crewed in the America's Cup one year," he admitted.

"Anything else?" She was smiling.

"A game of tennis now and then."

"Now and then?"

"Well," he allowed reluctantly, "I was in the quarter finals of the juniors at the U.S. Open years ago."

"I see."

"And you?"

"My accomplishments hardly compare. I ride, I can rope. I can throw a calf and brand it, give it a shot, neuter it."

"Ouch," Graham winced.

Jane gave him a quick, humorous sidelong glance. "I jog a few miles from time to time. I race quarter horses. Just hometown stuff. Indigo here won a race last week." She patted his shiny black neck and Graham wished she was caressing him so lovingly.

''And then there's the stuff I learned at ISA. But you've seen all that on my application.''

''You're quite a woman, Jane Manning,'' he said sincerely.

''And you're quite a man, Mr. Smith.'' She laughed, then touched her heels to Indigo's sides and took off across the range, scattering cattle, a graceful figure on the flying black horse.

Graham watched her for a minute, enjoying the sight, then he kicked Pard into a canter. ''We better catch up, old boy. I've got a feeling that a lady like that could leave us in the dust.''

After the ride he and Jane put the tack away and let the horses go out onto the fields to graze.

''Thank you for the ride,'' Graham said, meaning every word of it.

''Wouldn't you show me the Empire State Building,'' she asked playfully, ''if I were in New York?''

''Without a moment's hesitation.'' He was aware of the warm pungent smell of horses, cattle, oiled leather and the nose-prickling aroma of sweet alfalfa hay. His muscles were sore and strained and he'd lay odds he had a black and blue mark on one hip but he felt good—cleanly, physically tired.

The setting sun hovered on the horizon, big and orange, and its rays reached across the earth to enter the huge double-door opening of the barn. In its gilt light swallows swooped, insects buzzed, dust motes hung like tiny golden snowflakes. And within the glow Jane walked, unselfconscious and full of grace, a woman with an inner beauty and strength that Graham found novel, intriguing, exciting.

The sun brushed her skin with gold dust, touched her small nose and strong cheekbones and dark lashes as Graham would have liked to touch them: softly, delicately, reverently.

"Nice night, isn't it?" he remarked inanely, just to hear her husky voice.

"It always is in the summer," she replied.

They walked on toward the lighted ranch house. She wore jeans that fit her slim hips like a second skin. Graham could see her long flank muscles working as she moved. Wonderful. His head whirled.

He'd woken that morning one man and now he felt like a whole different person. He noticed things more acutely: the feel of the warm air against his face, the sound of horses snorting and stamping off in the dark, the scent of Jane Manning's smooth, tan skin.

The darkness hid her expression but he knew she must be feeling the strength of his emotions. She *must* feel them. He'd kiss her in a minute if it weren't for the fact that he was supposed to be there on business. Hah, business! And, of course, there were still four big Manning men waiting in the house—and Joe probably not far off.

Come to think of it, there had been something between him and Jane from the first moment. A certain tension, a constant pulse of attraction. And one totally unlike what he'd felt for any woman before.

Something special.

He'd just have to convince Lew to hire her. Not that he'd be doing either Lew or Jane a disservice. And then he could see Jane often. He'd love to take her out on the *Renée*…

What was he thinking? Jane Manning might not get the job, she might not *want* the job—although she'd said she did. He might never see her again. The thought was sobering, like a dash of cold water in the face. Never see Jane again? Unthinkable.

The house was full of light and talk. Joe had come over with his wife, Trish, and their son, Joey. It was a family gathering, complete with a whiskey bottle, cigars and bowls of popcorn.

"Heard you rode Pard," Joe said, rising and holding his big hand out to Graham.

"I tried."

"Did more than that," John put in. "He put ol' Pard through his paces."

The atmosphere had definitely lightened. Graham guessed he'd passed his test. Somehow that made him feel good, which was ridiculous. Why should he care if this family accepted him?

Jane took Joey from his mother's arms and cuddled him. "Oh, he's grown since last week! And he's getting hair." She nuzzled his fat cheek.

A crazy picture popped into Graham's head: Jane holding a baby, but he had strawberry-blond hair. It was *his* baby and hers and they were—he snapped the image off as if it were a television program he didn't like. What was the matter with him?

"Come on, Graham," Tom was saying. "Set yourself down and have a drink. Cigar?"

"Sure, thanks," he answered automatically. The whiskey was old and mellow and went straight to his head. The cigar made him slightly dizzy. He felt himself sinking into the leather armchair in which he sat as if he'd never be able to get up again. He was content to sit there forever listening to ranch talk, admiring the huge beams and stone fireplace and Navaho rugs of the ranch house's living room, watching Jane's face change expression, watching her slender neck and brown arms and gorgeous strong legs. And that adorable crooked tooth...

"You look sort of sleepy," Jane finally said to him.

His heart thumped and he forced a dopey smile onto his lips. "I guess I am. I feel like something hit me over the head. It must be the altitude."

Graham had recovered some of his self-possession by the next morning. He'd slept like a log and woken up with the fleeting memory of a dream about Jane, something about trying to hold her hand to convince her of a terribly important fact but he'd been on Pard who'd been bucking and her hand kept slipping out of his grasp.

The Manning men were already gone but the littered breakfast table attested to the fact that they'd been there— in force.

"Good morning," called Jane from the kitchen.

Graham nodded briskly but he still remembered the feel of her hand in his dream. "Morning, Jane."

She looked glorious. Jeans and a white shirt rolled up at the sleeves. A wide leather belt with a silver buckle around her slim waist. Lovely swinging, shiny brown hair. Her hands were small and square and capable, with short fingernails. The freckles on her nose were charming.

"Eggs?" she asked.

"If it's no trouble."

She had a cup of coffee while he ate. "I stayed behind to see you off. The boys want me up on the plateau to help them with some calves later."

"You didn't have to wait."

"Why, sure I did. I couldn't let you get off all by yourself."

"Well, I'm glad you did."

She smiled. She liked him, he thought happily. But how *much* did she like him?

He collected his bag after breakfast and started out to his muddy car. Jane walked at his side.

"So," she said in a straightforward manner, "what do you think? What are my chances of getting this job?" No fawning, no false modesty, no beating around the bush. This woman knew her own worth. "Do I measure up?"

Graham looked at her for a long moment, wanting to memorize her features, knowing he would see her again. "Lew will want to interview you, of course. I'm sure you'll be hearing from him soon. But on *my* yardstick you measure up just fine."

She held out her hand. Her grip was warm and firm. Her touch made his stomach roll over deliciously. And

when Graham got into his car and started it, he knew he'd
held her hand just a touch too long.

And Jane Manning knew it, too.

CHAPTER FOUR

THE FOLLOWING WEDNESDAY, Jane's flight made its approach to La Guardia and she finally had her first glimpse of Manhattan. As the plane banked, she pressed her nose to the glass and gazed at the sprawling city below her. The Statue of Liberty stood tall and majestic amidst the many ships and boats dotting the Hudson River. Beyond that were the twin towers of the World Trade Center, the Empire State Building, the lushness of Central Park. The buildings, packed close, piled up, new and strange and yet so wonderfully familiar, filled her vision and seemed to stretch to the horizon and beyond.

"Your seat belt, please," came the stewardess's reminder and Jane buckled up, feeling her stomach twinge with excitement and trepidation.

She was here at last, eager and prepared and yet nervous about whatever challenge the city and her new life offered. In her purse was the address of the Gramercy Park Hotel on Lexington Avenue, the street number of Mercury Courier and fifteen hundred dollars in traveler's checks. There was no return ticket to Denver, however. Jane was going to get this job or else. Optimism sprang in her heart as the plane's landing gear thumped down onto the runway.

Her first impression, oddly enough, was of the hot damp air of the East coast, which hit her in the face when she emerged from the terminal. It was funny, Jane decided, as her bus carried her into the heart of Manhattan, but all her preconceived notions of New York had been wrong. It wasn't sophisticated, sleek and glossy, not at first glance. Nor was it dirty, criminal and brutal, as she'd heard. New York was made up of individuals and there seemed to be no norm, only exceptions. The variety dazed her. On one street corner stood a pasty-skinned woman carrying two big shopping bags wearing all black: black shoes, black textured hose, black dress, even a black floppy hat. In the oppressive July heat no less. And there were foreigners from everywhere dressed in saris or robes or odd European styles. Businessmen, gorgeous women, students with huge Afro hairstyles, poets, actors, shoppers, orthodox Jews in black hats and beards. Fat women who sweated and screamed at pale children, writers, artists, messenger boys on bicycles, bums asleep on benches.

New York.

Everywhere Jane looked there was a person with a new eccentricity, a mark of uniqueness. A mark of being a New Yorker. Would she look that way after a while? Jane glanced down at her neat outfit and grimaced. Well, she certainly wouldn't fool anybody yet. And, she noticed, she was too tanned. Everyone she saw had a distinct city pallor.

Then she couldn't help recalling that Graham Smith had been ruddy and healthy looking. Idly she wondered where he was at that exact moment. In the city? Off on an assignment somewhere in the world? All the way to New York on the airplane Jane had imagined that Graham would be at the airport to meet her. It was a silly, impossible notion but one she couldn't dismiss. She'd imagined him standing in the terminal, waiting for her, his strawberry-blond hair a little unruly, an expensive summerweight sport coat hanging loosely, carelessly, off his broad shoulders, his blue eyes dancing, welcoming her.

Of course, it had merely been a pleasant fantasy. He'd no idea that Jane had arrived that day. Heavens, her appointment with Mr. Rapp wasn't even till Friday.

Jane glanced out the bus window again. New York, she

was here at last, she mused, her heart beating just a little faster as she craned her neck and looked up, not even able to see the tops of all the skyscrapers. And then, on a whim, on an impish impulse, Jane turned to the business-man seated next to her. He was rocking back and forth with the motion of the bus, his eyes half closed, an ex-pression of utter boredom on his face.

"It's a far cry from Rifle," she said with a smile, guess-ing that this obvious New York native had never before been spoken to by a complete stranger on a bus.

"Pardon me?"

"It's not much like Rifle, Colorado, I said."

"Rifle?" He looked alarmed then very concerned then a bit dazed, but by the time they'd sat chatting for a half hour in the heavy city traffic, Jane had his card—he was a dress designer who worked in the garment district—and had promised to look for his labels at Macy's.

And who said New Yorkers were unfriendly?

SAFELY OUT OF THE AFTERNOON HEAT and checked into her air-conditioned room in the Gramercy Park, Jane glanced at her watch: 3:00 p.m. Plenty of time to ex-plore—or shop. She opened her suitcase and eyed her clothes, then stood back with her hands on her hips. They were all wrong. Her summer slacks had no pleats and were hopelessly too wide in the leg; her skirts were two inches longer than she'd seen the nicely dressed women on the street wearing; her two dresses, left over from col-lege days, were just plain out. And the A-line khaki skirt and Hawaiian-print camp shirt she'd worn on the flight made her look fifteen.

How did a person find Bloomingdale's?

Jane took the subway uptown from her hotel, which was on 21st and Lexington. The desk clerk had told her that the train was a safe bet at this hour and would actually stop in the basement of Bloomingdale's. Unbelievable! The subway was already crowded with commuters so she stood, marveling at the new sights and smells, feeling the damp closeness, hearing the unearthly roar of the train, holding onto the swinging handle over her head and rocking back and forth with the car's motion, knocking companionably into other passengers. On one side of her stood a well-dressed Arab businessman whose dark eyes never left her. On the other side was a Puerto Rican boy in a baseball outfit. Seated at knee level was a transvestite whom she tried not to stare at but whose matching red pumps and red purse were hard to ignore. He had on twice the makeup she did! Jane tore her gaze away and looked up at the graffiti.

She had fifteen hundred dollars, Jane thought, as she pushed her way through the throng and out the doors to exit at Bloomingdale's basement. How much could she afford to spend and still be able to eat until payday?

A couple hundred. She could afford that much. Sure, why not?

Up the escalators, into the air-conditioned levels she went, strolling past elegant displays of every imaginable designer. Anne Klein, Halston, Christian Dior, Gucci, Ungaro. So many clothes! Jane wanted everything she saw. But the price tags! Her two hundred dollars wouldn't even buy her one outfit. Finally she did find a few summer-sales racks and bought a pair of white linen slacks—with pleats—for seventeen dollars. *Smart buy.* She patted herself on the back mentally.

Jane took the escalator up again. There had to be more sale racks, probably scattered all over the store. She felt dreadfully out of place in her provincial outfit among the beautifully attired shoppers with their fashionable dresses, wide belts, scarves and glittering jewelry. And how *did* they walk on those high heels?

At last Jane found a dress. It was jade-green and white and had a full skirt—wide green belt included. The bodice had a double-breasted overlay with big buttons, and the

sleeves were elbow length and cuffed. She knew she
looked good in it and her white pumps would go fine.

Oh gosh, that multicolored scarf over there. How much
was it? Twenty-five dollars? Oh well... She signed another traveler's check, got her change and figured she
could spend another ninety dollars. She found a beige,
below-the-knee skirt for twenty-eight and a soft yellow
cotton top with a scoop neck and short sleeves. The
brightly colored scarf would go beautifully.

Down one escalator. Why, she hadn't even seen this
part of Bloomingdale's. There was nothing she could afford here, though. Down again. Oh my, what exquisite
perfumes. She was in cosmetics. Miles of makeup were
dramatically spotlighted, set off by smoky-black mirrors
behind every display. Nearby stood counter after counter
of sparkling jewelry. What heaven!

"Hello," said the saleslady behind the Elizabeth Arden
counter, "have you smelled our new fragrance today?
Here, let me dab a little on your wrist. Isn't that lovely?
What pretty skin tones you have."

"Thank you," mumbled Jane.

"But you've been in the sun a great deal. I wonder, are
you wearing the right protection?"

"I use a sunscreen...."

"With alcohol, I'll bet." The saleslady's red, glossy
lips parted in concern. "Could I show you a product that
will bring back the elasticity in your skin while protecting
it at the same time?"

"Well..."

Jane let her apply the whole gamut. Astringent, mois-
turizer, base, blusher, three colors of eyeshadow blended
expertly to highlight her "lovely green eyes," two shades
of peachy lipstick, eyeliner, dabs of goo to soften those
tiny lines at the corners of her eyes, smoky brown mascara. Oh, my gosh, her reflection in the mirror was certainly...well, amazing!

"What do you think?" asked the bejeweled saleslady.

"I, ah, it certainly is different."

"I'm glad you're pleased. A change in cosmetics can alter one's whole outlook, can't it?"

"That's the truth," replied Jane.

"Would you like me to write this up?"

"Oh." Jane thought quickly. She'd bet all these products would run a hundred dollars. "Well, tell me how much it would come to."

Five minutes later Jane had her answer. "That will be $378." The woman smiled again pleasantly. "Plus tax." Jane swallowed hard. She escaped the Elizabeth Arden counter finally, minus fifty-odd dollars, with a blusher and a lipstick and a night cream.

She fell into bed that night full from a Chinese meal, her new clothes hung carefully in the closet, night cream smoothed sparingly on her face and delicious guilt curling in her belly.

The following day she called home and told her father all about her impressions of New York. "The sirens go all day and night," she said, trying to remember the quiet of the ranch, trying to relate, to grasp her two divergent lives. Before her interview the next day, she had plenty of time to explore the city. She visited Times Square, marveling at the crowds, walked through Greenwich Village, took subways all over because she couldn't resist exploring. She strolled by the Plaza Hotel, read the menu in the window and decided tea would cost her twenty dollars. She avoided the department stores like the plague.

Friday morning she put on her new jade and white dress, more makeup than usual, sprayed her hair until it looked full and luxurious, and took a cab to the offices of Mercury Courier. It was exactly 8:58 when she took in a lungful of sooty, heavy summer air, pushed open the door to the four-story building and marched in.

"Good morning, you must be Jane Manning," said the receptionist who had been typing away at an astounding speed considering the length of her purple nails. And she was chewing gum as fast as she typed.

"Yes," replied Jane, feeling nervous perspiration bead her upper lip. "I'm supposed to see Mr. Rapp. At nine," she added needlessly.

"Why don't you sit over there a sec and I'll see if he's off the phone. By the way," said the girl, "I'm Donna. Donna Lippman." She swiveled in her chair and checked the blinking light on the telephone console. "He's still talking away...." Donna shrugged. "Want some coffee?"

"Do you have a glass of water?"

"Sure."

Jane glanced around the office. It was old, Victorian. The windows were big and the walls were papered and there was dark oak trim around the high ceiling. From the reception area Jane spotted several doors down a dim corridor. There were polished wooden steps leading upstairs and no elevator that she could see. The building must have been a house once, or had apartments, and been converted into an office.

"Like the place?" asked Donna, returning with the glass.

"Oh yes. It's very comfortable-looking."

"Lew bought the building three years ago and did some renovations. It used to be a house. All the couriers have their own offices."

"How many couriers are there?"

"Five right now. Well, four really, but Norma has an office, too."

"Norma?"

"Norma Stedman. She's the other bodyguard. An ex-cop. She's really something, a tough old broad." Donna turned in her chair again to check the console. "He's still talking. Sorry."

Jane couldn't help liking Donna. The girl had a heavy Brooklyn accent, dark brown twinkling eyes and was probably four or five years younger than Jane. She had black frizzy hair to her shoulders, a tiny little nose and painted mouth, long fingers with bright purple nails, clothes straight out of a punk shop in the Village—lots of purples, blacks, drapes and folds and tons of silver jewelry.

And then, as Donna continued to ignore her typing, Jane couldn't stop the question from coming to her lips. "Is Mr. Smith around?"

"Quicksilver?" Donna grinned knowingly.

"Excuse me?" said Jane.

"We call him Quicksilver around the office. He's the real elusive type, you know, hard to pin down."

"Oh," Jane replied. "Is he here?" she repeated casually.

Donna shook her head, her long silver earrings swinging. "No. Haven't seen him for a couple of weeks. He doesn't really work here much, just does odd jobs for Lew. You know, he and Lew go way back. I think he and Graham's dad are old friends or something."

"Well, well, hello!" came a loud, heavily accented voice from the front door. "And who do we have here?" If forced to put a label to his accent, Jane would have chosen Russian.

"This is Jane Manning," Donna said. The man was huge, at least two hundred and thirty pounds, all solid muscle, with a short dark crew cut. The buttons of his tan suit strained across his chest. "Jane is interviewing for the other bodyguard spot," Donna was explaining. "Jane, meet Lukas Yurchenko, one of our couriers."

"Pleasure to meet you, Jane," he said, holding out a beefy hand, his ridiculously small blue eyes gobbling her up.

Jane took his hand and felt the crushing pressure of challenge as his grip ground the ring she wore into her fingers. "Nice to meet you," she replied sweetly, her back stiffening. How rude, she thought, he wanted her to wince. Well, she wouldn't.

"Oh," said Donna, "Lew's free at last. I'll take you on up, Jane."

Lukas Yurchenko released her hand. "You have a telephone number?" he asked bluntly, the tone of his voice uncomfortably demanding.

"No," said Jane, taken aback. -

"An address?"

"No."

"Then how am I going to take you out?"

It was her turn to smile. "You aren't." Behind her she could hear Donna's chuckle.

Lew Rapp couldn't have been kinder. He had a fatherly image, the type of man whom everyone would warm to and trust instantly. He was on the short side, overweight, with graying hair combed over a large bald spot on the crown of his head. He had soft brown eyes, a genuine smile and an easygoing manner. The perspiration finally dried on Jane's upper lip.

"Graham recommended you highly," he was telling Jane in his second-story office. "And he went on at length about what a good time you and your family showed him."

He talked to Jane for an hour. They discussed her background and compared it to life in the city; they chatted about current world affairs and the amount of violence going on in America and in the center of Paris. He spoke openly of Jane's youthful appearance and how he was pleased because she would be highly unlikely to be pegged as a bodyguard.

"Do your couriers ever run into trouble?" she asked.

"I wish I could say no," he replied, his gray brows drawing together. He sat back in his leather chair and folded his arms across his chest. "Mercury is three years old now," he told her. "And up until last April we never had a robbery. But since then my couriers have been hit four times." He frowned. "I'm afraid, the robberies were successful, too. I hired my first bodyguard in June. That's

Norma Stedman. But Norma can't be everywhere at once and two weeks ago, Peter, one of my couriers, was robbed crossing town with some jewelry from a safe-deposit box.''

''That's awful.''

Lew Rapp nodded. ''I couldn't agree more, young lady. And it's going to stop. I haven't put my life's blood into this business to see it go under because of some thugs.''

''Mr. Rapp,'' Jane ventured carefully. ''My training is quite extensive and I'm sure hoping that you'll give me a shot at this job.'' Had she been too forward, too pushy?

''Well, Miss Manning—Jane,'' he said, ''I intend to do just that.''

''You do!''

''Yes. Starting Monday, in fact. I hope you came prepared to stay.''

''I'm all set,'' breathed Jane, elated, not even trying to control her joy and relief.

''I think you'll fit in just fine,'' Lew said, ''and Donna can introduce you around and show you the ropes on Monday. I won't give you an assignment, though, for a few days. I think you should get to know the men and spend some time with Norma. She's got twenty years' experience with the NYPD, the New York police, and she can fill you in on the routes the couriers use, the airlines we take, all those details.'' He stood, came around the desk and shook Jane's hand firmly. ''Welcome aboard, Jane Manning.''

''Thank you,'' she said brightly, ''I'll do a good job for you, Mr. Rapp.''

The weekend was filled with more sight-seeing and some shopping as Jane would be on the payroll starting Monday. She sampled the good food in the neighborhood restaurants near Gramercy Park. She even caught a matinee of *Chorus Girl*, which Jane adored.

Her weekend also brought moments of musing. Where was Graham Smith? she couldn't help wondering. He had gotten to her. And yet Jane was quite aware that a man as attractive and compelling as Graham Smith—Quicksilver—must have dozens of ladies drooling over him. Even if she did see him again, it was highly unlikely he'd ask her out. Yet there had been something between them—a spark. And a woman could hope, couldn't she?

New York City grew on Jane. She loved the bag lady at the corner of 20th and Third Avenue, the wino who slept on the second bench in from the west entrance to Gramercy Park, the vendors in Union Square and the weirdos in Washington Square. She chalked up the miles on foot and her blisters grew apace but nothing daunted Jane Manning, soon-to-be official bodyguard at Mercury Courier.

On Monday, Donna helped Jane get settled in. She took her up to the fourth floor, to a cubbyhole of an office. "It's weensy in here, and stuffy, but at least it's a place of your own."

"It's great," said Jane, turning around in the six-by-eight space, wondering if it hadn't once been a walk-in closet.

"Lew keeps saying he's going to have a window put in but you may have to bug him about it. At least there's a desk and a phone."

The desk was simply a piece of painted wood jutting out from one wall. The chair was serviceable; there was a burgundy metal wastebasket.

"Maybe a few posters or something," said Donna, "on this wall." She stood with her weight on one high heel, cocking her head, a small white hand on her chin. "And a fishbowl, a plant or two. Y'know?"

"I'm sure it can be fixed up just fine." Jane didn't mind the tiny, stark space one bit; it was *hers*.

"You got a place to live yet?" asked Donna.

Jane shook her head. "I checked the newspapers all weekend but the prices..."

"I know. You could try the Barbizon."

"The what?"

"It's a woman's hotel. Uptown, eastside on 63rd and Lexington. It's clean and safe and affordable. Tell you what, I'll go downstairs and give them a call. If they have space, you maybe could go and look at it during lunch." Donna smacked her chewing gum.

The morning sped by. Jane was introduced to the couriers who were not out on assignment. There was Peter Lerner, a handsome blond man in his midthirties, tall, lanky, bearded. He was friendly and mild mannered, welcoming Jane into the crew with a very attractive white smile. She was reintroduced to Lukas, the Russian—Donna said he'd been in the KGB and had defected—and to yet another courier, Rick Como, a short, stocky Italian with a mournful countenance who asked Jane, "Just how old are you, anyway?"

She knew her youthful appearance came as somewhat of a shock to the employees at Mercury. They thought she looked too innocent and too inexperienced to be taken for real. And yet Jane didn't mind, recalling Rob Dearborn's comment: "Your appearance is your best asset. It will give you the edge every time."

Jane's first impression of Norma Stedman was one of size. The woman was in her late forties, tall, large boned. She must have weighed a good solid hundred and seventy pounds but it was all muscle. Her features were also big and severe. Her hair, which she kept trimmed short was steel-gray. There was nothing motherly about Norma and yet Jane felt the older woman taking her under her wing immediately.

"I spent twenty years in the city with the police," she told Jane, "and there're a few things I've learned that I'd be more than happy to share with you."

"I'm all ears," Jane replied with gratitude.

"Good. I was afraid you'd be one of those uppity young women who thought she knew everything." Norma was straightforward and honest. Jane liked her from the word go.

At noon the sound of Donna's high heels on the steps reached Jane in her little office. "Oh," Donna breathed, "there you are. Listen, I called the Barbizon and they have a room available starting Wednesday. Want me to take you over and have a look-see?"

"Now?"

"No better time than the present, honey."

They rode the bus uptown, Donna with her ready tongue chatting the whole way, leaving Jane with a wealth of knowledge. "Norma's okay. She scares me, though. Big woman, isn't she? But you gotta give her credit, she's got an invalid husband she's been supporting since the sixties. Industrial accident, I think." Donna pulled a fresh stick of gum out of her big purse and Jane thought that from then on, whenever and wherever she smelled Juicy Fruit, she'd think of Donna Lippman.

"And that Lukas, what a god-awful oaf!"

Jane said nothing to that remark.

"Do you like Rick?" Donna asked as they stepped off the bus.

"I barely know him."

"I think he's sexy with those sad Italian eyes. Solid, you know. Of course Peter is a dreamboat, isn't he? Tall, blond and, oh, that beard! Umm..." Donna pushed open the door to the hotel and charged in. "Of course, Peter has a steady. He would."

Jane was pleased with the hotel. It was no luxury spot but it appeared to be clean and the price was certainly right. She was shown a room and told the clerk she'd take the next one coming up.

"It'll save you spending so much at the Gramercy," Donna said. "Where'd y'say you were from? Aspen?"

Jane shook her head. "Rifle. It's sixty miles from the ski resort. A ranching community."

"You're a cowgirl? Wow!"

"No," Jane said with a laugh, "I'm a bodyguard."

They ate at a deli near the Barbizon. Jane, at her new friend's urging, had corned beef on rye. "*Real* rye," Donna emphasized, "not like that phony stuff they have in New Jersey."

"Oh," commented Jane, lost.

On the bus back to Mercury, Donna told her about her boyfriend, Frank. "He's a long-distance truck driver. He owns his own rig, too. Cost him a hundred thousand."

"He must be rich," Jane said.

"Oh no. I should have said the *bank* owns the rig. Frank's lucky to meet his monthly payments. What with the highway taxes and the cost of diesel fuel these days." On and on she went. "You'll have to meet him, Jane. He's absolutely gorgeous! Maybe we could double-date sometime. Frank's got this friend who rides with him. Harve. He's real sexy. Maybe not so smart but a good-looker. Of course, you wouldn't have to marry him!" Donna giggled.

"I haven't met the fourth courier," Jane remarked in an attempt to change the subject.

"Oh, that's Kelly. Kelly McCall. He's on a job today. I heard he was taking documents to a Philadelphia court. A murder trial or something."

"That's interesting. Doesn't he need a bodyguard?"

"Naw. It's not a Mafia trial or anything like that."

"Oh," said Jane, "I get it."

"But you'll have lots of work. Norma hasn't been able to cover all the routes. And you know we've been robbed four times this summer. Lew is going to lose his insurance, I hear."

"Oh, no!"

Donna shook her head. "It's so sad. The police have gotten nowhere with the robberies. Not a clue. Lew thinks it could be an inside job," the girl stated matter-of-factly.

"A what?"

"You know—" she popped her gum "—someone who works at Mercury."

"One of the couriers?" asked Jane, aghast.

"Could be. Someone is giving out information. Can you imagine? The creep. Why, Lew is the sweetest man I know and I hope whoever is doing it gets busted and rots in jail!"

"Amen."

"So you think you might like to meet Harve?"

"Well, I, uh, would like to get settled some first."

"Sure." Donna shrugged, chewing. "Maybe next week."

"That would be better."

By Wednesday, Jane was itching for an assignment, but for all of Lew's fatherly friendliness, she decided it was best not to push too hard. He'd send her along with one of the couriers when *he* thought she was ready.

"No sense sticking your neck out too soon," advised Norma at lunch that day.

From Jane's tiny office, where she spent her time looking over maps of the routes used by couriers and some past job reports, she found she could hear the front door below opening and closing, its sound made possible by the echoing wooden steps. Jane couldn't help listening, imagining that the comings and goings below were clients or the couriers returning from jobs. But sometimes she found herself imagining that Graham Smith's self-assured footfalls were among those she could hear on the steps. It wasn't like Jane to spend so much time thinking about a man, trying to recall his features, the breadth of his shoulders or the color of his eyes.

She wanted to ask Donna a dozen times if he'd called or come in to see Lew but Donna was such an awful gossip. No, she couldn't ask her. Once had been enough.

But where *was* he?

Jane finally met Donna's boyfriend, Frank Hansen, that

afternoon when he returned from a run to Florida and stopped at the office to pick Donna up.

"Jane," exclaimed the secretary as she gathered up her purse to leave, "meet Frank."

He was big and blond and rumpled, very macho-looking. He was chewing tobacco.

"Nice to meet you. I've heard so much about you," Jane said graciously.

Sitting on the edge of the reception desk in his big work boots and faded T-shirt, he nodded at Jane and mumbled something.

"How was your trip?" Donna was asking him.

"Lousy. The I-95 was so crowded with old fogies driving back from Miami I had to crawl. How the hell can I make a buck if it takes me an extra day to haul a load 'cause of some old..." and he swore nastily.

Jane cringed.

"Poor baby," cooed Donna, who was obviously, uncritically mad about him.

"And the speed limits—ridiculous," he groused. "I got a ticket from those—" he swore again "—cops in Georgia."

There was a brutal aura surrounding Frank Hansen and Jane took an immediate dislike to the man. What on earth did Donna see in him? It was definitely time for Jane to make her exit. "Well, see you around," she said politely.

"Yeah, sure."

"Oh, is Harve waiting in the car?" Donna asked.

Frank nodded without enthusiasm.

Jane turned and glanced out of the tall, old-fashioned window. Sitting in a beat-up '72 Ford, double-parked, was a large dark man, with lots of chest hair showing above the neck of his shirt. He had a beetle brow and thick arms, she could see, but his face was essentially turned away so Jane was unable to tell much more.

"Wanna come out and meet Harve?" Donna was asking hopefully.

"Well, I...I promised I'd call my father after work," Jane lied. "You know, he worries."

"Oh. Well, maybe tomorrow then."

"Sure, maybe," replied Jane, wondering how she was going to get out of that one. "I guess I better get on up to my office and put some files away. See you." She disappeared up the stairs, relieved to get away from Frank's uncomfortable presence, wondering, once more, what a sharp girl like Donna could see in a man like that.

The last days of July slipped away. The heat in the city was unbearable in the beginning of August, the humidity reaching close to ninety-five percent some days. Jane found that she had to shower often, twice a day anyway, to stand it. It seemed like she was grimy all the time from the soot that hung in the thick city air. The police reported an increase in domestic violence those early August days and Jane stayed in her Barbizon room at night.

It wasn't all that bad, though. Norma had her over to dinner one evening and Lew finally allowed Jane to body-guard—locally only—until she got the hang of it.

Her very first assignment was to guard Peter Lerner while he took the plans of a revolutionary new hull design to the docks of the New York Yacht Club.

"The new hull is for a boat that'll race in the America's Cup," Peter told her.

"The design is *that* valuable?" asked Jane as she drove carefully through the heavy city traffic, keeping a watchful eye on things.

"You bet. Wait till you see the dock area. It's got more security than Fort Knox."

Then there was an assignment in which she and Peter transported artwork from Manhattan to Westport, Connecticut, and another job with Kelly McCall, who was in his fifties and could have been Lew's brother, carrying the contents of an elderly woman's safe-deposit box from one New York bank to another. Jane's jobs went, thankfully, without incident. Norma's, thus far, did too.

Only once more did Jane allow herself to ask Donna about Graham. ''Oh,'' she said casually one afternoon, ''have you seen Quicksilver lately?''

Donna shook her head. ''Not a word. It's funny, too, because he usually calls on Lew every couple of weeks or so.''

''Oh, well,'' said Jane, feigning disinterest, ''I'm sure he'll come around sometime.''

At night in her hotel room Jane allowed herself to think about Graham. She recalled him with utter clarity yet there were huge, empty gaps in her memory. Had his nose been straight or hooked? Was he as tall as she remembered? Was his voice as pleasantly modulated? Good Lord, was he married? No, she decided, he wasn't. Had Jane imagined his interest in her?

She was dying to see him again, to test her feelings for him. How would he feel about her in this different environment? Would he even notice her here in New York, his home?

Impatience ate at her sometimes when she thought of Graham. She'd known him less than a day, a ridiculously short time. He'd probably forgotten her but, darn it, she wanted to know if he had or not!

At Mercury she found herself listening automatically for the downstairs door to open and each time it did, her heart gave a little expectant jump. It could be him, it could be Graham. But it never was. At the Barbizon she leaped every time the phone rang, then had to take a deep breath and wait for the second ring in case it was Graham and she would appear too anxious. It was, however, either her father or Donna or Norma Stedman when it did ring, which wasn't often.

Graham Smith, Quicksilver, where are you? she asked the darkness at three in the morning or the watery sun at eight as she descended into the bowels of the city to catch the subway to work or the green, green grass in Central Park as she jogged in the awful humidity.

And then one day she was coming down the stairs at work and there he was. Tall, devilishly handsome, his strawberry-blond hair catching the golden summer light from the high window as he leaned over Donna's desk chatting.

Jane froze for a moment and then he looked up and noticed her. She was struck dumb by his presence, just as she feared she would be. There was something more to this man than just good looks. There was some indefinable magic in his blue eyes, in the insouciant tilt of his lips, in that delightfully expressive face that was so full of unspoken promise.

"Well, hello, Jane Manning." He stood up straight and grinned at her.

"Hi." She found her legs again and walked down the steps to take his hand. Oh, yes, indeed, it was still there, that current between them; it was in the warmth of his touch, in the way his fingers closed over hers, possessive somehow, yet smooth as silk and gentle.

"Long time no see," he was saying as he gazed into her eyes. "You'll have to fill me in on everything, how you like the city, et cetera."

"Sure," said Jane, releasing his hand, glad she'd worn her best dress that day and done her hair. What did he *really* think of her, though? Did he find her out of place in the sophistication of Manhattan? Did she still measure up?

"I've got to see Lew for a few minutes," he said then. "Do you think we might have lunch?"

Jane was about to say yes when Donna's voice stopped her. "Don't forget you have to go to Jersey City with Lukas at eleven-thirty, Jane."

"Oh," replied Jane, momentarily flustered, "I guess I can't make it for lunch today, Graham. I'm sorry."

He grinned, his deep, mellow voice echoing pleasantly. "So am I. But we'll do it another time."

"You're in the city for a while?" she ventured.

''Could be. Never know.''

''You ready to go, lady?'' came Lukas's voice from the head of the staircase.

''Oh, yes, anytime,'' replied Jane, tearing her gaze away from Graham reluctantly.

''I'll see you, then.'' Graham began to head up the steps and she watched his form until he was out of sight. She'd forgotten what a great physique he had. Those long, muscled legs, a nice rear end, the tapered hips beneath the white linen sport coat, and his easy, confident carriage made for one hell of a package.

Jane stood staring after him like a lovesick puppy, feeling as if it would almost have been better if he had not come back into her life at all.

How much time had they spent together? Two minutes? And his promise of lunch—had it been just words, polite bantering? Perhaps she should have pinned him down. ''What *day* do you want to have lunch, Graham?''

But really, who could pin down a man with a name like Quicksilver?

CHAPTER FIVE

WHEN JANE LEFT THE OFFICE that afternoon Donna was standing on the curb in front of the building waiting for Frank to pick her up.

"See you tomorrow," Donna said brightly, snapping her gum. "Boy, it sure looks like rain. Hope this heat spell is over soon. Gawd, it makes my hair frizz up like cotton candy!"

"I love your hair. Mine just goes straighter in the humidity."

"Say, maybe Harve'll be along. I mean, you want to meet him? We were going out for pizza."

"Ah, gee, thanks, Donna, but I, uh, have a date."

"Oh, neat! Who?"

"Oh, you don't know him. Someone from, uh, Denver."

"Well, have fun." Then she stretched up to her tiptoes and waved a purple-tipped hand. "Oh, there's Frank!"

This time he picked her up on a monstrous black and chrome motorcycle, a Harley-Davidson. It didn't faze Donna; she merely hiked up her skirt and swung a leg over the seat. She waved goodbye as Frank revved his machine up and lurched forward into the one-way traffic but Frank himself hadn't even turned his head. Well, thought Jane in relief, at least Harve hadn't been along.

She took the subway uptown. By now she was so used to the urine odor that permeated the stations she didn't even wrinkle her nose. And she read the want ads as she stood swaying, not even hearing the clickity-clack racket

of the train. The usual places were for rent: co-op on Park
Avenue $1,500 per month; studio in the Village, good
lighting, $950 per month; shotgun apartment in German-
town, $1,200. She folded the paper up in disgust. How
would she ever find a decent, affordable place to live?

When Jane emerged from the stuffy, echoing tunnel she
felt a breeze lift her hair and there was a muted rumble
of thunder. Astonishing. It was the first fresh air she'd felt
since arriving in New York. The leaves on the trees in
front of a gray stone building fluttered weakly. Poor trees.
They were encased in concrete—and their roots? Did their
roots stretch down to the subways and sewers underground?

Then Jane saw that the sky had turned dark gray, lightning flashed behind a building, and when she rounded the
corner to her hotel a real wind buffeted her, sending grit
and dust and a few stray papers ricocheting off her. It *was*
going to rain.

By the time she got up to her room the first drops were
splattering on the hot sidewalks, sending up that tarry wet
pavement smell, and people were rushing for cover and
windshield wipers began swishing in the rush-hour traffic.
Jane threw open her window and breathed in the fresh air,
getting her face wet in the process. She thought of the
afternoon thundershowers at home on the ranch, of the
black thunderheads boiling up from the west, releasing
their burden, then moving on to leave the land refreshed,
the air cleansed, the sky a perfect blue. And she and her
brothers, so often caught out in the rain, would have to
race for the barn. "Me first!" James would always
scream, bent low over his horse's neck, his horse flying
over the ground, throwing clods of mud up from its
hooves.

A momentary nostalgia flooded her. Then she pulled
her head in and sighed. Memories were good but she'd
always have them and right now she had to experience a
new existence, a new city, unfamiliar people and different

feelings. Then, some day, she'd probably feel nostalgic about *this* period of her life.

And, oh, how exciting New York was! It breathed, it shook with life. It rattled and honked and screeched. It smelled wonderful and horrible. It presented enough weird sights in a day to fill *Ripley's Believe It or Not.* And every neighborhood was different—Wall Street, Fifth Avenue, Washington Square, Chinatown, the Village, the Palisades. Each one was a city in microcosm, with its own smells and noises and sights and customs. New York.

Jane sat on her bed and listened to the rain and the thunder. Out there was the whole city waiting for her to explore it. It was teeming with people, promising adventures, beckoning. On the other hand, she wasn't foolhardy. To go out alone—in the pouring rain... Maybe she'd wait until the storm let up and then grab a bite to eat at the deli down the street. Or she could go to a movie, except that men in shabby trench coats had a way of sitting next to her in the theaters. It wasn't that she was afraid of them, it was just unpleasant. If she had her own place she could do so much more....

She lay back, kicked her shoes off and put her arms behind her head. Graham. Quicksilver. The thought of him came into her mind unbidden. Had he really meant that lunch invitation? Or had he known she was busy? Was he just being polite. He *had* liked her back in Rifle, she knew he had. But this was his home ground and here he was in control whereas there he'd been at a disadvantage. Actually, not really so much at a disadvantage. He'd handled things pretty darn well. She smiled to herself at the thought of Graham on Pard. Well, at least he had a sense of humor. And a long lean hard body and bright blue eyes and that firm, narrow jaw and—

The phone rang. Her father? Donna with Harve panting in the background?

"Hello?"

"Jane?"

She sat bolt upright, speechless for a heartbeat of time. She'd conjured him up in her mind and this was a phantom voice.

"Jane Manning?"

"Yes," she said breathlessly, "I'm here."

"Oh, you sound funny. This is Graham."

"Oh, I...I just ran up the stairs."

"Listen, I've been thinking of you a lot. I wish I'd been in town when you arrived but I was off on a job. There's this crazy writer in England...well, you don't want to hear about it. So, can we get together this evening?"

"I'd love to." Her heart thudded against her ribs.

"I *did* say I'd show you the Empire State Building, as I recall." His voice promised fun and she could picture him standing insouciantly—where?—someplace elegant, talking to her. "Donna told me you're at the Barbizon. Right?"

"Yes."

"I'll pick you up at 6:30. Is that okay with you?"

She glanced at her watch: 5:35. Oh my, her hair! "It's fine. Great."

"Good. See you soon."

"See you, Graham."

Jane gave herself a minute to dance around the room in her stocking feet. She grinned to herself and whistled a tune and twirled on the gold-and-brown patterned carpet. Then she stopped, gasped, and looked at her watch: 5:45!

It took her twenty minutes to wash her hair, then blow-dry it. Darn! And her hair was straight as a stick. Pulling on her white pants—thank heavens she'd bought them— buttoning the yellow blouse, she raced around her room like a madwoman. More deodorant. She'd sweat in this heat. Was the Empire State Building air-conditioned?

Then a little blush, the expensive stuff from Bloomingdale's. Mascara, but her eyes kept blinking and she smeared it. Six-fifteen. Would he be late? Sandals or the beige heels? Would they be walking much?

At 6:20 she had to stop and pat her face dry. It was still raining and thundering out. What kind of jacket should she wear? She didn't own a raincoat. He'd think her a hick. No raincoat!

Then a thought struck her—would he call up or expect her to meet him in the lobby? Should she wait in her room, dancing with impatience, or appear to be too eager and go down to the lobby?

Oh, damn, this was all so new, so difficult. At home Branch just drove up in his pickup truck and she hopped in and they went to Tilly's Café or the local Elks lodge or a movie in Glenwood Springs.

She waited until 6:35, then couldn't sit still another second. Riding down in the elevator she had a moment of panic. What if he called her room and she didn't answer and he left?

The elevator doors swished open and she stepped out. A flash of lightning illuminated the dim lobby for a split second. She looked for Graham's tall figure. Was he there yet? The front door opened and let in a gust of air, a spattering of raindrops, and he was striding across the lobby toward her, a broad smile on his face, the shoulders of his exquisitely cut sport coat dark with rain.

"Jane? Sorry I was late. Couldn't find a place to park." He gave her a rueful expression. "It's raining like crazy and I don't have my raincoat."

"Neither do I," she admitted.

"It's good to see you again," he said then, his eyes resting on her face.

"You, too." She gave a nervous little laugh. "It's different."

"You mean New York? Sure, but I'm the same and I'll bet you are, too." He took her hand; his was wet but it didn't matter. "Let's go. Hungry? Thirsty? I'll take you anywhere you want. This is my town and I want to show it to you.''

Graham's car was double-parked. They ducked their heads and ran. It was a little red Porsche, its hazard lights blinking while a policeman stood next to it calmly writing up a ticket as the rain cascaded off his yellow slicker.

"Officer, please," Graham said. "This is my fiancée and she just arrived in New York. You wouldn't want her to get the wrong impression, would you?" And he pulled Jane close while they both got wetter and wetter. "Come on, give me a break. I'll never do it again, officer." He bent his head to Jane. "Will I, honey?"

"No, certainly not," she told the policeman solemnly.

The officer stopped writing and peered at them from under the brim of his dripping hood. "Okay, buddy, I'll make it a warning this time."

"Thanks, officer, really," Jane said, smiling. Graham chimed in with, "We appreciate it, I'll never do it again."

"It was entirely my fault," Jane added. "I took too long getting ready. Thank you ever so much."

Graham held the door of the car while Jane slid in, still smiling at the policeman, then he ran around to the other side, got in and pulled out into the traffic. He started laughing at the first stoplight. "That down-home charm'll do it every time! Jane, you were terrific. I owe you one."

"No problem. Next time, though, tell the guy I'm your sister or something." She was laughing too and trying to wipe the rain off her face without smearing her mascara. All that frantic getting ready and she was soaked, her hair hanging in ratty strands, her linen pants creased, her blouse sticking to her.

"My sister? Hey, lady, there's no way on earth he could have mistaken you for my sister."

There was no answer to that remark. She got her comb out of her purse and tried to do something with her hair. While she pulled and tugged at the wet snarls, she could feel his gaze slide from her profile down to her clinging wet blouse. Why was it that a mere glance could be as intimate, as sensual as a caress?

Finally the traffic light turned green, and she saw him turn his attention back to the road.

"Sorry you got drenched," he said.

"Oh, well, I've been wet before. At least it's a relief from the heat."

"You're a good sport, Jane." He weaved through the traffic and turned onto a side street. "First we're going to get something to eat and dry off, then we'll go up to the Empire State Building like I promised. The rain's letting up and I know it'll stop by then. Is that okay with you?"

"Sounds wonderful." Actually, Jane didn't care where they went. It was exciting enough to be with Graham. He moved, it seemed, from one adventure to another and she was dying to see what would happen next.

He took her to a little northern Italian place in Chelsea on Ninth Avenue. They sat at a tiny table in a dark corner with a candle stuck in a Chianti bottle for light. The waiter had a dirty apron and a thick accent but the food was marvelous. Jane never remembered exactly what it was because she was so aware of Graham, so involved in their conversation, so bombarded with sights and sounds and smells.

"So, how is the Big Apple treating you?" Graham asked, sipping his wine, his blue eyes dancing in the candlelight.

"Wonderful. I love it. And Lew is great and so is my job," she replied enthusiastically. "This city is so, so *exciting*." Then she hesitated. Did she sound like a hick? Too easily impressed? But, what the heck, she *was* impressed. Why try to act otherwise?

But he was smiling at her without condescension. "I love to hear you talk. You've got just the slightest Western accent, did you know that?"

She put her head to one side and said, deadpan,

"Funny, I thought everyone *here* had a funny accent, Graham."

He burst out laughing.

Jane leaned forward and asked him, more seriously, "Graham, tell me the truth. Just how much did you have to do with getting me this job?"

"As much as I could manage," he said frankly.

"Why?"

"Two reasons. I thought you could do the job and I wanted to see you again."

"You did?"

"What do you think I'm doing right now, Jane?" he asked, grinning.

"Seeing me," she said quietly.

"Now, tell me about yourself," Graham coaxed. "Everything before you decided to become a bodyguard."

"Gosh, that's boring."

"Not to me. I'm insatiably curious, you know, like the baby elephant in the *Jungle Book*."

"And look what happened to him. Didn't he get his nose stretched out by a crocodile?"

"Ah yes, but that was all for the best—for elephants, anyway."

Jane looked at him and sipped her wine. He was fun. Witty, sharp, handsome. Full of knowledge and experience and good at so many things. What was he doing with a girl like her—from Rifle? He must have his pick of hundreds of women. Or did she provide variety? And yet there was this feeling she got from him. "Vibes" they were called. He liked her, he really did. Maybe more than just *like* but she shied from putting it into words. And she felt the same. Oh yes, she *liked* Graham Smith a lot.

"Well," he said. "I'm waiting with bated breath."

So she told him about her mother dying when she was ten, about being raised on the ranch by her father and four brothers. About being dissatisfied, in limbo, until she read about the ISA and how women make good bodyguards.

"Then I knew what I wanted to do. Like one of those light bulbs you see in cartoons. You know, *eureka*!"

"And are you still glad you did it?"

"I sure am." She nodded resolutely. "Now it's your turn."

"You positive you want to hear? It's not very interesting."

"That's my line. Go ahead, tell me everything. I'm another elephant's child."

She ate while he talked. He spoke well and used his hands a lot. His voice was smooth and deep, his accent nonspecifically East Coast. He described things well. His upbringing had been in various European cities where his father had been posted as a consul for the foreign service. "That's where he met Lew, who also worked for the service for years. They go way back. And that's why my French is so good. I went to a lycée in Paris for a while. And besides my mother is French Canadian and used to speak it at home." He told her about foreign studies at Georgetown University, a year of law school and two years with the foreign service. She felt as if she was beginning to know the elusive Quicksilver, as if those gaping holes in her knowledge of him were filling in.

"You've had a pretty exciting life," Jane said.

He shrugged. "It's all what you're used to. To me your ranch is about as exciting as I've seen. And you *raced* quarter horses?"

"I was raised on a horse. That's not the least bit interesting."

But Graham leaned forward over the little table and said in a soft, caressing voice, "I love to watch you eat."

Jane's hand stopped, her fork halfway to her mouth. "What?"

"You're beautiful when you eat."

She put her fork down and stared at him. "When I *eat*?"

"You enjoy your food. And your mouth is pretty. And you have some tomato sauce on your chin."

Quickly Jane raised her napkin to wipe her chin off. She felt herself blushing. "That's mean, Graham."

"I like a natural woman. You look great even when you're wet."

"Or covered with tomato sauce?"

"Then too."

"Graham…"

"Yes?" he asked, mock-innocently.

When they had finished dinner and left the restaurant, it was still light out and the rain had stopped. "See?" said Graham, "I told you it would stop raining."

"Are we really going to the Empire State Building?"

He took her hand as they started out and she shivered with delight at his touch. "Yes, we are. It's open till late. And the view really is spectacular."

"The Empire State Building," mused Jane. "I never thought…"

Graham pulled her hand up to his mouth and kissed her fingers lightly. "Ah, but one never knows what life holds, does one?"

She felt her insides grow warm and ticklish and glowing. "No," she agreed softly.

She felt as if she were—what was that awful cliché?—being swept off her feet. A strong current was sweeping her along; it was wild and exciting and irresistible. It was Graham and it was happening too fast. She couldn't think; he wouldn't let her. She was scared and thrilled and full of a breathless, warm, melting sensation.

Graham Smith, the logical part of her mind told her, was a rogue, an adventurer, a man who took the world by the tail and shook it. He went at things so aggressively that she wondered if he ever took the time to stop and evaluate, to really figure out what he wanted from life.

Another part of her was fascinated by his dynamism and sense of humor, by the softness of his voice and the genuine caring he emanated and the way he could make Jane feel as if she were the only female on earth. His spirit matched hers in some ways; they were both people who wanted more from life than a steady job or security or a nice house. They both wanted some kind of stimulation, something different.

They walked to the Empire State Building. Its silhouette was so familiar it seemed as if Jane must have been there before—the grand decorative lines, the way it climbed from its base in irregular steps to the sky, its upper layers smaller than the ones below lifting in perfect symmetry to the needlelike spire. And it was elegant inside, in the ornate, Art Deco fashion of the thirties. What struck Jane was the fact that it was, after all, an office building, a place where people came to work every day.

The elevators rose so quickly Jane couldn't believe they were up to the eighty-sixth floor. She even had to pop her ears.

They walked around the observation platform while Graham pointed out various landmarks. The atmosphere was cool and hazy and she could barely make out Central Park up to the north or the World Trade Center to the south. But the city itself was stretched out at her feet, miles upon miles of gray thrusting buildings, arrow-straight avenues, the green of trees and parks, the rivers, the tiny antlike cars crawling endlessly along the streets. It was a beautiful sight.

"It's so big," breathed Jane.

"London's bigger and Mexico City and Tokyo, I think."

"But they're not like...not like *this*."

"No, they're not. There's only one New York."

"Oh, Graham, thank you for this. I never realized. I mean, being down there—" she pointed "—you don't get the full picture."

It was windy on the eighty-sixth floor. Jane's slacks and blouse flattened against her and her hair blew into her

eyes. The sun was setting off beyond New Jersey but the
haze made it appear to be merely a yellow glow. So different from the diamond-bright clear Colorado sky where
the sun shone in all its glory.

"Had enough?" he finally asked. "I'm afraid it's going
to rain again."

By the time they left the building it was pouring.

"Want to get a taxi?" Graham suggested. "My car's
pretty far away."

But they got wetter standing at the curb waiting for an
empty cab than if they'd walked.

"Damn!" Graham yelled, shaking his fist at the hundreds of suddenly filled taxis, "you can't ever get a cab
when you need one in this town!"

They finally walked, splashing through oily puddles,
half running, laughing like two children whose mothers
had told them not to get wet. Graham gave her his jacket
but it was already so damp it didn't do much good. Still,
she liked the feel of it and it smelled faintly of him.

Once they reached his Porsche and clambered inside,
the windows promptly steamed up. Jane took her handkerchief and wiped at them while he drove. "That's two,"
she warned playfully. "Where are we going now?"

"To get dry," he said lightly and her heart bounded in
her chest.

"Where?" she asked.

Graham was looking straight ahead. "To my place."
He hesitated. "That is, if you want to." His voice was
carefully noncommittal, as if he were allowing her the
chance to back out gracefully. And she knew she could
back out. Graham would never pressure her; he wanted
her to go with him but if she declined he wouldn't argue.

Jane realized suddenly what his invitation signified.
They were two adults. They liked each other and there
was something profound between them, an undeniable af-
finity. They needed to learn more about each other, much
more. They needed to explore their feelings, and if that

led to an intimate expression of their love, so be it. If she
said yes now there would be no turning back, no playing
coy games. As an adult Jane owed him that much. And
if she said no Graham would, as an adult, take her home.

Panic seized her momentarily. It was too soon. The city
was overwhelming her, and Graham… It was all too
much. And yet, strong and definite, there was this bond
between them. It had flared into being the moment they'd
met and was blazing stronger with each second. It was
real and important and unique in her experience.

"I'd love to," she said clearly and Graham broke into
a broad smile, turned downtown on the Avenue of the
Americas and stepped on the gas.

His apartment was on 10th Street close to the heart of
Greenwich Village in a very nice neighborhood, a brownstone that was surprisingly charming and substantial for a
single man, Jane thought. Graham parked in a nearby underground garage and while he walked around to open her
door, Jane had another moment of apprehension. What
was she doing?

But then he was holding his hand out and smiling, and
she knew that she and Graham could have something very
good, very special together. Jane drew in a deep breath,
took hold of his hand and they walked to the street and
then up the steps to the shiny dark-green door.

It was still raining and the thunder seemed to be rever-
berating off the buildings of Lower Manhattan. Jane shivered a little in her wet clothes.

"Well, here we are," said Graham, opening his door.

Jane stepped in and looked around. The foyer led into
a living room that had a gleaming parquet floor, an Au-
busson rug and several upholstered chairs and a couch
done in floral patterns. There were gilt-framed mirrors and
a few very large, very ornately framed oil paintings on
the walls. Wainscoting, painted white, covered the bottom
half of the walls and above that they were done in a deep
forest green. There were green velvet drapes, a marble-

topped sideboard and a finely carved mantel on the far side of the room.

"It's lovely," said Jane.

"Thank you. My decorator is very inexpensive, though."

"Your decorator?"

"My mother. It's old family stuff."

"Oh. Well, she did a marvelous job."

"I'll tell her."

"Does she live in New York?"

A shadow passed over his face, Jane thought. "No, in Montreal."

Of course, he'd said she was French Canadian.

"Now, let's see. You need to get dry. Follow me." He led her upstairs to his bedroom. It was plainer than the downstairs—a double bed, a serviceable dresser, a rocking chair. Maybe his mother had run out of "old family stuff." He took a blue terry cloth robe from the closet. "Put this on and we'll dry your clothes."

"What about you?" she asked.

"Ladies first."

She changed into his robe and, barefoot, carried her blouse and pants downstairs. "Your turn," she said. "Do you have a dryer? I'll just put these in…"

"Right through there." He pointed toward the kitchen. "And I'll be back in a minute."

When he returned he wore jeans and a white polo shirt that emphasized his lean physique.

"Tea?" he asked. "Or coffee? Or maybe a bit of brandy to warm you up?"

"Nothing, thanks. I'm fine." She was a little constrained with him now. What should she do next? She wondered if he felt awkward, too, or if he was used to entertaining women in his apartment.

She walked to a window and pulled back the heavy fabric. The rain streamed down the glass endlessly, making the street outside and the buildings waver. The city lights were merely globes of diffused brightness. She sensed Graham coming up behind her.

"Are you nervous being alone with me, Jane?"

She turned to face him. "A little. This is all real new to me."

"I feel like I've known you forever," he said softly. "I can't imagine not knowing you." Then he put a hand out and touched her cheek. "You know, I've been wanting to kiss you since that day in Rifle. Did you know that?"

"No," she whispered. Her breath came too quickly and her heart was bursting with excitement and fright and happiness. "Did you really?"

He nodded, his blue eyes holding hers, mesmerizing her. His other hand reached out and she could feel his fingers, warm and strong, cupping her face, turning it up to his. She closed her eyes and his lips came down over hers, at first gently, as light as a bird's wing, then harder so that her mouth opened under his.

Her arms went around his neck and she pressed herself against his body. Her blood sang, her senses quivered with the wonder of his nearness. His lips felt familiar, as if she'd known them before, as if she hadn't just met this man. She breathed in his scent as his breath mingled with hers.

He pulled back and looked at her. "That was even better than I thought it would be," he said.

Jane searched his face. It reflected pleasure and a kind of quiet awe. She sighed and laid her head against his chest. His arms tightened around her and he kissed the top of her head.

"I can't believe I'm here, I can't believe I met you," murmured Jane.

"I know what you mean." He tilted her face up and studied her so long she began to feel uncomfortable.

"Is something wrong?" she asked.

"No...I just wondered about...well..."

"What?" she asked, puzzled, leaning back in his arms.

"Gosh, I feel like a fool asking. But I was wondering about you and...Branch Taggart."

"Oh."

"Look, it's none of my business, I know, but he seemed to know you real well and..."

She looked down and smiled to herself. "Don't worry about Branch. It's long since over."

"You sure?"

"I've known Branch for years and he'd like to think there was something between us. But there never really was. At least, there sure isn't anymore."

"I'm very glad to hear that."

"Now, should I ask you about any of your lady friends?" she queried teasingly.

"No. Besides, there isn't one as big and strong as Branch. You don't have to worry about a thing." His blue eyes were laughing at her again and she felt happy and excited and nervous. Her pulse thumped and leaped and she could feel his hands on her waist. When his mouth covered hers once more, she gave in to the feel of his lips on hers, his smell, his touch, the moist, velvety feel of his tongue. Delight raced through her body in shivery waves. She sighed when he pulled away.

"You're not regretting this, are you?" he asked softly, his lips moving in her hair.

"No," she said into his chest.

"I don't think you're afraid of anything or anyone," he said. "I love that in you."

She raised her head. "You don't find it...intimidating? Lots of men would. Lots of men *have*."

He laughed. "Hell, no, Jane. I like a woman who knows her own mind."

She leaned back in his arms and asked soberly, "What's happening, Graham? I mean, what's really happening between us?"

"Something special," he answered just as solemnly, his mouth coming down over hers once again.

Upstairs in his bedroom he pulled the blue robe off her shoulders and kissed the skin he uncovered. "So beautiful," he murmured. Jane wanted to tell him she wasn't really beautiful at all but it didn't matter, not as long as Graham thought she was.

Then she helped him off with his clothes and gasped at the wonder of his nude body. He was a remarkable piece of work—long and lean, broad shouldered, with strong legs and sinewy arms. He was gentle and fierce, a practiced lover, a man who knew how to please a woman. His hands found all the secret places on her body and made them tingle in response.

He pulled back the covers on his bed and Jane saw that his sheets were a leopard-spotted pattern. She giggled and ran her hand down his bare flank. "Sexy," she whispered into his ear as they fell onto the bed together.

"Yeah, me Tarzan, you Jane," he growled, biting at her earlobe. Then he stopped and looked at her as she lay under him. "You *Jane*, get it?"

She started to laugh, burying her face in his neck. "How original!"

"Any man said that to you before, I'll break his neck," Graham murmured into her ear.

She could feel his hardness against her belly and the sensation filled her with warmth. She closed her eyes and pulled him close. "Oh, God, kiss me."

His tongue savored her mouth, his breath mingled with hers, his hands stroked her back and hips and buttocks, the inside of her thighs. Jane squirmed with pleasure, the heat building within her. Small cries came from her and he whispered quick, panting questions. "Here? Oh, yes," and "Slow, my darling," and "Is that good, is that it?"

She was ready; she wanted to feel him inside her, wanted to be one with him. "Now," she urged, "Graham, quickly!'' and he took her almost harshly, stabbing swiftly and sure, filling her until she cried out.

Jane had never before felt the intensity of this joining. Graham fit her perfectly, molded to her body, touched all the right places. Her senses expanded and she seemed to float with him above everything. The world receded and there was only the two of them, alone, rocking, filled with the same pure, electrifying jolts of sensation that drove them both onward. Then she felt him grow rigid, bigger, within her and he groaned and she felt the same heat burst within her.

Jane was aware only of her breath, rasping in and out, the sweat that beaded her forehead and Graham's weight on her. It seemed to her that she'd come back from a distant place, a place where feelings were stronger, reality more real, sensations more pure.

''Jane,'' she heard Graham say, ''Janey, my Janey. Ah, girl, you've done me in.''

She put a hand on his thick, wavy hair and felt the lassitude that held her. ''I hope it isn't permanent,'' she breathed.

''God, so do I,'' he said fervently then laughed. ''You're wonderful. I love an uninhibited woman. There's even more to you than I suspected, Jane Manning.''

She smiled into the darkness. ''Was I disgraceful?''

''Delightfully so. Noisy as the devil.''

''Graham, you're embarrassing me.''

But he only rolled aside and flung an arm across her bare stomach. ''I must be getting old,'' he teased.

Her head fit perfectly into the hollow between his neck and shoulder, his other arm went around her. Jane had never felt so content in her life. She slowly trailed her fingertips across his chest.

''That was special, wasn't it?'' she finally asked. ''I mean, it's not just my imagination, is it?''

His arm tightened around her. He thought for a minute

and she was afraid that he'd tell her it had been ordinary. But he said softly, "It wasn't your imagination, Janey."

And she snuggled up to him, happy, and breathed in his scent and listened to his heartbeat until she fell asleep.

CHAPTER SIX

"TEN MILLION IN DIAMONDS," Lew was saying to Graham. "Our biggest job to date."

"A lot of money," Graham remarked distractedly, unable to concentrate on their conversation about the diamond delivery Lew wanted him to make. Between the prospect of a trip to Amsterdam, not to mention his large fee, Graham should have been all ears. But it was all he could do to pay attention.

There was a jetlike roar running through his head and a heavy pounding in his heart. His raw silk shirt caressed his skin and he felt an idiotic smile trying to curve his lips. It was almost as if he were coming down with the flu but it was a wonderful illness because he knew there was a sure, instantaneous cure: Jane.

"Detective Sorello says it's only a matter of time before the police nab the robbers." Lew stood and walked to the window in his office. "But I don't have the time to wait for the police, Graham. One more substantial loss and Lloyd's will never renew my policy. If they drop Mercury, no bonding or insurance company will touch us."

"It's bad, Lew, I know. I'm sure there's a way, though...." *Come on, Graham,* he told himself, *pay attention.* It certainly wasn't as if it were the first time he'd been with a woman. Hell, he'd had plenty of experience! But there had never been a woman like Jane Manning.

He sat in front of Lew Rapp's desk and images of Jane flew around in his head like butterflies—her husky voice like sweet music in his ear, her satin-smooth peachy skin, her small capable hands that drove him wild. They had both been wild, a fine wildness. He wondered if it had been as good for her as it had been for him.

Where was she now? In the office, out on an assignment? *Where are you, my adorable Janey?*

"Graham, are you listening?"

"Oh, yeah, sure I am, Lew. You were talking about my handling this job coming up in September. In, uh, Amsterdam. Yeah. That's right."

"Are you okay, son?"

"Oh, I'm fine. Better than ever, in fact."

"You could have fooled me."

Lew Rapp had known Graham's father before Graham had been born. Lew and Smedley had gone through foreign service training together and over the years, in their various postings, they'd kept in touch. Graham had known Lew since both the older men had been stationed at the American Embassy in London twenty years before. Lew was like an uncle to Graham, a beloved family friend, and he was in trouble. At the moment, Graham wished Lew had retired like his own father because he was having a terrible time concentrating on Lew's troubles.

Graham straightened his shoulders and with great effort, cleared his head. "I'll be glad to pick up those diamonds, Lew. No problem. And I promise you, they'll be perfectly safe with me."

"I hate to ask," Lew said. "I've got four top men here who could handle it. Especially if Norma went along. But I don't know if one of them is setting up these thefts. *Someone* in this office is."

"It does look that way," Graham agreed.

"The thieves seem to know exactly where my couriers will be. They're even *waiting* for them. And, of course, no one who's been guarded by Norma has been hit. It's got to be an inside leak."

"Must be," Graham mused.

"Another thing," Lew continued, "the crooks have only gone after stuff that's easy to fence like jewelry, cash, securities. It's a nightmare."

"I'll say. And I suppose if it isn't one of the couriers himself, someone here has friends on the outside doing the dirty work for him."

"Detective Sorello is sure of it."

Graham frowned. "Has he tried lie detector tests?"

"Not yet. But everyone is willing."

"Anyone too willing?"

Lew shook his head. "Sorello tried that ploy. It didn't work. Unfortunately," he added, "those tests are far from foolproof, anyway."

Graham sat lost in thought for a few minutes. "I've got an idea," he stated finally, "and if you don't like it, just say so. But I think maybe we could kill two birds with one stone."

"How's that?"

"I pick up the diamonds, like we talked about, and at the same time we nab the thieves."

"Easy to say," Lew said in a doubtful voice.

"Now wait a minute. It's not as crazy as it sounds." Graham sat forward in his chair eagerly. There was a glint in his blue eyes.

"I don't like that look…"

"Listen. Suppose you *don't* try to keep this diamond shipment under wraps around the office. Suppose you let, say, Donna know about it. Now we all know Donna is an ace gossip and before you could blink the whole Mercury crew would know about the diamonds. Hell, they'd probably know my flight number!"

"What's your point? My God, Graham, that would be like handing out an invitation for someone to steal them."

Graham grinned wickedly. "Exactly."

"You mean…lure them deliberately?"

"Yup. Right into a trap."

"I see…but what about actually catching the thieves? I mean, my God, what if the diamonds *did* get stolen?"

"Have some faith, Lew!" He laughed, looking cock-sure. "I haven't been twiddling my thumbs and sitting on my butt these last few years. And I'll have Norma with me. Between us these would-be robbers will be lucky to get off with jail terms. Hey, how can we fail?"

"Oh, sure. Sounds great sitting here. But what about the danger to you and Norma?"

Graham leaned back in his chair, crossing one foot over the other knee and folding his hands behind his head. "The odds are with us, Lew. You know my training. And Norma's as well."

"But you can't carry guns to Amsterdam."

"I detest guns. They're for thugs and amateurs. And besides, even if your thieves were dumb enough to try to follow us carrying weapons, which I seriously doubt with the tight airport security nowadays, they'd still have to get close enough to take the diamonds and then we'd collar them. In that situation, the hands are far more effective than any weapon."

"I just don't know." Lew frowned. "The whole thing gives me a whopping case of indigestion."

"Look, why use my services at all if you don't take full advantage? Do you want to go on getting hit and lose everything?"

"Certainly not."

"But that's exactly what might happen. Say we keep the shipment hush-hush and I bring the stones back to New York safely; eventually, whoever is behind these thefts is going to strike again. The difference is, you won't know where or when or who. Listen," he urged, "let's nab them *now*. When the element of surprise is on our side for a change."

Lew paced to the window and back to his desk. Finally he put both hands on the smooth, polished surface and leaned toward Graham. "All right, I'll go for it. Logically

I know you're right but I sure don't like the idea of using my best friend's boy like this.''

"Dad would insist you do. He trusts me. He knows I can handle myself, Lew."

"Oh, damn," said Lew abruptly. "We've got a problem."

Graham raised a curious brow.

"The Picassos."

"What Picassos?"

"Peter and Norma are picking up a real valuable set of Picasso sketches at the National Gallery in Washington and delivering them to the Met here in New York. It would make a perfect hit and it's the biggest thing I have coming up between now and the diamond job. If those Picassos get ripped off I'm in real trouble."

"When is this planned for?"

"A week from this coming Monday. I'm positive the word is already out around the office."

"Picassos would make a good hit," Graham agreed. "There're dozens of collectors who'd pay plenty to hang them in a private gallery. Some of them just about advertise in the *New York Times*!"

"*You* could get them. If you honestly think there could be a theft attempt, and if you want to handle it."

"Done. I'll drive on down to North Carolina the Friday before. Spend the weekend at the beach with Dad. No problem." Then suddenly Graham cocked an eyebrow. "Norma. Would she be upset if she's taken off the job?"

"Unfortunately the insurance company would insist on you having a bodyguard for this one."

"Well, I can't take Norma down to the beach for the weekend. Somehow I can't see her and Dad…''

"She prefers not to work weekends, anyway. Because of her husband. He's in a wheelchair and it's hard for him to get out."

"So, no Norma." Graham's blue eyes brightened and he hit his fist into his hand. "Hey! I'll take Jane!"

Graham left Lew's office ten minutes later. He was glad he wouldn't be going to D.C. with Norma. Not that he didn't appreciate Norma's experience but the old battle-ax made it plain she didn't like him. For some unknown reason she had always eyed him speculatively when he was around her. It was clear that she disapproved of him but for the life of him Graham didn't know just why.

He and Lew had compromised finally, Lew insisting that they lessen the possibility of the priceless sketches being stolen by spreading word around Mercury that the job had been canceled. Graham had argued that they should try to catch the thieves this time but Lew had been adamant: "I don't want to risk it, not with Jane going in Norma's place. She's still pretty inexperienced."

Only Graham and Jane would be privy to the knowledge and Lew would prefer—as Donna and Jane seemed friendly—that Jane not really know about the job until after they left New York. Graham, who had been itching at first to get a shot at the thieves, was forced to agree. Then, too, Lew was right: Jane was relatively new to the job and to put her in danger, on purpose, was pushing things.

He went upstairs to Jane's office, eager to see her but she wasn't in. Once more he wondered where she was.

THE SUN WAS OUT in New Jersey; steam was rising up from the Garden State Parkway as Jane and Rick drove. It had been raining in Atlantic City where they'd gone to pick up packets of new playing cards—cards, Rick Como told her, that the casino owners thought might have been tampered with.

"How could someone mark brand-new playing cards?" asked Jane from the driver's seat. "They're still sealed, for heaven's sake."

"I suspect the owners of the casino figure it was done in the factory. Maybe a factory worker was in league with someone on the outside, a gambler, and they're running a scam on the card tables.''

"What people won't do to make a buck," observed Jane, shaking her head.

The pickup in Atlantic City had gone without a hitch. But the casino had warned Rick that there could be an attempt made to grab the packages of cards and destroy them. Rick's job was to deliver the cards to an independent forensic expert who'd been hired by the casino to check for fingerprints. Should there have been tampering, it wouldn't be too difficult to lift a set of fingerprints from the cards and nail the cheaters.

Jane was quite aware of her duties. She remained vigilant for a car trailing them or for an out-of-place vehicle when they stopped at the toll booth to pay their ticket. She had great respect for her ability to outrun a pursuing car, however, and felt confident as she drove through the marshy flats of northern New Jersey.

"You're a good driver," commented Rick.

"Thanks, I took an evasive driving course and it must have helped some."

"Evasive driving. Sounds dangerous."

"It can be." She smiled. "But I thought it was kind of exciting."

"You're quite an unusual lady, Miss Manning."

Jane colored a little and said nothing.

The forensic man had a small office in the city, downtown near the docks on the west side of Manhattan. Jane pulled up in front of the nondescript building and turned the car off. This was, in her judgment, the most dangerous part of the job. Anyone could be waiting for them—in that alley or behind that pile of garbage, in any of the parked cars along the curb, in a store across the street. She was ready, all senses on the alert, her muscles ready to react to any subliminal signals she might get from an abnormal presence.

She checked the area carefully, then stepped out of the car and locked her door. Blast it, her hands were a little shaky. Rick waited for her all-clear sign. It was 4:00 p.m. The street wasn't very crowded and no one looked out of context in the normal flow of people.

Satisfied, Jane motioned to Rick who unlocked his door, stepped out and headed quickly to the entrance of the building where he moved aside to allow her to go in first.

"Just in case," she said crisply, watchful for the slightest movement ahead of her on the stairs. The halls in the old building were dark—too dark, Jane decided— moving up a flight of stairs, still ahead of Rick. At the top of the steps she scanned the dim corridor. There were several doors, all closed, and she walked slowly down the hall until she found the one they were looking for. In another five minutes they were leaving the building, the job done, but that keyed-up sense of danger still held Jane in its grip.

"I'm always glad when I make a delivery," said Rick as he got back in the car. "Especially lately. You just never know when someone's going to jump out at you. I was one of the couriers robbed back in June," he added. "I'll tell you, it was goddamned scary!"

"Did you have a chance to stop them?"

"No way! I was alone and one of the men waved a gun under my nose."

"You did the sensible thing," Jane declared. "Nothing is worth getting killed over."

"You can say that again. And another thing—" he looked over at her in earnest "—I'm real glad to have you along today."

"My pleasure." She put the car in gear, headed down the street and wondered if Rick noticed that her hands had finally stopped shaking.

"WHEN IS SHE DUE BACK?" Graham was asking Donna.

"About five, I guess." Donna put a fresh stick of gum in her mouth. "She went to Atlantic City with Rick."

"Oh?" Was there anything Donna didn't know?

"Yeah. To a casino there. They were picking up some marked cards, taking them to a guy over on Eighth."

"Interesting."

"Oh, well, we have lots of exciting cases here. Maybe not as big-time as you do, though." She smiled and winked at him. "When are you going to quit traipsing around the world on your own and settle down?"

"Why, Donna, I didn't know you were interested." He shot her a rakish grin.

"I've got a boyfriend, Mr. Quicksilver. And besides, you are definitely not the stable kind. A girl would have to go through hell trying to get you to the altar!"

"Yes," said Graham, winking, "but wouldn't it be fun?"

He left a note for Jane.

Dear Jane,
I'm cooking in tonight. If you're free how about eight o'clock? If you'll recall, I'm a dynamite cook. Please come.

Love, Graham.

It was a dozen blocks or so farther downtown to his apartment. Graham usually walked, as he loved the city and the crowds and the unique pulse of New York. Besides, he kept his Porsche in a rented garage because to leave it on the street—even for the few minutes he'd spent with Lew—was a sure way to lose his hubcaps at the very least.

He whistled a nameless tune as he walked the street in long, easy strides, his hands in the pockets of his linen jacket, a smile curving his lips.

What to cook for Jane? It never occurred to him that

she might not come. He was sure Jane wanted to be with him as much as he did with her. They fit together, as if some unknown hand had molded two bodies decades ago for the single purpose of their eventual, inevitable union.

What a grand scheme life was!

He shopped at a neighborhood market, a small, cramped store with ceiling-to-floor shelves loaded with every imaginable item, pyramids of fresh fruits and vegetables, foreign specialties and a great butcher section. Safeway had nothing on Alfredo's market.

While he picked over the fresh vegetables he put Jane from his thoughts momentarily and mused over the plan he'd presented to Lew. It was a sound idea. And with Norma along in Amsterdam—forget that their time together would no doubt be uncomfortable—they were sure to thwart Lew's robbers. How could any crooks resist the temptation of grabbing ten million in diamonds? It would be a cinch to fence them. Of course, the fence would take a big cut, at least sixty percent or better, but diamonds were essentially untraceable and the thieves would come away with well over a couple of million. They *had* to try for the stones, didn't they?

"Good evening, Mr. Smith," said Alfredo, grinning his stained, uneven smile, his white butcher's jacket smeared with the day's labors. "I have nice fresh tomatoes today. Picked in Jersey this morning. You want some?"

"Sure, pick me out three."

"I have no seen you for a while, Mr. Smith. You been away? The heat is bad this summer, yes?"

"Terrible," agreed Graham when in reality he hadn't actually noticed it. He guessed his thoughts had been too consumed with other matters. Matters like Jane, for instance.

"How about finding me a nice plump chicken?" asked Graham. "Real fresh."

"I got just the one for you."

Carrying his grocery bag, Graham took the steps up to

his place by twos. He felt great, like a new man, one who had the world at his feet. It was, he supposed, all due to Jane.

He put his groceries away and got out the good linen and china, then went to shower and change. His body still damp, he slipped on a clean pair of pearl-gray linen trousers and a loose, blue cotton shirt, which he rolled up at the sleeves, then went to the kitchen to start the dinner. In the background the stereo was playing classical music at the moment. As he deftly sliced the tomatoes, he wondered if Jane liked that kind of music. He'd have to ask her, maybe take her to the Kennedy Center one night. Then, after a late supper…

Graham's pot simmered away on the stove while a glass of white wine sat half empty on the tile countertop. He glanced at the time: 8:00 p.m. Surely if Jane had other plans she'd have called him by now. So she must be on her way. The evening's scenario filled his thoughts. They'd dine by candlelight, talk for a while. He'd have to ask her about spending the following weekend at his dad's place but how could she refuse him when they had to be in Washington that Monday, anyway? Of course, *she* didn't know that yet.

Jane. What a stroke of luck—or fate—that they'd met. Jane, with those long legs and nice curves, those clear green eyes with the dark lashes, the bridge of freckles across her nose, those beautiful soft lips. And that slightly uneven tooth. Could Jane be the one he was waiting for? Was he actually falling for the girl from Rifle, Colorado? What told a man that he'd met his lifelong mate? Sure, Graham loved dozens of things about Jane; he adored the way she moved, lithely and with self-assurance. And her honesty appealed to him. There was no fear whatsoever in Graham that she might someday turn into a nag. Not Jane. But how was he supposed to know that she was the one?

Again he glanced at the clock: 8:10. Maybe he'd been too overconfident in expecting her to come over.

At 8:12 the door buzzer sounded. Graham rose quickly from his chair and felt his heart begin a heavy, pleasant rhythm.

CHAPTER SEVEN

THE NOTE WAS TAPED to Jane's office door. Donna, she thought. Who else? She scanned the paper, smiled to herself, then read it again slowly, savoring each word, trying to read between the lines, noting Graham's slapdash slanted writing. She plunked herself down in her office chair and wiggled her feet out of her shoes while she reread his note, lost in thought, remembering. Then she jerked back into the present and checked the time. Oh boy, almost seven!

Should she call him right now and ask if she could come over early, just as she was? But, after all, she didn't know him *that* well. Besides she felt grubby after the long day in the car. She wanted to be fresh and clean and fragrant for Graham.

She took the subway to her hotel and raced around her room getting ready. He was waiting for her in his venerable old brownstone, chilling wine perhaps or tossing a salad. How would it be between them now, after they'd made love? Would they be awkward and uncomfortable with each other? No, she thought, shaking her head. What had happened between them was natural and wonderful.

She ran out to the busy corner to hail a taxi, hopping with impatience as one after another flew by with fares inside. Eventually one stopped at her frantic waving. "I swear," she said to the cabbie, "I was ready to throw myself in front of the next cab that didn't stop."

"Lady, you get a ticket for that kinda stunt," was all he replied as he headed downtown, jerking forward, slam-

ming on the brakes, mumbling at other drivers, rolling
through red lights.

But Jane didn't notice. A familiar excitement gripped
her. Graham. Her knees felt weak at the thought of his
lovemaking. She'd put aside those notions for the day
because her job allowed for no distractions but now she
was free to think about him, to recall the feel of his lips
and every word he'd said and how he looked. She dared
say the words to herself: *I love Graham Smith,* but then
quickly retreated from them. How could she love a man
she'd only known for a few days? Love had to grow and
there hadn't been the time for that. But there could be.
Why not? And if he turned out to be other than lovable,
well then, she'd count their affair as experience and keep
looking. But she couldn't imagine finding a man as stimulating, as gorgeous, as fascinating as Graham Smith.

When the taxi pulled up in front of his brownstone,
Jane paid the driver and got out. She was nervous all of
a sudden. This dating game was unsettling, and she didn't
really know Graham well enough to feel at ease. There
was the green door just up those stairs, the windows with
their heavy green drapes. And Graham.

Had she dressed properly? It seemed in New York that
you could wear anything under the sun but there was still
a certain, intangible big city flair to women's fashions.
Even the teenyboppers in their jeans and sweatshirts had
that *look.* She'd worn her tan skirt and an emerald-green
crocheted top with a V neck. The back of her neck felt
damp in the overcast, muggy weather and she thought
maybe she looked small-townish and gauche.

Oh well. Jane squared her shoulders and climbed the
stairs. He'd asked her to dinner so he must want to see
her. She used the brass knocker and the door opened almost instantly.

"Janey," he said and her breath caught in her throat.
She'd forgotten how handsome he was, how strikingly fair
and tall and bursting with vigor. He pulled her in and

kissed her on the mouth, hard. "I thought you'd never get here."

"We were late getting in," she said breathlessly, remembering once again the night they'd shared, the naked skin, the moans and touching, the intimacy. She knew she was blushing and she saw in Graham's laughing blue gaze that he remembered every vivid detail only too well.

He held her away from him and studied her face. "It went all right? The job, I mean?"

"Oh, yes, no problems."

"Good. Come in. I'm starving. How about you? Wine?"

Jane wrinkled her nose and sniffed the air. "Mmm, that sure smells heavenly."

"Chicken cacciatore. Old family recipe." He laughed as he poured her a glass of wine. "Actually it's out of the *Single Man's Cookbook*."

He led the way into the living room and they sat down on the sofa. "We'll eat in a minute," he said. "I want to hear all about your day. You were with Rick, right?"

"Yes, Rick. He's very nice. He told me about his son's braces and his daughter's bad grades. We drove to Atlantic City, we drove back. Routine."

"In this business routine means success. Remember that, Janey."

He'd set the dining table beautifully: Waterford crystal, fine English bone china, white linen tablecloth and napkins, brass candlesticks with tall white candles.

"Graham, you went to so much trouble," Jane protested.

"I'm only trying to impress you. Next time it's paper plates on your lap, lady."

He lit the candles and turned the lights down. A recording of a jazz quartet played mellow rhythms in the background. A slice of delicate green honeydew garnished with dark red, rolled-up prosciutto sat on a glass plate before her.

"This is wonderful," she said, leaning across the table and putting her hand over his. "I do appreciate it."

He turned his hand, grasped her fingers and lifted them to his lips, kissing each one in turn. "My pleasure, Janey," he murmured, holding her gaze.

Jane's stomach flip-flopped and her skin felt hot all over. "Let me go or we'll never get to eat," she whispered.

He grinned, gave her hand another quick kiss and released it. "Dig in," he said and picked up his fork.

They talked ceaselessly, making very slow going of the dinner. There was so much to catch up on. It almost made Jane mad that there was an enormous amount of Graham's past that she still didn't know about.

"Foreign affairs?" she asked at one point. "That must have been interesting."

"I *thought* it was going to be interesting. You see, I wanted to be a spy and I figured that was the way to do it."

"So why aren't you a spy?"

"I found out it was too much trouble. You have to lie a lot. I hate to lie."

"Me, too." She went on cutting up her chicken breast with its tangy sauce. "Umm, this is good."

Graham chewed some pasta and swallowed. "So what was it like going to the University of Colorado?"

"Fun. It's a party school. But I learned a lot. I loved fine arts and history."

"Then you went to vet school?"

"I love animals, too."

"A Renaissance woman."

"Hardly. I'm a ranch girl." She emptied her wineglass.

"More?" He poured without waiting for her answer, filling her glass with a sparkling dry Italian red wine.

Jane wondered how many women he'd had over to dinner, how many women he'd wined and dined and bedded on the leopard-spotted sheets. She felt no jealousy, merely a keen curiosity. The knowledge would help define Graham Smith, but if she asked he might get the wrong idea.

"Do you date a lot of women?" she inquired carefully.

"I told you there was nothing to worry about, remember? I *have* dated a lot of women. Right now I'm not interested in anyone but you."

"Graham..." she began.

"Hey, that's no line. I mean it. I hate games, Janey."

She smiled tenderly. "I believe you."

"Good. What about you? You must have been the belle of Rifle."

She shrugged. "There was really never anyone serious, aside from Branch, and even that petered out. In college there were a few, you know, the usual. I guess I was practicing."

"For what?"

"For you." She watched as his expression softened. She wanted to touch him, to hold him close and feel his heat and his strength.

"Jane..." he started to say but the phone rang. "Damn."

"Go on. I'll still be here when you get back."

She couldn't help but hear his side of the conversation. "Dad, how are you?" It was obviously his father calling.

He paused as if listening. "No, I can't make it this weekend. Next weekend, for sure. I'll drive down Friday."

Jane idly watched Graham's tapered back in his blue shirt. She wanted to walk up behind him and press her body all along the whole length of him. "Yeah, no problem, it's convenient," he was saying. "Oh, did that carburetor come in yet? Great. Maybe I'll get a chance to put it in the boat. Then we can do some fishing."

He had a boat. Where? Oh yes, his father lived on the shore in North, or was it South, Carolina?

"Dad, think you could clean the old place up a bit?"

He paused. "Well, because I'm thinking of bringing a guest down with me."

Jane's ears perked. A guest? Who?

"Yes, female." He sounded exasperated. "I think you'll like her a lot, Dad." Then Graham laughed. "Okay, good. See you next Friday. Late afternoon probably. Bye."

Graham came back to the table and sat down across from Jane. "You'll come, won't you?" he asked.

"What?"

"You'll come down to my father's. Please. Next weekend."

"You mean that was *me* you were talking about?"

"Who else?"

"You want me to go down to your father's with you for the weekend?"

He grinned. "Chicken?"

"Well, no but…are you sure?"

"Are *you*?"

"I'd love to."

"Fantastic. More wine?" he asked, holding up the bottle.

"Sure. I'm off tomorrow. Did I hear you say you have a boat?"

"Yes. Actually it's my dad's but I use it more than he does now. It's an old wooden job, named the *Renée*."

"*Renée*," mused Jane.

"That's my mother's name. The boat was built for their honeymoon over thirty-five years ago. It's a beautiful thing. No fiberglass hulls in those days."

"A boat," Jane said with a sigh. "I've always wanted to go out on the ocean."

"We will, okay?"

"Oh, Graham, that'll be great. You're sure your father won't mind?"

"Janey, sweetheart, he'll adore you. Don't worry."

"Well, you met my family, so I guess it's my turn," she said, laughing.

"I wish you could meet Mom, too," he went on, wistfully, Jane thought. "But she's up in Montreal."

"Are they...divorced?"

Graham sighed. "No, not yet. They're separated. I may as well explain it all. They split up about a year ago, after Dad retired. They were driving each other crazy. I guess they both sort of had middle-age crises."

"Oh, that's too bad. After all those years together."

"Yes. Well, anyway, they're trying separation. I guess they're both at fault although I tend to side with Dad, maybe because I'm a man. But Mom tried to make him over. She'd been trying for thirty years but when he retired and started doing just what he wanted she went sort of nuts. She made him so miserable—and herself." He paused to drink some wine then swirled the ruby liquid in the glass and stared at it thoughtfully. "Women always seem to make men over, don't they?"

"What do you mean?"

"They want men to work harder or not work so hard. To eat less or drink less or dress better or help more in the house. Whatever. It's always something. A woman marries a man because she loves him, or says she does, then proceeds to make him over."

"Now wait a minute," said Jane quickly. "You're generalizing. A lot of women think their men don't need making over and a lot more know it's a waste of time to try."

"Really?"

"I mean, sure, people will argue. You'd argue with anyone you lived with long enough. Take my brothers, for instance. Holy cow, did we argue! And don't think men don't try to make their wives over just as much. Why, there's this one poor lady in Rifle who got breast implants because her dear hubby liked big boobs!"

"Holy Toledo, Janey, I didn't mean to get you going..."

"Well, you did. Sorry. I think maybe you're a little sensitive on the subject."

"Maybe."

"Really, I'm sorry." She tried to smile. "Did we just have an argument?"

"Sort of. A mild difference of opinion, anyway."

"Oh, my. You're upset about your folks and I start preaching." She sat back in her seat and fiddled with her napkin. "Sometimes I have an awful big mouth."

"I love your mouth."

"Are you going to say things like that in front of your father?" she asked, smiling with relief that he wasn't angry.

"Maybe. Would you mind?"

"I'd be embarrassed."

"Listen, Smedley—"

"*Smedley*?"

"That's my dad's name, Smedley. His father was Smedley, too. It's an old Quaker name. Anyway, I was going to say, Smedley is a bit eccentric. Operates on his own wavelength, so to speak. A brilliant man, mind you, but he's a free spirit. He probably wouldn't notice if I grabbed you and kissed you right in front of him. He'd just ask something like, 'Why do you suppose people put their lips together to show affection? Now, dogs are much more sensible. They...'"

Jane started giggling. "Stop," she said, "I'm afraid of what you might say."

"And you'd have a right to be. How about a safer subject: dessert. I've made brandied fruit with whipped cream."

"Sounds absolutely delectable. But first I have to use the bathroom. I'll be right back."

"It's upstairs, on the..."

"I remember," she said, feeling flushed.

"Oh, sure."

Was it the wine that was making Jane feel so warm, so

full of anticipation, so absolutely relaxed? But she hadn't had that much. She made her way up the stairs to the bathroom. The mirror showed a face she almost didn't recognize—bright-eyed, pink-cheeked, lips curved with a lazy, secret kind of smile. She fluffed her hair, washed her hands and stepped out into the hall. Curiosity nudged her to peek into the half-open door across from Graham's bedroom.

There was a dark wooden four-poster bed with a mauve-and-white patterned spread, a dressing table with filigree boxes, gilt brushes, bottles and tubes and flowered china containers. Very feminine. She couldn't resist—the closet door was ajar. Inside were several clear plastic garment bags of women's clothes and one containing a full-length dark brown fur coat.

A woman lived in that room. Or *had* lived in that room. It still smelled faintly of lavender and mothballs and expensive perfume.

Jane withheld judgment carefully. She found Graham humming a tune, serving up the brandied fruit into cut glass bowls. He lifted his head at her appearance. "Just in time. There's espresso, too."

"Graham, whose room is that across from yours?" The question came out more forcefully than she intended, and she was afraid she sounded demanding and strident—and nosy.

He stopped what he was doing, the spoon in his hand suspended in midair, dripping brandy. His eyes crinkled up in mirth. "Would you believe a live-in maid?"

"No."

"Smart girl." He put the spoon down and approached her. "My God, Janey, this is the first crack in your unflappable aplomb I've seen. Should I believe my eyes?"

"Graham, I just…"

"You're jealous," he said, softly, wonderingly.

"I just…"

"I can't bear your suffering. Alas! I must confess…"

"Graham, I'm not jealous, just curious. Whoever it is she sure has darn good taste."

"It's my mother's room, the famed Renée."

"Oh."

"She comes to shop and likes her surroundings—shall we say—compatible. It's very handy for her."

"I'm sorry I'm so nosy."

"Janey, I have nothing to hide. Ask me whatever you want. Ask away. God, you're wonderful. You really weren't jealous." He came closer and smiled down at her. "I'd grab you and kiss you right this second but my hands are all sticky from the fruit."

Jane took one of his hands and deliberately, slowly, turned it over and licked the sweet syrup off one finger. Then another. Their eyes met and she could see that his were filled with heat, with need, mirroring her own. Then she was in his arms, breathing in his scent, feeling the hard strength of him, tasting the nectar of his mouth.

"Do you still want dessert?" he finally breathed in her ear.

"Later," she whispered back.

She slid her hands under his shirt and kneaded the taut muscles of his back. Graham was pulling her top over her head and then kissing her neck and her shoulder, tickling her unbearably until gooseflesh appeared all over her skin.

"Upstairs," Graham said in a strangled voice.

They started toward the staircase but stopped on the way to kiss, to clutch at warm, bare skin, to breathe in each other's scent. Jane's skirt fell by a table, her shoes were kicked off at the bottom step. Graham's shirt was thrown over the banister.

"I can't wait," he said and when Jane laughed softly, he swooped her up in his arms and started up the stairs, bumping into the wall in his haste.

"I'm too heavy, put me down," she protested, hanging onto him.

"No, you're not. You're light as a feather." But he was gasping, stumbling up the stairs.

"You're crazy, we'll both fall down the steps!"

"You're not being romantic, Janey," he panted.

"Graham, put me down. I promise to be romantic." Laughter bubbled up in her as she ducked her head away from the wall.

"Okay." They were halfway up the stairs, both nearly naked. It struck Jane so funny she buried her face in his chest and shook with merriment.

"It's not nice to laugh at me," Graham pointed out as he settled her on her feet.

"Sorry," she replied.

"Come on then, walk if you're so damn heavy." He took her hand and pulled her along to his room.

They stopped once more at the foot of his bed and Jane undid his pants so that they slid to the floor. "Umm, you're gorgeous," she whispered, kissing his face, his neck, his hard chest, nibbling at his skin with gentle little bites.

The leopard-patterned sheets awaited them. They lay facing each other, locked together, mouth to mouth, hip to hip. His hardness ground into Jane as she stroked his thick hair and kneaded his shoulder. Her breath came faster in exquisite anticipation. Then Graham bent his head and kissed one breast. His tongue found her nipple, his mouth closed over it and he sucked gently. An electric shock of pleasure shot through Jane and she moaned and pulled his head nearer.

"Now," she breathed, "please, now," and he rose over her and entered her swiftly, filled her, pulled back slowly, then filled her again. She moved under him, meeting his thrusts, her hands urgent on his back and his buttocks, her cries mingling with his harsh breathing.

They climbed together, slowly and sensuously, then more quickly and harder, rocking as one entity; they were a match, fitting together in utmost perfection, striving in unison for release.

When it came Jane cried out and shuddered with the powerful ecstasy of it and she felt Graham deep in her, sharing the glory with her, giving, receiving, adoring her with his body.

"Oh," she said breathlessly a moment later but then there was nothing else to say, no words with which to express her pleasure, her wonder.

Graham lay over her, supported on his elbows. "Is that all—*oh*?"

"That's all. I haven't energy for anything else."

Silently he traced her eyebrow with one finger, then moved down her nose, around her lips, feather-light, sweetly, reverently. She nibbled at his finger and sighed deeply.

"Happy?" he asked.

"Totally."

His finger kept sketching the lines of her face: jaw, forehead, ears, eyebrows again. "You're absolutely lovely," he said.

"You're prejudiced," she murmured.

"Of course. Would you want me any other way?"

"I'd want you any old way," Jane said into the darkness, turning toward him once again.

CHAPTER EIGHT

"What, exactly," asked Jane, "are these Outer Banks that your father lives on?"

Graham glanced over at her, smiled, then moved his eyes back to the country road that followed the coast of North Carolina. "Basically, it's a ninety-mile long sandbar. Only about a mile wide, though. The Atlantic is to the east, and there's a scattering of sounds, or bays, to the west."

"Oh," said Jane. "A far cry from Rifle, Colorado." The top was down on Graham's red Porsche and the hot summer sun of the South was beating down on her head and shoulders. It was a steamy heat the likes of which Jane had never felt before, a fierce, wet heat laced with salt from the ocean. She could even taste the salt on her lips and her body felt sluggish and covered with a fine sheen of moisture, as if she'd just bathed. No wonder the North had been first to industrialize while the South had lazed the long summer days away in slow self-indulgence.

They'd driven down from New York through New Jersey to the squat peninsula dividing Chesapeake Bay from the Atlantic Ocean, taken the twenty-one-mile long Chesapeake Bay Bridge-Tunnel from Cape Charles back onto the mainland of Virginia and kept the sports car pointed south along the farm-dotted coast.

Jane had done her best to listen to Graham as he gave her a guided tour from the hustle and bustle of the North into the ageless serenity of the South. From time to time one of his hands would leave the leather steering wheel and he'd indicate a landmark. "Over there across from the bay is Norfolk, where all the big naval carriers come in," he'd say and she would follow the direction of his hand, unable to see anything but the strength of his muscled forearm and its crisp blond curling hairs. She could shut her eyes and almost feel that arm encircling her, drawing her close, pressing her naked body to his.

Every move Graham made as he drove isolated itself in her mind. She'd never noticed how strong his neck was or that his shoulders beneath the light green polo shirt were wide and square. And his thighs as he braked or used the clutch—they were long and tapered and powerful looking.

"About ten more miles and we'll cross a bridge and be on the Outer Banks," Graham explained. "You'll love it there. Everyone does."

"I love anything different," she said cheerfully, blotting her damp brow with her wrist. "But, Lord, this heat!"

Graham, however, didn't seem one bit bothered. He'd kept the top down the whole way—an eight-hour drive—and his strawberry-blond hair had blown into a mass of wind-beaten strands. His forehead was burned a deep reddish brown, and his cheeks and nose, even though he'd already had a tan, were seared as well. Only his eyes, because he wore aviator-style sunglasses, had been spared. Of course, she could have asked him to put the top up, but he was enjoying himself so much and, she had to admit, so was she.

The road, which had been flanked by cornfields, hog farms, stands of pines and oaks, maples and magnolias, finally opened up to marshland and there was the bridge of which Graham had spoken, arching up gracefully over a sparkling bay. And beyond, the Outer Banks.

"It *smells* like an ocean," Jane said.

"Of course!" He laughed good-naturedly. "Have you ever seen the Atlantic before?"

She smiled. "Only through some buildings."

The moment the Porsche sped onto the bridge, Jane felt an immediate, welcome drop in the temperature. Maybe she'd survive the heat after all. And then with a swish of tires they were on the barrier island, flying past the reeds lining the bay, cresting a sandy hill. And there, spread majestically before her was the deep blue Atlantic as far as she could see to the north and south, the sun sparkling off distant whitecaps, lines and lines of them that disappeared over the curve of the eastern horizon.

"It's beautiful," she murmured.

"I know," he agreed. "I fell in love with it the very first time I came down here."

"When was that?"

"Fifteen years ago or so. When my parents built their house as a vacation home."

"How long has your dad lived here year-round?"

"Close to four years now, I guess. Since retiring from the service."

"It's so...so remote," said Jane, feeling the wild quality of her surroundings as Graham turned onto a broken beach road and raced along the coast. She could only see the ocean now and again as there were sand dunes covered with sea oats barring her vision and a house or two, some even built on stilts.

"I take it there are floods here," she said.

"Sure. Especially during a hurricane but a good strong nor'easter can bring the waves in as well. It's the time of year for them. Maybe we'll brew one up for you and *then* you'll get a sight of wild ocean."

"No thanks."

He gave Jane the Cook's tour. "There's quite a story behind those sand dunes. Back in the forties the Army Corps of Engineers used bulldozers to form them but maintaining them proved to be too expensive, so now the natives just let the waves do their damage. The locals down here kind of shrug their shoulders at most everything. Especially the sea. They've learned you can't tame it so they let the ocean do its worst, then get out their shovels and rebuild all over again.''

"Sounds like a lot of work.''

"Maybe. But there's no fighting nature, Jane. Better to let it take its course.'' He glanced at her slyly out of the corner of his eye. "You know, like us.''

"Is that what it is with us,'' she asked archly, "simply Mother Nature?''

His right hand left the steering wheel and reached out to stroke her knee lightly while his eyes stayed on the road. "Janey, sweetheart, I can't even begin to tell you how much more I feel for you. Of course, the nature stuff isn't half bad,'' he teased, "for lapses in conversation.''

"You're awful.''

"I'm not, you know I'm not. As a matter of fact, I distinctly remember you calling me wonderful. Now, when was it? Wait a sec, I'll get it in a minute.'' He gave her a quick grin.

"Stop teasing, Graham.'' But Jane couldn't help the heat from flushing her cheeks nor could she stop her heart from pounding against her ribs. There was something special about Graham Smith, something she found difficult to put into words. He possessed a unique hunger to really live, to enjoy each moment no matter what. It was a kind of drive, a physical thing. His craving to see and do everything, to take the world by the tail and shake it reminded Jane of traits she'd seen in a lot of rodeo-circuit cowboys; they just kept moving, kept challenging their surroundings, pushing their limits.

And yet, she thought, as he pulled into a long sandy driveway, Graham did not scare her with his zest for life. Rather, it drew her, compelled her to find out what he was all about. To live life with him.

Sitting atop a dune was a silvering, wood-framed house that had rather a strange shape. "Your dad's?'' asked Jane.

He nodded, downshifting in the sand, sliding around a curve and kicking up gravel. "It's supposed to look like a ship's prow. Does, if you're on the beach side and looking up at it."

"I like it," she stated.

"And I hope you like Dad, too. Although, like I warned you, he's a bit offbeat and takes some getting used to."

She wondered just how weird his father was. Would she like him at all? Would he like her?

They got out in front of a garage and Jane smelled the strong, salty air and felt the sand sift into her sandals and between her toes.

"Dad's car's here but I don't see him around. Must be—" But his words were cut off when Jane heard a growling sound. She turned to Graham questioningly but her attention was diverted by two lean Doberman pinschers bounding toward Graham from around the corner of the garage.

Instantly, her training making her reaction automatic, Jane threw herself between Graham and the vicious dogs who were still racing toward them, barking wildly, pink tongues flapping, sharp white eyeteeth gleaming. She crouched, putting one arm up to fend off the attack, while she searched the area desperately for a club or a rock or anything to use as a weapon.

"No! Jane, don't!" came Graham's voice from behind her and she froze, uncertain, poised between aiming a blow at a dog's head and obeying Graham's command, but then it was too late to do anything because suddenly the animals were leaping through the air, knocking Graham clean off his feet and... Amazingly, their short tails were wagging and Graham was gasping and laughing and pushing the beasts off him.

"It's only Heckle and Jeckle," he was telling her as he tried to avoid their sloppy tongues, "Dad's watchdogs."

Jane straightened, put her hands on her hips and cocked a brow. "Why didn't you warn me?" she asked, hovering between irritation and amusement while she watched Graham struggle to get up.

"I forgot. Now give me a hand, will you? These stupid mutts…"

She slapped her thigh and called forcefully. "Here, Heckle, here, Jeckle. That's enough, you two bad dogs!"

They obeyed, turning toward her, their ears alert and upright, their noses testing; then, tongues flopping happily, they trotted toward her, ready to renew the game.

"My God, these are the worst trained animals I've ever seen," she said to Graham. "Get down!" she snapped at the dogs but they were bent on leaping up at her now, their sandy, salty paws leaving smudges all over her white shorts. "You two wouldn't last a day on the ranch. My dad would shoot you and hang you out to cure!"

"He wouldn't," said Graham with assurance.

"He just might," Jane replied under her breath.

With the dogs at her heels, she followed Graham inside. "Are they allowed in?" she asked, trying to close the door in their faces.

"They have the run of the house." Graham shrugged, then laughed at Jane's expression of disgust.

"The least you could do then," she said, "is teach them some manners."

He tried to check his laughter. "We did. But they were smarter."

"Very funny."

Jane followed Graham into the living room while one dog playfully chewed at her ankle.

"Anyone home?" Graham called. "Dad?"

"Out here, on the sun deck!" came a slightly accented voice.

For a moment Jane stood in the center of the room and looked around, bemused. The place was as close to the interior of a ship as an architect could make it. Triangular in shape, two walls were wood-paneled, while the other, which faced the ocean, was entirely glass. On one of the wood walls was a large fireplace and on the other hung paintings of seascapes, adding color to the room. Beneath her feet was a blue rug, recently vacuumed, Jane noted. The furnishings were serviceable and looked comfortable: a big couch with lots of pillows facing the fireplace, several floor lamps, a glass coffee table with sea shells scattered on its top. In front of the glass wall sat an antique dining table, its rough wood faded and bleached, an old whaler's lamp sitting in the center. There were benches on either side of the table. No chairs.

"What a great room," Jane declared.

"Dad thought it up. I like it a lot, too." One of the dogs hopped up onto the couch. "Get down, Heckle," Graham said, glancing at Jane sheepishly.

"Oh, brother," she mumbled, giving in and, against her better judgment, petting Heckle's head.

"Maybe I'll give them to you for Christmas," Graham said, leading the way out onto a spacious deck that faced the ocean.

Jane's first sight of Graham's father was startling. It was hard not to stare.

Smedley Smith, all six feet two inches of him, was maneuvering on some strange contraption made of what appeared to be old beach junk: gray rotted wood planks; rusty bolts and nails; a rubber tire; faded, stretched cords; a vintage bicycle speedometer.

If forced to put words to the homemade *thing*, Jane would have said it was a rowing machine but that would have been stretching the imagination.

"Dad," Graham was saying, "this is Jane, Jane Manning."

"Hello!" he called cheerfully, pumping his sunscorched arms and legs madly, gasping while the contraption creaked and protested.

Her first impression of Smedley was one of beautiful clear-blue eyes and a strong, masculine face. His hair, which was silvering strawberry-blond and on the long side, was being whipped around from the strong ocean breeze. He was still well-built, but his clothes—Jane tried not to gape—were not at all what she had expected from a well-educated, purportedly sophisticated gentleman. Whereas Graham dressed impeccably, his English-American father was wearing old worn madras shorts, sixties' vintage; a torn, faded T-shirt that read Wink's Groceries; and Topsiders without socks, with a big toe showing through one of them.

"From...Colorado," he breathed, "Graham tells...me. Great state, that."

"Yes," Jane replied awkwardly, "I was born and raised there."

"You can...tell me all...about it at...dinner, Jane. For now—" gasp, pump, pant "—why don't you...two go for a...swim." Jeckle stuck out his drooping tongue and licked Smedley's ear with a slurp. "Go...away!"

"Hey," said Graham, "a swim sounds great. Are you game, Jane?"

"Sure, why not?" Anything to collect herself for a few minutes. This place was...unusual.

Before fetching their suitcases, Graham showed her to a guest room down the hall from his own. It was a small tidy room, sparsely furnished. On two sides were windows, one facing north toward the sand dunes, the other facing ocean. Both windows were open and Jane went to one to close it as she was unused to the constant, roaring drone of the sea. As she tugged it down, she noticed a wire hanging out of the window, leading down into a small puddle. She wondered what it was there for, then shrugged, dismissing it.

There was a double bed, a low dresser and shaving mirror, a rocker and a plant stand. In spite of all the sunlight, the plant was as dead as a doornail.

"Here's your suitcase," Graham said, placing it on the floor. Coming over to her, he pushed her playfully down onto the bed, then bent over and covered her lips with his. "Umm," he groaned against her mouth, "you taste good."

But Jane was embarrassed. What if his father… "Stop it," she protested, albeit unconvincingly. "Your dad."

"He's still exercising." He slipped his hands up under her shirt and unsnapped her bra.

"Graham!"

Then his fingers were on her breasts, lightly tracing teasing circles around her nipples, and Jane knew that if he didn't stop in a minute she'd be lost. She pushed him away. "Not in your father's house. Promise me."

"Ah, come on, Jane."

"No." She stood and straightened her shirt. "Promise me."

"Oh, all right," he relented, his eyes twinkling. "But I'll bet you've never done it in the ocean."

"Graham." She tried not to smile.

"Okay. I guess I better let you change, huh?"

"Uh, Graham, what's that wire doing hanging out the window?" She had to ask.

"You'll never believe it if I tell you."

"Yes, I will. Please tell me."

"Well, during thunderstorms Dad runs the wire into the large puddle that forms outside the window. Then he hooks the inside end up to a battery charger." He hesitated. "It's really strange, Jane. Sure you want to hear?"

"Go on."

"Well, then he hooks himself up to the charger and—"

"Hooks himself up?"

"He uses pads covered with aluminum foil and tapes them to his chest. Then he regulates the current, you know, he gives himself electrical shocks."

"My God, you mean like…*Frankenstein*?"

Graham tried to look casual. "Sort of, I suppose. Dad claims the electricity is good for his heart. Keeps it in balance, he says."

Jane was utterly speechless.

"I warned you," he said, making a hasty exit.

She put on the new lavender swimsuit she'd bought especially for this trip. It was cut high on the thigh and plunged rather daringly in front and back, but she was pleased with the effect. Pulling on an oversized shirt and slipping into her sandals, she went to join Graham and his father on the sun deck.

"Hello again, Mr. Smith," she began uncertainly, unable to forget the wires and the battery charger.

"Call me Smedley, please." Without asking he handed her a glass of thick, reddish liquid. "V-8 juice. Good for what ails you."

"Thank you," said Jane dubiously. She'd have preferred an iced tea or a lemonade in this heat. She drank it anyway and was surprised. "It tastes good."

"Perfect on a hot day. It gets the juices flowing."

"I certainly hope so," replied Jane, "because I'm so hot I feel like I can't move."

"A swim will do you good. And then we'll all fish for our dinner."

She cocked her head. "You mean, you can swim right alongside your dinner out there?"

Smedley and Graham laughed, their deep male tones drifting on the offshore breeze. "I suggest you take your ring off, though," said Graham, sobering. "The bluefish have been known to take a shiny finger as bait."

The dogs were running in and out of the surf, barking wildly, as Jane and Graham swam. But this was no lake, she was discovering. There was a strong undertow just beneath the surface of the water.

"Don't go out any farther!" Graham called and Jane moved into shore a few feet, noticing that there were no lifeguards nor was there another living soul anywhere up or down the beach. They could have been marooned on a deserted island. Cooled off, they got out the fishing poles and Graham taught Jane how to cast out over the breakers.

"What if I get a shark?"

"We'll eat it and call it scallops. Plenty of people do."

"Say, where's your boat?" asked Jane.

"It's down the coast at a marina."

"Can we go see it?"

"Sure, we'll check out the old girl tomorrow."

Neither Jane nor Graham had put their shirts back on. She glanced sidelong at him often, too often, enjoying the sight of his strong legs flexing, his feet embedded in the soft sand, the muscles of his thighs and back moving fluidly as he cast his line. And she knew he was looking at her as well, in her lavender suit that hid absolutely nothing. Her legs were sandy, her skin salty, her hair stiff and brushed back off her forehead and she felt totally natural and uninhibited, as wild as these Outer Banks of Graham's, untamed and ready for anything.

They fished in their wet swimsuits while the hot afternoon sun gilded their skin. Her senses were keen and aroused, the world narrowed down to a universe of simple, totally physical sensations. She could feel the cool water sucking the smooth sand out from under her toes, the reflected heat of the beach on her back, the pull of the rod against her arm muscles. And there was Graham standing next to her, tall and carefree. Sinews stood out on his arms as he threw the line out, his thighs tensed, his hair tossed in the breeze. There was something about Graham, something special and innocent and vital. She wanted him right then, fiercely.

Evening fell over the Outer Banks with a red sun setting behind the dunes and lighting the waving sea oats to a golden color. They fried Graham's fish outside on a grill and Smedley, an expert chef, watched over the charcoals. "Tomorrow you'll catch a fish," he told Jane. "Graham's had lots of experience. You have to know when the blues are just sniffing around and nudging your line or when they've actually bitten. You'll master it." He took the spatula from Graham. "Here, you're not doing it right."

"Geez, Dad," said Graham, "do you ever think I'll be old enough to fry fish?"

Jane laughed and sipped on a beer. "My dad is the same way. It was only last summer that he let me take the trash out because he said I didn't know how to put the lids back on the cans right!"

"Really, Jane," said Smedley, turning the fish, "I'm not that bad," and Graham winked at her from behind his father's back.

They ate the meaty bluefish out on the deck and Jane had an extra helping of corn on the cob. The butter dripped from her fingers and chin. They cleaned up in the kitchen, then went back out onto the deck to sit and enjoy the evening. Smedley entertained Jane with his knowledge of local folklore while Graham rested easily in his chair, his feet propped up on the rail surrounding the deck.

"Ten miles down the beach," Smedley was telling her, "is what's called Nags Head."

"Nag? Like in a horse?" asked Jane.

"Exactly. Three hundred and some years ago pirates used to inhabit the coastline here. They'd wait for a storm to brew, then tie lanterns to the necks of donkeys and let the animals loose to walk up and down the beach. The treasure ships that passed here on their way to England would get blown off course in the storms. The lookouts would see the lanterns and think they had spotted a safe port but instead, the ships would get wrecked on the terrible shoals out there. The next day," Smedley told her, "the pirates would hop into their small boats and collect the booty."

"Is that true?" asked Jane dubiously.

"Absolutely. In fact, they've charted over a thousand old wrecks out there. The coastline here is called the Graveyard of the Atlantic."

"That's a wonderful story," she said.

"And their children's children's *children*," concluded

Smedley, "still live here. But today they rob the tourists instead!"

"Tell her about Virginia Dare," Graham suggested lazily, his hand reaching over to Jane's arm and trailing a feather-light touch across her flesh.

"Virginia Dare," Smedley explained, "was the first white baby born on the continental U.S. Long before the pilgrims dreamed of sailing for Plymouth Rock." He snorted at his inside knowledge. "Yes, indeed, she was born on Roanoke Island just south of here. The colony disappeared into the mists of time, my dear, but today the state of Virginia still celebrates her name and the county here is called Dare County."

"But I didn't know half of that," said Jane wonderingly.

"You wouldn't," Smedley was quick to tell her, "since they wrote the first history books up north."

"Don't get Dad going on politics," warned Graham.

The sky grew dark and a haze formed over the ocean. On the horizon, ships passed northward silently, heading toward Chesapeake Bay, their lights twinkling in the darkness. The moist night air embraced Jane and her fingers glided over her arms to fend off the chill damp from the ocean. Even her own touch was somehow arousing.

Smedley slipped inside and reappeared with a silver tray, three snifters and a bottle of cognac. Over his arm was a jacket for Jane.

"Thank you," she said, smiling up at him.

They sipped their cognac in companionable silence. The setting was so terribly evocative that Jane could have sat there forever, feeling the ocean air moisten her skin, hearing the distant call of a foghorn from a lighthouse, listening to the never-ending roll of the tide. Perhaps she would reopen the window in her bedroom.

Eventually Smedley disappeared inside.

"Is your dad going to bed this early?" asked Jane.

"Probably not. More than likely he's out in the garage

fiddling. If you can believe this—'' Graham chuckled ''—he has an old screen door set up in there and he uses it to filter sand from the beach.''

"What on earth for?"

"Gold, diamonds, who knows?" He shrugged. "He thinks that the ocean, from beating against the coast when it was rocky, say, a million years ago, crushed the rocks into sand and that there are plenty of precious stones just waiting to be filtered out of the sand."

"Well, it makes sense in a way, doesn't it?"

"I suppose. And he does have a few old pill bottles full of what he *tells* everyone is gold dust."

"You sound skeptical," said Jane. "Maybe it is gold."

"And maybe not."

"Don't be so hard on him."

"Oh, I'm not really. I like to rib him, though. He *does* take some getting used to."

"Well, I like him."

"And," said Graham, leaning close, "I can see you like Heckle and Jeckle, too." He glanced down at her hand. She was toying idly with Jeckle's ears while the dog practically purred. "I wish you'd play with my ears like that."

Jane sighed. "Back in New York, Graham. Not here. You promised."

"I did, didn't I? But I've got a plan. You did say, 'not in your father's house?'"

"Yes..."

"Ah, my sweet Janey, now you're curious! You know I've been scheming away but I'm going to torture you and not tell. You'll have to wait till tomorrow."

"Graham," she said, mock-angrily.

Later he saw her to the guest room door. "Just a good-night kiss?" he asked softly.

"Well, the light *is* still on in the garage. Maybe just one," she conceded.

His arms came around her waist and he pulled Jane

close. "This is becoming a pleasant habit," he murmured, his lips covering hers finally in a slow, tender kiss.

A few minutes later Jane turned out her light and lay on the bed in the darkness listening to the drone of the ocean. She thought about the long day, about all the new sights and sounds. About pirates and their donkeys and a baby named Virginia who had passed ages and ages ago into the dark unknown. And of Graham who was a part of all this as much as he was a part of the throb of the city. A man with many faces. And *that*, Jane decided as sleep crept up on her, was what was so exciting about him.

Not surprisingly—at least not anymore—Jane found Smedley on the beach at 6:00 a.m. He was on his hands and knees, with a magnifying glass, searching for stones in the early light.

She brought him a cup of coffee. "Find anything?" she asked against the roar of the tide.

He pulled an interesting turquoise stone out of his frayed pants pocket. "This is a beauty. I'll have to drop it in some acid and see what I've got here." He exchanged the cup of coffee in her hand for the stone and they took a walk together.

"That son of mine," said Smedley about half a mile down the shore. "If he'd get his lazy bones up out of bed, he'd find there's a beach full of treasures out here. But if you wait too long to go beachcombing, a tourist is apt to get there ahead of you. You always wake up early?"

"Yes," said Jane. "On the ranch we had to. And now I jog sometimes in the city before all the cars are out."

"City's no good for you. Bad for the lungs and heart."

"I'm sure you're right," she commented, thinking once again about the wires hanging out of her window.

"This is the place, Jane. Out here in the wilds. Why, most of the ninety miles of beach here are still National Seashore. Protected. The government says it's to preserve the bird life, but I say it's really to preserve the people!"

As if to underscore his words, a group of gulls swooped down ahead of them and began scavenging a dead horse-shoe crab. "Birds do just fine," said Smedley, his strawberry-blond hair aflame in the first rays of the sun. "Yes, the animal life is going to take over the earth as it is. Especially the bloody insects! By God, North Carolina is already mosquito capital of the world!"

"What about baby harp seals?" asked Jane mischievously.

"They're in Alaska," she got as an answer.

Graham was on the deck when they returned, a coffee mug in hand, an early morning sleepy look to him. "In the city," he said, "this is positively an indecent hour."

"Lazy," said his father, grumbling. "Now Jane here, I like this young lady. She knows what's good for her."

There was a sudden commotion at the screen door. The dogs were whining and scratching to get out, pressing against the screen, enlarging an already respectable hole.

"Stop that!" hollered Smedley. "Confounded dogs! That does it, I'm going to drown them!" But as he opened the sliding screen door and let them out, his angry expression changed and soon he was tossing an old tennis ball down onto the beach for them to chase.

"It's really quite interesting around here," said Jane in an aside to Graham.

"Oh, I've seen worse," he commented. "But for the life of me, I can't remember just where."

All morning long Jane couldn't forget Graham's teasing promise of the previous evening—that he had a surprise for her today. It couldn't have been the visit they made to the Wright Brothers' National Memorial near Kitty Hawk. Nor did she think his surprise was their stop at the purported site of the Lost Colony where Virginia Dare had once walked the gently wooded land. And she seriously doubted that a stroll out onto a fishing pier to see what the locals were catching could have been his ultimate scheme. But when he pulled into the marina and parked in front of the lovely old mahogany sailboat, the *Renée*, Jane was beginning to get a glimmer of his plot.

It was a scorching morning on the Outer Banks, the radio in the Porsche calling for a heat wave throughout the South and possible afternoon thundershowers. Jane felt the perspiration soaking her head and the back of her tank top was plastered to her skin.

"Ever been sailing?" asked Graham as he maneuvered the twenty-two footer out of the bay and through the narrow, shallow inlet into the ocean.

"Never," replied Jane while she fumbled with ropes and tried to follow his instructions. Lord, this was complicated stuff, much worse than hitching up a team of six horses to a wagon.

The bay was calm, the inlet a bit tricky with waves going both east and west, meeting, crashing, sending plumes of sparkling white spray high into the air. Once they were actually out on the ocean, the water calmed again and the *Renée* glided smoothly over the rolling sea, her white sail billowing out and snapping before the northerly breeze.

The freedom of sailing struck Jane; the boat depended on nothing but the wind. And, oh boy, was the wind a powerful force out there on the ocean! It filled the sail and tilted the whole boat over with its force, skimming it along on the surface of the water. Once Graham let Jane hold the wheel for a while and she could feel the living energy of the wind quivering in her hands as the keel dug into the water to keep the boat upright and the sail fought it, urging the *Renée* onward.

"This is fabulous!" Jane called later through cupped hands, bracing herself against the cabin on the slanting deck, watching as Graham tacked backward and forward to make progress against the wind. The word "tack" suddenly took on new meaning. It was a different world, a wonderful new experience that thrilled and excited Jane. Another gift given to her by Graham. "I love it!" she

yelled to him over the hiss of the hull on water and the
crack of canvas.

"It's okay now but we have to watch out for a change
in wind this afternoon. And storms as well. You can climb
the mast and be my lookout!"

Graham was near the prow of the boat, leaning over
the side, fiddling with a rope. He was wearing cutoff
jeans, a faded blue shirt and Topsiders to keep his footing.
His hair blew in the cool breeze, catching the sun and
gleaming like gold. His arms and legs looked tan and
strong and capable as he worked. His expression, Jane
saw, was alive and happy.

"You'd have made a perfect pirate," she said.

"And that's exactly what I would have been doing...three hundred years ago."

"No qualms about stealing from the poor, innocent
ships?"

"None." He laughed and a devil-may-care gleam appeared in his eyes. "The old ships were stealing the natives blind in the name of their kings. At least I'd have
been keeping the booty in North America."

About three miles offshore Graham swung the sail out
of the wind and the *Renée* lurched, rolling and drifting.

He turned to Jane. "I hope you don't get seasick."

"I feel okay. Why are we stopping? Are we going to
fish?" But even as she asked, Jane knew the answer; it
was written all over his face. It was in that rakish grin
and the gleam in his eyes.

"Fish?" he said casually. "Maybe later." He pulled
off his shirt and tossed it on the deck. Then he caught her
arms and pulled her against him almost fiercely, his lips
covering hers in a passionate kiss, bending her head back,
crushing her breasts against his bare chest.

Graham had never been rough with her. And certainly
this was not rough, exactly, but his urgency, the demand
in his eager hands, the force of his manhood pressing
against her was a new experience for Jane and her re-

sponse was immediate and strong. He was playing her pirate and she loved it. Her arms went around his back, her hands kneaded the rippling, corded muscles of his shoulders.

They discarded their clothes on the deck then stumbled, laughing and excited, below to the single, narrow, pull-down cot. It was even hotter down in the cabin and the air was dead and salty, close. Both of them broke out in a sweat and when Graham poised on top of Jane, their legs and bellies glided smoothly together.

He spent very little time on preliminaries. His hands stroked her breasts, pushing the flesh beneath upward to meet his lips, flicking her taut nipples with his tongue until she could no longer stifle a cry. He kissed her neck, forcing her head back, kissed her shoulders, her nipples again and a hot ache coiled deep in her belly and her hips rotated against his, longing, craving, desperate to be filled by him.

Graham slid his hands beneath her buttocks and pulled her upward until her back arched and her legs parted, quivering, tense, expectant. Then he drove into her, filling her completely for a long, exquisite moment until he pulled out. He plunged again and again. She felt her body tightening, the blood pounding in her ears. Then she was gripping his shoulders and her hips lifted, straining, press-ing, rolling against his until it was there, so near, so near...

Jane cried out and shook, her limbs straining, her body rocking, and then slowly the sweet ache abated and she felt his climax come, a pulsing throb deep inside her as he gasped and clutched her to him.

When it was over they lay together sweat-slicked and sated. "I hope I didn't hurt you," he breathed in her ear.

Jane laughed softly and nuzzled her face against his damp neck. "I hope I didn't hurt *you*."

They swam alongside the boat, holding onto a rope, cooling down. Then, dried off and dressed, Graham turned

to her. "Okay, first mate, it's time to earn your keep. Out
with the fishing poles."

"Aye, aye," she said, determined that today *she* was
going to catch dinner.

By three o'clock Jane had caught two sea trout and one
small yellowfin tuna. Graham, she was delighted to point
out, had not caught a thing.

"Want me to show you how I did it?" she couldn't
help saying but Graham suddenly had a sober expression
on his face and was paying no attention whatsoever to
her. Instead, he was looking over her shoulder out to sea.

Jane turned around curiously. Moving in from the north
was a black bank of clouds, with lightning streaking the
huge mass. "Oh, no," she said, alarmed. "What do we
do?"

"We set sail and beat a path to the inlet. Pronto."

It was only a minute or two after Graham raised the
sail that the wind rattled and shook the *Renée*. It was a
cold, ominous wind that brought goose bumps to Jane's
flesh. The *Renée* responded to the gust and leaped forward
into a swell, rolling to one side. Jane stumbled, frightened
suddenly, recalling Smedley's stories about the Graveyard
of the Atlantic.

"Are we going to make it?" she called to Graham who
was working with the rigging, straightening out a rope.

"We'll make it, all right," he assured her, "and in
record time. But I want you to hold on tight, Jane. I mean
it."

The wind was growing stronger, the black mass ad-
vancing on them and yet, strangely, the sun was still out
bright and hot on her shoulders. She could see whitecaps
ahead of them and behind them as the sea responded to
the oncoming storm and kicked up spray and foam into
the sun-drenched air. The *Renée* flew across the waves,
pitching, heaving, the sail full and cracking like a shot
and Jane was abruptly afraid it would tear into tatters and
they would be stranded.

"I thought it was supposed to be hot and calm today," she shouted to Graham from where she hung on, helplessly watching him scramble around the deck.

"They've never been able to forecast these quick storms," he called back. "I should have been paying more attention to the horizon."

Jane put up a hand to shade her eyes and strained to see the shore. The inlet was there, all right, but it looked so far away. "We'll make it in, won't we?"

"Sure, sure we will." He flashed her a reassuring smile. "Come on, don't look so forlorn! This is fun!" And she could see that Graham was truly enjoying himself. She wished some of his confidence would rub off onto her. He'd said he loved the fact that she wasn't afraid of anything. But that was on *land*!

The inlet to the bay was treacherous. Behind the *Renée* were huge swells, pushing the boat, threatening to swamp it, and ahead were the smaller waves from the bay, rushing out to meet the sea. Graham was working the sail feverishly by then, trying to avoid the collision of waves that could capsize them with no trouble whatsoever. Then, finally, mercifully, the *Renée* dipped into a trench, came out of it with her bow nosed into the sun and *plop*, the water smoothed out and she glided sure and sound into the sparkling blue bay.

"Wow," breathed Jane, "for a few minutes there..."

He tipped his head back and laughed heartily. "Had you worried, did it?"

"Oh no, not at all." She laughed along with him, relieved, happy, feeling very much alive and glad that she'd shared the adventure with him.

WHILE THE STORM WHIPPED AROUND the sides of the house and spattered the windows with salt and rain, Jane helped Smedley cook the fish.

"Someday that boy of mine is going to push it too far," Smedley was telling her.

"Didn't you ever get caught out on the sea in a storm?" asked Jane. He had, after all, owned the boat for thirty-five years.

"Sure I did. But I never had my wife along with me."

"Do you think she'd have been any happier waiting at home?"

"Well, I don't really know. The point is, young lady, I had the good sense to make her stay onshore."

He was a hard man to reason with, Jane decided. He had strong opinions; he was unbendable and not a little eccentric. Nevertheless, she was growing fond of him, enjoying his stubborn banter. He reminded her of her father in some ways. Strong, old-fashioned men, they both did and said exactly what they wanted and damn the rest of the world if it didn't like it.

Graham built a fire and they ate at the old wooden table, sitting on the benches with the whaler's lamp lit. Graham's knee was pressed up against hers familiarly. Her fish was excellent, broiled to tender perfection, swimming in butter and lemon and parsley. Outside the wind howled and behind their backs the fire blazed. The dogs lay near the hearth. One of them—Jeckle, Jane thought—was snoring, his mouth sagging, twitching as he dreamed.

She went to bed that night with a book from Smedley's collection of mysteries. Her room was cozy and secure and she allowed Jeckle to rest at her feet until he took up too much of the bed and was banished, groaning, to the floor with Heckle. Finally she put the book on the nightstand and snapped off the light and lay there with her arms behind her head, thinking.

There was an otherworldly, untamed quality to this long barrier island of Graham's. It was in the air, in Smedley's lore of long-ago times, of pirates and graveyard shoals. It was in the way the sea wind tore through Graham's hair and lit his eyes to the color of aquamarine, in the way his gleaming teeth were bared as he worked, grinning, daring nature to test his mettle.

Graham Smith, she was beginning to realize, was everything she'd ever wanted in a man. She wouldn't change a thing about him. But as the weathered gray boards of the house creaked in the wind, Jane had to wonder if *she* was everything he'd always wanted in a woman.

CHAPTER NINE

JANE WAS IN HER ROOM, just pulling a tank top over her head on Sunday morning when she heard both dogs start barking hysterically. The frantic scratching of canine claws on the screen door filled the brief moments when Heckle and Jeckle paused for breath.

Running barefoot out into the living room to see what the commotion was all about, Jane got there in time to catch the dogs' glossy black backs disappearing through the front door, which had been opened by someone, someone who was scolding the dogs by name in a loud, imperious, feminine voice.

A neighbor?

The dogs' barking subsided and the door opened again to admit the caller. Jane's first impression was of a tall woman in, perhaps, her late fifties, marvelously well-preserved, with artfully streaked silver hair and classic features. She wore a simple peach-colored linen dress with such perfect lines to it that Jane immediately sized it up as a Halston original, like the one she'd seen in the window of Saks Fifth Avenue that cost a mere three hundred dollars. White pumps and coral beads—two long strands—a straw bag and a large diamond winking on her ring finger completed her ensemble. Her stance was elegant as she halted in surprise upon the threshold and her eyes were a frigid blue that pierced Jane with an arrow of appraisal. "And just *who*," demanded the woman, "are you?"

Jane drew herself up, trying to ignore her hastily

combed hair, bare feet and casual attire. After all, Jane had been invited to Smedley's house while this woman certainly had not. She was about to ask the lady just who she thought *she* was when Jane was aware of Graham coming up behind her. She turned to him for help when she saw his face light up.

"Mother!" he exclaimed. "What a surprise!"

"Graham," said the woman breathlessly, "I had no idea *you'd* be here! How wonderful to see you! Oh, you've gotten too much sun again and...have you lost weight?"

Jane remained where she was feeling decidedly out of place. And to think that she'd been about to accost Graham's mother as an intruder. Thank heavens Graham had come when he did!

But he was pulling his mother toward Jane and saying, "Mom, I want you to meet a very special friend of mine. Jane Manning, Renée Smith."

Renée's dark blue eyes had softened. She held her manicured hand out to Jane. "You'll have to excuse me— I was very surprised, you understand."

Jane clasped her hand. "It's so nice to meet you, Mrs. Smith. Graham's told me a lot about you."

Renée's curved eyebrows rose. "So my son talks of me, his mother, when you two are together?" There was a slight lilt in Renée's voice, a shadow of inflection that made her speech musical and graceful.

Graham laughed, "You know me too well, Mom. Do you have some luggage in your car? Did you drive down this morning?"

"Yes, I flew into Norfolk last evening and got up very early this morning. Graham, *mon chéri*, there are a couple of things in the car, if you don't mind..."

"Two steamer trunks, I bet," Graham said, rolling his eyes.

"But of course not, two very small—"

"*Renée*." The voice came from behind Jane. She

turned to see Smedley in the hallway, one hand out, touching the wall as if groping for support.

Renée nodded, expressionless. "Hello, Smedley. You're looking well."

"Renée," Smedley repeated, making his way into the living room. He seemed stunned.

"*Oui, c'est moi*, it is I," she said.

"But you...you should have called," said Smedley. "I mean..."

"I did not, I just came. If I'd phoned you, you would have given me an excuse and told me you were busy or something."

"Renée—"

"Do you have some coffee made?" the woman asked, interrupting him. "I started very early this morning."

"Coffee? Coffee. Oh, not yet. We all just got up."

The dogs were whining and pressing against the door from outside now. Renée let them in and they tried to jump on her, stubby tails wagging, tongues lolling.

"No!" she cried, shaking her finger at them, then she pointed to a corner. "Go sit! Naughty boys!"

Meekly, Heckle and Jeckle slunk to the corner, turned a couple of times each and thumped down, panting. Jane was impressed.

"Those dogs," Renée said in disgust. "So, shall I make coffee and, perhaps, some crepes for breakfast? I can see that no one has begun anything. You have flour and butter and eggs, Smedley?"

"Yes." Smedley seemed to be recovering.

"*Mon Dieu*," Renée said, "this place is a mess. Don't you clean the stove, Smedley?"

"Mother," Graham said gently.

"Oh, sorry. I must not say a word. You may live like a pig if you like. You have my permission."

Smedley ran a big knuckled hand through his mussed hair. "Renée, it's clean."

She shrugged and turned toward the kitchen. "Graham,

my things? And perhaps, Jane, you might help me set the table."

Wow, Jane thought. She was beginning to see what Graham had been talking about. Renée was a controller. But Jane didn't want to make too hasty a judgment. The woman's officious manner *could* be a guise for nervousness. Arriving unannounced like that must not have been the easiest thing Graham's mother had ever done.

Graham came back with two large leather suitcases. "Where do I put them?" he asked, a little embarrassed.

Jane realized that both guest rooms were filled. There was only Smedley's room. Oh dear, how awkward.

Smedley had retreated to the deck. "Put them in my room," he called through the screen door. "I'll sleep on the couch," he mumbled.

"No, don't be ridiculous. *I'll* sleep on the couch," announced Renée.

"Renée, you're my guest. I'll take the couch," he yelled.

"Hey, I've got a great idea," said Graham brightly. "Jane and I will sleep on the boat and you two can have the whole house to yourselves!"

Renée gave him a look of disapproval. "Certainly not! That's indecent and I won't consider it!"

Impasse.

Graham diplomatically left the bags in the living room and they all sat down to breakfast. Renée had brewed coffee, thawed orange juice and was in the process of cooking wafer-thin crepes, which she deftly rolled around dabs of jam and then sprinkled with powdered sugar.

Renée was the grand hostess, Graham was witty and charming, Jane tried to keep up her end of the conversation and Smedley gradually relaxed and started to be his old self.

"So, Renée, how is Montreal?" he asked cautiously.

"Rainy. My sister had a soirée last week. The prime minister and his wife came. And do you remember Ian

Pembroke from the London embassy? He was there with his *new* wife. She was not a day over thirty.''

"Ian remarried?''

"Yes, and Catherine Baldwin asked after you.''

"How nice.''

Renée finally turned to Jane. "And how long have you known my son?''

"Let's see. About three weeks, isn't it, Graham?''

"You met in New York?''

"Well, no, Mom. We met in Colorado. Jane just moved to New York for her new job.''

"Ah, your new job. What do you do, my dear?''

"I'm a bodyguard at Mercury Courier,'' Jane said proudly.

For a moment there was an acute silence.

"Did you know that Jane's family raises rodeo stock on their ranch?'' Graham put in hastily.

"Rodeo stock,'' Renée repeated tonelessly. "And do you ride this stock?''

"Yes, I ride the horses. I raced a little. Nothing serious.''

"I ride in Montreal,'' Renée said, obviously relieved to have found some common ground. "Do you jump?''

"Well, a few irrigation ditches from time to time.''

"Oh.''

"These are *Western* horses, Mom,'' Graham explained.

Renée looked at him blankly and Jane hid a smile behind her coffee cup.

"How is Lew?'' Smedley asked expediently.

"He's fine,'' Graham replied. "Having a little trouble with the business.''

"What kind of trouble?''

"Oh, I'll tell you later. It's boring stuff.''

Boring? thought Jane. But he probably didn't want to get into it at the table.

"And is Fiona doing well?'' Renée asked.

"That's Lew's wife," Graham told Jane. "She's fine. Still complaining about her weight."

"And so she should," Renée sniffed.

"Did you know I got an invitation to George Mondragon's retirement party?" Smedley said to Renée.

"You mean he is just now retiring?"

"Yes, at seventy. There's going to be a big bash at his house in Hamilton. Formal. You know Eleanor."

Graham explained to Jane: "George is an old friend of Dad's and the consul general for Bermuda. Eleanor is his wife."

"Oh," Jane said, her head whirling with all the names.

"And so, are you going?" asked Renée, studiously casual.

Wouldn't George have invited both Smedley and Renée? Jane wondered. After all, they were not divorced.

"I don't think so. Seems a lot of hoopla for the old geezer's retirement. Still, it might be fun."

"Have you kept the moths out of your dinner jacket?" Renée asked with asperity.

Smedley looked down at his plate and began cutting up a crepe into many tiny pieces. Jane could see that Renée was *dying* to go to this George's party and was angling for an invitation. How uncomfortable.

Jane and Graham did the dishes while his parents wandered out on the deck, arguing about who would sleep where.

"You see what I mean?" asked Graham.

"I sure do," replied Jane. "What a shame. Your mother is very beautiful."

"Yeah, I guess she was a real knockout when she met Dad. He always told me how gorgeous she was."

"Still is."

"Not as gorgeous as you," Graham said with a glint in his eye. He bent his head and nuzzled her neck while soap dripped from his hands onto the floor.

"Graham, your mother might come in."

"Bashful, aren't you?"

"I don't know your parents very well. I mean, would you like me to grab you and kiss you in front of *my* family?"

His eyes lit up with merciless merriment. "Only if their shotguns were unloaded."

"See what I mean?"

"I missed you last night," Graham said. He wiped his sudsy hands on his shorts and pulled Jane close to him, his hands on her waist, so that she leaned out from his embrace and looked up into his face.

"Me, too," she admitted, "but I did have Heckle and Jeckle to keep me warm."

"I'm jealous."

"Don't be. They both snored and twitched all night."

"Damn mutts."

"Let's get the dishes done. I want to get out onto that beach," Jane said. "It may be old hat to you but to me it's an adventure."

So there was another day of heat and sun and swimming in the rough water, a stroll on the beach, throwing driftwood for the dogs, laughing together at their antics, finding seashells in the sand.

Late in the afternoon she and Graham drove down to Nags Head to get some groceries that Renée wanted. The top of the Porsche was down and Jane's hair was wind-blown and sticky with salt but she didn't care. The island offered total freedom and a time apart from the real world.

"I think," announced Graham on the way home, "that Mom is tired of living alone. I *think* this unscheduled visit is an attempt at rapprochement."

"What about your dad?"

Graham thought for a minute. "Once the shock wore off I noted a hungry stare in his eyes. I *think*."

"Maybe they'll get back together," said Jane, sensing that Graham wanted to hear that.

"Maybe," he said. "I just wish Mom would lighten up sometimes."

"She was probably nervous. It was hard for her to just show up like that."

"Um, I guess so. She tends to get real bossy and real busy when she's upset."

"If your father would have welcomed her, I mean really seemed glad to see her, I'll bet she would have melted."

"It's true. Smedley has a problem with intimacy. It's that old stiff upper lip routine. He went to an English public school, you know."

"Well, *you* sure don't have an intimacy problem," Jane quipped.

"No, it's that hot Gallic side of me," he said lasciviously, putting a hand on her bare thigh and squeezing.

A few minutes later they pulled into the driveway. Renée met them at the door and took the groceries from them. She'd changed to beautifully cut pale lavender slacks with a white silk shirt. Jane wondered how she was going to cook dinner without ruining the outfit.

"Where's Dad?" asked Graham.

"Looking for stones on the beach," Renée answered. "I think he's trying to avoid me." She said it lightly but Jane sensed the pain behind her words.

"Now, why would he do that?" asked Graham.

"Because, *mon cher*, your father is an abject coward."

"Mom…"

She bent and rattled pans in a low cupboard. "He is and always has been," Jane thought she heard Renée say amidst the clatter. A second later the woman straightened and, holding a pot by its handle, she shook it in Graham's direction. "At least I didn't raise you to be a coward like your father, *mon Dieu!*"

"Hey, Mom, give the guy a chance."

Renée stopped brandishing the pot. She stood tall and

said, very clearly and deliberately, "But that is exactly what I am here for."

Before dinner, Jane and Graham strolled down the beach. His arm was around her, his head bent close as they walked along the receding tide line, bare feet splashing in the sliding water.

"What a wonderful place," Jane said with a sigh. "I could stay here forever."

"Lew wouldn't like that."

"No, he wouldn't."

"But we can come again. It's wonderful in the fall when all the tourists are gone."

"I'll never manage to get four days off again. I'm lucky Lew gave them to me this time."

"I guess you just know the right people." Graham grinned.

Jane disengaged herself from his arm and faced him, hands on hips. "Did you get me those days off? Graham, I will be so angry with you if you did!"

"I confess."

"That's not fair!"

"But there's method to my madness."

"What *method*?"

"I'll tell you tomorrow. I needed you."

"Graham, you're disgraceful!"

"Yes—and no. Reserve judgment until tomorrow morning."

"I *hate* mysteries!" cried Jane.

He put his arm around her again and started walking. "You're beautiful when you're angry. Did anyone ever tell you that before?"

"No." She started to finally laugh, unable to sustain her temper. "Mostly they just hightailed it and ran when they saw that look in my eyes."

Frantic barking came from beyond a dune. Two dogs.

"We've got company," Graham said wryly as the two black and tan beasts bounded over the hill, spraying sand, barking, flinging themselves at the receding water and biting at it.

Smedley trudged into view, hands behind his back, head bent, eyes fixed on the ground.

"Hi, Dad!" Graham called.

"Oh, it's you two. Did Renée send you?" he asked warily.

"No, she's busy whipping up something spectacular for dinner."

Smedley's eyes lit up. "Do you suppose she's making shrimp Newburg? She knows I love it."

"Well, shrimp was on the shopping list."

"Haven't had it in a year. And those little round rolls she makes?"

"I did buy some yeast," Graham admitted.

"Um," came from Smedley as he kicked sand with one bare foot. "Suppose I'll have to show up for dinner."

"It would be a good idea." Graham eyed his father speculatively.

"Although, *confound it*, she has no business just popping in here unannounced. And now she's taken over the kitchen. I'll never find my pots again." He bent to examine a pile of stones, fingering one with a reddish tint. "I'll tell you, it's been peaceful around here without her constantly nagging and organizing."

"I think I'll walk on ahead," Jane said meaningfully, catching Graham's glance.

"You can stay right here, young lady," Smedley was quick to say. "I haven't got any secrets. And you know something else," he went on without pause, "she emptied my jars of diamonds out onto the sand!"

"I'm sure she—" Graham began.

"She *knew* I'd been collecting them for years! I had to spend an hour picking up what I could out of the sand. Now I've got exactly one jar left!"

"I'm sure she—" Graham tried once more.

"And don't think I don't know she'd like to go to that party in Bermuda."

"It seems natural to me that she—"

"Sure, sure, Renée comes flying back into my life and takes over again. Well, if I go to Bermuda, it'll be alone!"

"*Dad*," Graham said, exasperated, "I think you're being unfair just because Mom dumped out a few jars of beach junk."

"Beach junk! That's how much *you* know!" And he stalked away, growling under his breath.

"God, he can push my buttons!" Graham said heatedly to his father's hunched, retreating form.

"He's confused, that's all. Can't you see how strained everything's been since your mom got here?" Jane noted Graham's frustrated expression and felt sorry for him; it was clear he would like nothing more than to see his parents reunited. "These things take time."

"Sure," he replied then smiled. "I know."

"Come on," Jane urged, "let's finish our walk. There's nothing we can do to help your mother and father. Come on, where's that old Graham who doesn't let anything bother him?"

"Beats me." He took his hands out of his pockets and cocked his head. "Wanna race back to the house?"

"I've never run in sand. You'll beat me."

"Exactly what I was thinking." Graham took off ahead of her. Jane smiled to herself and continued walking slowly, enjoying the feel of the foamy tide at her feet, watching his footprints disappearing swiftly along the edge of the water, looking up and shading her eyes while she watched a gull screech overhead and swoop down to pick at a ripple in the surf. She arrived on the sun deck ten minutes after Graham.

He was still breathing hard. "Cute trick."

"I never said *I* wanted to race."

Somewhere Renée had dug up a cut glass decanter and filled it with wildflowers. And she'd located matching glasses. There were even candles stuck in bright pottery holders and shrimp Newburg, rolls and a crisp Caesar salad. Smedley had changed into khaki pants and a clean white shirt and looked very handsome at the head of the table. It was obvious to Jane that they were all trying very hard to be a family.

"This is a wonderful meal, Mrs. Smith," Jane said. She noticed that Graham's mother did not request to be called Renée.

"Thank you. I wonder sometimes if Smedley sees to eating properly."

"I do just fine, Renée."

"You look well," she admitted grudgingly.

"Are you two going to take the boat out tomorrow?" Graham asked. "Jane and I have to leave and someone should use the poor old thing."

"Old thing?" objected Renée.

"Old for a boat. Come on, Mom, where's your sense of humor?"

After a couple of glasses of wine Renée did loosen up. She told Jane stories of Graham's childhood. "Oh, but he was an enfant terrible! The trouble he got in! He used to invade my parties in his Ninja costume, screaming in Japanese and throwing darts."

"Mom…"

"What a time that boy gave us," mused Smedley, catching his wife's eye.

"Must we tell *Graham* stories?" asked Graham, looking down at his plate.

Renée folded her hands, elbows on the table, and gazed at him lovingly. "But your father and I adore these memories, *mon cher*." She glanced at Smedley. "In high school he locked himself in the office and took over the school's public-address system. I can't tell you how humiliated I was!"

"Sounds like Graham. Did he tell you about his ride on Pard at our ranch in Colorado?"

"Pard?" asked Smedley.

So Jane had to repeat the story. Graham laughed louder than anyone at her description of his fall, as seen through the kitchen window.

"So you *did* see that," said Graham finally.

"I was waiting for it," Jane quipped. "You think I was brought up by the Manning men to be dumb?"

When the meal was over, they all helped to clear the table. Jane was carrying in the last of the clutter when she heard Renée say to Smedley in the kitchen, "I am so sorry about throwing away your gems today," and Smedley's reply, "Oh, er, no harm done. Here, let me scrub that pot. You'll ruin your nails."

"Good sign," Graham said when Jane told him, "I *think*." They were sitting on the deck, watching the sun's rays slant across the water. It was a peaceful time, the only sound the muted soughing of the ocean as it sucked at the shore. Jane half sat on the railing, her back against the house and Graham was in his usual chair with his feet propped up. A warm breeze laden with a salty ocean smell and moisture blew her bangs off her forehead. She was so terribly aware of Graham nearby, of his long lean body that was so relaxed, of his lazy smile as he watched the dogs fighting over a stick on the beach. She was acutely conscious of every sensation, every harsh call of a sea gull, every glint of the setting sun on a whitecap. She wanted to touch Graham, to feel him close; she craved his mouth on hers, his whispers in her ear. But his parents were there and they couldn't...

Graham reached out and took hold of her hand. "So now you've met my folks. And they've revealed to you the true me. What do you think?" Idly he played with her fingers and watched her from under sandy eyebrows.

His touch made her draw in her breath. What sweet torture it was to be so close to him. "I think I like your family very much," she said.

"And me?"

"You, too."

"You *like* me, that's all?"

"Well, I like you a lot."

"Janey, Janey," he said with mock-despair, "I guess that'll have to do for now."

She closed her eyes and leaned her head back against the rough silvered wood of the wall. What did he want from her—a declaration of love? It was too soon, wasn't it?

"Down-to-earth Janey," Graham mused as if reading her mind. "You're very good for me, you know."

"Am I?"

"And I'm very, very good for you," he murmured, and their eyes met and locked and spoke eloquently to each other.

Renée and Smedley joined them and the talk was quiet for a while, about the weather and the ocean and fishing. It was hard to imagine Graham's parents were separated and hurting each other. They seemed so well suited but Jane supposed that could merely be the habit of years. Maybe they could work things out, she thought hopefully.

Dusk fell and the drone of the ocean seemed to grow louder, to fill the air. That huge body of water was a powerful entity, Jane was beginning to realize, as powerful as the sun was back home, an entity affecting the climate and way of life and mood.

Graham stood up and announced, "I think I'd better check out the *Renée*."

"What? At night?" asked his mother.

"Yes, I'm not sure I secured her properly yesterday." Then he grinned self-consciously. "I need company. Jane, will you come?"

Jane was beginning to follow the direction of his plan. "Sure," she said, trying to hide a smile.

"Good. Well, see you later," he said lightly to his parents.

"That was embarrassingly transparent," Jane commented, as they drove through the hot night.

"But you're here, aren't you? Look, this way we kill two birds with one stone. We give them time to be alone together and we get the same thing. I thought I was brilliant."

He was right. Jane's heart was pounding. She couldn't wait to be alone with Graham, to breathe in his sweet scent. When she closed her eyes and felt the hot wind on her face she could imagine it was the illusory touch of his fingers.

The *Renée* rocked gently in a strip of luminous, moonlit water and the cabin was close and dark. He pulled her into his arms. "God, I'm crazy about you," he breathed. "I couldn't sit there another minute. I thought I was going to leap on you and growl, like a tomcat."

She kissed him, melting against his chest and he crushed her to him, hard. They found the bed in the darkness and sank down onto it, still holding each other. His body was familiar to her now but each time was a new experience, a new adventure. He thrilled her and fulfilled her and she couldn't get enough of his mouth and his hands and his passionate murmurings.

The boat rocked lazily as they came together in wild tenderness, crying out, sweating in the stuffy cabin, lost in each other until the moon stood overhead and washed the *Renée* in bright liquid silver.

RENÉE AND SMEDLEY stood together on the steps to see Graham and Jane off on Monday morning.

"Drive carefully," Renée was saying. "That little car goes too fast."

"Don't worry, Mom," called Graham, throwing the bags in the trunk.

"Thank you again," Jane said, poised by the car door. "I had a wonderful weekend. I'm so glad I met you both."

"Come again anytime," said Smedley.

They drove away and Jane looked back one last time to wave to the attractive couple. Renée was gazing at her husband, and Jane could swear there was a wistful expression on her face. How sad, Jane thought, turning away, that Graham's parents, while growing older, had become dissatisfied with each other. They were looking for more but failing to see that there really wasn't *more* out there; they already had what they needed. She vowed to remember this lesson if she ever got restless after years of marriage.

"I wonder how they're going to get along," Graham mused. "I feel like I'm a rat deserting the sinking ship."

"Maybe not sinking," Jane replied. "You did notice your mother's suitcases were gone last night, didn't you? And they weren't in *my* room."

"Nor mine," Graham said lightly. "So that means they were—"

"In your dad's room."

"Well, what do you know," he said.

"Do you think your father will take your mother to that party in Bermuda?" asked Jane. "I just know she'd give anything to go."

"Oh, she'd love to arrive dripping in jewels with a new creation on and see all their old buddies," agreed Graham. "It all depends on my father's nerve. In some ways he is a coward."

The miles flew by; a white haze burned off the surface of the ocean and the sun blasted out of a heat-bleached sky. They got held up at a drawbridge on the Inland Waterway and Graham leaned over and kissed Jane. "Sorry I didn't sneak into your room last night?" he asked, his warm breath sending rippling shock waves down her hip. She leaned against him, feeling the whipcord strength of his body, loving the nearness of him but a little afraid, too. She was falling in love with this man, this Quicksilver, and it was all happening much too fast.

In Virginia, Graham turned west at the sign that read Washington, D.C. "Are we going a different way?" asked Jane.

"Sort of. This is the surprise I told you about."

"Oh, I'd forgotten about that."

"I'm going to pick up some Picasso sketches at the National Gallery and deliver them to the Met in New York."

Jane sat straight up. "You mean you're on a job?"

"And so are you. Lew assigned you to me as my body-guard."

"Graham, why didn't you *tell* me?"

He shrugged and pulled out to pass a truck. "Lew told me not to tell anyone till I'd left New York."

"We left New York three days ago!"

"We did, you're right. But I didn't want you worrying. It was supposed to be a vacation."

"Oh, Graham! You should have told me!"

"Why? Would you have practiced karate on me all weekend if you'd known?"

"No, it's just that…oh, I don't know. You can be re-ally…infuriating sometimes."

"And you love every minute of it."

Some time later they pulled up to the rear service en-trance of the national Gallery. "I'm going to check out the area," said Jane, stepping out of the car.

"There won't be any theft attempt," Graham was quick to tell her. "Lew was very careful to make sure no one in the office knew about this job."

"Nevertheless," Jane retorted, "I'm going to treat this like any other job. And, besides, someone in Washington could have talked about it."

She found it to be a typically deserted parking lot with trash Dumpsters and cars and piles of empty boxes. There were a million places for someone to hide. Graham still sat in the car, smiling sardonically, but she ignored him.

She wasn't going to take a chance on anything going wrong.

Finally she let him go inside while she waited at the door to keep an eye on things. He was accompanied to and from the storage room by a museum guard and the curator and returned shortly with a one-foot square box that had been sealed very carefully.

"That's it?" she asked.

"They're small sketches, I guess," he said. Then he thanked the two men and stepped toward the door.

"Hold on," said Jane. "I have to secure the area. You wait here."

He looked at the guard and they exchanged smiles that clearly said, "Oh, boy, look at the amateur, following all the rules in the book."

Nevertheless Jane checked the area thoroughly: behind Dumpsters again, around the corners of the building, in the bushes, everywhere people could conceal themselves. She was ready to call Graham out to the car when she heard a squeal of tires and a horn honking behind her. She jumped as if she'd been shot and whirled around.

There was Graham in his red Porsche, grinning like crazy. "Come on!" he yelled. "I'm hungry for lunch."

"That was stupid!" she blurted out angrily as she got into the car.

"But you were so busy securing the area I knew I'd be safe."

"Where are the sketches?"

"Locked in the trunk."

"Damn it, Graham, *you* may not take this job seriously but I do!"

His smile faded. "I'm sorry, Jane, I could see you had everything under control," he said contritely. "I'll never do it again, I promise. Forgive me, my beloved bodyguard. Gee—" he brightened "—Beloved Bodyguard, isn't that a great name for a book?"

Jane snorted in derision. He was impossible. He wasn't

Get 2 Books FREE!

Get 2

HOW TO GET YOUR
2 FREE BOOKS AND FREE GIFT

1. Peel off the 2 FREE BOOKS seal from the front cover. Place it in the space provided at right. This automatically entitles you to receive two free books and an exciting mystery gift.

2. Send back this card and you'll get 2 "The Best of the Best™" novels. These books have a combined cover price of $11.00 or more in the U.S. and $13.00 or more in Canada, but they are yours to keep absolutely FREE!

3. There's <u>no</u> catch. You're under <u>no</u> obligation to buy anything. We charge nothing – ZERO – for your first shipment. And you don't have to make any minimum number of purchases – not even one!

4. We call this line "The Best of the Best" because each month you'll receive the best books by the world's hottest authors. These authors show up time and time again on all the major bestseller lists and their books sell out as soon as they hit the stores. You'll like the convenience of getting them delivered to your home at our discount prices…and you'll love your subscriber newsletter featuring author news, horoscopes, recipes, book reviews and much more!

5. We hope that after receiving your free books you'll want to remain a subscriber. But the choice is yours – to continue or cancel, anytime at all! So why not take us up on our invitation, with no risk of any kind. You'll be glad you did!

6. And remember…we'll send you a mystery gift ABSOLUTELY FREE just for giving "The Best of the Best" a try!

MIRA®

SPECIAL FREE GIFT!

We'll send you a fabulous mystery gift, absolutely FREE, simply for accepting our no-risk offer!

Visit us at
www.mirabooks.com

® and TM are trademarks of Harlequin Enterprises Limited. © 1996 MIRA BOOKS

Books FREE!

DETACH AND MAIL CARD TODAY!

HURRY! Return this card promptly to get
2 FREE Books
and a
FREE Gift!

The Best of the Best™

YES! Please send me the 2 FREE "The Best of the Best" novels and FREE gift for which I qualify. I understand that I am under no obligation to purchase anything further, as explained on the opposite page.

Affix
peel-off
2 FREE BOOKS
sticker here.

P-BB1-00
385 MDL CY2W

185 MDL CY2X

NAME (PLEASE PRINT CLEARLY)

ADDRESS

APT.# CITY

STATE/PROV. ZIP/POSTAL CODE

The Best of the Best™—Here's How it Works

Accepting your 2 free books and gift places you under no obligation to buy anything. You may keep the books and gift and return the shipping statement marked "cancel." If you do not cancel, about a month later we will send you 4 additional novels and bill you just $4.24 each in the U.S., or $4.74 each in Canada, plus 25¢ delivery per book and applicable sales tax, if any.* That's the complete price, and — compared to cover prices of $5.50 or more each in the U.S. and $6.50 or more each in Canada — it's quite a bargain! You may cancel at any time, but if you choose to continue, every month we'll send you 4 more books, which you may either purchase at the discount price...or return to us and cancel your subscription.

*Terms and prices subject to change without notice. Sales tax applicable in N.Y. Canadian residents will be charged applicable provincial taxes and GST.

If offer card is missing write to: The Best of the Best, 3010 Walden Ave., P.O. Box 1867, Buffalo, NY 14240-1867

POSTAGE WILL BE PAID BY ADDRESSEE

BUSINESS REPLY MAIL

FIRST-CLASS MAIL   PERMIT NO. 717   BUFFALO NY

THE BEST OF THE BEST
3010 WALDEN AVE
PO BOX 1867
BUFFALO NY 14240-9952

NO POSTAGE
NECESSARY
IF MAILED
IN THE
UNITED STATES

capable of sticking to rules. She was beginning to understand his nickname, Quicksilver. And yet, she wondered, as they peeled out of the parking lot and darted through Washington traffic toward the beltway, wasn't that a part of Graham that attracted her?

But the romantic interlude was over for Jane. She was on the job, acutely aware of every car on the road, every broken-down vehicle on the shoulder, every possible hiding place for a pursuing vehicle. Graham insisted on stopping for lunch although Jane would have gladly gone without to avoid the possibility of problems. She was well aware that they were safer on the road, moving.

"But I'm hungry," Graham complained.

She insisted he stay in the car while she went into a McDonald's. Walking out of the place, Jane was brought up short by a hard poke in the ribs and a voice whispering harshly, "Stick 'em up!"

Adrenaline flared in her veins and she dropped the bag of food, smashing her elbow into the hand at her back, knocking it aside, then spun around, ready to slam a knee into the assaulter's groin.

"Graham!" she gasped.

"Damn it, you were ready to emasculate me!"

"You're right! Oh, darn you! *Darn you*!"

He picked up the bag of hamburgers. "I think your drink spilled," he said mildly.

She insisted on driving.

"Okay." Graham gave in. "Okay, do whatever you want. I've been a bad boy."

Silently Jane took the keys from his outstretched hand, got in and started the car, waiting without saying a word.

"Okay, so you're mad at me. But you're forgetting that I used to work in security. Everything was safe, Janey. I wouldn't have jeopardized the Picassos just to tease you."

She shot him a hard look as she pulled back onto the interstate. "I'm not putting down your capabilities, Graham. I'm only trying to do my job. I simply can't take things as lightly as you do. And you can't just keep apologizing like a little child, then turn around and pull stunts like that." She caught his glance and decided that he wasn't taking her seriously. "From now on," she said, determined to drive home her point, "I'll just tell Lew that Norma has got to go on jobs with you."

"You wouldn't!"

She fell silent, satisfied.

The delivery at the Metropolitan Museum of Art at Central Park went smoothly. Graham got all his papers signed while Jane scouted the area and he *did* behave himself.

"Can I drive now?" he asked as they stood on the curb together.

"Of course."

"The keys?" He smiled, a mixture of devilry and sincerity tilting his handsome mouth.

She handed them over. "I'm sorry I got so mad back at that restaurant," Jane began as he pulled out into traffic. "You've just got to understand how seriously I take my work."

"Okay. Friends then?"

She nodded.

"Lovers, too?" He tipped his sunglasses up and winked at her.

Graham pulled up in front of the Barbizon Hotel, double-parked, swiveled in his seat and took her chin in his hand. "Jane, that was the best weekend I ever had. Can we do it again?"

"I'd love to."

"You did have fun? Even with the dogs and Mom and Dad and all that stuff?"

"It was wonderful."

"Gosh, I'm going to miss you. I have that Amsterdam job coming up shortly. The diamonds. Norma's going this time—Lew's orders. I wish it were you going along, Janey. What a wild time we could have." He kissed her gently and her stomach rolled, quivering with delight. "Norma's an old grouch."

"Norma's a great lady and I'll bet she's a terrific bodyguard."

"Not like you, Janey." He kissed her again. "Come over for dinner in a couple of days?"

"Um, I will. But I'll cook this time."

"Anything you want."

A car honked furiously behind them.

"Uh-oh, I gotta go," said Graham. "Bye, I'll call you."

She got out quickly, waved at the angry driver and blew Graham a kiss.

Riding up in the elevator, Jane started to daydream. What if Norma got sick—oh, nothing serious, maybe a sinus attack or something—and she had to go to Amsterdam with Graham in Norma's place? She closed her eyes and imagined the trip. Wow. The old-world charm of Europe, millions in sparkling diamonds and Quicksilver, all to herself.

CHAPTER TEN

WHEN NORMA SWEPT INTO Jane's tiny office it felt like the woman was sucking all the air and a few of the loose items from the rest of the building in with her. "I found you an apartment," was her pronouncement.

Jane's head snapped up. "You *did*?"

"You're still looking, I take it?" Norma asked briskly.

"You bet! But I haven't found anything I can afford."

"'Course not. You have to *know* someone. I know someone. An old friend of mine is the landlady of a building up on 84th and First Avenue, East side. Somebody moved out on her and she needs a tenant—quick."

Jane felt excitement stirring but tried to bank the embers against disappointment. She couldn't help the grimace on her face when she asked, "How much?"

"Two hundred and fifty. A steal. It's rent controlled."

"Holy cow, that's cheap!"

"It's a one-bedroom shotgun apartment. She'll let it for first and last, no damage deposit. It needs a little fixing up."

"If it's got walls and a door and indoor plumbing I'll take it."

"Call her. Give her that old 'I'm-a-great-tenant' routine. I'm sure she'll let you have it but there'll be the usual lecture on her waiting list." Norma thrust a scrap of paper at Jane, then turned to leave.

"Gosh, Norma, *thanks*, I mean it."

"No problem." Norma disappeared down the hall and Jane felt the urge to kick her heels in the air.

"Oh, boy," she whispered to herself. An apartment, a home, her first bachelor place all her very own. Graham would love it; he hated that old Barbizon that wouldn't let him go beyond the lobby. She could clean and fuss and cook for Graham. She could have friends over and if one of her brothers wanted to come and visit, there would be a place for him to stay. She'd be a New Yorker, not a hotel dweller but a real, live, bona fide New Yorker!

Wait a minute. She had to call and get the place. What if someone got there first and snatched it away from her? What if she didn't hit it off with the landlady? Fingers shaking, she dialed the number on the scrap of paper. A hoarse voice answered.

"Lily Sypnewski?" asked Jane, stumbling over the last name.

"Yeah."

"This is Jane Manning. Norma Stedman told me you have an apartment to rent."

"Who'd you say this was?"

"Jane Manning. I work with Norma Stedman."

"I *do* have a waiting list."

"Yes, I'm sure you do, but I'd be such a good tenant. I'd always pay my rent on time, I'm a good housekeeper. I have a steady job and—" Jane thought quickly "—and I never make any noise."

"Well..."

"Oh, please, Mrs. Sypnewski, I'm absolutely desperate." There was a long pause on the other end of the line and Jane did not breathe once.

"Norma's friend?" the woman asked rhetorically. "Well, I suppose for Norma's sake. Five hundred is what I'll need up front. And a little elbow grease on your part. I suppose you'll want to see it first?"

"No, it'll be fine, I'm sure. I'll take it. Can I bring you over a check today?"

"Sooner the better," rasped Lily.

"I'll be there after work, by six," said Jane firmly.

Of course, she couldn't think of anything but the apartment all day. She and Lukas had to deliver some new perfume samples that afternoon to a plant way out in Hoboken somewhere. They got lost and hit the Lincoln Tunnel on the return trip during rush hour. She sat behind the wheel fretting and impatient as they crawled along, in the traffic.

"I'll never make it," she muttered, checking her watch again.

"Make what?" asked Lukas.

"Look, do you mind if we take a quick detour? I have to drop off a check for an apartment I'm going to rent. I'm afraid I'll be late if we go all the way to the office first."

Lukas shrugged his heavy shoulders. "I am a gentleman. Besides, this way I know where you live." He leered at her.

She shot him a disgusted glance. "I thought we had all that straightened out, Luke."

"We do, sure we do. You got a boyfriend. A little skinny, maybe, but he's a nice guy. So, I make a little joke."

Shaking her head, Jane headed crosstown. The address. She rummaged around in her purse with one hand until she found the piece of paper—84th off First Avenue. Damn, every street she passed seemed to go one way, the wrong way. New York was laid out simply but it worked only in theory.

The building was small and old, in the center of the block. Someone had tried to grow geraniums in a window box but they had wilted in the heat. It was a nice residential neighborhood in Germantown, quiet, with a deli on the corner. Jane left Lukas in the car, ran up the front steps and pushed the button marked Super. Her heart pounded so hard she put a sweaty hand on her chest as if to still it. It was 6:05 p.m.

The door buzzed open and Jane stepped into the hallway. A voice came out of the dimness to croak, "You're late."

Jane blinked and strained her eyes in the weak light. "I'm sorry, the traffic..."

"Sure, I know. You're Jane, huh?"

"Yes. Mrs. Sypnewski?"

Lily was under five feet tall. She was dressed in a conglomeration of gauzy, silky clothes, layers of skirts and blouses and scarves in bright colors, giving her a gypsy-like aura. Her hair was dyed jet-black and pulled back into a bun and her face was soft and velvety with tiny wrinkles. Her minuscule feet were shod in black patent leather Mary Janes and in her hand—perpetually, Jane was to learn—was a king-sized cigarette.

"Come on," Lily said, jangling a ring of keys, "I'll show it to you."

The door opened directly into the living room that opened directly into the kitchen that led to the bedroom that... "Shotgun apartment," murmured Jane to herself.

"Yeah, if you shot a gun at the front door it'd go straight through to the back," put in Lily.

There were a few basic pieces of furniture, the kitchen was old-fashioned, the stove desperately needed cleaning, the mattress had seen better days, the bathroom was...ugh. Jane saw what Norma had meant: it needed "a little fixing up."

"It's a rat's nest, isn't it?" Lily was commenting. "Poor old Mrs. Singer, her son finally had her carted off to an old folks' home up in Yonkers."

Mrs. Singer hadn't been too spick-and-span, Jane noted. "I'll take it," she repeated firmly, pulling out her checkbook and scribbling out a check quickly, as if afraid she might change her own mind.

Lily handed her three keys. "It's all yours, honey. No pets, no dope, men are okay as long as they don't make noise. I get up late so don't bug me until I've had my cigarette and my coffee, okay?"

"Okay, Lily." But the tiny figure had scurried out and all that remained was the scent of cigarette smoke mixed with baby powder.

"My Lord," breathed Jane. Lukas was waiting in the car. She closed her eyes, hugged herself and spun around in the center of her new living room then rushed out, struggling with the three different locks on the door, wishing she could stay and start cleaning and planning....

"GRAHAM!" SHE SAID BREATHLESSLY into the phone that night when he called. "I've got an apartment!" Then she had to tell him the whole story, about Norma and Lily and the heavy traffic.

"Janey, that's wonderful! When are you moving in?"

"Well, it needs some work. It's a mess. Probably this weekend."

"Want some help?"

"Oh, yes, would you mind?"

"No, sweets, I wouldn't mind a bit. I even know this great Goodwill store where you can get everything you need. Make a list."

"I'm so excited I don't know what to do!"

"I'm jealous," he said mock-seriously.

"Now you can come over to dinner at *my* place," she replied proudly.

"And you'll let me in past the lobby?"

"I certainly will," she said, laughing. "As long as you don't make too much noise!"

"Noise?"

"Lily's rule. Men are okay if they're quiet."

"Sensible woman," he agreed. "Janey, I miss you, babe. And I can't wait to see your apartment but I'll be out of town until Friday. Okay? Saturday morning we'll go to work on that place, I promise."

"You're too good to me," Jane said softly, "and I miss you, too."

"Damn, Janey, I wish you were here!"

"Me, too."

"See you Saturday."

"Bye, Graham."

It was so hot and humid on Saturday morning a person could cut the soggy air with a knife. The apartment smelled moldy and looked dingy when she ushered him in.

Jane had taken care of the utilities and phone during the week; she'd done some scrubbing in the evenings and hung some clothes in the closet. Lily had lent her a vacuum cleaner. But still it had been discouraging.

Graham changed all that. He rubbed his hands together, grabbed Jane and kissed her soundly. "It needs a little work is all," he said cheerfully. "I've seen lots worse."

He whisked her off to the Goodwill store. "My mother showed me this place years ago. One half of New York donates stuff to this store; the other half buys the stuff from it."

The store was housed in the basement of an old warehouse near the East Side docks in lower Manhattan. Jane had never seen so many things crammed into an area she estimated to be the size of a football field. It was dark and dusty and smelly in the brick building and there was no air-conditioning. She held on to Graham's arm, feeling uncharacteristically insecure, expecting wharf rats to leap out at her from the shadowy corners.

"Ugh," Jane said once as they meandered in and out of aisles that had stacks and stacks of used clothing, enough clothing to outfit an army. "I don't know about this."

"Nothing like it in Rifle?"

"That's for sure. Listen," she suggested, "maybe I could go to a department store, use my new credit card or something. I only need a few things, really."

"Nothing doing. You're getting too used to Bloomies and Saks. A bad habit. This place is for the real folks, Jane, the needy and the ones just starting out—like you."

"I'll bet *some* start out in Bloomies," muttered Jane as she twitched her nose over a pile of very worn sheets.

"Snob," said Graham good-naturedly.

It did take a full hour of shuffling through the piles of sheets and towels but eventually Jane was handing Graham a stack of linens. "These are in good condition. I'm amazed."

"I take it I get to do all the carrying."

"It was your idea to come here."

There were piles of chipped dishes and china—real china—and aisles and aisles of pots and pans and toaster ovens and vintage blenders. Everything. There were rows of furniture, piles of the old stuff stacked to the ceiling. There were chairs and tables and bed frames, even a brass one.

"I should get it," Jane exclaimed. "A real brass bed."

"There's a perfectly serviceable bed in the apartment."

"I know, but brass..."

"Come on," he said, shouldering her past the aisle, as his arms were filled, "I'd never be able to look myself in the mirror again if I let you overspend at the Goodwill."

"It was your idea."

"So you keep reminding me."

It was a silly old thing—an early sixties' clock radio, in dirty white plastic with a round clock face and a metal alarm tab that was missing its plastic knob. Jane fingered it thoughtfully and cocked her head. "You know, I had this same one, I swear, when I was a kid. The *same* one. Oh, Graham, it's even missing that clear knob for the alarm. Mine was, too."

"Must be yours then." He smiled and studied her face.

"It couldn't be. You're teasing."

"Maybe I am and maybe I'm not."

"Should I...? I mean, do you suppose it works?"

So they plugged it into an outlet behind the counter and lo and behold, WOR, New York, blared away. "I can't believe it!" breathed Jane. "It *is* my radio."

The price tag, no doubt placed on it fifteen years before, said a dollar fifty. The mountain in Graham's arms grew.

By eleven-thirty, they were both tired and grimy and sweaty as the temperature in the basement edged toward ninety degrees. "Can we go?" asked Graham hopefully.

"In a minute."

"I thought you hated this place."

"I never said that." And she stopped to dig through the stacks of moth-eaten blankets, adding, "There *must* be a winter here sometime."

By noon, the back of his Porsche was piled with pots and dishes, silverware, the sheets and towels, a few small tables, lamps and the old radio. They stopped at a hardware store and bought paint—white for the living room, pale green for the bedroom and bright yellow for the bathroom.

Lunch was thick ham sandwiches on pumpernickel and vinegary potato salad from the corner deli and they ate on Jane's new mismatched plates on her new table. She'd never tasted anything so delicious.

Jane put on an old T-shirt of Graham's that he'd thoughtfully brought along and they painted all afternoon as the old radio played. Graham sang along with the music, did an impromptu dance step once in a while, paintbrush in hand, and managed to get paint in his hair, on his jeans and on the floor.

Jane was happy. She loved being busy, having something physical to do. She loved having Graham there as if they were decorating their own place together, as so many married couples did. *Married couples.* What was she thinking? She and Graham...well, it was too soon. They'd only known each other a few weeks really. But still...

By late afternoon the windows were wide open in an attempt to let the paint dry. Jane put dishes in the cupboards and made up the bed with her "new" sheets and blankets. The watery sun threw lines of light across the freshly painted walls.

"I love it," Jane said. "My own apartment. Oh, Graham."

"I'd grab you and throw you on that bed but I've got paint all over me," he said.

"You could take a shower in my bathroom," she pointed out.

"So could you," he said, his eyes lighting up. "Sort of christen the shower."

"What would Lily say?"

"From what you've told me of her, nothing." He took her hand and led her through the bedroom to the small sunny bathroom. Pulling her T-shirt over her head, he bent to kiss one soft shoulder. "Lovely."

"There's paint in your hair," Jane murmured, running her hand through his thick, fair waves.

"I know."

The shower felt cool and soothing to her skin. She soaped Graham's body, scrubbing with a washcloth at the splotches of paint. She washed it out of his hair while he stood with his eyes squeezed shut and the warm water running down the flawless, tanned satin of his skin.

Then it was his turn. Gently he shampooed her hair and ran a soapy washcloth over her body until she shivered with pleasure. They both stood under the spray, locked together, hands slippery on wet skin, lips searching, pressing, as the warm water sluiced over them and the old pipes clanked and knocked on the walls.

Soaking wet footprints led to the bedroom, dripping bodies dampened the freshly made bed. "So what," whispered Graham. "I'll get you more sheets."

His kisses excited her, his hands intoxicated her. The newly painted green walls spun before Jane's eyes as Graham took her on an incredible journey with him, an odyssey of sensation and emotion.

"This bed is well and truly christened," Graham murmured some time later.

"Mmm," Jane said, running the sole of her foot up and down his calf.

"Isn't this better than the Barbizon Hotel?"

"Mmm," she repeated.

Graham rolled over on his back and put his hands behind his head. "We owe Norma one for this."

"I know." Jane stretched lazily, catlike. "I've been trying to think of what to do." She sat up suddenly, the sheet falling away to her waist. "I know! I'll have a party! A real party. I'll invite Norma and her husband and Donna."

"Don't forget Frank," said Graham.

"Frank. Of course," agreed Jane. "Saturday night."

"Am I invited?" Graham asked softly, stroking her side, his hand moving over her ribs to her hip and then lower…

"What will I make? I mean, I've never had a party like this before."

"Have it catered," he suggested wryly.

"*Graham.*"

"Am I invited?"

"Yes, silly. I couldn't have it without you."

Saturday night came too soon. Jane had cleaned all day, arranged flowers in a vase she bought at Woolworth's, cooked her chicken and chili casserole, bought ice cream, paper plates, plastic cups and beer and wine. She wore her green and white dress and prayed for an evening breeze to stir the stagnant air in her apartment.

Norma and Martin arrived first, buzzing the door at seven sharp. Jane gasped in dismay, remembering Martin's wheelchair and the front steps but Norma muscled the chair up the steps as if she were a longshoreman. Martin held a wrapped package carefully on his lap.

"Oh, you shouldn't have!" admonished Jane. "This is a party to thank *you.*"

The box contained a set of long-stemmed glasses. "I figured you wouldn't have any," stated Norma.

Donna and Frank arrived next. Donna wore red parachute pants, white high heels and a purple, orange and red filmy blouse that came to her knees. She looked, Jane thought, like a particularly bright, exotic flower. Frank appeared sulky and wore jeans, a Western-style shirt, a belt with a rather large silver buckle and his name etched on the back of the leather: "Frank." Jane had a sneaking feeling Donna had made him come to the party.

Donna brought a big box of Godiva chocolates that was immediately opened and sampled.

"It doesn't look half bad," Norma admitted, glancing around critically. "You've done a good job."

"Graham helped a lot."

"It's terrific!" said Donna, snapping her gum enthusiastically. "You lucky thing!"

Lily arrived next. Jane had invited her because her landlady knew Norma. She brought a bottle of Jack Daniel's. "I knew you wouldn't have any," she rasped, blowing out a stream of smoke. "Mind you, this is my bottle. I'm only lending it for the evening."

The buzzer sounded. It had to be Graham, but when he didn't appear at her door, Jane peeked out into the hall. The outside door was filled with a large, untidy lump.

"You weren't supposed to look," she heard Graham saying. "Dammit all, I'm stuck!"

He was trying to drag something inside. It was huge—taller than him and bulging against the door frame. Frank came to help and, with a few minutes of wrestling, it popped into the hallway.

"A horse!" exclaimed Jane. It was a horse, a stuffed horse, a *huge* fur animal with a pale, fuzzy coat, a bristly mane and tail and patent leather hooves.

Graham stood, hands on hips, puffing a little. "It's been hell getting it here."

They pushed and tugged some more and finally got it into Jane's apartment so that everyone could see.

"Helluva waste of money," grumbled Norma. "Impractical."

"I didn't want you to be homesick," explained Graham. "I thought he looked a little like Pard."

Jane stroked the soft neck. "I love him. Oh, thank you." She felt her eyes fill with tears at thoughts of home, the fragrant barn, her brothers and the big old, comfortable house. And her new friends, too, her new life...and Graham.

Donna patted her on the back, Frank downed a plastic cup of Lily's bourbon, Lily blew smoke rings in the air and Martin chided Norma for grumbling.

"He'll keep you company," Graham was saying and she gave him a brilliant, grateful smile through her tears.

Dinner was a success. Lily trailed the corner of one of her scarves into the salsa, dropped ashes in the salad and told hilarious jokes.

"How many Californians does it take to change a light bulb?" she asked.

"I don't know," said Jane dutifully. "How many?"

"Five. One to screw in the bulb and four to experience it." Then she laughed and laughed so hard that she went into a coughing spasm.

Everyone ate on paper plates on their laps and talked across one another. Even Frank loosened up—maybe it was the booze—and smiled at one of Lily's off-color jokes about bikers, but he seemed to be ill at ease and kept a hand on Donna's arm or waist or knee, as if for security. By the end of the evening Jane still couldn't figure out what Donna saw in him. Oh well, to each his own, she told herself.

Graham was charming, even engaging Frank in conversation—about cars, Jane decided, as she overheard "carburetor" and "turbo" and "horsepower" from that corner of the room.

So what if her ice cream was melted because the old, chugging refrigerator didn't work too well or if the pipes banged and grunted for ten minutes after someone used the bathroom? No one seemed to mind.

Martin told hair-raising stories of his former work on the high rises in the city. It was fascinating, Jane thought, to hear him talk about walking a six-inch steel beam a thousand feet above the ground.

"How could you do it?" asked Donna, wide-eyed.

"I'm half Mohawk Indian," Martin said. "All of us Mohawks are great high-rise workers."

His accident had not been due to a fall, he told them, but to a truck backing up into some equipment that had collapsed on him. "I paint pictures now," he said, without self-pity.

Norma patted her husband on the shoulder with her big hand. "He does paintings of the buildings he's worked on. He's getting real good, too. Sells 'em to the buildings to hang in the lobbies."

Everybody was gone by eleven-thirty and Jane settled back on the couch with a sigh. She felt tired but good, a successful housewarming, a pleasant evening with friends behind her. Inside the air was finally cooling off a degree or two; outside the summer city throbbed, sirens wailed in the distance, horns honked occasionally, New York beat like a heart full of anticipation. This was what she'd always wanted and daydreamed about when she'd been riding the desolate range with her brothers or tapping a pen against her teeth in class at Fort Collins. She'd made her choice—her *own* choice—and it had turned out perfectly. No, better than perfect because in her wildest imaginings she could never have conjured up someone as wonderful as Graham.

"It was a real nice party," Graham said, breaking into her thoughts as he dumped paper plates into a trash bag.

"Was it? Do you think everyone had a good time?"

"Absolutely."

Jane sighed again and rubbed at some ashes Lily had spilled on the coffee table. "My first party."

"But not your last, Janey."

She smiled at him. "I love Pard, Graham."

He sat next to her and pushed her damp bangs off her forehead. "I thought for a minute there, you were awful homesick and I thought maybe I'd just made things worse."

She ran a finger down his shirt front. "No, Pard is sweet and so are you and I'm very, very glad I'm here with you."

Graham stretched out his legs in front of him and yawned. "I'm getting old, I guess. Not even midnight and I've had it."

"Ancient," Jane agreed. "Will you stay?"

"I'm too tired to go anywhere," Graham said lazily, resting a hand on her knee.

"That says lots for my charms," Jane answered dryly.

"I can't say enough about your charms, Janey, my love," Graham murmured, walking his fingers along her thigh.

"Should I do the dishes?" asked Jane, looking around at the party litter.

"Later, Janey, later," said Graham, turning to her and pulling her into his arms while outside the city pulsed steadily on into the night.

CHAPTER ELEVEN

ON MONDAY JANE SLEPT right through her alarm and leapt out of bed when she realized the time: 7:35!

No time to jog or even shower.

What had gotten into her? Had it been that last-minute trip to Cleveland with Lukas the day before? They *had* gotten into La Guardia late. Then an impish smile curved her lips; perhaps it had been Graham's after-midnight phone call.

She was ready to leave, snatching up her purse, feeling guilty and harassed, when the telephone rang.

It was her father. "Jane, glad I caught you."

"Daddy, I've got to run. Can I call you later? I'm sorry."

"I was only checking to see how you're coming along. Haven't heard from you for a week. I was getting worried. Is that new apartment of yours safe?"

"Yes, there are three locks and I'm perfectly safe."

"Nice neighborhood?"

"Very nice."

"Well, Jane, honey, are you enjoying your new place?"

"I love it, Daddy…"

"Well, I was just wondering."

"Oh, Daddy, I'm sorry. Really I am. I've been so busy."

"You're all right then?"

"Fine. Honestly."

"Well, try to call more often, Jane. Reverse the charges if you like."

"Daddy," she begged off, "I have to go. I'll call you later. I promise."

She left her apartment thinking there was some truth to the words that you could never go home again. But whereas a month ago Jane would have felt a twinge of homesickness, now there was only a peaceful kind of acceptance.

It was pleasantly warm outside, certainly not like September in the Rockies with that cool, crisp, high country air, the light morning frost on the range, the breath pluming from the horses' nostrils. But New York would do just fine.

At 8:45, fifteen minutes late, Jane hurried up the steps to Mercury's offices, planning in her mind the excuse she would give Lew.

But nobody noticed her tardiness.

When Jane walked into the office it was in a turmoil. Donna grabbed her and cried, "It's Norma, they shot Norma!"

"What?" Jane gasped, bludgeoned by shock.

"Oh God, Norma's been shot! She was on a job with Peter. He just called from the hospital."

"How bad is it?" Jane asked, abruptly feeling ice-cold, her mind flying in a dozen directions.

"I...I don't know!" wailed Donna.

Lew strode up, his round face drawn in grim lines. He kept slicking his scanty hair back in a nervous gesture. "Where did they take her, Donna?" he asked. "Calm down. What hospital?"

Donna cried harder and searched blindly through papers on her desk. "I wrote it, I wrote it down...."

No one seemed to know what to do. It was as if someone had cried "fire" but not a soul remembered the drill.

"What did Peter say?" Jane kept pressing Donna for a

straight answer. "Is Norma alive? Donna, you've got to tell us. Which hospital?"

"Oh, God! Here it is!" Donna held up a scrap of paper.

Jane grabbed it. She had no idea where Bellevue Hospital was. "I'm going," she said. "I don't have a job this morning. Anyone else?"

"Peter said she was going into surgery, emergency surgery," sobbed Donna.

"So she's still alive," said Rick. "Maybe it's not so bad. I'll go with you, Jane."

They caught a cab to the hospital while the others stayed behind to keep some semblance of order in the office. "Call us," Lew had ordered. "Keep me informed."

"God damn it," Rick swore as their taxi weaved in and out of traffic. "It shouldn't have come to this. Poor Norma."

But no one was more upset about Norma than Jane. A cold lump of guilt was sitting in her stomach like lead. She couldn't forget what had crossed her mind when Graham told her about the Amsterdam job: if something happened to Norma then Jane could go to Amsterdam with Graham.

They entered Bellevue through the emergency room where even at this early hour there were patients being wheeled to and fro on carts and children crying in their mothers' arms and white-jacketed doctors and nurses scurrying about.

Rick tried to find out Norma's status from the desk nurse but got very little out of her. "You'll just have to wait, sir, until Mrs. Stedman's doctor is through operating."

"What kind of injury is it?" asked Jane.

"I don't know," said the nurse. "Really I don't."

Tears burning in her eyes, Jane tried again. "Can you tell us anything? Please..."

And amazingly the sympathetic woman said, "All

right, I'll see what I can do. Just please wait in the room over there. Go on now. I'll do what I can.''

It was at least fifteen minutes before the nurse poked her head in the door. "It's a chest wound. Right lung." She started to leave.

"Wait!" cried Jane, leaping to her feet. "Is she going to be all right? What did they say?"

The nurse shook her head. "I don't know what's going on in the operating room, miss. Now, please, I've got work to do. You'll simply have to wait."

Jane turned to Rick and swallowed a sob. "Poor Norma. Oh, God, this is so awful."

It turned out that Peter had been at the hospital but the police had driven him over to the station house to make his report. "I wish to hell he'd get back here," Rick said. "I'd sure like to know exactly what happened."

Rick left shortly thereafter to get them some coffee and call Mercury. When he disappeared down the hall and into an elevator, Jane felt suddenly, horribly alone. She tried leafing through last month's *Smithsonian Magazine*, in between pacing, then peeking down the hall as if somehow, miraculously, Norma would be standing there, sound and fit as always. She kept telling herself that Norma was in excellent physical condition. The woman didn't smoke, drink or have an ounce of fat on her body. That counted for something, didn't it?

But still, a chest wound, a lung...

Nervous adrenaline pumped through Jane's body, making her eye twitch and her knees rubbery. Her heart was pounding and her mouth felt as dry as cotton. Where was Rick? Had anyone notified Martin, Norma's husband? Would Martin be able to make it to the hospital on his own? Maybe she should find a phone and call Mercury to make sure someone had thought to call Norma's husband.

No, no, she decided. She'd better wait right there in case the surgeon came in.

The minutes ticked by slowly. Through the glass-paneled window in the waiting lounge Jane could see one of those round, white-faced generic clocks like the ones in her old high school. The sweeping second hand seemed to be moving in slow motion.

Where was Rick?

God, what she wouldn't do to get to a phone, call Mercury and then Graham. Graham should know, too. And, besides, Jane wanted him there, *needed* him to be with her. This waiting, the not-knowing, was ghastly.

Rick swung open the door at 10:20. Coffee sloshed unnoticed from two plastic cups onto his hands and trouser leg.

"Did you tell someone to get in touch with Martin Stedman?" she rushed to ask.

He nodded and handed her a cup. "Lew went to pick him up. They should be here shortly. Any word yet?"

"None. I wonder how long this sort of surgery takes?"

"I haven't the slightest idea. I imagine a while, though, what with having to go into a chest." Rick shrugged helplessly.

"And her lung... Oh, God." Jane fell silent, trying to remember details from her year at vet school but unable to think, blocked by her stress.

"Rick," she said, getting to her feet shakily, "I need to call someone. I'll be right back."

But Graham was not home. "Darn," she said, waiting and waiting for the phone to be picked up. After fifteen rings, Jane finally hung up slowly and sagged against the wall.

Why had she had those thoughts about Norma? How could she have been so mean and selfish? And where the devil was Graham?

Martin Stedman arrived, his wheelchair pushed by Lew, at 11:30. His frail, seamed face was the color of ashes.

"Have you heard anything?" asked Lew.

"Not a word," replied Rick.

Jane crouched by Martin's chair and took his hand gently in hers. "I'm sure Norma's going to be okay."

Noon came and went. Still no word. Martin kept asking: "Is it a good sign when it takes a long time?"

And Lew would reply: "I'm sure it is."

At 12:15 the door swung open and Graham stood there, tall and strong, self-possessed, his face creased by uncharacteristic concern. Jane's heart gave a great glad leap and she left Martin's side to run to Graham.

"I tried to call," she said in a whisper. "Oh, Graham, this is so terrible. Poor Norma..." And her broken voice trailed away.

Graham took both her hands in his. "I stopped by the office to see if you wanted to go to lunch. Donna told me." He gazed at her soberly. "How long has Norma been in surgery?"

"Since...9:00, 9:30. I'm not exactly sure." Jane wanted desperately to tell Graham, to unburden herself of her awful guilt—wishing Norma would get sick—but she couldn't. Not there, not with Lew and Rick and especially Martin all looking at them.

"Do you want to walk down the hall or something? Get some air?"

"Well..."

"Come on. I'm sure nothing is going to happen for five minutes." His hand squeezed hers reassuringly. "Come on." He pushed open the door with his shoulder and gently led her along.

They got coffee; Jane had decaf because she already felt too shaky. Sitting at the cafeteria table, she lowered her eyes. "I feel like this is my fault," she confessed in a whisper. "I know it's crazy, Graham, but I wished Norma would get sick."

"But why? I don't understand."

Her face grew hot. "Because I thought if Norma were sick, I'd be asked to go to Amsterdam with you." There, it was said. But she felt no better.

"Janey." His voice was soft and caring, caressing. "Are you really blaming yourself? Come on, that's absurd."

"No, it's not. Well, of course it is *logically*, but in my gut I've always thought that if I wished for something hard enough, it would come true."

"What you're saying is that you've been able to set high standards for yourself and you've lived up to them. But this is different."

"It is and it isn't. But I can't help it if I feel miserable and guilty, Graham." She finally looked up at him.

"It's okay to *feel*, Jane. And if you feel guilty then go ahead. It'll pass. You're just upset right now and Lord knows you have a right to be. Norma has been very kind to you these past weeks."

"Almost like a mother."

"I know. And believe me, when she wakes up from surgery and you tell her all about how you wished this on her—" he smiled and leaned close "—Norma will have a good laugh along with you."

"Is she going to wake up, Graham? Is she?"

Of course, he had no answer. They left the cafeteria and headed back up to the third floor. There was still no news, nothing save a quick word from the desk nurse after her lunch hour.

"It's been over three hours," Martin said with a sigh as he wheeled his chair around the confined space of the lounge. "Why don't they let us know something!" He stopped moving and put his face in his hands.

The waiting was terrible, as if they were all being tested for some kind of masochistic endurance. But it didn't stop; there was no letup of emotion or the pain of their nerves being scraped raw.

Donna showed up at 1:30 p.m. Frank, amazingly, was with her, clean shaven, in a decent sport shirt, looking as solemn as the rest of them. "Peter just got out of the police station," Donna told everyone, "and he offered to

man the front desk for me. He looked awful," she said,
chewing her gum madly, as nervous as they all were.
"And he's worried sick about Norma."

"Was Peter able to tell the police anything?" Lew
wanted to know.

"Not much," she replied. "There were two of them.
Big men. Oh, yeah, they were wearing those ski-type
masks. Black and red, I think Peter said." She shrugged,
tucking her arm into Frank's. "They got away with the
jewelry, though," breathed Donna. "He said Norma
should have just let them go."

"It was her *job*!" Martin Stedman came half out of his
chair until Jane managed to calm him down.

"Peter was only worried, I'm sure," Jane said. "He
didn't mean anything by it. Really."

"She's a hero," Lew was quick to add.

"A *heroine*," said Jane, patting Martin's arm.

The schoolroom clock crawled along at a snail's pace.
2:10. 2:15. At 2:19 the door swung open and a tall man
in blood-splattered greens with his mask hanging around
his neck stood on the threshold.

They all froze.

He pulled off his cap showing thick sandy hair and his
lips split into a smile.

THAT HAD BEEN ON MONDAY. By Thursday Norma was
moved from the Intensive Care Unit into a private room.
Several of Mercury's employees were waiting down the
hall for the nurse's okay to visit her. Jane was one of
them. So was Graham, who had barely left Jane's side
since the morning of the shooting. Even Lily Sypnewski
was there, having been informed by Jane as to Norma's
condition. Her diminutive figure was dressed in a mauve
flowered caftan that dragged on the floor in the back. She
kept muttering that she hated hospitals and reaching for
her cigarettes, then remembering the No Smoking sign,
she muttered some more.

"Damn fool job for anyone," she said to Jane, her fingers twitching toward the sagging pocket where she kept the cigarette pack.

"Now, you can't stay too long," the nurse admonished the eager entourage.

The first thing that met Jane's eyes was the oxygen tube, then a wire or two hooked to a blood-pressure apparatus and a heart monitor. Jane was intensely relieved to see Norma propped up and smiling, even though there was no color in her cheeks.

"Well, hello," she said, faintly embarrassed by all the to-do. "My, my. Everyone is here."

There were flowers all around and everyone chatted with Norma, making careful, cheerful small talk.

Graham said, "It's great to see you out of Intensive Care."

Lew asked, "Hey, when are you going to quit faking it and get back on the job!"

Peter chimed in with, "You know, you took a shot aimed at me."

"Nonsense," Norma responded. "I was stupid enough to chase those thugs down that alley." And then Peter and Norma had to rehash the whole incident while the others listened raptly. It seemed that while the two of them were making a crosstown jewelry delivery for a store that was moving, the robbers appeared as if from thin air, wearing ski masks, shoving Peter and Norma back in their car while wresting the briefcase from Peter.

"One of them had a gun," said Norma. "I should have let him go but all those years with the police... I just couldn't."

"Norma chased them down an alley," put in Peter. "But what gets me is why the thieves made a hit on us when there was a bodyguard along. They've never done that before."

"Norma was assigned to go along at the last minute,"

Lew said slowly, as if coming to a profound realization. "Maybe the crooks expected you to be alone."

All the talk about the robbery and Norma chasing the men down the alley and getting caught by a stray bullet barely scratched Jane's consciousness. She was thinking, instead, that it could have been *her* accompanying Peter that morning except that she'd been late getting to the office.

Had Norma gone in Jane's place because she'd been late to work? Oh, no…

"I really blew it, Lew," Norma was saying. "You could tell those two jerks were amateurs by the way they moved and handled the gun. I should never have underestimated them. I'm very sorry."

"Norma," Lew said, "it could have happened to anyone. It's not your fault. Hell, and don't get me wrong because I have the utmost respect for New York's finest, but Detective Sorello should have come up with a lead by now."

Norma nodded.

"But don't you worry, we'll get them. They'll pay for what they did to you."

"I worry about your insurance, Lew," Norma said. "It was bad enough and now this…"

"It's all going to work out in the end," answered Lew, "and I'll get my policy renewed. Now, you just rest and get better. Hear me?"

Norma smiled and nodded and the nurse came in, wagging her finger. "You'll have to leave now and let Mrs. Stedman be."

"Nurse," said Norma, "can I have a minute, please." Then she looked at Jane. "You stay, Jane. Just for a minute, please."

The nurse looked disapproving but did leave the room with the others, calling over her starched white shoulder, "I'll be keeping track of the time."

"Are you sure you shouldn't be resting?" Jane cautioned.

Norma beckoned Jane closer. "Later. I can sleep later. I had to talk to you alone." Then, when Jane was about to say something, Norma raised her hand. "I want you to hear me out. And remember, I've got a lot of years of experience and I'm not going to tell you this lightly, Jane. You just be brave for me, won't you?" Norma sounded a little breathless.

"Of course."

"Someone at Mercury is tipping off the robbers, Jane. I'm positive now. You see, I was asked to go with Peter only that morning—a last-minute decision on Lew's part because this other job I was supposed to go on was delayed."

"Did you go with Peter in my place?" Jane blurted out, unable to let the question rest another moment.

Norma raised a brow and looked at Jane for a second. Then she frowned. "Good Lord, girl, has *that* been on your mind all along? Listen to me now. My stupid mistake was none of your doing. Just get that bee out of your bonnet, you got that?"

Jane felt a surge of welcome relief. She squeezed Norma's hand and felt a reassuring, surprisingly strong clasp in return and smiled widely at her. "Boy, does that make me feel better! Now, you get some rest, Norma. The nurse said—"

"Wait a minute, Jane. Damn! These painkillers they dose me with make me so fuzzy. I hate them!"

"Norma—"

"Listen to me. We've got a problem to take care of. Jane, those thieves hit Peter because they'd been told he would be alone. And they were waiting for him. It was real obvious to me that they were hesitant the minute they saw me along. Surprised was the impression I got."

"So you think one of the masked men is a Mercury

employee or getting information from a Mercury employee.''

"Exactly. And, believe me, this is no news at Mercury, either. Detective Sorello questioned all of us, even asked if we would take lie detector tests. I wasn't sure if you were aware…'' She grimaced in pain.

"Oh, I heard the scuttlebutt. Donna, you know. Now, Norma, maybe you better take it easy.''

"Never mind my aches and pains. Anyway, we can eliminate you as a suspect because you weren't around for the earlier robberies,'' said Norma with assurance. "And it isn't me. Now, Donna we know was on the switchboard and Kelly, I'm told, was in Boston. Lukas, as well, was at Mercury all morning, and Rick showed up late for work but I doubt if he could have gotten across town and back that fast. You see, I've had plenty of time to think about this.''

"Okay, maybe that's all true," Jane conceded, "but that sure doesn't mean one of them couldn't be in cahoots with the robbers.''

"No, it doesn't. I'm merely eliminating possibilities. My old police brain working away.'' She cleared her throat roughly.

"Are you all right?''

"Fine. Now, let's see," said Norma, "there's Lew.''

"But Lew *owns* Mercury!''

"So what? If he's in a financial bind he wouldn't be the first to rob his own place, collect the insurance and still have the goods to fence. It's done all the time, believe me.''

Norma moved restlessly, as if searching for a more comfortable position. It made Jane terribly anxious and, besides, the nurse would be back any second. "Can I do something, Norma? Your pillows? A glass of water? I think you've talked enough.''

"Listen to me," Norma said hoarsely. "You're the only one I can trust.''

"I can't accept that it could be Lew."

"Hmm. Well, then, you won't like this, Jane, but there's always Graham Smith."

"Graham?"

"Yes. I know you two are—let's say, close—but, Jane, there's something funny about that guy. He's too slippery, too charming. Too sophisticated."

"No." Norma must be crazy, Jane thought in confusion. The drugs they were giving her...

"Think about it. The robbers were both big men. Graham's six one or two, isn't he? And he wasn't around that morning, was he?"

Jane's heart stopped, remembering the phone ringing and ringing at his place.

"I can see him as the Gentleman Thief. Oh, yes, he'd fit the bill exactly. And these old instincts of mine are rarely wrong."

Norma's voice was weaker. Jane should leave but she couldn't, not now. She had to convince Norma that she was wrong about Graham. She turned her back so Norma couldn't see the anguish on her face. "You're wrong, it's not him. He'd never hurt Lew. He wouldn't harm a fly, I know him too well."

But Norma wasn't through. "Jane, I realize this is the last thing you want to hear, but in my book, he's a prime suspect. And he may not even think he's hurting Lew. He might think the insurance company can afford losses."

"Not Graham." Jane came back around to face Norma. Her chest was aching. "You're my friend, Norma, and God knows I respect you. But on this one you're wrong."

"You're a sharp girl," Norma was saying, "and..."

But she couldn't finish because the nurse had pushed open the door and was ordering, "Out now, miss. I left you too long as it is!"

Jane turned to leave, her brain spinning.

"One more second," pleaded Norma. "Jane, you'll be going to Amsterdam now, you realize. You've got to be careful. It's all on your shoulders. Please, be careful. Watch Graham Smith!''

"You're wrong about him," reiterated Jane shakily. "I'll be perfectly fine. I've got to go. Take care, Norma." And Jane was out the door. For a long moment she leaned her back to the wall and breathed deeply. Poor, poor Norma! The shock, the wound, all the drugs they were pumping into her—no wonder she was suffering delusions.

Graham was standing down the corridor, talking to Lew while he waited for her. She studied him carefully from afar, saw the way he stood with his feet planted apart and his hands negligently in his jacket pockets. She took in the tilt of his head, the strong neck and shoulders, the thick strawberry-blond hair that she'd run her fingers through so lovingly, so often. He was a good man, a wonderful, loving man who simply liked to live life to its fullest.

Norma was sure reaching! Poor woman.

Jane collected herself, calmer now, and went to join the two men.

"Is Norma all right?" asked Lew, his graying brow furrowed.

"She's very tired, I think," said Jane, trying to sound casual. She felt Graham taking her hand. "She only wanted to tell me to be careful from now on." Jane smiled. "But you know me, I'm always careful."

"Yes, of course you are," Lew replied. "But Norma is right. You're going to really have to be on your toes now, Jane Manning." He made a grumbling sound in his throat then added, "I'm off to the police station. It's time I start pushing them for some answers. See you all later." And he disappeared into the elevator.

"Well," began Graham, "it's been a rough few days, hasn't it?" He reached up and pushed the bangs away from Jane's forehead in an affectionate, possessive gesture. "Can I buy you dinner, pretty lady?"

"Sure," said Jane staunchly, "a pizza. From Mario's."

"Mario's it is."

They walked onto the next elevator hand in hand and Jane allowed herself to mull over Norma's wild accusation. And, Jane decided firmly, that was exactly what it was: wild.

CHAPTER TWELVE

"I DON'T LIKE IT," said Lew. "Jane is very new to this profession. We're pushing her too fast and too hard."

Graham fiddled with a pencil sharpener on Lew's desk. "Yeah, I know the diamond job is risky." He glanced up at his friend and frowned. "And it's not that I don't trust Jane. Hell, she's good and her training is tops.... It's just that Norma has had twenty years' experience...." His voice faded and he and Lew exchanged expressions that said: and look what happened to Norma!

"I don't see where there's a choice, though," said Lew. "Everybody in the office knows about the job now and Jane is all we've got. I can't hire someone and have him, or whoever, ready before you leave. There's no time."

"Lew, I don't know. I'd really rather do this job by myself. You know Jane and I—"

"Yes, I know," said Lew humorously.

"Well, it's not such a great idea to be emotionally involved with your bodyguard, for heaven's sake."

"I've taken that into consideration. You're a professional, Graham. I trust you. And if it doesn't work, you always have the option of sending her back and finishing the job alone."

"Okay, okay. But I think you're wrong about one thing, Lew. Jane should be in on the whole plan."

Lew shook his head. "I can't allow you to tell her. Oh, as soon as you leave New York you can let her know that you're hoping to lure the crooks and nab them—it would be madness *not* to tell her that."

"And unfair."

"Very. But I won't have you telling her about the rest. I know it's your contingency plan and it's a damn solid one, clever. But in this office only the two of us are going to be in on it and that's final."

"But who could Jane tell? Especially after we leave for Amsterdam?"

"How should I know? I just want it that way. I'm going by the book and the rules say the fewer who know the better. And besides," said Lew, "you and Jane are going to catch those crooks long before your contingency plan is even needed."

"I never knew you to be such an optimist," said Graham teasingly.

"Well, you are going to get them, aren't you?"

"Sure, like I said, they're apt to be unarmed on this one because they won't be able to get a gun through airport security. Unless, and it's a possibility, they wait to snatch the stones until we get back to New York but I'm betting a hit will happen in Europe. The diamonds are worth too much to pass up and if they wait till we're back in the city to go for them, they'll have to figure they've got fewer options. In Europe," Graham mused, "they'll be able to bide their time and pick the most opportune moment."

"And if they don't," Lew said, "you put into effect plan B."

"Exactly. I'll make it so damn easy to steal the stones they won't be able to resist!"

"Hell," Lew said with a chuckle, "they'll probably think you're stealing them yourself."

Graham's face dropped. "That's an ugly thought."

"Just joking, son."

"Real funny, Lew."

All the way home to his apartment Graham mulled over this new development: Jane was to accompany him to Amsterdam. The notion unsettled him and it must be because there was the possibility of danger to her. Certainly he was not feeling his usual carefree self as he strode along Seventh Avenue.

Of course, everything would go as smooth as silk. The crooks would try for the diamonds and he and Jane would thwart their attempt with ease. Heck, even Norma had said the creeps were amateurs! It was only Norma's mistake that had gotten her shot. Why, if the woman had known how to use her hands, she never would have had to chase the thieves down an alley! "Guns," he mumbled to himself, "useless hunks of metal."

Now, Jane was an expert with her hands. No problem there. Well, it wasn't going to do any good to stew over the situation. They'd do just fine in Amsterdam, he decided, feeling better.

Taking his apartment steps by two, Graham thought of Jane inside his place, cooking their dinner at that very moment. It was like coming home to a wife, being greeted by succulent aromas and a loving smile. How pleasant, how *right*.

"Hi, Jane!" he called, tossing his linen jacket carelessly onto the couch. "I'm home!"

"In the kitchen," came her reply.

"Mmm, what smells so good?" He gave her cheek a kiss, picking up the pot and pan lids. "Spaghetti?"

"Yes."

He opened the fridge and took out a Heineken and searched his junk drawer for the opener. "How did your trip with Kelly go?"

"All right." She wiped her hands on a dishtowel and began pressing garlic for the bread.

"What's the matter," he said lightly, "did Kelly make a pass? If he did..." Graham came up behind her and wrapped his arms around her waist, pulling Jane back against him.

"Stop it," she said, "I'm trying to clean up this garlic mess."

He nibbled her ear until she squirmed away. *"Graham."*

"Oh, all right." He let her go and backed off, leaning against a counter and sipping on his beer. Something was wrong. "What is it, Jane?"

"Nothing," she replied offhandedly. "I'm a little tired."

"Then we'll clean up here and go out to eat. You should have said something earlier."

"Everything's nearly done."

"So we'll eat here and I'll do all the cleanup."

"You're always so accommodating."

Of course, thought Graham, it was her time of the month. That must be it. He smiled, relieved, but then remembered: she'd had it last week. His mood flip-flopped. Frown lines deepened around his mouth. "Any trouble delivering those fashion designs?" he asked in a neutral tone.

She shook her head. "Everything went smoothly."

"Are you feeling all right?" He took a long swig of beer and watched her over the neck of the bottle.

"You're asking a lot of questions, aren't you?"

"Just making conversation. If you want, we don't have to talk." Maybe some music, some soft, easy listening music. Barry Manilow. Graham went into the living room and put on a cassette. There, that was nice and relaxing.

Having had an early lunch, Graham stuffed himself with the pasta and garlic bread. Jane, however, toyed with her spaghetti and barely looked at him. Then, when they were clearing the table, Jane dropped a dirty fork on the carpet and burst into tears.

Graham had had enough. He took the rest of the dishes from her, set them down roughly on the kitchen counter and pulled her into his arms. "Out with it," he said. "I know you too well and something's very wrong."

"It's just…Norma." She tried to free herself but he was having none of it.

"What about Norma?"

"Oh, Graham…she…" And he thought Jane was about to say something profound but instead she said, "I'm worried she won't recover."

"What?"

"You know. She could have a relapse."

"That's ridiculous, Jane. Now tell me the truth."

This time Jane managed to pull away from him; she was strong and to keep her imprisoned would have been a real struggle, one Graham wasn't so sure he'd win.

"Jane," he tried again, "I know you too well. I wish you'd be honest with me. Is it the trip to Amsterdam? Are you getting nervous?"

She stood several paces from him and put her hands on her hips. "I am *not* getting nervous. Now you're being ridiculous."

"Then what is it?"

"I'm—" she looked away "—not feeling well. Maybe a cold coming on or something."

"That's it?"

She nodded. But Graham didn't really buy her explanation. Jane was not the type to let a few sniffles get her down. He let it drop, however, deciding that she was feeling anxious about the upcoming trip and didn't want to admit it. Sure, that was all there was to it.

Jane seemed better as they did the dishes together, even slopping soap suds on his shirt once when he got in the way and laughing. It was good to hear her laugh. Then, after everything was tidied up they took brandies into the living room and sat close together on the couch.

"Listen," began Jane, relaxing back onto the cushions and curling her feet beneath her, "I'm sorry about earlier. That's not like me."

"All is forgiven."

"You're too good to me."

"Don't I know it!" He rose, put on another cassette, a mood setter, a slow, easy James Taylor recording, and turned down the lights. "Feeling sexy?" he teased, sitting back down and taking her brandy from her.

Jane wore a skirt, no stockings and a loose bittersweet-red shirt with buttons all the way down the front. He began with the first button, unfastening it, exposing the top of her bra, kissing the soft, satin-smooth flesh of her breasts. Moving on to the next button and the next, he kissed her each time languidly, his lips silk against her own smooth skin. Her belly. He felt her quiver.

"Janey," he whispered.

He reached around her back and unfastened her bra; it sagged below her breasts, which he cupped in both hands and caressed with his lips, one breast at a time, slowly, savoring her taste, flicking his tongue across her nipples until they hardened. This was going to be a long, delicious night, he decided, feeling himself pulse with expectation.

He kissed the softness of her belly above the waistline of her skirt and eased her shirt off her shoulders, his hands returning to cup her breasts, his mouth moving up again to taste her. As she moved and began to twist, her skirt hitched itself up and Graham brought a hand to her thigh and traced tiny, teasing patterns. A moment later, his hand slipped beneath the elastic of her panties, cupping her gently while his other hand kneaded a breast and his mouth drew a peak into its hungry warmth.

"Oh, Jane," he groaned against her, "I can never get enough of you."

Deciding that they couldn't wait until they got upstairs, he rose for a moment and began to undo his shirt. She looked so lovely lying there, half-dressed, her skin glowing peachy in the dim light, her mouth rosy and parted. And yet, somehow, as she watched him shed his shirt and unfasten his belt, there was a kind of sadness in those green eyes, a sadness and…indecision.

But why? What had happened between them? If only he could reach her tonight. He sat down beside her again

and pushed her hair back behind one pale perfectly
formed ear. "Are you okay, Janey?"

Her face was averted and he could only see the plane
of her cheek, her little nose sprinkled with freckles, her
eyelashes fanning out on her cheek. She straightened and
pulled her blouse together then shook her head. "I guess
I'm not feeling too great," she said in that throaty voice
of hers. "Are you mad?"

"Of course I'm not. You should have told me, though.
I want our lovemaking to be special for both of us."

"I know. Me, too." She reached up and pulled his head
down and kissed him. "I'm just feeling off tonight. You
know."

"Sure, I'm being a selfish lecher."

"Would you...mind taking me home?"

"Of course not," he replied, lying through his teeth.
He minded very much but if Jane wasn't in the mood,
well, he'd have to respect her wishes.

A half hour later they kissed good-night. It was a
strained leave-taking, unlike any of the others they'd had.

"I'm sorry," Jane whispered. "I'll be better tomorrow."

"Sure, I'll call you, okay?"

She nodded and Graham watched her walk away from
him to the door of her apartment building. Janey, tall and
lovely. Was she really coming down with something?
Maybe it was family trouble or an old boyfriend, that one
she'd mentioned. Something at work? He wished she'd
confide in him. Well, maybe it was just a matter of time.
After all, she hadn't known him very long and he had no
right to pry.

He waited until she was safely inside before glancing
in his side mirror and pulling out into the traffic. A light
rain began to fall and he turned on his wipers, idly watching them swish back and forth as he waited at a stoplight.
How many women, he wondered, had he known in his
thirty-three years? A few, anyway. And how many had

stayed around? None. Was it because he'd scared them all off? Or because he really hadn't loved any of them? It was both, he decided, staring, hypnotized, at the bleary red stoplight.

Oh well, he was damn glad they'd all flown. If they hadn't, he'd never have found his Janey, his solid and steady lady who knew where she was going and realized her own worth and who was not in the least intimidated by his life-style.

Ah…Janey.

Another light. The drizzling rain continued, streaking his side windows, causing the city lights to diffuse colorfully in the glass.

Green light. He let the clutch out and moved with the flow of traffic. He knew—or at least hoped—he'd be involved with Jane for a very long time. Forever would suit him. Of course, there would be marriage, a couple of kids. He'd like one with clear green eyes just like Jane's. Naturally, he'd still travel as the courier business suited his need for action and diversity but he'd be able to pick and choose his jobs, stay home if he liked. That was okay; plenty of husbands had families and traveled. No problem…

Husbands!

Graham's mind exploded with the notion as the light turned yellow, then red. Husband! Quicksilver—in love and married? Holy cow.

He never braked for the light nor did he hear the scream of the siren behind him—not for two blocks, anyway.

JANE ROUNDED THE CORNER of 59th and Madison and made for Central Park. Already a half hour into her jog, the oxygen level in her brain had lowered, leaving her with a sort of euphoric well-being in which thoughts came at random, some crystal clear, others fog-bound and quickly lost. Every so often she remembered Graham. A spaghetti dinner, the smell of garlic and onions cooking, a beer in his hand. Her well-being fled.

She looked at her watch as she entered the park: 6:36 a.m. How *could* she have been so curt with him? Sure, anyone would have been upset by Norma's accusations and her warning but a sensible adult would have confided in Graham. A razor-sharp thought sliced through her head: *unless that sensible, reasoning adult no longer trusted him a hundred percent.*

"Damn," she said, breathing heavily. It had dawned cloudless and pleasantly cool in the city. It should have been a beautiful morning to Jane because she could add an extra few minutes to her run when the humidity level was lower. Instead she was beginning to feel sluggish.

6:39. At this rate she'd be dragging by the time she made her way back to the apartment. It was funny, Jane realized, but negative thinking affected every muscle, every bone and fiber of her body.

Why had she let Norma get to her? Graham had tried to make love to her. Yes, on the couch. Jane had a vivid mental picture flash in her brain of him standing above her and she recalled the feeling of reluctance that had swept her even as her insides seemed to be melting.

6:44. Another jogger passed her going the opposite way. He waved, breathed, "Morning," and his dog followed Jane for a few feet until the jogger called him away. At this hour the park was never truly empty. A bum or two slept on a bench, a bicycler sped by. There were always joggers and stray pets on the path. She circled the reservoir on her usual route. Sweat was now soaking her headband and the back of her T-shirt flapped against her skin wetly. She stayed close to the perimeter of the park, saw a mounted policeman, waved at him.

But if she trusted Graham, say, ninety percent, what exactly comprised the other ten percent? Doubt, of course. A small seed planted by Norma Stedman that had begun to swell by the evening before when Jane had cooked dinner.

Oh, boy! What if that seed grew and blossomed and became full-blown mistrust? She couldn't let that happen. My God, she was falling head over heels in love and she wasn't going to let a silly warning ruin a great relationship when she knew in her heart Norma was dead wrong.

6:56. Jane took a curve in the path and headed toward one of the park's many exits. She decided that by tomorrow morning—when they were to fly to Amsterdam—she'd have this unsettling doubt erased from her thoughts. It was all a matter of perspective, getting things straight. Very simple.

6:57. From behind her came the scratching sound of branch moving against branch, a twig breaking underfoot...

Jane spun around instinctively in time to ward off a blow with her forearm. She ducked, stepping backward to brace herself for another blow, then knocked the stranger's arm away, sidestepping agilely, cat-quick, panting evenly. The strike from the big man's fist had missed its mark entirely, causing him to stumble and Jane, arms thrust out for balance, kicked out and upward with a foot and caught the mugger squarely in the groin.

There was a deep, throaty groan of pain as he bent over and clasped at his crotch. He was backing off, staggering toward the bushes and Jane started after him. No way was this creep going to escape!

"Hold up there," came a command. Jane glanced quickly, afraid for a moment her mugger wasn't alone, but it was the park policeman, mounted still, trotting along a grassy embankment. "Hold it right there!" he called again but already, in the instant Jane had turned to look at the policeman, the mugger had ducked into the bushes and was out of sight.

"Damn!" she said, still panting.

"Stay where you are," called the policeman but Jane

knew it was completely useless to pursue the thug—the horse couldn't make it through the undergrowth and Jane was winded. Her attacker had gotten away!

"Just swell," she grumbled, her hands on her hips, sucking in a lungful of air.

The police at the uptown station let her call Mercury. "Donna," she said, "I'm going to be running late. I'm with the police and have to make a report. No, everything's fine. I was jogging and almost got mugged.... Yes, I hurt him pretty good.... No, he got away. Listen, I have to go.... Okay, see you in a couple of hours. Bye."

Jane thought she was being helpful to the police but the sergeant, a tall, thin, wiry man with kinky hair and horn-rimmed glasses, obviously thought otherwise. Lazily, with apparent unconcern, he took down the information given him by Jane.

"Anything else?" he asked, sounding bored.

"A nylon stocking mask, long-sleeved checkered shirt... I did tell you blue and white with shots of rust in it?"

"Sure, yeah, I got that down. Go on."

"Khaki trousers, Wilson tennis shoes."

"Yeah, Wilson, got that, too."

"I told you he was six feet and about two hundred pounds."

"Sure."

"Oh, and his hair was very dark."

"You could tell that under the nylon?" asked the sergeant with deliberate sarcasm.

"Yes, I told you, I've been taught to observe."

"Isn't that nice."

Jane tried to keep her temper in check. "Are you really interested in this, sergeant," she snapped, "or am I wasting my time?"

"Now, now, miss. I'm doing my best. You know how many muggings there are in this city on an average day?"

"I read the papers. Now you tell me, how many victims can remember so many details?"

He finally relented and grinned at her. "Very few, miss."

Jane sat back in her chair smugly. "So what now? Is there any hope of apprehending this man?"

"To be honest, no. But if he ever gets caught, the information you've given me will come up out of the computer and we can always call you in for an ID."

"I guess you never know."

"Never do, miss."

Jane rose to leave. "You know," she said pensively, "what I can't figure out is what he wanted from me. I mean, I wasn't wearing any jewelry, or carrying a wallet or purse."

"Rape, most likely, miss."

"Maybe," said Jane, without conviction.

It wasn't until she was back home, in the shower with shampoo dripping in her eyes, that it occurred to Jane the mugger might well have been after *her* specifically. First Norma—of course, that had been an accident—but was there a connection somehow? Norma was out of the way. Did someone want Jane laid up in a hospital as well? And if so, that would leave Graham very much alone and without protection in Amsterdam.

And then on the heels of that supposition came another, causing goose bumps to rise on her flesh despite the steaming hot water. Did Graham himself want to get his bodyguard out of the way?

CHAPTER THIRTEEN

THE 747 ALTERED COURSE SLIGHTLY and the sun, fiercely brilliant at forty thousand feet, speared into the windows on the right side of the plane and struck Graham dead in the face. He opened his eyes halfway and watched Jane from between his lashes. She was no longer reading but was sitting very still, staring out of the window, her face turned away from him. He could see the curving fan of her dark hair against her cheek, the sweep of her jawline, the corner of her mouth, that sweet, clinging mouth. Her hands were in her lap, small, strong hands with no-nonsense short fingernails. Those hands, Graham knew, could gentle a horse, break an assailant's wrist or drive him crazy with their touch.

He loved to watch her, sometimes at night waking to stare at her asleep or, if she wasn't there, to imagine how she looked in her own bed. He was getting awfully used to her, liking her more and more. He dared not say he *loved* her, not even to himself, but he couldn't imagine life without her. Graham knew himself well enough to know he wasn't about to turn down what fate had offered him and the idea of settling down didn't seem so dull anymore, at least not with Jane Manning.

She sighed and looked down at the book in her lap. Her brow was creased. He didn't blame her for being nervous; this was her first big job. Ten million in diamonds even made *him* nervous.

It was darn near impossible to think of Jane as his bodyguard. Although he'd die before admitting it to her,

Graham felt very protective of Jane, as if the roles were reversed. Now, Norma, okay, he'd go along comfortably with her guarding him, but not with Jane. It must have been some old-fashioned previously buried instinct inside him but there it was—Jane was his lady and it should be him taking care of her.

Nevertheless he had a job to do for Lew. He supposed it was high time he let Jane in on the fact that they were to set themselves up as bait. She had to be forewarned and she had to cooperate. He had a feeling, however, that she wasn't going to like it one bit. And what on earth was he going to do if he ever had to fall back on his secret contingency plan? She'd like that even less.

He swallowed hard and broached the subject.

"You mean you told everyone in the office deliberately?" she asked in alarm when he had finished.

"We had to. Lew wants the thieves to follow us." If he blamed everything on Lew maybe she'd be easier to convince.

"That's *insane*."

"But don't you see, the idea is to force them into making a try for the diamonds so we can catch them."

"The police are supposed to catch criminals," she said coldly.

"They've been trying for months and have come up with nothing. Lew doesn't have time to wait. By the time the cops find the thieves Mercury will be history."

She was stubbornly silent.

"So we're supposed to expose ourself a bit and keep a sharp eye out."

"I'd keep an eye out, anyway," she muttered.

"I know you would. But forewarned is forearmed, they say."

"Look, Graham, my job is to *prevent* attacks, not *allow* them. Rob taught us that if our charge was attacked, we'd already failed." Her voice rose a little.

"In this case we have to bend the rules a bit. You can see how important this is, Janey."

"Don't you Janey me! I don't like this. I don't like it at all. Lew should have told me himself if he wanted me to do it."

The man in the aisle seat had an ear cocked to the conversation, Graham was sure. He put a hand on Jane's arm to quiet her down. "Maybe Lew should have told you. That's my fault. I told him I'd take care of it," he lied.

"You figured I'd just go along without a question? Graham, you should know me better. My job is to protect you, not to set you up like bait."

A little boy's head popped up over the seat in front of them and the child stared curiously, thumb in mouth, until he was snatched down by his invisible mother.

"Jane, please, we'll discuss it later," Graham said quietly.

"Don't patronize me!"

Someone across the aisle leaned forward and stared over at Jane. Graham flinched inwardly.

"I'll send you back on the next plane," he said half-jokingly, trying to defuse her indignation.

"Try it!" Jane snapped, her small freckled nose thrust into his face.

This was awful. What had happened to his sweet, loving, passionate Janey? "Listen," he tried, "if you'd just think about the plan, you'd realize—"

"I know my job, Graham, and nothing is going to change my mind!"

In a minute, he knew, a full-fledged argument was going to erupt. Everyone on the plane would know their business and the thieves could even be on this flight!

"Shh," he said, smiling, putting a finger to his lips, "everyone's listening."

"So what? I can't believe you're worried about your image at a time like this!"

He'd seen it in an old Cary Grant movie; it had worked then, why not now? Graham leaped to his feet, unintentionally bumping his head on the luggage rack and said loudly, "All right, you win! I'll apologize to your mother, just put the blasted ring back on. We can't postpone the wedding again, Thelma!"

Up and down the aisle of the plane giggles broke out while Jane sat in her seat, frozen in mortification, her cheeks flaming scarlet. It was half an hour before she spoke. "I'll get you for this, buster," she warned. But she was trying not to smile.

They checked into a hotel near the diamond exchange, within the ring of concentric canals that encircled the city. It was a tall, narrow, gabled hotel called the Canal House, small and homey and charmingly Dutch.

"I really prefer this hotel to the big modern ones. I hope you like it, Jane," Graham said, watching her reactions as she stood in front of the place, looking up at the fanciful gables and staunch, rosy, seventeenth-century brick and baroque window motifs.

"It's beautiful, it's wonderful, Graham!" she exclaimed and he was inordinately pleased that she liked it.

The Canal House was even more picturesque inside. Narrow and cozy with ruffled lace curtains, dark beams and knickknacks, antique oil paintings on the walls— Dutch masters, naturally—and the gleam of a well-beloved old home.

"Do we need two rooms?" he asked, only half teasing.

"One will do," she said, straight-faced. She was getting nervous again. He wished he could get her to relax, to enjoy Amsterdam, at least for tonight. And he wished, too, that he could muster the courage to ask her if she'd decided to go along with his plan but he'd better give her more time to mull the whole thing over.

"Come on, now," he ventured when they were in their room. "Don't worry about a thing, at least until tomorrow. I want to show you this city, Jane. I want you to

enjoy it.'' He pulled her close and kissed her forehead.
''You've never been to Europe before. This is a special
time and, just think, we can share it.''

She tilted her face up to his, searched his eyes deeply
and smiled wanly.

Graham put his hands on her shoulders, leaned close
and kissed her freckled nose. ''You know,'' he said, ''I'm
dying to hold you, Janey. I can't stand this tension between us.''

''Neither can I.'' Her voice was so sincere, so soft and
full of pain that his heart turned to putty.

''Well, what are we going to do about it?'' he asked.

Her emerald-green eyes still held his with deep sadness
then dropped. ''I don't know. Maybe after the diamonds…''

He continued to hold her but it was as if he could feel
her flesh shrinking away from him. He let his hands fall.

Jane gave a short, constrained laugh. ''It's getting dark
in here, Graham. It's getting late. If we're going to see
the city…''

It was 7:00 p.m. and quite dark out, due to Amsterdam's northerly latitude; outside their narrow, lace-
curtained window the night was damp and cool, the city's
endless, self-indulgent nightlife illuminated brightly by
streetlights that reflected on the canals.

Jane put a thin, rust-colored sweater and tweed wool
blazer over her corduroy skirt, brushed her hair, redid her
mascara and lipstick. Graham merely slipped on a navy-
blue crewneck sweater under his gray herringbone sport
coat. They'd both packed extremely lightly, using only a
small carry-on bag each. There was nothing worse for a
courier than to have to wait in a large, noisy, unruly crowd
for luggage to be unloaded from a plane.

''Have I got a surprise for you!'' he said as he locked
the door behind them.

''Oh, no, not another one of your surprises!''

There, that was better. She was beginning to relax now. "Ever hear of *rijsttafel*?"

"No, what is it?"

"Well, it's a kind of meal. It means, literally, 'rice table' in Dutch. But it's Indonesian. The Netherlands ruled the East Indies for hundreds of years and this is one of the few remaining customs."

"There are Indonesian restaurants in Amsterdam?"

"All over. We're going to a very special one. It's called the Bali."

There were slim, sloe-eyed waitresses in sarongs, fake palms and heavy wooden, Dutch-style tables in the restaurant. Jane took a menu and looked at it, then laughed. "You order. I'm lost."

He got the "deluxe combination." "Now watch out, some of this stuff is hot."

The waitress brought seemingly dozens of tiny, delicate porcelain bowls, each one filled with a spicy, delectable dish, each one with an odd Indonesian name: *saté babi*, bite-sized morsels of skewered pork cooked in a mouth-watering peanut sauce; *loempia*, a mixture of bean sprouts and vegetables wrapped in waferlike pastry and deep-fried, *kroepoek*, a large, crunchy prawn cracker. And rice, of course, to accompany every dish. Some of the flavors were vaguely reminiscent of Chinese food, some of East Indian. It was a mélange of delicacies.

"Where do I start?" Jane wondered aloud.

She exclaimed over each different flavor. "Chilis and peanuts?" she asked. "Fish with something..."

"Coconut milk and coriander," Graham supplied and she looked at him with respectful surprise.

He delighted in her pleasure. She was discovering something new and he loved her lack of sophisticated veneer. She showed her enjoyment. She was real, absolutely true to herself.

"This is almost better than Colorado beef!" she joked, tasting the suckling pig in a spicy sauce.

He watched her chew and swallow, watched the tip of
her tongue flick a bit of sauce from her upper lip. Her
face shone in the dim overhead lighting, her green eyes
sparkled and her freckled nose wrinkled experimentally
over each new dish. "Um, this is wonderful, some kind
of shredded beef and ginger. And lots of garlic."

She held the fork out to him and he tasted it. What fun
he and Jane could have together, years of fun, traveling,
exploring, sailing the *Renée*, raising a family.

"Aren't you hungry?" she was asking.

"I've eaten plenty," he said with a smile.

"I was afraid I'd stuffed it all down. What a pig I am,"
she said without self-consciousness. "James always
claimed I out-ate him two to one."

"You'd never know it to look at you," Graham answered.

"Let's walk around some," Jane suggested as they left
the restaurant. "I want to see this city up close."

"Too bad we don't have longer. I'd love to take you
to the Rijksmuseum—to see the Rembrandts—and Rem-
brandt's house. The van Gogh Museum, too. And then,
outside of Amsterdam, are the windmills and tulip fields
and dikes."

"Next time," she said wistfully.

Graham took her hand as they walked along the Her-
engracht, "Gentlemen's Canal," the most important of
the three canal rings built in the 1600s. Trees lined the
banks. Tall, narrow, gabled houses, all four stories high,
stood in sober ranks along the street, throwing wavering
squares of light into the water. A motor launch chugged
by and, in its rippled wake, the houses' long reflections
in the water suddenly fractured into splinters of liquid
luminescence. Jane drew in her breath in wonder and Graham squeezed her hand. "Nice, huh?" he murmured into
her ear.

"It's so different," she replied, "so pretty. These

houses, why, they've been lived in so long, so much longer than I can even imagine.''

"Europe *is* old," he agreed.

The buildings lining the canals reflected the nature of the people: conservative, cautious about wasting precious space, but not above demonstrating their success. The upper stories of the houses had been used for storing tea, spices and furs, the riches of the Dutch colonies. Graham pointed out to Jane the heavy beams that jutted out from their topmost gables. "All that's missing are ropes and men to pull aloft." Then he smiled and added, "It's hard to believe that the red-light district is only a few blocks from here, next to the oldest church in the city."

Jane turned to him in disbelief. "You mean... prostitutes?"

"They're legal here. They even take traveler's checks."

Jane stopped short. "How do you know?"

"Oh, I've heard, you know, from, ah, friends."

"Friends," Jane repeated, "hmm."

"Right."

He turned up another street. "It's a nice city, isn't it?"

"Lovely. Oh, I wish I was just a tourist here."

He squeezed her hand and rounded another corner. "This is Prinsengracht. Anne Frank's house is on the next block."

"Anne Frank. Oh, that poor girl. I read the book when I was twelve, I think. I cried and cried." She started walking faster. "I want to see it, Graham."

They stood together in front of the narrow brick house that was indistinguishable from all the others. Jane was silent for a long time. "She must have stayed up there on the top floor," she finally said in a hushed voice. "Oh, Graham, I can't believe someone went through that, a little girl." And he felt her hand tighten on his.

Jane wanted to walk some more since it was her only chance to see Amsterdam. Tomorrow they'd go straight to the diamond bourse, pick up the stones and head to the airport. Not much time for sight-seeing. He led her toward the oldest part of the city and showed her the church of St. Nicolaaskerk, dating from 1306.

"1306!" gasped Jane.

"Ah, but in the next block is a still older profession than Christianity."

"Can we go there? I mean…"

"Sure." Graham was amused by her interest. "It's a tourist attraction."

Girls posed half-nude in picture windows. Others knitted or painted their nails while awaiting clients. Garish neon signs lit the ancient streets of the red-light district, the Oude Zijds Voorburgwal. Graham held back a chuckle as he watched Jane's face turn an embarrassed pink when they passed the lovely old canal houses and their residents of easy virtue.

They arrived back at the hotel late and left a wake-up call for seven. Jane sank into a chair in their room, sighed and slipped off her shoes. "It's still early in my head."

"I know the feeling." He started massaging her shoulders, loving the feel of her taut muscles under his hands. "Feel good?"

"Sure does." But then she was quiet for a time, finally turning to look up at him. "Graham, we've got to sleep in separate beds tonight."

He felt as if he'd been splashed with cold water. "Why?" he asked, confused.

"I'm on a job. I just don't think it's right. I don't know, it's a feeling I have that I can't shake."

"Janey…"

"I don't want to be distracted."

"Well, sure, okay." Was there something else bothering her? Or perhaps it was just this job. "I'll be awful lonesome."

She gave him a crooked smile and mumbled, "Me, too." Then, after a pause, she asked, "How come they call you Quicksilver?"

thieves, he'd be holding her in his arms at that very moment. And now, even if he did tell her everything, maybe it was too late to smooth over these hard feelings. Would this breach in their relationship be permanent?

He nearly groaned out loud, feeling wounded and sad and alone in his torment. And there she was, lying three feet from him in the darkness, her skin all warm and silken beneath the pretty blue nightgown, the scent of her perfume lifting from between her breasts and wafting the small distance to his nostrils, driving him completely out of his mind.

CHAPTER FOURTEEN

THE BUILDING WAS OLD AND VENERABLE, brick, with tall windows, an imposing portal and an unobtrusive sign that stated it was the Beurs voor Diamanthandel, the Diamond Bourse. It was one of sixteen bourses, or clubs, in the world and the thought of all that glittering wealth inside and her own responsibility made Jane very nervous. She took a deep breath and looked around as Graham signed them in.

Plainclothes guards abounded. Actually they looked like businessmen but Jane recognized them in a flash. She also noticed the electronic surveillance devices that were everywhere.

"This way, *Als 't blieft*, if you please," said a stolid-looking Dutch burgher as he led Graham into a high-ceilinged room, past wooden tables at which sat scores of dealers, in pairs, studying white paper packets of gems with their jewelers' eyeglasses or haggling or shaking hands over transactions.

My God, thought Jane, how many millions of dollars were changing hands at that very moment? The dealers came from everywhere: Europeans in neat suits, orthodox Jews from Antwerp or Tel Aviv or New York in black coats and hats and beards. A babel of voices filled the antique chamber, a clamor comprised of dozens of languages. Bright sunlight flooded the place from the tall, unobstructed windows. Of course, Jane concluded, they all needed natural light to study the stones.

"You okay?" asked Graham as they entered the hallway leading to the high security area and eventually to the vaults.

"Don't be overprotective," Jane whispered back. "I'm fine."

Their companion unlocked a heavy iron grill door, studied the instructions Graham had given him, passed everyone's identifications to a uniformed guard, then ushered Jane and Graham farther into the bowels of the closed area where there were chairs and a table and beyond that, the huge gilded vault door.

Jane took a seat while they waited in the small room. "How much do you think is behind that door?" she whispered to Graham.

"More than we'll see in a lifetime," he replied with a wide grin.

The man returned in a few minutes while a guard reclosed the door to the vault behind him. Then there were papers to be signed by Graham, the counting of the packets to be done, the emptying of them into a wide leather courier belt that Graham had buckled around his waist beneath his sweater and sport coat. Handshakes were dutifully exchanged.

Jane felt a tremor of excitement seize her. She was on the job now. This was what she'd been trained for. And yet she knew that the risk on this delivery was greater than normal. Graham was sure the thieves, with their inside knowledge of this diamond pickup, would try to steal them. He *wanted* them to try. Jane was confident of her ability to protect Graham but the thought of deliberately putting him and herself in danger went against all her common sense and training. And that matter had never been settled between them.

They returned to the front door, accompanied by their guide who said, "*Dank U wel*, thank you," several times in the extra polite Dutch manner before turning them over to the guard posted there. The guard signed them out, phoned for a taxi and handed them back their overnight bags, which they'd checked with him. It was all done efficiently, precisely, automatically. Jane was impressed.

A cab pulled up at the curb and the guard opened the door of the bourse for them. He said, "Goodbye, sir, *dank U wel*," nodded at Jane, saw them out and closed the door behind them.

"Well," said Graham, grinning, "now it begins."

He loved the danger, Jane knew. He absolutely thrived on it. "Wait a minute," she said, scanning the area for anything out of the ordinary, a person loitering, a movement out of place on the street, a vehicle too close to the taxi. Everything looked normal, ordinary, perfectly safe. But, naturally, a crowded city street in broad daylight was an unlikely choice for an ambush. Even amateurs would know better. The thieves might, however, be watching them, waiting for the perfect moment. Still, there was nothing in this Amsterdam street scene that sounded an alarm in Jane's head.

"Okay," she said and followed Graham to the waiting cab. He was taking this all very casually, she saw. Was that merely to put her at ease?

"Schiphol Airport," Graham requested while Jane was busy looking out the back of the cab window, then in front, along the quaint poplar-lined street. She even watched the taxi driver; he *could* be a plant. Every possibility had to be taken into account.

It was five miles to Schiphol Airport, one of the most secure airports in Europe. This leg of the trip constituted the weak point of their journey. Despite heavy traffic, they could be waylaid somewhere along the route. Jane wished now that they'd rented a car so that she could drive. Her evasive driving techniques, she'd bet, were better than their taxi driver's.

"There's the Rijksmuseum." Graham was pointing to a solid, imposingly Dutch building on the right. "Sure wish we had time..."

"Is your door locked?" she asked, leaning across him to check it.

They had to stop for a red light. She glanced around, not exactly nervous, but attuned to every movement near her, on guard, ceaselessly vigilant.

"Hey, take it easy." Graham put a hand on her knee. "Look, there's the Van Gogh Museum. And the Heineken Brewery is not far from here, just to the left."

She ignored him. Craning her head around just as the taxi started up again, she peered out of the back window. Her heart stopped for a split second, then pounded heavily. That man, three, four cars behind them, had a familiar look to him. Had it been only his too-quick maneuver, cutting in front of another car, that had caught her eye? Maybe. But she'd seen something, a jawline, a set of the head under a hatbrim, a glimpse of a familiar movement. Or had she? Was it only her oversensitive imagination? She kept looking out the back window but the car—a nondescript gray sedan—was no longer in view. It was almost as if the driver had realized that she had caught sight of him.

One man, not two?

"Graham," she said quietly, "there could be someone following us. I'm not sure."

"Oh, really?" He turned and looked behind them.

"He's gone now. It could have been, God, I hate to even say it, it could have been the jerk that tried to mug me in Central Park."

Graham watched her carefully. "You sure?"

"*No*, I'm not sure. There was something about the driver I just saw...but he had a hat on and I couldn't tell..."

Graham patted her knee. "Good," he said, "I hope they're onto us."

"You're not starting *that* again."

"Jane, nothing's changed. My orders stand." He

seemed utterly cool, totally in control, enjoying the hunt, even though he was the quarry.

"I want my objections noted," she said firmly, angrily. "I was not hired to be the cheese in a mousetrap!"

Graham sighed and held her wildly gesturing hand in both of his. "A lovely cheese you make, sweetheart," he murmured.

"How can you...how can you," she stammered, "be so casual?"

He shrugged, still holding her hand, raising it to his lips to nibble at her fingers. "It's a job."

Schiphol Airport was crowded. The worst possible scenario for confusion, ambush, attack. And yet Jane could see the many guards, both armed and in plainclothes, that airport security demanded these days. Would anyone dare try for the diamonds under these circumstances? She stayed close behind Graham as he forged his way to the check-in counter; she was coiled tense inside, watching carefully for that one nervous gesture, that one sweat-covered brow. She remembered so plainly Rob Dearborn's lecture on the profile of an attacker. He was a male, usually, between the ages of nineteen and twenty-six, a dogmatic, bitter, confused person who believed fervently that he was right in what he did.

"We have over an hour before we board," Graham was saying. "Lunch! I'm starved."

"No, I couldn't eat a thing."

"Mind if I grab a doughnut or something?"

"No, but I'll have to check out the restaurant."

"Okay," he said with a laugh, "I'll eat on the run and get a stomachache."

But she hardly heard, being too busy watching, her eyes scanning, her muscles ready to react. That man over there, reading a newspaper; was he only hiding behind it? Or that woman pushing a stroller? In practice at ISA Rob had set up a woman with a baby carriage in a park—innocent, perfectly ordinary—but there had been guns under the pink blanket and all the students had been caught red-handed, including Jane.

Graham bought a flaky raspberry pastry. "It's good. Want a bite?"

Jane looked at him blankly.

"This way," he said finally, leading her down a concourse, to their gate, she supposed.

But the concourse quickly turned into a construction site with piles of materials and ripped-up tiles. It was practically deserted.

Jane stopped short.

"Come on, it's a shortcut to our gate."

"It's too dangerous," she said, putting an arm out to hold him back.

"That's *good*, Jane. The thieves are running out of time if they want to steal these diamonds."

"Graham, I can't let you."

"Look, there're a few yards of this mess, then the new concourse." He pulled gently at her arm. "Come on, we're ready for them, Jane. They don't know that. We've got surprise on our side. And there are dozens of security men within calling range. It's perfect for us."

"No." She shook her head vehemently. He was carrying things too far. She sized up the odds if they proceeded farther down the concourse and didn't like them. Hands on hips, she squared off to him. "No," she repeated.

"Damn it, Janey, it's our job!" He tried to push past her.

She had no choice. It was almost as if her body moved of its own volition, smoothly, swiftly, instinctively. Her right hand reached out, found its hold, twisted slightly and Graham was yelping in surprised pain, bent over, neutralized. Whichever way he moved the pain increased, his own weight used as leverage against him.

"Ouch!" he complained. "Come on, Janey, let me go. This is embarrassing. Now, come on, we've got to help

Lew!'' He tried to wiggle his arm out of her hold. She tightened her grip. He grimaced and stopped in his efforts. ''Please, Jane,'' he attempted.

''You said Lew wanted us to deliberately lure the robbers, not to commit suicide in some deserted—''

But she never finished. Her eye caught a sudden movement. A man was stepping out from behind a pile of construction debris, swiftly followed by another. Her mind saw them, took in their hats and the scarves over their faces and registered threat in a split second.

''Will you let me go *now*?'' Graham was asking tightly.

''Very funny,'' she breathed, dropping his arm instantly.

The two men were big, Jane noted. They wore army surplus fatigue jackets, jeans and longshoremen's caps pulled low. They advanced steadily but warily because Jane and Graham had both whirled to face them, knees bent in ready positions.

''This is it,'' Graham said out of the corner of his mouth. ''I'll take the guy on the right.''

Jane could practically feel the sparks of excitement that Graham gave off. *He loves it,* she had time to think, and then the man on the left—her man—pulled a pistol out of his pocket. A blunt, ugly 9-mm pistol.

All her lessons came back to Jane then. She could hear Rob talking: ''Get the guy close. If you can reach the gun without moving you have it made. First, you draw his attention some way. That gives you a quarter of a second. You have another quarter of a second before he can pull the trigger. That's a half second. If you can't knock the gun aside in half a second you deserve to fail this course.''

Okay, she told herself, *let him come closer.* He did, as if obeying Jane's silent command. He was very close, trying to back them up against a wall, his buddy at his side.

''Hand 'em over,'' came his muffled voice, pure American in accent.

''Sure, pal,'' Graham was saying, as if to pacify the

man, "I don't want any trouble." Out of the corner of her eye, Jane saw Graham reach inside his jacket. She knew he was up to something. But first, the man with the gun...

The weapon with its black Cyclops eye was pointed at her middle. It was time. Jane faked a cry of fear. "Please!" she yelled, "don't hurt me!" His eyes swung to her, his attention, for that fraction of a second, was total. Her hand, fingers stiffened, shot out and snapped his gun hand aside so fast he had no idea that it was coming until his weapon clattered onto the concrete floor out of his reach.

With satisfaction Jane saw his eyes fill with shock. *Amateurs,* she thought, *Norma was right.* But then she was aware of Graham grappling with the other man, of grunts and thuds, and her man was going for his gun where it lay on the floor. She tripped him expertly and leaped toward where he sprawled on the hard floor.

Suddenly Jane was aware that there were more people on the scene: a woman, blond, scared, carrying a toddler. Two other children holding hands, eyes wide. Oh, Lord, she thought, they'll get hurt!

The gunman scrambled up with surprising agility, grabbed one of the children and held the screaming youngster up in front of him like a shield.

Jane was paralyzed, one eye on the gun on the floor, one on the thief and his hostage. Graham had the second man down on his knees, held securely with an arm lock.

Then everything happened at once. The first man lunged for the gun, his young prisoner kicked him in the shins with drumming heels, the child's mother screamed and threw herself at the thief. Jane tackled him but got tangled up with the hysterical mother. Graham shouted, losing his prisoner in the process; the baby wailed, the first thief swore, the gun was knocked beyond anyone's reach.

And then Jane was holding the baby, the mother was

grabbing her two children, Graham was cursing and the two thieves were racing away down the torn-up concourse, around a corner.

"Here!" Jane said, handing the crying baby to Graham. "I'll get them! Call security!"

Graham thrust the baby at its mother. "No," he snapped, "It's too dangerous! They're gone, anyway."

"For God's sakes, Graham, call security!" She tried to pull out of his grasp and it became a tug-of-war.

"Forget it, Jane, forget it this time! You did fine."

"But I can get them!" she cried, incensed.

"Jane, not this time."

They faced each other, panting. Graham's coat sleeve was ripped, his hair mussed.

"How could you? How could you stop me?" She was hopping mad. "It's too late now!"

Graham only said, "See if the kids are okay, Jane."

They were, all three of them, wailing and runny-nosed, while their mother cowered against the wall, white-faced and shaken to the core.

And then there was a whistle and uniformed men were running toward them, and Jane was standing in the middle of the concourse, trembling with reaction and anger, while Graham put a serious businessman's look on his face, one she'd never seen before, and went to meet them.

A half hour later, Graham had somehow managed to make the head of airport security believe that he and Jane were total innocents, merely on vacation, and that the muggers had simply been after his wallet. They left the security office and strode down the long echoing hall back to the main terminal. Jane kept waiting for Graham to explain why he'd lied to the officials but he was uncharacteristically silent.

She finally broached the subject. "Why didn't you tell them about the diamonds, Graham? It would have explained everything."

"I don't want them getting in my way."

"Maybe they can help."

"They'd just foul the whole plan up."

Jane was confused. She walked next to Graham, wondering about many things. First he invited danger, then he appeared to be worried about her safety. He stopped her from doing the precise thing she was hired to do. It was as if he *wanted* the thieves to get away! And then he deliberately lied to the Dutch police.

She glanced up at him but, for once, could read nothing on his handsome features. What, Jane asked herself, did she really know about Graham Smith? He seemed to live on the surface of life, ever moving, as elusive as quicksilver. Norma's warning echoed in her brain: too charming, too carefree. *Watch Graham Smith!*

Jane felt a chill seize her innards, a terrible, tearing doubt. Had Graham's plan gone wrong just now? Could he be planning to steal the diamonds himself?

CHAPTER FIFTEEN

"OKAY, JANE, LET'S get you on that flight to New York now," said Graham.

"You mean, let's get us on the flight," Jane said automatically.

"Just you, Janey," he said carefully.

She stood in the concourse, hands on hips, her face sagging in disbelief. "This is some kind of joke, isn't it?"

His gaze was studiously sober. "I'm afraid not."

"Well, you've lost your marbles, mister. We're both getting on that flight. It's my job to protect you."

"I don't know who's protecting whom," he was quick to answer. "If I hadn't been so darned worried about you, I could have taken care of those thieves myself and they'd be in jail by now."

"Oh, boy, what a lame excuse! It was *you* who wouldn't let me chase them! Oh, if you can't see that, Graham, what's the use of standing here arguing?" Jane sighed. "Now let's get on that plane."

"I'm not going."

"This is no time to make bad jokes."

"It's orders, Jane. Lew said that if we didn't get the crooks by flight time, I was to go it alone."

"You're telling me this is *Lew's* idea?" asked Jane furiously.

"Lew's...and mine as well. Don't worry, the diamonds will be perfectly safe."

It occurred to Jane as they stood there facing each other, ignoring the stream of travelers having to step around

them, that Graham might very well be planning to rendezvous with the thieves, claim he got robbed—who was
to say otherwise?—and split the take three ways. Oh yes,
Jane thought darkly, it would be so easy for him to pull
it off. Quicksilver. She wished she had the nerve to confront him with his perfidy.

Graham was looking at the time. "Ten minutes, Jane.
You have to be on that plane."

What in heaven's name was she supposed to do? Let
him—God, how the thought twisted in her stomach—steal
the stones himself? Oh damn, *damn*!

He took Jane's arm and began to steer her down the
concourse. Her indecision carried her along in silence.
What was she going to do?

"I hate for you to be going back alone, Jane. Honest I
do. It's a long flight and I know you'll worry.... Wait a
minute. Stay right here." He disappeared into a shop and
Jane remained rooted to her spot, thinking frantically,
knowing that she absolutely couldn't get on that plane and
leave him.

An awful image invaded her mind: Graham behind
prison bars in a zebra-striped suit, cap and all, and Jane
visiting, holding onto the tattered fabric of her love, waiting, waiting all those long years. Then she was angry with
herself. Graham was no thief! She was the one who'd
gone nuts, who'd listened to a drugged woman's ram-
blings and taken them to heart. Besides, Graham had just
told her that this was Lew's idea. Nevertheless, Lew had
not told *her*. And Jane was going to do her job. She was
going to stay with Graham and that was that.

But how? He sure wasn't giving an inch.

He came striding out of the shop carrying a plastic sack,
a silly grin on his handsome face. What was he up to
now?

"Here," he said brightly, "to keep you company,
Janey."

She peered down into the bag. "Oh, Graham..."

"I couldn't find one with the right color fur but it's close." He forced the sack on her, put his hands in his pockets and rocked back on his heels.

Jane pulled out the teddy bear and stifled a smile. It *was* awfully cute and was kind of a reddish brown, though certainly not the color of Graham's hair. "Thanks," she said, momentarily relenting, tucking the bear under her arm. She tried again. "Look, Graham, I have no orders from Lew and I just can't go back to New York."

"You'll have to, Jane," he said softly but with absolute resolution. "Or I'll merely sit here and not move until you do."

"You wouldn't."

"I would."

"Graham, can we call Lew right now? I'd feel better asking him."

"It's too early in New York. He's not even awake yet."

"I can't leave you!"

Graham glanced at his watch pointedly. "Five minutes, Jane."

What could she do? He obviously meant it. Indecision tore at her. She needed more time to think.

"Jane…"

"Oh, all right!" She pretended to give in; it was the only way to manage the situation. Let Graham think she was inexperienced and dumb; let him think she'd follow his orders without using her own judgment!

His hand was at her elbow, hurrying her along to the gate. Anger seethed within her, along with a terrible disappointment.

"Now you've got Teddy there to keep you company. I'll see you in a couple of days," said Graham, smiling now.

"If I get in trouble with Lew…"

"I'll take the blame, I promise. There's your gate. Don't worry yourself another minute, Janey. I'm having a ball."

"It's no laughing matter."

"I know. I'm sorry." But he didn't look in the least contrite.

"Just what are you planning?" asked Jane.

"I can't tell you."

"Lew's *orders*?"

"Yes." He put his hand up. "Scout's honor, Janey."

"Are you leaving Amsterdam?"

"Yes."

"But you won't say where to."

"I can't. But I will call the office, Jane, and let them know. As soon as you're back in New York you can find out."

"What do you think I'd do with the information at forty thousand feet over the ocean?"

"Parachute out, of course—" he winked "—to follow me."

She narrowed her eyes at his levity but he ignored her expression, pulled Jane up against his chest and kissed her thoroughly. "I wish we could be together," he murmured. "I'm going to miss you."

For a moment she went weak all over and sagged against him, unable to resist the magnetism of his touch. But it was all wrong; she steeled herself, put her hands on his chest and pushed him away, catching a fleeting look of regret on his face just before he masked it.

The last boarding announcement sounded over the speakers in several languages and Jane stepped back. "Well, goodbye," she said, smiling falsely. "Take good care of yourself and the diamonds."

"I will." He stood there, though, not leaving.

"Well, bye."

"Bye, Jane. Better get on board."

"Um…bye." Oh, brother, what was she going to do now? He'd wait there, all right, until the airplane's door was closed. Graham was taking no chances.

Lugging her overnight bag with Teddy still tucked under an arm, Jane boarded and walked toward the back of the plane, her brain working feverishly. There had to be a way to get off without Graham spotting her.

Then she saw it. The food service elevator was still attached to the side of the big jet. If she could somehow ride down on it... Oh, how silly. She'd never have the nerve. On the other hand...

"Please take your seat, miss," said a stewardess politely.

"I, uh, have to use the lavatory."

The woman frowned. "You'll have to be back in your seat before we taxi, miss."

"Oh, I will," lied Jane.

Ducking into the flight crew's service area was easy, as they were busy checking overhead compartments, seat belts and passing out magazines and pillows. But, oh my, it was going to be a tight squeeze fitting in between those two stainless steel carts. She started to squirm around one of the carriers so she could hide and felt a tug at her leg. Looking down, she discovered a hole in her panty hose the size of a silver dollar. Darn.

What was she thinking! There she was, worrying about a three-dollar pair of hose when she might get caught at any moment! What would she say, what absurd excuse could she come up with? *I was hungry. I hate flying.* Oh, Lord, how embarrassing.

The elevator, which was loaded with the trays of the last flight's leftovers, finally jerked and whined and began its descent to the tarmac.

Heck, this wasn't so bad after all. *Clever,* Jane thought, smiling to herself. Oh, boy, was Graham going to be surprised!

The elevator faltered briefly, causing Jane to reach out for support. Her hand came away from a tray all gooey with red sauce and stringy cheese. Lasagne! Someone's cold, half-eaten meal.

The elevator came to a halt a foot above the ground.

The noise outside was deafening, jets pulling in and out of the gates, their engines screaming. She had to find a way back inside somehow. Through the luggage area?

Jane straightened, still hanging onto Teddy, hoisting her bag with sticky fingers. She was stepping onto the tarmac, picturing herself riding up the conveyer belt with the luggage to get inside the terminal when she heard a noise behind her. Spinning around, Jane found four guns aimed at her and four airport security men staring at her without a hint of amusement.

"THE CLOTH YOU REQUESTED for your hand, Miss Manning."

It was the chief of security, the same man who'd interviewed Jane and Graham a short while ago. But this time Jane was the suspect. How humiliating.

She took the damp rag thankfully, grateful for the relatively friendly face of Captain Vermeer. They'd taken her bag, even Teddy, from her immediately, and she had not seen either since. Only these unsmiling, ramrod-straight guards who stood at attention against the sterile white walls of the room in which she'd been sitting—on a hard wooden chair—for hours it seemed. Jane wiped her fingers, thought about removing the spot of red sauce from her skirt but decided not to, and looked up at the captain. "Why are you holding me?" she asked innocently, as if she didn't know that they had taken her belongings to search for a bomb.

"Come, come, now, Miss Manning. You cannot be so naive! You will explain this very stupid thing you have done, please."

Jane did her best, realizing that no matter what she told him she would sound as if she were accusing Graham of stealing the diamonds himself. Why hadn't Graham said he was a courier before? Now he'd really gotten her into trouble!

"I will check this story, naturally," the man finally told her, rising.

"Are you going to call New York?" Jane asked.

"Of course, but it is very early there, I think."

"Will you find out if Mr. Smith checked in at Mercury, please?"

"I shall find out all the facts, miss. And then we shall see what is to be done with you, eh?"

She was allowed to use the bathroom down the hall and one of the guards brought her tea. It was another thirty minutes, however, before Captain Vermeer returned. There was a grim expression on his face.

"What you have done is very serious. And you have caused us much trouble and expense. Do you understand?"

Jane nodded.

"We," he really said, "vee," "have searched your bag and I am afraid the animal is no longer in one piece. Your story has been confirmed by your employer."

"Thank God!"

"Yes. *Dank Gott* you are who you say you are."

"You are going to let me go?"

His eyes pinioned her. "I could hold you, however, for many charges."

"I understand. Really I do. I acted rashly and stupidly."

"Among other things. Go back to your New York, miss, where perhaps such odd behavior is better tolerated. No?"

"Uh, yes." She stood up. "Did they say if Mr. Smith left Amsterdam or where he might have gone?"

"Your Mr. Smith has flown to Bermuda."

"*Bermuda*," breathed Jane, the agony of her suspicions striking her like a blow.

"To London, then Bermuda. I had these flights confirmed. I should not like to find this Mr. Smith sneaking down food elevators, eh?"

Two guards escorted Jane from the room, then handed her the overnight bag and Teddy's sad remains, which she chucked into a trash can. She was angry and humiliated and placed the blame squarely on Graham's shoulders. How dare he put her through such an ordeal!

Bermuda, she mused. Smedley had been going to Bermuda! What was going on here? Jane found a telephone, noticing that she was still being followed by a guard. She could hardly blame them for being cautious. After ten minutes she had Donna on the overseas line. "Graham's gone to Bermuda?" asked Jane.

"That's right. He checked in about an hour ago. What's going on, Jane?" The sound of gum snapping carried across the ocean.

"I'll tell you later. For now, tell Lew that I'm going to follow Graham. I think I know exactly where he is."

"You wanna talk to Lew?"

Jane thought. "No. Just tell him that. Bye, Donna." She hung up quickly in case Lew got on the line and tried to put a stop to her plans. Graham *could* have been telling the truth about Lew's orders although Jane had grave doubts. It was, however, in Graham's favor that he'd checked in with the office. But, of course, he thought she was safely on the plane back to New York.

She had to haggle with the airlines over her unused but marked-up ticket, then she discovered that the only flight available to Bermuda connected through London. And it cost more. She pulled out the brand-new VISA card she'd gotten from her bank in New York and charged the difference. If and when she caught up with Mr. Quicksilver he was damn well going to pay for her ticket!

After a stopover at Heathrow in London, Jane was finally heading west into the setting sun toward Bermuda and hopefully toward some answers to the questions that had been darting through her head ever since she'd talked to Norma.

How could she have fallen for a thief? Jane's judgment

had always been sound but now she felt as if her world had somehow tipped and nothing was right anymore. She went over and over the facts. Graham was either truly engaged in an elaborate scheme to lure the thieves or he was in league with them and pulling the wool over everyone's eyes, Lew's included. It didn't seem possible for Graham to be so underhanded and devious—not the man who laughed and teased and touched her with gentle, caring hands, and lived life to the fullest. It couldn't be her handsome man whose strawberry-blond hair caught the light like gold, whose China-blue eyes twinkled with devilry, whose deep voice caressed her ears.

Oh, yeah? thought Jane, sitting bolt upright in her seat and spilling coffee on her sweater. The jerk! Look what he was putting her through! The selfish, cruel, horrible man was engaged in the worst sort of crime. Forget the diamonds, forget all the other goods he'd stolen—to Jane it was far worse that he was deceiving and using his friends.

How could Graham be so crooked?

He's not, her heart shouted, *he's kind and considerate and fiercely loyal.*

Or was that all a facade?

Hour after hour Jane's thoughts vacillated, flip-flopped, drove her half out of her head. She fidgeted in her seat, spilled some soup on her skirt and used the lavatory six times.

"Perhaps you should refrain from more coffee," said the Englishman sitting next to her, the man whose knees she'd bumped every time she passed him on her way to the aisle.

"Sorry," was all Jane could say.

"Hmm. Quite." He rattled his newspaper and turned a shoulder to her.

The Boeing jet touched down on Bermuda at 6:35 p.m. local time. For Jane, however, it was hours later. She was hardly an experienced traveler, and the effects of being bounced from one time zone to another and back again were wearing her thin.

She knew she looked awful. Her hair was stringy and oily. Her makeup had not been touched since early that morning in Amsterdam and her clothes...

Jane glanced down at her stained skirt and rumpled sweater. Real cute. She could change in the ladies' room at the airport into her wool slacks but wool, on Bermuda? So she pulled off her sweater and crammed it into her bag and tried to straighten her white blouse. Of course, she couldn't see that there were rust-colored balls of wool from her "On Special" sweater stuck to the back of her blouse. Nor had she remembered the hole in one leg of her panty hose or the run up the side of the other. And even if she had been mindful of her appearance, Jane's anxiety overshadowed all else.

Now she had a task before her: find the consul general's party. And finding the party did not necessarily mean she'd find Graham there!

Bermuda was paradise in the middle of the Atlantic where British grace mingled with island languor. Jane's taxi sped on the wrong—British—side of the road, across an elevated causeway, along the northern coast toward the capital port city, Hamilton.

The scenery went practically unnoticed. *George,* Jane was thinking. What was his last name? Oh darn, she should have listened better! Some funny name. An animal. George...George...Mondragon! Consul general of Bermuda. Someone would know where his party was, wouldn't they?

The taxi passed beautifully landscaped homes, their stucco exteriors painted in eye-pleasing pastels: pink, cream, violet, blue to match the sparkling water, coral, yellow. Every dwelling had intricate wrought-iron grillwork around the deep-set windows and doors. The profusion of brilliant tropical flowers that glowed in the evening sun finally touched Jane's senses. The plant life was so green, so utterly, overpoweringly verdant, so unlike the dry sparseness of her home that she couldn't help gaping.

Hamilton was a tightly clustered, picturesque town of elegant shops and stucco hotels and international restaurants along winding streets above a colorful harbor where clean white cruise ships nestled alongside private yachts.

The British Consulate was pastel with a surrounding, vine-covered stone wall and a tall white wrought-iron gate. It was, of course, locked at this hour. Jane asked the taxi driver to wait and rang the quaint bell at the gate. No one answered. She stood there, hot and tired and increasingly impatient. Angry tears pricked at her eyelids. "Isn't anybody here?" she mumbled to herself.

How was she going to find Graham? She rang again, waited another minute, shifting from foot to foot. Should she find a phone and see if the consulate had an emergency number? She could always look up George Mondragon in the phone book, she supposed. But the party might not be at his house.

She rang again. Her driver leaned out of his open window and called to her. "They'll all be at the grand affair, miss."

Jane whirled on him. "George Mondragon's party?"

"Sure, miss. The whole island's been buzzing with it for weeks. I took some folks out there already."

Jane closed her eyes and whispered a thank-you. "Can you take me there? Is it far?"

"Hop in. It be about fifteen minutes."

The coastline twisted and dipped, following old stone walls and fertile embankments. The road was so narrow in spots that the cab had to slow to first let other vehicles go by, but more often the taxi driver bullied on past, jockeying for the right of way. The ride was hair-raising but speedy.

The sun was making its lazy low arch in the west, turning the ocean to the color of copper, casting long shadows across the road as they sped on their way.

Why couldn't she be enjoying this new adventure with Graham? How had things gone so wrong? And *what*, wondered Jane for the hundredth time, was she going to do if he wasn't at George Mondragon's? Call Lew at home and tell him the bad news, that Graham had disappeared with the diamonds, she guessed.

Damn you, Graham Smith!

The taxi passed by lavishly foliated hills rising from pink-tinted sandy beaches and estates nestled in junglelike growth. Jane was suddenly struck by the astounding aura of wealth on Bermuda. She was a fish out of water, a cowgirl, duped by Mr. Charm himself, duped and *had*.

What was Graham doing on Bermuda? Luring the thieves, he would no doubt tell her. Hogwash, thought Jane. More than likely he'd come to Bermuda to join forces with Smedley! This little jaunt of his was no coincidence!

It was nearly eight by the time she was deposited at the end of a sandy, palm-lined driveway that led up to a pink villa snuggled into the lush hillside. A beautiful home, an enchanted castle where anything could come true.

She began walking up the drive, her bag slung recklessly over her shoulder, her appearance very much the worse for wear.

There was a gate—wrought iron, wonder of wonders—and a bell. Jane pulled on the cord, peeking through the curlicued grill to see dozens of shining, sporty cars parked in the driveway. Beyond that, off to one side of the house were ladies and gentlemen milling about the lawn, the women in gauzy, glittering formal gowns, their jewelry winking in the gilded evening light; the men in handsome, crisp white dinner jackets.

Jane reached up and slapped at a mosquito that was biting her grimy neck as violin music, haunting and beckoning, sounded from the villa.

Damn you, Graham Smith!

CHAPTER SIXTEEN

GRAHAM GLANCED AT HIS WATCH. Jane must be safely home in her apartment by now, he decided. He felt vastly relieved; he'd telephone her first thing in the morning and reassure her that everything was okay and maybe, he thought grimly, he should bring up the subject of her distrust and clear the air between them before it was too late.

"You look better every time I see you," Eleanor Mondragon was saying. "One of those men who ages so handsomely."

"Why, thank you," replied Graham, forcing precisely the right smile, boyish and flattered. "And you look beautiful tonight. Of course, you always do." She did look quite spectacular, he had to admit: the Grande Dame was dressed in flowing black chiffon, her gray hair wound into an intricate coiffure interlaced with pearls, real pearls. But then it was her husband's final social fling and should be recalled by Bermuda's society for decades.

With his mind still on Jane, Graham sipped on his champagne and viewed the elegant assemblage that spilled from terrace to terrace to the flawless green lawn. Japanese lanterns were strung all around. Uniformed Bermudian waiters and waitresses mingled, carrying silver trays of hors d'oeuvres and drinks. A violinist played lilting tunes next to the splashing tiled fountain.

Eleanor waved to someone across the pool and blew him a kiss. "It was so wonderful to see your mother and father arrive together," she said softly, tapping Graham's sleeve. "We had heard that they separated, dear, and it seemed such a tragic thing for two people who had always been such a close couple.''

''It was...*is*...well, I don't exactly know what their status is right now. All I know is that my mother flew in from Canada.''

''Oh, they do seem happy,'' exclaimed Eleanor and Graham followed the direction of her gaze. There was Smedley, up on a terrace, tall and distinguished in his dinner jacket, in a circle of equally distinguished men, arguing happily. British and American politics, no doubt. And over there on the lawn was Renée, radiant in a flowing rose creation, jewels sparkling from her ears and neck, laughing and apparently carefree, engaged in women's talk with several other ladies.

He couldn't help but feel glad, in spite of his concern over his own romantic problems, to see his parents together again, just like in the old days.

''And you, my dear boy, when is some smart young lady going to steal you off the circuit?''

The subject of Jane was on the tip of his tongue when he felt a tap on his shoulder. He turned quickly to see the Mondragon's butler standing behind him, his old face expressionless, his white gloved hands folded properly in front of him.

JANE SAW HIM MATERIALIZE out of the semidarkness as if he were a wraith. So he *was* there! She didn't know if she was relieved or unnerved to see him again. On one hand, a thief didn't let his boss know where he was going; on the other, he could already have handed the stones to an accomplice and be planning to say he'd been robbed.

Jane wiped at a trickle of sweat on her temple and waited impatiently as Graham said something to a man—the butler, she supposed. She wanted to laugh wildly, standing there in the soft hot twilight: the *butler*!

But Graham was approaching, his face a mask of incredulity. "Janey!" he gasped. "What on earth are you doing here?"

He wore an exquisitely tailored white linen dinner jacket, formal black trousers, a ruffled shirt, patent leather shoes. In any other circumstances Jane would have drawn in her breath, spellbound by the handsome picture he made. As it was, she could barely keep her temper under control.

She thrust her face up to the wrought-iron bars. "Did you think I was going to get on that flight and forget about the diamonds? No wonder they call you Quicksilver!"

"But, Janey, I saw you get on that plane. I thought you were in New York!"

"I won't even begin to tell you what I went through to follow you!" She felt ridiculous talking to him through the metal bars as if she were a prisoner. "Will you get that *person* over here to let me in?"

"Uh, sure."

She stalked in and dropped her bag on the ground. "Look, Graham, I'm hot and tired and thirsty. I tracked you down because I have to do my job and now I want to see the diamonds. Are they here?"

"The, uh, diamonds. Ah, yeah, they're here."

"I want to see them. Now."

Graham snapped his mouth shut and seemed to gather himself. "Lord, Janey, you do take a man aback."

"The diamonds."

"They're in George's safe." He looked at her sharply. "You thought I was running off with them. Janey..."

"You're darn right I did."

"You don't trust me," he stated sadly.

"After what you pulled in Amsterdam? No, I don't trust you. That's why I sneaked off the plane you put me on."

"*You what*?"

"Down the food elevator. And then they thought I was

a terrorist or something and Captain Vermeer was furious.
It was all so horrible.''

"Janey, sweetheart, do you mean to say our nice security man in Amsterdam *arrested* you?''

"Only until he got Mercury to vouch for me. And then
I had to go to London and…you owe me seventy-five
dollars for my ticket to get here!''

"But how did you know where I…? Of course, Vermeer called Mercury. Oh, Janey, you should have gone
home.''

"And let you skip off with the diamonds and ruin
Lew's business and make a fool of me and…and everyone?''

"I told you—oh, damn it, it wasn't supposed to happen
like this. If we didn't get the thieves in Amsterdam I was
to go on alone, so they'd be sure and try again.''

"Oh, yeah?'' She waved an arm toward the lawn. "At
a party on *Bermuda*? That's how you'd lure the thieves?
Inside a locked gate surrounded by dozens of people?''
She eyed him assessingly. "A party where your father just
happens to be?''

"Well, sure, that's why I stopped by, to see my folks.
Lew knows. It's all approved, Janey.''

She folded her arms.

"I told you, we had this contingency plan.…''

Could he be telling the truth? Oh, how she wanted to
believe him! Her whole mind and heart and body craved
his innocence. Please, she prayed silently, let it be the
truth.

"Believe me, Janey, everything's under control.'' He
looked at her pleadingly. "Truce?''

She glared at him for another second, then her face
crumpled and she felt as if she was going to cry. But that
would never do. She was on a job, her biggest, most important assignment to date—Norma's assignment, really—and to be failing so miserably made her feel sick to
her stomach. She had to get control of herself. In as level

a voice as she could manage, Jane finally said, "Graham, you've got to understand that I want to believe you, that I'm trying to believe you. But either way, I've got my job to think about and I can't let you go running around making me look like a complete fool." Surely he could see things from her point of view.

Tentatively he reached out and patted her back, then trailed a finger up her neck and hooked a lock of damp hair behind her ear. "Everything's going to be fine, really. You did a great job."

She shuddered with the pleasure of his touch. Here she was, trying with every fiber of her being to get back in control and the mere brush of his fingers was sending her straight into that miasma of confusion again. Sudden anger exploded within her and Jane lashed out against him in the only way she could. "And look at you. Look at you! All spiffed up in a…in a dinner jacket! Oh, I suppose you just happened to have it in the zipper compartment of your overnight bag!"

Graham glanced down at himself. "Well, actually, my father brought it along with his stuff."

"Oh, so he knew you were going to be here. And why didn't I know?"

"It was only a possibility. If we'd nabbed those guys in the airport I would have gone straight back to New York with you. Now I'm not in any hurry. This was an alternate route."

"Oh, I see," she said sarcastically. He had an answer for everything. He could be telling the truth. Maybe Lew really *had* told him to send her back. But could she rely on that possibility? Her mind told her no, her heart pleaded with her to trust him. She stood there in the warm, perfumed darkness and felt as if she were going to fly into a million pieces. "Can I see the diamonds, Graham?" she asked, trying to keep her voice level, trying to stave off the misery that would drown her if she let her guard down for an instant.

"I told you, they're—" But he clammed up then. "Okay. I'll go get George to unlock the safe. But really, Jane Manning, you do try a man's soul, my sweet."

"The diamonds, Graham."

Ten minutes later Jane was apologizing to George Mondragon. "I just had to see them, you understand."

"Are you happy now?" Graham asked, leading her out of the den.

"Very."

"Well, now maybe we can get you fixed up and forget about the blasted stones for a little while."

"Fixed up?"

Graham stopped and looked at her. "I assume you want to stick with me, right?"

"Right."

"Well, it would be terribly rude to show up at the Mondragon's big event in that outfit."

It was Jane's turn to look down at herself: creased corduroy skirt, rumpled white blouse, torn panty hose. "Can't we leave? Go somewhere?"

"That would be even ruder. Janey, I just can't, at least not yet. It would look pretty ridiculous—you showing up and hauling me off."

Jane sank down onto a rattan bench and rubbed her forehead with grimy fingers. "Oh, I don't know what to do." She wanted to cry; she wanted Graham to comfort her but she didn't dare weaken. It would be folly to let him touch her or let herself feel anything. What on earth was she to do?

Cautiously Graham sat down next to her. "Poor Janey," he said tenderly. "I would never have put you through this if I'd known you were going to follow me." He touched her hand with gentle fingers but she pulled away.

"Graham, you should know me by now. How could you have thought I'd just let you go?"

"Wishful thinking?" he offered, not very successfully.

Their eyes met and held. Jane felt a deep sorrow grip her. Her love for Graham was tarnished, dirtied. Even if he were innocent, would he ever trust her again?

As if he knew what she was thinking, Graham stroked her cheek. "Come on, sweetheart, let's get you something to wear. My mother will help. And Eleanor. You'll see, you'll feel much better when you're all fixed up. Here I am forgetting that you're probably thirsty and all. I'll get you something. Champagne?"

Jane sighed. "So it's Cinderella and her fairy god-mother? Graham, really…"

"You'll be the belle of the ball, Janey."

"And at midnight my gown will turn into rags. Graham, I'm really not in the mood."

He smiled his twinkling, mischievous grin and pulled her up. "And I'm Prince Charming and we get to live happily ever after."

"Do we, Graham?" was all Jane said.

RENÉE AND ELEANOR MONDRAGON stood in front of three dresses that hung on hangers. Their heads were cocked, their brows drawn.

"The yellow," said Eleanor.

"The shoes won't go."

"Perhaps the green then. It's bigger in the waist. And she could wear the white satin slippers…"

"Hmm," said Renée, "now that I see her coloring, maybe the gold. What size shoe do you wear, dear?"

"Mrs. Smith, really, I…" Jane began.

"Now, now. Try these on. We weren't sure of the fit. Pamela is smaller and Bea is bigger."

"Pamela and Bea?"

"My daughters," answered Eleanor graciously.

"Oh."

"She has a lovely figure," said Eleanor, studying Jane as if she were on the auction block.

Renée held up the yellow dress. It was strapless, tucked,

with thousands of crystal beads sewn on the bodice. "No, too fussy."

Then there was a taffeta with winglike shoulders. "Overpowering," said Renée, shaking her head.

Eleanor held up another dress. "Try it on, dear," she said.

"Yes," said Renée, studying Jane with her head cocked to one side.

"Yes," agreed Eleanor.

"My gold sandals," mused Renée.

"The clip for her hair," said Eleanor decisively.

"See if my shoes fit," suggested Renée.

They were a touch narrow but Jane, wishing she could crawl into a hole and die, said she didn't mind a bit. "It's only for a few hours, after all."

Eleanor stuck the gold and rhinestone clip in Jane's hair, pulling it back on one side. "Try that."

Jane felt like a mannequin, a ridiculous role for a body-guard to play. She wanted to laugh and cry at the same time but the two older women were taking their handi-work so seriously, she couldn't insult them.

"Take a look," said Renée triumphantly, pushing Jane toward the mirror.

Jane stared, blinked, then stared again. The gold dress fell from thin straps to the floor, a sleek, metallic, shimmery tube, its curved lines touching her bust and hips in its flow. It was loose yet clinging, terribly simple yet gor-geously complicated. "It's beautiful," she breathed, re-volving in front of the mirror.

Graham obviously thought so, too. "Good God, you're an eyeful! How am I going to keep the men off you?" He put a warm hand on her bare back and pulled her closer. "See? I knew you'd feel better."

"Only until midnight," Jane reminded him firmly. "then I turn into a cowgirl again."

The party was in full swing by the time they joined it. Night had fallen and the palm trees swayed softly in the tropical breeze. Frangipani, hibiscus and oleander bushes crowded the emerald lawn and the lighted turquoise pool. Japanese lanterns bathed everyone in a flattering glow. Jane tried to imagine what it would be like to be a real guest at the party, someone who could enjoy the beauty, the music, the gowns and jewels and fine conversation. As it was, she felt both she and Graham were playing a part.

She drank a glass of champagne—too quickly—and smiled and nodded and shook innumerable hands, not remembering a word or a face. And all the time questions and awful, tearing doubts crashed in her head. Graham appeared to be totally in his element, relaxed and debonair, but was he truly as comfortable as he seemed? It could be an act. Jane *hoped* it was an act. But was Graham so caught up in acting that he no longer knew reality from make-believe?

Smedley, looking very handsome in his formal attire, came over to join them. "Have you seen your mother?" he asked Graham.

"Oh, yes, we've seen her. She looks wonderful and she seems to be having a great time."

"You think so? She did perk up quite a bit when I asked her to join me here. Did I do the right thing?"

"Absolutely," put in Jane.

"You better watch out, Dad, or some young attaché will snap her up and you'll be left in the lurch," Graham joked.

"Do you really…? Oh, you're teasing me." Smedley swallowed the last of his champagne. "Perhaps I'd better go find her," he said too casually and wandered off.

There was a midnight buffet set out on the patio. Tables were heaped with seafood salads, caviar, roast beef, fruits of all descriptions, mouth-watering desserts and a luscious six-tiered cake that sported tiny figures of George and Eleanor atop it.

Graham brought Jane a plate piled with samples of everything. They sat beside a pink frangipani bush with the fountain tinkling nearby. A string quartet played a lovely assortment of Mozart and Bach and the sea breeze rustled leaves as background. It should have been idyllic, the fulfillment of any Cinderella's dream, but the props were the only reality in this fairy tale; the prince and Cinderella were false, empty characters, going through the motions, unsure of their next lines or the final act.

The party broke up about four in the morning. The weary revelers left for their homes or hotels or rooms at the Mondragon's huge villa. George and Eleanor said goodbye and thank you hundreds of times. Food and glasses and napkins lay all over the grounds as if Sherman's army had tramped through. One lone party goer was peacefully asleep in his formal attire on an air mattress in the pool.

Smedley and Renée danced obliviously in a corner, totally out of step with the music.

"See you in the morning, Mom," Graham said, tapping her on the shoulder. "The party's over."

Smedley blinked owlishly and looked around. "Who cares," he muttered.

"Good night, *mes chers*," said Renée expansively.

Leading Jane across the littered lawn and into the house, Graham said, "Eleanor told me that you could have the room next to mine." He stopped in front of his door in the dimly lit hallway and took her hands.

Her heart thudded too heavily. It had been a long, long day and she was upset and tired and trying desperately to keep her equilibrium, yet this man's touch still made her heart pound and her knees weak. She looked down. "I'd prefer to stay with you, if you don't mind."

"Janey, ah Janey." He let go of her and shook his head sadly. "I have a feeling that you're on the job."

"I am," she whispered. "Someone here has to remember this is business."

"Business, Janey? Everything between us can be reduced to business?'' He didn't sound like the Graham she knew; he sounded older and careworn. ''Look, Jane—'' he tilted her face up ''—can we get everything straightened out when we get back to New York?''

''Oh, Graham.'' She felt her eyes filling with hot tears. ''Oh, how I hope so!''

He opened the door to his room and waited for Jane to enter. She brushed so close to him she could smell the scent of his after-shave. Desire rose within her.

''Well, here we are,'' he said, attempting levity, trying to regain his normal jauntiness.

Jane could see the two of them reflected in the mirrored closet door—two beautifully dressed people standing close together in an elegantly furnished bedroom. He with hair gleaming golden in the faint light from the bedside lamp, tall and broad shouldered and heartrendingly handsome in his white dinner jacket; she with diamonds sparkling in her hair, her eyes too big, shadowed darkly, her body a column of glimmering golden curves. She hugged at her elbows, feeling empty and cold despite the tropical night air.

What would she do if Graham pulled her into his arms?

CHAPTER SEVENTEEN

JANE KNEW she was asking for trouble by spending the night—no, morning now—in Graham's bedroom. Her body ached with exhaustion, every muscle crying out for rest; her eyes were scratchy and a yawn pressed up from somewhere deep inside her chest. She could see that Graham was subdued as well. He peeled off his dinner jacket, threw it over a chair and started unbuttoning his ruffled shirt.

"For Lord's sake, Janey, relax. I'm not going to bite," he said testily.

"I'd rather be in my own room, believe me," she said with a sigh.

Graham ran a hand through his hair. "Sorry," he mumbled. His shirt was half undone and she could see the fine golden hairs of his chest. "Aw, Jane, don't be mad at me. I can't stand it. Come on over here."

"No," she whispered.

He stared at her silently, his sandy brows drawn together. "I'm not going to let you do this to us," he finally said.

"It may not be entirely up to you, Graham," she answered slowly.

"All right, I'll put all that aside for now, until the job's over. Why don't you at least get undressed? I could use some sleep myself." He yawned widely, the cords in his strong neck stretching.

Jane picked up her overnight bag from the corner where she'd dumped it and went into the bathroom. There was no sense in pushing things by undressing in front of him. Had it only been a few short days ago that she'd been utterly unself-conscious with him, running around his apartment stark naked, laughing, playing hide-and-seek, loving him?

Her filmy blue nightgown was not going to help matters much, she realized, assessing herself in the bathroom mirror. Standing on the cool tile floor, she saw the details of her body beneath the soft nylon. The fabric deepened in color over the hollow of her stomach, lightened and glistened over her breasts and nipples. The material touched her so lightly, yet in her exhausted, keyed-up state, her skin was as sensitive to it as if she had a fever.

Mustering her courage, holding the gold dress carefully over one arm, Jane left the bathroom. Graham was calmly getting into bed, nude. He always slept nude, Jane remembered. His pale, muscular buttocks disappeared under the covers as Jane averted her eyes, flushing with discomfort, unable to banish the images that crowded her mind, images of Graham poised over her, lying beside her, holding her, kissing her....

"Come on, Janey," he said softly and her heart gave a great uncontrollable leap of fear and excitement. Turning her back, she hung the dress carefully in the closet.

"It didn't turn to rags at midnight, did it?" Graham asked drowsily from the bed.

"No, guess I'm just lucky."

"You were beautiful, you were a beautiful Cinderella."

"Thanks," she murmured, putting off the inevitable— getting into bed with Graham.

Finally she padded across the carpet and slipped very carefully into the queen-size bed, as far from him as she could manage.

"Look, Jane, I'm not going to force myself on you. That's not my style," Graham said dryly. "Just go to sleep."

"I'm sort of wound up," she said. "Please turn the light off."

Click. Darkness enshrouded them. Jane lay there stiffly, staring into the night, her heart pounding so hard she was sure Graham could hear it.

His hand moved across the bed, a phantom disembodied entity that came to rest on her hip. Every fiber of Jane's body snapped rigid with expectancy. She tried to find her voice but swallowed instead, her mouth dry and cottony. The word "please" finally crossed her lips, forced up through a constricted throat. She felt on fire suddenly.

"Janey, you'll never get to sleep if you're going to be so tense." His voice came lazily out of the blackness. He rolled over toward her and she was terribly aware of the bed sagging beneath his weight, of the rustle of the bedclothes. "Let me rub your shoulders. You're overtired. You need to relax."

"I'm all right." She didn't sound very convincing.

"You're not. Let me..." His hands touched her neck and began kneading her muscles expertly, warm and strong and knowing, his touch unbelievably pleasurable. He moved down to her shoulders. "Turn your back to me, sweetheart." She did. His fingers found every tired muscle, every spot of tension. She sighed and felt the tautness ebb from her body. She'd let him continue, just for another minute. The sensation was delicious; she felt herself slipping away on a tide of comfort.

"There, that's better," he said quietly, his voice a caress as much as his touch, his fingers massaging, probing, drawing the tightness from her.

She'd stop him in a second, Jane thought, in just another second. But his touch felt so marvelous after her long, dreadful day. So marvelous... She had a moment's realization that she was floating away, her eyes were closing, her body giving up, and then even that faded....

Something was hot on her face. Jane turned her head

on the pillow and rolled over with a sigh. Now the heat was on the back of her head. She began to awaken and realized that it was the sun warming her, pouring in through the window and lying in wide swatches of brightness across the bed.

"Mmm," she said, licking her dry lips and stretching her legs. She rolled onto her back and opened her eyes. Graham was standing by the open window, gazing out at the scenery. He looked relaxed, one hand on the casement, the other scratching through sleep-tousled hair that was lit to the color of gold. He was wearing briefs and nothing more. He finally stretched, the corded muscles of his shoulder blades flexing, his flanks long and lean as his arms rose above his head.

He turned away from the light. "Oh, hi," he said, smiling. "Hope I didn't wake you."

Jane averted her gaze and started to sit up. "What time is it?" she asked casually, feeling a slight headache as she moved.

"Around one."

"One! In the afternoon!" She swung out of bed.

"Whoa there. What's the panic?"

"But Graham...the diamonds."

"All is well, my sweet." He moved toward her and she retreated suddenly until the back of her legs bumped into the bed. "Did I ever tell you," he murmured, "that you look beautiful in the morning?"

Then he was standing in front of her, legs apart, reaching up to push her bangs out of her eyes with a gentle hand.

"Don't, please," said Jane.

She wondered how she could want him so desperately in the midst of such doubt. Was it love that allowed for the incongruity of her emotions? Was love really so blindly forgiving?

He lowered his head and kissed her, a soft brush of his lips against hers, warm and provocative. Jane felt her stomach flutter with pleasure even as her mind insisted that she push him away. Graham's arms slipped around her back slowly, soothingly, the way an experienced horseman would handle a skittish colt. He drew Jane toward him until the thin fabric of her nightgown touched the breadth of his chest. His hands moved down her back and spanned her waist, pulling her against him with more urgency. She could feel his hardness then and an ache coiled in her belly.

With every ounce of willpower Jane could gather, she pulled back. Her eyes searched his face as her chest rose and fell too quickly. What was the emotion written in his solemn expression? Was he deceiving her still, using their overpowering attraction as a weapon to confuse her?

Jane stumbled away from him and rushed for the safe haven of the bathroom but his words lingered after her and hung heavily in the air: ''You know there's something special between us, Janey.''

A half hour later Jane was dressed in clean slacks and blouse, her hair blown dry, her makeup hastily put on. She zipped up her bag, looked around the empty room and then glanced at the golden evening gown still hanging in the open closet. She sighed wistfully and turned to leave.

She found Graham on a sunny breakfast patio, coffee mug in hand, chatting with a few guests who had also slept in.

''Coffee, miss?'' asked a maid as Jane stepped onto the patio.

No one was bright-eyed that day. One lady sat in a corner alone, near a tall potted palm, with sunglasses on. Her face was pale. Too much of a good thing, Jane thought wryly.

''We'll be taking off shortly,'' Graham was saying to his host. ''Great party, George.'' And Jane noticed that of all the people there, Graham was the only one who looked as if he'd gone to bed early with a good book. How did he manage it?

"Are your folks up? I'd like to say goodbye," Jane remarked.

He turned to her nonchalantly. "They already left."

Something was fishy, Jane decided, as their taxi sped toward the airport. It wasn't the diamonds—she'd poked her nose into the belt to reassure herself on that score— and she supposed Smedley and Renée could have risen earlier and not bothered to wait for their son, although it seemed odd, their rushing off like that. And what had happened to Graham's plan to nab the thieves? Had he given up that easily? Did he expect an attempt in the Bermuda airport or perhaps at Kennedy?

"Do you suppose," ventured Jane, "that the thieves followed you to Bermuda?"

"I'm sure they thought of it. If they're not here, they know every move I'm making."

"So your plan is still in effect?"

"Yes, but it would be better if you weren't along."

"Forget it, Mr. Quicksilver, I'm sticking to you like glue."

The argument commenced near the phone in the airport. Graham dialed New York. "Donna?" he said into the receiver while Jane studied faces in the crowd, "it's Graham. Yes, I'm fine.... No, I can give you the message. Tell Lew I'm heading to my dad's place on the Outer Banks—"

"What!" cried Jane, spinning around.

Graham cupped his hand over the receiver. "Quiet, will you? Yes, just for the night," he told Donna. "I'll be arriving back in New York tomorrow... No, Jane and I won't be flying into National...Norfolk, Virginia. Tell Lew. I'm renting a car.... No, no, I'll be fine. It's just that my dad isn't at the beach house and there's a problem there.... You know, the place is really deserted and... Well, never mind, see you late tomorrow. Yeah, bye."

Jane was standing with her feet apart, hands on hips, her jaw thrust forward. "You've really done it now!" she snapped. "The whole office will know every move we're making!"

"Exactly. You know—" his eyes glinted "—you're nose is so cute and freckly when you're mad."

"Oh, stop it! Let me think!"

Short of hog-tying him, there was no way of stopping Graham from pursuing this insanity. Or was it insanity? Maybe it was just a well thought-out scheme to "steal" the diamonds from himself with the help of his father. Why else would they be going to North Carolina? Why else had Smedley left so early that morning? But Graham *did* have the stones—she'd seen them—so how was his father involved?

It was too much for Jane. She slumped sullenly in the plane seat and tried to catch Graham's expression out of the corner of her eye. All he did was turn to her and smile openly and charmingly and pat her hand as the plane lifted into the cloudless blue September sky.

In Norfolk Graham rented a bright red Mustang convertible. "They won't be able to miss us in this number!"

They drove for an hour south to the North Carolina coast, Jane recognizing landmarks along the way: The Chesapeake Crab Company, the Wishart's Hog Farm featuring fresh Virginia ham, the Island Motel with its Triple X films available. Of course, Graham had the top down.

"You realize," said Jane, "that if your thugs *are* following us they could blow either of our heads off with a rifle?"

"It'd be a helluva shot though, wouldn't it?" He looked over at Jane, tipped up his aviator glasses and winked.

"Nothing ever bothers you, does it?"

"Nope. Well, it does bug me that you're doubting my credibility."

Jane fell uncomfortably silent.

There was a long stretch of open country road just before they crossed the bridge to the Outer Banks.

"Well, well," said Graham, his head tilted to look in the rearview mirror.

"What is it?"

"That car. Back there behind the camper. He's been moving up fast and was ready to pass the motor home but then pulled back into his lane."

"You think he spotted us and fell back?"

"Could be."

If this was a farce, Jane thought, it certainly was an elaborate one.

By the time Graham pulled into the sandy driveway leading to his dad's house, the car that was following them—that was *maybe* following them, Jane corrected herself—had disappeared. Not that it couldn't have been a quarter of a mile back up the road. How difficult would it be to spot a shiny red Mustang in Smedley's driveway?

At first Jane didn't notice that the elder Smith's car wasn't there. But when Graham tilted a pot beside the garage and produced a house key, she asked curiously, "Where is your dad, anyway?"

"Maybe he and Mom stopped at the Island Motel," he said humorously.

"That's ridiculous." Jane took her small bag from Graham and put it in the guest room. "So what now?" she asked when she returned to the living room. "Do we just sit and wait or would you rather go for a walk on the beach and leave the diamonds here, with the door unlocked, of course."

Graham patted the belt under his shirt. "We sit and wait."

Jane sank miserably onto the couch, keeping an ear tuned to Graham's movements and musing on the frailty of love and trust.

Graham. He *was* a daredevil. And she loved that part of him, cherished the adventurous spark that had never left him. But that trait of his had a dark side as well, one that might easily get him into trouble, such as now, when he imagined he was outsmarting them all—challenging, daring, seeking that singular thrill.

Could he be as guilty as he looked to her? Wouldn't stealing the diamonds and getting away with it be the ultimate dare, like shaking his fist at the world and walking away victorious?

Oh, he was capable of doing anything he pleased, Jane knew. The question remained: was he capable of a criminal act?

Just then there was the sound of a car in the driveway. Graham came out from the kitchen where he'd been rattling around in cupboards. "Don't tell me that's Dad." He strode to the window.

"It must be," Jane replied, following him.

Renée was there as well, swinging her legs out of the car gracefully, waiting for Smedley to unload the trunk.

"I never expected Dad today," Graham muttered, "much less Mom. I thought he was going to put her on a plane to Montreal." Graham dropped the curtain and turned to Jane, shaking his head in disbelief.

"Oh, here you are!" Renée exclaimed as she swept into the house. "I thought you were headed home to New York, *mon cher*." She gave Graham a kiss on the cheek. "And Jane, too." Renée stood looking at the two of them, then shrugged. "So we are all here. How lovely."

"You're staying?" asked Graham tentatively.

"Perhaps. We shall see." Renée smiled charmingly, in a manner reminiscent of Graham's.

But her son was frowning, a hand rubbing the afternoon stubble on his chin. "Where's Dad, anyway?"

"Fetching the dogs from the neighbor's."

"I, uh, thought you were going to Montreal," Graham said carefully.

"Oh, I *was*. But then I said to myself, why not spend some time at the beach? And the boat. You know, I have not been out on the boat in so long,'' Renée said nonchalantly, but Jane read between the lines and realized that what Renée meant was, ''I wanted to spend some more time with Smedley and see how our tentative truce works out.''

A moment later the dogs bounded in, jumping and barking and leaping, knocking the sliding screen door half off its track.

''Settle down!'' yelled Smedley, huffing up the steps behind them.

''Hi, Dad,'' said Graham.

''Oh, you're here already,'' said Smedley.

''And so are you,'' replied Graham elliptically.

''I will freshen up,'' Renée was saying gaily, ''and then we'll see what there is for dinner.'' And she disappeared down the hall.

''I *tried* to get her to go to Montreal,'' Smedley said in a stage whisper, ''but you know your *mother*.''

''What are we going to do now?'' asked Graham. ''I don't want her around tonight.''

''Your father knows…?'' put in Jane.

''Of course,'' replied Graham distractedly.

''I tried,'' said Smedley again.

''The boat,'' said Graham decisively. ''You get her on that boat tonight, Dad.''

''What if she won't go?''

''She'll go if you ask her nicely. And I mean *nicely*. Hearts and flowers and all that.''

''I don't know if she'll listen.''

''She'll listen, don't worry. She went to Bermuda with you, didn't she?''

''So,'' said Renée, bustling back in, ''now for dinner.''

''Wait a sec, Renée,'' said Smedley, catching a silent directive from Graham. ''Why don't we go out on the boat tonight?''

''Tonight? But…''

Smedley looked down at his feet, and Jane could have

sworn she saw him scuff a toe as if he were an embarrassed schoolboy. "We can fish and cook dinner there. All by ourselves. You know you love the ocean at night." He glanced up to see how she was taking it.

"Why, Smedley…" Renée said, for once nonplussed.

"Then we can, uh, sit on the deck and watch the moon." His voice wavered on the last phrase but he plunged bravely on. "And talk about things."

"Mom, really, I think it's a great idea to go out on the boat," urged Graham. "A great idea! And soon, too, before it gets dark. Don't you think so, Dad?"

"Oh…oh, yes, sure, before dark. Renée, shall we get ready?"

"Well, I don't know. I have to pack, you realize. I cannot *go* just like that." And she snapped her fingers.

Graham rolled his eyes.

"And I wish to talk to you, Smedley, alone." Her back as straight and stiff as a ramrod, Renée disappeared out onto the deck. Smedley followed, looking pained.

Graham sank into a chair and rubbed the bridge of his nose. "The best laid plans of mice and men…"

"What if they don't go out on the boat?"

"I'll make them go to a motel."

"You really think…" began Jane.

"Yes, damn it, I think this house is *not* going to be the safest place for a second honeymoon tonight!" he snapped.

"And I'm supposed to go along with you, whatever crazy thing you plan to do?" Jane retorted angrily.

He put up a hand to silence her. "Yes, and let's drop the subject. I'm positive everything will be cleared up by tomorrow and, boy, you better give me one huge apology, lady, and I mean *huge*."

Jane was about to say that she hoped she could when the raised voices of Graham's parents filtered into the house.

"Is this some kind of plot?" Renée was asking. "I'm

not stupid, you know, and I know my son and his mad notions!''

''I would merely like your company, Renée,'' said Smedley.

''After a year?'' came her sharp query.

''Yes, damn it, after a year.''

''Don't you talk to me like that!''

''Then, for Lord's sake, Renée, come out on the boat with me!'' shouted Smedley.

''You really want me to?'' she asked, suddenly sounding vulnerable.

''Yes, damn it!''

''Sh! The children will hear!'' warned Renée.

When his parents came in, Graham was studiously occupied reading a magazine and Jane was busy getting herself a soda from the refrigerator.

''Graham,'' said his father, ''your mother and I are taking the boat out before it gets dark.''

''Terrific!'' said Graham innocently.

''Will you please go pack,'' Smedley said to his wife, none too gently. ''And for God's sake, Renée, just a small bag!''

Renée said over her shoulder, ''I shall bring whatever I require. It might be a trunkful, *mon cher*.''

A half hour later, the dogs yelping in the drive and scratching the paint on the car with their jumping, the couple was ready to leave. Renée had not taken along a trunk, Jane noted, but a bag that would have sufficed most people for two weeks.

Smedley swore as he put the case in the trunk of the car and pinched a finger when he closed it. Renée ignored him, waving and blowing them both kisses.

''Be good!'' she called. ''Please, *mes enfants*.''

Jane smiled dutifully and waved back, thinking these two were going to make this reconciliation work yet.

''They're off at last,'' stated Graham, standing there

with his hands in his pockets, the setting sun catching his hair and setting it aflame.

A pirate, Jane thought. He would always, no matter the outcome of their night, be her buccaneer.

"Well—" he turned back toward the house and grinned at her "—we're all alone now, Janey."

CHAPTER EIGHTEEN

JANE UNWRAPPED A FROZEN PIZZA and crammed the empty box into the trash can. "What I really can't figure out," she said to Graham casually, "is why you're so all-fire sure the thieves will make a try tonight." *There, that was put calmly,* she thought, proud of her control.

It *could* be true, after all, that he was actually being honest with her. Paying lip service to his story wouldn't hurt. No matter what, though, she planned to watch his scheme unfold and be ready to foil any attempt of his to make off with the stones.

Graham was busy turning on the oven, opening and closing cupboard doors, mumbling about the missing pizza pan.

"Well?" she said.

"Oh. The thieves have to try. Can you think of a better setup than this? A deserted house, nighttime, no witnesses..."

"But *us*," Jane reminded him.

"I meant there are no witnesses in the area, no one to notice them or their car." He put the pizza on a cookie sheet and stuck it into the oven. "Remember, no one's seen their faces yet. No one can identify them."

Jane frowned. "I know there's something familiar about one of them. It makes me so mad that I can't put a finger on it but everything happened so fast in Amsterdam. But I'm sure...there was something—that man in Central Park that day..."

"Don't worry, we'll find out soon enough, Janey."

"I don't know how you can be so sure."

"Call it experience or a gut feeling or intuition." Graham chucked her under the chin. "Now come on and help me put the dogs away. With those two buffoons loose no one would get within a mile of this place."

Jane followed Graham out to the deck where he whistled for the dogs. They came eventually, galloping up from the beach, tongues flapping, stubby black tails wagging. Heckle jumped up, sandy paws square on Graham's chest, and almost knocked him over. He laughed and pressed the dog down.

"Someone should take those dogs in hand," grumbled Jane. "They're the most ill-behaved, useless mutts I've ever seen."

"They're enthusiastic," corrected Graham. "My mother gave them to Dad for Christmas one year and he'll never get rid of them, believe me."

Finally Heckle and Jeckle were locked safely away in the guest bedroom with bowls of dog food and water, which they were lapping up and spattering the floor with when Jane last saw them.

"Now what?" she asked.

"We eat the pizza."

"I mean what do we do about setting the trap?" Jane asked impatiently.

"We act natural, as if we don't have a care in the world. We eat, we go to bed—together—and we turn the lights off and leave the doors carefully unlocked."

"Then we lie there and wait."

"Yes," Graham said. "Together. With hours to waste."

Jane checked the oven, turning her back on him. "What if we fall asleep? And where will the diamonds be?"

He patted his waist. "I'll take the belt off and leave it on the dresser."

"Do you think they're watching us now?" asked Jane uneasily.

Graham shrugged. "Probably. I certainly would if I were them."

Jane shuddered. *Was* he one of them?

"Aw, Janey, don't be nervous," Graham said, misinterpreting her tremor. "You could see they were absolute amateurs. You and I can take care of them without so much as a broken fingernail."

She turned, leaning back against the kitchen counter, and studied his face. Could he be desperate beneath that easy facade? Could Smedley be involved in this, too? After that blatantly coincidental meeting in Bermuda, Jane had to consider that possibility. Was Smedley planning on receiving the "stolen" diamonds and splitting them later with the two mystery men and Graham? Or was Smedley going to sneak back and help steal the diamonds himself? Did he need money? Renée must receive an allowance from him and she did have *very* expensive tastes…

Jane thought about what Graham had just said. He was right; she and Graham could take the two thugs—if they were working together on the same side. "Boy, I hope so," was all she replied.

They took their sloppy pieces of pizza out onto the floodlit deck and watched the ships' lights slide across the black satin water.

"It's beautiful," Jane said with a sigh. "I wish I could enjoy it more. Just the thought of somebody out there watching us makes my skin crawl."

"It is too bad," Graham agreed.

"You mean it makes you nervous, too?" Jane asked hopefully.

"Well, no, I mean it's too bad you aren't enjoying yourself."

"Oh."

"You know," Graham said after a while, "I miss those two galumphing brutes. Things aren't right without them spraying sand all over and bringing me rotten fish heads."

The night breeze carried sea odors on it: salt water and

seaweed and wet sand. It was getting seasonably cool out. Soon a person would need a sweater, Jane thought.

"It's hurricane season," Graham said unexpectedly.

"Sure doesn't seem like it," mused Jane.

"It can change in an hour. But nothing's headed our way right now, don't worry."

"Nothing but trouble."

Graham was fiddling with something at his waist.

"What are you doing?"

"I'm taking this damn belt off. It makes me sweat." He pulled it out from under his shirt and gave a sigh of relief. "And if they're watching us this'll give them even more incentive."

Jane sat up straight. "Put that somewhere safe!" she whispered.

"Not too safe, Janey. They have to think they can get at it. You don't hide the cheese in a mousetrap—you load the trap with the biggest, juiciest piece you can find."

"I hate this! I'm a bodyguard, not a mousetrap!"

Graham tossed the diamond belt carelessly on the patio table and leaned over Jane. "If you're upset, I'll drive you to a motel or even the Norfolk airport. You know I would have preferred to do this alone. I don't want anything to happen to you, sweetheart." His voice reflected his concern; he was worried about her peace of mind. She had to believe he cared.

"Oh, no, I'm staying," she said. "After all this, I'm sticking with you to the end."

He ran a finger along her jawline. "I was afraid that's what you'd say. It's that stubborn streak of yours, Janey. But then I wouldn't want you without it, would I?" He straightened. "Time for bed," he said briskly. "Let's retire and await developments. I'd just as soon get it all over with."

"So would I," Jane said fervently.

Halfway to Graham's bedroom, she froze in horror then

whirled on him. "The diamonds!" she cried. "You left them on the deck!"

"So I did," he said unconcernedly. "I'll get them."

But Jane pushed past him, raced out through the door and pounced on the belt where it still lay on the table. "Thank heavens!" she breathed. She felt the small, hard shapes inside the belt with her fingers, just to make sure. The diamonds were there.

"Sorry," said Graham behind her. He sounded sheepish. "That was dumb."

"Inexcusable," Jane said between clenched teeth. "Unless you *want* the thieves to get them!"

He hesitated a moment, as if there was something he wanted to say but then shook his head and repeated, "Sorry."

"This is Lew's business," Jane said, shaking the belt in his face. "And my job. And Norma's and Peter's and Donna's and everybody else's jobs! These diamonds are precious for a lot of reasons!"

But Graham just turned away and went back toward his bedroom without responding. Jane was filled with disappointment and pain. She wanted to run after him and shake him and pummel him and scream at him: *Why, Graham, why? What are you doing? Tell me, confide in me. We can fix it somehow. Bow out before it's too late. If our love means anything to you, please, make this come out right!*

But she couldn't. Her only hope lay in keeping quiet, in going along with his game, in being totally ready to react to whatever happened. "Never give your opponent a hint of what's in your mind," Rob Dearborn had taught. "That way you always have the edge."

Abruptly Jane realized that she was all alone on the floodlit deck, surrounded by black ocean and empty sand dunes. The sea oats waved in a night breeze, their dark, spindly shadows reaching toward her. Her mind played a nasty trick on her and she believed, for a moment, that someone really was out there, waiting and watching. She shivered, hurried inside, slid the screen door shut and stood in the living room, her heart pattering like the tattoo of horses' hoofs on a race track.

Graham was already in bed, still fully dressed, propped up with a *Gentleman's Quarterly*. "Want the lights off?" he asked pleasantly.

"Yes." Jane noted the diamond belt on the dresser. How would they come for it? Through a window? Would they create a diversion and hope Jane and Graham left the diamonds unguarded?

"Tired?" He looked at her over the magazine.

"Yes. No. I couldn't sleep a wink."

"Well, we have to turn the lights off eventually. If you want to get some sleep, you can. I'm used to staying up."

She glanced at him sharply. Oh sure, he'd love that! Jane peacefully, conveniently asleep when the diamonds disappeared!

"Come on, sweetheart, it's warm and comfy in here."

Gingerly she slipped her shoes off and slid into bed next to him, leaving as much space between them as possible. It was only last night that they'd been in the Mondragon's guest room and she'd gotten into bed with him there, as well. This was getting ridiculous. If Rick Como had been sent on this job, would Jane have had to share a bed with him? Or was this all Graham's doing?

"Lights out," Graham said as he snapped off the lamp.

The bedroom was plunged into darkness. Jane felt her heart constrict. Would the thieves come soon? She lay there stiffly, listening, straining to hear in the blackness. When Graham's hand touched her clenched fist she gasped.

"Hey, it's only me. Relax. They'll wait a good long time before they try anything. They'll want us to be asleep." He pried her fingers away from her palm. "You can't lay there like Chuck Norris all night."

Jane saw a glimmer of humor in the situation. She tried to relax.

"That's better," came Graham's disembodied voice. His hand played with her fingers. "You want to talk?"

"Talk about what?"

"Anything. You start."

"I can't think of anything." What Jane wanted to talk about was not idle chatter. "You first."

"Hmm, let's see." He was silent for a while. "Do you want funny stories or life history or philosophy?"

"Funny stories." Jane settled herself more comfortably, one ear cocked for trouble. It was going to be a long night.

"Did I ever tell you about the time my roommates stole my clothes and left me naked in the girls' dorm...?

It was a funny story. Jane laughed and found herself feeling easier about everything. Graham had a way of making the best of a situation. He was a nice person to be around and he took the edge off unpleasant circumstances. He made life fun.

The night ticked on. Once Jane heard a loud thump and sat bolt upright. "Shh!" There was another thump.

"It's the dogs," Graham said.

But Jane had to get up and tiptoe down the hall to listen at the guest room door. There was another thump, then the slurping of water and a long whining yawn. Yes, it had been the dogs.

"Your feet are cold," Graham said when she climbed back into bed.

"How do you know?"

"I can tell. Should I warm them up for you?"

"No." Jane felt a sudden irrational spurt of fear. If he touched her she was lost. "Talk some more."

He was lying on his back, an arm behind his head, one leg crossed over the other. She could see his profile now that her eyes were used to the dark. A flood of images piled one upon the other in her mind, a photo album of mental snapshots. Graham naked, poised over her, making love to her. Graham on the *Renée*, fluid and efficient, fearless in the storm. Graham at the hospital, enfolding her in his arms, comforting her after Norma had been shot. In his apartment in New York cooking. At the top of the Empire State Building. At the ranch in Rifle in Jared's jeans and boots...

"You know, I'm not so young anymore. Thirty-three," he said in a pensive tone.

"The venerable old age of thirty-three."

"Now don't tease, I'm trying to be serious. You see," he said then hesitated, "I think I...fell in love with you, Janey, way back that first day in Rifle."

Jane lay frozen, unable to breathe. Did he mean it? Her suspicion wove ugly threads into the fabric of Graham's words. Was he only trying to put her off guard?

His hand reached across the blanket to take hers. She felt the warmth of his grasp and something within her melted.

"A man shouldn't be alone. Or a woman. I'd hate to grow old alone. I guess my parents' separation affected me more than I thought. I'm awful glad they're trying to get together again. I imagined them alone, my dad here and Mom in Montreal. Lonely and getting older. It hit me. It's time, Janey. I want to settle down. I want to marry you."

Silence filled the room to bursting. What could she say? She wanted to kiss him, to whisper, "Yes, I'll marry you. I love you," but she couldn't. Her awful suspicions had to be quieted first.

What a dreadful mess.

"Janey?"

She licked her lips and tried her voice. "Yes?"

"You're shocked."

"Yes, no. I don't know."

"Well, will you?"

"What?"

"Marry me?"

"Oh God, Graham, I'll have to, uh, think about it. This is really a big decision."

"You love me, don't you?"

Her answer was instant and truthful. "Yes, I love you."

"Well, then, that's all I need to know. Take your time, Janey, and let me know when you're ready. Hey, I know this is a lousy time to ask you. You're all tense and tired and worried about the diamonds." He squeezed her hand. "Trust me. Nothing will happen to them."

Trust me, he said. Oh, how she wished she could throw herself at him and cry, "Yes! Let's get married right now!" But first she had to trust him. "I'm sorry, Graham. It's just that I have to get used to the idea." Horrible, trite words lifted from some bad Gothic novel. She was a liar. She'd been thinking about marrying Graham since the first day she'd met him.

"Sure, sure, scary, isn't it? A whole life together? Kids. Babies crying and all those little problems. Fights and doing the dishes and the flu and getting old together. But I love you, Janey, and we'll be a wonderful couple."

He was right. They were meant for each other. Graham couldn't be a thief, not her handsome, dashing, fun-loving buccaneer, her romantic hero, not Graham.

A second later he was telling her about how he hated kids' toys in the living room. "We'd need a family room, don't you think? City or suburbs? And we'd go to the ranch in the summers. Your dad can teach the kids how to ride. And my dad can teach them how to sail..." He leaned over and brushed her cheek with his lips. Her heart squeezed with love and pain. "You want to go into the other room and get some rest?"

"No," she said quickly. "I'm fine."

She must have dozed off a while because she found herself jerking awake. But Graham only told her to go back to sleep and patted her hand again. Instead she half sat up, pounded the pillow behind her into a hard ball and dug her fingernails into her palms. *No sleeping,* she told herself. To pass the time she imagined a life in which she was Graham's wife. They'd go on wonderful vacations, everywhere in the world. They'd ride and sail and have fascinating friends. Around every corner would be an adventure. And they'd love each other so much. She could work part-time when they had children; she'd be at home waiting for him when he got back from his assignments.

She was lost in the brightly colored fairy tale of Graham and her and two amazingly beautiful children on a picnic in a delightful sylvan setting when she became aware of Graham stiffening beside her. Simultaneously, down the hall, the dogs began to bark and throw themselves against the guest room door.

Jane found herself on her feet, every muscle alert. "Where are they?"

Graham was beside her in the darkness. "In the living room," he whispered grimly. "Let's go."

"Get the diamonds," she said quickly, then she edged out into the hall. The lack of light would hinder the thieves more than her and Graham, who knew the layout of the house, and the dogs' barking would cover the sound of their movements.

"Careful, Janey," came Graham's quiet voice. "I'll try to get around behind them. They must have come in—" But his words were cut off by a splintering crash, and before Jane realized that Heckle and Jeckle had broken through the door she saw their fleeting shadows dart into the living room.

Instantly there was pandemonium: furniture overturned, thumps, cries of fright, dogs growling and yelping.

"The light!" Jane cried, "I'll get the light." She edged around the wall toward the switch. A voice was cursing in the darkness, a familiar voice. *Who was it?* She reached the light, readied herself for movement and snapped the lamp on.

A tableau of chaos met her eyes when they adjusted to

the sudden brightness. Graham was moving between the two men and the sliding doors, the dogs were leaping about, chairs were knocked over, lamps broken. The thieves stood stock-still in the center of the room and Jane immediately recognized the faces, but then things moved so fast that she didn't have time to put names to them.

The two men started edging toward the open door to the deck. Graham said something and stood in their path. Jane was on her way to grab one of them while Graham took the other. The first thief tried to push past Graham. A dog streaked through the air after the man, slamming into Graham's shoulder, knocking him sprawling into the fireplace. There was a thud and Graham lay motionless. The thief stopped, snatched the diamond belt from where it had fallen out of Graham's hand, flashed a look of utter fear and hate at Jane, then fled out the door. His companion hurried after him.

Chase them or see to Graham? Jane's mind screamed. The dogs were at full cry down the beach after the two men. She kneeled by Graham, terrified, but he was already trying to sit up. Thank God, he was all right.

He looked dazed and there was blood on his forehead. "Go after them," he croaked. "Janey, get them. I'm okay."

She had time for a split second of relief, then she was out the door, following the uproar Heckle and Jeckle were making. A pink mother-of-pearl light washed the sky behind the ocean. Dawn. The night was over. She could see deep footsteps in the sand then smaller dog prints overlaying them. She couldn't let those men get away. They had the diamonds! This shouldn't have happened! It was those dogs, those damn, misbehaved dogs!

It was difficult running in the loose sand, frustrating, like the awful slowness of a nightmare. She pushed herself, panting, and the sounds grew closer. Just beyond the next dune she spotted several dark struggling figures in the quickening light.

One dog had a man by a trouser leg, snarling and pull-ing, while the man tried to kick at him. The other dog was playing tug-of-war with something in the second man's hand, his legs braced as he tugged and growled and shook his head. My God, it was the diamond belt!

Jane ran up and without stopping knocked the first man down with a roundhouse kick. Jeckle let go of the man's pant leg and cocked his head at Jane in question, sniffed at the fallen form curiously then stood guard over him. The second man—it was Frank Hansen, she realized, fi-nally putting name and face together—was panicked, ter-rified of Heckle but not letting go of the belt. He gave a mighty yank and Heckle released it with a yelp; Frank flew backward to land in the sand, the belt flying out of his hands. Jane leaped on him and got him in a joint lock.

"The police are on the way," she said panting, praying Graham *had* phoned them. But at least she had the two men—Frank and his friend, Harve—and she wasn't about to let either one get away, no matter what!

Crouching there in the pale light, her heart pounding like mad with triumph and nervousness and anxiety, Jane wondered how long she'd have to keep these men under control.

Was Graham all right? Had he called the police yet?

Heckle was busy with something down by the water-line. The belt. He was tossing it about, worrying it as if it were one of his raggedy toys. "Heckle!" she called. "Come!" He stopped and looked at her, undecided. The first rays of the sun were spilling across the ocean, reach-ing toward Jane over the tips of the waves. "Come, Heckle!" she called again.

The dog started toward her, growling and flinging the belt. She took her eyes from her prisoners for a split sec-ond and yelled at him. "Dumb dog! Come, Heckle!"

He galloped toward her, still shaking the belt, and with horror, Jane saw the gems tumbling from a tear in the fabric and Heckle was gaily shaking more out. They glittered and winked as they arched up into the pink sunlight then fell to the wet sand.

Jane couldn't move and, oh Lord, the tidal surge was sucking the stones out into the ocean and the stupid dog wouldn't stop cavorting and miserably, horribly, Jane had to watch the foam carry ten million dollars in diamonds out into the Graveyard of the Atlantic.

CHAPTER NINETEEN

THE DIAMOND CAUGHT THE LIGHT and shot blue fire. Jane moved her hand so that everyone could see it better.

"Well, when's the big day?" asked James, the brother closest in age to Jane, a joker, a teaser, as open as the Colorado sky.

Jane turned in the circle of Graham's arm and tilted her head up to him. "Well, we thought we'd leave it up to Daddy. We want to have the wedding here, don't we, Graham?"

Tom Manning rubbed the gray stubble on his chin thoughtfully. "Is this gonna be a big shindig or something we can handle?"

"Small," said Jane promptly. "Renée and Smedley will want to come, of course. And all of us and…" She was counting on her fingers and looked up, surprised. "That's not so small."

"How 'bout Thanksgiving?" Tom peered at Graham. "You ready, boy?"

Graham laughed. "Yes, sir, Mr. Manning, I'm as ready as I'll ever be!"

"Brave fella." Tom nodded in admiration.

"You got guts, mister," Jared said, slapping Graham on the back.

"Think you're up to a bachelor party?" asked John.

Graham cleared his throat. "You men really are going to have to take it easy on a city slicker like me," he said humbly.

"Quit shufflin' your feet," ribbed James. "Jane told us about you. You're puttin' us on."

They all laughed. Jane was thrilled that everyone seemed to be getting along so well. She'd been nervous as she and Graham drove up the long dirt road to the ranch, and a little choked up at the memories that came rushing back at her. But Graham had put a hand over hers and she'd known he understood and that he'd always be there for her.

There she was, a woman who was all grown up, had gone out into the world and succeeded. A woman who was coming home with the man she was going to marry. It was all a little overwhelming and emotional but she had her anchor, Graham, so she would never be adrift.

There was a big dinner waiting for the Manning clan, a homecoming celebration. Trish, Joe's wife, was setting the table with John's fiancée. Little Joey, fat-cheeked and content, was being passed around from burly arm to burly arm.

"Boy, has he grown," said Jane.

"He's gonna be a big boy," said Tom proudly.

There were two extra places at the table, Jane noticed. "Who's coming?" she asked curiously.

"Rob Dearborn and his wife," said James. "We thought he'd like to hear all about your job."

Jane was ecstatic. "Oh, Graham, you'll be able to meet them! Isn't that great?"

"Wonderful," Graham said wryly. "Maybe he can give me a few pointers on how to get out of that arm lock you got me into in Amsterdam."

"She put you in an arm lock?" asked Tom suspiciously.

"Was that to make you marry her?" asked Jared, hooting with laughter.

Jane snapped something rude to her brother.

"It's a long story." Graham grinned at Jane.

"I think we better hear it," said Joe. "Sounds interesting."

"Oh, it's interesting, all right," replied Graham.

Rob Dearborn and his wife arrived shortly. His smile was reserved, his manner as quiet as usual. He gave Jane a warm handshake and turned to Graham as Jane introduced them. "Good to meet you. I'd like to talk to you sometime...."

His wife smiled apologetically and pulled on his arm. "Later, dear."

"You folks going on a honeymoon?" asked John.

"Well, we'd like to sail the *Renée*," began Jane. "That's Graham's father's boat."

"I thought Renée was Graham's father's *wife*," said Tom, puzzled.

"She is. The boat's named *Renée*, but we're having a little trouble reserving her—the boat, that is."

"My parents don't want to get off her," Graham explained. "They're on about their fifth honeymoon by now."

"Hey, we'll have to go see this boat of yours," said Jared. "I've never been on anything but a rowboat."

Jane pictured the Manning men crewing the *Renée*. "You'd all sink her," she groaned.

"Dinner," called Trish.

The conversation around the big dining table was animated, the Manning men interrupting one another loudly and frequently, the women talking across broad chests about the coming wedding. Tom Manning stood at the head of the table and carved the roast and looked content while Graham took the inevitable teasing in stride in spite of Jane's retorts—"Stop that Jared," and, "That's cruel, John!" and, "Not at the dinner table, Joe." More than once her face turned the color of ripe apples.

"Are you going to give up your job then?" asked Trish.

"Oh, heavens, no," Jane was quick to reply. She put

a forkful of potatoes down and looked around the table. "Lew, my boss, was thinking of selling Mercury. We may buy it."

"You and Graham?" asked Tom.

Jane glanced at her father. "Yes. Graham thinks we make a good team."

"You can't deny it, Janey, we *do* make a good team," remarked Graham, taking her hand and smiling proudly at her. "The best ever."

Jane looked down at her plate, embarrassed and thrilled, adoring Graham, loving and ruing her position in the spotlight.

"What about children? I mean," said her father, "you'll be a married woman."

"When we decide it's time for a little one—" Graham looked at Jane "—well, I guess we'll work that out, too."

"Sounds like a tall order," Tom said.

"Daddy," chided Jane, "don't be old-fashioned."

"Umph," came a sound from her father's chest and a debate over working married women sprang up hot and heavy around the table.

"Is it always like this?" asked Graham of Trish Manning.

"Every time we all sit down to a meal together." She shrugged and smiled. "You'll get used to it."

"I hope so."

"Tell us about this arm-lock thing," said Joe, wisely changing the subject. "You've got our curiosity ticking."

"Go on, you tell them," Graham urged. "They'd never believe me."

Jane took a deep breath. Where to begin? With Amsterdam or even further back, with the mugging in the park, or Norma?

"Well," she said, "Mercury Courier was having trouble..." She went on to tell them about the thefts, Lew's suspicion that they were inside jobs, Norma's shooting.

"My Lord," her father thundered, "and you're telling me this work isn't dangerous?"

Rob and Graham spent a good five minutes calming him down.

"Do you want to hear the story or don't you?" Jane finally asked.

"All right," muttered Tom, "get on with it."

She explained about Amsterdam and the theft attempt at the airport, including the infamous arm lock Graham couldn't break. Her brothers nodded, having been the subjects more than once of Jane's arm locks—in practice, of course.

"So that move we practiced worked well against the man with the gun?" Rob wanted to know.

"Perfectly," Jane replied. "He didn't have a chance to pull the trigger."

"Go *on*," said James.

"Okay, so the two guys got away at the airport and…" She told them, shamefaced, about her suspicion that Graham was trying to steal the diamonds, about her chasing him to Bermuda, carefully leaving out her near-arrest by Captain Vermeer—that was *too* embarrassing—and about the party.

"What did you wear to the party?" asked Trish, wide-eyed.

The men mumbled scornfully as Jane started to describe the gold dress.

"Janey, my love," said Graham, leaning close, "I think you'd better get on with the action."

She told them about the beach house and how they'd set a trap for the thieves. "But the dogs ruined everything."

"The dogs?" John asked.

"Heckle and Jeckle. Smedley's two Dobermans."

"Dobermans, you mean, watchdogs?"

"Well…" said Graham.

"Dumb mutts," said Jane. "Crazy dogs." She told

them about the chaotic confrontation in the house, Graham getting knocked out and the chase down the beach.

"And I was staggering around in the house trying to remember my own name," said Graham. "It only took me a little while, though, and then I called the police and went looking for my bodyguard." He shook his head and chuckled, remembering. "I'll never forget the sight. There was one man on the sand out cold and the other afraid to move because of Jane and the dogs and my sweet little Janey, jumping up and down, mad as a hatter, watching the diamonds wash out to sea."

"So who were the thieves?" asked Jared.

"Frank was Donna's boyfriend and Harve was his partner. See, Donna was the receptionist at Mercury." And Jane had to describe that whole part of the story, about how Frank had known every move the couriers made because of Donna's penchant for gossip. "And Harve was the man who tried to mug me in Central Park that morning. I knew one of the thieves in Amsterdam looked familiar. It was driving me crazy because I couldn't remember—"

"You got mugged?" Tom Manning rose from his chair and hovered over the table again.

"He tried," said Jane. "Rob, that roundhouse kick took him right out, worked beautifully."

Tom sank back silently, shaking his head.

"The *diamonds*, Jane, what happened to the diamonds?" asked John. "Did you get them back?"

Jane exchanged a glance with Graham, who looked down modestly, hiding a grin. "You tell them, Jane."

"No, it was your idea," said Jane.

"Come on, squirt," shouted James, "tell us!"

"There weren't diamonds, they were rhinestones," said Jane. "Glass."

"You mean you went through all that to deliver *rhinestones*?" Jared demanded.

"I exchanged the real ones on Bermuda with my dad.

We'd planned it a few days before with Lew's approval,'' explained Graham.

"So what I saw in the safe there,'' Jane told them, "were rhinestones. Then Smedley delivered the real ones to New York the next morning and was back on the Outer Banks before dark.''

"A sleight of hand,'' mused Rob. "Very clever.''

"Very transparent,'' said Graham, "but it worked. The real diamonds were never really in any danger except for a short time in Amsterdam and Jane and I always had the edge.''

"But,'' she said, "Lew didn't want anyone to know about the switch.''

"And rightly so,'' put in Rob. "The fewer who know a plan, the more likely it is to work.''

"I sure was mad, though,'' reflected Jane.

"And all along poor Janey thought *I* was stealing them myself,'' said Graham.

"That's dreadful.'' Trish shook her head.

"Oh, it was.'' Jane turned to her sister-in-law. "From now on, though, it's all on the up and up between us. No more tricks. Graham—'' she swung around and caught his eye "—promised. Didn't you, dear?''

"You bet, my sweet,'' he hastened to say.

Dessert was hot apple pie à la mode. Jane ate a fair portion then settled back in her seat, her arms folded across her stomach. "I do feel sorry for Donna,'' she told them. "The poor girl had lousy judgment.''

"This Frank sounds like a real winner,'' said Rob.

"Well, it's history now,'' said Graham, serving himself a second helping of the pie. "They go to trial next month and the D.A. thinks they'll each get twenty years. It would have been life, or worse, if Norma hadn't made it.''

"Will she be all right?'' asked Rob's wife.

Jane nodded. "She'll be back on the job by Christmas. She's even promised to brush up on her karate.''

"It will serve her better than any weapon," said Rob with assurance.

"I think," Jane mused, "that her mistake in judging Graham hurt her more than the bullet."

"But she apologized," said Graham. "She's a real lady."

"And as for Donna," Jane went on, "they aren't prosecuting her because she didn't know a thing about what was going on. She did get fired, though. And I don't blame Lew one bit. It will be a good lesson for her. Heck, she's already got a new spot in Macy's. Accounting department."

"What about your apartment?" asked her father. "Seems like you just moved in. And your landlady, what's her name?"

"Lily," said Jane. "No problem. Lew hired a new receptionist and she's desperate for a place. She'll even buy all my pots and sheets and everything." Jane stopped and glanced over at Graham. "Everything but Pard."

Tom Manning looked bewildered. "Can't says ol' Pard was ever for sale."

Jane had to explain. Even after her explanation of the huge stuffed horse the Manning clan looked vaguely perplexed.

After dinner Jane and Graham announced that they were taking a walk, all the while trying hard to disregard the knowing smiles directed their way. A brilliant canopy of stars spread overhead as they headed toward the barn, arms wrapped around each other. The air was sharp and cold, and snow had dusted the hard ground.

"That's quite a clan you've got there," Graham said in an amused tone of voice.

"Think you can handle 'em, pardner?" she replied, laughing.

"As long as they don't get the shotguns out."

"Graham, you aren't really mad at me, are you? I mean because I thought you were stealing the diamonds?"

He tipped her chin up. "You were doing your job, Janey. I admit it, I looked guilty. I wanted to tell you a hundred times but Lew—"

"I know, he made you promise not to tell me."

"Listen, if it had gone on another minute, I'd have told you, Lew or no Lew."

She snuggled up against him. "Okay, just so there are no more secrets between us."

"Never again," Graham swore. "It's too much trouble keeping a secret from you." He smiled down at her. "Come on, let's go see my ol' buddy, Pard."

"Your *buddy*?"

"Sure, after all, we were pretty close there for a while."

Jane laughed. "For a little while, anyway."

They walked to the barn, holding each other close. Graham's lips brushed hers. "Cold," he murmured, "but I bet I can heat them up."

The barn was warm and dark and echoing, filled with the smell of animals and hay and leather, a familiar, welcoming odor to Jane. She flicked on the light and blinked in its brightness. A whinny came from a stall down the line and Graham tugged on Jane's sleeve. "There's Pard." They stopped at the horse's stall and Jane held her hand out.

"Come here, boy, that's it. Remember your old *buddy* here, Graham?" Pard chewed affectionately at her glove.

"I'll tell you something, Janey," said Graham as he put an arm around her shoulder. "I'm new at this love business but I honestly believe that marriage has to be able to survive a crisis. Lots of them probably."

"Like your folks."

"Yes, like them."

"I love you very, very much, Graham Smith," said Jane.

"And I love you," he whispered, taking her into his

arms. Then he looked over at Pard. "Think the old boy'll be jealous?"

"Never mind," murmured Jane, pulling his head down.

It was several minutes later when they broke apart. Jane leaned back in Graham's arms and studied his face, his beloved, familiar face. His eyes were laughing, full of fun, shining like steel in the light.

"Who says you can't catch Quicksilver?" breathed Jane lovingly.

Pard lifted his head and gave a long, satisfied whinny.

Adam knew that Robin was going to ask
about his secret sooner or later.
And then it would be game over....

Firecloud

CHAPTER ONE

IN TWENTY MINUTES it would be too late, Robin Hayle thought as she unlocked the door to her shop. It was already 6:05 a.m. and shortly the sky would turn from pearl to pink then gold, and the shadows in the plaza would be all wrong. She switched on the lights in the back of her photography studio and hurriedly loaded her camera, snatching up a long telephoto lens just in case.

"Good morning!" came a voice from the front. "Miss Hayle? You here?"

"In the back," Robin called. "I'm heading out in a minute, though." Picking up an extra roll of film, she went to greet her salesgirl, Ericka. "What on earth are you doing up at this uncivilized hour?"

Ericka was already behind the counter, her round pretty face as cheerful as usual. "It's Indian Market, isn't it?" She began to wipe down the display cases. "I knew you'd be busy, so I figured I'd get here early."

"Early is right. Listen, I'm going to try to get some shots of the plaza before the hordes arrive."

"Go ahead, I'll get everything set up."

Nineteen, Robin reflected, and already the girl was efficient. Her own teenage years were receding into a comfortable haze, but she was darn sure she hadn't been as responsible as Ericka Dalton. She'd certainly never gotten up before six in the morning and gone off to a real day's work.

Robin's photography shop was located in the Sena Plaza right in the heart of Old Santa Fe. A short half block from her store was the nearly four-hundred-year-old core of the city, the Santa Fe Plaza, a tree-lined square that was bordered on one side by the Governor's Palace, the *Palacio Real*.

The *Palacio* had been built in 1610, Robin thought as she walked beneath the cottonwoods toward the plaza. Even by European standards, that was an old building. The Pueblo Indians still sold their rugs and pottery, their jewelry and trinkets beneath its shaded portal.

Robin stood on the corner of the plaza and checked the light meter on her camera. In the mother-of-pearl dawn she was a study in casual elegance, tall and graceful, dressed in a full calf-length blue chambray skirt and an oversize white silk blouse tied in a knot at her waist. A string of bright turquoise beads hung around her neck and swayed as she moved.

Usually at 6:15 a.m., the plaza was silent; only the occasional fluttering sound of a pigeon rising from a church belfry broke the morning calm. But not today. It was the last weekend of August, the weekend of the Santa Fe Indian Market, an affair that brought buyers from all over the world into town; already there were dusty pickup trucks and vans unloading their wares, and Indians in brightly colored shawls moving around, setting up their booths.

Robin walked in her usual long-legged stride toward the far end of the plaza. The Sangre de Cristo Mountains that rose to the east of town could be seen in the quickening dawn, their tall peaks turning rose in the champagne-clear morning light. With the low portal of the palace giving depth to her pictures, Robin shot half a roll of film of the mountains. A pigeon lifted from the palace's flat roof; she caught the peaceful portrait on film.

She moved around the plaza, snapping pictures of the women at work, trying to capture the shy yet proud demeanor singular to the Pueblo Indians.

"There you are." Shelly Dalton, Ericka's mother,

crossed the brick street and walked toward Robin. She was carrying a white bakery bag. "Want a squishy, low-cal doughnut?"

"I ate already, but.…" Robin shrugged and took one. "Can you believe these crowds?" she asked rhetorically. "I know I've only lived here a year, but still, I've never seen so many people in the plaza all at once.'

Both women glanced around. Even though it was barely light enough to see, early-bird tourists were milling, handling intricately patterned Navaho rugs, eyeing the turquoise and silver jewelry, exclaiming over the pottery and stylized ceramic animals.

"Maybe I should wear a sign on my back," said Shelly. "Shop at the Dalton Fine Arts Gallery."

"You've had a good summer, haven't you?" Robin asked as she licked sugar from her fingers.

"A record season. And yesterday, with the annual market going on, we sold more than we did the whole month of June. I'm going to *make* Chuck buy me that Volvo I want."

"Must be nice," Robin said flippantly to her friend.

"Some got it, some don't," Shelly quipped good-naturedly. "Ericka's at your shop already, isn't she?"

"Bright and early. In fact," said Robin, "I better get on back. I've got a nine o'clock."

"What is it this time?"

"It's a lady from Los Angeles who wants a picture of herself selling jewelry with the Indian women under the portal."

"I *love* your stories," replied Shelly. "You meet the neatest people."

"Isn't that the truth? Sometimes I feel like a psychiatrist. Dealing in people's fantasies." She shook her head mock-seriously. "You know, I should probably sign an oath, like a doctor, never to divulge my clients' secrets."

"Don't do that. I'd miss your tall tales." Shelly laughed.

Robin specialized in portraits in which any fantasy of her clients was met. A client might want to be photographed as an Indian warrior, a Hell's Angel, Aphrodite rising from the sea or a local Spanish noblewoman from the 1600s. To Robin, anything went, so long as her client's fantasy was indulged. She saw to every detail: costume—even if it had to come all the way from Denver—makeup, hairstyling, props. It was exhausting work at times, but since Robin had moved to New Mexico from Illinois a year ago and opened her own shop, she'd been a great success. She was thirty-two years old; things could be a lot worse.

"Guess I better get these doughnuts on over to Chuck," Shelly said. "We left the house so early he didn't get a chance to eat."

"Can I have just one more?"

"Honest to God, Robin Hayle, I don't give a hoot *how* tall you are—how can you eat so much and stay so skinny?"

"One hundred and forty pounds is *not* skinny." She snapped a picture of Shelly, catching her friend with no makeup on and her shoulder-length, permed brown hair still in damp coils.

"Thanks. Now please destroy that film."

"Sure."

The plaza was bathed in gold, the sun just peeping over the rim of the Sangre de Cristo Mountains, and the old dun-colored adobe buildings glowed in the warm rays of light. Robin shot another roll of film, trying to capture that lucent sense of peace, that contemplative mood peculiar to the City of Holy Faith, Santa Fe. There was no place else where man and landscape came together with such mutual advantage, where the landscape was brought to human measure.

Robin had first fallen in love with New Mexico three years ago when she'd come for a visit. Like the hundreds of various artists who'd preceded her, she'd been mesmerized by the unique light found only in the Southwest, a clear, precise light that made every pine needle stand out with purity and far-distant objects appear with clarity against the sky. She'd known then that Santa Fe would become her home.

And she'd made her move at the right time; this particular corner of the Southwest was a cultural center, but unlike Paris or New York, New Mexico had space—lots and lots of open space. She had traveled all over the state and taken thousands of pictures, yet she felt that she could explore the land for the next fifty years and still only see half of it. The Land of Enchantment, read New Mexico's license plates. And that was exactly what it was, Robin thought.

Shelly had once said, "I can tell how much you love it here from the photographs you take."

Robin was glad it showed. Although she mostly did portraits of clients, she also sold lots of landscapes. Every square inch of the walls in her shop was covered with studies of the land: the tortured red buttes and great mesas, the gentle, rolling grasslands, the blinding sand dunes and the sun-bronzed cliffs that had been inhabited long before the time of Christ by the Mysterious Ancient Ones, the Anasazi Indians.

Many peoples had come to New Mexico over the centuries. And each new group that had settled there had become assimilated, had found its niche, its style. The Anasazi Indians had left their mark, the Navaho and Apache raiders theirs, the Spanish, the Mexicans and finally the Anglos.

As each successive wave of newcomers had found their home in the Rio Grande Valley, so Robin hoped she would. Having lost her parents in an airplane accident when she was nine, she had always craved that feeling of belonging, of being secure, of being loved. True, she had been raised properly by her aunt and uncle in Waukegan,

Illinois, and they had loved her, but it just wasn't the same as having a mother and a father.

In Santa Fe, Robin felt she was on an equal footing with everyone else, as all were new to this ancient, evocative land.

Robin snapped one more picture before returning to her shop. It was the face of that particular child that drew her camera like a magnet. An Indian child, a dignified, secretive face, a quiet moment in which the child sat beneath a booth twisting a string of silver jewelry in his fingers slowly, his mother close by. What thoughts, Robin wondered as she threaded her way through the gathering crowds, were behind those silent black eyes?

When Robin arrived at the shop, playfully named Robin's Nest, there were already a dozen customers in line waiting to buy film. "Oh, Miss Hayle," Ericka called, "can you give me a hand?"

Ericka was a delightful young college student. Her parents, Chuck and Shelly Dalton, had moved to Santa Fe from Ohio fifteen years before. They'd opened an art gallery in the Sena Plaza and scraped by for years until Santa Fe had become a mecca for art collectors.

Robin had been luckier in a way. Her parents, even though they'd died early, had left her financially secure, although not with enough to buy that adorable adobe house on Canyon Road that Robin craved. She had modeled part-time while in college, not because she was forced to, but because photography fascinated her. And she did, of course, have that five-foot-ten-inch frame, not to mention a great head of shoulder-length, thick, curling ash-blond hair that she helped along with a yearly frosting job. Her eyes, a dark blue, were striking with makeup. She could have modeled for years, but the other side of the camera had begun to lure her and before Robin knew it, she was taking pictures of everything and everyone, eventually studying the art in school.

True, the Daltons had struggled to make it, but at least

they'd always had one another. They'd had family holidays, family squabbles, warmth and loving and belonging. Robin often felt cheated of those things and admitted to herself that she harbored a stockpile of insecurity because of it. Oh, she hid it well, always seeming to be in control of her life, always ready with a joke, a witticism, a funny story. She tended to talk too much, but deep down inside there was that sense of being an outsider, of wanting to belong.

She hated to leave Ericka on one of the busiest days of the tourist season, but Robin's client from Los Angeles walked in shortly after nine.

"Ericka, honey, I've got to go for about a half hour. Can you manage?" Robin asked apologetically.

"No problem, Miss Hayle." The young woman went back to selling film without a word of complaint. Tomorrow morning, even though it was still Indian Market, Robin thought, she'd let Ericka sleep in and come into work at noon.

And in a couple of weeks, when Ericka was off to college again, Robin planned on writing her a large bonus check.

Robin's client, a Mrs. Hartmann, was a very short, stout woman of about sixty. She was well dressed, her rust-colored purse and her high-heeled sandals matching, her jewelry strictly from Tiffany's.

In the back of Robin's Nest, Mrs. Hartmann changed into the traditional Pueblo outfit Robin had provided: a sleeveless green striped dress caught at one shoulder over a blouse, a blue shawl patterned with roses, long necklaces of red and jet beads, silver earrings and bracelets. Robin helped her into a black wig that had thick bangs and a blunt pageboy cut.

When Mrs. Hartmann was dressed, she looked in the mirror and practically jumped up and down with satisfaction. "Oh, this is wonderful!" she exclaimed.

"Mrs. Hartmann," Robin said, standing back and viewing her handiwork, "you look positively gorgeous."

Mrs. Hartmann's life story came out as the two women walked up Palace Avenue. "I *always* wanted to be an Indian. You know, dear, for a day. Like *Queen for a Day*, the old TV show. You see—" Mrs. Hartmann nudged aside some shoppers "—my grandfather was a full-blooded Navaho Indian. He got into oil."

Robin didn't question that one.

"And you, Miss Hayle? Surely you have a fantasy."

"About a trillion of them," replied Robin. "My biggest, if you can keep a secret, is to find a *really* tall man."

Mrs. Hartmann tipped her head back and looked up at Robin. "I see what you mean."

The sun was already hot in the eastern sky by the time they crossed the street to the Governor's Palace and sought the shade beneath the portal. It was crowded. Hundreds of tourists pushed and shoved, fingered the Indian wares, exclaimed over the high prices.

Mrs. Hartmann chatted away with two Indian women, then Robin asked if her client could sit by their jewelry-laden blankets, her back against the old *Palacio* wall. The Indians giggled shyly behind their hands and nodded.

Robin shot a full roll of film. She had to admit that Mrs. Hartmann looked the part and was having a grand time.

"When do I get to see the pictures?" she asked excitedly when they were done.

"The proofs will be ready Monday morning. About eleven. I'll go over them with you and we can pick out the best. Okay?"

"That will be fine, Miss Hayle." She led the way back to Robin's shop, turning and saying, "Now, about that tall young man of yours..." By the time Mrs. Hartmann had changed and was gone, Robin had an earful of information on the advantages of short men. But Robin could

just see herself at five foot ten on the arm of a short man—
like back at those junior high school dances.

Before lunch, Robin had one more client coming; he
was a young student from a seminary in New York State
who was vacationing with his brother. He wanted to be
photographed in front of the Cathedral of St. Francis
dressed in priests' robes of the sixteenth century. Robin
had had a devil of a time finding the robes but finally had
managed to talk one of the fathers at the church into lending the boy the antique clothing and only because he was
of the faith. She arrived at Robin's Nest starving and hot,
her feet tired from hours of standing on the hard bricks
of the streets. But Ericka obviously needed help.

The young woman's big blue eyes, with those heavenly
dark fringes of lashes, implored Robin. "Just an hour? I
really promised Shane I'd have lunch with him and—"

"Say no more." Robin took over for Ericka behind the
counter. "When true love calls, one must follow. Or
something like that."

"Geez, thanks, Miss Hayle." She was off and running,
the energy of youth propelling her out the door. Ah, wondered Robin, when was the last time she had run to meet
a beau?

The customers kept coming until Robin was, for the
first time in a year, sold out of thirty-five mm film. And
she wasn't about to go into her private stock in the back,
not with yet another portrait to do that day. She sold two
silver-framed color landscapes she had taken herself. Both
were quite expensive, too. And she sold her favorite print
of autumn wildflowers with the Taos Pueblo in the background. She'd won an award for that one, first prize in
the New Mexico State Art Fair last spring. Of course, she
could print as many as she liked. Signed and numbered,
she might end up selling dozens of them. Oh, that adobe
house on Canyon Road—what she wouldn't do to get out
of her downtown apartment.

Finally, when the local restaurants filled up for lunch,

the shop quieted down. Robin walked to the open door
and took a deep breath, stretching her arms over her head.
Then she leaned against the doorframe and sighed. Her
shop was situated on a picturesque street. Like all the old
streets in Santa Fe, its twisting, narrow path was lined
with adobe walls and tall cottonwoods that formed a lush,
cooling canopy overhead. On both sides of Robin's shop
were art galleries and shops that sold Indian jewelry and
rugs in a profusion of color, baskets, pottery, oil and wa-
tercolor paintings, posters.

Shelly popped her head out of her shop, as well. "Hi!"
she called from two doors down and gave Robin a wave.
"Busy?"

"It's slow right now," Robin called back.

"It'll pick up." Shelly made a tired face.

Santa Fe was experiencing a renaissance. Indian art was
in demand in collectors' circles, and the city was the center of one of the largest concentrations of Indians in the
country. There were the Pueblo Indians, heirs of the Anasazi cliff dwellers of a thousand years ago, a placid, com-
munity-centered people who lived in tiered adobe dwellings.

And there were the Navahos and Apaches, totally different tribes, relative latecomers to New Mexico, nomads,
then herders, but above all fierce warriors.

The art of the Indians stirred Robin's senses. Their pottery, their silver and turquoise jewelry, their rugs and
blankets—all came from Mother Earth herself: the clay,
the wool, the metal and stones, the dyes, even their paint-
brushes of yucca fiber.

What had the Indians thought when the first conquis-
tadores had made their hot and dusty way into New Mexico? It had been exactly four hundred years ago, and
they'd come from Mexico, looking for the fabled Seven
Cities of Cibola, which supposedly had streets paved with
gold.

Robin opened a bag of potato chips and munched,

watching the tide of people in the street. There, bent over
an Indian's handicraft, was a classically Spanish face, a
woman with dark hair, huge dark eyes and a high-bridged
nose. Perhaps one of her ancestors had been given a land
grant from the Spanish king back in the 1600s.

And next to her was a blond man, sweat stains under
his arms, arguing ferociously with the Spanish lady over
a piece of silver jewelry that they both wanted. The Indian
artisan watched them both with timeless patience, waiting
for their quarrel to subside.

History repeats itself, Robin thought with a smile, popping another chip into her mouth.

The Anglos had been the last to arrive in New Mexico,
forging the Santa Fe Trail through the wilderness, only to
find the city, already centuries old and quite pleased with
itself.

But the Anglos stayed. And the Indians, Spanish and
Anglos warred, finally tiring, until an uneasy peace came
to New Mexico and the trinity was complete, ungainly
but enduring.

Robin stood in the door and drank a can of Coke, polishing off the chips. The restaurants began to empty and
the streets became crowded again. She decided to get out
her stock of film, after all, and was in the back sorting
through cartons of thirty-five mm film when the bell over
her door tinkled. She turned automatically to see if the
customer was in need of assistance. Suddenly she stopped
still. A thought winged through her mind: *Oh, Mrs. Hartmann, he's definitely not for you.*

For an indecently long time, Robin stood undetected in
the back of her store observing the man. He was tall, very
tall, maybe six three or four. He was big and broad and
well-muscled, strong-looking from his neck down to his
well-shod feet.

He didn't appear to need any help at the moment. He
was probably browsing, most likely waiting for his wife,
who must surely be window-shopping nearby. Still, the

stranger seemed quite interested in a window display Robin had recently arranged. Maybe he had a fantasy and was thinking about having a portrait done. What would this man's wish be? Her mind was filled with vivid images just thinking about the possibilities.

As if setting up a shot, Robin studied him with a professional eye. He was about forty years old, she guessed, and obviously Indian in descent. His skin was copper colored, smooth as satin. He had the most perfectly shaped head, and his cheekbones were high, powerful, framing his strong, slightly hooked nose as if sculpted by expert hands. From Robin's angle of view his shadowed, deep-set eyes looked as black as a moonless night.

He has to be married. A strange, disturbing jealousy shot through her. Why couldn't she have a man like that? Of course, maybe he was all looks and dull as dishwater.

There was a vitality to him, though, emanating from that well-set body, an unquestionable force. There appeared, from his carriage, to be pride as well, but not necessarily arrogance; rather, this man exuded competence and self-esteem.

He was an Indian, yes, but his attire told her a different story. He was wearing a forest-green polo shirt and khaki trousers, and on his wrist was an expensive-looking European watch.

Robin had him completely framed for a portrait when suddenly he turned and caught her studying him. Embarrassed, she dropped her gaze to her hands.

But he fixed his attention just as quickly on her display, and then she wasn't sure if she was relieved or insulted. Moving out to stand behind the counter, Robin saw him not only studying the display in her window but fingering it as well. Before she could object, he was pulling a framed photograph from the arrangement. Darn it all, she'd just finished setting that up!

"Excuse me," she said.

He turned abruptly and faced her full on, his black gaze

falling directly on her for an unsettling moment before he looked again at the picture. "Where," he asked finally, "did you get this photo?" His tone was polite, but demanding a response in some indefinable way.

Robin's hands felt curiously empty; she placed them on her hips. "I shot that photo myself. Is there something—"

"And do you recall exactly *where* you shot it?" He sounded businesslike, but now she sensed a note of urgency in his voice.

"I took it at San Lucas Pueblo. I think it was two weeks ago. Why?"

The stranger strode over to her and tapped the print with his finger, indicating a lovely clay pot she'd used as a part of the background. "This pot is a counterfeit," he began, "a blatant forgery. The real one is in the Peabody Museum at Harvard University. You see that?" He pointed to a blemish on the pot. "I recognized the piece by that dark marking. It's what we call a firecloud, a smudge made when the piece was originally fired. That pot is unmistakable."

"Oh," replied Robin, at a loss. Of course, she distinctly remembered taking that portrait. She'd taken a client up to the pueblo for background and, as they arrived, a potter had been firing his work outside in the open, in the traditional way, so they'd stopped to watch. She'd asked the man if she could use one of his pieces in her picture; she'd tipped him and he'd been very proud and cooperative.

What was this stranger getting at? "Listen," she said, her head cocked to one side, "I don't quite understand…"

He regarded her for a long time with those Indian-black eyes then finally said, "I should introduce myself, Miss…"

"Hayle, Robin Hayle."

"Robin's Nest," he mused aloud. "Then you're the owner."

"That's right."

"I'm Adam Farwalker," he said, "from the University of New Mexico in Albuquerque, the archeology department." He tapped the picture once again, and Robin noticed his long-fingered brown hands. "I saw this photograph as I was walking by. I couldn't believe it at first, this copy being displayed right out in the open."

Robin was still puzzled. What was he trying to tell her, this man from the university, this archeologist?

He leaned against her counter, his strong arms folded across his chest, a knee bent so that their eyes were on a level. "Antique pieces, *true* ones, are bringing outrageous prices these days, Miss Hayle. The original of this piece—" he indicated the photograph "—is priceless. And, I might add, against the law to sell."

"The one in the picture is a fake then?" Robin asked.

"A very good one."

"And my kindly potter in San Lucas is really a crook?" Robin shook her head; it was hard to swallow.

"He could be. Or he could be innocent." Adam Farwalker's jaw tightened almost imperceptibly, but Robin saw the tension beneath his smooth skin. "The Indians are often exploited. They're given some cock-and-bull story about making a reproduction for a museum. It's been done with oil paintings for years, and now that Indian artifacts are in such high demand, we're starting to see these kinds of forgeries springing up like mushrooms. It's big money for unscrupulous art dealers. You see, it's harder nowadays to get hold of prehistoric pots. You can only sell pottery found on private land since the Archeological Resource Protection Act was passed."

"I see," said Robin thoughtfully. She glanced up at Adam Farwalker's chiseled face and wondered if he was a Pueblo Indian. He didn't really *look* like the Pueblo Indians she'd seen... Curious, hoping he didn't take offense at her ignorance, Robin asked, "You seem to know an awful lot about this pottery. Are you, uh, a Pueblo Indian?"

A corner of his mouth lifted; he was obviously amused.
"I'm an Apache," he said with quiet dignity. "Prehistoric
pottery is my field. In fact, I'm on a dig right now in
Chaco Canyon." He paused then went on. "Would you
recognize the potter again?"

"Well, sure. He was middle-aged, kind of thin..."

Ericka returned from lunch then, interrupting them.
Robin introduced the young woman and assumed that the
subject of the forged pot was closed. She was very wrong.

"If Miss Dalton can watch the shop now," Adam Farwalker said, "we could get going."

"Excuse me?" said Robin.

"Get going to San Lucas Pueblo."

"I..."

"To find this pottery maker of yours." Robin was so
stunned, so taken aback by his suggestion, that for a minute she merely stood there.

"You've got an appointment, Miss Hayle," came Ericka's voice. "It's at three, I think."

"Oh," said Robin, snapping back to reality, "I *did* almost forget. I'm awfully sorry, Mr. Farwalker, but I can't
really be of any help."

"Of course you can," he replied easily, as if asking
her to drop everything was the most natural thing in the
world. Oh, he was the perfect gentleman, and obviously
very professional, but there was something else, too,
something hidden in that calm expression. "After your
appointment," he continued, "we can drive up to San
Lucas. I assure you, Miss Hayle, this matter is vital."

"Well, I..."

"I'll wait for you in the plaza."

"But I don't know how long this shoot will take,"
Robin protested, amazed at how easily this man had taken
control.

"No matter. I'll wait." And then he was gone.

Robin stood unmoving, watching the vacated space, staring into nothingness until Ericka's voice tugged her reluctantly back to reality.

CHAPTER TWO

ROBIN HAD A DEVIL OF A TIME keeping her mind on Mr. Norgard's photography session. He was a large, blond, muscular man who posed as a Viking. It was for his girl-friend's birthday, he explained somewhat sheepishly. Luckily the shoot didn't take long, and Robin was soon telling him when to stop by for the proofs, glancing at her watch and wondering if Adam Farwalker was actually still waiting for her. Should she go meet him? He was, after all, a complete stranger. Maybe he wasn't who he said he was...

It was Ericka, however, who set Robin's mind at rest. "Aren't you supposed to meet Mr. Farwalker?" she asked. And then it came out. "Oh, sure, I know him. Well, I know who his family is, anyway. They have a big ranch south of here."

"A ranch?"

"Yes, they're a real old family in these parts." Ericka shrugged. "I don't know them personally, but everybody says they're really nice people."

"I guess it's okay if I go meet him then," reflected Robin.

"Oh, sure," said Ericka.

"You'll lock up at six?"

"No problem. I'll see you tomorrow, Miss Hayle."

"At noon. You sleep in."

"Okay, you're the boss," Ericka said eagerly.

Robin grabbed her shoulder bag and camera, ran a hand through her mass of hair, pulled her skirt straight and stepped out into the hot yellow sunshine of midafternoon. Although the plaza was half a block away, she could hear the noise from the crowds at Indian Market, and the sidewalk in front of her shop was jammed with people who jostled her as she walked along.

What if she couldn't find Adam Farwalker in the mass of humanity? It struck Robin suddenly: she wanted to see him again. There was something about that man, Adam—she even liked his name—something very special, but hard as she tried, Robin could not put a finger on what it was. He was certainly the cerebral type, but there was nothing dull behind that implacable expression and those courtly mannerisms. What excited him, what pushed his buttons? She crossed the street, threading her way through the stalled traffic, and craned her neck to see. What if he had grown tired of waiting and had left already?

But she saw him instantly, just as she reached the shaded portal in front of the *Palacio Real*. He towered above everyone else in the crowd, yet it was his aura of stillness, of imperturbable calm that caught her eye. She started toward him then stopped, unable to resist studying this stranger who had just barged into her life.

She stood beneath the cool, shaded portal and observed Adam while a sea of people ebbed and flowed around her. His head was bent; he was talking to someone. He shifted his position and she saw who it was—Julien Cordova. He knew Julien, then. Well, of course he did. Julien had been born and raised in Santa Fe and was the curator of the *Palacio Real* Museum. It would be odd if Adam *didn't* know him.

A lady burdened with parcels bumped into Robin. "Excuse me," she mumbled, shouldering her way past.

When Robin looked back, Adam was smiling at something Julien had said. How handsome he appeared, his teeth flashing white against his copper skin! She would dearly love to do a series of portraits of Adam Farwalker, to see if she was skilled enough to capture on film that

poise, that self-containment. His was a face that belonged
on the cover of a magazine. In black and white, she decided, so that color did not interfere with the line and
shadow of his features. It was a face that was seasoned
but without blemish, full of strength and energy, proud,
the face of a warrior, containing a harsh beauty and a store
of secrets—like the land from which he came.

Robin shook herself; he was only a man, after all, and
he was waiting for her. She started toward the pair of men,
comparing them in her mind. They were so different—
Adam big and dark and quiescent and Julien small, elegant, animated, with the pale skin and sad eyes of his
ancestors, the Spanish noblemen who had settled Santa Fe
nearly four hundred years ago.

She knew Julien well. He was the president of the
newly formed Santa Fe Business Association, of which
Robin was a charter member. He'd been elected unanimously, because his knowledge and leadership abilities
and political acumen made him the only logical choice.

"Hello, Julien," she said, a little more breathlessly than
she would have liked. "I see you know Mr. Farwalker."
Glancing at Adam, she said, "Sorry I took so long."

Julien was lifting Robin's hand to his lips, kissing it in
his intimately continental manner, but all the while Robin
was aware of Adam, sensing his gaze on her.

"My dear Robin," Julien was saying, smiling with
charm and a total disregard for the four inches she rose
above him. "I do hope you're getting some additional
business this weekend to tide you over the quiet times."

"Oh, yes, Julien, the studio's doing fine, thanks."

"Good, good." He glanced humorously around at the
hordes of buyers who were grabbing at Navaho rugs and
silver jewelry and pottery and paintings from the booths,
or even snatching at things before they were unloaded
from the vans that had been driven into Santa Fe for Indian Market from hundreds of miles away. "I must leave
you. Today is one of the most loco of the whole year. No

doubt there are dozens of crises I must attend to, and I've been shirking my duties." He laughed and shook Adam's hand. "So good to see you again, Adam. And I'm looking forward to your mother's fiesta tonight."

"She couldn't put it on without you," replied Adam genuinely.

"Oh," Julien added, turning to go, "good luck finding the man who made that counterfeit pot."

"You told him about it," Robin said when Julien had left.

Adam Farwalker shrugged. "It's bound to get out. And Julien's in a position to warn people about this sort of thing."

"So you really think it's that important?"

"Look, Miss..." He hesitated.

"Hayle. *Robin*," she said firmly.

"Miss Hayle. The economy of this area depends to a great extent on the art collector's dollar, especially the collector of Indian art. Aside from being against the law, counterfeiting pottery—or any kind of art—could ruin the reputation of every honest gallery owner in the state."

"I see what you mean," she said ruefully.

He took her elbow then, and she could feel the strength of his hand as it enclosed her arm. "Let's get out of this mob scene," he said impatiently. "Did you bring the picture along?"

She patted her fringed leather bag. "It's in here, don't worry."

It was amazing how easily Adam made his way through the throng. It was like the Red Sea parting for Moses. Was it his size or merely the determined look in his eye? Whatever, she was content to be swept along next to him for three blocks, to where his mud-caked Land Rover was parked.

"San Lucas, you said?" he asked as he unlocked the passenger door for her.

"Yes, that's where I took the picture." She couldn't

help but notice that, as she climbed in, he stood by her
door, ever the gentleman, until it was closed.

When he was seated, he asked, "And you don't know
the name of the man, the potter?"

"No, I never asked. It just sort of happened, you know.
I saw some people firing pots and we started talking."

Adam pulled the vehicle out into the busy street, winding his way through the traffic until they were headed out
of the city on the main highway to the north. They passed
DeVargas Mall, a modern shopping center named for the
Spaniard who succeeded in the reconquest of Santa Fe
after the Pueblo Revolt in 1692. It always tickled Robin
to consider what Don Diego DeVargas would say about
this monument to his name.

She would have liked to share this pleasantry with
Adam Farwalker, but his drawn brows and silence stopped
her. She shivered deep down inside somewhere, drawn by
this man but a little wary of him, too. This wasn't like
her at all. Robin could usually laugh and joke and talk a
blue streak. She had a tendency, she knew, to talk too
much, to overpower people—men, anyway. But not this
man.

"That pot is extremely valuable. Priceless, actually. It's
held up as the archetype of Anasazi black-on-white
ware," he finally said. "There's only one like it in the
world. There are collectors who would pay in the six figures for it."

"For a pot?" Robin asked in astonishment.

"It's nearly a thousand years old. If a collector really
thought he'd found an original, sure, he'd pay that."

"But he wouldn't be able to show it to anyone, would
he? I mean, he'd know he got it illegally."

"Well, possibly. Some collectors are content to just
own a piece and never show it to anyone. And there *are*
some valuable pieces for sale. You see, it's only illegal
to sell the artifacts found on federal land. If a piece is
found on private land, it's fair game."

Robin pulled the photograph out of her bag and looked at it once again. Her client was dressed as a conquistador in armor, helmet and tall leather boots. He stood in front of the pueblo, the stepped adobe cubicles making lovely checkerboard squares behind him. On the ground was an artful display of pumpkins and cornstalks, red chili peppers and the graceful round pot with its narrow neck and black geometric shapes on a white background.

"It's a beautiful piece," she said. "It even looks old. I could swear I see a crack in it. And some chips."

"It was very well done," Adam admitted.

"You're sure there couldn't be another one like the original? Maybe somebody found one...."

"I'm sure," he said and then turned his attention back to the road.

The harsh dry land sped by the window of the car as Robin stared ahead. It was parched by the August sun, but there was still a subtle array of color: ocher, vermilion, orange, sand, yellow. And a sky so blindingly blue that she always wore sunglasses. There were mountain peaks to the east of them, a dark, beckoning green mass that shimmered distantly in the heat haze. It was disquieting, untamed country, full of enigmas—hidden spots of startling beauty and dangerous barren stretches like the one named the *jornada del muerte*, the journey of death. It was a land that could bear men such as Adam Farwalker, professor of archeology, all man, all Indian. Something primitive stirred in Robin.

"So you teach?" she ventured.

He nodded, his eyes on the road. His profile was vigorous and blunt, the swell of his lips perfectly carved. He was a powerfully attractive man.

She tried again, determined to get him to talk. "Are you on sabbatical? I mean, if you're on a dig in Chaco Canyon..."

"Yes," was all he said.

"Is your university funding the dig?" she pressed, not one to give up easily.

"Partly. The university and *National Geographic* both. It's a follow-up to the Chaco Project of the seventies."

Well, at least she'd gotten something out of him. "Are you there year-round?"

"No. Usually just summers, but this year I'll be there until the second semester begins."

"Beautiful country up there," Robin found herself saying.

He finally had a reaction. "Have you ever been to Chaco Canyon, Miss Hayle?"

"No, but..."

He was smiling skeptically. So she'd finally pushed one of his buttons. "The canyon is in brutal country. It's a dry spot in the driest state in this nation. The sun drains the water from a man's body faster than he can drink it in. Beauty, Miss Hayle, as they say, is in the eye of the beholder."

She smiled to herself. Ignoring his tone, she said, "Please, call me Robin."

He turned to flash her a glance. "Robin it is, then."

Fifteen miles north of Santa Fe in the mesquite-covered red hills was an enclave of several pueblos. Following the sign, Adam pulled off the highway to drive the twisting mile to San Lucas. A sunlit plaza shaded by dusty cottonwood trees was the stage; the backdrop was the adobe dwellings piled one upon the other, built of the earth itself as the Anasazi had learned to build in this arid region devoid of forests. Indian children played under low trees; dogs barked; women in bright shawls and colorful skirts went about their daily business. The scene was timeless—except for the several pickup trucks parked nearby.

Adam pulled up alongside the trucks and switched off the Land Rover. He turned to her, his dark head inclined slightly in her direction. "Where to?" he asked.

"I told you," Robin began, "I met the man purely by accident, behind the pueblo where they were firing pots."

"Then we start there."

But the area behind the buildings was deserted, and the fires were out that afternoon. Only a skinny dog lay panting nearby in the shade.

"Now what?" inquired Robin.

"We ask around, show the picture. This is a small community." He stopped in the middle of his long stride. "I *am* sorry about dragging you away from your work, Miss—Robin. But this is very important."

"That's okay," she said, grateful for his sudden concern, realizing that this man did have other sides to him.

Adam approached an elderly Indian whose chair was tipped back against the wall of an adobe house. He asked the man in English, "Do you know who made this pot?" He motioned for Robin to show her photograph.

The man stared at him. Adam tried the same question in Spanish, but the man continued to gaze unblinkingly at him as he inhaled deeply on his cigarette. Finally his head moved from side to side; he blew smoke out of his nose in a stream.

Adam asked him in Spanish if there was a headman of the pueblo that he could talk to. Robin caught the impatient tone of Adam's question and wondered if he were making their job harder. They were, after all, practically in a foreign country, as Indian pueblos, like reservations, were autonomous bodies governed by their own tribal councils.

The man said something; Robin caught a few words of Spanish. She wished she could talk to him. She'd try smiles and charm and persuasion, but he seemed not to understand English.

"We'll try the headman. He speaks English," Adam told her. "This fellow knows nothing."

But Robin wondered.

She followed Adam's broad back up stairs and around

corners to a door painted bright blue. Adam knocked. A heavyset woman answered, then called her husband.

"I am Reynaldo Sanchez. How can I help you?" the headman asked, and Robin heaved a sigh of relief that he spoke English. Maybe *she* could talk to him.

Adam explained their problem, showing Robin's photo to the Indian. "I'd like to locate the artisan who made this pot."

The man looked wary. "Do you wish to buy the pot?"

"No, not exactly, I'd just like to talk to the man who made it."

Oh, no, Robin thought. *Now we'll never find out.*

She was right. Reynaldo went stony-faced and called something in Tewa to his wife. He turned back to them and smiled deliberately. "I am sorry. I have never seen this pot, nor do I know who it belongs to. Perhaps this picture was taken in some other pueblo, *señorita*?"

"Oh, no," Robin was quick to say. "It was right in the plaza under that big tree. I'm sure—"

A little boy, probably the headman's son, scurried out the door, brushing Robin's skirt. He was in a hurry, intent on some errand. Robin didn't give the incident a thought—until later.

"I can't help you," Reynaldo said, closing his blue door in their faces.

They went back to the square, and Adam showed the photograph to a couple of women. They stared at him blankly and shrugged their shoulders.

"Let's ask in that store," suggested Robin, pointing to a small grocery on one side of the square. "I bought a Coke from the man. He'll remember me, I'm sure."

But he didn't. And Robin was sure it was the same man: she remembered his concho belt with its turquoise sunburst design. "No, I have never seen that pot. No one in San Lucas makes pots like that. Maybe you should try Cochiti or Acoma."

"The lady says she took the picture right over there,"

said Adam irritably. "Look, we just want to talk to the man who made it."

"Nobody here made that pot," the store owner said patiently, unmovably, enveloped in the obdurate privacy of the Pueblo Indian.

Leaving the store, Robin glanced sideways at Adam. He was angry, his dark brows drawn together in a bar. "Why won't they talk to us?" she asked.

He muttered something, a swear word, she suspected, in a strange language. Apache? "Because they're afraid and stubborn and secretive. They don't trust anyone outside their community," he finally said.

"But you're—" She stopped short.

"Yes, I'm an Indian." Adam halted and turned to her. "But I'm the wrong kind. Apache and Pueblo have been hereditary enemies since before the Spanish came here." He shrugged, his broad shoulders stretching the fabric of his polo shirt. "Unfortunately, they don't trust me any more than they trust you."

"Oh, dear."

"Yes. I'm afraid we won't find out a thing here. They've closed ranks."

"But how did they all know so fast? Oh, the little boy..."

"Probably." He grimaced and made a fist, hitting it into the other hand. "I should have known. If we'd come up here asking to *buy* the pot maybe we'd have gotten somewhere."

"Well, now what?" Robin asked, wondering if she should return to San Lucas without Adam and make some more inquiries. But no, they knew who she was now.

"I'll take you back to Santa Fe. It's getting late."

The sun was low, its rays long and bronzed, reaching across the plaza, lighting the adobe cubicles. The pueblo appeared to be a golden pyramid set against purple mountains. A boy drove goats home through clouds of gilded dust.

"Do you mind?" Robin said, pulling out her camera. "The light is irresistible."

"No, go ahead."

Flashing him a bright smile, Robin shot some pictures of the goats, of the pueblo itself, of some women dressed in traditional Indian garb, of a tree with the sun slanting through its branches. Several children, brown and round-faced, gathered to watch her curiously. She captured the array of childlike expressions, too: open, friendly, shy, impatient.

Adam waited for her, his shoulder against a rough adobe wall, his hands in the pockets of his well-cut trousers. She wanted to ask if she could photograph him, but she lacked the nerve. Maybe some other time—if she ever saw him again.

It was funny, but in her shop, when she'd first seen him, she had only noticed his sporty clothing and his self-confident demeanor. But now, as he stood there against the old pueblo wall, he looked Indian to her. She could see him mounted on a pinto war horse, the arid, unforgiving mesa lands behind him, his ebony hair in thick braids, his painted, sun-coppered skin gleaming in the harsh sun. An unaccountable chill crept down her spine and tingled in her scalp.

She had to shake herself, realizing that he'd been watching her. Finally something flashed in Adam's eyes—anger, amusement, disdain?—and he moved away from the wall and squatted to talk to two of the children. What did he tell them? They giggled and he smiled in return, his face relaxed and open, as he'd been with Julien. Why was he so guarded with her? Why couldn't he laugh and joke with her that way? What was there about the man that made him seem so...so mysterious, so closed to her?

Secretly, while his attention was on the children, Robin snapped a picture of him. She couldn't resist. It wasn't even an artistic shot, nor was she sure she'd focused properly. She just wanted his image; it was as if she possessed something once she'd photographed it. It was an odd concept but one Robin had always felt was the reason she became a photographer. Once she captured something on film she owned it forever.

Dusk dimmed the stark hills around them, softening their harshness, as Adam drove toward Santa Fe.

"Thanks for waiting for me," Robin said, still trying to break the ice. "I just can't bear to let a single scene go to waste."

"Will you use all those shots?" Adam asked.

"Oh, no, some will turn out lousy. Others I'll file away. A few I may enlarge and frame and put in the shop. The tourists buy photographs of the Southwest like mad."

"Interesting," he commented.

"Well, it's a living. No, I shouldn't say that. I love photographing things. I used to model in college, but I was always much more interested in the other end of the camera," she said, realizing that she was talking too much. "Photographs can capture something, a mood, a place, a personality. And I love fulfilling people's fantasies."

"Their fantasies?"

Robin had to explain about her studio and the costumes and props. She was half tempted to tell Adam how she saw *him*, but thought better of it.

He smiled as he listened to her stories. "You must have fulfilled some very bizarre fantasies," he remarked.

"Well, sure, but those are the fun ones. Once I had to arrange for a man to dress as a gorilla, but he wanted to be photographed in the zoo, with the gorillas."

"Did you do it?"

"Of course." She laughed. "It took all kinds of arranging and I was scared half out of my wits, but it's my job."

"Mine seems pretty dull compared to yours."

"Oh, no! I think it's fascinating. Ancient artifacts and

ruins and figuring out how people lived thousands of years ago have always fascinated me.''

''Have they?''

''Oh, yes. I'd love to see your dig. I mean, is it possible...well, for me to see what you're doing out there some time?'' Oh, dear, there she was, being forward again, inviting herself.

''You'd like to see Chaco Canyon?''

''Oh, yes. And I could get some great shots, I bet.''

''I'm sure it could be arranged,'' Adam said noncommittally, but Robin couldn't tell whether he meant it or not.

She changed the subject, not sure she really wanted to know. ''Gosh, I'm starved. I'm always starved, it seems. Do you think we could stop?'' She noticed that Adam glanced at his watch. Darn it! She was pushing again. His wife—or girlfriend—was probably waiting for him at that party Julien had mentioned. ''Listen, I'm sorry. Maybe you have to be home for dinner or whatever.''

He looked at her for a moment, as if considering something. ''There is no one at home, Miss Hayle—Robin— waiting for me. I'd be glad to stop somewhere,'' he finally said.

Relief flooded her. So he wasn't married. Wonderful. Although why it was wonderful, Robin didn't even begin to explore. ''Well, I eat like a horse so I insist we go Dutch treat.''

''Sorry, Robin, I really do have to draw the line somewhere. I dragged you up here. It's the least I can do to buy you dinner.''

''All right. I give up pretty easily, don't I? How about Maria's? She makes the best burritos.''

''Maria's it is,'' he said.

Maria's was situated on a hillside just on the outskirts of Santa Fe. Adam and Robin were seated outside, facing the west, where the last pink glow of the sunset still stained the sky. Strings of lights surrounded the patio, twinkling spots of brightness that complemented the candles on their table.

Over her menu Robin studied Adam's face in the gathering darkness. Inadvertently, unable to escape habit, her mind conjured up yet another image of him: Adam on his haunches by a camp fire, dressed in leather leggings, his thick coal-black hair held back by a strip of cloth, his eyes searching the darkening land, his visage reddened in the fire glow.

Yes, he belonged to this land. She decided what it was about his people that held her fascination. It was their uncompromising yet utterly secure sense of belonging to the natural world, a unique gift granted to the Indian. Or, perhaps, a gift that had been given to all of humankind once but lost by Robin's own race.

She'd very much like to know Adam better. She'd like to break through his impenetrable constraint and see him laugh. She screwed up her courage, took a deep breath and said, "Maybe tomorrow, after work, I could drive to the pueblo with you and look for the pottery maker again."

His eyes lifted to hers, so still, so dark, reflecting twin points of light from the candle. Once again he seemed to be weighing up her words. "All right," he finally replied with equanimity, and Robin realized that he'd missed the invitation in her voice completely.

CHAPTER THREE

ADAM HAD NOT MISSED the invitation at all. On the contrary, it tempted him with exquisite irony. From the first moment he'd seen Robin Hayle standing in her shop, he'd been much too aware of her, uncomfortably aware. She had a way of looking at a man with frankness, her emotions surfacing vivaciously like rushing water flashing with sunlit jewels. And she met his eyes nearly on a level when they stood together, a singular experience for Adam, but he found himself liking it.

Robin Hayle.

He tried to withhold judgment, to suppress the attraction he felt. The Middle Way of the Apache was to avoid all excesses, even of happiness, and he had found the Way useful in his life.

"So," she was saying, "tell me some more about your dig."

Oddly enough, he wanted to tell her. "I'm doing follow-up research on Pueblo Bonito.... Are you familiar with any of the ruins there?"

She tilted her head and regarded him with her dark blue eyes. "Well, just the usual stuff."

"Pueblo Bonito is the best known community in the canyon, but there are a dozen others. What I'm trying to do is date the pottery periods more specifically, tie them to the few facts we know. Uh, Robin, I must be boring you."

"No, not at all." She was resting her chin on her fist,

elbow on the tabletop, watching him closely, studying him as if she wanted to take a photograph of him.

He leaned back in his chair, as if to distance himself from her, aware of the disquieting interest he felt. "Well, that's all, really. I teach at the University of New Mexico in Albuquerque in the archeology department. Southwestern Indians and their pottery are my area of specialty."

The waitress arrived, and they ordered. Robin *did* eat a lot; she asked for the "grande" platter, and she wasn't a bit self-conscious about it.

He eyed her across the table surreptitiously. What attracted him to her so much? Was it her lighthearted manner? Her beauty, her long, lean body? Was it her quirky way of making a living?

"Tell me about how you happened to end up in Santa Fe," he said, a little surprised at his curiosity.

"Ah, so you can tell I'm not a native." She hesitated then flushed. "I'm sorry, I seem to be full of thoughtless remarks."

"Don't apologize. I'm a native, yes, but not so far back as you might think. It's the Pueblo tribes that were here a thousand years ago. We Apaches are newcomers; as nomads, we only arrived in the fifteenth century, just ahead of the Spanish. Almost everybody is an immigrant here."

"Thanks," she said wryly.

The dry hills around them were dark, their own oasis of light standing out like a beacon. Warm air caressed Adam's face and arms. He watched Robin eat while he picked at his own food; his mother was expecting him for the annual barbecue. He was late already, but just now that didn't matter. He folded his arms on the table. "And how did you come to live here?"

"Oh. Well, I visited once with a friend from my hometown, Waukegan, Illinois. That was three years ago. I fell in love with the place. The possibilities—" she waved her hand, gesturing around her ''—for my craft are endless. And the people. You know how it strikes someone from the Midwest? Like a foreign country. Exotic.''

''So I've been told.'' He liked her enthusiasm, the way she smiled with fun and humor. Yet when she was quiet she seemed almost like a vulnerable child, a woman who should be treated gently. The parody struck Adam; here was a person full of life, a tall, confident woman, and yet she was definitely hiding something. He could discern it in her eyes, behind the humor, could sense it from a stolen glance when he'd caught her off guard. Instinct and experience told him that there was pain somewhere in Robin Hayle, and if there was one thing Adam could recognize in another human being, it was pain. He wondered what had happened in her past.

Adam caught himself and smiled sardonically. This curiosity of his about a woman he'd probably never see again was futile. Nothing was going to happen between them; he wouldn't allow anything to come of this meeting. They were as far apart in their separate worlds as the sun and the moon.

She pushed her empty plate away and sighed. ''That's better, I feel human again.'' Then she folded her hands in front of her on the table and said, ''Do you mind if I ask you about yourself? I'm terribly curious. You see, I've never really met an Indian before.'' She stopped and pressed her lips together. ''I sound so dumb, but I don't know how else to ask.''

He smiled at her candidness. ''Sure, what do you want to know?''

''Everything,'' she said then laughed at herself.

''That's a tall order.''

''Well, how about the Apaches then? What are they like?''

Adam was finding that he wanted to talk to Robin, to explain things to her. He felt as if he hadn't conversed with an interesting woman for ages. What harm could come of a simple conversation?

"Everyone always thinks of the Apaches as warriors, you know," she was saying, drawing him out. "But I suspect they're a lot more."

Adam nodded. "They fought because they had to. Although," he admitted, "my tribe, the Mescalero Apache, did have a terrible reputation. The Eastern newspapers loved to play it up, of course. But the truth is, to us, the family and the clan are everything. We even introduce ourselves by who we're related to."

"So a hundred years ago," said Robin, "the Apache got a bum rap from the press?" She smiled faintly, challenging him.

"Well," said Adam, "I will admit that the name Apache comes from a Zuni Indian word, *ápachu*, meaning enemy."

"Aha."

"But believe me, the welfare of the clan was, no, *is* the focal point of our existence. We call ourselves the Diné, which means the People. It makes us sound very self-centered, and perhaps we are. And we call this land Dinetah."

"Dinetah," Robin said, savoring the word, "I like that."

"The U.S. Army fought us for fifty years. But before the Spanish or the Americans came we were peaceful farmers and herders."

"Farmers," she said, "I never would have guessed."

"Well, we're good with horses, too. And we never lie."

"Never?"

He shook his head. "You might find this interesting," he explained, "but the Apaches are what you could call the original women's libbers." Adam had to smile at her look of curiosity. "We're a matrilineal society, meaning that the mother is the hereditary head of the family. When the daughter marries, she brings her husband home."

"Amazing," said Robin, "and all along I thought the Apaches were warlike, you know, an all-male society, machoism at its height."

"Apache warriors *were* fierce in their day, but contrary to popular belief, they never took scalps. Apaches have a horror of mutilation, even of their enemies."

"Are you fierce?" Robin asked.

He looked at her blankly for a minute then cleared his throat. "Me? I'm one of your civilized Indians. College degree and all. I've made a compromise of my life. My subject allows me to stay in touch with the past of my people."

"You look like you could be fierce," she mused.

"Isn't that a strange thing to say to someone you hardly know?" he stated flatly.

"I suppose it is, but, you know, I can't help imagining people in photographs with costumes on, and backgrounds. Silly, isn't it? I see you in buckskin with long braids, on a horse, a fierce warrior."

"You've seen too many movies," he said dryly.

She disregarded his statement and leaned forward. "What is your fantasy, Adam Farwalker?" she asked, staring at him intently.

He went all cold inside. What had happened to their innocent conversation? "I don't deal in fantasies," he replied.

"But you should. Come on, think about it. How do you *see* yourself?"

He turned his face away from her and stared out into the darkness. The muted voices of the other diners, the tinkle of silverware, the sound of a cork popping from a wine bottle reached his ears. He was aware of her, still scrutinizing him, expectant, curious, attentive. A sudden urge to tell her everything washed over him. He could unburden himself, be rid of hiding, of pretending. It was as if this strange woman had seen into his heart and knew his war name, Changing Man, the name given him when he was a child, a secret inside his family. Changing Man, an apt description, he'd always thought. And this woman, this Robin Hayle, who dealt in fantasies, would accept and understand.

No. No woman would understand what was wrong with him. *Fierce.* He wanted to laugh at her assessment of him.

"Come on, you must have imagined yourself in some kind of scene. Everyone does," she urged.

"I hate to put a damper on everything," he said, "but I think we better go." He glanced at his watch. "I'm expected someplace."

"Oh." Her face fell, and he hated himself for being the cause of it. "I'm sorry. You should have told me. Really. Maybe I should call a taxi," she said.

"I dragged you out to San Lucas, Robin, and I'll get you back to Santa Fe. It's still early."

"Okay, if you're sure. I mean, sometimes I go on and on. My friends've learned to tell me to shut up when they've had enough." She was gathering her bag and pushing her hair off her shoulders as she rose, flashing him a too-bright smile.

The night wind flowed in the open window of the car as Adam drove toward the city. He could smell the pungent odors of sage and creosote bush and piñon, all mixed with dust, a familiar aroma.

He wondered again if Robin saw through his coolness. She couldn't, she hardly knew him. He'd learned to control himself, to consider every gesture, every expression, every word when he was with a woman. He'd had years to school himself in the hard lesson of keeping his distance from women. He'd had to.

"It's really too bad we couldn't find the man who made that pot," Robin said. "What are you going to do now?"

"I could try asking around at San Lucas again," he answered.

"Is there anything else you can do? Can the police help?"

"Not really. I have no proof, nothing but your photograph. That's not enough to convince them to do anything."

He sensed her hesitance, as if she wanted to say something but was not sure if she should. He wished he could joke and laugh with her, lay a hand on her arm, feel the thick silkiness of her ash-blond hair. He wished he had the freedom to still do that.

Adam stared at the road, at the lights of cars coming toward him. He wondered how he would act with this woman if he were a whole man.

Ridiculous. The entire situation was laughable, senseless. Ten years ago he'd caught the mumps from a young cousin. The mumps! A grown man with a ludicrous childhood disease. But in adult males the mumps could be devastating, causing clinical sterility. The doctor had shaken his head gravely and informed him he could never father any children.

He had the normal urges and his performance was not affected; in all outward respects he was perfectly normal. He'd made a conscious decision to avoid serious commitment, though. Oh, he'd had a few superficial relationships, but the women to whom he was attracted seriously were all looking for something he couldn't give them. So he spared them the decision, threw himself into his work with a fervor and masked his shortcoming with aloofness. He was aware that he appeared to be arrogant at times, and prideful. But hidden, like a worm in an apple, was the bitter ever-present knowledge. What woman would accept that knowledge without derision or, worse, pity?

Robin's voice intruded into his thoughts. "Are you, um, from Santa Fe originally?"

"Yes, born and raised. My parents live here, just outside of town."

She sighed, and he wondered what it meant, then she drew her knees up under her full skirt and turned sideways toward him, one arm resting on the back of the seat. He was acutely aware of her, of her scent, of her hair catching the flashes of outside light like ribbons of silver, of her tilted head and questioning eyes. "You're so lucky," she was saying in a soft voice. "You belong to this place, you know. You have roots, your family lives here. Sometimes I feel so unattached that it's scary. My parents died years ago. I hope you appreciate what you've got."

There was the trace of pain he'd noted. She was lonely, that was all. Where were all the men that surely must be interested in her? Why wasn't she married? Against his will he glanced over at her; she was staring out the front window of the car, her neck long and lovely, her profile classic. Regret seized him like a fist.

Adam pulled up in front of Robin's Nest. "Thanks for dropping everything and going up to San Lucas with me," he said.

"Even if we didn't find anything. Oh, well, we could try again, couldn't we? Thanks for dinner, anyway," she said, smiling. "And I got some great shots."

He went around to her door and opened it while she gathered up her shoulder bag and camera from the back seat. Her breast pressed against the white fabric of her blouse as she reached behind her, and Adam flushed and looked away.

She slid out of the car and turned to him. "Thanks again," she said genuinely. "I enjoyed this afternoon.... That is, it was good to get away for a while, from Indian Market. You will let me know if there's anything I can do to help?"

"I will," he replied, making an instantaneous promise to himself never to see Robin Hayle again. She was too disturbing to his hard-earned peace of mind.

"Well, bye," she said, turning away. Then she stopped, cocked her head and looked at her shop front. "I wonder why Ericka pulled the blinds?" she mused.

"Excuse me?"

She kept staring at the shop. "We never close the blinds, it messes up the displays. Why would she…?"

He looked. The blinds were all the way down. "You mean, you never close them like that when you lock up?"

"No." Robin turned to him, a frown creasing her forehead. "Did Ericka forget? But why on earth…?"

Then she rummaged through her big bag for her keys, pulled them out and started toward the door.

The sixth sense is only the other five senses working to their limits, noting anything out of harmony. Adam's brain tested his impressions, listened to his five senses, the way his father had taught him when they went hunting, listened to his instincts. "Wait," he said, putting a hand on her arm.

She stopped abruptly and peered at him through the dimness. "Yes?"

"Is there a back door, a window, something like that?"

She frowned more deeply. "Sure, there's a door to the studio on the alley, and my office window. Do you—"

"I'm going to take a look," he said. "Stay here."

"But what do you think happened?"

"I don't know," he said tightly, "I'm just going to take a look."

When he got to the back of her shop he saw it immediately. Someone had broken the window, knocked the glass out and entered the building. The back door was open, too. Could whoever had done it still be inside? He stuck his head in and listened. Utter silence greeted him.

"Adam?" he heard from the alley behind him. "Oh, there you are. What…?"

"I told you to stay—"

"What happened? Oh, my window!"

"Someone's broken into your store."

"Oh, no!" She brushed past him and flicked the lights on inside the back door. He heard her gasp.

Stepping inside, Adam understood why. Her shop was in a shambles. Every drawer and cupboard had been

opened and the contents dumped out on the floor, every
picture pulled off the wall, every camera and roll of film
tossed helter-skelter, many unrolled, exposed, ruined.

"Oh," she said in a distraught voice. He could see her
sag, her hand going out for support. He took her arm
quickly and led her to the nearest chair he could find. She
held onto his hand tightly and stared around at the mess.

"Are you all right?"

She looked at him, tears welling in her eyes, then she
seemed to shake herself. "Yes, sure, I'm just... Oh, boy,
I don't know."

"Have you ever been burglarized before?"

"No."

"Any of the other stores around here been robbed?"

"Not since I opened the shop." Her head rose. "Did
they steal the cash? It's in a drawer..."

He left her there and checked beneath her cash register.
The day's cash, checks and credit-card receipts had been
neatly stored by Ericka in a bank deposit bag, with the
register tape. He handed her the bag silently, watched as
she checked the contents then looked up at him, bewildered. "It's all here," she said, "just as Ericka left it. I
don't understand."

But Adam was beginning to. There was evidently nothing missing in her shop—even the cash had not been disturbed. It was as if this ransacking were a message of
sorts.

"I just don't get it," Robin was saying.

"I do," stated Adam, his mind working logically and
clearly now.

Robin looked at him anxiously. "What's going on
here?" she asked. "Why didn't they take the money?"

Adam folded his arms and looked at her upturned face.
"I'm beginning to think this was not a simple burglary,
Robin. It's too coincidental. It's a warning."

"What *are* you talking about?"

"Somebody found out you were at San Lucas today,

asking about a forged pot—the lady photographer who was there two weeks ago. Word must have spread like wildfire. Did anyone at San Lucas know your name?''

She thought for a minute. ''I gave the man, the potter, my card, in case he wanted a copy of the picture.'' Then she stared at him openmouthed for a second. ''What are you saying?''

Adam felt a sudden burst of anger at himself for getting an innocent person involved in what was already a messy situation. ''Damn it,'' he muttered. ''Look, your potter at the pueblo, or someone working with him, probably did this to warn you off.''

''Oh, come on,'' she said skeptically.

''Robin, I'm not sure you realize what we're dealing with here. Some of these art counterfeiters run huge rings. There are hundreds of thousands, maybe millions of dollars at stake. Apparently they don't take kindly to investigations.''

Adam stalked out to the front of the shop, regarded the clutter once again and cursed himself. He'd marched through that pueblo like a blundering white eyes, and in his wake had left an entire community suspicious and doubting. Why hadn't he been more subtle; why hadn't he used his head? It couldn't have been because he was with Robin, uncertain, ill-at-ease, not thinking quite straight. He couldn't be that careless.

''Adam,'' came her voice behind him, ''I think I should call the police and report this.''

''I suppose so. Can I do it for you?''

''Oh, no, that's all right. I'll do it. But I would like to ask a favor of you. I know you have a…a date, but maybe you could stay and face the police with me. I…I have this awful feeling they won't believe me. Can you call and say you'll be late?''

She was so shaken, so apologetic, so terribly vulnerable that all Adam could do was stand there, helpless. ''Sure,'' he replied softly, ''my appointment doesn't matter.''

"You can use the phone…"

He wanted to hold her tight, stroke her thick silver-blond hair, tell her everything was going to be fine. He trembled with his need, steeled himself against it and kept his distance from her.

He watched while she phoned the police, saw her gather herself together and look around at the chaos in her little shop. A gleam of anger shot from her eyes when she hung up.

"Those *slobs*," she said. "No wonder they closed the blinds!"

"I'll help you clean up," he offered.

"The police said not to touch anything."

"Perhaps later then. Tomorrow."

"I won't say no," she answered wryly.

She heated the day's coffee on a hot plate, and they sipped while they waited. It wasn't more than five minutes before an official car drove up. Robin unlocked the front door for the policeman, who introduced himself, flashed his badge and grimaced at the mess.

"Detective Cordova," Robin said, "are you any relation to Julien?"

Adam's head snapped up. "Rod!" he called. "Well, I'll be damned!"

"Adam, that you?" The two men shook hands. "It's been a few years," said Rod. "Now, what's this burglary all about? You say no money's been taken?"

"I'm sorry, Robin," said Adam. "Rod's an old schoolmate of mine. Julien's younger brother—well, one of his *many* younger brothers."

"You know Julien?" Rod asked. "Sure, everybody does." He laughed, answering his own question. He was a trim man, small like Julien, but not so elegant. He gave the impression of sharpness, of being in control, of seeing to the bottom of things. He pulled out a pad, fixed his eyes on Robin and said, "Okay, what's the story here?"

Robin told him about the pot, about their trip to San

Lucas that afternoon, about Adam's theory. Adam added
a few of his own comments but mostly let Robin vent her
anger and confusion on the patient Detective Cordova.
Rodriguez wrote quickly, nodded, listened, asked a few
pertinent questions.

"I'll send my fingerprint man over on Monday," he
said when he was through writing. "Maybe they left some
prints."

But Adam could tell he was doubtful. "You don't
sound like you're convinced, Rod," he remarked.

"Well, it's like this, Adam. I have to go on facts. So
far the facts are clear: nothing's been stolen. The window
was broken, yes. Probably some teenagers getting into
trouble. You know." He shook his dark head. "There are
a few nasty gangs around."

"But why *my* shop?" asked Robin.

"You've got a teenager working for you, don't you?"

"Ericka?"

"I'll question her. Maybe she has some friends, they
heard her talking. You know how it is, Miss Hayle. Happens all the time."

"Ericka Dalton had nothing to do with this," Robin
said defensively.

Adam put a hand on her arm. "Rod's only doing his
job. I'm sure Ericka had nothing to do with it; it's only
that Rod's got to check."

She said nothing more, but Adam could see that she
was still hot under the collar. Rod was not taking this as
seriously as Adam would have liked. Of course, if you
looked at the break-in from an outsider's point of view,
it was merely a petty crime.

"Look, Rod, keep the pottery angle open, okay? There
could be a connection," Adam suggested.

"Until I find otherwise, I'm open to any and all possibilities," Rod answered. "Stranger things have happened. Good night, Miss Hayle. Sorry about the mess."

He grinned at Adam and said, *"Buenas noches, amigo.* See you around."

"Well," said Robin when her door was closed behind the detective.

"He's just doing his job."

"Of all the nerve! Accusing Ericka." She turned around, made an angry gesture with her hands. "I wish *he* had to clean this up!"

"I was afraid the police would react like that."

"He wasn't much help, was he? But it does sound crazy. I hardly believe the story myself." She looked imploringly at him. "Maybe it's just a coincidence, a group of teenagers, like he said. Maybe somebody broke into the wrong shop. It could be that, couldn't it?"

"Robin..." He didn't want to upset her any more than she already was; neither did he want to give her false hope. "I don't know for sure who did this. I don't want to scare you, but if we disturbed a ring of forgers, this may not be the end of it."

She stared at him with those wide, dark-blue eyes, then she strode across the littered floor, her sky-blue skirt swirling around her long legs. "Oh, I don't know," she said, "it just seems like someone should do *something* about crime these days. It's as if no one cares. Even the police."

She was brave, he'd give her that. Too brave, maybe, for her own good.

"You know," she stated emphatically, "if I could do something myself—like find out who did this—I'd confront them. I swear I would."

She was angry, and she sure had a right to be. But there was something Adam had kept from her, something he'd remembered when Rod Cordova had been here. It had happened in Albuquerque two, maybe three years ago. A local policeman had gotten a lead on one of the counterfeiting rings. The papers had been full of stories of art counterfeiting back then. But it had all ended abruptly—

the police officer's body had been found in the desert alongside his car. Some had called it an accident; others were not so certain. Needless to say, the follow-up investigation had led nowhere.

Good God, what had he gotten Robin involved in?

CHAPTER FOUR

SUDDENLY ADAM LONGED to take off for Chaco Canyon and bury himself in his work, to turn back the clock to that morning before he'd passed by Robin's window and spotted the photograph. But firmly imbedded in his genes was the Apache sense of honor, of duty and fairness. He had gotten Robin into this ugly situation, and he could not conceivably walk away from his responsibility.

"You better stay at the ranch tonight," he said.

"Oh?" she replied and, by the tone in her voice, he decided he'd better rephrase his suggestion.

"I want you to be my guest at my parents' place, Robin. Of course, I can't force you to stay there, but for safety's sake, I'd feel much better. I'm sure, if you think about it," he added carefully, "you'll agree."

"I couldn't. I don't even know your parents."

"They won't mind. There's plenty of room. I'm sure they'd want you to stay with them under the circumstances."

"I feel so foolish. My goodness, you make it seem as if we're involved in some cloak-and-dagger plot."

"Perhaps we are," he replied gravely.

She put a finger on her chin and tapped her foot for a minute, thinking. "Can I be back early in the morning?"

"As early as you like." He glanced around the shop. "And I *am* going to help clean up in here."

"Oh, I didn't really mean that. You don't have to."

"I insist."

He drove Robin to her apartment on Bishop's Lodge Road, which was only four short blocks from her shop.

"I believe," she said tentatively, "that there's an affair going on tonight at your folks' place. I'm afraid this is a really bad time for me to intrude…"

"The annual fund-raiser, yes. But you won't be intruding in the least."

"Are you sure? I feel awfully silly about this. I mean, it isn't a formal sit-down dinner, I hope."

"Not at all."

"What is the fund-raiser for?" she asked.

"The proceeds go to the Native American Art Museum here in Santa Fe. My mother likes to stay active in local affairs."

"Is it dressy?"

Adam parked his car and glanced at Robin for an instant. "You look fine," he said. "It's not formal, like I said. A mesquite barbecue, an auction." He shrugged, climbed out of the Land Rover and went to open her door. "May I have your key?"

Robin looked at him askance. "You're not thinking someone might have broken into my apartment, too?"

"It's a possibility." He took the key ring and walked up the narrow flight of stairs ahead of her. He could sense her reluctance to believe him, to comprehend the danger she might be in. There was a stiffness to her now, a hesitance. He only hoped she was not making more of his invitation to the ranch than was meant.

Cautiously Adam tried her doorknob. It was locked. He inserted the key and let the door swing open noiselessly, listening, trusting his senses.

"Well?" she asked from behind him.

He found the light switches inside her door and flicked them on. Good. No one had made a mess in her apartment.

"Oh, thank heavens!" she breathed, starting to go in.

"Wait a minute," he warned.

He poked his head into the kitchen and the bedroom then, satisfied, he told her to come in.

"I'll just change and throw some things into an overnight bag," she said. "I should only be a couple of minutes."

As Adam stood in the middle of her living room alone with his impressions, an acute sensitivity, a peculiarly Indian sense of environment, of place and time, surfaced in him. There was, of course, the scent of the place, of Robin in particular: a female scent, neither sweet nor flowery but simply natural. Then there were her surroundings and, to Adam, surroundings revealed a person's inner self. The white man called it taste—so and so's taste was good or bad—but to the Indian the things a person gathered were either for utility or reminders of their heritage. Robin's possessions told nothing of her upbringing in Illinois. They were new, all of them, and traditionally Southwestern in style.

So, Adam thought, she'd left her past behind, the past that he surmised was clouded by some sort of pain. There was a feel to these possessions, however, that was not lost on him. Robin had collected Navaho rugs and lovely baskets and intricately woven coverings for the cushions on her couch. On the clean white walls were prints of Hopi Indians and pueblos, of striated tabletop mesas gilded in afternoon light. There were framed, limited-edition posters advertising the Santa Fe Opera. Pots of lush plants and bunches of chilies and ropes of rosy garlic hung from the beamed ceiling. Beige, moss green and muted pastels caught the eye. A pleasant place. Oddly, though, there seemed to be none of her own fine photographs on display. Adam wondered why. It was as if she'd grasped a feel for his land and his heritage, but somehow she had not yet fit her own self into the scenario.

"I'll be out in a sec," she called. "Fix yourself a drink if you like."

"No, thank you," he replied, his hands in his trousers

pockets as he stood, rigid, uneasy with his thoughts. She was just behind that door, only steps away. He tried not to let himself dwell on Robin in there, changing her clothes, brushing her hair...

Despite the fact that his back was to her, Adam sensed her presence in the living room the moment she entered. It was as if she had suddenly brought life to an inanimate place. He turned to face her. She was lovely, like sunlight sparkling; she brought with her a freshness and vitality that filled his being with a unique longing.

"Well," she said, "how do I look?"

"You look fine," he remarked noncommittally, taking her overnight bag from her hand, but his eyes stubbornly refused to leave her. She had put her hair up with combs, the effect of which was informal yet elegant, feminine and sensual all at once. Adam experienced a stirring in his groin and suddenly he felt closed in, as if he needed to run for miles in the cool night air.

"Hold on a second," Robin said, then she strode purposefully into the kitchen where she began to write something on a notepad. Adam watched as she leaned over the spotless countertop. She certainly looked better than *fine*. She wore a salmon-pink, calf-length skirt with a matching blazer whose sleeves were pushed up to the elbows. Underneath was an off-white top with a low scoop neck. And he couldn't help but notice as she finally straightened and the fold of her jacket parted, Robin wore no bra beneath the shimmering material.

He was seized by sudden regret.

"What do you think?" Robin asked, handing him the note.

Adam looked at it. "Don't bother wrecking this place," he read, "I got the message loud and clear." He glanced at Robin's amused expression and found himself smiling.

"You're putting this on your door?" he asked.

"I sure am. I've no intentions of cleaning up in here, too, *if* your theory about the counterfeiters is right." She brushed past him and tacked up the note, and he was gripped by her scent as it floated in the air. It was her perfume, of course, a light, unfamiliar aroma that filled his head. It was as if she were tormenting him on purpose.

"Let's go," Adam said, turning away.

The drive to the ranch didn't take long. His family's old Spanish hacienda sat at the end of Canyon Road only a few miles from the center of the city, enfolded in hills above the Santa Fe River.

"I never realized there was this much open land so near Santa Fe," remarked Robin from her seat in the darkened car. "I mean, it's really *big* up here."

"The ranch," said Adam, glad to slip into his role as professor, "has been in the family for over three centuries." He heard her mild gasp of surprise.

"But…but you're an Apache," she said. "I mean, Apaches didn't have ranches here three hundred years ago. Or…did they?"

"Well, no, they didn't. The ranch was originally a Spanish land grant to an ancestor of mine—and this is purely family legend—but my mother says the Spanish king gave it to one of his bastard sons."

"Then you're not entirely Apache."

He shook his head. "I'm about ninety percent Indian, though. My great-great-grandmother, Cassandra, married a wealthy American after her father died. By doing so, she saved this ranch when the United Sates won the war against Mexico. Most all the other Mexicans lost everything. But not her."

"So," said Robin, "that's all fine, but how did the Apache get into the family?"

"Cassandra's husband died of wounds from the Civil War and she married again, a half-breed Apache."

"I see," answered Robin.

"Yes. His name was Adam."

"So you're named after this illustrious ancestor. How wonderful."

"My mother liked the story. Of course, there's a question as to how illustrious he was. He was a wild sort, off in the mountains half the time, but his children inherited the hacienda. And from then on they kept the land, but they all married Apaches."

"Wow, what a story," said Robin.

"I often wonder how much of it's true, although the original land grant is on file in the historical library. This is one of the few haciendas that survived American taxes and surveying laws."

"Cassandra," mused Robin, "a strong woman. I would have liked her."

"She probably would have liked you," he found himself saying.

"What a remarkable inheritance," Robin said softly.

And Adam felt like adding: *But it's all going to end with me.*

Before them spread the rolling hills of the ranch. Cattle, mere shadows in the moonlight, dotted the countryside above the Santa Fe River, which in the late summer was a mere trickle. And beyond several camel-like humps of land stood the sprawling hacienda, Las Jaritas—the Willows—lit like a strand of diamonds on the hillside.

"If you listen," Adam said, "you can hear the music." Indeed, when the night wind shifted, they could hear faint guitar music as if it were being played in a distant time and carried on the breeze through the decades.

"Oh, that's beautiful," Robin whispered. "It gives me goose bumps."

Carrying her bag in one hand, Adam took Robin's arm with the other and led her across the crowded, lantern-lit courtyard to where his mother stood talking. Christina Farwalker looked charming; she was a small, plump woman who wore a calf-length, full skirt, a conch belt and peasant blouse and lots of turquoise jewelry. Her lustrous black hair was cut in a modern style, feathered

and swept back—the perfect combination of ethnic and
chic.

Adam was aware the moment his mother saw him. Her
black eyebrows raised, she excused herself from the man
to whom she was talking and made her way through the
crowd toward him. He'd have to explain to his mother;
she'd think he'd brought a date and be thrilled to death.
Abruptly he released his hold on Robin's arm.

"Hello, Adam," Christina said, stepping forward to
greet him. "You're awfully late."

"Hello, Mother," he replied. "This is Robin Hayle.
She owns a photography studio in town and due to some
rather peculiar happenings today, I've asked her to stay
in the guest house. That's why I'm so late."

"Nothing's wrong, I hope," said his mother. "But, my
dear—Robin, is it?—you're most welcome here." She
was looking back and forth from Robin to Adam, obviously puzzled.

"Robin got involved with a crazy idea I had…" Adam
offered. "I'll explain later."

"I *am* glad to be here, Mrs. Farwalker," Robin was
saying brightly, shaking the shorter woman's hand and
taking control of the conversation.

"Call me Christina, please. And Adam, take Robin to
her room and then get her something to eat."

Robin laughed lightly. "I know I look like I'm starving," she said. "I always do. But Adam already bought
me dinner."

"I won't tell a soul." Christina laughed, and they were
friends already. Somehow the notion disturbed Adam.

The low, one-story hacienda spread along the hillside
behind an aged adobe wall. Built onto and expanded
countless times over the centuries, it was an intricate jum-
ble of adobe walls and small, square windows covered
with the ubiquitous wrought-iron grills of the Southwest.
A century-old chapel still stood apart from the main structure. Nearby was a building that had once been the ser-

vants' quarters, but now, newly renovated, served as private guest housing.

"I'll get lost coming back to the party," joked Robin as Adam swung open her door.

"Just follow the noise. The louder it gets, the closer you are." He placed her bag on an armchair and turned to leave.

"I'll be ready in a second."

"I'll see you there," he said quickly. "There's someone I have to talk to for a minute. Do you mind?"

"Oh, no. Of course not." But she sounded disappointed. A pity, he thought, as he closed the door and fled into the shadows, but he was doing her a favor.

There actually was someone Adam had to see. He threaded his way though the throng and found his mother again. He had every intention of warning her off before she said or did anything embarrassing to either himself or Robin.

"Got a minute?" he asked his mother, tactfully steering her away from the group. Quickly he explained Robin's situation and how he had gotten her involved.

"And you're convinced that there really is a counterfeiting ring and someone deliberately broke into Robin's shop to warn her?" asked Christina.

"I'm going to act on that theory," said Adam. "I want to make sure Robin is safe."

"Of course. She can stay as long as she wants."

"Mother, you do understand that's why I brought her out here? For her own protection?"

"Such a lovely girl," Christina observed with a sigh. "Don't you think so?"

"Yes," Adam said impatiently. "But if she'd been a hag I still would have done the same thing."

"Well, son, I see you finally got here. A little late. You've missed the auction," came his father's voice.

"Adam's had a little problem," offered Christina, and then she repeated the story to her husband. "So that's why he's so late. But you must meet Adam's friend, Robin. She's absolutely delightful. She's a photographer, Ray, and that's how this whole thing got started.''

Ray Farwalker was an exceptionally tall, rawboned man who wore a studded, Western-style shirt, boots and dress pants and kept his long, graying hair tied back in the old way, in a ponytail. He was a quiet man who worked hard every day of his life, and he had an aura of peace to him, a peace Adam had come to envy. Soberly he asked his son, ''You reported this to the police?''

''Rod Cordova's taking care of it.''

''Good,'' said Ray. ''Now where's this lady of yours?''

''She is *not* a lady of mine,'' replied Adam tightly. ''I just felt responsible after what happened to her shop.''

''And well you should,'' said Christina. ''Poor girl. Why don't you go get her, Adam? Your father would like to meet her.''

''Mother…'' Adam warned.

''She's a *guest* in my house,'' Christina pointed out. ''I do think we owe her certain courtesies, Adam.''

''I'm sure I'll get a chance to meet her later,'' Ray said.

''Well, I better get back to the party,'' Christina exchanged a meaningful glance with her husband, a glance Adam caught. Anger coiled within him. She was doing it again—assuming, pushing, *hoping*.

''Mother, don't read anything into this,'' he warned again.

''Son,'' Ray said, ''your mother—''

But Christina laid a hand on her husband's arm to silence him. ''Adam,'' she said quietly, ''you have been taught to adjust yourself to remain in harmony with life. If nature withholds children from you, it is up to you to seek the pattern behind it, to find its beauty and accept it. Not to fight nature, as the white man does.'' Then she stood on tiptoe and kissed Adam's cheek. ''You and Robin enjoy the party.'' She took Ray's arm and the two

of them disappeared into the noisy, laughing crowd while
Adam watched, his face devoid of expression.

ROBIN SAT, SLUMPED, her hands on her cheeks, contemplating the situation. She wished Adam had never paused
at her shop window. She wished she'd never seen him or
talked to him. He was someone she could like, a lot, but
it seemed he had no interest in her.

She looked around the guest house. It was typical of
the charm of old Santa Fe she'd come to love. The furniture was simple and spare, with cleanliness and a Spanish flavor. On the four-poster bed was a black and red
Indian blanket, on the floor a Navaho rug. The bathroom
was utterly modern. The room itself, she decided, was a
trinity of cultures. Like Adam Farwalker.

She really didn't feel like joining the party. Sighing,
she stood and walked to the open window, drawing aside
the curtain. Guitar music lifted from the courtyard and
floated along the paths to her room. Everywhere she gazed
there were potted flowers, dark in the night shadows. Over
near an old chapel was a lonely little bench resting against
the high adobe wall, a wall, Robin guessed, meant to keep
out intruders. She felt suddenly lost, out of place, out of
her time.

Leaving the guest house, Robin strolled aimlessly toward the chapel. She couldn't help thinking about the
story of Adam's ancestor, Cassandra. The woman had
walked these same paths, smelled this exotic profusion of
late summer flowers. Of course, the walls had probably
been new then, and the chapel in better repair.

A soft footfall behind Robin made her turn. It was
Adam, tall and broad-shouldered in the dark. She put a
hand to her throat in an unconscious gesture. "Oh, you
startled me."

"Sorry. I was worried you'd actually gotten lost."

"I was poking my nose into corners. This place is so
fascinating, so old. I think it's marvelous your family still

lives here." She wondered who would inherit all this. "Are you the eldest son?" Robin asked casually.

"Yes," he replied. "I have two younger sisters."

"Then your children will be the ones to carry on your name and live here."

Adam stood leaning against the adobe wall of the old chapel. He folded his arms. "Apache society is matrilineal, as I told you. My sisters should be the ones to bring their husbands home to this place. Unfortunately, they've become so thoroughly modernized they both moved away with their husbands. My mother isn't happy about it."

For a long moment Robin stared at him pensively. Why had he sidestepped the issue of his children inheriting? Didn't he plan on *ever* marrying? "You know your heritage is worth preserving," she said softly, trying to draw him out. When he said nothing, she couldn't help but add, "It's beautiful here, Adam. I'm very jealous. I wonder if you know how valuable your inheritance is."

"Oh, I do know, Robin, I do," he said simply, almost bitterly, she thought.

They stood in mutual silence, history embracing them. Yet Robin felt that distance Adam was purposefully cultivating.

"You must be hungry," he stated after a time. "Shall we join the party?"

She would have preferred to say there in the darkness with Adam, but how could she possibly tell him that? "I suppose we should," she said, chiding herself for being a fool.

As they passed by the solitary wooden bench against the wall, Robin slowed her pace. Had Cassandra once sat on that very seat and secretly kissed her wild Apache lover? she wondered.

"Are you coming?" asked Adam and she nodded quickly, tearing her mind from the past and following him toward the gathering.

On the lamp-lit central patio the party was in full swing.

A wonderful mélange of faces greeted Robin: elegant Spanish grandees whose families had lived in New Mexico for centuries; heirs to East Coast fortunes in town for Indian Market; collectors in their own right; Westerners with sun-faded eyes, snakeskin boots, string ties and Stetsons; stoic Indians who were local artists or friends of the Farwalkers.

Dutifully Adam left Robin's side for a minute to get her a plate of ribs and chicken from the mesquite grill, coleslaw and salad from a long trestle table. She looked around, wishing she could take some photographs in the flickering light.

It was then that Christina took the opportunity to speak to her. "Are you enjoying the party, Robin?"

"Very much so, Mrs. Farwalker."

"Christina," she said easily. "This is my favorite event of the year. It's my way of bringing the Indian and the white communities together."

"It's very generous of you."

"My husband writes it off our taxes," replied Christina with good humor, and Robin laughed along with her. How different the Farwalkers were from most Indians, she thought. They chose to bridge two worlds, and obviously they did it very successfully.

"My son told me about the photograph," Christina was saying, "and about your shop. It's terrible."

"It makes me furious," Robin answered.

"You know, these rings of counterfeiters can be very dangerous. You have to be careful. I don't know what my son was thinking when he dragged you out to that pueblo. Usually he's very levelheaded—"

"I realize I should have consulted you first, Mother," Adam said lightly as he returned with a plate for Robin and one for himself.

At that point a couple from New York who owned a gallery joined in the conversation. Robin couldn't help but notice how easily Adam talked with them, how alive he became while discussing his role as one who treasured and preserved history, who protected the marketplace as well as the museum. He even laughed once, his black eyes dancing in the soft light. How could he be so at ease with others, barely acquaintances, and so stilted with her?

Nonetheless he was a perfect host, escorting Robin from group to group; taking her arm occasionally, introducing her to so many people she knew she'd never remember all their names.

Julien Cordova was there, talking animatedly to a group of collectors. "How nice to see you again, Robin," he said. "I must say, Adam, this meeting you so often is becoming a pleasant habit. Delightful party."

And then they drifted on, pushed here and there by the eddying throng. The music grew lively, and a young man sang in Spanish, a lilting song about *amor* and *la vida*, love and life.

Two effeminate men who owned a Western art gallery in Scottsdale, Arizona, were talking to Adam, but Robin wasn't listening. Instead, she was staring at Adam's face unashamedly, at the strength of his bone and muscle, at the strong set of his chin and those finely molded lips.

He caught her staring at him and turned away slightly, his animated expression closing as if the door to his soul had shut. Maybe, Robin told herself, it was the Indian in him, the innate privacy he used to protect himself from outsiders. In time she might come to know him, to understand.

She was probably kidding herself about that, though. He was so distant with her, he was obviously just not interested.

By midnight guests were starting to leave. The music quieted; unobtrusively servants cleared tables; the flames in the gas torches were lowered. A few night owls still hung around, however, sitting and chatting over wine spills on the tablecloths.

Robin was tired. She'd been sitting talking to Ray Farwalker about a portrait she'd shot on the Apache Reservation near Santa Fe, but he'd had to leave her and say his farewells to some visitors. She felt suddenly alone, an alien in Adam's world, a place she had no business being.

Self-consciously she sought out Adam. He was saying goodbye to Julien on the far side of the courtyard. He stood tall and erect, yet he appeared to be relaxed. He ought to be married, she decided. A man with his looks and education shouldn't have been allowed to go unattached all these years. Maybe he really was a cerebral bachelor type after all, content with his teaching and sabbatical digs out in the middle of nowhere.

Yet she doubted it. He was undeniably a red-blooded male, and he was at ease in society. Surely he had women friends, maybe even a girlfriend or a fiancée. She studied his face as he spoke to Julien; she could look at him forever.

"Robin," came Christina's voice at her shoulder, "I thought you'd gone to bed."

"Not yet."

"You must be exhausted, dear." Then, before she could stop her, Christina was calling Adam over and chiding him gently for leaving Robin unattended. "See her to the guest house, Adam, she's very tired."

Robin's cheeks flushed as she stood and felt Adam's hand encircle her arm.

"Oh, that's all right, I can find my way," she managed. "Really, I can…"

"Nonsense," he said. "Mother's right."

It was all so polite between them, so artificial. Feeling foolish, Robin let him walk her along the paths while silence seemed to ring in the cool night air.

They passed the bench. The image of Cassandra flashed without summons through her brain; the woman was crushed to her Indian's smooth bare chest, her back arched, her lips hungrily moving against his. Robin felt dizzy and weak, almost able to hear their soft, forbidden moans of passion.

Why wouldn't Adam hold her like that, or kiss her? But his hand fell away as he pushed open her door. "Good night," he said, his deep voice uninflected.

She felt ashamed then, knowing how much she longed for an intimate touch, a word, a warm glance from him. But she wasn't going to get it. Not from this man, Adam, the man who walked far and—apparently—alone.

CHAPTER FIVE

IT WAS A DAY of frustrations.

Robin woke up with the sun, far too early, still tired but unable to sleep any longer. It was her obsession with Adam Farwalker, the anticipation that she would soon see him, that was making her jittery, as if she'd had too much coffee.

He was a strange, alluring man. Partly because he was Indian, and she admitted to herself that his heritage *was* terribly intriguing, but also because she could sense something powerful and significant behind his reticence.

It was pointless lying there. She rose, showered and dressed in white leggings and an oversized bright red shirt that hung practically to her knees. Of course, after cleaning up her shop she'd be filthy, but she couldn't show up at the Farwalkers' breakfast table in jeans and a work shirt.

She found her way along the paths to the main hacienda and entered quietly. Was anyone up yet? After last night…

She half expected to find Adam having coffee or already eating when she poked her head into the kitchen. But it was empty. Even Christina Farwalker was nowhere to be seen, although a fresh pot of coffee sat on a hot plate. She helped herself.

It was curiosity that propelled Robin to wander through the main rooms of the house. This was Adam's birthplace, the place where he'd run and played as a child. But it was hard to picture Adam young and carefree; it was as if the man had always been tightly contained.

As she explored, that ever-present sense of being an outsider struck Robin with a heavy hand. Since the loss of her parents, she'd often felt left out when confronted with a warm family scene, a large, inviting house that was occupied by loving parents and lots of squabbling children. And this house, this hacienda, impressed her with those feelings of close family ties.

It was a charming old place, in typical Santa Fe style. It had the casual plainness of architecture, the sharp contrasts between light and shadow and massive solidity of walls, doors and heavy, dark ceiling beams. There was a spareness in decoration and furniture, and an integrity of materials: smooth adobe and clear, polished pine, natural wool rugs and bright tiles. Each piece of Spanish colonial furniture, each stylized Navaho rug and graceful Pueblo pot had been placed by a loving hand.

Robin was fingering a three-foot-tall intricately woven basket that sat next to a corner fireplace when Christina found her. "And how do you like our house?" she asked cheerfully.

"I love it," replied Robin. "It's so...so warm."

"Would you like to explore—or perhaps you're hungry?"

"I already looked around," she admitted. "And I *am* hungry, thank you."

Adam, she was told, was not yet up. She felt a small stab of disappointment but forced it aside while Christina served her a plate of *huevos rancheros*, eggs on tortillas, smothered with a piquant sauce of tomatoes, peppers and onions.

"So, my son tells me you indulge people's fantasies," said Christina, leaning her elbows on the pale wood of the table.

"Oh, did he really?" Robin wasn't sure how she felt about Adam having discussed her with his mother—good, she guessed. Then she had to explain about her portraits and costumes and tell her stock of funny stories.

Christina was laughing over what Robin called the Lady Godiva incident when Adam walked into the kitchen. He hesitated when he saw her, as if he'd forgotten she was there and was chagrined to be reminded. She had to admit that his rebuff hurt. But she couldn't be so ridiculously sensitive, she told herself, and besides, Adam looked so darn handsome that morning, she could forgive him almost anything. He was dressed casually in jeans and a red and black plaid shirt rolled up at the sleeves. And he looked younger somehow, well-rested perhaps, or at ease in his parents' house. She glanced at him and nodded and smiled, but in her mind's eye she couldn't help imagining him on a horse with a lance in his hand and a bright band holding back his thick black hair.

"Did you sleep well?" he asked.

She gave a self-deprecating shrug. "Oh, sure."

Christina dominated the conversation. She had an easy, affectionate relationship with her son. She made him smile and joked with him; she bullied and meddled, Robin guessed, and gave advice a little too freely. But Adam took it in stride, indulgently, towering over his small mother, letting her think she was in control.

It would have been nice, Robin thought, to have Adam that free and open with her. Of course, she didn't believe in miracles, but still, he *could* give her one of those rare, white-toothed smiles of his, couldn't he? Instead, he made her feel as if she were the outsider, the intruder.

Eventually Ray Farwalker joined them for breakfast. He was awfully kind to Robin and she was made to feel very much at home. "Did you find the coffee I made?" he asked Robin and then told her about his morning, how he and some ranch hands had found a stray calf. The conversation turned to family stuff then, Christina reminding Adam about his sister's birthday.

"I'll try to make it," replied Adam, "but the team out

at the dig has to be back in school soon and we've got a lot of work.''

"An afternoon won't kill you, Adam," Christina pointed out.

He gave her a smile and downed the rest of his coffee. "I better be going," he said, getting to his feet. "Robin's got to get back to her shop, and I've got work to do, too."

Christina walked them to the door. "Robin, you phone anytime, I mean that. And you're welcome to stay here whenever you like. Really, I want to hear more about your clients. You bring her out here again, Adam, you hear me?"

Did Christina notice that Adam didn't answer her? Did she feel the abrupt prickle of strain in the atmosphere? But Robin said something inane, talking too much as usual, to cover the uneasiness, and followed Adam out to his car.

"That was quite an affair last night," she commented.

Adam pulled his big Land Rover onto Canyon Road and turned it toward Santa Fe before answering. "My mother loves doing it. She gets to see everybody she's missed during the year."

The vehicle was headed east, and Robin put on her sunglasses as the early morning sun glared right in her eyes. The wide valley, from the Sangre de Cristo Mountains in the east to the Jemez range in the west, was bathed in brilliant, clear light, striped with the long shadows of hill and tree and fence post. Robin's fingers itched for her camera; the light was perfect. She could possess these images forever.

The city took shape as Adam drove into it; the streets narrowed, the buildings crowded in, the walls and trees created privacy where it had no right to be. "You can drop your stuff at your place," he said. "Then we'll head to the shop and put it back into order."

"You don't have to," Robin protested. "I can call Ericka and we'll manage just fine."

He only glanced at her as he pulled up in front of her building. Of course, Adam checked the apartment, then, satisfied, told her to come in. "I wish you'd stay at the ranch," he said. "At least consider it, Robin."

She put her overnight bag in the bedroom and called, "Thanks, really. But I have too much work to do and honestly, we can't be positive that the mess in my store has anything to do with your forged pot." He said no more about it, but Robin could tell, by the way his brows drew together in a dark bar of concern, that Adam was not pleased.

They brought along what few tools Robin owned, a hammer and two screwdrivers. Then while she began to sweep up the floor in the front, separating damaged goods from still usable ones, Adam scavenged the alleyway for old boards, which he used to nail over the broken window in her office. Robin savored the early morning time they had together without his family or her customers constantly interrupting. As she glanced around her shop and assessed the damage, she decided something good had come out of all this. She could spend a few more hours with Adam.

"You better save the damaged frames and film," he called over his hammering, "for the insurance adjustor."

She made a sign, Open at Noon, and then the hard work began. The trouble was, the streets were filled with eager shoppers, Sunday being the last day of Indian Market. Faces kept peering through the front windows and hands continually rattled the doorknob.

Adam came into the front of the shop once he had the window temporarily repaired. He stood, hands on hips, and surveyed the place. "I still can't believe someone had the nerve to do this," he said grimly.

"Oh, come on," said Robin, trying to be cheerful, "it could have been worse." As they worked together, straightening, rearranging, tossing out, she decided to press him, to see if he would open up a little and satisfy her curiosity. "Tell me about your sisters," she said while they picked up film cases and cameras and lenses.

"They're both younger than I am." He paused, studied a coil of ruined film pensively. "Married. Felice has two children and Amanda has three."

"Oh, so you're an uncle. What fun. I would love—"

Someone was pounding on the door. Irritated when the person would not leave, Robin went over and unlocked it. "Mrs. Hartmann, well, hello."

"Are the proofs back?"

"I said Monday, Mrs. Hartmann."

"Monday? But…" Mrs. Hartmann thrust her face into the shop. "What happened here?"

"Burglars," said Robin swiftly, to forestall a long story. "Now, about those proofs…"

"Tomorrow. All right, I'll be back."

Robin locked up again and turned to Adam. She started to ask another question about his sisters, but someone else was knocking on the door.

"Lady, I need some film," called a man. "You opened up for that woman there."

Trying to be polite, Robin unlocked for a moment. "I'm closed till noon. I don't have any film. Can you come back—"

"Honey!" The man's wife had sidled in past Robin. "Look at that photograph! How much is it?"

It was a study of some buttes against a rainbow. Robin liked the picture herself, but right now its glass was broken and it was lying on the floor. Nevertheless the lady stepped daintily over the clutter and studied it.

"How much is it?" the man asked.

"Fifty-nine ninety-five with the frame. But the glass is broken…"

"How much without the glass?"

Robin gave up. "Oh, say fifty even."

"It's a deal." The man looked around. "Say, what happened here?"

"A burglary," replied Robin.

"Huh. Terrible mess." He looked down at his feet. "Hey, there's some film. I need just that kind."

She picked up the photograph and film and made her way to the counter. "Sorry, Adam, I'll just be a minute," she said over her shoulder. She started to remove the few remaining glass shards from the frame. She must not have been paying attention, because she felt the cold, numb slice of the glass across her finger and, before she realized what it was, a line of blood was welling up in bright ruby droplets.

"Oh, darn, I've cut myself.

Adam was at her side immediately.

"How dumb," she said. "I don't want to touch the picture; I'll ruin it."

"I'll do it," Adam said. "Just tell me…"

"Are you two married?" asked the man. "Nice shop you've got here. I'm a meat wholesaler myself. Pittsburgh."

Adam was wrapping his handkerchief around her finger, his dark head bent over her hand. Robin felt her cheeks redden. *Married*. How could this be happening? "We're not married," she said quickly.

"Young folk these days," the man went on. "Don't say a word, I got it. Listen, do you folks know beef—"

"Adam, could you ring up the purchases?" She felt really flustered now. Her finger was throbbing; the man was going on about how nobody ate meat these days; his wife was sifting through the mess on the floor, examining photographs and cameras.

Robin told Adam what to do, and he managed quite well, even remembering the sales tax. He wrapped the photograph, smiled at the people, thanked them and deftly got them out of Robin's Nest.

Then he turned to Robin, who was still standing behind the counter, her wrapped finger in front of her. "I wonder if the sale was worth the cut," she quipped.

"Let me look at it."

She felt quite foolish standing there with Adam unwrapping her finger as if she were a child. Then he was going into the back for a Band-Aid and she stared after him, her embarrassment transforming into a kind of floating elation. It had been ages since a man had taken care of her. She'd lost her father so early and her uncle, with whom she'd lived, had been a salesman always on the road. Robin had been forced to maintain her independence, to rely only on herself.

What woman wouldn't want a big strong man taking care of her once in awhile?

Adam was coming back, peeling away the paper on the Band-Aid, very businesslike, very quiet. Yet there was an energy to him that seemed to fill her small shop, a strange but soothing power that held her silent. Was it the Apache in him? Was that why he was so mysteriously attractive to her?

He looked up then and caught her studying him. For an instant there was a kind of communication in the glance, as if he were about to tell her something, to let himself go.

"Hello!" came a voice at the door and the handle rattled. "Hello in there, Robin!" Then a man's face appeared, pressed to the glass.

"Julien," said Adam. "Shall I let him in?"

"Sure," replied Robin, taking the Band-Aid herself and wrapping her finger.

"Oh, my, oh, my, what happened?" asked Julien, his high, intelligent forehead creased in concern. "*Dios mío*, what a mess!"

Robin sighed and put a smile on her lips. "We're not really sure."

"My brother told me some crazy story," he said, "about this being connected to that counterfeit pot. What is going on, Robin?"

She told him the whole story again while Adam interjected details here and there. She wondered if Julien was ever going to leave, to let them finish their work. Julien was a kind, sweet man, caring and concerned, but didn't he know it was still Indian Market?

"You must let me help you," he was saying. "What can I do?"

"We're managing," replied Adam as his eyes met hers over Julien's head.

"Yes," said Robin taking the cue, "we'll be done soon."

"Well, then... But tonight, Robin, at the association meeting we simply must discuss this matter."

"Of course," she answered, casually ushering him to the door. "See you then, and thanks, Julien."

Julien took one last look around and frowned. "A pity," he said, "truly a crime..."

By noon Robin's Nest was sufficiently back in order so that she was able to open the door to customers. Adam was in the back still putting a few things on shelves, but she knew he was anxious to leave. She hated the thought of his going; he'd be so far away. She'd probably never see him again.

He emerged slapping dust off his hands.

"Can I buy you lunch?" she offered.

"No, thanks, I've got to get going. I want to drop by San Lucas again. Maybe I can find out something more." He hesitated. "Look, Robin, I'm not trying to run your life, but I'd feel a lot better if you stayed out at my folks' at night, for a while, at least."

"I couldn't, really. Adam, I'll be fine. Obviously these creeps pulled their stunt and they're done. And besides, Detective Cordova knows about it now."

He stared at her, as if he wanted to say something else, but the moment passed. "I can't force you, of course," he finally said.

"No, you can't."

"But you will let Rod know if anything at all peculiar happens?"

Dutifully she nodded.

He began to move toward the door. *So this is it,* she thought. *I'm never going to see him again.*

For a moment Robin was about to ask him when he was going to be back in town, to tell him she'd like to hear from him sometime. But she didn't. If he'd wanted to see her again he would have said something already.

"Well," she said as they stood together beneath the cottonwoods, "thank you for last night and helping me clean up today." She held out her hand, feeling foolish and strangely shy. "It was nice meeting you, Adam."

"Yes," he replied taking her hand awkwardly, "it's been an interesting twenty-four hours. Well…"

"Well," she said as the tense handshake ended, "guess I'll see you around."

"Oh, Robin! There you are!" It was Shelly Dalton. She was hurrying along the street toward them.

Oh darn, thought Robin.

"Oh, my gosh," Shelly was saying, "Ericka had this call from the police about your shop being wrecked or something…" She glanced at Adam. "Oh, excuse me, I didn't realize…"

Robin sighed and made the introductions.

"So nice to meet you, Mr. Farwalker," Shelly said. "I believe I've met your mother."

They shook hands. Robin could have strangled Shelly for the coy looks she kept flashing at Adam then at Robin and for the inordinately long time she left her hand in his.

Then Chuck came out of the gallery and also had to be introduced. "Your mother does the auction every year, doesn't she?" he asked Adam. "Terrific idea."

Adam glanced at his watch as Shelly was saying, "You've *got* to tell me what happened! Ericka was telling us about the police thinking teenagers were involved or something. Anyway, I got busy."

"Just a second, Shelly," Robin said quickly, "and I'll fill you in."

Adam was anxious to leave, she could tell, and it made her nervous. Maybe if Shelly hadn't come over she would have pressed him a little to see if he planned on ever contacting her again. As it was…

"I do have to go," he said, "and take care, Robin, I mean that."

"Oh, I will." Then, aware that her voice had an edge of urgency, she said, "If you find out anything more you'll let me know, won't you?"

"Of course."

Then he was gone, his tall, dark form disappearing into the crowds. Shelly and Chuck were both talking at once, and Robin guessed she was giving the right answers but she could barely concentrate, her eyes still futilely searching the throng as if he'd reappear—her devastatingly handsome Apache Indian.

"And he helped you clean up?" Shelly was asking. "Robin, are you listening?"

She was and she wasn't. A part of her was wondering if she could find out more about the counterfeit pottery. Wouldn't that be an excellent excuse to contact Adam Farwalker?

CHAPTER SIX

"THE MEETING WILL PLEASE come to order," Julien Cordova said at seven sharp, and the murmuring and shifting in the conference room of the La Fonda Hotel settled into quiet. "I apologize for calling this meeting on a Sunday, but as you all know, after Indian Market and the end of the summer season many of you will be out of town, and I wanted to get the association organized before that. Now, for the first item of business, will the secretary please read the minutes of our last meeting."

Robin crossed her legs and sipped the coffee that was still piping hot in its Styrofoam cup. She hoped the caffeine would keep her awake during the meeting, as she was feeling bored and sleepy and wished she could just go home, collapse in bed and forget the past twenty-four hours.

"I'm not sure it's prudent to spend ten thousand dollars on a full-page and in *Travel and Leisure*," Chuck Dalton was saying. "Everyone knows Santa Fe's here. It's overkill."

Robin sighed. The arguments were commencing and probably wouldn't end for hours.

Thad Mencimer, a heavyset, fair young man whose face was red with aggravation, shot to his feet. "That's assuming an awful lot! There are thousands of people out there who don't know what Santa Fe has to offer. We need to reach a broader market. Why, last month's figures show a drop in sales tax—"

"One percent," scoffed Chuck, "and that's because we had a week of lousy weather."

Someone else stood and shook a finger at Chuck. "One percent means a drop in my gross receipts. *I'm* not about to ignore it. Everyone always blames the weather..."

"Has anyone considered a half-page ad?" asked Chuck Dalton.

"Ridiculous!" retorted Thad, and Robin saw Thad's wife, Lorraine, pull at his sleeve. Poor woman, she was young and very pregnant and embarrassed by her husband's ill-considered comments.

Robin shifted on the hard seat. She wondered idly where Adam was—back at Chaco Canyon? She pictured him crawling into a little pup tent. How did he live out there? In a trailer? A cabin? She wanted to know so that she could think about him, imagine him in the correct setting. Had he found the potter at San Lucas? Would he let her know if he had?

"...good Indian Market this year," Julien was saying. "I think we all did as well as can be expected given the economic climate."

"Not good enough!" someone called out. Thad Mencimer, Robin noted. Sometimes the man was a pain. "A full-page ad is absolutely necessary," Thad repeated. He shook a handful of papers. "I have figures here on how many people an ad like that would reach."

"We've neglected the overseas market," someone else said. "Japan, West Germany. That's where the bucks are."

"The *New York Times* travel section. Can't someone do an article?" another member asked.

"You're all getting off the subject," piped up Thad. "I call for a vote on this issue right now!"

Robin drank the rest of her now lukewarm coffee. It was going to be a long evening.

"Now, ladies and gentlemen, we're all friends here and we all have the same goals in mind." Julien was holding out his hand. "I must beg you to speak one at a time. Let's not get confrontational." Then he grinned. "Don't you love that word?"

He got a laugh, defusing the situation neatly. Thad Mencimer, however, still glowered, while his shy wife whispered earnestly into his ear.

After a few minutes more of discussion, the motion to put a full-page ad in *Travel and Leisure* passed. Julien had convinced everyone there was enough in the treasury to cover it, and Chuck Dalton acquiesced gracefully. One hurdle over with, thought Robin, trying to decide whether she should stay or get up, go to the ladies' room and splash cold water on her face.

Shelly Dalton stood then and said she had an important announcement to make. "Do you all know what happened to Robin Hayle's shop yesterday, folks?"

Expectant murmurs rose from the group.

"Well, I think Robin should tell us the whole story and we better think about it real hard."

"Robin, come up here and tell the association what happened. I was going to bring it up myself," said Julien.

Thanks a lot, Shel, Robin said to herself as she rose dutifully and went to the front of the room to tell her tale. She tried to be quick and clear, but she felt a little presumptuous rehashing Adam's theory about a counterfeiting ring. "And that's it. I still don't know for sure who or why someone broke into my shop. Julien's brother, Rod Cordova, thought it could be teenagers, but I really don't think so. Anyway, I've considered installing a security system like some of the galleries have."

"It's a disgrace!" a gallery owner in the back of the room said bitterly. "We're not safe anywhere."

"My insurance rates are too high now," said another.

"What do we pay the police for, anyway?"

"All right, everyone," said Julien, frowning, "let's keep this orderly. Comments, please, one at a time."

Thad Mencimer popped up, a red-faced jack-in-the-box.

"If there really is a person or a group making fake pots and selling them to collectors, every art dealer in Santa Fe is compromised. No big collectors will trust us. We have to do something about this!"

"How about your brother, Julien? Can Rod help us?" asked someone.

"No police," came a voice from the side of the room. A statuesque woman stood. "If the police get into this there'll be publicity. How will *that* look? It'll be all over the art world in a couple of weeks. I can just hear it now, Santa Fe inundated with fakes. Then watch your business go downhill!"

"Madeline's right," said Shelly Dalton.

A voice came from the corner of the large room, "I can see our ad in *Travel and Leisure*," said the man. "Come to Santa Fe and get ripped off!"

"Right on!" called out a woman. "We *can't* let the police in on this. My God, every newspaper in the state will file a story."

"No police," agreed Julien. "Any other suggestions?"

"But Rod already knows," Robin pointed out. "Although he was skeptical about the reason for the break-in."

"I'll make sure Rod is discreet," said Julien. "He'll understand. But I think we should discuss methods of dealing with this problem, just in case you were being warned off, Robin."

The discussion was hot and heavy. Suggestions ranged from a vigilante committee to a registration system for each piece of artwork. Robin got herself another cup of coffee, sat down and wiggled her toes in her shoes. So far nobody had come up with a practical idea.

Julien stood, elbow cupped in his hand, fist to his chin, listening, soothing, directing. He was the perfect president for the association, intelligent, cultured, familiar with every facet of the city's business, history and people. He'd been elected unanimously at the first organizational meeting, and Robin thought he was doing a terrific job.

"All right," Julien finally said, "I'm beginning to see a pattern here. What we need is more information. We can't decide what to do until we have all the facts. I suggest we form a special subcommittee of, say, five or six people, to go into this matter. I make a motion to set up said committee. Any seconds?"

A hand rose. Thad Mencimer's. "I second."

"All in favor."

The ayes had it.

Before Robin knew what was happening she had been volunteered as a member of the subcommittee along with Chuck Dalton, Thad Mencimer, Madeline Lassiter and Ben Chavez, a longtime art dealer. Julien himself would also attend their meetings to help out.

It crossed her mind then, the promise that she'd made to Adam, her word that she would bow out of this forgery business. Now here she was, albeit innocently, involved again. Deeply involved. *Darn.*

"Well," Julien said, "I think we've made great progress. The new committee will meet three times a week—how about in the library of the Governor's Palace?—and will report back its findings to the association at the next meeting. Meeting adjourned."

Robin grimaced. Three times a week. Oh, well, maybe this committee she was on would actually come up with some ways of guarding against forged artwork, or at least find out for sure if her shop had been wrecked as a warning. So many questions still remained to be answered.

"See you Tuesday night," Madeline said. "Bring that photograph of yours, the one with the pot in it."

"Sure, see you," Robin agreed, smothering a yawn.

She walked back to her shop, where her car was parked, with Chuck and Shelly.

"Boy, am I beat," she said, letting the yawn finally take over.

"I bet," said Shelly. "Why didn't you bring your friend Adam with you tonight? I mean, he's involved, isn't he?"

"Oh, Shel, he has to work. It's a long drive out to Chaco Canyon. He can't indulge himself in the luxuries of civilization very often. Besides—" she yawned again "—I really don't think he was interested in me."

"Why not?"

"How should I know? Heck, I hardly know the man."

"Okay, okay, but what if he calls you again?"

She shrugged in the darkness. "I'm not holding my breath."

"What a guy!" said Shelly. "And tall, wow, is he tall."

"He certainly is that," muttered Robin.

"Oh, to be young and single and sexy again." Shelly sighed.

"The only one of those that applies to me is single," said Robin dryly.

As they approached the Sena Plaza, a thought flashed through Robin's mind: what if the blinds were drawn again when she reached her shop, what if they'd broken in again, smashed everything all over again? What if...

But Robin's Nest sat undisturbed, blinds up, window displays intact. She breathed a sigh of relief and swore to herself to get a security system installed no matter the cost.

Shelly and Chuck got into their green van and Shelly waved out the window as they passed Robin. "Night," she called. "See you *mañana*!"

Robin walked to her own car, a sporty white Japanese import, and started it up. When she flicked the lights on, they caught a shadowed movement under one of the spreading trees. Robin felt her heart leap, but it was only a tomcat, a big, gray one, who was calmly patrolling his territory, stalking from tree to tree with unhurried dignity.

"Oh, boy," she mumbled to herself, "are you a nerd.

Jumping at shadows.'' Then she turned her car toward home and sped through the empty streets, whistling loudly to herself.

She hated to admit it, but she was a little nervous as she opened the door to her building and looked up the dim flight of stairs to her apartment. Last night she hadn't even thought about the possibility of danger, but last night Adam, big, strong, capable Adam, had been with her and had gone up there first.

She hesitated at the bottom of the stairs, fingering her keys. She could hear the television from one of the downstairs apartments. Well, somebody was home. She could knock on their door, ask to use the phone and call Christina Farwalker. It would be safe out there at the hacienda, safe and secure and...

Forget it, kiddo, Robin told herself angrily. She couldn't live her life jumping at every sound, every shadow, every locked door. She took a deep breath and started up the steps. Her heart pounded a little too hard, and she felt shaky. What if someone were waiting for her inside? That was ridiculous. How would they get in? She could see her door, and it was untouched, closed, just as it always was. Even that silly note she'd tacked to the door was still in place. Everything was fine.

She clenched her teeth and climbed doggedly to the landing. *Oh, Adam,* she thought, *where are you when I need you?*

The doorknob didn't turn; it was still firmly locked. Robin felt an enormous sense of relief wash over her. She unlocked the door and stepped inside, reaching out to turn the lights on. As Adam had done last night.

Light flooded the living room, glinting off the white walls, the tile floor, the familiar posters. ''Whew,'' said Robin. No one had been there, no one had broken in to steal or make a mess. She'd been silly to even worry about it.

She threw her shoulder bag on a table, kicked off her

shoes and took a deep breath to relax. Suddenly she realized she was starving. Wasn't there a package of cookies in the cupboard? And a glass of milk. That sounded good. Then she'd go to sleep; she always slept better on a full stomach. Oh, boy, she was sleepy.

She opened a cupboard door. Yes, chocolate-chip cookies. She popped one into her mouth, chewed, turned toward the refrigerator.

She froze.

From that angle she could see around the corner to her sofa and coffee table. There was something on the low, glass table, a pile of jagged pieces. What?

Slowly Robin approached the coffee table. Her eyes shifted around the room, her heart pounded again. What was on the table? What?

It looked like black and red pieces of something, scattered, broken. And when she was closer she could see that there were fragments all over her floor and her sofa and rocking chair. Red and black fragments all over, like spots of blood flung from an explosion.

When she finally stood over the mess she knew what it was, and then her heart nearly stopped and she gasped and felt sick to her stomach.

It was a red and black clay pot that had been smashed onto the table and broken, deliberately broken, so that shards had spattered all over. Yes, a pretty red and black patterned pot, an Indian pot—but not hers. Robin didn't own a pot like that.

Someone had brought that piece, gotten into her apartment and deliberately broken it on her table.

Why? *You fool,* her mind answered, *to warn you.* Adam had been right.

She backed away from the table, trod barefooted on a sharp fragment, hardly felt the stab. Someone had been in her apartment. How? Who?

"Oh, my God," she whispered.

She ran into the bedroom. The windows were shut. Nothing was disturbed.

The roof. Robin's apartment had a roof patio with stairs that led up from the living room. But that door, too, was shut and locked, just as she'd left it.

She sank into a chair and noticed that she was still clutching the bag of cookies. Her hands trembled. What should she do?

She tried to think. Whoever had done this knew everything about her, where she lived, when she was out. Had they picked the lock? Hadn't the neighbors noticed? But the intruder might have looked like a deliveryman or a friend.

She should have listened to Adam. Should she call the Farwalkers, pack a bag and drive out there? It was too late, she didn't have the nerve; she hardly knew them.

Rod Cordova.

But the association didn't want the police involved. Damn the association. Someone was *after* her!

Rod Cordova wasn't on duty on Sunday night. Of course not. A nice young officer with a faint Mexican accent spoke to Robin. "Miss Hayle, please explain to me again, what crime do you say has been committed?"

"Someone got into my apartment and broke a pot on my coffee table."

"Someone broke a pot that belonged to you?"

"No, not *my* pot. I don't know whose pot. But they got in…"

"Is there damage to your door?"

"No."

"I would send someone over, Miss Hayle, but my report must say what crime has been committed. Is it breaking and entering? Burglary? Destruction of property?"

"Breaking and entering, I guess," said Robin. "I'm frightened. Somebody got inside here and I don't know how."

"All right. I'll send someone over."

Robin paced nervously until the officer arrived.

"See," she said, indication the fragments of pottery, "someone got in here while I wasn't home and smashed it on my table."

"Do you have a cat, ma'am?"

"No, darn it, it isn't *my* pot. Someone brought it here."

"Someone brought you a pot and then broke it?"

Robin felt helpless. No one would understand. It sounded crazy. She tried again. "I made a report to Detective Cordova yesterday. The same thing happened in my shop. Someone got in here, too."

"Did you have a fight with your, er, boyfriend, ma'am?"

"I don't *have* a boyfriend," she said too loudly. "I don't know who did this!"

"Yes, ma'am, I'll let Detective Cordova know about this when he gets in first thing tomorrow morning."

"Thank you, but what about tonight? What if this person tries to get in again?"

"I'll tell the officers on duty to swing by here every hour or so. You lock your doors and windows now, ma'am."

"They *were* locked."

"Yes, ma'am."

Just before he left, the officer looked over his shoulder at the pile of broken pottery on her table, shook his head and commented, "Too bad about your pot, ma'am."

It was almost funny, *almost*. When the polite policeman had left, Robin wedged chairs against both her doors and checked every window. She went into the bedroom, put on her nightgown, brushed her teeth and got into bed, the usual nightly routine, except that tonight she lay there in the dark with her eyes wide open.

The night was utterly quiet. Only occasionally, outside, was there the sound of a car passing on Bishop's Lodge Road. She counted each one. The glow from their lights would hit the far wall of her bedroom then crawl slowly

across the smooth paint. Then it would be dark again for
a minute or two. In the corner of her room was a brass
hat rack, which she could just make out in the blackness.
When the car lights crossed the wall, the spindly object
cast a skeletal shadow, creeping along with the lights. To
top it all off, she'd left her closet door open; a childish
fear made the roots of her hair tingle.

After fifteen minutes of desperately trying to calm herself, Robin sat bolt upright and turned on her bedside
lamp. Purposefully she reached for her telephone and
pulled it into her lap, dialing information. She felt better
already.

"Chaco Canyon Visitor's Center," she said firmly into
the mouthpiece.

They wouldn't be open this late. She dialed, anyway;
clicks sounded in her ear. It rang five times. A recorded
voice came on. "This is Chaco Canyon Visitor's Center.
We are open to the public from nine to five every day. If
necessary, you may leave a message at the sound of the
beep. Thank you for calling the canyon."

Robin waited, tapping her short nails on the bedside
table, her heart beating furiously. Sleep—sure, she'd get
some sleep tonight...*Beep.*

"This is Robin Hayle," she began, "and I have an
urgent message..."

CHAPTER SEVEN

ADAM WAS LOOKING OFF into the distance in the photograph. She'd caught his face at an angle, so that the artfully sculpted line of brow and cheek and jaw was made manifest. He was leaning against the adobe wall in San Lucas Pueblo, hands in his trouser pockets, frowning slightly. Not award winning, she thought, but even on paper that sense of mystery was present in his carriage, in the pitch of his dark head, and Robin formed in her mind the word *Indianness* to describe it, because that's what it was to her. She and Adam were of the same human mold, but there were vast dissimilarities between them.

She looked once more at the picture she'd secretly snapped. What had Adam been thinking just then; why was there that distant look to him?

Robin could have sat in the back of her shop and studied the image of Adam all night. But it was nearly six, almost time for the special committee meeting to begin.

Adam was coming to the meeting. Knowing that in a few short minutes she'd see him again made her stomach feel queasy. Of course, she'd phoned Chaco Canyon on Sunday night in a state of panic. Then, when Adam had gotten hold of her Monday, she'd been relieved to hear that he wanted to help, to at least address her special committee meeting. He'd sounded genuinely concerned and anxious to be involved. And he'd seemed worried about her, and angry over the broken pot. But now she was beginning to feel foolish. It was a long drive into town from the canyon; surely this was a terrible inconvenience for Adam. Even Rod Cordova, when he'd finally gotten in touch about the smashed pot, had told her not to worry. "Keep your doors locked and leave the forgery business to the police," he'd said, "and I'm sure everything will be okay."

She could have called Adam again and told him not to bother coming into town after all. She *should* have. But she wanted to see him again.

Robin went into the bathroom and brushed her hair. She smoothed her short black denim skirt and tugged at her pink and gray striped top. Not that Adam would notice, but she couldn't help wanting to look her best. A little perfume, mascara, lipstick...

The harsh bright light above her head was not in the least flattering. She could see dark circles under her eyes, and the soft grooves framing her mouth seemed deeper. She was getting old. Thirty had come and gone and her youth with it. She'd never had a husband, not even a fiancé, really. Why not? Everyone loved Robin Hayle. She was lively and vital and *fun*. No party or gathering was complete unless she was invited and brought along her camera and told her crazy stories. But the men sensed that insecurity in her, that almost frantic need to belong. And they got scared off. Who wanted a desperate woman?

Adam also had seen through her carefree facade instantly and discounted her. He probably wouldn't even come tonight.

She snapped off the light and took a deep breath. She told herself that thirty-two was still young and that she had plenty of time to have a family. And she told herself that Adam was going to be there—he was probably already waiting, wondering where she was.

By six sharp all the committee members had gathered in the library of the *Palacio Real*. Julien announced that Adam Farwalker was expected and would make a presentation about prehistoric pottery and how to detect a forgery; there were a few murmurs and curious glances exchanged. "I'm certain Adam will arrive shortly," said Julien, but Robin wondered, and her heart beat a little faster.

She kept glancing at the clock: six-fifteen, six-twenty, six twenty-two. At six twenty-three, she crossed one leg over the other and pulled at her short skirt. Her palms were damp against her knee.

At six-thirty the library door opened and a cool breath of air swept in. Robin's head swiveled, a ready smile on her lips. But it was only a janitor, pulling his mop and bucket along. She turned back to the meeting and sighed.

It was six forty-three when the door opened again. This time Robin merely stared ahead. No point in revealing her disappointment. But then the empty chair next to her, the one she'd been saving, was being pulled aside and Adam was sitting down. "Sorry I'm so late," he whispered, "but something came up."

"Oh, that's all right," Robin said casually. "We're still hashing over old business. This will probably bore you to death. I shouldn't have gotten you into it."

"Nonsense," replied Adam. "I want to help in any way I can."

On the other side of her, Thad Mencimer nudged Robin. "Who's he again?" he asked loudly.

"My name—" Adam leaned forward and spoke across Robin's chest "—is Adam Farwalker."

Robin rolled her eyes and shot an annoyed glance at Thad.

"I think," Julien was saying, "that we should concentrate on suggestions as to how we can stop these counterfeit pieces from reaching the marketplace." He glanced around the table. "Any suggestions?"

So Adam had come after all, Robin mused, relieved and happy, a dozen pleasant emotions buffeting her simultaneously. She glanced sidelong at him, as if shifting naturally in her chair, a smile glued to her lips. He looked great. His strong features were set in an impassive expression, as if carved in stone, eternal and beautiful. Wearing a lightweight khaki sport coat with a yellow polo shirt beneath, he appeared relaxed and comfortable. Robin sighed.

Yet as happy as she was to see him, a part of her was ill-at-ease, feeling guilty for her alarmist tactics in getting him to come.

Now he had to sit and listen to the committee's problems. And he'd told her not to get involved in the question of the forgeries in the first place. He hadn't smiled at her or seemed pleased to be there; he was probably boiling inside. She could feel his body next to her as if it radiated heat, as if it were pressed up against her.

For all her obsession with Adam, it was not lost on Robin that the heavy lady, Madeline Lassiter, hadn't taken her eyes off him since he'd slipped into the room. Obviously Robin was not the only one who was captivated by him. But Adam himself seemed oblivious. Was he really so unaware of Madeline's attention—or Robin's?

Her anxiety grew. Maybe she shouldn't have called and left that message at Chaco Canyon. Maybe it would have been better if she'd never seen him again. She uncrossed her legs and sat there feeling brittle, as if she'd break if somebody dropped a pin. Everything was turning out all wrong.

Chuck Dalton was speaking. "The first thing we've got to do is lobby the state legislature," he was saying. Robin tried to concentrate.

"Lobby?" scoffed Thad. "Oh, *that's* really going to help. Brilliant idea."

Chuck shot him a look. "If you'd let me finish, I was going to say that the laws pertaining to the sale of artwork could be clarified and broadened."

"Oh, come on," piped up Thad.

"Now, Thad," said Ben Chavez, "I think Chuck's got a point."

On it went. There were some good ideas thrown up to

the committee, and some outlandish ones. Thad, always argumentative, came up with the suggestion that the police check all the artwork on sale in the local shops and carbon-date it, and even Robin had to laugh along with the rest of them. Only Adam sat there, unspeaking, glancing from one member to the next, his face utterly devoid of expression. Was he amused, interested or bored silly?

"Robin," said Julien, "surely you have an idea or two."

Jolted from her reverie, she sat a little straighter in her seat, aware that Adam's head had turned in her direction. She'd love to come up with something really clever. She folded her hands on the tabletop and cleared her voice. "There is something I believe might work as a starting point," she began. "I've been thinking along the lines of gaining the cooperation of the Indian artisans themselves. You know, go to the root of the problem."

"Oh, sure," said Thad, interrupting. "We don't even speak their language!"

Robin gave him a sharp glance. "Listen, Thad, why don't you let me finish?"

"Hear, hear," said Chuck, grinning.

"My suggestion is," Robin continued, trying to ignore Thad's unpleasant stare, "that we try to get the Indian community to organize. They could form their own association."

"I get it," chimed in Ben Chavez, "they could *police* themselves."

"Great idea," commented Madeline. She swiveled with amazing grace in her chair. "Mr. Farwalker, what do you think?" She held his gaze for an embarrassingly long time.

"Robin's idea is a sound one," he stated. "The Indian artisans have never been organized before. And like she pointed out, it's a start."

"Humph." Thad was impatiently checking his watch. "Are these meetings going to take all night or what?"

"Perhaps," said Julien, "we should break for dinner. I'd like Adam to have enough time to address us. After we all get a bite, we can meet back here at, say, nine?" All but Thad were in agreement, but no one moved for a moment, unsure and uncomfortable with Thad's rudeness.

Adam stood, turned toward the man and said in a deep, smooth voice, "I believe, Mr. Mencimer, that the majority rules." Then he took Robin's arm and led her out onto the street.

"Well," Robin said, "you sure told *him*."

They were standing beneath the portal of the *Palacio Real*, deserted now that the Indian women had packed up their wares and left for the day. September was just around the corner and the evening air was already crisp. In the mountains to the east, there were a few aspens whose leaves had changed and the last rays of the setting sun struck them, making them appear to be ablaze. The sun caught Adam, too. Robin gazed at him for a moment, watching the last light of day play on his strong face, turning his skin to a deep copper hue, his eyes seeming to glow with fire.

She felt that guilt sweep her again. He didn't really want to be there; he was merely living up to what he believed was an obligation. "Look," she said, "I feel really rotten for getting you into this. And now you'll have to stay in town till God knows what time…"

"Robin, listen," he said, his dark eyes coming to rest on her, "I would have driven into town just to see that broken pot alone and make sure you were all right. Don't you understand, this was all my doing? I'm the one who should apologize."

"I guess we could argue that one all night," she admitted. "So let's just say we're both at fault. Still, you'll have to let me cook you dinner or I'll really feel awful."

"I'm not too hungry, Robin; you don't have to go to any trouble."

"Maybe you're not," she stated, "but I'm starved. As

usual.'' And finally, as if she'd been waiting her whole life for it, Adam smiled at her warmly.

"That'll get you a three-course dinner," she said.

"What will?"

"Oh, never mind, let's just say you have a nice smile, Adam Farwalker, when you relax a little." She tucked her arm into his and led the way.

Of course, Robin had planned all along to fix a meal for Adam. She'd hurried to the store at lunchtime while Ericka had watched the shop, and she'd organized everything, even set the small table in her living room for the two of them with candles and dusty-rose linen, her good Lenox china and her mother's sterling silver. She unlocked her door and switched on the lights. Yes, the place was neat and tidy, the atmosphere intimate.

"Would you like a drink?" She tossed her purse on the couch and turned to face him, her hands on her hips. "I have some vodka and gin, there's tonic and some red wine, and, let's see…"

"A glass of wine will be fine," he replied. "But first, Robin, I'd like to see that broken pot."

She was sorry she showed it to him. On the walk over to her place he'd been almost jovial with her, talking about the meeting and even laughing once when Robin had asked if he'd noticed the attention Madeline had paid him. "I think the woman likes you," Robin had said, and he'd thrown back his dark head and laughed.

But now he stood fingering the shards of clay and looking grim. "You shouldn't be staying here alone," he said. "I don't like it at all."

"Oh, Adam, it's a warning, like you said. Nobody's going to hurt me."

"And now you're on that committee." He looked at her with a grave expression. "You should have told them no."

"I couldn't. I'm just not the type to turn tail and run."

"Still…"

"Still, what's done is done. Let's forget it and have dinner. Come on, please, you'll spoil my appetite."

"I doubt that," he replied, his attempt at humor not in the least lost on her.

When Robin had the time, she loved to cook. While Adam sat on the couch and leafed through a book on Southwest Indians, she whistled and hummed and popped in the oven two individual casseroles of blue corn tortillas filled with beans and cheese and smothered in her own hot salsa. The lettuce and tomatoes were already chopped for the topping, and the bowl of sour cream sat in the fridge. Bread, swimming in butter and garlic, rested on a baking sheet.

She began to cut up a cantaloupe for dessert, wondering if he liked real whipped cream with it as much as she did. "Dinner will be ready in ten minutes," she called then glanced in his direction.

He'd been watching her; he looked down at the book too quickly and flipped a page. Her heart gave a glad little leap. *So he isn't totally impervious to me.*

She began to whistle again and glanced at him once more but this time he was buried in his reading.

Robin checked the casseroles: the salsa wasn't yet bubbling. She leaned her elbows on the counter and tapped her foot. "Do you think that book is accurate?" she asked.

"It's pretty superficial," he commented.

"So it doesn't catch the flavor?"

Adam shook his head. "It's what the tourists want to believe."

"What's it really like then?"

"Being an Indian or living in the Southwest?"

"Well, both, I suppose."

"I can only speak for the Apache, you understand," he said, "but for the last hundred years it's been a struggle."

"A struggle?"

"Yes. Between the old ways and the new. Very few of

the young people make a success leaving the reservation. Many of them go off to college and find that they can't make it there.''

''But *you* did, Adam.''

''Not easily. The difference is that my family has never lived on a reservation. But the problems still exist. We have our tradition, our own way of thinking, and we like our freedom.''

''But you're free.''

''An Apache is free, Robin,'' he said, ''when he can roam a land where there are no fences, no housing developments, no malls...'' Adam smiled darkly. ''It can never be the same again.''

''You'd be happier hunting and fishing and wandering the hills?''

''Me? I don't really know. I can only speak for my race as a whole. We were far better off before the white eyes—'' and at that Adam laughed ''—came to the West. We're born hunters. We're closest to our true selves when out in the open. It's in our blood.''

''Adam,'' she said carefully, ''are you happy, then, you know, doing what you do?''

He thought for a minute, turning pages in her book idly. ''I am happy, I suppose. I'm one of the few who has successfully bridged the two worlds. I don't think for a minute I could survive on the land as my ancestors did.''

But she wondered about that.

''There's no easy solution,'' he added. ''Time marches on, and the Apache as a nation are going to have to march with it or disappear as a race.'' He looked thoughtful for a moment, then continued. ''An Indian feels as if he's betrayed himself and his people if he lives in the outside world, yet he can't have success in terms of that world if he stays totally within his tradition. Most opt for tradition. My family has tried to live with a foot in each. It can work, but sometimes it isn't easy.''

"It must be challenging," Robin agreed, but he only nodded then went back to his book.

The candles were lit, the music turned low as Robin served her dinner. She sat down, put the fine linen napkin in her lap and gave Adam a smile. "I hope you like this recipe," she said.

Adam was pensive during the meal. Oh, she drew him out about his two sisters and their families and his uncle, his mother's brother, who lived on the reservation and was a "singer." He used the Apache word; Robin got the impression that it meant a combination of doctor and religious leader.

"A man's maternal uncle is a very important figure in his life. My uncle taught me a lot about myself and my clan," Adam explained.

"Do you have a big clan?"

A corner of his mouth lifted in amusement. "I think there are about a hundred in New Mexico, and that's just my mother's side, the turtle people."

"Wow," said Robin, "a family like that must be a real nice thing to have. Someday I'd like to have a big family, too…" When he said nothing she shrugged and went on. "So your uncle is sort of your mentor."

"I guess you could say that. He gave me my secret name, my war name."

"What is it?"

"I can't tell you."

"Oh."

"Only my family knows it."

"Now you've got me curious," she remarked lightly, but she felt the stab of rejection—she was the outsider again, not privy to the secrets that bound Adam's people together. It only brought home to her how far apart their cultures stood. She wondered what the odds were of two such different people ever getting together.

He had fallen silent and become contemplative. She certainly hoped that she hadn't been the cause of his withdrawal. Maybe she shouldn't have brought up the subject of Indians; maybe Adam wasn't adjusted to both worlds as he let on.

"So you studied archeology in Albuquerque?" she asked nonchalantly.

"A long time ago," he replied.

"Was it difficult for you? I mean, the change?"

"Sure. I had my problems. A lot of white kids do, too."

"Oh, I didn't mean..."

"I had to take all that my uncle had taught me, the myths, the stories of coyote men and ghosts and taboos, and reduce them to rational terms. Like the dietary laws of Jews and Moslems or the demons of Christianity. But educated people do that every day."

Adam went back to his meal. She'd tried and tried to get past the superficial conversation, but it seemed the more she delved, the more he fell back to lecturing, as if she were one of his students. It made her want to gnash her teeth. He wasn't this way with everyone, either. No, she'd seen him animated with others, even warm. Why couldn't she elicit that reaction from the man?

Robin looked up from her plate and once again caught him staring at her with those Indian-dark eyes. She felt her breath catch and was suddenly inclined to talk a mile a minute, but something in those expressionless eyes held her silent, aware only of the tension pulsing between them. What was she seeing in his face? Was it sadness? Pain?

The urge to come right out and ask him became overpowering. She had to swallow convulsively to keep quiet. She even reached for her wineglass and took several long drinks, hoping the urge to pry into his private life would pass. What had she thought to accomplish by asking him to dinner?

She glanced at the wall clock in her kitchen. Eight-twenty, it read. My God, how could it be so early? The minutes were crawling by, as if bogged down in a mire.

Maybe if she broke a glass or pounded the table, it would break the sticky silence.

Robin sat there demurely, the food gummy in her throat, those horrible minutes slugging along at a snail's pace.

It was finally Adam who put down his fork and spoke. "Robin," he began, holding her gaze, "there's something..." But he never finished and she couldn't find it in herself to press him.

She must have been wearing her distress like a red flag, because several long moments later he said, "Look, I guess I'm pretty lousy company right now."

"Is something wrong, Adam?" she asked, her voice scratchy and dry.

"Nothing's wrong. Let's just say I'm worried about your safety."

"But I'm fine, honest, I am. If someone wanted to harm me they'd have already done it. You know that, don't you?"

"It may look that way," he said, "but I still feel you shouldn't be taking risks."

"I'm not."

"Just being on this new committee is risky."

"I don't believe that."

"Then you're only being stubborn."

Robin raised a brow. "Maybe I am, at that."

She did notice one thing, however; Adam had eaten his whole dinner, not to mention three pieces of garlic bread. For a not-too-hungry man, he'd done fine.

He even said, "You know, your tortillas are better than my mother's." Then, giving Robin one of those rare smiles, he added, "But don't tell her I said so."

"I won't. And thank you, I enjoy cooking." With another man, she would have quipped that the way to a man's heart was through his stomach, but Adam probably wouldn't appreciate her stab at humor. Instead, she poured herself half a glass more of wine and searched her brain frantically for an avenue that might lead to comprehending the man.

Over dessert he looked at her more and more; it seemed as if he was weighing something in his mind. It made Robin squirm restlessly and chatter too much again to ease that persistent feeling of discomfort. And yet, she slowly discovered, her tension was not entirely unpleasant; rather it was tinged with anticipation. Her stomach fluttered and her skin felt too sensitive, as if the air in the room was scraping it. And still he watched her, questioning now, deciding.

Finally, mercifully, it was time to clear the table and go. Adam helped. They each made several trips into the kitchen, back and forth, carrying plates and glasses, napkins and the bread basket. Robin dropped a fork, bent to retrieve it, and so did Adam.

"Here, I've got it," he said, and she found herself still stooped, staring directly into his eyes, their faces only inches apart.

For a flash of time she thought he was going to kiss her. It was in his eyes like a fire; it was on his parted lips and in the set of his shoulders. She held her breath, feeling a weakness in her limbs, a delicious pounding in her ears. And he did take her hands in his, but instead of drawing her to him, he helped her to her feet.

"Oh...thanks," she mumbled as he handed her the fork, "I could have gotten it," and she gave a nervous little laugh that was hideously transparent. She nudged past him and into the cramped kitchen where she hid her face for a moment, running water in the sink, busying herself.

She was wondering desperately how she was going to deal with her embarrassment when suddenly he was behind her, so close she could feel his breath in her hair. She shut her eyes, expectant, afraid, trembling. He was touching her lightly, his fingers on the curve of her waist, and she leaned back against him and drew in a ragged breath. His other hand was in her hair then and he was lifting it to one side.

Robin felt his lips on the back of her neck, softly tracing a path to her earlobe. She could feel her breath quickening, and little stabs of pleasure deep in her stomach. He whispered something, but she barely heard it, wanting only for him to turn her around, to feel that sensual mouth on hers, to taste him.

She was never certain how long they stood there like that in her close kitchen or if she actually answered. The flow of time seemed to have paused, as if it, too, awaited Adam's decision. And Robin could only sag against his strong body and yearn to feel those arms around her, pressing her to his chest.

Somewhere she could hear the tap water running but his lips were still brushing her neck, and she only thought of Adam—he had taken over her senses, the space they stood in, time.

It must have been her confusion that kept Robin from realizing he had moved away from her. The running water was slowly coming into focus and there were the dishes just as she'd left them—hours ago, it seemed.

Feeling crept back into her limbs and she was aware of a strange, acute sense of emptiness. Where was he? But there he was, in her living room, standing at the window, gazing out into nothingness. She leaned her whole body weight against the sink and felt the cold stainless steel press into her belly.

Adam turned away from the window eventually and she heard him say, "It's almost nine, we better be going." Her heart sank like a stone to her feet.

He behaved in every way as if nothing whatsoever had happened back in her kitchen. He was polite, unerringly so, and proper to a fault as they walked together back to the library at the Governor's Palace. It took every ounce of strength Robin possessed to stride alongside him in silence. But she knew if she opened her mouth all sorts of things would come tumbling out—things she would surely regret.

"Ah, there you are," said Julien, who had waited out front for them. "Adam, I hope you didn't take offense at Mr. Mencimer's rudeness earlier."

"Not at all," said Adam.

"How glad I was to see you put him in his place! What a delight." Then Julien turned to Robin and took her hand in both of his. "You are such a clever woman, Robin Hayle, for thinking to bring Adam along. We are all most grateful and anxious to hear him. *Gracias*, my dear." He lifted her hand to his lips and kissed it.

When Adam stood to speak everyone was attentive, even Thad. Robin, able to be more objective again with Adam at a distance, was proud of him, childishly proud.

"Is anyone here familiar with the Archeological Resource Protection Act?" he began, and everyone was eager to comment. He had them eating out of his hand in short order. Robin was impressed. She sat without fidgeting, totally attentive, unable to keep from recalling the feel of his lips on her neck. She had an almost uncontrollable urge to lift her hair and touch the spot that still tingled, but he'd see, he'd know.

"A true Socorro pot in good condition," he was saying, "can bring up to twenty-four thousand dollars. Of course, anyone with skill can paint a black-on-white design over an unpainted antique that's all but worthless. And there you have a forgery."

"The paint's new," said Thad, "you'd think any idiot could spot it." He folded his arms across his chest and grinned.

"You would think so, wouldn't you?" countered Adam. "The trouble is, if the pot's been fired by a clever artisan, and aged with the right materials, it's very hard for even an expert to identify."

"There must be tests or something," said Madeline.

"Sure," put in Chuck, "there's acetone, for one. It won't take off really old paint."

"That's correct," said Adam, "and black light can be used to detect a forgery, but there again, it would take an expert. There's a lab àt Los Alamos that tests a lot of artifacts. Unfortunately, it's time-consuming and costly."

"Maybe we could test our own stuff," said Thad.

"But," Adam interjected, "do you have the equipment for thermoluminescence testing, Mr. Mencimer?"

"Well, no, but..."

Julien stood for a moment. "I think Adam has a point here. Running our own tests on artifacts is impractical, and expensive, I'm sure."

"Well, I, for one," Chuck stated, "intend to stick with baskets and rugs. They're easier to verify as authentic."

"And the profit is better, too," Madeline said. "Gosh, a real old Navaho rug can sell for up to a hundred thousand."

"If you can get your hands on one." Thad made his humphing noise. "I say, let's get our artwork checked by a museum expert or something."

Robin saw Adam raise a dark brow. "I hate to put a damper on that," said Adam smoothly, "but there are very few true experts working in the museums. Maybe one or two in all New Mexico could spot or run tests on a forg-ery. It's an exacting science."

"So Adam," said Robin, "what *do* we do?"

He looked at her for a second and she thought she detected a softening in his expression. "There are positive steps the business community can take," he said, his attention back on the group. "For one, I would suggest a pamphlet be printed and distributed. On it could be a list of agencies and labs who run the tests we were discussing. And also I'd include a list of reputable independent art dealers, people who can be trusted thoroughly. The pamphlet," he went on, looking each committee members in the eye for a moment, "should also make broad suggestions that could be followed. Things like only dealing with licensed, reputable middlemen, and spending those extra dollars to have a so-called valuable antique tested for authenticity.''

Adam's words flowed easily over Robin as she sat listening, almost transfixed. He was such a vital man, so efficient, so self-contained. It was the Apache part of Adam that made him so fascinating to her, so *different*. And it was, paradoxically, the Apache in Adam that made him impossible for her to reach. Was there a place they could meet, a common ground?

She couldn't take her eyes off his face, his strong brown neck, his capable hands when he made a significant gesture.

Body language, they called it. And Adam's was gentle but commanding. Even Thad had shut up and quit interrupting. Amazing. Wouldn't it have been wonderful, mused Robin, to have had Adam as a professor?

"Also," he was saying, "I think Robin's idea should be pursued. Help the Indian artisans to organize their own association. The majority of the artists are honest, hard-working people and have reputations to maintain. The few rotten eggs in the basket could be located and, once found out, no one would deal with them.''

"Oh, excellent!' said Julien.

"It's an idea.'' Adam put his hands on the lectern, relaxed, casual, in complete control of the group.

He spoke until well past ten. And then, when the meeting was adjourned, Chuck and Julien both kept him tied up talking for some time out in front of the *Palacio*. Robin hung back; she'd said all she needed to at the meeting. In fact, her idea, along with the pamphlet, had gone over better than any. So she stood beneath the portal, hugged her pink and gray shirt around her and leisurely studied the man who, only a short time ago, had put a hand on her waist and kissed the back of her neck.

She could almost feel that sensual mouth brushing her

earlobe as she stood waiting in the shadows. At that moment in her kitchen he'd wanted her. So what had stopped him?

"*Adios*," she heard Julien saying.

Chuck, too, was moving away. He waved at Robin. "See you tomorrow. Maybe you and Shelly can get up a tennis game now that the town's quieting down."

"I'd like that," replied Robin as she watched him head toward his van.

Alone at last, she thought. "Well," began Robin, "that was a long night. But productive. Don't you think so?"

"I hope I was of some help," he replied.

"Oh, you were," she said enthusiastically. She wondered just how long they were going to stand there on the deserted street and discuss business. Had Adam forgotten that brief, wonderful moment of intimacy between them? "Well," she said again, "it is getting late. I should probably…"

"Of course. I'll walk you home."

"You don't have to, I mean…"

"I want to, Robin. At least I'll know you're safely inside."

"You're not still thinking someone might be in my place waiting?" asked Robin, striding next to him.

"What I'm thinking," said Adam, "is that I wish you weren't staying there alone."

"But Rod is still sending a car around to check and besides, you know how I feel on the subject."

"I certainly do," he replied and because of the light tone of his voice, she could imagine that warm smile of his. He ought to smile all the time, she mused.

It felt *right*, strolling beside him in the darkness. It felt as if the most natural thing in the world would be to go home together and let their emotions have their way. In fact, she decided, everything just now felt exactly perfect. The brisk night air fanning her face, the sound of their footfalls on the brick street, that singular, embracing smell of Old Santa Fe, a mature aroma of aged adobe and century-old trees, of grass and dry earth. His hand touched her elbow as they rounded a corner, and her knees felt as if they were about to buckle.

"Are you driving back to Chaco Canyon?" Robin ventured. She glanced over at him and saw his profile, dark and shadowed, strong, evocative.

"No," he replied, "it's too late."

Her heart lurched in her chest.

"No," he repeated, "I guess I'll drive up to the hacienda instead."

"Oh."

Dutifully Adam unlocked her door and looked around inside. "Just in case," he said. Then they were standing in the entranceway—close. She knew that in a moment he would leave. She had to do something, to let him know, to hold him there somehow, even for only a minute more. To let him go, to see him disappear down that narrow staircase, was inconceivable.

She took a very deep breath. "Stay," she said. "Stay here with me." She knew her cheeks were flaming and her plea had been too bold—she didn't care. Suddenly, as if he'd only just registered her words, a tide of emotions played across his features: surprise, indecision, finally, amazingly, need.

He said absolutely nothing. But Robin barely had time to think before his hands came up and grasped her arms, urgently, almost painfully. Then, before her heart could beat again, he'd pulled her to him and was crushing his lips to hers. The bursting forth of his passion seemed to drain her of all emotion, all thought—she knew only a primitive urge to be possessed by him, to possess him herself.

Robin put her arms around his back and gripped his shirt with her fingers, feeling his muscles ripple beneath her touch, savoring him. The entire long length of her body was pressed to his, molded to it, fitting perfectly.

She felt as if they were already in bed, locked together as one, and yet it was just a kiss.

Adam kissed her and held her and moved his strong hands along her hips, the curve of her breasts, into her hair. Her body quivered in anticipation, melted against his shamelessly.

She was lifted off her feet, held suspended by the force of his awakened passion, when abruptly she seemed to be falling, stumbling, reaching out for something to grasp onto, reaching out for Adam.

He'd let her go. Suddenly and without warning, he'd dropped his hold and backed away. She saw him as if through a haze, his big body seeming to sag, a look on his face she was helpless to decipher.

"Adam," she whispered.

When his voice emerged it sounded totally alien, a stranger's voice, strangled and in pain. "I have to go," he got out. "Robin...Robin, I'm so very sorry." And then he was gone, silently, swiftly, swallowed by the night shadows.

CHAPTER EIGHT

ROBIN STOOD STARING at the closed door. Tears welled up in her eyes—tears of want and need and frustration. The question hammered at her again: *why?* He'd wanted her. She knew that. A woman didn't mistake an outburst of desire like that. He'd touched her with a desperate urgency and then…and then he'd just turned off, as if a wellspring of gushing water had been quenched.

Why?

Slowly, painfully, she walked into her bedroom. She was ashamed and humiliated. Rejected. She wished she could feel angry; perhaps that would come later. Anger would be a step up from the misery that entangled her like a sticky web.

She turned off the lights and lay down in bed with her clothes on, staring into the darkness. Tears trickled out of the corners of her eyes, sliding into her hair. She hadn't the energy to wipe them away.

Sleep finally came, a relief, a sodden, restless time of forgetting.

Things, of course, looked different in the morning. The lemon-yellow sun slanted into her apartment, the weatherman called for another clear day in the seventies, and Robin whistled to herself in the shower: "I'm gonna wash that man right outta my hair."

"Good song," she said to herself staunchly, scrubbing shampoo into her hair.

She'd made up her mind. Life was going to be much simpler from now on. She was going to drop the whole subject of forged pottery; she wasn't even going to think about it again. She was going to quit that damn committee. They'd have to find someone else. Enough was enough.

And—above all—she was going to forget Adam Farwalker, erase him, wipe the slate clean and start over.

There were lots of men in Santa Fe. Tall ones, too, she'd bet. Men who appreciated a fun-loving, warm-hearted lady and who communicated on her wavelength.

Sure.

She was still whistling as she drove to her shop and parked right in front in an empty spot, which never would have been there in the busy season.

She had an appointment after lunch. Ericka was coming in at noon to take over, as the portrait was going to be shot outside. Thank heaven for Ericka. Robin wondered what she was going to do when Ericka went back to college. Oh, boy. But then, it wouldn't be very busy, so she'd just manage on her own.

"I'm gonna wash that man right outta my hair!" she sang as she unlocked her front door and let herself in, turned on the lights and flipped the Closed sign to Open.

Things were definitely looking up.

Robin's appointment was with a man from New York who had bought a second home in Santa Fe. He was a small, pale man with tinted glasses, a clothing manufacturer, straight from Seventh Avenue—Gary Kahn.

He'd always wanted to be a cowboy. Robin had the outfit ready: chaps, plaid shirt, boots, rope, hat, even tattered long underwear. Gary wanted to be photographed on a horse, lariat in hand, rifle in the scabbard of the saddle. The works.

Robin had everything set but the location and the horse. The outskirts of Santa Fe abounded with dude ranches and stables where Robin knew she could rent a horse.

She had a better idea, however. She told herself firmly

that the shoot would be more authentic this way, so she picked up the phone and called the Farwalkers' number.

Christina answered. "Robin, how nice to hear from you. Nothing's wrong, is it?"

"No, no, it's not that at all." Robin explained about Gary Kahn's portrait. "So I wondered if I could use one of your horses. I'd pay you, of course."

"Oh, what fun! Could I watch? Oh, Ray will be delighted. My dear, I must have you do a family portrait one day. Goodness, there won't be a charge for the horse. It's our pleasure."

And so it was all set up for one o'clock and Robin hung up with a ridiculous feeling of satisfaction, as if she'd put one over on Adam. Well, at least his mother liked her!

At noon Ericka arrived, adorable in a Western-style blouse with piping around the yoke and a full flower-print prairie skirt. "Wow," she said, "did Mom tell you I had a call from the police again?"

"Again? But I thought all that was cleared up."

"I guess not, Miss Hayle. This Detective Cordova still thinks teenagers broke in here. Why does everyone always blame teens?" Ericka pouted, two dimples appearing in her cheeks.

"I don't know," admitted Robin, "but when you're all grown up, remember this incident and don't be in too big a hurry to pin the blame on some poor kid."

"Boy, I'll *never* be as creepy as those cops," said Ericka firmly. "I can hardly wait until I'm out of here and back at college."

Robin smiled. "What about Shane?"

"Oh, Shane goes to the University of Colorado up in Boulder. It's only about fifty miles away from my school."

"Sounds like fun times ahead," said Robin and finally got a big grin out of Ericka.

Gary Kahn came in early, and Robin could tell he was

excited. He changed into his cowboy outfit in the back of
her store and emerged a changed man; he walked taller,
his spurs clanked aggressively, his shoulders were
squared. His shirtsleeves were rolled up negligently, allowing just a bit of ragged underwear cuff to show.

"This is great," he said eagerly. "Now, where's the
horse?"

"The horse, Mr. Kahn, is a real working cow pony on
a ranch run by some friends of mine. Shall we take your
car or mine?"

Gary was impressed, but he handled it well with his
newfound macho image. He shook hands gravely with
Ray Farwalker, remarked upon the beauty of the weather
and Santa Fe and expressed interest in Christina's yearly
fund-raising dinner.

"Well, next year, Mr. Kahn, you and your wife will be
on my list," said Christina. "You give me your address
before you leave today. And be prepared to bid high."

"Oh, I will, Mrs. Farwalker. It's a worthy cause." Then
Gary Kahn added, "And thank you, ma'am."

Robin spent about an hour taking photographs of Gary
on horseback. Ray and Christina watched; a few ranch
hands gathered around and gave Gary pointers on how to
hold the lariat. One of them whistled so that the horse's
ears would perk up nicely for the shots. Another adjusted
the bandanna around Gary's neck just so.

"Great shots, Mr. Kahn," Robin said, folding up her
tripod. "The proof's will be ready the morning after
next."

"I'll be there. I'm flying back to New York next Monday, so I'd like to have them all picked out before then.
What a kick. Say, do you think these folks deserve tips?"

"Well, not the Farwalkers, but I'll bet the hands
wouldn't say no."

So Gary dispensed good cheer and twenties and Robin
drove him back to Santa Fe while he grinned and slapped
his Stetson on his knee like a pro.

"Robin," said Ericka, when they got back, "a lady was here looking for you."

"Mrs. Hartmann again?"

"No, an Indian lady. She was very sweet. I told her you'd be back about three."

"An Indian lady?"

"I guess so. She didn't say what she wanted. So, how'd the shoot go?"

"Great. I'm dying to see the proofs myself."

Gary came out of the back, a small, pale man with thin hair and tinted glasses on. A hint of his former expansiveness still remained in his walk and his smile. "See you day after tomorrow. Thanks, Miss Hayle." He shook her hand, grinned and left. Robin looked down; a hundred-dollar bill lay on her palm.

"Wow," said Ericka softly.

"Split it with you," said Robin, "and don't argue."

Ericka went home at four. The afternoon was as hot and still as summer—siesta time. Robin took out her copy of *Santa Fe Style*, a book of wonderful photographs of her adopted city, and began to study it.

She was examining a photograph of an old Santa Fe kitchen, white-walled, clean, spare, its typical corner fireplace raised so that the hearth turned into a bench, a bunch of ears of dried corn hanging from a post, when the bell tinkled and someone came into her shop.

She looked up, put a welcoming smile on her face and was about to say, "May I help you?" when something held her.

The woman stopped inside the door as if reluctant to go on. She was elderly, a Pueblo Indian, dressed traditionally in a calico skirt and blouse, a brightly colored shawl over her shoulders and many strings of beads and turquoise around her neck and wrists. Her thick, straight hair was streaked with gray, cut into blunt bangs, a Dutch-boy style that was immensely flattering on the Pueblo women. Her outfit, in fact, very much resembled that of Mrs. Hartmann, but this was no costume.

"Excuse me," the woman said. Her voice was slightly accented and timid, her sweet face creased with lines of worry. Was she lost?

"May I help you?" Robin asked, her finger still marking a page in her book.

"You are Miss Robin Hayle?"

"Yes." Robin cocked her head in question.

"You do not know me, Miss Hayle, but I know who you are."

Robin put the book down on the counter. "Oh, you're the lady who was looking for me earlier. I'm sorry, I was out on a job. Did you want a portrait done?" Somehow, even as she said the words, Robin knew this gentle Indian lady had not come to be photographed.

"Oh, no, please, that is not why I am here. I only wish to talk to you." She was shy yet dignified, proud, with a handsome bone structure under velvety, lined skin. Her hands, Robin noted, were small and square, work worn, with short fingernails and rough knuckles. Hands that had seen toil.

"Well, you seem to know me. May I ask your name? You know, you'd take a lovely picture. Are you sure you're not interested..."

"Oh, please, Miss Hayle." The woman held up a hand. "I have come to see you on an entirely different matter. My name is of no importance to you, but what I have to tell you may be."

"Okay. Come on in back and sit down and tell me. Would you like some coffee? No? Tea then?"

The woman followed her into the small office. Robin turned the hot plate on while her mind rattled with curiosity. "Please sit down," she said, indicating a chair, fussing with tea bags and cups. "I really am curious."

"You were in San Lucas Pueblo looking for a man," said the woman.

Robin nearly dropped a spoon. Her heart squeezed with sudden excitement. Casually she said, "Oh? You live there?"

"No, no. I live…somewhere else."

"I'm sorry, I don't understand." She handed the woman a cup and sat down facing her.

"Of course not. I will start at the beginning." Nervously the lady played with her spoon handle. She looked straight into Robin's eyes and her gaze darkened. "You see, I am a potter myself."

Of course, her hands…

"I know the man you were looking for," said the woman in her soft, apprehensive voice.

Deliberately Robin set her own cup down, afraid that she might spill it in her agitation. "Oh, I see."

"I have known this man for many years. He is a fine potter. He is very afraid now, because you and…a man were asking about his pot, one you took a picture of some weeks ago, and it is said his work is a copy of a very famous one."

Robin let out her breath slowly. It was hard to believe, but this stranger was telling her the whole story. She had to take great care not to scare the woman off.

"This friend of mine, he is innocent. He did not know the pot was going to be sold. He was asked only to reproduce it. Truly. He never knew he was breaking the law."

"I believe you," Robin answered.

"He is innocent, but he is very afraid that if he goes to the authorities they will not believe him."

"Yes, I understand." Robin pushed her hair off her shoulders. "But maybe he would talk to me."

"I don't know."

Robin drew in a lungful of air. "What is his name? How would I contact him?"

The woman looked down at her strong, blunt hands. Her voice was so soft Robin had to strain to hear. "He is

John Martinez. He remembers you. He does not want any trouble, but he might talk to you.''

"You'd tell him I mean him no harm? I only want to find out who asked him to make the pot."

The woman met her gaze and nodded slowly. "I want to stop these men, too. I told John… These people exploit us. It is not fair. But we are afraid to go to the police. So many years and still we are not always treated fairly…''

Robin reached out and put her hand over the woman's. "I know. I understand. Change comes slowly. But if you could tell John Martinez that I won't give his secret away. I can help. Please. I'd love to speak to him."

"I don't know. Maybe. I will tell him." Then she held her head high. "If you try to find him yourself he will disappear. You must wait. I will let you know."

"Yes, sure, whatever he wants."

"You will tell no one?''

Robin shook her head. "No, I won't."

"John is sorry he ever made those pots, and all the trouble he went to in order to make the firecloud appear in the right spot. He is afraid." The woman was growing perturbed, her fingers nervously plucking at the fringe on her shawl.

"Please, don't worry. You can trust me," Robin said fervently. "How do I get hold of you?''

The woman rose, shaking her head. Her heavy earrings, butterflies, swung gracefully under her curtain of hair. "No, no, please, you will wait."

"Okay."

"John does not know I am here." She started toward the front of the shop, striding quickly, wanting to be gone.

"Tell him not to worry, okay? I'm harmless." Robin tried a joke, following the woman out into the front of her shop. "Well, thanks for coming. I really appreciate it. You will get in touch again, won't you?''

But the lady never even turned around; she walked

straight to the door, slipped through it and disappeared around the corner.

"Whew!" Robin said aloud, trembling in reaction. And then she realized in dismay that she had no idea who the stranger was or where she was from. She should have tried harder to find out.

Intrigue, danger, mystery. *Wow,* thought Robin, *I've solved the case.* Well, part of it, anyway.

John Martinez. She had a name now to put to the face she recalled from that first day at the pueblo. A middle-aged man of medium height, thin and sinewy, with the large, strong-looking hands of an artisan. His English had been accented, but he'd been proud of his work, and friendly. He must be innocent, Robin reflected. Otherwise, why would he have let her see that pot, much less photograph it?

So…who had requested John Martinez to make the copy? And how was she going to find out?

It occurred to Robin that she was being very naive. Perhaps there was no other party who had hoodwinked John Martinez into making counterfeits. Wasn't it much more likely that he was doing it on his own? That sweet old lady who'd just left could have been his sister or aunt or something, and might have been sent deliberately to throw Robin off Martinez's trail. Wouldn't that scenario better explain his fear and reluctance to show himself or go to the authorities?

The bell tinkled. Robin looked up. "Oh, hi, Shel. How's it going?" She had an urge to tell Shelly the story of her visitor, but something stopped her, some ill-defined, vague feeling that she better get it straightened out in her own mind before telling anyone else. Besides, she'd promised the woman not to talk about it.

"Slower than molasses. Chuck's reading magazines and I'm bored."

"Go home and get caught up on your housework."

"Are you kidding?" Shelly made a face. "You know,

Chuck was really impressed by your friend's little talk last night. He checked every pot we've got in the store. He'd like to get them all tested at Los Alamos, but it'd cost an arm and a leg." She walked around, ostensibly studying photographs. "He said you and Adam went off together for dinner."

"You're fishing, Shelly."

"Unabashedly."

"Nothing happened." Robin turned away, not wanting to meet her friend's curious gaze. "I told you he wasn't interested. Now will you just drop it?"

Shelly held her hands up. "Okay, okay, sorry. I just have this awful urge to be a matchmaker. I can't help it. And you've got to admit that man is a catch if I ever saw one."

"Maybe for somebody else."

Shelly stared at her for a moment then came close and put a hand on her arm. "He hurt you, didn't he?"

"Oh, for goodness' sake, I hardly know him, Shel."

"Funny, he didn't strike me as a woman-killer."

"Oh, it's probably me. I have a tendency to be a little pushy. Men run screaming in fright from my attentions." She tried to be witty, to brush it off, her usual reaction to being hurt. Funny girl.

"They're all cowards. Never mind," said Shelly kindly. "They just don't appreciate a good woman."

Shelly's departure left Robin in a strange mood. On one hand, she wished Shelly had not brought up the subject of Adam again, because it brought back all the anxiety, focused and in sharp relief. On the other hand, her mind was still working on the problem of John Martinez and what to do about *that*. Restlessly Robin puttered around her shop, answered the phone and went through the motions of closing up at five.

On the drive home, Robin toyed with her choices. She could report John Martinez to Rod Cordova. But that thought was dismissed as quickly as it came; Rob would think her a lunatic by now. Martinez would disappear; there would be no proof of her story. No, that was not the thing to do. Besides, she'd promised the woman. What if she convened her subcommittee? The one she'd decided that morning she was going to quit, she reminded herself. But what, really, was she able to tell them? And what could they do about it? After all, she had no way of getting John Martinez to show up and give them his story, did she?

She had to do *something*. She had to get some kind of help, advice on the next logical step.

It came to her suddenly, as she pulled up in front of her building and parked. It hit her with logic and clarity and no small measure of spite—she'd dump this problem right where it belonged, in Adam Farwalker's lap.

CHAPTER NINE

THE LAND GRADUALLY FLATTENED, growing browner and drier, a stark, barren expanse of high mesas slashed by jagged arroyos. Off to the north a large bird—a hawk, a buzzard?—circled ominously, hunting.

Why was she doing this?

To solve a crime? To see that justice prevailed? To protect innocent people? To see Adam Farwalker again?

The sun pressed heavily on the parched land; Robin wondered how hot it must have been in midsummer. How did people live here? Yet there was a harsh beauty about this bleak corner of the world, a beauty of clean lines, of spareness, of wide vistas, of subtle colors and sharp-edged shadows.

She sped along the empty highway toward Chaco Canyon in her car. It was farther than she'd thought, nearly two hundred miles. Checking her road map, she calculated that she'd be there in an hour or so.

What would Adam do when he saw her? Would he smile, or would his face close, rejecting her, uncomfortable with her presence? Well, she told herself, she had a darn good reason to seek him out this time.

She stopped for gas at a lone station in Pueblo Pintado.

"Goin' to Chaco Canyon?" asked the bearded old-timer, as he cleaned her dusty windshield with a stained cloth.

"Uh, yes, how did you…?"

"Yer from the city. What else would you be doin' out here?" he said, chuckling. "It's forty-five minutes from here, that is if you don't stick to the speed limit too close.''

Although Robin was anxious to get going, she couldn't resist an opportunity. ''I wonder,'' she began, ''if you'd mind doing me a favor?''

He raised a bushy gray brow. ''And what would that be, miss?''

''Well, as you can see, I'm new to the area and I'd love to get a picture or two...''

''There's plenty round these parts to photograph, miss. You can leave your car right here, if you like.''

''Well, I was hoping I could take *your* picture.''

''Me?'' He poked himself in the chest with a grimy finger.

He had that kind of lived-in face, Robin knew, that went with the land, that had been weathered and lined and turned to leather by a lifetime under the Southwestern sun. She shot an entire roll of film, using the mesaland to the south for the background. He was quite a subject, puffing up for Robin, posing, tugging on his old sweat-stained brown hat for her. Through her lens she saw at least two great shots, which was a blessing, because a truly good photo might only come at the rate of one in a thousand.

''That it?'' he asked when they headed back toward her car.

''That's it.'' Robin pulled out a twenty and forced it on him. ''Take it,'' she urged, ''you earned every penny of it.''

''Well, okay, then. Now you drive careful and enjoy the canyon, hear?''

When Robin started her car up she was tempted to turn around and head back to Santa Fe; it was only the old man's cheerful smile that kept her headed northwest. The truth was that she was too embarrassed, after their conversation, to make a fool of herself and turn around.

Was she disgraceful, she thought once again as she raced along, only using the Indian lady's visit as an excuse to see Adam? How could she so easily have forgotten her promises to him to play it safe, to not get involved? How could she have forgotten the warnings she'd already received?

At times she wondered if there were someone watching her, following her. She glanced in the rearview mirror; the road stretched for miles behind her, ending in a shimmering mirage, as if a lake had appeared where seconds before there had been only dust and rocks and clumps of mesquite.

Adam. He was like a mirage. Sometimes he was there, a welcome, refreshing sight, and then he was gone and all that remained was emptiness, barren ground.

Why?

To the west, a line of pewter-colored storm clouds moved along the horizon. Perhaps there would be one of those late afternoon thunderstorms that were so common in New Mexico, although it was so perfectly, exquisitely blue overhead it was hard to imagine rain. But the clouds could rush in like a conquering army, drop their loads and hasten on, leaving a rainbow and an incredible sunset behind.

Nothing could survive on this sun-baked terrain, thought Robin. Yet it did: brush, mesquite, sage and bunchgrass. Squat twisted trees grew along the dry river beds and piñon on the hills. There were no animals that Robin could see, not even a prairie dog or a rabbit, nothing but the occasional snake carcass making a question mark on the road, sizzling in the unforgiving sun.

It was a relief to drive up to the visitor's center. A sign announced that she was entering Chaco Canyon National Historical Park, under the auspices of the National Park Service. A pleasant-looking man answered her question: "Oh, Adam, yes. They're working at Pueblo Bonito. Just follow the road. It's a few miles, on your right. You can't miss them."

Getting in her car again, Robin noticed a butte off to

her left, a tall column of eroded rock standing all alone like a sentry guarding the entrance to the canyon. She was momentarily tempted to get out her camera but then smiled to herself ruefully. If there had been one shot taken of the rock column, there had been two million. Santa Fe postcard stands abounded with good photos of not only this unique site, but of all Chaco Canyon. She might as well leave her camera right in its case.

It was hot, in the high eighties, she guessed. She felt wilted and tired, grimy and more nervous by the second as she followed the road up the canyon. The sand-colored walls rose on either side of her, not close, but still there, delineating her world, reflecting heat onto the dry river bottom.

Some ruins appeared at the base of the canyon walls, but the signs still directed her onward. Pueblo Bonito, pretty village, she translated. That, of course, was the name given the place when the white man discovered it, but what had the Anasazi called their town? And why had they built it here in this godforsaken wilderness?

Adam. He would know. He knew this broad canyon intimately, far better than he knew Robin. He was committed to his work here, he *belonged* here. Jealousy shot through her, then quick self-reproach. Jealous of a *place*; how ridiculous.

Ahead of her Pueblo Bonito loomed into view, a huge, semicircular area enclosed by walls made of stone, the afternoon light etching each square, picking out the neat patterns of the masonry. The city rose from the valley floor, sitting patiently in dignified decay, crumbling slowly, inevitably in the sun. Hundreds upon hundreds of cubelike rooms, desiccated husks now, piled one upon the other, their collapsed roofs open to the sky like empty eye sockets.

Robin stopped her car next to a pickup truck that was parked near a break in the walls. She could hear voices in the distance, and a sort of tent city had been set up to one side. Adam's Land Rover was parked in front of one of the tents. She stepped out of her car, taking a deep breath. The wind was hot and strong, whipping her tan skirt against her legs, lifting her hair off her damp neck. An eerie feeling settled in her bones, as if the wind carried on it the whisperings of others who had walked this land before her, an unthinkably long time ago. The Ancient Ones.

They'd built these walls and rooms, worked, sweated, laughed, died here. And something was still left of them—a spirit, a memory, an intangible presence.

She walked inside the walls, fighting her feeling. *Superstition doesn't suit you,* she told herself. People visited this place every day. It was just a pile of rocks, an archeologist's playground.

And yet...

The ground was rough and strewn with stones, so she had to watch her step carefully. The voices grew closer, and she saw a stable set up containing broken pottery. A roped-off area appeared; two boys crouched on the ground.

She saw Adam then and stopped. He was resting on his haunches in a trench, a small brush in one hand, an artifact in the other. His concentration was total. His shirt was off, his hard, lean muscles glistening darkly with sweat. He wore shorts, and the muscles in his legs glinted like molten copper in the sun. His jet-black hair was held back by a strip of cloth. Just as in her imagined portrait...

He hadn't seen her yet. An overwhelming urge struck Robin to run, to hide from her feelings for this man. He could never belong to her; he was a part of this time-worn land, and an insurmountable distance stood between them, a million miles and a thousand years.

But his head turned. She could see his body stiffen; he'd spotted her. It was too late to retreat. For a moment he remained unmoving, the object in his hand forgotten, his eyes boring into hers while she stood there helpless and self-conscious. His torso was coppery, hard-muscled, practically hairless, gleaming with decisiveness and strength in the harsh sunlight, and she couldn't take her eyes off him. The wind was gone, yet those ghostly whisperings of the past, of a people long gone, still sang in her ears, making her sway with dizziness. Maybe Adam himself wasn't even real…

He straightened then, his muscles bunching fluidly; he said something to one of the boys, handed him the brush and artifact and came toward Robin, dusting off his hands against his shorts. There was no welcoming smile on his lips.

"Adam, I'm so glad I found you," she babbled, nervously taking off her sunglasses. "I…"

"What are you doing here?" he asked quietly.

Her courage fled, her anxious energy drained from her body as if a plug had been drawn. She averted her face. "I came to tell you something, about the counterfeiters. I'm sorry, I shouldn't have disturbed you, but I thought… It's important, Adam."

For an unbearably long time he stood contemplating her, his hands on his hips, his black Indian eyes pinning her. Wild, uncontrollable thoughts flew around in her head. For a moment she felt terrified of him, like a pioneer woman of a hundred years ago confronted by an Indian warrior. But that was absurd; Adam was perfectly civilized; it was just her crazy imagination playing tricks.

She heard him sigh, a long, deep expulsion of breath escaping him. She shouldn't have come.

"Okay," he said, "let's go someplace a little more private. Are you thirsty?"

"Yes," she managed to say gratefully. "It's a long drive."

He took her arm and led her over to a couple of chairs and a water cooler that sat in the shade of a curved wall. A faded blue shirt was flung over one of the chairs, and Adam picked it up and pulled it on, leaving it unbuttoned so that his sun-bronzed skin showed in a smooth vertical stripe. Silently he handed her a paper cup and she sat down and drank the cool water.

"So you drove all the way out here to tell me something," he began.

"Yes." A small anger flared in her. *He'd* started this whole thing! "You certainly aren't making this easy for me. I thought you'd want to know…"

"I do want to know. You'll have to excuse me. I was a little surprised to see you," he said carefully.

"I know who made the pot," she blurted out. "His name is John Martinez and he does live at San Lucas."

His black eyes rested on her, unsurprised, expressionless. She turned the paper cup in her hands. "A woman came into my shop yesterday. She never told me her name, though. An older lady, a Pueblo Indian. She said she was a potter. She knew all about us looking for this John Martinez and the pot and everything."

Adam folded his arms across his chest and watched her unflinchingly. "Go on."

"Well, she said this Martinez is innocent, but he's afraid to go to the authorities. He doesn't want to be involved. Neither does this woman, but she wants the forgeries stopped. She said maybe, *maybe,* this John Martinez would talk to me. You see, it's whoever asked him to make the pot that we want. They're the guilty ones."

Adam walked a few steps, as if thinking, then turned to her in a sharp motion. "This woman, the one who told you this, you have no idea who she was?"

"No. But she was very sweet and gentle and scared, I think. About sixty, dressed in a pueblo dress and shawl. She was well-spoken and wore some beautiful jewelry. She had silver earrings, butterflies, that were lovely."

Adam rubbed his jaw with a long-fingered hand. "How are you to get in touch with her again?"

Robin shook her head. "She said she'd get in touch with me, that I shouldn't go back to San Lucas. I got the idea that if anyone looked for this Martinez character he'd disappear again.''

"This woman, was she from San Lucas, too?"

"No, at least she *said* she wasn't. She didn't say where she was from, though. Then she left, in a hurry, like she'd changed her mind about talking to me."

Adam was staring beyond her, arms folded. His face showed nothing, not interest or curiosity or triumph. Yet Robin had the distinct impression he knew something more than she did, something more about the Pueblo woman. Perhaps it was his lack of surprise that made her think so, or the slant of his questions.

"John Martinez," Adam said, half to himself.

"Do you know him?" Robin asked quickly.

He looked at her. "No, of course not."

"What, what do we do now?"

"We?" Adam stepped toward her, his brows drawn into a frown. "I'll take care of it from here, Robin. I don't want you involved."

"But I *am* involved. That woman may come back. Maybe Martinez will talk to me. I can't just tell her to forget it, can I?"

"I'll take care of it, Robin. I know enough now. The proper steps can be taken. I promise you, you won't have to be involved at all."

She stood quickly. "But I *want* to be involved. You got me into this and now, just like that, you say I have nothing to do with it. I can't just drop it. I want to know what's going on, and what's going to happen. Adam, I can't just forget about it!"

She stood facing him, their eyes practically on a level. For a moment Robin thought he was going to relent, to tell her something, but his glance shifted to a place beyond her, and she knew he'd decided against it. "Adam..." she began.

"I do appreciate your driving all the way out here to tell me this. It was good of you." He smiled at her for the first time then, but it was forced, deliberate, signaling an end to the conversation. "As long as you're here, would you like to see what we're doing?"

"Oh, I'd love to but—"

"As a photographer, you'll be interested to know that William Henry Jackson photographed these ruins in 1877. Unfortunately the film was ruined, but he publicized the existence of Chaco Canyon."

She gave up. Adam obviously had closed the subject of her mysterious visitor and her own involvement. How easily he switched his moods, as if he were a TV set with remote control. On this station was Adam, aloof, private, self-contained. And on another was Adam, friendly, suave, the perfect gentleman and host. Then there was Adam the enigmatic Apache. And now he was the professor, archeologist, highly intelligent, well-versed and eager to educate.

Luckily Robin was interested. She had to admit she could listen to him forever—and stare at him like an infatuated coed.

He was still gazing a little past her, as if readying his thoughts. "As you can see," he said, finally catching her eye, "I'm hardly the first to work here in the canyon. There were excavations as far back as the twenties, funded by the National Geographic Society, and then there was the Chaco Project in the seventies. A lot has been done, but there're thirteen sites just in Chaco Canyon itself and thousands all over the Southwest."

"Thousands?"

"For some decades around 1000 A.D. there was a relatively wet spell in this area, so the land supported a larger population. Drought set in and eventually the Anasazi from all the settlements left, migrated."

"So they're all gone? The Anasazi died out?" she asked, following Adam out to the great semicircular central plaza of Pueblo Bonito.

"They were the predecessors of the Hopi and Zuni and

Pueblo tribes of today," he said. "You know, the modern descendents of the Anasazi have kept many of their ancestors' customs. When an anthropologist or an archeologist has a question, say, about what a certain prehistoric artifact was used for, they go to the present-day tribes and ask. Often they get an answer to the puzzle, too." He looked at her. "Are you up to a walk?"

"Oh, sure. Where?"

He pointed. "Up there, to the top of the canyon wall. There's a great view. You'll understand the overall plan of the ruin better."

It was a tough climb. But Adam was always ready with a hand, in case she slipped. They scrambled up the rocky path, climbing over boulders. It was hot, too, but Robin didn't mind; it was an adventure, and Adam was talk-ative now, a different person, both the professor and a thoughtful companion. Every time his hand touched her arm or her back or her shoulder, she felt that jolt again, that exciting heightening of her senses. She could see rivulets of white salt on his skin where sweat had dried, and she smelled the man scent of his body.

"Whew! I feel like a mountain goat," she said once, stopping for a moment and breathing hard.

"There used to be stairs up here. Look, you can still see some of the stones."

She saw them, stones placed by ancient hands to make the climb easier. It touched her somewhere deep inside.

They reached the top. The high mesa stretched away from them in undulating brown waves; below, Pueblo Bonito lay in its precise semicircle, spread out for examination. Robin got her breath back and turned around slowly in a circle. "How did they *live* here?" she finally asked.

"They were experts. They built a sophisticated water-collection system, ditches, dams and holding tanks, on these canyon walls to collect every drop of moisture that fell, and diverted it to their fields on the canyon bottom. It was a highly organized society.''

"How many people lived here?'' she asked, seeing the other pueblos scattered along the canyon floor.

"Well, there's a debate about that going on. At first it was believed the population ran to the tens of thousands, based on the number of rooms in the pueblos here. But lately a new theory is being considered, that these huge pueblos with their many kivas, the ceremonial rooms, were not actually dwelling places, but centers of religion and trade. In other words, a kind of ancient convention center, nearly empty except during ceremonial occasions.''

"So the Anasazi people came from all over to attend these, uh, services?''

"Probably. They built roads—'' he pointed out over the land to the north ''—all centering here, on Chaco Canyon. Thirty feet wide, straight as arrows, cut through hills and across valleys. You can just see a faint trace there. It was called the Great North Road.''

Yes, she could see lines on the arid earth, faint markings, as straight as any surveyor could lay out. "Oh, my goodness. But I can't believe they could have undertaken such huge projects.''

"They must have had skilled labor groups. Like I said, it was a tightly structured, highly organized society. There's still so much to find out. I could spend a lifetime here.''

"What about your classes?'' she asked.

"Yes,'' he said wryly. "Well, my grant only lasts until the end of this semester. And most of these kids working for me have to leave soon to go back to school.''

"I can understand why you're so fascinated by all this,'' Robin said, gesturing out over the canyon. "It's so...so mysterious, so beautiful.''

"Yes.''

They stood together in companionable silence for a

time, looking down at the ruined city. A sudden breeze
plucked at Robin, a cooling caress at this height, molding
her skirt to her. It ruffled Adam's hair and made his shirt-
tails flap against his sun-bronzed skin.

"A storm," he said, shading his eyes and gazing off to
the west. "But it may pass by us."

The thunderheads Robin had seen earlier were advanc-
ing toward them in a distinct line, pushing the wind before
them, whipping up dust devils and bending the sparse yellow grass. They both watched, fascinated, as the black
clouds billowed and grew, like a speeded-up film.

"Will it rain on us?" Robin asked. "Should we get
back?"

"I think it's going to the north," Adam said. "It usually does."

The sky turned dark and brooding; dust blew into
Robin's eyes. Thunder growled distantly, and she could
see jagged flashes of lightning far away.

"Are you afraid?" Adam asked. "We can go down."

She glanced at him. "No, it's exciting. I'm not afraid.
I wish I had my camera set up, though." She smiled.
"Shouldn't we be doing a rain dance? Wouldn't the In-
dians have been praying for rain at a time like this?"

He gave her a sharp look, as if measuring her, seeing
if she were poking fun. "Probably. I know a few words
of a Navaho chant, but I'd rather you heard it from a real
singer."

"Oh, I'd love it. Sometime," she said, holding her hair
out of her eyes. She felt free up there on the rim of the
world, the wind buffeting her, a strong, handsome man at
her side, a man who belonged to this time and place.
"This land is owned by the Indians now, isn't it?"

"Not according to the Department of Interior," he said
dryly. "There are Apache reservations, two in New Mexico and one in Arizona. But when the Spanish came to
New Mexico there were Apache herders all over the
state."

"Here?"

He shrugged, the wind tugging at his shirt. "Probably. The Navaho and Apache are very closely related and got here about the same time, in the 1400s. They found these ruins here. As a matter of fact, the name Anasazi is a Navaho word."

"And what did they think of these ruins when they saw them?" Robin asked.

"They knew a very powerful race had lived here. They respected the Ancient Ones and stayed away from their dwelling places. They never molested the ruins, or lived in them." He paused and scanned the sky. "Yes, it's going to the north. It won't rain here, not today." Then he continued: "There's a legend about Chaco Canyon that explains how the People came to live here in Dinetah."

"Oh, please tell me."

"It seems that when my people, the Navaho and Apache, the Diné, found Chaco, the Ancient Ones who lived here were slaves of a supernatural gambler they called Never Loses. The Ancient Ones bet everything they owned against him and lost, so they bet their freedom and lost that, too. The spirits of the Diné—Wind Boy, First Man, Coyote and the rest of them—devised their own games full of deceit. They won the Chacoans their freedom and sent an angry Never Loses into exile."

"What a great story. But how did your people explain the disappearance of the Ancient Ones?"

"They simply said that they went away. That's all. And so far, that's all we can say."

"An interesting mystery," said Robin.

"I like to stand here and look down and wonder. Here's an insignificant valley in the middle of nowhere. Civilization flourished here on a grand scale and then was lost. What did the last group of people who deserted this canyon see as they straggled along, burdened with their belongings? Where did they go? What did their gods tell them about their leaving?'' His voice faded away on the wind.

Suddenly there was a closeness between them, a new and joyful sharing. It was as if Adam had opened that closed door of his for a precious moment, so that she could see inside his mind to the Aladdin's cave of treasures he kept so well hidden. The wind was dying, and a shaft of late sunlight speared through an opening in the storm clouds. A rainbow formed on the far side of the valley, a lovely refraction of light and color. A moment later the brooding clouds seemed to swell and part, and sunlight spilled into the canyon, illuminating the rim with a bright golden light that was washed clean by the rain. It shone on the hard chiseled lines of Adam's face, on his glowing copper skin. He was so beautiful, Robin thought, like one of his ancient Indian gods.

''Adam,'' she said after a moment, ''I want to help you find the counterfeiters. Please let me help.''

He studied her for a long time, and her heart pounded too heavily. ''It could be dangerous,'' he finally stated, ''but there's no putting you off, is there, Robin Hayle?''

CHAPTER TEN

ADAM TURNED HIS FACE to the west, toward the setting sun, where streaks of light blazed across the valley beneath the fading rainbow and struck him with their warmth. For a moment he closed his eyes, searching for equilibrium, summoning the enduring bounty of nature to enter him and fill his spirit with harmony. When he opened his eyes she was still there, tall and long and lovely, soft and womanly. The last light reached out for her, too, and her windblown hair caught the rays like threads of yellow-gold.

She was strikingly beautiful, but she was more than that. She had an openness of mind, a sensitivity that most white people lacked. Perhaps it was due to her photographer's eye, which saw more deeply into things. And he sensed a vulnerability in her, a too-ready smile, a tenseness. He would love to scratch her surface and find the source of her discord.

What was he thinking? Why in the devil had he told her she could help? Had he forgotten the danger to her, the risk? He could easily have taken the information she'd given him and contacted Martinez himself. Or he could have insisted on calling in Rod Cordova to have the police handle it, in spite of the promise Robin had made to her mysterious visitor. So why hadn't he?

Adam knew the answers already. Despite the fact that nothing but ruin would ever come of a relationship between them, he could not quite let her go. He'd walked out on her the other night—because then he'd still had the strength to do so. It had been a cruel act, selfish and cowardly. If only she'd stayed out of his life. He hadn't the strength to let her go again; the spirits of his forefathers had stripped him of his powers and left him helpless and alone to face this woman.

"It's getting late. We better go down now," he said.

They were both quiet as they began the steep descent. He'd deliberately withdrawn into the reserve and silence, his cloak of aloofness, afraid that he'd revealed too much of himself to Robin. For a moment, he'd let his true self show, and he knew she'd recognized it. *Careful,* he warned himself, watching her long slim back in a silky turquoise blouse as she walked down the rough path ahead of him.

Something else was bothering him, too: the Pueblo woman who'd visited Robin. There was little doubt in his mind who it was—Josefina Ortega. He was angry with her for dragging Robin back into this affair. Why in hell was Josefina meddling in it?

"Can I see more?" she asked then.

"More?"

"Yes, of Pueblo Bonito. There's still plenty of daylight."

"Sure. Yes. Have you ever seen a kiva?" He knew he was distracted, and that his thought of a moment ago about Josefina was unkind. She was a wonderful woman, a lifetime friend of his mother's, in fact. She was also one of the great Southwestern Indian artists of this century, her pottery proudly on display in homes and galleries all over the world.

It hadn't taken Adam more than a few seconds to guess the identity of the woman when Robin had described her. The earrings alone had been a dead giveaway. Her visit to Robin was completely out of character for Josefina; she'd always been timid and retiring, finding fulfillment in her pueblo, her family and her craft. Going to Robin with her knowledge had shown great courage.

Of course, surmised Adam, his very own mother was
no doubt the cause of Josefina's visit to Robin. Who else
had known about the forged pot in San Lucas Pueblo, and
also of Robin's involvement? Yes, his mother must have
spoken to her friend Josefina, and Josefina in turn had
found out about John Martinez. The trouble was, Josefina
should have come to *him* and kept Robin out of it.

"A kiva," Robin was saying. "Isn't that a ceremonial
room?"

"Yes, it's where the Anasazi and the modern-day Hopi
men hold their religious ceremonies. They're often dug
into the ground, to allow the initiates to get closer to the
Mother Earth. Women were never allowed in kivas."

"Well, let's hope they don't find out about me," she
said lightly.

He helped Robin over a pile of rubble, his big hands
spanning her waist, half lifting her. And as he touched her
in the waning light that was turning her eyes the color of
wild violets, he felt that ache in his groin again. How he
would have loved to feel the curve of her soft bosom
against his chest, to savor her full lips and twist his fingers
in that heavy mass of spun-gold hair...

He must have hesitated too long, because she stopped,
still in the curve of his hands. "Adam," she began, her
voice a whisper, "I..."

"Let's go," he said quickly, snatching his hands back.
"It'll be too dark to see soon."

How was he supposed to think with Robin around? Yet
he welcomed her presence, as if he were a dying man
whose thirst was being miraculously quenched. But she
was young and vital; surely she was looking for marriage
and children. She *should* be looking for that, for God's
sake.

Damn Josefina. It was her fault he was faced with this
uncomfortable situation. Had his mother's friend really
believed she'd stay anonymous? Highly skilled, sweet and
kind and endearing as she was, Josefina was nevertheless

painfully naive. And eventually, if indeed Robin stayed involved, she would have to be told everything. So much for Josefina's anonymity.

What *was* he thinking? *If* Robin stayed involved? Was he crazy?

"What were these rooms?" Robin was asking, and he had to drag his attention back to reality.

"It's believed they were family dwellings," he answered. "The women would have cooked over here—" he pointed "—and there, through that doorway, they probably slept."

"How do you know all that? I mean…"

"The earth tells us." He stooped and picked up a handful of loose pebbles. "If I found, say, a fragment of straw here, then I'd look for more in the area. It takes a microscope, sometimes, to determine what's there, but eventually the earth would give up its secrets."

"And if you found enough straws?"

"I'd surmise that women wove baskets in this area, you understand?" He let the dirt sift through his fingers.

"And in a kitchen area, do you know what they actually cooked?"

He nodded. "With the sophisticated techniques available to us now, we can tell exactly what they ate."

"That's amazing," said Robin, running her long slim fingers across a smooth stone seat. "I can almost see a woman sitting here, grinding corn."

"You can see all kinds of things here," he replied. "That's what my job is all about, to breathe life into these cold stones."

They passed the worktable containing the day's find of pottery shards. Robin stopped by it momentarily to look at the pieces then lightly fingered a sharp-edged fragment that lay there. "This is from a pot?" she asked.

"A very old pot," he said, "from around the tenth century." Then he put a fingertip on the surface of the shard and felt its familiar smoothness. "It's what we call a black-on-white. You see the lines here? This one had geometric designs on it. You can make out the corner of one here. I think this piece was from a mug. See? There's a part of the handle.'' He picked it up, turned it over in his fingers and showed her the design.

"Will you find the missing pieces and be able to put it together?'' she asked, touching the black lines with a pink fingernail.

He shook his head. "Probably not.''

"What a shame," she said.

"See this blemish?'' he asked, pointing to a round black smudge on the curve of the shard. "It's a firecloud. Prehistoric pots commonly have them. They come from the pot being imperfectly fired. Just like modern Pueblo potters, the Anasazi fired their work in animal dung. The mark is from an incompletely burned fragment.''

"Is this spot like the one on John Martinez's pot?'' she asked.

"Yes. The blemish makes a piece less valuable to a collector.''

"Oh, I think it makes it even *more* fascinating," Robin said, cocking her head. "I imagine an Indian lady and how mad she was when her mug came out of the fire with that mark on it.''

"That's a minority opinion," he replied, watching her stroke the black smudge on the shard. And he couldn't help comparing that ancient piece of clay to himself: Changing Man, fragmented, imperfect, blemished. Quickly he turned away from her and began to move on.

That night at her apartment, Adam recalled painfully, he'd left and driven away and promised himself that he wasn't going to see her again, that a relationship between them was fair neither to him nor to her. There were so many reasons: their different cultures and beliefs, his own inadequacy, fear for her safety. But here he was again, allowing her sweet stubbornness to bulldoze him, permitting her to believe she could help uncover the counter-feiters.

He indicated a recently excavated set of steps that led up to a wide, flat stone platform. "Climb on up," he said, pointing the way, "but take care, the stones might be loose." He followed her closely, unable to take his eyes from her slim ankles as she held her full skirt aside with a hand.

"Oh, Adam, this is the kiva, isn't it?" She sounded so excited, so truly interested, that he hadn't the heart to bring up the subject of the black marketeers just then. But he would, and soon.

"Yes, this is it. One of many, in fact. But this one happens to be under excavation right now." Inadvertently he touched the small of her back, feeling the cool fabric slip over her warm skin. He suggested she approach the opening in the ground. "You'll be one of the first to see it."

"Me?"

He couldn't help it. He smiled. "Yes, you. Other than a few of my workers, no one's been in here for centuries."

"God, how spooky," she whispered, craning her neck to look down into the inky black pit, where countless centuries ago mythical rites had been performed by the Ancient Ones.

The kiva, which sat below the platform of stone, was not entirely excavated yet. There was loose masonry on at least one side of it, and Adam wasn't too certain of the ceiling. "Here," he said, leaving her side for a moment, "I'll get a lantern and you can look down inside."

"But can't I go in?"

He stopped and glanced at her for a moment. "It's not all that safe, Robin. I really would rather you..."

"Oh, please. There's a ladder and everything. Just a quick look. I promise I won't touch a thing."

Ordinarily Adam would have stuck to his guns. Ordinarily. But she looked so lovely, so enthusiastic, standing there in the fading golden light. "Well, I guess if I go down first... But just a quick glance, Robin. It's not in great shape."

As the deepening shadows reached across the twisted land, Robin held the lantern over the pit while Adam descended, then she handed it down and climbed onto the ladder. He was instantly aware of the cold in the kiva, a dry cold, and the odor of crumbled stone and dirt that was distinct in the air. There was even a faint, aged smell of dung left from the long extinguished fires of dried droppings that had once illuminated the pit.

Even to Adam the place was eerie. He had never entered a kiva without feeling the touch of the long dead who'd once performed their secretive, magical rites there with the firelight blazing in their dark eyes. If he stood very still, he could almost hear their chanting, a song like his uncle could sing: sensual, primitive, filled with the call of the spirits and the flesh.

"Wow," Robin said as Adam held the lantern shoulder high, bouncing its light off the aged walls and the fire pit in the center of the chamber. "So this is a kiva," she said, her voice a reverent whisper. "It's so strange, so mysterious."

He stood close, aware of the new scent in the lamp-reddened kiva—Robin's scent—fresh, womanly, very much alive. The stirrings began in his belly again and his head rang with the chanting, but this time it was his own song and was undeniably real. His senses had never been so charged with life, so in tune with the powerful force of the place. He wanted Robin with a kind of mindlessness; he wanted to possess her in every way, to own her body and soul, and he wanted to perform his rite in this haven, this magical place.

Adam felt her hand touch his arm. The pain was excruciating, tender and burning at the same moment. She said nothing, but he could hear her swallow, and the pulse in her fingers where they lay on his arm quickened, steady and strong. The blood began to pound in his head. He turned toward her, his eyes dark and shining in the lamplight, filled with his overpowering need. He placed the lantern on the hard earthen floor and cupped her face with his hands. There were only the two of them in this ancient kiva, on this lonely planet.

It was then that he became cognizant of the dust sifting down from the curved ceiling. He was confused for a moment, then he saw Robin look up and blink, and the air was filled with dust.

He heard it a split second later. Immediately he snatched Robin to him and dived for a corner of the chamber, covering her body with his. The ceiling seemed to crash down on them, dust and rock battering his back and head, suffocating, painful. Then suddenly, as quickly as it had begun, it was over. He could hear a few loose stones strike the floor, and dirt was still drifting down onto him, but it was over.

Robin was gasping and terrified beneath his weight. He shifted quickly, pulling her to his chest, rocking her. "It's over now. It's over," he said, coughing, his shallow breathing matching her own. "Are you all right?"

"I think so," she said weakly. "Oh God, what happened?"

"The ceiling. Part of it caved in."

"Can we…"

"Yes, I can see the hole. I don't know where the ladder is, though. Will you be okay for a minute?"

"Sure, yes, I'm okay."

He came to his knees, testing for injuries, and then to his feet. It was pitch black, and he had to feel his way over the fallen rock, stumbling once, finding his way like a blind man.

"Adam," he heard her say. "Where are you?"

"Over here." He coughed hard then, the dust choking him, gritting against his teeth. "I can't find the ladder." A moment later, he tripped against it. It was lying on its

side near a wall. "Here, I got it," he called, rasping.
"Hold on, I'll set it back up. You all right?"

"Yes."

By the time Adam had the ladder up again, he could
hear footfalls on the stones above them. His workers.
Then someone, it sounded like Jack, called into the opening.

"Mr. Farwalker! You down there? Adam!"

"Here! Help me with this ladder, grab the end of it."

In only a matter of minutes he had Robin on the surface, her weight leaning against him; she was still trembling and shaken, but unhurt, thank God. The student
workers by now had all gathered around, asking questions,
stunned by the sudden, unaccountable cave-in.

"Here," one of the girls offered, "drink this." It was
Linda, holding out a plastic water bottle. "Oh, Mr. Farwalker," she said, "you might have been killed!"

"We're both okay," he assured her. Then he looked at
Robin, who sat close to his side, hugging her knees to her
chin. "I never should have taken you down there," he
said in a hoarse voice. "When I think what might have
happened…"

She gazed at him then gave a weak smile. "I *wanted*
to go down there, Adam. I made you do it."

"Yeah, Mr. Farwalker," said Jack, "it's not your fault.
Why, we've all been in there. Lots of times, in fact. It
just happened."

The six young people stood around, obviously wondering, thinking about their own safety. Adam couldn't blame
them. He'd worked on digs for many years, though, and
had seen some cave-ins. Yet he'd thought this kiva was
relatively safe.

He felt Robin's hand on his shoulder. "Come on,
Adam, stop blaming yourself," she urged. "I'd have
sneaked in there when your back was turned, anyway.
Come on." Then, amazingly, he heard her giggle. "Besides," she said, "I look pretty good compared to you."

He glanced at her dirt-smudged face then down at himself.

"See?" said Robin, "you look like a chimney sweep. And your hair's gray."

A few of the students laughed nervously while Robin sat smiling and expectant. He had to give in. Adam, too, smiled. She was right, of course; no one was really at fault, and they were both unharmed.

"And excitement makes me hungry," Robin said sheepishly.

It was good, walking beside Robin, her lean body molded to his in the dusk. He kept his arm around her shoulder—merely a protective gesture—but he could imagine the silky softness of her bare skin. He'd bet her whole body was velvety smooth, and warm, yielding.

"You're not still feeling guilty, are you?" she asked as they made their way toward the students' campsite.

"I should be," he replied, wiping his mind clean of his thoughts.

"You know, guilt is such a wasted emotion. I mean, anger, now there's an acceptable one. Or happiness."

He stopped and looked down at the path, trying hard not to smile. "You're something, Robin Hayle," he found himself admitting. "Nothing ever daunts you, does it?"

She was quiet for a moment then said, "Some things get me, Adam Farwalker, you bet they do," and there was that insecurity again, that wistful tone of voice.

Nancy and Linda had been cooking dinner when word of the accident had spread throughout the camp. The students took turns over the stove. Too bad, Adam thought, because it was Jack and Craig who were the good cooks of the group.

So packaged macaroni and cheese it was, with a can of tuna or two thrown in. "Why, this is delicious," Robin said kindly, and a few friendly arguments broke out among the crew.

The talk finally turned to the cave-in. Adam sat quietly

and listened to the reactions of his students. Nancy said, "I think we should begin restoring the kiva first thing tomorrow."

Craig concurred with Jack's statement: "It's going to have to wait for spring next year. We'd only get about half of it cleared out before it snows."

"And it snows in October around here sometimes," Linda was quick to point out.

"Plus we all have classes in Albuquerque," put in Jack.

"I don't," said Nancy, "I graduated, remember?"

"Well," said Robin, coming to her feet, "this has been one heck of an afternoon, but *I've* got work tomorrow. Bright and early."

Adam stood quickly, confused. "But you're not driving back tonight?"

"Of course I am."

"Robin—"

"Hey," interrupted Craig, "be careful driving that highway alone at night. There've been some strange people around here today."

It was only a small alarm, but nevertheless a bell sounded in Adam's head. "What people, Craig?"

"Oh, this Indian I saw. He was drinking or something, stumbling around in one of the roped-off areas." The young man shrugged. "Then he got into a junky old pickup truck and drove off like a demon."

"Roped-off areas?" asked Adam, the bell sounding louder.

"Yeah. It was right before the cave-in, I think. Or maybe…"

"Right *after* it?" asked Adam in a quiet voice.

CHAPTER ELEVEN

ADAM STOOD ALONGSIDE Robin's car and frowned. "I don't like you making this drive tonight," he said as she started up the motor. "You won't be back in Santa Fe till midnight as it is."

"I have to get back," stated Robin, "I've got appointments tomorrow. Work calls."

"I still don't feel right about it."

Robin gave him one of those big bright smiles of hers and turned on the headlights. "I'm going to be fine. Just because one of your students saw some man nosing around doesn't mean he had anything to do with the cave-in."

Maybe she was convinced of that, but Adam had his doubts. No, more than doubts; he felt there was a connection. But Robin was putting the car in gear...

"Well," she was saying, "I'll let you know the minute I hear anything more about this John Martinez. I honestly believe my Indian lady will be back in touch. Goodbye, Adam," she said, "I hope I see you soon."

He put his hands in his pockets and watched grimly as she pulled away, her tires kicking up loose gravel on the road. At that rate, Robin Hayle would be back in town well before midnight.

Why hadn't he tried harder to stop her? Was it because she was getting to him, chinking away at that armor he'd so calculatingly donned ten years ago? Or maybe Robin was as resilient as she seemed and not in the least vulnerable. Maybe she didn't need or want a strong man telling her what to do. He wondered about that, though. In certain respects, they were very much alike despite their different backgrounds.

It was an utterly cloudless night. Above the canyon walls the immense canopy of stars gleamed with a pristine beauty, the air so rarefied and clean that the Milky Way seemed to be made of white gauze. Adam could almost reach out and touch it. As he stood there, hands still in the pockets of his shorts, he felt a closeness to nature that steadied him, that made him feel whole again.

He was ready to turn, to walk back up the stony path to his camp, when some vague apprehension held him. His glance followed the curving road below. He could see where the dark highway flowed with the land's contours, and yes, there were Robin's lights, glowing, turning the pavement to silver ribbons in front of her car.

He stood immobile, watching for a moment as the twin tunnels of light grew smaller. A part of Adam's mind said she was okay, driving a bit too fast, but all right. Another part, that nebulous place in his brain that reacted purely by instinct, noting anything out of order, any dissonant element, argued against complacency. Everyone had that place, but it was the Indian who was trained to listen to it.

And there it was, the cause of Adam's disquiet. His heart pounded heavily as he watched another set of headlights pull onto the highway just behind Robin. At this time of night, in that isolated part of the canyon, the car tailing her was far too coincidental...

Suddenly he was all muscle and bone and nerve reacting. Crossing the parking area at a dead run, Adam was in his Land Rover in seconds, backing out onto the highway, stripping the gears, forcing the sluggish vehicle to leap forward like a scared cat.

He pounded the steering wheel with a fist. Damn it! Why hadn't she listened to him? Why hadn't he insisted she stay?

Catching up to Robin would be impossible. At best, his
Land Rover could do fifty, and it was a nightmare at that
speed on the sharp curves. The road dipped and twisted,
sometimes climbing, sometimes dropping down to the
canyon floor where his lights picked out roadside objects
eerily from the shadows.

Fifty, fifty-three miles an hour—the vehicle's motor
strained like a beast of burden hauling too heavy a load.

For a moment the road straightened on top of a rise.
He could just make out the two sets of lights, far ahead
of him, as they disappeared in tandem around a sweeping
curve. Robin must have been aware of the car following
her, Adam decided, and probably had the gas pedal to the
floor. He'd never catch up in time.

Images floated unbidden through his head. Robin lying
along the roadside with a gunshot wound to her breast.
Robin in her burning car, a pillar of orange flames reaching to the heavens. She was screaming for help, her deep
blue eyes filled with terror.

For several miles Adam could see nothing whatsoever
ahead. Only the huge, massive humps of rock stood on
either side of the road, dark, forbidding sentinels. His engine was beginning to heat up now, waves of acrid-
smelling heat radiating from the metal floorboards. The
vehicle couldn't be pushed this hard... It occurred to
Adam that he was about to crack the engine block but
that it made no difference. He was never going to reach
her in time, anyway. A horrible, wrenching sadness
gripped him, a sadness for what they could have had together. He recalled with strange clarity her last words: "I
hope I'll see you soon." There had been promise in her
voice and expectancy in her eyes. He'd chosen to ignore
it then, but now it seemed the most important thing in the
world.

Several miles before the main highway, Adam thought
he saw the cars but perhaps that was only fear and wish-
fulness.

He came around a sharp bend in the road then and
definitely spotted taillights in the distance. They seemed,
however, to be sitting, unmoving, at an odd angle.
Robin's?

The red lights grew in his vision as the temperature
gauge in the Land Rover rose into the danger zone. Then,
as he neared, the taillights took on an otherworldly quality, as if a primitive animal was staring at him with glowing, fiery eyes; he pushed on the gas pedal even harder
until he thought his foot was going to go through the floor.
God, if that was Robin's car... He could make it out now,
tilted onto its side in a ditch, its headlights turned sky-
ward, askew, crazily searching the night.

Adam pulled up and came to a stop. The car was
Robin's, all right. His chest tightened, and he was vaguely
aware of his racing heartbeat, as if he'd been running to
catch up to her. Leaving his door swinging, he was tugging on Robin's within seconds, calling out her name,
yanking on the handle.

She was inside and moving, although moving as if she
were drunk, moving very, very slowly, her head lolling
from side to side. He heard her moan when he finally
jerked the door open, and he crouched, putting his hands
on her shoulders gently. "Robin, it's Adam," he said, his
voice a harsh whisper. "Come on, Robin, we've got to
get you out of here."

Again she moaned.

"Come on, there... Okay? Can you stand?" But she
couldn't. She sagged against him, dazed, hurt, but he
couldn't see an injury.

He scooped her up in his arms and saw it then in his
headlights, the blood that had spattered her turquoise silk
blouse and matted her spun-gold hair. Carefully bending
down onto one knee, he propped Robin against the back
of her car where he could see better in the light. She was
pretty well out of it but still breathing steadily, though
very deeply, and moans escaped her.

"I'm going to get the first-aid kit out of my car," he said softly. "Just sit here." Of course, she wasn't going anywhere, but he felt so protective toward her, so worried, that he didn't care how foolish he sounded.

The blood was coming from a beaut of a gash on her forehead above her right eye. The deep cut still welled blood, though with gentle but firm pressure, Adam soon had it stopped. "Robin," he kept saying, "can you talk? Can you understand me?"

He did the best he could to clean up the wound; then, holding back her damp hair, he placed a wad of gauze on the cut and taped the edges. It was all he could do for now. "You need stitches," he said. "Robin, please, can you hear me?"

"I can hear you," she said after a frighteningly long time.

He whispered something that could be translated as "thank God" in his native language.

"What?" she mumbled.

"Nothing." Adam smiled and felt tension drain from his body. He was crouched in front of her, knees splayed, his hands on either side of her head. "Do you think you can make it to my car?"

"Oh...sure."

She was not at all steady on her feet, but she was coming around. She even said, "Aren't you supposed to ask me what day of the week it is or something?"

"What day of the week is it, Robin?" He helped her into the passenger seat of the Land Rover.

"It's Monday," she said groggily.

"Try Thursday."

"Okay, Thursday then. And my name's Robin Hayle. I got that right, didn't I?"

Adam closed her door and touched her shoulder with his hand. "You're doing great. Now hold on a minute and I'm going to get your car keys. Okay?"

"Oh, my car..."

"It'll be all right. The tire rim's bent, you've got a flat. The driver's door sticks."

"It always did." Then, when he was finally in the driver's seat, she said, "Where're we going?"

"To Cuba. There's a doctor I know there."

"Cuba? I've never been there."

"Cuba, New Mexico, Robin. It's right up the road."

"Oh." She turned in her seat and grimaced. "Do I really need a doctor?"

"Yes. And that's the last word on it. Don't try me again, lady."

Dr. Ernest Lopez was that rare commodity known as a country doctor. He still made house calls, although he did urge the Mexican and Indian population of Cuba to come into his clinic. Sometimes they did; mostly they didn't.

Adam pulled up in front of his small adobe home. The lights were on in the living room. "Hold on," he told Robin, "and I'll find out if Ernest can see you here or at the clinic."

"Adam," she said, "about how I got off the road back there…"

"We'll talk about it when you're fixed up, okay?"

"Okay, I guess."

Robin was semi-brave as she sat in Dr. Lopez's kitchen and was stitched up. "Oh, I hate this," she complained, squeezing her eyes shut as Ernest injected Novocain around the wound. She put out her hand, groping for Adam's, and he found her fingers and gently held them. "Ouch," she said. "Good thing I have bangs. I'm going to look like the bride of Frankenstein."

"Oh, I don't think you'll look *that* bad," he offered.

Adam forced Dr. Lopez to accept payment for his services. "If you don't, Ernest," he said as they were leaving, "then next time I'll take my business elsewhere."

"And where else would you find a clinic, Adam, around here?"

"Good question."

Soon Robin was seated in the Land Rover, Adam's old blue jean jacket, which he kept in the car, around her shoulders. "My blouse is done for," she said lightly, but he could see her glance down at the blood stains and tremble in reaction.

He turned on the cooled-down vehicle. "I'll buy you a new one."

"But you don't—"

"Yes, I think I do."

Even though he drove slowly, watching the temperature gauge, they were halfway back to Santa Fe before she wanted to talk about the accident. "You know my car's stuck way out there," she began, "and I don't know how I'll get along without it."

"Don't worry about your car," said Adam, "I'll take care of it."

"That maniac." Her hand went gingerly up to her forehead.

Adam wanted to be very careful how he approached the subject; after all, Robin had damn near been killed tonight. "What do you remember?" he asked in a soft voice, and he looked sidelong at her for a moment.

"Not much." She shrugged then held the folds of the jacket together with her fingers. They were shaking. "He followed me, you know. It was no accident."

"Yes, I know."

"Of course you do... He even bumped the back of my car a couple of times."

"Robin, if you'd rather not—"

"It's okay. I'm starting to get mad, actually. Can you believe it? That guy would have killed me! And, Adam, it *was* an old pickup."

He said nothing.

"He kept following and following. So close I couldn't even see his lights in my mirror... And then, oh, hell, he pulled alongside in that old, souped-up truck and forced me into that ditch."

Anger flared within Adam, red-hot and boiling. "He's going to pay," he said between clenched teeth.

He could feel Robin's gaze on him, questioning. "And just how is he going to pay? We don't even know who he is."

"Oh, I'll find out."

"You seem very sure of that."

"I'm calling in Rod Cordova," Adam said firmly. He heard Robin's intake of breath.

"You can't," she protested. "I gave my word to that woman, Adam. I *promised*."

"I understand. But do *you* understand, Robin, someone tried to…to kill you tonight? Do you realize that?"

She only nodded.

"I'm sure your visitor, that Indian lady, would understand."

"I don't know… I really don't."

"Well, I do." He knew his voice had risen and that he was no doubt scaring her. "Look, I'm sorry. I didn't mean to shout. I just know what has to be done. Someone knows every move you're making."

"But how?"

Adam shook his head. "If I knew that… And I have to guess the reason you were attacked tonight is because of that special committee you're on."

"That's crazy."

"I don't think so. Why else would someone still be after you?"

"I don't know."

"The other possibility is that you're being watched every minute of the day. If someone saw your visitor…"

"The Indian lady?" asked Robin.

Adam nodded. "I've got a very bad feeling about her visit. It was unwise, to say the least."

"But she couldn't have known I was being watched."

"Maybe," he said pensively.

"Oh, my gosh!" cried Robin suddenly. "My committee meeting was tonight!"

"I'm sure," said Adam, "they'll understand completely why you missed it. And I think that you're better off out of it now. It's time to hand this over to the police."

"But calling in Rod..." Robin said doubtfully.

"I'm *going* to call Rod. He can locate your John Martinez and maybe come up with some leads."

"And if Martinez won't talk to him?" asked Robin slowly.

"Then I'll talk to him myself."

"Adam, I don't think—"

"The subject's closed." For an instant he regretted his authoritative tone, but then when she fell silent he decided not to relent.

It crossed Adam's mind as he drove to tell Robin about her mysterious Indian woman—Josefina Ortega. To let her know that Josefina would probably call the police if she knew the trouble her visit had caused. But maybe the less Robin knew right now, the better.

"I want you to stay at my folks' for the next few days," he said as the lights of Santa Fe illuminated the horizon.

"It's so inconvenient," she replied. "Not just for me, but for them, too."

"Actually," put in Adam, "I'm not asking. I'm telling." Again, taking command seemed to work. It was amazing, he reflected, how incredibly protective he felt. And over a strange woman, a white eyes, a foreign creature. And yet, how quickly she had gotten under his skin, like sand fleas. Always there, always making him itch.

Maybe, he thought suddenly, as he steered up Canyon Road, she didn't even like him and all these mental acrobatics were for nothing. But no, a man did not mistake those signals that had been running between them since that first day when she'd come from the back of her shop and their eyes had met. And at dinner that night, at Maria's, with the setting sun striking her golden hair and catching in those blue eyes… Yes, it had been there since the beginning, and, damn it all, he'd done nothing whatsoever to stop it.

"I'm afraid we're going to upset your mother," Robin was saying. "It's really late, Adam. This is unfair to them."

"Nonsense. My parents would have a fit if I *didn't* have you stay out here."

"I can't stay forever, you know. I mean, I have my own place and I can't go around like a scared rabbit. I won't go—"

"Robin," he said, pulling up in front of the hacienda, "let's take it as it comes. Tomorrow Rod may be able to get to the bottom of things."

"Do you really believe that?"

He didn't. But he merely said, "Here we are. Wait, I'll come and get your door."

Adam was careful not to awaken his parents, as it was nearly one o'clock. Of course, they were relatively used to his coming and going at odd hours; whenever he was in Santa Fe during the summers, he used his old bedroom at the hacienda. Christina and Ray would find out everything in the morning, anyway.

He led Robin along the dark twisting path to the guesthouse complex. She was still not entirely steady on her feet, and Dr. Lopez had suggested strongly that she see her local doctor. Concussions were nothing to fool with, but Robin, Adam surmised, would no doubt ignore his advice.

"I'll turn up the heat," he said as he swung open the door and switched on the lights. "It gets downright cold up here in the beginning of September."

"Thanks," she replied. She plumped herself down on the side of the bed, then looked at her hands and blouse. "I'm a mess. I look like a creature out of a horror movie."

"I better find you something to sleep in," he said.

"Maybe you could, um, rinse out your blouse or whatever while I'm gone. Mother's clothes will never fit, I'm sure."

Robin only nodded tiredly, looking like a lost little girl sitting there.

He hesitated at the door. "Will you be all right while I find something for you to put on?"

"I'm fine. Just pooped."

He made his way along the path and quietly entered the main house. His sisters, he knew, had long since moved all their clothing out of their old bedrooms. So what was he going to get for Robin to sleep in?

Adam walked silently down a long, narrow hall and entered his own room. He could give her a shirt to wear, but didn't he have pajamas somewhere—a Christmas present, never worn? Sure he did. In the bottom dresser drawer.

For some reason it was terribly awkward pulling them out of the drawer. He always slept in the buff, but standing there dangling the blue pajamas from his fingers made him feel foolish. Robin could have slept in her underwear or whatever. This was absurd and embarrassing.

Yet he could see her in them. The V at the neck would hang low because she was really very skinny. And the waist would droop down over her lean hips. Inadvertently he wondered how the new, stiff cotton would feel against her soft skin.

"God, man," said Adam, grumbling at himself, "they're only pajamas!"

He knocked on the guest-house door when he returned. But there was no answer. Was she asleep already? He opened the door quietly and heard the sound of running water coming from the bathroom. Crossing the room, he tapped on the door, clearing his throat. "Um, Robin, here's something to wear."

"Oh, thanks," she called and the door opened a crack. Her hand came out. "I'll be right out."

"I, ah, better get going," he said.

"Hold on, I'm almost done."

He sat in an armchair, feeling ridiculous. He ought to get back to the main house and get some sleep. Yet a part of him refused to move, envisioning Robin in those pajamas. What a desperate old lecher he was becoming.

When she came out she was holding her crumpled wet blouse in one hand. "I need a hanger."

He was on his feet in a flash. "Here, there's some in this closet. Go climb into bed," he offered, "I'll get it." Hanger in hand, he took her blouse, shook it out and hung it near the heater to dry. It seemed so small to him, so feminine, so damp and smooth, silky cool to the touch... Robin was pulling up the coverlet when he turned around and, just as he'd imagined, the neckline on his pajamas was far too large, exposing her neck and the faint swell of her breasts.

He took a deep breath.

"Thanks for your pajamas," she said, smiling, looking absolutely beautiful to him.

"They've just been sitting in a drawer," he managed to tell her. "You know, Christmas stuff. I never wear... Oh, well, they're new."

"Oh," she replied and he could see a twinkle of amusement in her tired eyes. She yawned then, and he forced himself to remember the late hour. He had a lot of things to do tomorrow, not the least of which was to contact Rod Cordova. Adam would have loved to have questioned this John Martinez himself, but he didn't trust himself not to murder the man. It was, after all, an Indian whom his student had seen nosing around near the kiva and then driving off in a battered pickup.

"Adam," said Robin, breaking into his dark thoughts, "I wonder..."

"What?"

"I wonder if you would stay here awhile. I mean, just to be here, nothing...nothing else..." Her usually bold glance fell to her hands, which held the coverlet.

He felt himself swallow hard. He shouldn't stay—God, he didn't have it in him to stay and not touch her. But to just leave...

As if an unseen entity, the Apache trickster Coyote, propelled him forward, Adam found himself sitting on the side of her bed and then Robin's golden head was on his shoulder and she let out a contented sort of purr. ''Thank you,'' she whispered.

He had to get out of there. In a minute he'd do something they'd both be very sorry for, and Coyote would yip in laughter.

Somehow he managed, though. And when her deep rhythmic breathing reached his consciousness he rose carefully and turned off the lights. When he sat back down on the bed, he put his feet up and gently rested her head in the crook of his arm, his fingers softly moving through the hair that he had been forbidden to touch for such a long time. Yes, it was like silk, yellow-gold silk.

Several times over the next hour he lowered his head and his lips brushed the hair that his fingers caressed. His senses, in spite of his weariness, were acute. He was aware of the scents filling the room, the rough wool of the Navaho rug, the clean sheets, the powder-scented soap in Robin's laundered blouse. And of Robin herself, a warm, earthy, womanly scent. His eyes, adjusting to the dark, stared out through the parted curtains, and he could see the pinpoints of light in the night sky, the star warriors that guarded the world until Father Sun came out again to rule. The heater groaned quietly, almost in tune to his own breathing, and Robin's chest rose and fell softly.

Regret sat in his stomach heavily. He wished he weren't so keenly aware of his surroundings or so honest with himself. It was, of course, the Indian blood that pounded through his veins. In many ways, his heightened senses were a curse. He'd prefer to run from himself at moments—like now, as he held this woman to him, all the while knowing he could never really have her. When this

was over, when the police found the counterfeiters and
Robin Hayle was safe, and she was gone from his life, he
would have his uncle, his mother's brother, the singer,
sing him a cure and set his mind at rest. When this was
over.

He closed his eyes for a minute then opened them and
looked down at Robin's peaceful face. She was so brave.
So perfect. And the only thing he could do for her was
to protect her from this terrible situation he had gotten her
into. It seemed too little.

He must have slept then, because when he again opened
his eyes the moon had passed overhead and dawn was a
promise in the eastern sky. And he knew he'd slept, because Robin was in his arms now, her firm breasts pressed
to his own chest, her mouth dangerously close to his.

CHAPTER TWELVE

THE ROOM WAS EMPTY when Robin awoke. She knew that even before she opened her eyes, but there was still the impression Adam had made on the bed and, in the air faintly, his scent, male and erotic.

He'd left silently sometime in the night. She lay in the bed, stretching voluptuously, and remembered the feel of his arms, the warmth of his skin, the hardness and smoothness of his body. She wondered where he was and when he'd knock at the guest-room door to say that breakfast was ready. He'd no longer be closed to her, not after the intimacy of last night—he couldn't be.

Sitting up, Robin felt her head throb; automatically her hand went to her forehead. "Ouch," she said, feeling the sore bump under the bandage.

She climbed out of bed and padded barefoot across the floor to a mirror. The white square of adhesive should have been a sobering reminder of her accident, but somehow she couldn't muster up angry sentiments, not this morning. She felt filled instead with cheer and optimism, as if the sun were always going to shine in a cloudless sky and never, never again was there going to be a drop of rain to spoil a perfect day.

Of course, it was Adam who had done that to her. And how crazy it seemed that it had taken a brutal jolt to awaken him. An accident was nothing to take lightly, but nevertheless Robin was smiling. What a changeable man he was, she thought again. It seemed miraculous that suddenly he'd opened that door to his private world. It was miraculous and glorious, and she felt warm all over—warm, and she knew now, decidedly in love.

Where *was* Adam? Oh, probably sleeping in. They'd both been up late last night. Wonderful Adam. She imagined him asleep—oh, if only she'd seen his room in the hacienda so she could really picture him. His face would be relaxed and young-looking, his body stretched out—those lovely long, muscular thighs and calves. The hard flat stomach, the broad, hairless, coppery chest.

She'd never met anyone like him. He was quiet about his feelings, careful with them, but when he decided what he wanted, he was gentle and caring. He'd be a passionate, considerate lover. They'd talk. Oh, how much they had to say to each other! How much they could learn from each other.

Robin took a shower, careful not to get her bandage wet, and dressed in the same clothes she'd worn yesterday: the full tan skirt, the dry, stained turquoise blouse. But they'd have to do. Looking at herself in the mirror again, she decided the white adhesive was not the least bit becoming, so she tore it off.

Her face two inches from the mirror, she examined the cut. Four neat stitches. Big deal. Experimenting, she discovered that her bangs covered the stitches up nicely. That was much better; she didn't need to look like a wounded veteran. Thank goodness she at least had some makeup in her purse. She *was* looking a little pale—nothing that blush wouldn't remedy.

It was almost nine o'clock. Was Adam still asleep? She'd love to just go on into his room and wake him up. But Christina wouldn't exactly condone that, Robin decided. She was dying to see Adam again, to bask in that loving expression on his face, to hear him say her name. Would he kiss her good morning? Well, maybe, if his folks weren't around…

He was old-fashioned; he'd care what his mother thought. He was overprotective and old-fashioned, but it

was only because he'd been alone too long—like Robin—
and somebody, something had hurt him once. She'd find
out what it was, and she'd love him, adore him so much
that she'd cure his hurt and he'd be happy all the time.
Whatever happened, however different the worlds they
came from, now that she knew he cared, she was going
to move heaven and earth to bring them together.

Christina was in the kitchen, reading the arts section of
the Santa Fe paper over a cup of coffee.

"Good morning, Robin. Are you feeling all right?"

"Oh, I'm fine. Is Adam—"

"Let me see that cut. Adam told us what happened."
Christina stood and pushed Robin's bangs aside, stretching up to look. "Oh, it's not too bad. No one will ever
see it." She shook her head. "This is terrible. Adam says
you're going to stay here."

"Is he up yet?"

"Oh, he was hours ago. He drove back to Chaco to get
your car fixed. He said for you to wait here."

"Oh." He was gone already. She felt absurdly disappointed. "He didn't have to do that."

"He didn't want to wake you. He'll be back this afternoon. Now, don't you worry, just relax and enjoy yourself
and eat. You're so thin."

Robin made an effort to smile. Christina was handing
her a cup of coffee. "Oh, thanks. As a matter of fact, I'm
starving."

"I knew it," said Christina.

There were eggs and refried beans, soft, tasty homemade flour tortillas and strong coffee. "This is great,"
Robin enthused. "I'd recommend this restaurant to my
friends."

Christina laughed. "Ray likes a big breakfast."

"This is all very gracious of you," said Robin, "but I
really do have to get back to my shop. It's Friday, and
I've got to get to the bank. And Ericka won't be coming
in till afternoon."

"Adam said you should wait here until he gets back with your car."

"My car." It struck her then. "But what's he going to do with *his* car if he drives my car back?"

Christina shrugged. "Now, don't you worry. He'll probably get one of his students to drive it. He'll figure something out. He also said he's going to see Rod Cordova and he doesn't want you wandering around alone until he talks to the police."

"It's so crazy," said Robin. "I don't believe any of this is happening." She stared at a rolled tortilla in her hand and shook her head. "Maybe it's a dream. Or maybe it's all a series of strange accidents."

"Adam doesn't think so."

"Well, anyway, I've got to get back to town. There's a man coming in this afternoon for a shoot."

Christina frowned slightly. "My son will be very angry with us if we let you go alone."

"Oh, I feel awful, putting you out like this. I'll call a taxi…"

"You wait until Ray gets back. He'll figure something out." Christina leaned her elbow on the light, clear pine table. "What fantasy does your client have? Can you tell me?"

"Let's see." Robin closed her eyes and thought. "Oh, yes, today's the man who wants to be photographed as a Confederate officer—up on Glorieta Pass. Oh, my goodness, I've got to get his costume!"

Christina clasped her hands. "I love your stories!" she said. "Of course, you have to meet this man. Ray will take you."

"I couldn't ask—"

"Nonsense. Now you get the man's uniform lined up."

What else could Robin do? She phoned the rental agency about the Confederate Army uniform and arranged for a horse, complete with cavalry saddle, to meet her at Glorieta Pass at five. All the time she was aware of Christina, moving around the kitchen, tidying up. Adam's mother. And what, exactly, did Christina think of her— the strange white woman whom her son had to keep rescuing as if he were a knight on a charger?

Ray came in from work and had a roll and coffee. "So, more adventures," he said to Robin. "My son seems to have turned your life upside down."

If only he knew, Robin thought.

Christina told her husband that Robin had to get into town. "She shouldn't go alone. You'll take her, Ray, won't you?" Then she called him a strange, caressing word that Robin guessed was Apache. An endearment. She wanted Adam to say that word to her, to explain its meaning. She'd ask him when he got back.

"I can take her into town."

"She can't be left alone," said Christina.

"Fine, let me get a few things done around here first. Give me an hour or so."

"Mr. Farwalker, wouldn't it be easier to lend me a car?"

"What if something happened?" He shook his head soberly.

"Oh, for goodness sake," said Robin, "I hate being a burden."

"My dear girl, relax and let yourself be a burden, just this one time. Enjoy it," said Christina kindly. "That's what families are for."

Whose family? Robin wondered. *Adam's family?*

"Can I phone Ericka? Just to open the shop until we get there?" asked Robin. "Then I'll relax."

Shelly answered. "You're *where*? And I thought you said he wasn't interested! Naughty girl."

"Shel, his *parents* are being very nice to me. His *father* is driving me in later."

"Oh, I get it. Mom and Dad are there. I won't say another word."

"Listen, tell Chuck I'm real sorry I missed the committee meeting last night. I was out at Chaco Canyon until late.''

"Chaco Canyon? What for?''

"Uh, photographs. Yeah, I got some great shots,'' she lied. "Is Ericka there?''

"Still in bed. You need her at the shop?''

"Well, yes. I can't get in for a while.''

"Okay, I'll roust her out and send her over there.''

"That'd be great. Tell her she can have the afternoon off.''

"Sure, will do. And, hey, you better talk to Chuck about the meeting. He came home raving about Thad Mencimer. Seems there was some sort of argument...''

"Terrific.'' Robin groaned.

Ray drove her into town in his big, roomy air-conditioned pickup truck. He had the radio tuned into a station from Gallup, New Mexico. The commercials were all in English, but the news was in Navaho, a curious sibilant language to Robin's ear.

"And you can understand Navaho?'' she asked.

"Enough,'' he replied.

"I wonder how many people know there's a Navaho radio station?'' Robin mused.

Ray Farwalker took his role seriously. He accompanied her to her apartment, which he insisted on checking out first. At last, she could change her clothes—to something deliberately frivolous, a blue denim jumpsuit with rhinestone snaps down the front. He went with her to the bank, to the rental shop to pick up the officer's uniform, to the grocery store for tea and bread and meat for the sandwiches that Robin fixed for Ericka and Ray and herself for lunch. Adam's father didn't say a whole lot, but he was a comfortable man, quietly competent, and he had a subtle, dry sense of humor.

There were practically no customers all afternoon; Ericka went home, and Robin perched herself on the stool behind the counter to pay the first of the month bills. By four, she was done and went back to see how Ray was doing. He'd gotten through *American Quarterhorse* and *Cattle Breeding* and *Western Rancher*, so they had a cup of tea together.

"I hope you aren't going out of your mind sitting around," said Robin. "You know, you really could go home now. Obviously I'm perfectly safe here."

"I'll wait for Adam. He wants you to stay out at the ranch again tonight, so I can just drive you on out there."

"Your son certainly does like to manage things," she replied, exasperated.

Ray looked at her, his dark eyes giving nothing away but, she knew, judging her according to some inexplicable Apache standards that she could never understand. "And you are a little the same, I think," was all he said.

The bell over her front door tinkled. "Oh," she said, "a customer. Thought I'd never see one today. Excuse me."

It was Adam.

He looked hot and tired and impatient. Her heart went out to him—he'd gone to so much trouble for her. "Adam…" she began, but something in his expression stopped her, some unfathomable anger.

"Is my father here?" he said in a curt tone, dismissing her, making her shrivel up inside. And all she could do was gesture with her head toward the back of the shop.

What had happened? Her mood swung abruptly from cheerfulness to anxiety and all she could think was that she'd said or done something terrible. But what?

In a few moments both men appeared from the back; they had their dark heads bowed and were speaking in Apache. Robin pressed her lips together, refusing to give into paranoia. Finally Adam met her gaze.

"I talked to Rod Cordova this morning," he told her.

Robin sighed. "I still wish you hadn't. I promised that woman and…"

"You promised her," said Adam sharply, "before you were damn near killed."

There wasn't much she could say to that. "So I suppose you told Rod all about John Martinez."

Adam nodded slowly. "I had to. And I *am* sorry about the promise you made to your Indian friend, Robin, but making you swear to keep quiet was…frankly very childish of her."

Robin felt her cheeks flush with irritation; even Ray Farwalker put a hand on his son's arm. "She wasn't being childish," said Robin, "she was just scared."

"Sorry," said Adam, running a hand through his hair, "it's been a long day."

"Okay, I understand. What did Rod say, anyway?"

"He was very upset about your accident last night and when I drove out to Chaco, he went up to San Lucas."

"Did he find John Martinez?" asked Robin anxiously.

"Yes. I just got through talking to Rod again, in fact. It seems he got nothing out of Martinez, though. The Indian said he's never heard of you or the pots or an old woman with butterfly earrings. Rod even checked where Martinez was last night. He was home, according to everyone in the pueblo." Adam made an angry gesture with one hand. "But, of course, they would say that, whether it's true or not."

"You mean, you think John Martinez was out at Chaco Canyon yesterday and…"

"He has an old pickup truck."

"But so do most Indians—and a lot of white ranchers, too," put in Ray.

"I know, I know," said Adam. "It was worth checking out. But it didn't amount to anything. Damn."

"Adam," said Robin, "don't you think, now that you're here, your dad can go home?"

Adam raised a hand and tiredly massaged the back of his neck. "There's a small problem. Dad, I need you to drive me back out to Chaco."

"Today?" Robin asked.

"I've got to be out there tomorrow morning. And my car's still there."

"I can do that," said Ray. "Why don't we drop Robin off at the hacienda on the way? And your mother will want us to eat something first."

What a bother she felt, Robin thought. She absolutely couldn't bear the trouble they were going through for her. "Wait a minute," she said, putting her hands on her hips. "This is turning into an awful mess. Adam, *I'll* drive you out to Chaco. It's the least I can do."

"Robin, it's a long drive and your head—"

"My head is fine. Ask your father. I didn't pass out once today."

He watched her for a moment. "I'm not sure it's a good idea."

"Why not? Look, I'll just stay at a motel somewhere near Chaco and drive back here first thing in the morning." She looked from one man to the other. "Hey, I'm a big girl, you know."

Ray seemed noncommittal, but Adam was frowning.

"My car's fixed, isn't it? The only problem is that I have a five o'clock appointment. Could you wait a couple hours?"

A corner of Ray's mouth lifted in amusement. "Son," he said, "there's an old Apache proverb that says when a woman speaks wisely, even Coyote must listen."

"Well," said Robin when Ray was gone, "I have a great idea."

Adam quirked a brow.

"You need a nice, relaxing drink. I'm going to close up here, and we'll go over to La Fonda until my client meets us back here."

"I won't argue with that," Adam replied.

The atmosphere in the Conquistador Lounge was old world, very Santa Fe. The decor consisted of wrought iron, Indian adobe and bunches of bright red dried chili peppers; Anglo service and business acumen provided the rest.

Adam took a long swallow of his frosty margarita and sat back with a faint smile. "Not a bad idea, at that."

"You must be exhausted. Your mother told me you left very early this morning." She was being careful, speaking only of impersonal subjects. The man sitting across from her was not the same one who had held her tenderly last night. She didn't know what had gone wrong, what she'd done, to cause this drastic change in him; she only hoped it was due to his long day.

"Um," he said.

Julien came in just then, accompanied by Madeline Lassiter. They seemed to be looking for a table in the crowded lounge. He saw Robin and waved, then the two of them, an odd couple, made their way over to Robin's table. "*Buenas tardes, amigos.* Robin, you weren't at the meeting last night."

"Uh, no, sorry I couldn't make it."

"There was quite a row," Madeline said, eyeing Adam. "Why, Mr. Farwalker, how nice to see you again. You know, I wanted to ask you about a pot I have, a Hopi polychrome. The dealer I bought it from told me it was sixteenth century, but I have my suspicions it's newer than that."

"The laboratory at the university would be glad to help you, Miss…"

"Lassiter. Madeline Lassiter," she answered, beaming at him.

"I'm afraid I just don't have the equipment with me to help you," Adam said sidestepping gracefully.

"Is this the same fight that Chuck told Shelly about?" Robin asked Madeline.

"Oh, boy, it was hot and heavy there for a while. We discussed your plan to organize the Indian artists. Well, Thad—you know Thad—made a disparaging remark about Indians." She shot a glance at Adam. "I apologize for him, Mr. Farwalker. Anyway, Ben Chavez got up in arms. His grandfather was Navaho, you know. It was ugly, I'll tell you. So we left with nothing accomplished.''

"Thad, dear boy," put in Julien, "is hasty and misguided, but he's not a bad person."

"Oh, no?" commented Robin.

"He'll come around," replied Julien.

"Don't you think the committee would be better off without Thad?" asked Robin.

"My dear, we can't just kick him out of the group. That wouldn't be fair. We'll convince him."

"I hope so," murmured Madeline, eyeing Adam again. "What did you think of Thad, Mr. Farwalker?"

"I really don't feel qualified to make a judgment, Miss Lassiter," said Adam.

Robin looked from Adam to Madeline and back again. Her head was cocked, her brain working. "You know," she began, "maybe your mother, Adam, could speak to the committee. She'd be such a good liaison..."

"You'd have to ask my mother *that* one," remarked Adam dryly. "The Indian community, as I'm sure you know, is very closed. Your idea, like I said at the meeting, is sound, but getting the Indian artisans to organize may not be so easy."

"But it's certainly worth a try, isn't it?" put in Julien.

"Of course it is," replied Adam.

"Well," said Robin, "it can't hurt to ask your mother. The worst she can say is no."

"Splendid idea," Julien was saying. "Well, we'll leave you two. Madeline and I are meeting a dealer here. Enjoy yourselves."

"Good night, Mr. Farwalker, or may I call you Adam?" Madeline said.

"My pleasure," Adam replied, rising and taking her hand.

"Well," said Robin, shaking her head, "I think you have a new fan in the form of Miss Lassiter."

But Adam only finished his drink, pointedly not taking the bait. Yet he was pleasant company, despite his reticence and his weariness, and all the women in the bar noticed him. Robin liked the feeling of being with such a handsome man. She could pretend that they were a couple, that she belonged to him and to Santa Fe, that there was a place for her, a home.

"It's almost five," Adam said.

"Is it? Oh." She finished her margarita. "Back to work, I guess."

"Your head's okay?" he asked.

"Just fine."

Her client was Ted Butler, a shy, bone-thin Texan from Houston with such a strong southern accent Robin had trouble understanding him. He changed into his officer's uniform in her shop and strutted out to show them. "Ah shirley dew look shop," he said, which Robin translated as, "I surely do look sharp."

"You certainly do," she agreed, cocking her head, checking him for authenticity. His breeches were snug, his gray tunic flattering, his tall leather boots elegant. His hat brim was rolled precisely, with the emblem of the Confederacy in front.

Adam drove Robin and Ted the thirteen miles to the spot on the highway marked Glorieta Pass, the site of a Civil War battle. It was a place of broad vistas, rolling hills dotted with stands of evergreens, dry and brown this September day. The horse trailer was already there, and a sullen-looking driver leaned against the fender of the truck smoking a hand-rolled cigarette.

"Could you get the horse out of the trailer, please?" Robin asked the man.

"Not this horse, lady," he said. "She's nuts. I told my boss…"

"Oh, great," said Robin. And as if to punctuate her words, a loud blow came from inside the trailer—a hoof connecting with the wooden tailgate.

"Ah don't know," said Ted doubtfully, his brows arched. "Ah'm no great rider."

"Let me," said Adam, "I've handled a couple horses in my day."

"Oh, could you?" asked Robin.

He backed the horse out easily, seemingly unafraid of the mare's rolling white eyes and quick hoofs. He spoke softly to her in his native language as he led her around. His big hands caressed her sweat-blotched neck and withers until she stood quietly. Robin watched spellbound. *If only he'd touch me with the same love and indulgence,* she thought. *If only he'd talk to me like that.*

"Mr. Butler, you can mount her now. She was just excited," said Adam.

Gingerly Ted Butler mounted the horse. Adam held the reins still, his voice and hands soothing, the mare's ears flicking back and forth, but she stood quietly.

"She'll be fine now," Adam said, moving away.

Robin dragged herself back to reality and set up her tripod. The sun slanted over the hills from the west, making interesting shadows on Ted Butler's rather ordinary face. If she caught him at a certain angle, he looked broader than he was, older and more commanding.

"Put your right hand on the hilt of your sword, Ted. That's it. Sit up real straight. Good."

Robin pushed her hair off her brow and looked through her lens again. "No, Ted, toward me. There. Okay." She waved a hand at him. "Just a little to the left. Good. Now, tuck your chin a bit... Good. Good." *Snap. Snap.* "Okay, that's better." *Snap.* "Now look past my right shoulder. Too high... Okay. Perfect." In twenty minutes, her voice growing raspy from directing Ted Butler, the shoot was all wrapped up. Robin let out a long breath. Ted Butler wasn't the easiest subject, but she had seen a number of interesting shots through her lens.

"How'd ah do, ma'am?"

"Great, Ted. The proofs will be ready Monday."

Ted was grinning. "And just think," he said, "mah great-grandaddy sat on his horse right there, maybe on that very spot."

They drove Ted back to Robin's shop, stopped by her apartment for a few of her things and were on the road, supplied with a bag of fast-food burgers and milk shakes, by six-thirty.

"You were wonderful with the horse," Robin said, munching on a hamburger as Adam drove.

"It's only experience. The animals know." He glanced over at her, and she couldn't tell whether he meant to be serious or not. "They say Apaches were always good with horses. Maybe it's just in my genes."

For all practical purposes it looked like she was involved with her French fries, but Robin couldn't take her eyes off his hands as they grasped the steering wheel, the same hands that had gentled the mare as if by magic. Apache magic. "What were you saying to the horse?" she finally asked.

"Oh, the usual. Things like take it easy, calm down. But in Apache the words seem to reach the animals better. I can't really translate them."

"I think it's wonderful," she said, "I mean, that you have that kind of power with animals. Will you teach your children how to do that? Is it really difficult?"

He was so completely still that Robin looked over at him, wondering if he'd heard her. His profile was stern, his lips set. He pulled out around a truck, pressing the accelerator of her racy white car to the floor.

"Adam?"

"Um. Sorry, I was concentrating on driving. What did you ask me?"

Robin looked at her hands, closely examining a pearl ring that she'd worn for at least ten years. "Oh, nothing, it wasn't important."

His thigh swelled with muscle under the fabric of his pants as he drove. She watched it surreptitiously, itching to touch the smooth skin beneath the cloth, to feel the male strength of it. She sipped on her milk shake and tried not to stare at him, but it was just too tempting.

Finally Robin stuffed the crumpled-up burger wrappers, straws and napkins into a paper sack and turned to toss the trash into the back seat. She spied a pretty lemon-yellow bag from a downtown Santa Fe clothing shop lying on the seat. "What's this?" she asked, stretching to pick it up.

"Oh," Adam said, glancing over, "I forgot completely. When I got back into town this afternoon with your car, I stopped by this shop my sisters always use..."

But Robin was barely listening. She'd opened the bag and seen a lovely, pure silk blouse in it. A dark, shimmering blue color.

Adam was saying, "I hope you like the color. They didn't have anything in turquoise."

"But... Oh, Adam, you mean you *really* replaced my blouse? I don't believe it!"

"Of course I did," was all he replied, and she couldn't find a single thing to say in return—not one word in her abundant repertoire came to mind.

Robin knew not to make too much of a fuss; Adam would have been embarrassed. Yet she couldn't help fingering the silky material, touching the tiny round covered buttons. He'd gone into a woman's shop and picked this out all by himself. The enormity of the act was staggering. And she noted, as well, that the dark blue color of the silk nearly matched that of her eyes. She wondered...

"It's a very thoughtful gift," Robin said finally, putting it back into the bag and dropping the subject. But she still wondered, for a long time, about the color.

They left the foothills of the Jemez range behind as it grew dark. The vast, parched plateau stretched before them; they were heading right into the sunset, into a realm of purple and pink and orange that changed iridescently each second. A single small cloud, its silhouette black, hung unmoving in the sky.

"Beautiful," Robin commented.

"Desert sunsets, they say, are the best."

Silence fell between them, strained, expectant, too difficult to break. Finally Robin said, "I can drive, you know. I had a lot more sleep than you did last night."

"I'm okay."

"If you feel tired…"

"Sure."

She crossed her legs, cramped in the little car, her muscles unable to relax with Adam's proximity. "Do you think John Martinez lied to Rod?"

"Yes."

"How is anybody going to find out anything?"

"Sooner or later, either Martinez will have to admit to what he's done, or someone will make a mistake, give himself away."

"What if they don't? I mean, I can't camp on your doorstep the rest of my life."

"No, you can't. Well, if the authorities put enough pressure on the counterfeiters, the ring will either quit or move elsewhere. Your idea for an Indian association is good in that respect, too, because the crooks get pressure from both sides. We'll get them eventually."

The miles sped by; few cars were on the road. The sun sank below the horizon slowly, like a burning ship going down.

At Torreon, Adam pulled into a small gas station and topped up the tank. Robin went to the ladies' room and splashed cold water on her face. She wondered what Adam really thought of her. The constant curiosity nagged at her because she couldn't read him. Yet last night he'd cared; he'd touched her with gentle passion. What had changed between now and then?

When she got back he handed her the keys. "Your turn," he said.

She drove faster than he did, enjoying the power and control. It was pitch-black outside the beam of her headlights; the moon had not yet risen. Adam reclined his seat. ''You okay if I catch forty winks?'' he asked.

''Fresh as a daisy.''

Robin was aware of the moment he slept, the very second his breathing became slow and cadenced. She glanced over at him but could only see shadows, a dark form lit briefly by a lighted sign in a village. She barreled on through the darkness of the ancient land toward an even more ancient rendezvous, the man she wanted for a mate sleeping beside her, their roles reversed. Odd, disconnected images flitted through her mind: the lights of the pickup truck approaching too fast from behind her, John Martinez handing her his pot, Madeline Lassiter batting her eyelashes at Adam, Adam's hands on the nervous horse's damp coat.

Adam woke up as they passed Pueblo Pintado. He rubbed a big hand over his eyes, looking out the window then checked his watch. ''You driving or flying low?'' he asked.

''Feel better?'' she inquired.

''Probably will when I really wake up. You okay? Your head bothering you?''

She touched the cut with a finger. It was still tender. ''Gosh, I almost forgot about it.''

''I didn't.''

It was past ten when they turned at the visitors' center.

''Pull up for a second, Robin,'' Adam said.

Dutifully she stopped on the shoulder of the road. ''You want to drive?''

''No. Listen, Robin.'' He hesitated, and she knew he wanted to say something difficult. ''It's late. There isn't a motel for miles. I don't want you driving off alone.''

Her heart began a swift rhythm, knowing a decision was coming, anticipating it, before her brain allowed her the knowledge. ''Okay. What do you propose I do?''

He was looking, not at her, but past her at the rising walls of the canyon. "Stay here with me."

She wasn't sure she'd heard right. He'd asked her to stay with him. Was it possible?

He reached out and touched her shoulder. "Stay with me," he repeated softly.

"I..." Her heart was pounding so furiously that she thought he must be able to hear it, to feel the glad, frightened beat.

"You realize what I'm asking?" he said with incredible tenderness, his fingers stroking her shoulder, moving up to her neck, her earlobe.

"Yes," she whispered, her throat closing over the word.

CHAPTER THIRTEEN

SHE FOLLOWED HIM along the dark, stony path, her hand in his, her heart beating so hard that it was almost painful. Powerful feelings gripped her, excitement contradicting terror, her whole body quivering with anticipation.

"Do you want to slow down?" he asked, stopping once. "The path is hard to see."

Robin could only shake her head. She was breathless—but not entirely from the walk.

Nothing could have been more foreign to her than following a man along an ancient trail beneath an immense, startlingly clear night sky—knowing where they were headed—longing for it, yet somehow afraid of what was to come.

What am I doing? she asked herself. She was embarking on a journey, a journey she had sought and craved. But Adam, like his fierce ancestors, was strange to her. Did she really know what she'd begun? Shouldn't she have played it safe and waited until she knew him better? The myriad questions flew elusively around in her head, but with each step her commitment became more solid and defined.

"Why don't you camp near the students?" she asked.

She could see his shoulders shrug. "They're young, and they don't want a chaperone."

His camp was big and inviting. There was a tent large enough to stand up in and a canvas lean-to across from it that covered a worktable. Papers, held down by rocks, were scattered on its top and books sat in negligent piles.

Beneath the lean-to was a Coleman stove; a fire pit sat in the center of the area, and nearby were a woodpile and kindling. Adam began to build a fire for warmth.

"Make yourself comfortable," he said as he built a teepee of wood in the pit.

Robin glanced around.

"Oh," he said, "there's a canvas stool in the tent, folded up."

"Okay." She pulled back the tent flap and, using a lantern he'd lit, she found the stool. For a moment she stood there, inside the tent, aware of his scent in the place, his own singular scent mingling with earth and canvas and wood smoke. Her skin tingled.

Then she saw the air mattress that he slept on, that *they* would sleep on, and her heart lurched. She came out of the tent quickly, feeling a little dizzy and a little intimidated.

He was crouched on his haunches, feeding a small red flame that coiled up from the fire. He gazed up at her for a moment, his eyes reflecting pinpoints of firelight.

"Don't you get cold here at night?" she asked.

"No."

There was so much of the Indian in this man that she had a hard time at that moment envisioning him at his university, living in an apartment, surrounded by creature comforts. She sat on the stool and put her hands near the fire, rubbing them together. "Do you prefer living outdoors?" she asked.

He gave her a sudden glance. "You're so curious, Robin. I get the feeling at times that I'm a specimen and you're studying me."

She felt her cheeks grow warm. "I *am* interested in you," she said, deciding absolute frankness was the only way to go. "You're a complete enigma to me."

"Because I'm an Indian?"

She looked down at her hands. "Yes," she admitted, "that fascinates me. But you shouldn't take it the wrong way. It's part of you, just like someone's shape or size or personality.'' She looked up and saw that he was watching her intently. ''That's why you're attracted to a person, because of what he or she is, isn't it?''

''I admire your honesty,'' he said. ''I'm afraid I've been taught to know myself but not necessarily to communicate it to others. An Apache trait.''

''A person can learn to communicate.''

''Yes, if he has a good enough reason.''

She let that drop. Adam seemed willing to talk, and she wanted so badly to delve into his soul. ''Does my being white make me an enigma to you?'' she asked.

He smiled faintly. ''No one's asked me *that* before.''

''Well, does it?''

''Not really. Sometimes you do things that seem odd to me, but I can always figure out your reasons.''

''Like what?''

''Like pursuing this pottery scam,'' he replied.

''Justice and the good ol' American way, huh?'' she asked lightly. Didn't he realize that if it weren't for this pottery scam, they wouldn't be in this camp together? ''You know,'' Robin said, ''I really do envy you. I envy you all this.'' She made a sweeping gesture with her hand. ''You're comfortable in what you do. With your family, your job, your *self*.'' And then she laughed. ''Don't I sound well-adjusted?''

''You do to me,'' he replied, dead serious.

''Anyway,'' Robin continued, ''we poor whites have been searching and searching forever for those qualities that come so naturally to your people. But we've never even come close.''

''Most whites don't seem to notice the lack.''

''But I do. I always thought that if I belonged to a big family I could find that harmony.''

''And can't you belong?''

She shook her head then pushed her hair behind her

ears, a pensive gesture. "The only way I can belong is to have a big family of my own."

"You deserve that then," he said, resting his arms on his knees and meeting her steady gaze. The firelight, now blazing, burnished his face and hands. "So you feel that you aren't comfortable with yourself?" he asked.

"Me?" Robin laughed again, too easily. "As much as anybody, I suppose."

He was silent for a minute, his stare pinning her. Slowly he got to his feet and stood there, tall and commanding, his eyes bronze in the eerie glow, his jet-black hair gleaming. Her breath caught in her throat. "I have no business probing into your life, Robin," he said quietly, "it's enough that you're here with me." Without hesitation he moved toward her, reached down and took her hands in his and pulled her to her feet.

She was face to face with him, with the man she'd ached to know for so long now. She felt she could hardly function, her thoughts spinning too madly, her pulse racing wildly out of control.

Gazing down at her, he released her hands, placing his own on either side of her face. "I want you," he whispered as his eyes searched hers. She barely had the presence of mind to nod and follow him into the tent.

He turned down the lamp then faced her. The tent flap was open and the firelight flickered on his face and chest as he unbuttoned his shirt and pulled it off. He stood there, big and powerful, dark shadows dancing on his beautifully coppered skin, his muscles moving as he breathed deeply and silently.

Robin drew in a breath. She felt as if all her senses had suddenly sprung to life. There was no existence other than in this small enclosed place with Adam. Civilization was stripped from her, and she let it fall away as her eyes half closed in expectancy. Her own hands reached up to undo the rhinestone snaps on her jumpsuit.

"I want to do that," came Adam's voice. She let him.

His hands seemed to linger on each shining stone, his fingers brushing her flesh, leaving a blazing trail of sensation behind until her body trembled with yearning. Then he was slipping the suit from her shoulders and helping her to step out of it.

"You're very beautiful," he said softly as he unfastened her bra and it, too, joined the mounting pile of clothing.

Goose bumps formed on her skin as the cold night air enfolded her nakedness. It was not at all unpleasant, because she felt so alive, so uninhibited. Perhaps a young Anasazi couple had once stood on this spot near the pueblo and dropped their clothing to the hard earth...

Adam kissed her lips, her eyelids, holding her hair aside, turning her in his arms, kissing her shoulders and the nape of her neck while his hands moved along the curve of her hips and buttocks. He seemed to want to possess her entire body, to memorize each curve and hollow before they would lie down together. Her knees grew weak, so unsteady that she sagged against him and turned to put her arms around his naked back where her fingers began their own quest for knowledge of him.

Adam was all iron-hard muscle and sinew beneath that smooth, hairless skin. He was amazingly warm to the touch, warm and vital as her hands searched him, bringing life to his beautiful flesh. His lips met hers and she moaned gently as his tongue probed her mouth, slowly, luxuriously, as if time itself no longer had meaning.

Still in each other's arms, Adam urged her down until they were both on their knees on the mattress, holding each other, hands exploring more quickly now, more hungrily. Then Robin's head fell back and her spine arched; she clutched his shoulders as his lips found each breast and drew its cool silkiness into his mouth.

She felt a primitive need to join with him. It was primeval but human; her brain registered each touch, each nuance of body language, each breath. Each instant between them was burned into her memory deliciously.

He eased her onto her back and kissed her with exquisite tenderness, such loving, that she felt herself open like a flower. Then slowly, patiently, he filled her, moving on top of her in fluid motion, his body in control, beautifully tuned and in rhythm with her own.

It winged softly through Robin's consciousness that they were made for each other, that no other man or woman could come together this perfectly. But soon she was incapable of thought or reasoning as that place deep in her belly began to burn and seek release.

Adam's mouth moved against hers, lightly brushing it, his lips parted, his breathing shallow and quick. "Oh, Adam," she moaned and he knew she was ready. Her back arched, and her legs strained and together they cried out softly into the night.

For a time they slept. But Robin was restless. The fire outside dimmed and she awakened occasionally in Adam's warm arms inside the goose-down sleeping bag and listened to the crack of an ember or the chatter of a night creature in the canyon.

She wanted to awaken Adam, to tell him so many things, to listen to the sounds together, to watch the fire die out. But he was sleeping so deeply, an arm thrown over her breasts, a leg possessively over her calves.

It was dawn when Robin opened her eyes again. A faint pearl glow lit the land outside the tent and drove the deep night shadows back into their dens. She turned her head and met Adam's gaze.

"Good morning," he said quietly.

"Hi," Robin replied, smiling lazily, drugged with happiness as his arm moved across her chest and his fingers touched the side of her breast.

Their lovemaking was different this morning. It was slow and tender as it had been before, but now there seemed to be a kind of sadness to Adam's passion. He kissed her and loved her and stroked her as before, but in his touch she sensed a holding back, as if he gave all of his flesh but none of his soul.

That notion shot through Robin's head for only a moment, though, and then disappeared as pure sensation gripped her. Then there was only Adam, his superb body poised above hers, his dark eyes capturing her own as he entered her gently.

By the time their morning song had died down, Robin was covered in a fine sheen of perspiration, her thick curling hair clinging to her neck and forehead.

Adam propped himself up on an elbow and smiled. "God, you're beautiful," he said, pushing a damp lock from her eyes. Then he leaned over and kissed her brow.

He was so gentle and kind and loving, she thought, so very special. A joy filled her to bursting. Yet there was that *something*, that remoteness. Oh, she'd tried in dozens of ways to fathom it, but each time without success. It was as if he were trying to tell her something by holding back, almost as if he were issuing a kind of warning. But maybe it was only her imperfect understanding of him.

While she dressed, Adam brought her a pan of water. "It's freezing cold," he told her, "but I thought you might want to ah, wash up or whatever."

She smiled and took the pan and absolutely adored his shyness. He was old-fashioned, a true gentleman, a rare breed. She could spend the rest of her life with him, she dared to think.

To fend off the crisp morning air, Adam had built a fire. He was cooking breakfast, however, on the Coleman stove. She could smell bacon frying.

"They say this stuff's lousy for you," Adam said over his shoulder as he turned the spattering bacon strips.

"Totally rotten," Robin agreed, "but I adore it." She sat near the fire. The logs hissed and popped and warmed her. Over the rim of the mountain the first rays of sun were creeping across the canyon. In a matter of hours, the canyon would be blazing hot, baking beneath that relentless sun. Bitter cold at night, scorching by day. A cruel trick of nature.

"How do you like your eggs?" Adam asked. "Scrambled or scrambled?"

"Oh, scrambled, please." She watched him at the stove. He was wearing a green and black plaid shirt, blue jeans, work boots. His sleeves were rolled up and she couldn't take her gaze off those strongly corded forearms—the same arms that had held her so carefully only a short time ago. Her love was so strong at that instant that it was like fire running before a relentless wind, utterly out of control, unstoppable. She hugged her arms around her waist and smiled secretly.

"We have to talk about tonight," he said as he dished up the breakfast.

"Oh?" Of course, she couldn't stay there forever—Ericka had to take off for Denver, and the shop wouldn't run itself, for Pete's sake. But staying out at his folks', without Adam...

"There's the hacienda," he suggested.

She shook her head as she took the plate from his hands. "I suppose I'll have to ask Shelly. She has a guest room, two of them, in fact."

Adam shot her a grave look as he sat on the ground in front of the fire. "I hate to say this," he began, "but I'm not sure I trust you to stay at your friends'."

"Adam!"

"I'm serious. You take everything so lightly." He continued to study her face. "I'm not sure you remember what happened to you the night before last, Robin."

"Oh, I remember," she answered dryly. "I've got the stitches to remind me. I've learned my lesson."

"I hope so. Someone, somewhere, knows an awful lot about your movements."

"I'll think about it," promised Robin, "and I swear I'll

spend the nights at Shelly's until this business is cleared up."

"Even if it takes awhile?"

"No matter how long. I could even get a room at a hotel; it's off-season, cheap, you know." She almost added that she'd gladly make the long, inconvenient drive to Chaco every night, but she deemed it best to take things more slowly.

And there *was* something in Adam's demeanor that morning. It wasn't anything she could quite put her finger on, but it was present nonetheless, just hovering below the surface of his calm expression.

They ate their breakfast in relative silence. Robin felt happy, though, content just to be near him in this marvelous place of his. She was certain he'd never brought anyone else there, too; a woman knew those things.

She wondered if Adam felt the same way about her as she did about him. Did he love her? She knew him well enough to suspect that he'd not had too many flings in his life, so last night must have been as special for him as it had been for her.

Contentment filled her, and so did a new, alien emotion, that of belonging, feeling comfortable, feeling wanted and needed.

"It's a lovely morning," commented Robin. "Not a cloud in the sky."

He finished the last piece of bacon and looked over at her. He seemed to be contemplating something. "What did you say?"

"Oh, just that it's a perfect morning."

"Yes, it is."

For a few minutes Adam straightened the campsite, clearing the stove, setting the dishes in a bucket of soapy water. He restacked the woodpile and hung the sleeping bag to air in the sun. Robin tried to help, but he didn't seem to want her to do anything.

"Leave the dishes to soak," he said when she tried to

wash them. "I always do," he added as if to explain his curt tone.

"Well," said Robin, "It's already eight o'clock. I better get a move on."

"Oh," he said.

"And Adam, thanks, thanks for everything." She was picking up her big purse from the ground and then found herself saying, "For last night, too."

He didn't say a thing, not a single word. A faint alarm sounded in Robin's head.

"I'll, ah, walk you back to your car," he finally said.

"You don't have to."

"No problem."

He'd withdrawn from her. It was written in his closed expression; it was in his distant glance and in the set of his stride. She tried not to make too much of it, telling herself that he was preoccupied with his work, that maybe he was thinking about the cave-in at the kiva and trying to decide whether or not to work on it this fall. He couldn't be upset with her. He couldn't be.

Their vehicles were parked alongside each other. Robin stopped by hers and searched her bag for her keys. The sun was warm on her back already, and Adam stood with his hands in his pockets, his face catching the bright light, his expression hidden from her.

"Oh, here they are," she said, holding them up and rattling them.

"You will stay at Shelly's, right?"

"I promise," she replied, unlocking her door, tugging on it when it stuck. But Adam was there to help her, pulling it open. Then, when she was about to climb in, he put a hand on her shoulder, stopping her.

"Listen," he began, "about last night..." His touch was stiff. "Robin, I... Look, it was very special to me. And I do want to see you again." He paused for a long moment, his dark eyes reaching out to her, telling her something, something sad and frightening. Her heart began to beat furiously.

"What is it?" she asked softly.

He drew in a long breath. "I hope, Robin, that we can always be...well, that we can always be friends."

She stared at him in stupefied confusion for an eternity. *Friends?*

She knew that the blood had drained from her face and that her lips were quivering. "Is that what you call *friendship* Adam? I thought we made love."

His face tightened. "I'm sorry, Robin. I never meant to hurt you."

"Thank you for your good intentions."

"You deserve much better than I can give you. We're too different. It can't work between us."

"Is this some kind of *Apache* revelation?" she asked sarcastically, lashing out at him.

He shook his head. "Only human."

"Well, so that's that. And I liked you, Adam, I really thought..."

"Robin, don't..."

"Please." She shook her head in disbelief, desperately holding back tears. "I guess I better get going." Shakily she got into the driver's seat and somehow managed to start the engine. *Friends,* he'd said. She felt like laughing hysterically.

"You'll be okay driving alone?" he asked, his tone as strained as hers.

"Oh, sure, perfectly fine." She stepped on the gas, backing out with her tires screeching, then forced the gearshift into first and sped off down the road. In her mirror she could see Adam, still standing there, the dust from her tires settling onto him.

Friends. How could she have been so intolerably stupid?

CHAPTER FOURTEEN

THE WEEKEND DRAGGED BY. Adam classified dozens of pottery shards, relaid some masonry in the collapsed kiva roof and tried to read a new tome on Mimbres pottery discoveries. The physical work permitted him to forget Robin for a few relief-filled moments, but attempting to read turned out to be futile.

On Sunday afternoon, the students headed off for a restaurant meal in Farmington; Adam took a long walk. The clouds built up in the west and came rolling in, cutting off the sun, but this time it did rain. The heavy drops hit the dusty earth and bounced, then more came, and the ground turned damp; unable to drink anymore, it became muddy.

Still Adam walked, his head drawn between his shoulders, hands in pockets, rain dripping into his eyes, trying to realign himself with the earth's harmony, to walk in beauty, as the Apache would say. He was not very successful.

He should have told her.

He'd seen her expression Saturday morning, hurt, bewildered, begging for answers. *Friends,* he'd said. He couldn't blame her for running from him. He couldn't give her what she wanted, not emotionally or in any other way. He was a living lie.

His feet slithered on the muddy path; a trickle of water gurgled down the usually dry streambed of Chaco wash. Nine hundred years ago this life-giving fluid would have been caught and diverted. It would have kept communities alive. Now it just went to waste, sucked up by the thirsty earth to nurture only snakeweed, mesquite and rabbit brush. A wasteland, as empty and desolate as his life.

Robin had loved him with her whole being, body and soul. Why had he led her on; why had he let himself give in? Because he couldn't help himself, because he was weak and lonely, because he wanted a woman. No, not any woman; he wanted Robin.

Well, it was over and if he had any damn sense, he'd leave it that way.

Monday wasn't much of an improvement. Odd flashes of memory bedeviled him: Robin in his arms, her head bleeding, Robin laughing, her hands touching his back, sending electric shocks through his body, Robin telling one of her funny stories, drolly, with perfect timing.

He had an irresistible urge to drive to the visitors' center and phone her shop. Was she safe? Was she staying with the Daltons? Had Rod come up with anything? But he didn't give in to the urge, because that would mean starting in all over again, hearing her voice, wanting her.

He didn't notice his students regarding him strangely, exchanging questioning looks. It was as if a tight band encircled his head, pulled tighter and tighter each minute.

"Do you think this hole is a ritual one or is it natural?" asked Craig, holding out a curved section of a bowl that had a small hole in it.

Adam looked at the piece, but he saw only Robin's face and her blue eyes, shocked, hurt. "Uh, let's see." He took the shard, felt its sun-warmed surface and recalled the silkiness of her skin. "Ritual hole? I'm not sure."

"The Mimbres people punch holes in their funerary pots, but did the Chaco people?" asked Jack.

"The hole could just be from your pick," Adam said, handing the young man back the piece and turning away.

Monday night he took his sleeping bag and lay out under the moon. He tried to relax, to open his mind to the mighty forces that pervaded the universe. The Apache way might bring him peace of mind, he thought, because, surely, the white man's way was not working.

The moon was nearly full, the silver disk slightly lop-sided. The white man called the markings on the moon a face, but to Adam that night the bright globe in the sky was marked, flawed, like himself.

He wished once again he could go to his uncle on the reservation, undergo the ritual sweat bath, take part in a Blessing Way, invoke the spirits and be cleansed, healed. He didn't question the efficacy of the ceremony, nor did he judge it according to the beliefs of the outside world; he only accepted. But the ceremony was long and costly and needed weeks to set up. He would have to wait and bear his pain alone until a Blessing Way could be arranged.

Apaches despised a coward. Was he a coward? he wondered. Or was he merely a man trying to do the best he could under intolerable circumstances? He'd had no choice, either, none whatsoever, when he'd put off Robin that morning. Maybe if she hadn't told him so honestly, so adamantly, how important a family was to her, how she dreamed of one day having a *large* family. Maybe if she'd said she never wanted children—as some women nowadays professed—then he would not have felt the terrible necessity to distance himself from her.

But that hadn't been the case at all, had it?

He stared at the blotched face of the moon and craved the soothing Apache chants, the stamping dances, the fire and drums, the regalia of costume and mask, the intimacy with a world beyond the limited human one.

Could he exist without ever seeing or hearing or touching Robin again? His mind said yes but his heart cried out against the decision. He missed her already, more than he could have imagined. He missed her affection and warmth and the constant delight that emanated from her.

Did he really want to go through life alone?

A tiny dart of hope pricked at him. What if he told her

the truth? If she loved him she'd accept him. Lots of couples had no children. As for the family, his sisters had plenty of children between them; one of his nieces or nephews would want Las Jaritas. It could work out.

But inwardly he shuddered at telling Robin of his infirmity. What if she pitied him? Or what if she stayed with him from a misguided sense of duty and resented him forever?

Adam rubbed a hand over his face. No, time would heal them both. It was better this way.

By Tuesday morning his mind had turned on him treacherously. He'd been taking it for granted that she was safe, that she was keeping her promise to stay with her friends. And he'd left the question of the forgeries up to Rod. He'd ignored the fact that Josefina Ortega knew what was going on and that perhaps he, as an old family friend, could coax more information from her.

How easy it had been to remain in the canyon and pretend everything would work itself out. But this passiveness did not suit his character. It was too bad, because by facing up to his responsibility, it would mean seeing Robin again. He'd have to pretend they were merely acquaintances, turn his feelings off, somehow see this business to its conclusion without causing either of them more pain.

He drove to the visitors' center and reentered the world of the living by phoning Rod Cordova. And as he'd suspected, Rod had come to a standstill with his investigation. "Sorry, Adam, but I came to a dead end with your pal, Martinez. I'll keep the file open, but it's going to be damn difficult even proving there's a counterfeit ring."

"Okay," Adam replied, but there was one more thing he was going to try, and he wasn't going to mention it to Cordova. "I'll be in touch," was all he said.

His next call was to his mother. When he told her to telephone Josefina and explain about the danger Robin had been put in, his mother hesitated. "Look," said

Adam, "you're the one who told Josefina about the forgeries in the first place. Just call her and ask her to be
cooperative when I get there. She trusts you."

Christina was uncertain, admitting to her son that her
friend Josefina was scared of her own shadow, but eventually, reluctantly, she agreed. "You'll be careful though,
won't you?" she asked.

And now there remained the question of Robin. She
was the real key to Josefina's cooperation. Leaving the
visitors' center, he looked up into the sun, closed his eyes
for a moment and steeled himself.

ERICKA DALTON SAT ON THE STOOL behind the counter of
Robin's Nest. She looked up at the tinkling of the bell
and smiled. "Oh, hello, Mr. Farwalker."

"Is Robin in?"

"She's in back, doing a portrait." Ericka rolled her
eyes, then whispered, "The lady is dressed up like Marie
Antoinette. And she's got her two poodles with her.
French poodles, get it? I think Robin's going to throttle
those dogs."

From the back room came a sharp yipping and a lady's
admonishing voice. Ericka giggled.

Adam glanced at his watch. "She'll be awhile then?"

"Another half an hour, at least."

He told her he'd be back then walked down the street
and grabbed a bite to eat. The time passed in a strange
jerky fashion; seconds dragged endlessly but minutes
flew. He strode back into Robin's Nest before a half hour
was up.

Robin was standing talking to a lady in full eighteenth-
century costume: billowing satin skirt, low bodice, powdered wig. Two white poodles frisked, nipping and yap-
ping, around their feet.

"So, I can see the proofs on Thursday?" the lady was
saying.

"Yes, stop by at around eleven," said Robin, but her

voice caught when she saw Adam standing in the doorway. She looked shocked for an instant then seemed to
recover. "You can change in the back room, Mrs. Downing," she told the woman.

Robin was pointedly ignoring him. She had every right
to. "Ericka," he heard her say, "why don't you go and
get lunch now." The young woman glanced from Adam
to Robin and back then quietly picked up her purse and
disappeared.

With Ericka gone and Mrs. Downing in the back, the
shop was suddenly, utterly quiet. Adam crawled with discomfort. "Robin," he began as she headed around behind
her counter and started to sort through some papers. He
tried again. "Look, I've got to talk to you."

This time her head came up.

"It's about the Pueblo Indian woman who paid you that
visit. I'm afraid I've been keeping a few things from
you…"

Robin listened silently, with an impartial expression.
When he was done, she finally said, "I see." She pushed
her hair off her shoulders in a familiar gesture. "Why
didn't you tell me this before?"

"I wanted to keep you out of it, I guess. But now I
have to ask you to help again."

"Well, I don't really see what I can do," she said, still
standing behind the counter as if for protection.

"I'm going to see Josefina this afternoon. I'd like you
to be there. If you tell her what happened to you, I'm sure
she'll decide to cooperate. I'm hoping she'll take us to
John Martinez."

"Why should she want to help us all of a sudden?"

"I asked my mother to call her, to persuade her."

She stared beyond him, held by her thoughts. He knew
she was reluctant to go with him; he didn't blame her. He
was stupid to have come.

Finally she spoke. "All right, I'll go with you. Just this

afternoon, you said? I've got to get back by seven. Shelly and Chuck are having a dinner party.''

"Good. I really appreciate your help.'' He hated himself for mouthing the meaningless words. "Why don't I come back for you at two?''

She looked relieved, probably glad to escape his company until she had to endure it. "That'll be fine,'' she said.

Marie Antoinette, now dressed as an ordinary twentieth-century lady, came out of the back with her nervous poodles. "See you Thursday,'' she said, "and I can't wait! Are you sure they'll be ready? Now, did you say Thursday morning or afternoon?''

At two, Adam pulled up to the front of the shop. Robin was already outside, waiting for him, a tall, graceful figure in a slim beige skirt that buttoned down the front and a stylish emerald-green knit top with shoulder pads. She struck him the same way every time he saw her—she was beautiful, full of life and love.

"I forgot to ask where we were going,'' Robin said, settling into the passenger seat.

"San Claro Pueblo,'' replied Adam. "Josefina lives there.''

"Why didn't she go to you? After all, she doesn't even know me.''

"She didn't come to me or my mother for the simple reason she wanted to remain anonymous. It's the Indian way not to get involved.''

"She was so sweet. Did you think she'll be upset when we arrive out of the blue like this?''

"I hope my mother already phoned her.''

"Um,'' was all Robin said before quietly turning her attention out the window. The tension in the car pressed on Adam heavily. It seemed that a hundred questions lay buried below the surface of the silence, like lava in a volcano, ready to erupt. It was on the tip of Adam's tongue to tell her everything, to relieve the agony, but what good would that do now? He couldn't change the facts of life.

He glanced over at her. She was still sitting there, stiff and removed—utterly without her usual exuberance. Yet there was no point in kidding himself. He wanted her as much now as he had that night in Chaco. It was almost unbearable to sit so near, to smell her scent, to know what secrets lay beneath her clothing, the velvety softness, the curves and hollows and taste of her. And he couldn't have them, not again. Not unless he was willing to tell her everything, and then he'd lose her anyway.

He switched his eyes back to the road and this time kept them there.

San Claro was one of the oldest continually inhabited pueblos in New Mexico. It sat nestled in a fertile valley between low, rounded hills. Tall cottonwoods shaded the old Spanish chapel in the plaza, and the houses were more scattered than in San Lucas or many of the other pueblos.

They found Josefina firing pots outside her studio. Her son was assisting her, building up the pile of sheep dung over the pots so that it would burn evenly, smothering the fire with ash to make the pots turn the lustrous black for which Josefina was so famous.

Adam helped Robin out of the Land Rover and approached the smoking fire. Josefina saw him and stopped her work, holding her rake still, staring from his face to Robin's, uncertain.

"Josefina," said Adam carefully. "I see we've come on a busy day. Do you have a moment to talk to us?"

"Your mother called me," she said, almost in a whisper. "I promised her I would help you."

"You know Robin Hayle."

Robin smiled, stepped forward and took Josefina's hand. "It's good to see you again. I'm so glad to know your name," she said with genuine warmth.

Josefina led them inside her studio. Although it had been several years since Adam had visited Josefina in San

Claro, he smiled to see that nothing had changed. The big room held forty years of clutter from her craft: clay and unfired pots, brushes and paints, bundles of plants from which the paints came, tools, drawings, specially curved stones that were used to polish her work. And rows of exquisite finished pieces of all sizes and shapes, some in colors, but most the lustrous black-on-black style that had brought Josefina international acclaim.

"Oh!" breathed Robin, stopping on the threshold. "They're beautiful!"

"You like my work?" asked Josefina, obviously enjoying Robin's appreciation.

Robin went to a long table that was filled with pots, each one different, each one gleaming like a black jewel. She touched one with her fingers, stroked it. "Incredible," she was saying. "I've seen some like these in the galleries, but I had no idea you made them. I always wanted one, but they're far too expensive for me. How wonderful that you can create them."

"It has taken me a lifetime," said Josefina modestly. "But come, we can sit down and talk."

Adam could see that Robin had to pull herself away from the studio to follow Josefina's brightly clad form through a door into her immaculate house.

"So," Josefina began, putting a coffee pot on the stove, "Christina tells me that you are going to solve this crime of the false pots and that I am going to help you. But first, I want to apologize to Miss Hayle for not telling her who I was. I was only trying to help, but it didn't work out the way I thought it would."

Robin leaned forward, her elbows on the kitchen table. "Have you spoken to John Martinez since I saw you?"

The woman shook her head. "No. I left a message for him as he has no phone, but he has not replied."

Adam was relieved that Josefina didn't know that Rod Cordova had questioned Martinez; he knew she wouldn't like that at all. He felt vaguely guilty about using the harmless woman this way, but he had to find out more about John Martinez. "Josefina, we would like very much to talk to John. I'm sure he can tell us more than you know. He can help us nab these people that ordered the pots." *That is,* Adam thought, *if John himself isn't the guilty party.*

"I want to help. But I know so little. Perhaps I can convince John to see you. Perhaps not." Josefina brought a tray of coffee cups to the table. She looked tired and sad.

Adam felt another small twinge of guilt but suppressed it. "Josefina, let me tell you what happened to Robin last Thursday night, and then you decide if it's worth persuading Martinez to talk to us." He told Josefina about the kiva caving in, the suspicious Indian and the pickup truck that had pushed Robin off the road. He saw Josefina's face grow paler, her eyes wider.

The woman finally sank into a chair, visibly shaken. Adam took one of her work-worn hands in his. "The forgeries must be stopped. So that Robin is safe, but also because they'll ruin the reputation of all Indian potters."

"Like you, Josefina," Robin said softly. "What if someone copied *your* pots?"

"Oh," said Josefina, near tears. "What am I to do?"

"Take us to see Martinez. If you tell him we can be trusted, he'll talk to us, won't he?" said Adam.

"I don't know."

"We can try," put in Robin. "Isn't it worth trying?"

Josefina nodded, her hands clasped tightly in her lap, and Adam knew they'd won the first round.

Her son, Manuel, was left to watch the pots that were being fired. Nervously Josefina climbed into the back seat of Adam's Land Rover, and they began the short drive to San Lucas.

Robin turned around to say something to the older woman and Adam was uncomfortably aware of the way her skirt split and showed her long, lean brown legs. He stared straight ahead, following the winding road, half listening to the women talk.

"You're doing the right thing, really," Robin was saying. "Don't worry."

"John will be angry when he sees I have brought two strangers."

"But I'm not really a stranger," she explained gently. "I met him when I took those photographs. Remember? Now, don't worry, everything will be fine."

Then Robin started asking questions. Curious Robin, Adam thought, always wanting to know everything about everybody.

"So your whole family helps you?" she asked. "Those beautiful patterns, your daughter does them? Oh, she's *so* talented. I'd give anything to be able to do something like that!"

"I learned from my aunt," said Josefina, "but the black-on-black I learned myself. A professor digging up old pottery years ago found some black shards and came to me wanting to know how to recreate the black color."

"How did you do it?"

"Oh, I tried many ways. I found it was the kind of dung I burned and it was also the smothering of the fire with ash. I had many failures at first. And then, you have to rub the unfired pot with a special stone so many times, over and over." And Josefina made rubbing motions with her hands.

"Oh, I'd love to see how you do it," Robin enthused.

"I would be happy to show you."

"You know," Robin said, "you'd be the perfect person to organize the Indian potters. If you formed an organization, then all the members could be warned about people like the ones who had John making pots for them. You know what I mean? And if the police needed to be called in, your organization could do it, and you wouldn't have to go as individuals."

"An organization?" Josefina said doubtfully.

"Yes, it could work. All the pueblos could join. Like our association in Santa Fe. You'd be able to protect yourselves."

"I don't know…"

"It would be a great thing. Oh, Josefina, don't you see?"

"I wouldn't know where to start."

"I'll help you," said Robin enthusiastically.

"It's a good idea, Josefina," put in Adam. "The time is coming when the Indians are going to have to do it."

"I cannot think of such things. I am only one woman, a simple potter. I wouldn't know what to do. I don't think I could do anything like that," said Josefina.

"But you're so well-known. You're famous. Everyone would listen to you," pressed Robin.

"Oh, I don't think so."

Robin gave up then, wisely, Adam thought. Josefina needed time to get used to the idea.

Robin was wonderful with the older woman, warm and friendly, drawing her into conversation. There was so much love in Robin, and it showed in so many ways. But to Adam she was very stiff, very polite, very careful. It was best that way, he told himself. It was the only way. But it hurt.

At Pueblo San Lucas, Josefina directed them to Martinez's house. Parked in front was an old, rusty pickup truck with dented fenders. A pickup, reflected Adam, like the one that pushed Robin's car off the road. But how ridiculous to think that this could be the same one; there were probably twenty more just like it in San Lucas alone. Yet he saw Robin staring at the truck, too.

Josefina knocked on Martinez's door while Adam and Robin waited in the car. They didn't want to scare him off. This was going to be a ticklish situation as it was. It was possible, after all, that Martinez was guilty, despite what Josefina believed.

"Yes, that's him," Robin said excitedly when a man opened the door.

It took Josefina several minutes to calm John Martinez down. He kept glaring at Adam and Robin in the Land Rover and shaking his head and arguing. Then Josefina walked back to the car, looking very upset again. "He will see you, but he is angry, like I said he would be. I don't think he will tell you very much." She looked down at her feet. "I'm very sorry."

"You've done your best," said Adam. "Let's see what John has to say."

The adobe house was small and neat. John's wife grinned and nodded and served them all coffee, but she spoke only Tewa with Josefina and her husband. Then she left them alone, with a tortoiseshell cat curled up by the corner fireplace for company.

John was sinewy, about forty-five, Adam guessed. He was of medium height, with a weathered face and large-knuckled fingers, and there was clay still under his fingernails. He smoked unfiltered cigarettes incessantly, obviously anxious. He spoke to Josefina in Tewa, an angry tirade, Adam suspected.

"He says," Josefina translated, "that the men he made pots for heard about people looking for him and threatened him. He can tell us nothing."

"Threatened him!" said Robin.

"Explain to him he can do more good by telling us who these men are. He won't have to go to the police. We'll take them the information," said Adam.

Josefina spoke to Martinez at length. Adam could see the man's eyes darting from face to face, belligerent, uncertain, afraid.

When Josefina stopped talking, Martinez said something short and harsh.

"Tell him," Robin said, putting her hand on Josefina's arm, "what happened to me." And she lifted her bangs to show the cut on her forehead, while Josefina told the story in Tewa.

Martinez appeared shaken. He stared at Robin, and Josefina patted his hand, speaking quietly and persuasively. Adam felt hopeful; maybe it had been a good idea to bring Robin along after all.

There was a long silence when Josefina finished. It was so quiet that Adam could hear the big cat purring in its corner. John Martinez finally turned to Adam and, in accented English, said, "When a woman is hurt I am at fault, too. I will tell you."

"Oh, thank you, Mr. Martinez," said Robin.

"I want you to know that I made those pots because a man who said he was from a museum came to me." Martinez inhaled deeply on his cigarette. "He wanted me to copy some pots in pictures he showed me. This was to learn how the pots were made in the past. I believed him, and I enjoyed the...how do you say?" He spoke a word to Josefina.

"Challenge," she answered.

"Yes, I enjoyed the challenge. Even to making the fireclouds appear in the right spots. I do not make much money from these pots."

Adam listened silently, not wanting to disturb the man's narrative. He was terribly aware of Robin sitting next to him on the plastic kitchen chair, her face full of concern. She felt sorry for John Martinez; she believed him. But could this seemingly innocuous Indian potter have tried to kill Robin? Was he lying?

"Two men come every month to pick up the pots. I do not know them."

"The same men?" Adam asked.

"Yes, but they wear hats and I think false...." He said a word to Josefina again, "Yes, mustaches. They leave me money. That is all."

"How do you get hold of them?" asked Robin. "I mean, if you need to."

Martinez stubbed out his cigarette. "I am given a number. But I have to leave a message. It is one of those machines."

"An answering machine," said Adam.

"But I only called it once because I have no phone. I must use the one in the plaza."

"Do you have the number?" asked Adam cautiously.

After a moment's hesitation, John thrust his hand in his pocket, came up with a wallet and pulled out several scraps of paper. "Yes, this is it."

Robin had already gotten a pencil and piece of paper out of her shoulder bag. She wrote the number down, checking it twice.

"You will not say who gave you the number?" asked Martinez anxiously.

"Not unless you want us to," Adam replied. "And I think it would be best if you go on making your pots, for now, anyway. Just in case, you understand. You *are* our only link to these counterfeiters."

"And they'll have to get in touch eventually, won't they?" asked Robin. "To pick up your pots."

John sat there with his eyes still shifting cautiously from face to face.

"Can you tell us anything more, anything at all?" Adam's voice was quiet, in control, gently urging.

"Please," coaxed Robin, and Josefina nodded at the Indian man.

Martinez sighed deeply. "They come every month in a different car," he began. "But one I remember more than the others. It was a van, very pretty. It was green and silver with a painting on its side, a picture of the desert." Wistfully he said, "I would like a van like that."

But Robin was rising from her chair, her eyes wide. "My God," she said in a horrified whisper, "I know that van!"

CHAPTER FIFTEEN

ROBIN FOLDED HER ARMS across her chest tightly and compressed her lips. She turned her head and stared out the window of the Land Rover.

"Listen," Adam said, "I didn't mean to knock your friends. Maybe they are good people. But I think you're going to have to face the facts. Martinez told us about this state-of-the-art green van and the Daltons have just that van."

"Then Martinez is lying," she shot back. "He's just trying to pin this whole thing on somebody else."

"You don't know that."

"I know Shelly and Chuck are honest. I'm not that bad a judge of character. I mean, heck, they've got two grown sons, both college graduates. They've got grandchildren, for Pete's sake."

"And that makes them innocent?"

God, he was making her mad! First he gave her that friend business up at the canyon, and now he was trying to convince her that the Daltons were heading a counterfeiting ring. Well, she wasn't buying it.

"Robin," he said, "listen to me a minute, will you? I'm not trying to start an argument—"

"I'd say we *are* arguing."

"Come on. Face it. There's no other van around like theirs. It's custom made. I've even seen it myself, that night at your committee meeting when Chuck Dalton drove off."

"So what? That only means that everyone's seen the

van around, including John Martinez. I say he's lying. I say he's the one who ran me off the road.'' She crossed her legs, feeling as if she were going to break in two. ''And what's more, Martinez is an Indian and your own students saw an Indian near that kiva. *And* he owns an old pickup truck.''

Adam let out a long sigh. ''I know all that. I think we ought to give Cordova a call and let him do some questioning—''

''Of the Daltons? I absolutely won't let you do that. Adam,'' she said, turning toward him quickly, ''*please*. You just can't implicate them. It's too horrible. I absolutely won't let you do this.''

''He'd only question them.'' His voice had finally lowered. ''I'm sure they'd understand.''

''Understand what? That I've named them as suspects who tried to kill me? I can't. They're my friends, Adam. They're very special to me. My God, Ericka is practically my protégée.'' She put her face in her hands for a moment and then took a deep lungful of air, looking back at Adam. ''I only know one thing,'' she said, ''someone tried to kill me and no matter what else you want to believe of the Daltons, it wasn't them. Neither Shelly nor Chuck would be capable of it.''

Adam was quiet for a long time. As they drove through the outskirts of Santa Fe, she could see a frown creasing his forehead. Did he believe her?

Whether or not he trusted her judgment, Robin knew that she couldn't let him go to the police, not with what little they had, and certainly not on Martinez's word. She sat in silence, uncomfortable and nervous, knowing that she had to go lock up the shop and face Ericka. But even more awful, she had to stay at the Dalton's, and they were even giving that dinner party...

And then there was Adam. Enigmatic Adam Farwalker. Her *friend*. What a joke! Maybe she *was* a bad judge of character, after all. She'd sure gotten him all wrong. And

worse, ironically, pathetically, she still wanted him.
Would it always be there, every time she bumped into
him, that need to be held in his arms? She felt sick and
afraid, as if she were in a tailspin with no hope of pulling
out.

He stopped in front of the shop. It was nearly six
o'clock. She had only a few minutes left to convince him
not to go to Rod, not yet. She thought frantically, and
then remembered. "The number," said Robin, almost
desperately. "The phone number John Martinez gave us!
We've got to try it, Adam. Maybe the phone company
could give us an address."

He turned off the engine and nodded. "Okay," he
agreed. "But I doubt we'll get a thing. The minute we
started asking questions up at San Lucas last week, I'm
sure the counterfeiters began to cover their tracks."

"You mean the number will be disconnected?" Robin
was disappointed.

"Probably. And the address will turn out to be under
a false name anyway."

"You're giving them an awful lot of credit."

"And I'm beginning to wonder," said Adam, "if they
won't change the way they pick up the pots. They'll want
to be really careful now. Unless the money's too good to
pass up. Or unless they feel that they've scared us off."

Robin was quiet, thinking. If those men came this
month to collect Martinez's forgeries... "Adam," she
said, "*we* could be there. You know, when the men come
for the pots. We could watch John's place and see if anyone shows."

He looked at her for a long time before he answered.
"It's too dangerous."

"But it doesn't have to be. Not if we're just watching.
When we see who shows up—or *if* anyone shows up—
we call Rod. At least that way we'll be sure who the real
criminals are."

"Robin..."

"Look, it's the only way we'll ever know if Martinez is telling us the truth."

"It would be a lot safer if the police were waiting," said Adam.

"Oh, sure," she put in quickly, "except for one thing. We can't tell Rod the story and keep the Daltons out of it. And if we *did* tell him, and didn't mention the van, then we'd be lying. We can't do that, Adam, don't you see?"

He was studying her face, obviously skeptical.

"What harm would be done if we hid and watched Martinez's house? All we have to do is see if there really is a pickup and if so, we get a license-plate number. We go straight to Rod with it. It's foolproof."

"We'd need to know exactly when the pickup will happen."

"That's the only problem. John might not want to tell us. And if he's the one behind the black-market pots, he won't tell us. But if he's innocent..."

"Josefina might convince him to help us," suggested Adam.

"Would she?"

"She likes you, Robin. She might do it on that basis alone." He thought for a minute. "I'll talk to her. If she can get that information from John she could let you know."

"*If*," said Robin.

"I can try." Adam hesitated then asked, "And if it turns out to be the Daltons? Could you turn them in, Robin?"

It was a long time before she replied. "I could do it then, Adam, if I had to, if there was proof. But not now. Promise me you won't call Rod until we at least try this."

"I don't know. I suppose I could be at Martinez's myself..."

"No. I'm going, too."

Adam gave her a half smile then shook his head. "I

guess we'll be debating that one again," he said, relenting for the time being.

"Okay," she answered, feeling much better. "Should we go let Ericka off and try that number?"

As Adam suspected, the number had been disconnected. He tried the telephone company but got nowhere as the number had been unlisted in the first place. Short of obtaining a court order, there was no way they were going to get an address.

"Darn," said Robin, "you were absolutely right, these crooks are sharp."

They were standing together in her office, their shoulders nearly touching. Deliberately she stepped back from him. "Well," she said, hesitant, "there's that dinner party…"

"Come on," he said quietly, "I'll drop you at the Daltons'."

Robin had to direct him. Their house was only a few miles southwest of the city, built into the side of a dry, red clay hill in an exclusive country-club suburb. Like all the homes on the private circle, the Daltons' was a one-story sprawling adobe structure with natural gardens of cacti and wildflowers behind its low wall. It was a showplace.

"Quite a house," commented Adam and Robin knew just what he was thinking: it took a lot of money to own a home like this. She hoped to God he didn't notice the swimming pool.

To make matters worse, Chuck was in the driveway, getting something out of the van—the custom-made green van with the desert scene painted on its side. Robin felt a surge of nausea as they pulled up alongside and stopped. "They have a very successful gallery," she whispered, realizing how ridiculous she sounded and how nervous she was bound to be around the Daltons.

"I'm sure," replied Adam laconically.

"Hi, there," Chuck was saying, poking his head into

Robin's window. "Come on in, everyone's about to arrive. Good to see you again, Adam; I hope you can stay."

"I really…"

"Now, come on, Adam. Shelly's a great cook. At least have a cocktail and some of her pooh-poohs, or whatever she calls the stuff." He nodded as a car pulled in behind Adam. "There. Now you have to stay."

Robin had known that it was bound to be awkward staying with her friends. But she wasn't prepared for the doubts that plagued her mind. She kept remembering how shocked she'd been when Martinez had told them about the van, and the things that had flowed through her head.

How much money did the gallery bring in? Enough, really, for all this, and to send two sons and now a daughter through expensive, out-of-state colleges?

Shelly was dashing around, putting out plates and bowls of hors d'oeuvres, directing her maid. *Her maid,* thought Robin as she gave Adam a surreptitious glance to see if he was noticing.

"Oh, hi!" called Shelly from the sunny patio. "Come on out and fix yourself a drink. If you wait for Chuck, you'll die of thirst."

"Hi, Shelly," said Robin. "Everything looks delicious." She felt her heart sinking. She'd never be able to pull off this farce of friendship. Why had she let that business about the van get to her?

Adam crossed to the far side of the pool and fixed them both gin and tonics. Other guests were arriving, about a dozen or so of them. Julien appeared, and on his arm was none other than Madeline Lassiter. There were other familiar faces, a few acquaintances. Ericka's boyfriend was there, as well. Robin looked long and hard at the handsome young couple who stood by themselves, chattering away, totally engrossed in each other. What if Chuck were involved in this ring? What would become of his beautiful daughter if her father went to prison?

"Are you all right?" asked Adam as he handed her a tall, frosty glass.

"I can't do it, Adam, I just can't," said Robin.

"Do what?"

"Stay here."

"Then you'll have to stay out at my folks'. You can't go back to your place alone. Not until everything's cleared up."

"Great," she said. "But I can't stay with your parents. It's just too inconvenient for everyone concerned."

"Robin..."

"Seriously. I'll get a room in town."

"What will you tell the Daltons?"

Why should he care? she thought. "I don't know. Something. Anything. This is just too ghastly, having to face them like this."

Adam was studying her face. His expression mirrored hers; both were grim. "Do you want me to drive you into town?" he asked solemnly. She looked him in the eye. Why was he bothering? Was it his sense of duty, or did he still feel something toward her—something more than friendship? What had gone wrong? Maybe nothing at all; maybe he simply had had his fling and it was enough. At that moment she hated him.

"Do you want me to drive you?" he asked again.

Robin shook her head. "I'll get a ride later, with Julien or someone."

"Are you sure?"

"I'm positive," she said in a steady voice.

Adam did hang around for a few more minutes. He was obviously as ill-at-ease as she was, but Robin didn't know if it was because of her or the Daltons. And she couldn't ask.

"I simply love that sweater of yours," Madeline said in Robin's ear. "Where did you get it?"

"A catalog, I think," she replied distractedly. "I don't recall..."

"Doesn't Robin always look wonderful?" Julien put in as he approached, dipped his dark head to her fingers and shook Adam's hand. "It is so good to see you up and around," he said to Robin. "What a terrible, terrible accident you had."

"But how—" began Robin.

"Oh, my," Julien was quick to say, "my brother made a point of phoning me. Everyone has heard by now, of course, that your car was run off the highway. I've had nothing but calls from the association members. We were all very worried."

"That's right," agreed Madeline, staring at Robin's forehead where the stitches just showed beneath her bangs. "And I'm betting it was no accident, either. It's got to be connected to those forgeries, doesn't it? I mean, things like that don't just happen."

"Well, we think…" began Robin.

"It's difficult to say," Adam interrupted smoothly. It was apparent that he didn't want to discuss what they knew.

Why? wondered Robin. Hadn't he said a dozen times that it was another warning to her? He'd told Rod Cordova that, so why minimize it now?

"It's a dreadful business." Julien's pale brow furrowed. "And Chuck tells me that you are staying with them for safety's sake. I am so glad."

"It's a smart thing to do," agreed Madeline.

Then Shelly joined them, carrying a silver tray of deviled eggs. "Hi," she said, "has everyone got a drink yet?"

The group talked at length about Robin's situation, and Julien promised to speak to his brother. "Rod must be made to understand the danger to our Robin here. I don't care if he *doesn't* have any leads, Robin should have twenty-four-hours-a-day protection."

"Absolutely," said Madeline, flashing Adam a smile. "That's what we pay the police for, isn't it?"

"Well, I think," interjected Shelly, "that Robin's perfectly fine right here with us." And it struck Robin then: could Shelly have an ulterior motive for wanting her to stay here? Was it to watch her activities?

Oh, Lord, she thought in shame, here she was believing the Daltons were guilty! The seed of doubt had been planted and no matter how hard she tried she couldn't escape her doubts.

"I, for one, don't think Robin looks very well at all," Madeline pointed out. "Why, you're so drawn. It's the strain. I know, when I had that bad season two summers ago at my shop, well, let me tell you, I had one sickness after the other. It's stress, Robin, and if I were you, I'd drop this whole business about forgeries."

Adam shifted his weight and took a sip of his drink. "She *is* dropping it," he said. "In fact, both of us are. It's up to the police now."

"I'm so glad," Julien said, "for Robin's sake, of course. I think in our special committee we'll come up with a solution to this problem. And we must band together. Like an army, yes?"

"Exactly," said Madeline firmly, flashing Adam a winning smile.

It was at least another ten minutes before Robin and Adam were alone again. She was sick to death of this whole mess and only wished it could be erased, like chalk from a blackboard. "Sorry about cutting you off earlier," Adam was telling her. "I just think we better keep this Martinez business to ourselves. The fewer who know, the more chance we'll have to get a look at the men who pick up his pottery."

"I see," Robin answered without enthusiasm.

"Of course," Adam put in carefully, "we can always call Rod. This has been a nightmare for you." He sounded so concerned. But why not, she thought dismally, they were good friends, weren't they?

"I want to go through with it," said Robin. "I want to prove to you it's not Chuck and Shelly."

"All right."

"And I want to be there, Adam, I don't want to be left behind. Promise?"

"We'll see," was all he'd commit himself to. "Look," he added, "I've got to get going. And I'd like to take you to a hotel if you're bent on leaving here."

"I can't stay here," she said, "I'd feel like a traitor. Oh, I don't know…"

"Then let me give you a lift."

Robin gazed at her shoes. "I'll get a ride later." She was aware of their stiffness with each other, of the awkward moments as they stood side by side, not touching, surrounded by a dozen cheerful people. Suddenly she felt miserably alone. Robin against the world, she mused darkly. What had happened to that sense of comfort she'd once felt here in Santa Fe? She couldn't trust a soul, not anymore, except, of course, Adam. And where would that get her?

"Where will you stay in town?" he asked in a concerned voice.

"I don't know. I haven't thought about it. Maybe the Governor's Inn. Someplace close to my shop."

"Okay. I'll be in touch soon. And don't go to your apartment alone, Robin, I mean that. You just wait till we see who shows up at Martinez's place."

"Oh, sure. I hope it isn't too long." She knew she was sulking, childishly pouting. But she had a right to, darn it all—Adam deserved it. And she knew she'd much rather have him drive her to the hotel, but this was one way of showing him that she no longer cared. It was spiteful and devious, but it actually felt good.

He left shortly thereafter, promising to keep in touch as often as possible, expressing his belief that all this would soon be behind them. Robin hadn't the energy to respond. She never even said goodbye; she merely stared

at him, undisguised pain in her eyes, her heart aching for
what could have been.

"OH, BUT ROBIN, I WON'T HEAR of it," Shelly was saying. "You're staying right here."

"I appreciate all your concern *and* your hospitality,"
said Robin, unable to meet her glance. "But I just... I
guess I need to be alone. I'm like that, you know, at
times."

Shelly put her hands on her hips and frowned. "You
are not like that, Robin, not one bit. I know what you're
hiding, though. And it's absurd." Robin's heart stopped
and she felt heat soar up her neck. Shelly knew about
Martinez, about the van... "It's Adam, isn't it? He's got
you so upset you can't think straight," her friend said.

Robin suddenly felt like laughing. She let out a breath
she'd been holding. "You're right, Shelly," she said, "it
is Adam."

"Well, you don't have to leave because of him. You
could stay here, we could talk. Come on, Robin, this isn't
at all like you."

She couldn't look at Shelly, she just *couldn't*. "No,"
she said, "it's better if I'm alone. I can sort things out in
my mind that way. Honest, Shel, I need time to myself."

"Well..."

"I'll be fine. I'm going to get a room...in town," she
said, realizing that she didn't even trust her friend enough
to tell her where.

"You'll call me, though, won't you? We can talk?"

"Oh, sure, I'll call, and I'll see you at work."

"That rat," said Shelly under her breath, "he's nothing
but a womanizer. You poor kid."

By nine, Robin was checked into the Governor's Inn.
She would dearly have loved to have had Julien, who had
given her a ride, stop by her apartment so that she could
pick up a few things. And she would have, except she felt

utterly drained. She wanted only to drop into bed, to sleep and to forget.

She showered and pulled on her nightgown and thought about what a traitor she'd been to the Daltons. Some loyal pal she was!

She tried the TV. There was early news on a local channel, all bad news. She switched to a *Magnum PI* rerun, but then his tall, dark good looks reminded her too much of Adam. She switched that off, too. She sat in bed and tried to watch a sitcom, but it was terrible, the jokes stale and old, predictable. Finally she turned it off altogether and lay there, tired and shaky, in the darkness.

How could she have been so blind? Adam had always played it straight with her, but no, Robin had bulldozed her way into his life, stupidly, without thought of the future. Well, somehow she was going to have to get all those silly, naive dreams out of her head and go on living as before. Boy, had she been dumb—no, desperate was a better description, she decided. Her whole life she'd longed to belong to a close-knit family like his. And had she ever fallen for his heritage, the Indian stuff! How dumb could she get?

CHAPTER SIXTEEN

ROBIN HAD NEVER REALIZED how many times a day she and Shelly took a break from work and chatted. And if they weren't poking their heads into each other's shops, then it was a quick telephone call or a lunch date at the burrito house around the corner from the Sena Plaza.

The day began with doughnuts. "Hi," said Shelly, brandishing her white bakery bag, "how about some calories, Skinny?" And for the first time in years, since she'd had the Taiwan flu, Robin had no appetite. For her friend's sake, she forced one down anyway.

"Thanks," she managed to say.

"Still down?"

"I guess I am," replied Robin, hating the deceit.

"I swear, that man may be a hunk, but he's definitely a killer, Robin. It's just as well you're through trying to find those counterfeiters."

Robin knew that all the blood drained from her face. "Why?" she asked in a whisper.

"Oh, you know," said Shelly, "that way Adam won't be drifting in and out of your life. You'll be done with the cad."

"Oh."

"Do you realize that I'll be a mother without children this Friday? Ericka's driving back to school," said Shelly.

"I know. I don't know how I'm going to manage without her," replied Robin, but she was glad she didn't have to see Ericka every day and treat her as if nothing had happened and wonder...

"And she's in Albuquerque today spending that bonus you gave her. A new mall or something just opened."

"I hope she enjoys it."

"She will." Shelly rolled her big eyes.

It wasn't even noon when Shelly called again. "How about a game of tennis after work?"

"I, ah…"

"Oh, that's right, there's the business association meeting tonight. Darn."

"Maybe another time," Robin was able to say.

She spent most of the afternoon studying proofs and getting together with clients, but by four, she was sulking again, alone, resting her chin on her hands, staring, unfocused, into nowhere. She had no idea how she was going to get through the meeting tonight, or the trite chores of the next day, or the next. Life suddenly didn't seem too grand without Adam around.

Maybe she should see a shrink. Maybe a doctor could tell her where she'd gone wrong and how to cope with the loneliness. Or maybe there wasn't an answer at all.

"Hey," came a voice at her door, "it's five after six." It was Chuck. "You're going to the meeting, aren't you?"

She couldn't even look her best friends in the eyes anymore. How *was* she going to cope?

The three-month-old Santa Fe Business Association seemed, that night, to be falling apart. Robin was amazed. And it had all started because Adam Farwalker had strolled by her shop one day and seen that photograph.

Niles Warner, a local restaurateur, had started the fracas. "So I'm supposed to chip in my money for a pamphlet that this so-called special committee has dreamed up? The hell I will!"

"Now, Niles," Julien said placatingly.

"I'm going to have my say here," Niles went on. "I don't even sell pottery or art of any form! And let me tell you all another thing, they can't forge a steak or a head of lettuce. Maybe you good folks ought to think about switching lines of business.''

''I agree completely,'' piped up a lodge owner. ''There's no reason why some of us here should be penalized because a few collectors buy fakes by mistake.''

Good old Thad Mencimer was on his feet like a shot. ''Who said that?'' he shouted, red-faced.

''I did.''

Thad faced the lodge owner. The purple veins on his neck stood out. ''And I suppose if you need help with your lodge, like parking or whatever, you won't bring your problem in here?''

''I can take care of myself.''

Lorraine Mencimer tugged on her husband's sleeve. ''Thad, sit down, please.''

''Can we come to order?'' asked Julien from the podium.

It didn't work. ''This association is never going to make it,'' said a Western gallery owner. ''What we need is three or four associations.''

''Brilliant.'' Thad snickered.

''Please,'' said Julien. ''We are getting nowhere. We must come to order.''

Madeline rose to her feet and turned to face the group. ''Julien's right. The way to do things is to vote on them. Let's vote on the pamphlet and maybe we can work out payment on a sliding scale.''

''Now you're talking,'' came a voice from the rear. ''Let's hear more about this pamphlet, though. Let's find out what we'll be getting for our money.''

''*Your* money, you mean,'' Niles jeered, and his wife shot him a scathing glance.

Robin sat and listened, feeling as tense as the rest of them. The town seemed polarized between various factions, each grinding its own ax in the room that evening. Maybe it was good to air things out, she thought; then again, maybe it wasn't. She couldn't seem to get things straight in her head anymore.

It took forty-five minutes, but the pamphlet passed by a narrow margin, and only because the gallery owners were at the top of the sliding-scale payment plan, and the others, the restaurateurs and hotel managers, at the bottom.

"Yeah, well," said Niles under his breath, "it might take me months to pay, if I can even find the bill."

"I'll help you find it," said Thad boldly.

"All right," said Julien, "now let's get on to something less controversial, if we can. I'd like Robin Hayle to step up here for a minute or two and address the members on an idea she brought up at one of our special committee meetings. Robin?"

It actually took Robin a moment to even remember what her idea had been. Then she wished Julien had saved it for another night—any night.

Dutifully she rose to her feet and slid out through the row of men and women. A friendly catcall sounded from somewhere, and she pointedly ignored it as she stepped up onto the platform and Julien yielded the podium to her.

"Good evening," she began. "As Julien mentioned, I have another thought on how we might thwart these counterfeiters." Robin cleared her throat, trying to formulate in her mind what she was going to say. It was terribly difficult, not just because she detested public speaking, but also because her heart was no longer in it.

"I hope this isn't going to cost us anything," someone said.

"Oh, don't worry," Robin replied to the unseen voice, "it won't cost a thing. What I have in mind is an Indian artisans' association, patterned after ours. I've been told that the Indian community has never before been organized and that the artists work very independently of one another. An association," she said, glancing around the room, "would mean communication, and eventually, the honest artisans would police the not-so-honest ones."

"How do you know it will work?" asked a woman in the front row. "The Indians don't exactly have a good track record in organizing. They're real clannish. The Pueblo tribes still hate the Navahos, the Zunis distrust the Rio Grande tribes. And anything the white community suggests they're going to suspect."

"I realize that," said Robin. "But it's something we could work toward. And, as I said already, it won't cost anything to try."

Thad Mencimer stood. "I'm afraid I agree with that lady over there. I'm not sure the Indians *can* be organized. Won't they just think it's more interference from the whites?"

"I hope not," Robin put in. "I'm planning on speaking to Mrs. Farwalker—I think we all know how influential she can be—and soliciting her help. There's another person involved, too, an Indian lady," she said, not wanting to use Josefina's name. "The person I mentioned will be of invaluable help. I believe it can be done." Robin smiled at the group. "Well? Any questions, comments?"

There were some. Several members were dubious, many reiterating doubts about the Indians' ability to organize. But Ben Chavez and Chuck Dalton were very supportive—as was Julien.

Julien finally climbed back onto the platform and stood next to Robin. "I don't think we need a vote, do we?" Heads shook. "Okay, then. Thank you, Robin."

She received applause as she stepped down and took her seat. Julien then pulled up a tripod that was covered. When he unveiled the object beneath, it was the mock-up for the *Travel and Leisure* ad. Naturally there were comments.

"Santa Fe doesn't look like that," said someone. "That's just a bunch of mesas in a sunset."

"Well, I like it."

"I don't; it's the wrong image."

"The caption is a cliché. Everyone's heard of the land of enchantment. We've gotta change that, it's been used."

"How about come visit the old world?"

"That's stupid." Thad, of course. "This isn't the old world."

"Pipe down there, Thad."

Nothing was resolved that evening and the man from the printer's who had done the mock-up at his own expense left, gritting his teeth, before the meeting was adjourned.

As Robin sat there growing weary and bored, she glanced around at the faces. Of course, Martinez had described the Daltons' van, but he could have been lying. Couldn't any knowledgeable gallery owner be involved? Counterfeiting provided easily obtained, tax-free money, and there were a number of fine artisans to do the work, especially if they were fed a cock-and-bull story. Sure, any one of the members here might be involved, thought Robin. A chill crawled up her spine. Any one of them could have been responsible for her accident, could have hired an Indian to do it, in fact. But right now the finger sure pointed to Chuck and Shelly.

She and Adam were going to find out when the next pickup of Martinez's pots was to be. They'd know then who it was. She hoped that day came soon.

Adam, Robin thought, as the voices still discussing the ad flowed in and out of her consciousness. Adam. A man she wanted desperately. A man who ran hot and cold, a man who spoke her language but had strange hidden corners to him. What had gone wrong? What had driven him back into that private world of his?

"Hey, Robin... Robin?" It was Chuck, tapping her on the shoulder. "The meeting's over, kiddo. Where were you just then?"

She forced herself to smile. "Daydreaming."

"Hope it was nice. Say, are you all right staying here in town?" he asked.

"I'm perfectly fine, Chuck."

"Well, Shelly was sure disappointed. You know how fond she is of you."

In a minute, Robin was going to cry. "And I'm fond of her, too," she said genuinely. "I just needed some space."

"So Shelly said. Come on, I'll walk you out. You got your car here?"

Robin shook her head. "No. I'm staying in town... It's convenient, anyway."

"And you're okay?"

"Perfectly."

Members were still gathered in small groups outside the La Fonda Hotel. Robin saw the Daltons' van then, double parked, Shelly waving out the window at Chuck. "Come on," she called, "I've been waiting forever. Hi, Robin!"

Robin waved, but her eyes were fixed on the green van, on the desert scene artistically painted on its side. There couldn't be two vehicles like that within a thousand miles...

"Hey there, Robin." It was Thad Mencimer. "I don't think your idea's going to work out very well."

"Don't you think it's worth trying, though?" asked Robin irritably.

"If you need any help," offered Lorraine deliberately, "as soon as the baby comes, I'd be glad to pitch in."

"That's sweet of you," replied Robin as they all walked toward Chuck's van. "I'll call you."

"Do. I mean that."

"Well, how's business?" Thad was asking Chuck. "Say, I wanted to thank you..."

But Shelly was still waving, and Robin stopped for a minute to say hello. Later she would remember that she'd heard Thad say something significant, but everyone was

talking at once, small talk, unimportant stuff, and she
wasn't really listening. Only later would she remember
that casual statement Thad made to Chuck, something
very, very significant.

ROBIN TURNED the plastic clock hands to noon and locked
up. She had no appointments that morning, and now was
as good a time as any to start working on the Indian artisans' organization. Her first step, she had decided, was
to see Christina Farwalker. If she could convince Christina
to help her start organizing the Indians, she'd have the
task half done.

Robin wondered, though, in her state of mind, if she'd
make any sense at all to the woman. Maybe she ought to
wait to pay this visit, wait until she had this forgery business behind her, and Adam along with it.

But she had to get out and do *something*. It was far
better to act, to be productive, to solve a problem.

She drove up Canyon Road and turned onto the dirt
road that led to the Farwalker ranch. Her car bounced and
shook, and she felt as if her brain were rattling. She passed
the time by thinking about last night's meeting and all the
unsettling, petty arguments. And she thought about afterward when she'd been standing out in front of La Fonda,
exchanging pleasantries with Chuck and Shelly while staring at their van.

There was something about the van, too, something she
couldn't quite remember at the moment. Was it something
Martinez had said? No, there was something else. Hadn't
Thad been talking to Chuck about the van? He had, she
recalled, but Robin had been busy speaking to Shelly and
had only been half listening.

Thad. Yes, he'd been thanking Chuck, saying something about how, when his shop really got moving, he
was going to buy his own van.

Robin's brow furrowed. Suddenly she had it. Thad had

said, "Say, I wanted to thank you again for letting me use the van, Chuck."

Robin practically drove into the ditch. She stopped the car and gripped the steering wheel. Of course! Just because the van had been seen in San Lucas Pueblo didn't mean that the Daltons had been driving it!

Wow, it could be Thad behind the forgeries! And he had a motive, too; he was always complaining about money. He had a baby coming. And he was a terrible obstructionist at the association meetings. No wonder he'd put his two cents in about the Indians being difficult to organize!

A smile of relief curved Robin's lips. And what was more, she realized, maybe Chuck had loaned his van—innocently—to others. Almost *anyone* could have borrowed it; anyone who knew Chuck Dalton could be the guilty party. The suspect list was growing longer and longer, and now her plan to wait at Martinez's to see who showed up was even more vital. She'd have to tell Adam; then he'd believe the Daltons couldn't have done it.

Her smile faded. Tell Adam? How was she going to accomplish *that*? He'd said he'd be in touch, but would he?

Robin realized, as she parked in front of the hacienda, that she should have called ahead. When was she ever going to be able to think straight again?

But Christina was home, and welcomed her. "Oh, Robin, what a nice surprise. Do come in. I just made a fresh pot of coffee."

Christina had cleaning ladies at the hacienda, two short, almost identical Mexican women. But judging from the way Adam's mother couldn't pass a cushion on a couch without straightening it, it was difficult for Robin to tell who helped whom.

The two women were in the kitchen that morning. Three cups of coffee sat on the familiar pine table, and a pie plate of wonderful home-baked cinnamon rolls was just coming out of the oven.

"Maria and Pia, this is my son's friend, Robin," said Christina, and the two women giggled and exchanged meaningful glances.

"Hi," said Robin, "your rolls smell absolutely wonderful."

"*Gracias, señorita,*" replied Pia. "You will have one?"

"And coffee, please."

They sat out in the courtyard, the morning sun on Robin's back. Beyond the walls a faint, cool breeze bent the tall grass, but inside the protection of the aged walls it was warm; not a breath of air stirred.

"I'm so glad you've come to visit," said Christina, offering the butter to Robin for her rolls, "although I wish you would have accepted our hospitality until this business is cleared up."

"To be honest," said Robin, "I would have, it's so lovely here, but being in town is really convenient for my work, and my car could only take so many trips on that dirt road."

"So," said Christina, folding her small hands on the table, "you look like a woman with a purpose."

Unconsciously Robin averted her glance. Adam's mother no doubt thought that she'd come with some problem concerning her son or, perhaps, something to do with the forgeries.

"I'd like to talk to you about something," she began. Then she told Christina all about her idea to organize the Indian artists. Christina watched her soberly, her dark brows drawn together. "And so I thought that if you could help me contact the artists that you know, or point out the leaders, the ones that would be listened to, you'd be a great help. You'd act as a sort of liaison."

"I see," said Christina, looking at her small, plump hands, and Robin was disheartened. Then the older woman glanced up. "Oh, it's a good idea, a really good idea. I was just considering the difficulties."

"But would you help me?"

"Did my son put you up to this?" asked Christina astutely.

"He only said I'd have to ask you myself."

"I'd like to help. Let me think about it. You know, Josefina would be invaluable to a group like this."

"I know. I even mentioned it to her, but she wouldn't commit herself to doing anything."

"Well, it's not exactly up Josefina's alley, but she might be convinced," said Christina. "It would be a lot of work, a lot of traveling and talking and explaining. It could be very disappointing, Robin. It might not come together in the end."

"I've been told how private the Indians are. But wouldn't they see the benefits of an organization?"

"Maybe, if approached correctly."

"But you see, *you* would know the right approach."

"My dear, you flatter me," Christina said with a laugh.

"Well, you have influence with Josefina then," suggested Robin.

"To a point." Thoughtfully Christina sipped her coffee, then nodded her head. "It's a solid idea. All the artists: Navaho rug weavers, Hopi silversmiths, Pueblo potters, painters. Hm."

Robin relaxed a little. She could see that Christina's brain was already at work.

"We'd have to choose one person in each pueblo to contact. The Navaho would be more difficult, they're so spread out. Maybe flyers in the native languages and in English." Christina spoke as if to herself. "I'm afraid there would be resistance. Some of the older artists will be afraid of getting involved. The younger ones will fear white influence. It won't be easy."

"But I bet we can do it," replied Robin.

"Maybe I'll pull out my fund-raiser list and send off some notes to the Indians on it. Yes, that's a start."

"And Josefina?"

"I'll talk to her."

"Christina, you are a born organizer."

"Well, an Apache woman is brought up to manage a whole clan. This is just practice."

Things were definitely looking up, thought Robin.

Christina excused herself to get some more coffee, and Robin was left alone in the bright courtyard. She turned her face up into the sun and sighed. She'd been in this courtyard before, under quite different circumstances. Then, Adam had been the mysterious stranger who had only come into her life that day. She would regret that day, too, she guessed, for a very long time. Yet for one incredible moment, he'd brought hope to her existence. She'd been able to dream of being a part of something finally, of belonging. It was difficult and painful to imagine going through life so alone, but maybe that was her destiny.

Why couldn't she reach Adam, reach all the way into his soul, read his thoughts? Was it really just different backgrounds? Robin suspected that his mother could explain it to her. But she'd never have the nerve to ask. Never.

"More coffee?" asked Christina, holding the earthenware pot.

Robin opened her eyes. "Oh, sorry," she said, "I was off in space. It's so lovely here." She gave Christina a smile. "Sure, only a half cup, though. Thank you."

No, she'd never have the nerve to ask. It would be too embarrassing, too devious going behind his back like that. No, she couldn't possibly... "Christina," began Robin in a small voice, but then she stopped herself.

"Yes, Robin?"

She swallowed hard. "I was wondering... Oh, it's nothing. Really."

"Go on, dear, something's troubling you. What is it?"
Christina seated herself and looked earnestly at Robin.

"You'll think I'm terrible."

"I could never think that."

"Look," said Robin suddenly, her face on fire, "I
should be getting back into town." And she started to rise.

"This has something to do with my son," stated Christina solemnly. "Please...if I can help... We *are* friends."

Robin slumped back into her chair. "It is Adam," she
admitted wearily, feeling as if her heart were in a vise.

"Go on."

"Well, he's very hard to reach sometimes, you know?
Hard to get to." She tried to laugh, but it came out more
like a hiccup. Christina said nothing, however; she only
sat very still and looked pensive and sad. Robin knew
she'd begun to squirm. Why had she said anything? It had
been a hideous mistake...

"I can tell you one thing," said Christina slowly. "You
understand, don't you, that I am loyal to my son?"

"Oh, of course I do," Robin murmured, her stare in
her lap now.

"Adam is keeping something from you. That's all I can
say. You yourself must hear it from him."

Robin managed to nod, unable to speak past the lump
in her throat. A dozen things swarmed through her head,
unbidden, tormenting thoughts, possibilities. What *was* he
hiding, a family of his own somewhere? A woman that
he was secretly engaged to? A problem because he was
an Indian and she wasn't, something she couldn't foresee,
something Apache, a rite he had to perform?

"Don't," came Christina's concerned voice, "don't
torture yourself. Speak to Adam. Speak to him."

Finally Robin looked up. She knew that there were tears
brimming in her eyes; she'd never felt so humiliated in
her life.

"It's all right," said the woman softly. "We are
friends, it's all right."

"I feel so foolish," Robin was able to say, and she wiped at her eyes and sniffed. "You know, I *never* cry..." she laughed then, at herself, at the whole crazy situation.

"Everyone should have a good cry once in a while, don't you think?" Christina returned her smile.

"Well," began Robin, taking a deep breath, "I really do have to get back to town." She looked at her watch. "And I suppose I better get started with this association thing."

"And I'll speak to Josefina," said Christina, but they were interrupted then by one of the Mexican women.

"There's a telephone call for you, *Señora* Farwalker," Pia said shyly.

Christina excused herself and disappeared into the house and Robin was left to sit alone again, only this time she was beginning to get anxious about leaving.

How could you have done that? Asking Adam's mother! Yet Christina had answered one question at least: Adam was keeping something from her. But what?

She was thinking, frowning deeply, when Christina came back to the courtyard. For a moment Robin didn't notice the grave look on the woman's face or the fact that she was wringing her hands.

"Robin," said Christina, her voice shaking, "that call. It was Josefina."

Robin was on her feet quickly, helping Christina into a chair. "What is it?" she asked carefully, holding the woman's hand.

"Her pots...her studio," whispered Christina, "someone wrecked everything!"

"Oh, no!"

"But it's worse." Christina's frightened eyes met Robin's. "John Martinez has been beaten up. My God," she whispered, "is no one safe?"

CHAPTER SEVENTEEN

ADAM LOOKED UP FROM HIS WORK for a moment as an
odd sense of foreboding enveloped him, as if the raven
were hovering over him, flapping its wings. The eerie sensation persisted, growing in intensity. Something, somewhere, had happened—something that affected him pro-
foundly. But what?

"Oh, Mr. Farwalker!" came one of the student's
voices, "lunch is ready!" He climbed up the ladder in the
kiva and headed down the hill, but the feeling still held
him with an unearthly will.

It probably had something to do with Robin and the
fake pots, he told himself; neither subject was ever far
from his mind. He knew Robin was all set and raring to
play the detective. And if they *did* discover who was picking up Martinez's pots, everything would work out. *But*—
and it was a big but—he kept remembering that case in
Albuquerque, the counterfeiting ring, the investigating officer found dead, under mysterious circumstances. He remembered Robin's car lying in the ditch, and he knew he
should have been more forceful and made her leave everything to Rod Cordova.

That afternoon Adam and his few remaining students
worked on the collapsed kiva, excavating the fallen rock,
trying to make it safe to leave for the winter. A chill was
creeping into the air even during the day. Fall was on its
way, the harvest season, the time to hunt, to butcher one's
animals, to store supplies against the season of snows.

Adam, still held by that odd sensation, searched the

immense grandeur of the sky. No clouds yet. But perhaps, one weekend when the clouds descended, he could go hunting with his father. They'd take a couple of pack-horses and ride up into the hills. He would feel totally in harmony with the world then, and remember the wonder-ful hunting stories his uncle had told him about the moun-tain spirits called *Gáhan* and about Coyote, the shrewd trickster of whom a whole series of tales existed. Was it Coyote who was disturbing his peace that day? Was it merely a trick?

Adam was brought back to reality when he heard a shout from below where he was working. "Mr. Far-walker! Josh from the visitors' center is looking for you," called one of the students.

Dusting his hands off on his jeans, Adam picked his way down the slope.

"Adam, I was going by anyway, so I thought I'd drop off the message," said Josh, the park ranger in charge of the center. "It sounds important."

"Thanks," said Adam, taking the pink slip. "I appre-ciate it."

"See you around. Say, you going to the goodbye party for Craig tonight?"

"Huh?" Adam looked up from the note. "Oh, I don't know yet."

"Sure am going to miss all the kids when they leave," said Josh in parting.

Adam read the message again. It was from Christina, and it was very disturbing. "Someone broke into Jose-fina's studio and Martinez is hurt. Call me."

He felt chilled; why hadn't he listened to his instincts earlier? Now he'd dragged more people into this mess. He wondered if Josefina had been injured, but it didn't sound like it, and he wondered how badly hurt Martinez was. It occurred to him instantly that if Martinez had in-deed been beaten as a warning or punishment, then the man had not been lying to them.

Someone had been watching him or Robin, someone knew where they'd gone. Someone knew every move they made. My God—Robin.

He reread the note swiftly. There was no mention of her. Thank heavens she was staying in a hotel, but, still, "accidents" could happen anywhere. If someone were trying to warn Josefina and Martinez, they could do the same to Robin.

Ten minutes later he was dialing Robin's shop from the phone at the visitors' center, but there was no answer. He fought down panic. Hadn't Ericka Dalton been going back to college any day? Sure, she wasn't there, and Robin was out on a job.

On impulse he dialed her hotel. No answer. He even tried her apartment once, but there was no one there, either. He hung around until one-thirty, dialing her shop several times more, but it only rang and rang and rang.

Impatience ate at him—one of the white man's reactions he'd picked up over the years. Patience was nature's way, but this situation wasn't natural. Damn it, it was man-made and he felt irritable and worried. Finally he called his mother, wondering if Robin had decided to stay there after all. She could tell him more about what had happened to Josefina and Martinez.

"Adam? Well, you got *that* message fast. Isn't it awful?"

"How badly is Martinez hurt?" he asked.

"Josefina was hysterical. She didn't say. Just that someone beat him. She's half out of her mind. You know how timid she is, anyway. Adam, this is serious. I think you've got to go to the police."

"Rod already knows all the facts I have and neither Josefina nor Martinez will report these incidents. You know that," said Adam. "Mother, have you heard from Robin?"

"Oh, Robin. Yes, as a matter of fact, she was here this

morning. She wants me to help set up an Indian artists' association.''

Relief swept Adam.

''Well, I told her I would. Apparently she discussed it with Josefina…''

''When did she leave?''

''About three hours ago. I'm sure she's at her shop.''

''She's not there.''

''Oh,'' said Christina. ''You don't think…''

''I don't know,'' replied Adam grimly.

By two he'd given directions to the kids, thrown a small bag in his Land Rover and was headed toward Santa Fe.

He should have checked in with Robin. In fact, he had been planning to call her that night, but what did that matter now?

He stepped on the accelerator, willing the lumbering Land Rover to go faster, but it went uphill only at a stubborn, sedate fifty. In the middle of the afternoon he stopped at San Ysidro and phoned her shop again. Still no answer.

Why hadn't he stayed with her?

The Daltons. Could they have realized that they were suspect? Were they really behind the counterfeiting ring? Could they have done something to Robin, lured her into a trap? Or Martinez. He could easily have called Robin and said he had some new information for her. She would have gone to San Lucas for that—and Martinez could also have lured her into a trap. She could be visiting Josefina, commiserating with her. Sure, she could be *anywhere*. But with Ericka gone, she damn well should have been in the shop.

The cottonwood trees still shadowed the facade of the Sena Plaza. The cute wooden sign still said Robin's Nest. The display in the window was just as attractive as ever. On the door a round plastic clock face hung, with its hands pointing to five o'clock. The words ''will return at'' were printed on the face.

But it was after six.

He felt as if a fist was crushing his heart, squeezing harder and harder. Something had happened to Robin. He could no longer fool himself into believing she was still out·on a job. Not this late.

A small, calm voice told him to consider the possibilities, then his options. The possibilities he'd already been over—ever since he'd left Chaco Canyon. His options were to search for her himself, to ask her friends, to check every hotel in town in case she'd moved, to simply wait, or to call Rod Cordova. He went around to the back of the shop, in the alleyway, and looked through the blinds of her office window. The office was empty.

His next step was to check her apartment. He decided to walk, having spent too many hours in the car as it was. And, besides, it would kill time. She could show up any second, perfectly safe.

It was a lovely walk. The late afternoon sun warmed his face; a few trees were just touched with color, and the old city was smug and peaceful now that the craziness of the summer season was over.

He should have been enjoying the stroll, but his heart hammered too heavily, struggling to release the grip of that weighty hand. Her car was not in front of the building; no one answered his knock. The door was locked.

Swiftly he walked back to the Sena Plaza. Robin's Nest stood silent, staring back at him with empty eyes.

Okay, her friends were the next step. The Daltons' gallery was just two doors down. It occurred to him that the Daltons would lie about Robin's whereabouts if they were involved in the pottery scam, but he had to try.

Chuck Dalton was just closing up. "Hello, Adam. Silly to stay open this late in the off-season, isn't it?" He was the picture of innocence.

"Say, Chuck, do you know where Robin is? I just got in from Chaco and there's a notice on her door that she'll be back at five."

Chuck held his left wrist up. "And it's almost six-thirty. *Women.* Heck, I thought she was in her shop."

"Would Shelly know?"

"Hang on, she's at home. I'll give her a call." He went to the phone and started to dial. "I'd figure *you'd* know where Robin was, if anyone would." And Chuck winked knowingly.

Adam clenched his teeth to bite back a reply.

"Shel? Adam Farwalker's here looking for Robin. You know where she is?" Chuck said into the receiver. "No," he said to his wife over the line, "she's not in her shop. She was supposed to be back at five." He listened then turned to Adam. "Shel says she thinks Robin was going out to see your mother today."

Adam shook his head. "She left there this morning."

"She left there this morning, hon," Chuck repeated into the phone. He listened again then hung up. "Nope, Shelly doesn't know. Robin was at the association meeting last night, though." Chuck regarded him soberly. "You're worried about her. You think it has something to do with this counterfeiting thing?"

"I don't know," said Adam evasively.

"Did you try the hotel she's staying at? I think it was the Governor's Inn," suggested Chuck, looking at him oddly.

"I've tried."

"Hey, I'm sure she'll turn up. Tell you what, if Shel or I hear from her, where can we get hold of you?"

"Leave a message with my folks," said Adam, giving Chuck the number. "Would you mind if I used your phone for a minute to call her hotel again?"

"No, go ahead."

But no one answered in Room 223.

Chuck locked up and drove away in his bright green van. Adam stared after him, wondering, testing Chuck's reactions in his memory. His sixth sense told him Chuck was telling the truth, but this time he couldn't trust his senses. The Daltons would already be alert if they were involved with the forgeries.

He walked back to her shop. Would she bother coming here since it was so late? Was she staying with another friend somewhere? Damn, he should have kept in touch, insisted that she let him or Christina know where she was every minute of the day. He paced. He could try calling Julien or that Lassiter woman or…who else?

Or he could tell Rod Cordova that she was missing. Make it official. But *was* she missing?

The light faded to a dusty gold. Long stripes of brightness lay on the sidewalk, and the trees rustled in the evening breeze. He still paced in front of her shop, feeling helpless and anxious.

A car was coming down the quiet street. Automatically Adam looked up, as he had for every passing car. It was white, a little sporty white model, drifting toward him along the old brick street. A late ray of sun reflected off the windshield, making it difficult to see the driver. He stood with his fists clenched, keeping hope at bay. It seemed as though the car was driving toward him for a very long time, through a tunnel of trees, lit by the dying sun. And then it swerved, too fast, the sun flashed away as the car pulled up to the curb in front of him and he could see the driver.

"Adam! What are you doing here?" Robin asked, stepping out of her car and stopping short.

The fist released his heart at last, and his heart soared. A thousand questions flew around like a flock of birds in his brain. Ignoring them, he walked to where she stood by her car and pulled her into his arms in vast, unthinking relief.

Yes, she was there, unharmed, tall and graceful, smooth-skinned, glowing, sweet-smelling. He pressed her close then held her at arm's length, drinking her beauty in, a heady draught.

"Adam?" she said, cocking her head in that endearing way she had. "Is something wrong?"

He finally found his voice. "Where in hell have you been?"

"Working."

"This late?"

"I closed up this afternoon and went out to get some shots. Hey, do I have to tell you every time I…?"

"You're late."

She glanced toward the clock on her door. "So I am."

He still held her shoulders in his hands. "Mother told me about Josefina and Martinez. I got worried."

She searched his face in the semidarkness, her pupils so large that her eyes looked like dark pools. "I appreciate that, but really…"

He finally dropped his hands, but they still burned with the feel of her. He turned away, raking his fingers through his hair, and swore softly in Apache.

"I'm sorry," Robin was saying, "I didn't know you'd be looking for me."

"Robin," he began, turning back, then he fell quiet. A long moment of silence stretched between them like a strand of the thinnest glass, perfect but fragile.

Her voice broke the strand. "Are you…are you staying in town tonight?"

"I haven't even thought about it."

She averted her face. "I was just wondering… Well, it's only an idea." She faced him again. "I would dearly love to spend an evening in my own place. I've been eating out and I hate it. As long as you're here…" She gave a funny little laugh. "Well, you could spend the evening with me…" Her voice trailed off.

He should have said no, but the trickster, Coyote, took his tongue and he heard himself saying, "I'd like that," and he could see Robin's face light up.

"Oh, good! Let me put my camera away, and then can we run by the grocery store. I'll cook…"

"I'll take you out."

"Oh, Lord, I've had enough restaurant food. I feel like cooking."

He gave in gracefully.

She fixed fat homemade hamburgers and a big salad, and they had coffee ice cream with hot fudge sauce for dessert. Robin was as happy as a lark to be back in her own apartment. She left the dishes in the sink and flung herself down on the couch next to him, put her stockinged feet up on the glass coffee table and spooned melted ice cream from the bottom of the carton.

"I was starved," she said. Then she sat up and got a serious look on her face. "I almost forgot."

"What?"

"Yesterday at the meeting I heard Thad Mencimer— you remember him?—thank Chuck Dalton for letting him use his van."

Adam sat up straighter. "You mean Thad borrowed Chuck's van?"

"Yes." She frowned. "So I figured that meant it could have been Thad who picked up the pots from John Martinez. I'd sure rather believe it was Thad than Chuck."

"There's no proof either way."

"So we still have to stick to our plan, I know," said Robin, rising and pacing back and forth, still holding the carton and licking the spoon. "It could be Thad or somebody else entirely."

"You realize, don't you, that if John Martinez really *did* get beaten up, he may be so scared he'll never let us know when the pickup will happen?"

She stopped short and her brows drew together.

"And Josefina, she's not going to stand up to harassment, either."

"*If* Martinez was beaten?" Robin said then. "You think—"

"I haven't seen him. I don't know if Josefina saw him.

He could be making it up, a smoke screen,'' said Adam. ''He could have been ordered to say that.''

''But if he really did get beaten then he *is* innocent, isn't he?'' she asked. ''Can we find out somehow? Wow, this has really turned out to be a mess.'' She paced some more, her spoon stuck in the ice cream. Adam noticed that, for once, she wasn't eating. He would have been amused under different circumstances. ''How are we ever going to convince Martinez to let us know when the pickup is now?'' she said, half to herself.

''Okay,'' he said, ''let's say Martinez *is* innocent, then he might be too frightened to pass word along to Josefina now.''

''Oh, swell…''

''On the other hand, his pride must be on the line by now, so maybe he'll be willing to help us anyway.''

''If,'' said Robin, ''he's innocent. What if he isn't?''

''In that case, I'd say he has two choices. Either he can ignore us or he can get word to us through Josefina about a pickup but give us false information.''

''You know,'' she said, ''I wonder if we shouldn't—'' She stopped short.

''Shouldn't what?''

''I was going to say, call Rod Cordova with all this. But why should we? I mean, what's he done but practically call us crazy?'' Robin chopped away angrily at her dessert with the spoon. ''The heck with him!''

Adam smiled at her. She was quite a woman. She deserved happiness and that big family she wanted, and all the love and security and belonging that went with it. She deserved someone special to love her and protect and cherish her.

But not him.

She'd fallen silent, staring at the spoon as if it were going to tell her something significant. ''Adam?'' she said after awhile. ''Do you have to go soon? To the hacienda, I mean?''

He knew what she was getting at. A heat filled his body, a molten sweetness. He could stay with her. She was asking him to, and he desired her with a sudden force that shook him.

Adam stood and walked to a window, staring out over the lights of the city. How could he reject her beauty and her love? Yet how could he accept it?

"Adam?" she said, and he was aware of her behind him, moving across the floor.

He turned to face her and saw, deep in her eyes, the truth. There was nothing held back from him; her honesty stabbed at him with the force of a knife.

"What's wrong?" she asked. "Please, Adam…is there a problem?"

His heart dropped to his stomach like a stone, and the heat in him turned to ice, leaving a sheen of cold sweat on his skin.

"Tell me," she said in a passionate voice. "Whatever it is. I don't care. We can face it together. Please, let me help."

He swallowed. "It doesn't concern you, Robin. It isn't your problem."

"It is," she whispered, coming up close to him. "Whatever is bothering you is my problem, too. Don't you see? It's already hurt us both. Can't you tell me?" She laid her hand against his cheek.

He put his own hand over hers, feeling its softness, feeling the delicate bones under the silky skin. Feeling its strength. "Robin," he said hoarsely, "I don't want to hurt you."

A puzzled look crept into her eyes. "I don't understand."

Adam took a deep breath, lifting her hand from his face, holding it still, playing with her slender fingers. "Maybe it's because we're so different."

She stared at him for a moment. "I don't believe that."

"Maybe you should." His heart wouldn't stop hammering; it was pounding in his veins, in his head. She was so close. Her sweet scent wafted to his nostrils. He lifted her hand in his, turned it over and brushed it with his lips. He was filled with a vast sadness, a sweeping sense of loss, as if his clan had cast him out. For an instant he was going to tell her, no matter the consequences, but the moment stole off into the darkness beyond the window. She'd told him what it was in life she sought. He couldn't give her that, ever, and he knew in his heart that Robin would offer herself in spite of his failing.

She was terribly quiet, standing so close to him that her breath touched his neck. Then she was laying her head on his chest. "I'm sorry," he heard her murmur, "you don't have to say anything. Just stay here now, Adam, stay with me."

He knew he'd stay then. He'd stay and they would love each other and the sadness, for a short time, could be put aside.

Adam let the heat build inside him slowly, as if he were feeding kindling to a dying fire until small flames began to spark in his belly, his limbs. The warmth filled him, driving away the chill. She'd done that. Robin...

Her arms crept around his back and she raised her face to him and fire swept the blood in his veins. He lowered his head and kissed her, remembering abruptly the feel and taste of her. His arms tightened around her and the length of her body burned itself into his.

She leaned back in his arms then, her lips reddened from the kiss, her face shining. "Come on," she whispered, tugging at his hand.

Her bedroom was dark, with bars of light from the window lying on the bed. It was permeated with her scent and he breathed it in. She was unbuttoning his shirt, her fingers fumbling, tickling his chest, sending hot darts of pleasure shooting through him. Then her hands were caressing his bare skin and her lips covered his. He reached under her blouse and touched her warm smoothness and felt the ache in his body. "Robin," he groaned.

Then they were undressed and the faint light from the window striped Robin's fair skin in broad bands, touching shoulder and breast and thigh. He cupped her face in his hands and drank in her loveliness then softly brushed her lips with his.

"You're the most beautiful man I've ever seen," Robin murmured against his mouth.

He pulled her down onto the bed, caressing her, re-learning the special, hidden places of her body. He kissed the sensitive pulse on her neck, drew his mouth across her taut nipples, flicked his tongue across her belly.

The fire rose in him, almost uncontrollable, but he waited, wanting to give her pleasure. Her breath was ragged; small moans came from her throat. His hands stroked, feeling her pleasure grow, learning to know her.

Then he was inside her, and she gasped, drawing him close, rising to him, clasping him with her body. He was gentle with her, holding himself back, loving her small, incoherent cries, waiting until the time was right, until she was ready. Then he plunged quickly, harder, and she rose to his thrusts and cried out and they met on the pinnacle, their bodies one body.

She moved under him later, then she traced a line on his face with her finger. "Are you asleep?" she asked softly.

"No." He shifted his hips, rolling over, supporting himself on an elbow. Silver light touched her face, washing it in radiance.

"Can you stay?"

"Yes, Robin, I can stay."

She snuggled into his side. "You feel so good."

He pushed her hair back and leaned over to kiss her forehead. "In Apache you'd be called *di-yin.*"

"What's that?"

"A medicine woman. Powerful."

"I like that," she said seriously. "Would your clan need a new *di-yin*?"

"It takes years of study," he said mock solemnly.

"I've got years." She laid a hand on his stomach. "You see, I have no clan of my own. Everybody needs a clan, don't they?"

"Yes, they do. Otherwise they don't know where they belong."

"That's me in a nutshell." She sighed. "I don't belong to anybody."

A hint of morning paled the eastern sky as Adam stood by the window of Robin's bedroom. Pale gold touched the silent belfry of the time-worn chapel and filtered down to the plaza. He turned slowly and looked over to where Robin slept in the tousled bed. She lay curled on her side, her shoulders white as marble, her hair a great streaked mass half-covering her face. Yet even as she slept, a frown creased her forehead. He knew what was causing that frown. It was the wondering, the not knowing. It was the torment of not being able to trust, to commit, to depend on him.

The faint light outside took on a soft pearl glow, and with it, the room underwent a transformation as the deep shadows receded. She lay there so still, so perfect, so whole. He'd been unforgivably selfish to make love to her again.

For a moment he thought to awaken her and tell her that. He looked down at the shirt that dangled from his fingers. Somehow there had to be a solution, didn't there?

He pulled on his shirt and buttoned it up, recalling Robin's fingers on those same buttons. He knelt by the bed and placed a soft kiss on her cheek, padded silently out of the bedroom, pulled on his boots, let himself out of her door and closed it with a quiet snick behind him.

CHAPTER EIGHTEEN

By FIVE O'CLOCK ON MONDAY afternoon Robin was thankful to see Mrs. Vermeil take her daughter firmly in hand and usher her out of the shop. The girl had been adorable in her Alice in Wonderland dress, but children's portraits were always difficult. And the fact that she'd had to include her white rabbit in the photographic session made things harder, but how could Alice in Wonderland be authentic without a rabbit?

"Whew," said Robin to herself, flipping the sign on the door to Closed. She stood for a few minutes, looking out onto the street. It was a gray day, promising rain later in the evening and, perhaps, snow in the high country. The sky had been low and grainy all day, autumn's first onslaught, and it matched Robin's mood exactly.

She wondered what the weather was like in Chaco Canyon. Was Adam still working, discovering buried pottery shards? Was he thinking about her?

It had been three whole days, she reflected, and no word from him. On Saturday night, it was true, the desk clerk at the Governor's Inn had told Robin that a man had called long distance and asked if she were still at the hotel, but he'd left no message. So he cared, at least enough to check on her.

Robin leaned her shoulder on the door and idly tapped a pencil against her teeth. But he hadn't cared enough to be there the morning after they'd made love. God, how she hated that, waking up alone with not even a note. They'd been so close, too, so loving, touching each other emotionally and physically. Why had he run from her? Why hadn't she been able to reach him?

The weekend had seemed endlessly long. She'd gone back to her room at the inn reluctantly, feeling lonely, inclined to forget his warnings and stay in her own apartment. She'd even tried to get Shelly for a game of tennis on Sunday in spite of everything, but Shelly and Chuck had driven to Denver with some of Ericka's things. It was just as well, she'd told herself, because she still crawled with discomfort every time she thought about her friends and the counterfeiting.

Wind rattled cottonwood branches outside the shop, making the leaves shiver. The street was practically deserted except for a couple of cars and an Indian lady, whose bright green skirt was being swirled around her legs by the breeze. An Indian lady who moved timidly, looking for something, her heavy silver earrings dangling as she turned her head apprehensively.

Quickly, her brain churning with questions, Robin unlatched her door and stepped outside. "Josefina!" she called, waving a hand.

Even when she was inside and out of the cold wind, the woman looked chilled and pale, anxious, standing near the door and glancing up and down the street.

"It's okay," Robin said, "we're safe here. I promise." She used the same quieting tactics as she had the first time Josefina had come to the shop; she made her a cup of steaming hot tea and sat her down in the privacy of the office. But Robin knew the woman was there for a purpose, and she was itching to know what it was.

"I heard about your studio being wrecked," Robin began softly. "I'm so terribly sorry. They did the same thing to me, but all your beautiful pots!"

"Yes, it was a terrible shock. But, after all, my pots are only small parts of Mother Earth and she has more to spare. I will make new ones," said Josefina as she held the teacup in both hands. "I was very frightened, but my two older sons are staying with me now and guarding the studio, so I do not worry so much anymore."

"Oh, good, that must be very comforting. I wish I had a few big strong sons to guard me," Robin said ruefully.

"You will, my child," replied Josefina.

"And John? Is he hurt badly?" asked Robin.

"John seems to be all right. He was very angry, very upset. He has no sons to help, only daughters. He sent his family to his brother at Isleta to protect them. This is a terrible thing, Robin," said Josefina, shaking her head sadly.

"I know," whispered Robin. "Have you thought about going to the police?"

Josefina shot her a glance. "No, they can do nothing."

"Then *we'll* do it. It's got to stop," said Robin, rising and starting to pace.

"Yes, we will do it. John has sent me to tell you…"

"Yes?" Robin stopped short.

"The men contacted him again. He acted frightened and told them he would do this one last order then no more. They are coming to pick up his work at his place."

"When?"

"Tomorrow," said Josefina, "at three in the afternoon."

"*Tomorrow?* So soon?"

"John thinks they are nervous. They know someone is looking for them—you, Adam. They know everything. They know about me and they know we went to see John that day. They threatened him and he lied to them. He lied well and they believed that he told us nothing, but they beat him anyway."

"Josefina," Robin said, thinking, "was John, um, well, black and blue? Did he have cuts on him or marks anywhere? From the beating?"

Josefina shook her head. "He said they hit him here." She indicated her own ribs. "It hurt him to breathe."

"No marks," Robin muttered to herself. What if he was

supplying false information through Josefina? What if...
But he was the only contact they had, and Robin would
have to go with it.

"Tomorrow at his place," repeated Robin.

"You will get word to Adam?" Josefina asked.

"Yes," said Robin, "I'll tell him, and we'll take care
of it from here on out. You've done a wonderful job.
We'll find out who's doing these awful things to all of
us. They'll be arrested, I promise. They'll go to jail."

"And if they do not?" asked the woman doubtfully.
"Then my sons stay forever at my house like soldiers?"

"No, no, we'll get them. All Adam has to do is write
down their license plate number and call Rod Cordova.
Rod will do the rest." Robin put her hand on Josefina's
arm. "You've been very brave. You'll see. Everything
will work out."

But when Josefina was gone, Robin was not nearly as
confident as she'd sounded in front of the woman. There
were so many ways the plan could go wrong. Adam could
have changed his mind about going through with it—because of the danger he imagined, or for any number of
reasons.

Then, of course, there was the scenario in which Martinez had made up the mysterious men who came for his
pots each month. Then no one would show tomorrow. But
she couldn't think of that possibility, not now.

What if the men noticed her and Adam? They knew
her car and they knew Adam's car. She'd borrow a vehicle, or rent one. What if Martinez gave them away?
What if he'd set this up in order for the counterfeiters to
try to trap them? Could John Martinez be that devious?

Robin paced back and forth in her shop, thinking.
Maybe she just should forget the plan and notify Rod
Cordova. But as soon as the notion solidified in her head
she dismissed it. Both John Martinez and Josefina Ortega
were only going through with this because they trusted
her and Adam. To call in Rod now, to have him waiting

at Martinez's place in their stead, might well spoil everything.

No, Robin decided, they'd stick to the original plan and alert the police when they had concrete evidence.

Rain was spattering her front window, and the thick, boiling clouds had moved lower, making the landscape seem very small, very limited in scope. Robin would have to go back to her lonely room at the inn; and she couldn't even call her best friend for a little gossip. Oh, God, she thought, let Shelly and Chuck be innocent. Let this awful mess be over tomorrow.

Adam. It was nearly six, and the visitors' center at Chaco Canyon was closed, but she could leave a recorded message for him. When would he get the message, though? Sometime tomorrow, maybe too late to drive into Santa Fe by three?

Would he come at all? And how would they act with each other? Robin couldn't bear another rejection; she'd have to stay very cool, very distant. It was hard for her to act like that, though. It wasn't *her*. Every time she tried to act cold and reserved she detested herself. Yet, somehow, despite the fact that Adam was at the root of her unhappiness, Robin couldn't hate him.

She sighed and, picking up the phone, dialed the number of the Chaco Canyon Visitors' Center. He'd come, her heart told her. He'd come because he couldn't stay away any more than she could.

BY ONE O'CLOCK THE NEXT DAY Robin was jumping nervously every time the bell over the door tinkled or the phone rang. Adam couldn't have gotten her message before nine, when the visitors' center opened, so he couldn't get to Santa Fe much before one. She'd phoned earlier and arranged to pick up an unobtrusive rental car at the Hertz agency, and it was parked outside Robin's Nest, a gray Ford station wagon. She kept looking at the clock on the wall, wanting Adam to come, afraid to see him, craving him, wanting to throw herself in his arms, hating herself for her weakness.

Where was he? Surely he would have called if he wasn't coming. Or maybe he never got the message. She took a deep breath. She'd leave by one-thirty whether Adam was there or not. She had a strong feeling she'd better be in place, hidden, watching Martinez's house, long before the three o'clock pickup. She'd just close up the shop and go, and if Adam showed up… She'd leave an envelope with his name on it taped to her door. Yes, that's what she'd do. A note, telling him to meet her at San Lucas, describing the gray station wagon. And if he got there in time, fine; if he didn't, she'd handle it herself.

At one-fifteen, she started fidgeting. A man came in to buy film, and she almost pushed him out the door. The minute he was gone she turned her Open sign to Closed, locked the door and leaned back against it, breathing hard, as if she'd just been running.

The phone rang and Robin's heart jerked wildly. She rushed to it, snatched it up. "Hello?" she said breathlessly.

"It's Shelly, home safe and sound from Denver. Hey, did you have lunch yet? Want to go to La Cocina?"

Shelly. "I…uh, gosh, I already ate, Shel."

"You want to just sit with me then? I have some great gossip to catch you up on."

"Look, Shel, I'm expecting a real important phone call…"

"Oh, sorry, I'll get off the line. Sure you don't want even a teensy little taco? You're always hungry."

"I just can't. How about tomorrow?" asked Robin, one eye on the clock: one twenty-five.

"Okay, call me," said Shelly.

My God, thought Robin. Could Shelly have been trying to keep Robin occupied while the pickup was pulled off? No, ridiculous. Her imagination was working overtime. Shelly had nothing to do with pottery counterfeiters and merely wanted to have lunch with her friend, Robin. Her *friend*.

She scribbled a note for Adam, taped the envelope to her door, grabbed a jacket and headed out the door. She looked up and down the street. No Land Rover, no Adam. Should she wait a few more minutes? She couldn't. She'd go without him. He was on his way, surely he was on his way right now.

She drove the big station wagon carefully, not used to such a vehicle. It was another gray day, but only overcast, not raining. The landscape was subdued, its colors subtle, its sweep more monotone. The mountains hovered on the horizon, dark masses with a faint dusting of snow on their peaks. She passed Tesuque, the halfway point. Glancing in the rearview mirror, she checked again to see if Adam was following her; maybe he'd gotten to the shop just after she'd left, and there was only the one main road up to San Lucas.

Her heart thudded; she'd feel immensely better if Adam were with her. She was a little scared. These men had used violence already. What if they were waiting for her? Where was Adam? Her foot seemed to have let up on the gas pedal, because when she glanced at the speedometer, she was only going forty-five. It took all her willpower to press harder, to inch the needle up to fifty, then fifty-five.

A car horn honked behind Robin, making her start as if she'd been burned. What? She looked around, slowing down. Behind her. A big grill, a dusty windshield, coming up fast. A truck. The sound came again, loud, insistent. She looked in the rearview mirror and, without hesitation, pulled off the road and stopped, bowing her head on the steering wheel, feeling her hands tremble under her forehead.

It was Adam.

In a second he was opening the car door. She sat there, drained, suddenly exhausted, and stared at him. "I...I couldn't wait," she finally managed.

"Sorry I was late. I didn't get your message right away," he said quietly, his dark eyes searching hers. "You okay?"

She gave a small hiccup of a laugh. "Yeah, sure. I was a little nervous about doing this alone."

He stood there for a minute, as if he wanted to say something.

"We better, ah, get up there," Robin said, looking away.

"Yes. I'll leave my car here. We can pick it up later," he said. "Do you want me to drive?"

"Yes," she replied gratefully, moving over to the passenger seat.

They were parked in an alleyway with a clear view of John Martinez's house by two o'clock.

"We may have to wait here a long time," Adam said, "so make yourself comfortable."

"Oh, I'm fine."

There was a period of silence, as if each was waiting for the other to speak.

"I'm glad you made it," Robin finally said.

Adam looked at her. "Would you really have come here without me?"

She nodded. "If I had to."

He turned to stare out the window at John Martinez's door. Robin tried not to keep looking at Adam, but he was so close. She would have liked to reach out and caress his copper-colored cheek. One of his hands lay on his thigh and she would have liked to grasp it, to be able to touch him when she wanted, the way a woman touched a man she loved. He'd given her incredible joy and caused her wrenching uncertainty in equal measure, but perhaps it was only the strange circumstances that had thrown them together after all. If they'd met casually and parted, none of this would have happened.

He was not going to talk about the other night, nor was he going to explain why he'd left. Was it the Indian in him, the Apache training that did not allow for intimate communication? Yet Apaches were gentle and affectionate in their personal relations, she'd seen that. He was keeping something from her.

"How's the dig going?" she asked.

"All right. The kids are leaving, except for a couple of graduates, but we've got that kiva mostly rebuilt."

"The kiva." She recalled the weight of his body on hers and the stifling dust. "That's good."

"Um."

"Did it rain at Chaco yesterday?" she ventured.

"It threatened."

"Gosh, it sure will be nice to get back to my own apartment when this is over."

"I hope it'll be today," he remarked.

"I'm sure it will, unless Martinez is putting something over on us," she replied. "You know, Josefina will be awful upset if John turns out to be one of the bad guys."

He nodded gravely.

"I asked her if Martinez was cut up or bruised, and she said he'd been hit in the ribs. So nobody would be able to tell if he'd really been beaten or not." She tried to keep her tone conversational. Was she chattering too much? "I don't suppose he saw a doctor about—"

"Wait." Adam put his hand out to silence her. He was watching Martinez's house intently.

Yes, someone was emerging. It was John, carrying a large cardboard carton. He took it to his old pickup truck and put it in the back. Returning to his door, he glanced around furtively.

"What's he doing?" she whispered.

"I don't know."

Martinez came out with another box.

"He's got pots in those boxes," said Adam with certainty.

"Is he trying to run away?" Robin breathed. "It's too early for them to come here."

"Josefina told you three at Martinez's house? You're sure?"

"Yes, I'm sure."

"Either Martinez is trying to avoid them or us by sneaking away early, or he's been notified to meet them somewhere else," said Adam.

"What do we do? Should we call Rod?"

Adam shook his head. "No time, I'm betting."

"Adam, we *have* to follow him."

"Yes, I'm afraid so." He pounded a palm on the steering wheel. "Damn, this is exactly what I didn't want to get into."

Martinez loaded yet another box onto the truck, then another. He moved quickly, stealthily, glancing around as if looking for someone. Then he climbed into his truck, started it up with a great blast of black exhaust and pulled away.

"Go on," urged Robin, "he'll get too far ahead."

"Look, Robin, you get out of the car right now. I'll do this alone. Call a cab and go back to Santa Fe. Tell Rod—"

"No! Go on, he'll get too far ahead!"

"Robin, who knows where he's going or who might be there?"

"You're not going to have all the fun, Adam!" she cried impatiently.

He muttered some Apache words under his breath and started the car. John's old truck didn't go very fast, so it was easy to catch up. Adam's main problem was trying to keep as far behind as possible—so as not to arouse Martinez's suspicion—without losing sight of him on the winding country road.

"Don't lose him," said Robin, leaning forward in her seat.

"I can't get too close. But he could turn off anywhere. There're dozens of dirt roads around here," replied Adam.

The road they were on dipped and curved, following

an undulating ridge line. Stands of ponderosa pine, aspen and spruce dotted the brown hillside; there wasn't a house or a village for miles. It was a serene landscape, just touched with autumn's hand, tranquil under the gray sky, but Robin's heart raced and she only saw the hills as convenient obstacles to keep Martinez from spotting them.

The old pickup didn't go very fast, so there was no danger of him outdistancing them. It also left a trail of black exhaust floating behind it, so that even when the truck was out of sight they had no trouble following it.

"Where's he going?" muttered Robin, straining to see.

There was a long descending hill and a sharp curve ahead. When they reached the bottom the pickup was gone—and so was the black exhaust trail.

"Oh, no!" cried Robin.

"Maybe he turned off," said Adam grimly, wrenching the steering wheel around, turning the station wagon sharply on the narrow road. "Look for a dirt road."

Slowly he drove back around the curve and up the hill. "There," he said, pointing.

Yes, she could see it, a narrow track, merely two wheel ruts on the hillside. A faint blue of black vapor mixed with dust hung over its surface. "That's it!" she said excitedly.

Adam drove very cautiously on the dirt road, his tires catching the ruts occasionally, throwing the station wagon from side to side.

"Can't we go faster?" asked Robin, on the edge of her seat.

"We don't want to come around a bend and run right into him," replied Adam as he concentrated on the road. "In fact," he said, "we better stop and walk soon."

"Walk?"

"See the way the hills come together up there?" he said, pointing. "There's a canyon ahead. The road is going to end anyway."

"But Martinez—"

"Oh, he's up there somewhere," said Adam grimly, "but God knows what he's doing."

"Then we better stop, shouldn't we?" she said, starting to look for a spot. There was thick brush on either side of the road, a few trees, a rising bank on the left and a hillside sloping away directly on their right. "There's plenty of cover."

"I'll have to find someplace to park the car, a break in the bushes," said Adam. "I don't like this, Robin. It's too isolated."

"We'll be careful, and maybe we can see what Martinez is doing and then leave. Maybe he's just hiding out here. Maybe he's too scared to go through with the plan," she said. "We can't turn back now."

"You can," Adam said.

"And leave you here alone? Besides, we only have one car. I can't leave."

He steered around a fallen branch, bumping along slowly. The exhaust pipe scraped on the road, and the shock absorbers thumped alarmingly.

Robin noticed an opening in the thick growth on her side of the road. "Can you fit in there?"

Adam nosed the car off the road, pushing aside branches with the grill. The brush crackled and rustled and closed in behind them. When Robin squeezed out of her door, she found Adam standing in the road, hands on hips. "I guess that'll have to do," he said. "I hope we'll be gone before Martinez drives back out anyway."

They walked about half a mile, poised to dash into the bushes if they heard anyone coming. But there was only silence, broken by the occasional cheery call of a chickadee, and the crunching sound of their own footsteps.

Robin saw the smoke just as Adam put a hand out to hold her back. "A fire?" she asked.

"A house probably. Now we better get off the road."

Robin was thankful she'd worn pants and low shoes. She had to push through the prickly branches, trying desperately to be quiet, her heart pounding, her mouth dry. She followed Adam's broad back, thankful he was breaking trail. He moved effortlessly, silently, through the undergrowth, in his element. Suddenly he put a hand up and stopped.

Just beyond the scrub oak and gnarled mesquite was a house, an old Spanish-style adobe house, stained and crumbling at the corners. Its windows were broken and boarded up, its roof tiles cracked. The only new thing Robin could see was a shiny padlock on the door, which hung open. John Martinez's pickup was parked in front of the house, and off to the side was a brown van.

"He's meeting someone," Robin whispered.

They crouched down, watching the house. She tried not to breathe hard, but she felt terribly short of breath, excited, keyed up.

John Martinez appeared in the door of the old house, then went to his truck and reached into the back for a box. Two men followed him. They were too far away to see clearly, and they wore hats that were pulled low over their faces. Robin swallowed nervously.

A third man came to the door and spoke. His voice carried faintly, but she couldn't make out the words. He was very obviously directing them to take the boxes out of the truck.

"It looks like John is working with them," Adam said quietly.

"Yes."

"Look, Robin, someone's got to go right now and call Rod before these men disappear. It'd be best if they were caught in the act, but we don't know how long they're going to stick around. I'm guessing they only store the pottery here until they find buyers, so they may leave soon." He thought a minute. "I think I better stay and keep an eye on them. You go back and get the car. Chimayo isn't far along the main road. You'll find a phone there."

"I can't leave you here! You wouldn't even have a car to get away in," she protested.

"Don't worry, they won't know I'm here."

"What if they leave before I get back with the car?"

"I'll get the license number of that van. The police can trace it. Of course, it'd be a lot better to catch them here, like I said."

"And Martinez?"

"We know where to find him, that's no trouble."

"I hate to leave you…"

"I'll be fine. You hurry. Be careful. Can you find your way?"

"Sure. Oh, Adam…"

"Go on. Quietly," he said, handing her the car keys.

She pushed her way back through the branches and burdocks, trying to be quiet, feeling as if someone were behind her every step of the way. Once she hit the dirt road she ran until she was out of breath and had a stitch in her side. Had she passed the place where the car was hidden by mistake? No, there were no broken branches.

Oh, Lord, what if those men were driving along the road toward her right now? What if they caught her alone? She stopped and listened—no sound came to her ears but her own harsh breathing. Slipping into the station wagon, she gunned it backward out of its hiding place and took off down the dirt road like a madwoman.

Chimayo, she thought, racing along the main road. *Isn't there a gas station closer?* But there wasn't, only an isolated intersection, with a sign: Chimayo 2 miles.

The old pueblo was charming, but Robin didn't notice. She pulled up in front of the general store, slammed on the brakes and ran inside.

"A phone?" she gasped to the startled storekeeper. "It's important!"

He tilted his head toward the back. She hurried over to the phone, jammed some coins in and dialed the operator.

"This is an emergency," she said breathlessly. "Please get me the Santa Fe Police Department."

It seemed forever before there was an answer. "Detective Cordova, please," she said. "It's an emergency."

"Detective Cordova is not in today," came the reply.

"Oh, God, no! Then anyone, someone important! Please, this is an emergency."

A man came on the line. "Lieutenant Wilson here."

"Please, listen. My name is Robin Hayle. Rod Cordova has been handling this case. I'm at Chimayo…" And she had to tell the story, praying he believed her. "There are men with…with contraband goods. They're dangerous. Can you send some police up here?"

He was reluctant, she could tell. Her story sounded crazy. "Please believe me! We'll lose them if you don't send someone!"

"All right, Miss Hayle," he finally said. "I'll send a couple of cars."

"Hurry, please. And they're dangerous. I'm going back there right now."

"You stay clear of those men," warned Lieutenant Wilson. "We'll take care of it."

"Oh, yes, I will! Thank you! Please hurry!"

Robin hardly remembered the return drive. She pulled the car off into the same clearing and left it there, rushing up the road toward the house. Were the men gone? Was Adam all right? Would Lieutenant Wilson send the cars quickly, or would he dawdle, disbelieving her story?

A column of smoke was drifting up from the broken chimney of the house. Martinez's pickup was gone, but the brown van was still out front.

Adam was nowhere to be found.

Robin felt like crying. Had they discovered him? Was he being held inside the house? Squirming through the brush, she crept toward the house, worming her way closer. She had no idea what she was going to do, but she had to get near, to find out if Adam was inside, held prisoner—or worse.

She stopped, crouching, a few yards from the clearing, breathing hard, terrified, her heart racing uncontrollably. How long would it be before the police got here? Twenty minutes, half an hour?

A branch rustled behind her. As she half-turned, a hand covered her mouth and a strong arm drew her back against a hard chest. A scream welled up in Robin's throat; she stiffened and went wide-eyed with terror. "Sh!" she heard in her ear. "It's me."

She slumped with relief, falling back against Adam, shaking in reaction. "Don't ever do that to me again!" she whispered fiercely.

"Sorry, I didn't want you to make any noise," he said, steadying her, grasping her arms.

"Rod wasn't there," she explained. "A Lieutenant Wilson was. He said he'd send two cars. Adam, he thought I was crazy. I don't know if they'll get here fast enough."

"We've got to try to keep the men here. Martinez already left."

"The van. If we do something to the van so it won't drive," Robin suggested. "The tires?"

Adam fished in his pocket, came up with a knife and held it up; they exchanged glances over its sharp blade. "I'll have to get close to the house," he said, "but if I keep the van between me and them I should be okay. I'll try to get at least two of the tires."

"What if they see you?"

He shrugged.

"Adam…"

He was starting to make his way toward the van, but he stopped and turned to her, his dark eyes questioning.

"You'll…ah—" she swallowed convulsively "—be careful?"

He gave her an enigmatic smile and slipped off through the bushes.

Adam was beside the van before she could believe it. She could see him digging at the tires with his knife, but it seemed to be taking forever. The men could come out of the house any minute. She crouched there in the bushes, staring through the tangled branches, quivering with anxiety. *Hurry, Adam,* she thought, *hurry!* One end of the van settled slowly; Adam was moving to the front wheel. *Oh, good, halfway done!*

It was then that the door of the house opened, and the three men came out. Robin's heart stopped in mid-beat. Slowly, unsuspectingly, the men walked toward the van; they were talking, and one of them was laughing about something.

She could see Adam freeze—he heard them! Then he jabbed at the tire once more and the front of the van slowly settled. But it was too late. The men were splitting up, one getting in the driver's door, the other two heading around to the far side.

They'd see him! There was no time for Adam to reach the undergrowth!

Robin had no choice at all. Her mind was working clearly, logically. She stood and walked out of the mesquite into plain sight of the three men. Calmly, seemingly unconcerned, she strode toward them. "Yoo, hoo," she cried, "boy, am I glad to see someone! My car broke down out on the road and I—"

The three men stood there, paralyzed with surprise for a moment, and Robin got a good look at them.

Shock jolted her as if she'd been punched, and she could only stare stupidly and openmouthed at one of the men.

CHAPTER NINETEEN

ROBIN GASPED AND WHIRLED and started running, sickeningly aware that two of the men were shouting and chasing after her like hounds after a doe.

She was afraid to look back; if she did she'd trip. So she ran, her long legs eating up the yards, her face and arms sliced by the brush that crowded the road.

"Get her!" she heard from behind. The voice sounded close, too close. "You go that way! Head her off!"

Which way? wondered Robin frantically. *Which way?*

She braved a look over her shoulder, but just that quick move was enough to send her sprawling into a mesquite bush. But Robin wasn't down for long. She scrambled up and was off, her only hope to stay ahead of them until Adam caught up.

Where *was* he? Oh, God, had the third man gotten him? Did they have guns?

Breaking through the undergrowth was a nightmare, branches springing up around her like living creatures, reaching for her, grasping at her. She put her hands out in front and pushed furiously at the tangles, but they snapped back, striking her arms and shoulders, slashing at her head. And still, no matter how quickly she made her way through the growth, the sounds of crackling branches from behind grew nearer.

The police! Surely the police would come racing along the road at any moment, sirens wailing, frightening off her pursuers. *Oh, hurry, hurry!*

Robin's lungs felt as if she'd swallowed a ball of fire

and her legs were giving way; her feet were cast in cement. Blood trickled down her cheek from a cut and she could taste it at the corner of her mouth when she gasped for air.

"There she is! Cut her off!"

Oh, God! Adam, help!

She ran into a piñon tree then, one of its gnarled branches seeming to snatch at her, monstrous, huge, throwing her to the ground where she landed so hard that the breath was knocked from her lungs. She tried to roll over; she tried to get to her hands and knees, but there was no air, and her chest felt as if it were caving in.

"I see her! Get her!"

It was over. Even if she could have gotten up, Robin knew that she hadn't the strength to flee. Broken and terrified, she lay there watching the men approach like wolves surrounding a lamb. The question struck her only then: why, why him?

Robin wasn't sure how long she stayed on the hard ground, panting like a rabbit, immobile, staring at him. It seemed like many long minutes, but logic told her it was seconds. Somewhere she was aware of sirens but they were so far off, in a distant place, a place she was never going to see. If Adam were able to come after her, she thought, he would already be there. A horrible regret filled her, driving away the terror for a moment. Adam…

"You should have taken the warnings more seriously," he said as he stood above her. "I'm sorry. I liked you."

Robin ran her tongue across her dry lips. "Why?" she managed to say. "Why did you do it?"

But he didn't reply; he only nodded to the other man, his eyes unable to meet hers.

It struck Robin suddenly that she was going to die. This was it, this was all there was. Even the sirens had faded, as if in farewell. She felt, oddly, like laughing at herself— all those dreams, all the hope…

The horror was gone from her eyes then, replaced by

a sad kind of irony, a self-mockery. At first she didn't hear it. She was aware only of her mad thoughts, but then it came to her: a voice, a voice as if from her past. A deep, smooth voice, utterly in command.

"I wouldn't do that if I were you," the voice said, and it was a long moment before Robin could clear the cobwebs from her head to comprehend that it was Adam's voice coming from behind the two men. Relief washed over her.

He moved into her line of sight then, catlike, silent and ready. His feet were spread slightly, his arms hanging loosely at his sides. There was something deadly in his stance. A shiver crawled up Robin's spine.

Then the tableau exploded. One of the men, head down like a bull, rushed Adam. Robin cried out, shocked by the sheer violence of it, but Adam sidestepped deftly, grabbed the man by the back of the neck and swung him around, then slammed him against a tree. And it was over, just like that; the other man, cowed, gave up without a struggle.

After all, Robin was to think later, Julien Cordova was not at all a physical man.

IT TOOK ADAM A LONG TIME to explain everything to the police. And Robin guessed that the only reason they were buying his story at all was because of the evidence, the cartons of forged pottery, not to mention the fact that she'd been pursued and her life threatened.

"Look," said Adam, standing in front of the old adobe house, "why don't you just haul these three men into town and I'll follow. We can clear everything up at the station."

"Well," said one of the four officers, "the district attorney's got a case here, I guess, but Detective Cordova's not going to like this at all."

"I'd be surprised," said Robin, "if he didn't know

about it already. I'll bet he was in on the whole thing. No wonder he wasn't much help.''

"Now, lady, that's assuming an awful lot," began Lieutenant Wilson.

"She's right, lieutenant," said Adam quietly, and the man shut his mouth with a snap.

It was another few minutes before the three Cordova brothers and the boxes of pottery were all loaded into the police vehicles. Robin and Adam followed in the rented station wagon.

"You know," Robin said as they bounced along in the wave of dust from the patrol cars, "I was sure you were dead back there."

A corner of Adam's mouth lifted slightly. "Now, how could I have been in any trouble with you out there saving me? That was quite a little stunt you pulled."

"I rather liked it myself," she replied, "that is, until I saw Julien." She shook her head. "Amazing. *Julien.* But anyway, what happened to you when they were chasing me?"

"Oh, I stood up and said hello to Martin Cordova. We hadn't seen each other in years."

"What did he do, faint?"

"Just about." Adam gave her a sidelong glance. "Then following after the rest of you was really very easy. You were making as much noise as a three-ring circus."

"And here I thought I was being so quiet..."

The sun had already dipped below the western ridge of mountains by the time they reached the highway. Robin switched on the heater in the car and hugged herself with her arms. Suddenly she felt drained, scratched and bruised and exhausted. It was hard for her to even think.

"So it's over finally," she said wearily. "I never thought..."

"Didn't you? But you seemed so positive all along that we'd get them."

"That's me—" she smiled ruefully "—always the optimist."

"Um," he replied then fell silent.

Robin gazed out the window and watched the scenery drift by as if it were on a film. The adobe cubes of the pueblos looked dark now in the autumn light, as if they were a part of the earth itself, merely shaped more geometrically. And above them the willowy cottonwoods were already turning golden—soon winter would come, and the land would become brown and white, waiting, waiting those long cold months for rebirth. When spring came, wondered Robin, would she still be seeing Adam or were these to be their last few minutes together? She longed to ask him, but somehow the words just wouldn't come to her lips. It was too much like begging.

It was late by the time they left the police station. Even the district attorney, who had been called away from his dinner table, had told Robin to go on home and clean up. "Don't worry," he'd said, "we've got enough evidence to keep these men behind bars for a long, long while."

One last time, Robin climbed into the car alongside Adam. Was this it, then? Was this goodbye? "What about your Land Rover?" she asked as she drove toward her apartment.

"My father can give me a ride out to it tomorrow."

She would have offered, but he didn't ask.

"And I'll get this rental car back to the agency for you first thing in the morning."

Robin glanced up at the full moon, which hung huge and bright over the Sangre de Cristo Mountains. She sighed and looked over at Adam—strong, beautiful Adam. "You certainly are tying up all the loose ends, aren't you?" she asked, the hurt in her voice undisguised.

"I don't know what you mean," he said then fell silent. She could feel the tension, however, emanating from him like a terrible living thing. In the passing car lights his profile looked hard as marble, as if a sculptor had carved bitterness into his features. Adam sat only inches away, but he was a total stranger to her.

She was thinking frantically, searching her mind for a way to reach him, when suddenly he did an alarming thing. He spun the steering wheel violently and pulled into a parking space along the road. Robin was confused; her apartment was still three blocks away. "You won't let it go, will you?" Adam's voice was harsh, frighteningly so. *"You just keep pushing, Robin."*

"I—"

But he silenced her with a sharp gesture. "Don't say another damn thing. You've asked for this, you acted as if you really wanted to hear it, so here goes…"

Her heart began to beat furiously, and instinctively she knew that she didn't want to hear it at all—not now, not like this. He was so angry, so in pain. She wanted to run, to cover her ears, anything.

"Do you think I'm blind?" he said as if demanding an answer. "I know what you want, Robin, and I can't give it to you. You want a husband and a family. You want to be a part of some man's life, to belong—"

She pushed his hand away. "Not *any* man's life, Adam Farwalker," she said in an angry voice.

"Okay. But can you deny that you want to be a mother, raise a family?"

What was he getting at?

"Well, I can't give you that, Robin. I can't give you those children." He slammed his palm against the steering wheel, and the force of his sudden rage made her heart leap. "It's the stupidest thing in the world but there you are," he ground out. "I was thirty years old… I had the mumps."

Robin sat utterly motionless for what seemed like an eternity. The mumps. He was sterile. So *that* was Adam's secret. She had no idea what to say to him, and she was afraid that anything she said would be wrong. He was so hurt, so angry, so very, very alone with his pain. She prayed for words of comfort to form in her head. Nothing came.

The silence drew out between them, a hollow, bitter, empty silence. She felt more alone than she'd ever felt in her life, alone with the beating of her heart.

It was finally Adam who spoke as he started up the car. "I'll take you home."

She bit back her tears of frustration. He'd certainly hit the nail on the head, hadn't he? She *did* want a family— she'd be lying to him and herself if she said otherwise. Oh, God, what was she to do? She *loved* Adam!

"I'm sorry," he said as he pulled up in front of her place and turned to her. "You can't know how sorry I am. It could have been good between us."

"Adam," she began, a thousand useless words swarming in her head, beating at her, "can't we...isn't there something..."

He shook his head slowly. "Facts are facts, Robin. I wish to God it weren't true, but I can't give you what you want, what you deserve."

"Isn't that up to me?" she asked. "Shouldn't I have a say in this, too?"

"I'm afraid," said Adam gravely, "you've already expressed your feelings on the subject. Maybe you shouldn't have been so honest, Robin Hayle." And even as he kissed her cheek softly she was thinking about that remark, hating it, trying to deny it, but there it was: she did want a family. No wonder at all, she thought darkly, he'd run from her. Good old honest Robin Hayle...

For long, miserable days those minutes in the car with Adam played through her mind over and over, endlessly, like a phonograph needle stuck in a groove. Robin went about her daily existence, opening and closing her shop, reading in the paper the breaking story about the counterfeit ring but hardly able to concentrate on its significance. She felt so empty, as if set adrift in a void where there were no stimuli whatsoever. There was no sight, no smell, no touch—just nothingness.

Thank God for Shelly. When the story of the van finally came out, Shelly was incredibly understanding and even laughed. "You should have told me," she said, "and saved yourself a big headache."

"I couldn't, I was afraid to. How can you ever forgive me?"

"Oh, how about you buy the doughnuts for the next week and then we'll call it even."

That was Shelly, the best friend a woman could ever have.

One other thing kept Robin going those days. She started planning for the new Indian artists' organization. If there was nothing left of her relationship with Adam, *something* good had to come out of what Robin had started thinking of as her "great adventure." She phoned Christina, carefully avoiding the subject of Adam, and got the names of some prominent Indian artists of the pueblos. She asked Christina to call a few then started on her own list during the quiet hours in her shop.

It was discouraging. So many of the Indians were suspicious or doubtful. Some didn't speak English. But she kept at it, gritting her teeth at the rebuffs, determined to have something to show for her great adventure.

She called Josefina, too, begging the woman to lend her support to the concept of the organization.

"I am not sure," said Josefina. "Why would anyone listen to me?"

"You are one of the most famous, respected Indian artists in the Southwest," Robin said firmly. "Every Indian in New Mexico will listen to you, Josefina."

"That would make me very nervous. Who am I to tell others how they should act? Every Indian must search his own heart to know what to do," said the woman.

"But you agree this organization is needed?" pressed Robin.

"I think it is a good idea, but I do not know how you can make it work."

"With your help I can. I know Christina thinks it's a good idea, too."

"Yes, she was very persuasive. But, you see, Christina does not always understand…"

"But, Josefina, if I can persuade some of the artists to get together for a meeting, would you come? Would you give it your support?"

Josefina sighed. "I must think about it. I will talk with my sons."

"Oh, thank you. I know you'll do the right thing."

"The right thing for an Indian is not necessarily the right thing for a white person," replied Josefina quietly.

It was difficult, but it kept her occupied at least, the endless, frustrating phone calls, the attempts to penetrate an alien culture that was wary and guarded, having too often been betrayed by Anglos. But she kept at it tenaciously; Robin was, if nothing else, determined.

And she never heard from Adam.

It was finally Shelly who broke through her silence on the subject and got her mad. "Okay, kiddo," said her friend one morning as she popped in, "what gives?"

With much coaxing and hugging, Shelly finally got the whole story from Robin. "Go ahead and cry," Shelly advised, "you deserve it." Then, when Robin's sobbing finally subsided, she said, "So? What are you going to do? I don't see that this decision is entirely Adam's."

"Well, he *made* it his decision," replied Robin, sniffing into a Kleenex. "He thinks that all I want is kids."

"Do you?"

"Yes…and no." Robin felt an odd sort of anger begin to bubble up inside her. "I mean, they don't have to be *my* kids, do they? Shouldn't I have a say?"

"You bet."

"After all, hundreds of people get married every day

and then find out they can't have children, don't they? And that doesn't stop them from loving each other.''

Shelly shook her head emphatically.

"And I bet if they had known before they got married, they still would have.''

"They adopt,'' offered Shelly as she took a doughnut from Robin's white bakery bag.

"Oh, sure,'' said Robin, feeling alive again for the first time in days, "I'd like to have my own kids... But Shelly—'' she looked at her friend intently "—we can't have it all, can we? It might hurt at times, but I've got so much love stored up inside me, enough for Adam *and* a bunch of children.''

"Even if they aren't yours?'' asked Shelly.

"They'd need me even more, wouldn't they?'' replied Robin pensively. "There're so many kids without homes...''

"Thousands and thousands,'' agreed Shelly.

Robin stared at her friend. "Indian children, too. Can you imagine the wealth of knowledge a man like Adam could give them?''

Indian summer touched the land with a generous hand, flashing in the rivers, gilding the mountainsides, kissing the desert with a last, frantic bloom of colorful wildflowers. Day after day the sky was clear, the air cool and crisp. Robin felt peaceful and vibrant; for the first time in her life she truly knew what she wanted. And she came to a decision: even if she never again saw Adam, even if there was never to be *any* man in her life, she was going to stop waiting for love to come to her; she was going to go out and grab it and hold it to her. She was going to adopt a child.

Her decision made, Robin knew that there was one thing she had to do first: she had to see Adam one last time; she had to try to make him believe how much she loved him, how much she *would* love him even if he were missing an arm or a leg or an eye. But if she failed she was not going to bury herself behind her superficial, fun-loving exterior. Not ever again. But just how was she going to see him?

The opportunity finally presented itself, however, when Robin got an encouraging call from Christina late in the month.

CHAPTER TWENTY

THE GATHERING AT CHRISTINA'S was to be a preliminary organizational meeting for the New Mexico Native American Artists' Association. It was off the ground, at last, Christina had told her on the phone, and Robin had to be there. It had been all her hard work that had finally persuaded at least some of the Indians to consider the idea.

Robin drove out to Las Jaritas in an unsettled frame of mind. She was thrilled that some of the Indians were organizing, and she was gratified to be involved. So many benefits could come from the fledgling association, and Robin was to be a part of it all. She knew, also, that John Martinez was going to be there today, and she was looking forward to seeing him again, to thank him in person for all his help.

Everything had turned out for the best, just as Robin's eternal optimism had always led her to believe. Everything but her and Adam.

Would he be there today? It was a Saturday; perhaps he'd taken the weekend off.

Why should he be there? If he'd wanted to see her he would have called—he'd had days and days to contact her.

The familiar hills lay under the brilliant yellow sun, the horizon standing out as sharply as a cactus thorn. Indian summer. The summer of Robin's Indian. Was her great adventure over? Was it the end of their love?

But his mud-caked Land Rover was parked in the drive-

way, behind the dozen or so other vehicles. Robin's heart
gave a frightened thump, then a glad one.

She pushed her hair off her shoulders, straightened her
long, slim navy-blue skirt and belted blouse and closed
her eyes for a second, then walked to the front door and
knocked.

Adam opened it. Had he been waiting?

"Oh, hello," she said.

He stood in the doorway, gazing down on her. "Hello,
Robin."

"Ah…I'm, ah, here for the meeting," she said inanely.

"Yes, I know. Please come in." His face was expressionless, his voice carefully neutral.

Rigid, Robin walked past him then stopped. Was this
all there was going to be between them now, strained
politeness?

"They're all in the living room," he was saying, then
he moved past her, leading the way.

She couldn't help staring at him as she followed. He
had no right to look so handsome, so tall and dark and
beautifully put together. And yet, she knew, there was that
imperfection that scarred him. Suddenly she wanted to
reach out and touch his back, to tell him that it was okay,
that she would love him no matter what.

"Oh, hello, Robin!" Christina rose from her seat and
came to greet her. Then Robin was whisked away from
him and introduced to the assembled group, representa-
tives of the pueblos and of the Navaho and Apache tribes.
Robin had trouble concentrating, her whole being focused
on Adam, who took a seat in the corner of the room. But
she smiled and replied correctly to questions, she guessed,
because no one seemed to notice her preoccupation.

Josefina Ortega was there with her son Manuel. John
Martinez was there, as expected, and many other Indians
whom Robin did not know, but whom she'd spoken to on
the phone.

"We've been working all morning," Christina said,

"organizing. They've elected me president." Then she smiled. "But only temporarily, until things get going. Now, we have a few small problems, Robin. We have to decide on dues and we really need to see a copy of that pamphlet your association is going to put out."

The discussion went on for another half hour. Robin answered questions about her own business association, trying to help. She could see there were going to be a couple of factions, as there were in all such organizations. Some of the Indians were distrustful still, but, with Christina and Josefina's influence, she was convinced that they'd learn to compromise for the good of everyone.

And all the while she was aware of Adam's attention on her. Her skin felt oversensitive, as if she had a fever, as if his big hands were on her flesh, setting her on fire.

"Well," she was saying to an artisan from San Claro, "when we have a disagreement at our meetings in Santa Fe, we always take a vote." Why was Adam doing this to her? Didn't he know what torment it was for her to be so near without having the freedom to touch him?

"Will everyone pay the same in dues?" asked another artist.

Eventually Robin was handed a plate of Christina's *chiles rellenos*, cheese-stuffed green peppers, and found herself seated on the couch next to Adam's mother. During the lunch break, the conversation turned from the new organization to the recently exposed counterfeiting ring. John Martinez, of course, had to explain to the group his role in the scam.

"I was told," he said in English, "that the pots were for a museum. I was paid so little..." And then he spoke in Tewa to a few of the Indians.

Robin half listened to his words, but she was more aware of Adam than anything else. He'd pulled a chair up close to the couch and, with a plate of food in his hand, seemed to be engrossed in Martinez's explanation while he ate. Robin's appetite, however, was entirely gone for once; she couldn't seem to get the food past the lump in her throat.

Christina said something in Apache to a woman seated on her right then turned to Adam. "Many here today," she said to her son, "are still confused about the forgeries. Perhaps you can explain better than I can."

Adam put his plate down. As usual, when he began to speak, everyone paid attention. How did he do that? wondered Robin once again.

"As I'm sure you all know, it was Julien Cordova," he was saying, "who was the head of the ring."

"But why would a fine man like that do such a terrible thing?" Josefina shook her head, and a man sitting next to her patted her clasped hands.

"Essentially," replied Adam, "it was an act of revenge. The Cordovas were an old Spanish land-grant family. They lost their land, of course, years ago, but apparently they still harbor bitter feelings."

"They did it for the money," put in Martinez angrily.

"Yes," agreed Adam, "that, too. When they lost their land, they lost their livelihood. There was a lot of money to be made from the forged pots, more, as it turned out, than most of us realized."

"Julien and his brothers were very clever," said Josefina.

"And," said Robin slowly, "they were in the right position to pull it all off smoothly." She fell silent, uncomfortable, too aware that Adam's gaze had shifted to her again.

"Go on," he said, "you know as much about it as anyone, Robin."

"She was very brave," put in Christina, laying a hand on Robin's arm.

Robin laughed lightly. "I didn't *feel* brave, though. Not at the time." She took a sip of her water then looked around the room, avoiding Adam's eyes. "If you think about it," she went on, "Julien was placed perfectly to organize the ring. He knew everyone in Santa Fe and he's one of the foremost experts in the area of Indian art. Heck, he even had me telling him every move I was making. It was no wonder he was always one step ahead of us."

"Of course," said Adam, "he had his brother Rod in with him, too. It was just pure luck that Rod wasn't there when Robin called for help that day."

"I wonder why the Cordovas made the last pickup of John's work?" Christina asked. "It was their downfall…"

"They thought they had John completely cowed," said Robin. "Although they did get a message to him to make a delivery to that isolated house instead. They were still being cautious even then."

"The van," put in John Martinez, "I was very taken in by that."

"Anyone would have been," agreed Adam. "Julien, of course, had borrowed it from Chuck Dalton for just that purpose. In fact, Julien used a different vehicle every time he sent his brothers out to make the pickups."

"A very careful man," said Christina.

"It was lucky," said Robin, "that Adam threw him off the track, though, when he told Julien at the Daltons' dinner party that we were washing our hands of the forgery business."

"And my poor pots," said Josefina, "all ruined."

"Your pots," Adam said, "and John's injuries, not to mention Julien having one of his brothers follow Robin to Chaco Canyon and try to kill her."

"He dressed like an Indian," Christina explained to the group, "and made a roof collapse on my son and Robin. Then he ran her car off the road. A horrible man."

"No worse than Rod, though." Robin frowned. "As a policeman, it was so easy for him to follow us to John's house in San Lucas. He even had John watched by a stakeout team with the excuse that John was involved with black marketeers. And," she said, her tone growing angry, "it was Rod himself who broke into my shop and my apartment! The creep."

"And," interrupted Adam, "the police in Albuquerque did pick Rod up at the airport there. He had a ticket to Mexico in his pocket."

"What will happen to these men?" asked Tina Sanchez, a weaver from San Claro.

"There'll be a trial. The district attorney is working on the charges right now," said Adam.

"I will tell my story at the trial," said John Martinez. "I believe now that it is the right thing to do."

"Oh, good," said Robin. "Your testimony will help so much."

"I do not like these ways of your law," said John, "but I trust you that it is right to do. My family is back at San Lucas and safe. My wife tells me I should do it and that she will come and watch me in the court."

After lunch Christina asked Robin to explain to the group what the Santa Fe Business Association was doing to see that this kind of thing didn't happen again.

"Well, we're doing several things. We're going to print and distribute a quarterly pamphlet containing information of counterfeit artwork, ways of spotting forgeries, lists of reputable dealers and so on. We're also going to lobby the state legislature for stricter laws governing the sale and documentation of Indian art.

"And it's the first time the association voted for something without arguing," she reported with a smile. "People finally realized we have to cooperate to stop this kind of thing. And, oh, yes, we had to elect another president. It's Chuck Dalton—of the Dalton Gallery. Some of you may know him."

There was a murmur of assent. Robin sat back, feeling relieved that the forgery matter was closed and that she had been able to help. She was glad to see, too, that the Indian artisans were willing to organize. There was going to be a new trust between the whites and the Indians after this, a breakthrough. It was no small thing, either, that John Martinez had agreed to testify in a white man's courtroom.

"Thank you so much, Robin," Christina was saying, "for coming here today," and then the meeting was breaking up. Many people shook Robin's hand and spoke to her. John Martinez said goodbye gravely, but it was Josefina who came up to Robin with a smile on her seamed face and a box, which she held out.

"This is for your help," said Josefina shyly, "and for all the danger I put you in."

It was one of her black-on-black pieces, a large shallow bowl decorated with stylized feathered serpents and jagged lightning. Reverently Robin took it out of the box and held it. "Oh, it's *so* lovely. But Josefina…"

"It is the least I can do for you," said the older woman. "You will remember what happened whenever you look at it—and that is as it should be."

"I'll never forget *you*," said Robin. "And I can never thank you enough."

Carefully Robin put the pot back in the box. She hugged Josefina and smiled some more and thanked people and shook hands, but all the time she was still conscious of Adam, standing quietly in the back of the room, and she knew there was one more matter that was not quite closed.

It was terribly awkward. Robin didn't know whether to leave with everyone else or to say something to him, to wait around in case he wanted to talk to her, or to keep the last shred of her dignity intact and say goodbye firmly, once and for all.

Suddenly the house that had been overflowing with people minutes before was absolutely quiet. Even Christina had vanished. There was only Robin, who stood in the living room fingering her purse straps, and Adam, his stare resting on her, impenetrable and calm.

"Well," said Robin, "guess I better get back to the shop."

Adam came to life then, finally, seeming to cross the distance between them without actually moving. He stood so close to her that she was afraid to breathe. "Can you try to understand?" he said in a deep voice. "I wanted to give you time."

Maybe she said something, or maybe she only nodded. But she would always remember that sense of nearness, and the fact that she was gazing at him in bewilderment as his strong fingers found hers and entwined them warmly.

"Come outside," he said, "I think better there."

The four-hundred-year-old stones of the patio were sun-warmed; the air smelled of ripe apples from Christina's trees and the sharp, dry odor of mesquite and creosote bush and piñon from beyond the thick aged walls. They sat across from each other, Adam still toying with her fingers. Robin was afraid to speak, in an agony of apprehension.

"I've been taught to avoid excesses all my life," he finally said. "It's the way of the Diné. I've been taught to be careful of other people, especially outsiders, and to walk hand in hand with the natural world." He paused and studied her. "We're a selfish people, the Diné, very self-centered."

She listened, feeling that Adam was trying to tell her something vitally important.

"My uncle gave me my war name when I was three. It is Changing Man. Do you understand, Robin?"

"Changing Man," she repeated, "but you shouldn't tell me. I'm not..."

"You need to know."

What was he saying? She couldn't quite grasp the significance of his words. He couldn't mean...

"You know everything about me now. It's your choice, Robin. You, alone, have the right to choose."

She lowered her head over their joined hands and felt tears dim her eyes. "I only need to know one thing, Adam."

He raised her chin. "What is it? Anything…"

"Do you love me?"

"I love you," he replied solemnly.

"Well, then, there's no choice. I love you. I want you for my husband, forever. I want Changing Man, just as he is," she said, "for my clan."

"Robin…"

"Don't try to change my mind, Adam. I love *you*, not what you can give me." She smiled shyly. "I know I've got a lot of insecurities, and I'll probably drive you nuts from time to time. But, Adam, I love hard."

He pushed her hair back. "And you'll be happy without children?"

"We can have children. We'll adopt them. Lots of them. Indian children." She took his hand. "They need us so badly. It's as if someone planned this. Don't you see? And you can teach them to walk hand in hand with the world."

"And you can teach them to love," he said softly.

"They'll have the best of both worlds. It will work, Adam, we can make it work."

"I live in Albuquerque usually, you know," he said then.

Robin's face fell. "Oh," she said, "I guess I can…"

Adam smiled. "You'd move from your precious Santa Fe? You'd even do that for me?"

She straightened her back. "Yes, of course," she said staunchly. "I'd just forgotten."

"Something's come up, though," he went on, "just recently. The Governor's Palace museum is currently without a curator."

"Julien."

"Yes, Julien was the curator there."

"And?"

"I've been approached to fill the position."

Robin's eyes lit up. "Oh, Adam, wouldn't that be wonderful? We could live here, and we'd spend summers on the ranch, wouldn't we? I can see your father teaching his grandchildren to ride and hunt and speak Apache."

Adam laughed. "You have things all planned, don't you?"

"Oh, yes, we're going to be very busy," she said, her face shining, her joy swelling like a bubble in her breast, "and very happy."

Adam drew her close. "As your bride price," he whispered, "I demand a kiss," and the warm golden sun illuminated the embrace sealing their contract, the difficult but enduring bond between the trinity of Anglo, Indian and Spanish that was New Mexico, the land of enchantment.

All they wanted for
Christmas was...
each other!

DECK THE HALLS by

MARGOT EARLY   HEATHER MacALLISTER

**It was the season for miracles.
And they definitely needed one....**

When biologist Jean Young joined David Blade and his son on their
boat, she never dreamed she'd end up surrounded by scandal—
or desperately in love with this unsmiling man who had too
many secrets and a little boy longing for a mother's kiss.

Bankruptcy lawyer Adam Markland had earned a reputation for
getting what he wanted—and he wanted smart, sexy Holly Hall.
Little did he guess it was his reputation as a cutthroat attorney
that was keeping her permanently out of his reach.

2 Complete Novels

at the LOW PRICE of $4.99 U.S./$5.99 CAN.!

Look for **DECK THE HALLS** on sale in November 2000.

HARLEQUIN®
Makes any time special ™

Visit us at www.eHarlequin.com

PBR2DTH

If you enjoyed what you just read,
then we've got an offer you can't resist!

Take 2
bestselling novels FREE!
Plus get a FREE surprise gift!

Clip this page and mail it to The Best of the Best™

IN U.S.A.
3010 Walden Ave.
P.O. Box 1867
Buffalo, N.Y. 14240-1867

IN CANADA
P.O. Box 609
Fort Erie, Ontario
L2A 5X3

YES! Please send me 2 free Best of the Best™ novels and my free surprise gift. Then send me 4 brand-new novels every month, which I will receive before they're available in stores. In the U.S.A., bill me at the bargain price of $4.24 plus 25¢ delivery per book and applicable sales tax, if any*. In Canada, bill me at the bargain price of $4.74 plus 25¢ delivery per book and applicable taxes**. That's the complete price and a savings of over 15% off the cover prices—what a great deal! I understand that accepting the 2 free books and gift places me under no obligation ever to buy any books. I can always return a shipment and cancel at any time. Even if I never buy another book from The Best of the Best™, the 2 free books and gift are mine to keep forever. So why not take us up on our invitation. You'll be glad you did!

185 MEN C229
385 MEN C23A

Name _____ (PLEASE PRINT)

Address _____ Apt.#

City _____ State/Prov. _____ Zip/Postal Code

* Terms and prices subject to change without notice. Sales tax applicable in N.Y.
** Canadian residents will be charged applicable provincial taxes and GST.
   All orders subject to approval. Offer limited to one per household.
   ® are registered trademarks of Harlequin Enterprises Limited.

BOB00

©1998 Harlequin Enterprises Limited

You're not going to believe this offer!

**In October and November 2000, buy any two Harlequin
or Silhouette books and save $10.00 off future purchases,
or buy any three and save $20.00 off future purchases!**

Just fill out this form and attach 2 proofs of purchase (cash register
receipts) from October and November 2000 books and Harlequin will
send you a coupon booklet worth a total savings of $10.00 off future
purchases of Harlequin and Silhouette books in 2001. Send us 3 proofs
of purchase and we will send you a coupon booklet worth a total
savings of $20.00 off future purchases.

Saving money has never been this easy.

I accept your offer! Please send me a coupon booklet:

Name: _____

Address: _____ City: _____

State/Prov.: _____ Zip/Postal Code: _____

Optional Survey!

In a typical month, how many Harlequin or Silhouette books would you buy <u>new</u> at retail stores?

☐ Less than 1 ☐ 1 ☐ 2 ☐ 3 to 4 ☐ 5+

Which of the following statements best describes how you <u>buy</u> Harlequin or Silhouette books?
Choose one answer only that <u>best</u> describes you.

☐ I am a regular buyer and reader
☐ I am a regular reader but buy only occasionally
☐ I only buy and read for specific times of the year, e.g. vacations
☐ I subscribe through Reader Service but also buy at retail stores
☐ I mainly borrow and buy only occasionally
☐ I am an occasional buyer and reader

Which of the following statements best describes how you <u>choose</u> the Harlequin and Silhouette
series books you buy <u>new</u> at retail stores? By "series," we mean books within a particular line,
such as *Harlequin PRESENTS* or *Silhouette SPECIAL EDITION*. Choose one answer only that
<u>best</u> describes you.

☐ I only buy books from my favorite series
☐ I generally buy books from my favorite series but also buy
books from other series on occasion
☐ I buy some books from my favorite series but also buy from
many other series regularly
☐ I buy all types of books depending on my mood and what
I find interesting and have no favorite series

Please send this form, along with your cash register receipts as proofs of purchase, to:
In the U.S.: Harlequin Books, P.O. Box 9057, Buffalo, NY 14269
In Canada: Harlequin Books, P.O. Box 622, Fort Erie, Ontario L2A 5X3
(Allow 4-6 weeks for delivery) Offer expires December 31, 2000.

PHQ4002

This Christmas, experience
the love, warmth and magic that
only Harlequin can provide with

Mistletoe Magic

a charming collection from

BETTY NEELS
MARGARET WAY REBECCA WINTERS

Available November 2000

HARLEQUIN®
Makes any time special ™

Visit us at www.eHarlequin.com

PHMAGIC

THE SECRET IS OUT!

HARLEQUIN®

INTRIGUE®

presents

TEXAS CONFIDENTIAL

By day these agents are cowboys;
by night they are specialized
government operatives.
Men bound by love, loyalty and the law—
they've vowed to keep their missions
and identities confidential....

Harlequin Intrigue

Harlequin American Romance
(a special tie-in story)

HARLEQUIN®
Makes any time special ™

Three complete novels by *New York Times* bestselling author

Penny Jordan

Marriage of Convenience

Three tales of marriage...in name only

Claire accepted a loveless marriage of convenience to Jay Fraser for the sake of her daughter. Then she discovered that she wanted Jay to be much more than just a father....

Lisa and Joel were at loggerheads over their joint guardianship of her sister's little girls. So Joel's proposal of marriage came as a shock.

Sapphire had divorced Blake when she'd found he'd married her only to acquire her father's farm. Could she even consider remarrying him—even temporarily—to ease her dying father's mind?

Don't miss *Marriage of Convenience*
by master storyteller Penny Jordan.

On sale in November 2000.

HARLEQUIN®
Makes any time special ™